The Templar Agenda

CW01335678

John Paul Davis

The Templar Agenda
Third Edition

First paperback edition: © John Paul Davis 2016
Original ebook edition published 2011
ISBN: 978-1537016573

Reviews

John Paul Davis clearly owns the genre of historical thrillers. *The Templar Agenda* is a fast paced and absorbing tale that takes the reader on an exhilarating adventure from the first page to the last. This tantalizing story is intricately woven and stretches from the ancient secrets of the world's most powerful society to the modern behind-the-scenes brotherhood that still wields power on a global level
Steven Sora, author of The Lost Treasure of the Knights Templar, The Lost Colony of the Templars, Secret Societies of America's Elite, Treasures from Heaven, and The Triumph of the Sea Gods

A well-researched, original and fascinating work – a real page-turner.
Graham Phillips, bestselling author of The End of Eden, Merlin and the Discovery of Avalon in the New World, The Templars and the Ark of the Covenant, Alexander the Great: Murder in Babylon, The Moses Legacy, The Marian Conspiracy, Act of God, and The Chalice of Magdalene

Told at a pace that leaves the reader breathless, Davis has constructed a plot that flies across the planet . . . We follow the novel's protagonists, Swiss Guard Mikael (Mike) Frei and Gabrielle Leoni, daughter of a murdered banker, as they race against time to uncover the hidden secret that has already led to a series of assassinations, could wreak havoc in the world's banking capitals, and threatens the stability and integrity of the Catholic Church itself . . . . Davis is adept at managing several storylines, moving swiftly from one group of characters to another, as the novel progresses. But he is equally skilled at ensuring that the reader remains gripped by the central plot to its dramatic and surprising conclusion . . .
John Alcock, author, prize winning poet, and former Director of Open Studies Creative Writing, University of Warwick & sometime Exchange Professor in Dramatic Literature, Eastern Michigan University

Books by John Paul Davis

Fiction

The Templar Agenda
The Larmenius Inheritance
The Plantagenet Vendetta
The Cromwell Deception
The Bordeaux Connection
The Cortés Trilogy

Non-Fiction

Robin Hood: The Unknown Templar (Peter Owen Publishers)
Pity For The Guy – a Biography of Guy Fawkes (Peter Owen
Publishers)
The Gothic King – a Biography of Henry III (Peter Owen Publishers)

For more information please visit www.johnpauldavisauthor.com
And
www.theunknowntemplar.com

From the beginning, mankind has been divided into three parts, among men of prayer, men of toil, and men of war.
Gerard, Bishop of Cambrai (1012-1051)

Prologue

The decision to initiate the murders of the high-profile Swiss banker and the Chairman of the Federal Reserve was made by the same seven men who had decreed the murders of over a thousand others. Under normal circumstances eight would have been involved in the process. On this occasion, had it not been for the actions of the eighth, their deaths might not have been necessary.

All of the seven were men of considerable status, particularly in America and central Europe.

All seven were men of influence and wealth – had they not have had the wealth their influence could not have been possible.

All seven were men of God, each one Christian but only one a confirmed Catholic.

They were the only members of the world's most secretive society whose existence in the eyes of the common man remained nothing more than a myth. Every couple of decades or so an ambitious writer would connect them with the latest genocide, political conspiracy or economic meltdown, but their theories were usually dismissed and forgotten after a few weeks. On the rare occasions when someone did stumble across the truth they could never locate the individuals.

All seven were masters of discretion.

At just after midnight Eastern Time in America the orders went out to the usual recipients. One was stationed in Rome, carrying out his regular duties as a soldier guarding the Pope. The other was somewhere in America, successfully evading the attention of the CIA.

Both took the calls immediately and proceeded to go about their business.

*

Switzerland

The first of the assassins arrived in Zürich at 22:53 after an eight-hour train journey from Rome. The journey was an unexpected one; out of keeping with his usual routine. Had the phone call come any later, it would probably have been too late.

He exited the train at the Hauptbahnhof, the largest station in Zürich, doing his best to avoid attention by mingling amongst the bustling crowd. The station was crowded, as always, the main hall in particular alive with activity. Countless passengers travelled up and down escalators to one of the station's ground or underground platforms, while others frequented the cafés and shops or stood in line to purchase tickets. It was late January and the vibrant Christmas market was gone, its elegant stalls and oversized tree dismantled.

Everything had returned to normal.

At 22:58 he left the station at the Bahnhofplatz exit and walked in the company of the masses across the nearby bridge, deciding against getting a taxi. As the crowd began to thin he changed direction, heading south towards the Rathaus quarter. He walked quickly, keeping mainly to the side streets that were deserted at that time of night. Every aspect of the route was familiar to him.

At 23:09 he walked through the rear entrance of a sparsely populated nightclub and on entry headed straight for the office of the manager, his visit seen only by the man he came to see. Even if one of the locals or employees noticed his arrival, nothing of their conversation was overheard.

At 23:12 he departed unseen through the same door and left the city in a three-year-old BMW.

The orders he had received were specific. His target was stationed in the City of St Gallen and if all went well he would catch him before he left the office. He had never met the man personally but all the details checked out, at least based on his background research. He had heard rumours of the man's importance, but he knew hearsay was susceptible to inaccuracy – particularly coming from the mouths of strangers. The important stuff he never left to chance.

His position at the Vatican gave him a position of rare insight.

At just after midnight he pulled up on the corner of a well-lit street, an unfamiliar location directed by the GPS. The street, buzzing with the activity of entrepreneurs, bankers and other corporate figures less than seven hours earlier, was deserted, the buildings eerily silent – disturbed only by the sound of distant cars. There was a chill in the air but at least it was no longer raining. The torrential downpour that had fallen ceaselessly all afternoon had been replaced by the gentle falling of snowflakes melting on impact as they hit the pavement. He didn't mind the snow; nor did he mind the waiting.

Along the street, all of the streetlamps were glowing brightly but the buildings were mainly deserted. A lone office light was shining through a third storey window on the opposite side of the road, some thirty feet from the car. Like most buildings on that street it was four storeys of grey stone, 18th century in origin and in need of redecorating. Like most it was a bank but unlike most at least one person was still working.

Through the darkened windscreen of his luxury motor the Swiss Guard focused on the lighted window. A solitary figure occupied the room – his features veiled by a lightly coloured blind, making him appear as a dark silhouette. Although he could not make out the man's facial features, his demeanour was clearly restless.

Al Leoni's office was the largest in the building. In keeping with the offices of all senior staff, it was ornately furnished with a fine collection of art covering four large walls that had been painted white less than two years earlier. Despite being located on the street side of the building it was surprisingly quiet, even at rush hour. The stone construction and double-glazed windows provided efficient insulation from the noise of the traffic, and being on the third floor provided stunning views across the city on a clear day. No one begrudged him the location.

As the chief executive of Leoni et Cie International Bank he was entitled to it.

Forty-two years in the business had established his reputation as one of greatness. When he entered the fray he had been unprepared. Back then, he had been twenty-two, still suffering the hangover of graduation and still in the shadow of his father. The bank was his father's and prior to that his father's and his father's before that, going back eight generations. Ascending to chief executive at the bank known then as Banque Leoni was like a prince ascending to the throne. For as long as his father lived he would remain in his shadow.

A decade in that shadow had taught him everything he needed to know. He had survived the eighties without meltdown and prospered in the nineties and noughties without aggravation. Across the business world he had become renowned as one of the industry's most careful and astute businessmen, earning him special respect in the eyes of industry officials and the media. His was one of a dying breed. He was the last stalwart on the St Gallen circuit.

Three decades of running the oldest bank in St Gallen had taught him how to deal with the pressure.

But today was different.

The bank was in crisis.

Gripping the telephone tightly in his right hand, Leoni shouted down the line at the unseen listener and breathed out deeply as he listened to the response. He'd been on the phone for over an hour, his tone permanently urgent. His stomach burned, a rough sickening feeling, accompanied by a tightening sensation across his chest. His second heart attack seven years ago had nearly proven fatal and the symptoms were not dissimilar. At sixty-five he was beginning to feel the pace, but retirement, not for the first time, would have to wait.

At 2:05 a.m. he replaced the receiver forcefully. Wiping his forehead with his sleeve, he picked up the seventy-page document on the desk, nudging the desk lamp with his elbow, causing shadows to appear across the blind. With shaking hands he shuffled the document between his fingers as he carried it hastily towards the fax machine, located in the corner of the room. He placed the document down on a nearby table and inserted the first sheet into the feeder tray, dialling the number from memory. The red light that had flickered continuously on the power bar changed to solid green, accompanied by the hum of the operating machine. Within seconds he inserted the second sheet.

He glanced at the clock above the window and grimaced. The document needed to be sent.

It needed to be sent tonight.

Behind the wheel of the stationary vehicle, the man from Rome waited. For over two and a half hours he watched silently, his attention focused on the one lighted window. At 2:47 a.m. he looked with interest as the light in the office extinguished. A surge of adrenaline tightened his skin, a familiar feeling that always occurred as he anticipated the task at hand. Under the watchful eyes of no one he loaded his SIG P75 and placed it inside his jacket.

*

Al Leoni nodded briefly at the security guard as he left the bank through one of two revolving doors and came to a halt on reaching the street. The warmth inside gave way to a brisk wintry wind that penetrated unpleasantly down his spine. In his preoccupied state he had been unaware that it had been snowing. Beneath him, the concrete was slippery, the pavement appearing darker than usual as snow melted on impact, adding to the abundant puddles formed from the earlier rain.

He felt discomfort but not just because of the cold. He was worried: a rare sense of anxiety that turned more and more to anger with every passing second.

He cursed himself for being so stupid.

The banker removed a cigar from his pocket and lit it, exhaling a mixture of smoke and his breath. The familiar sensation felt momentarily comforting, yet today that was his only comfort.

Tomorrow would be another busy day.

The Swiss Guard watched his target closely. Even in the darkness he could see the man clearly – the glow of Al Leoni's cigar illuminated him like a lighthouse to a ship. The banker's appearance was familiar to him: a bearded man, dressed in expensive attire befitting a corporate executive. The man walked briskly, feeling cold and noticeably agitated.

Timing was everything.

He opened the door quietly, careful to avoid making any sound as he vacated the car. As the banker disappeared from sight, he darted towards the nearby alley. With his back to the wall he exhaled slowly.

He had not been seen.

From a secluded position he watched the banker turn the corner, heading in the direction of the employee car park. The area was well lit at this time but deserted. Behind the wall, a ramp led to the second storey of the car park, the second of four including the ground level. Seconds later the banker disappeared from sight.

Slowly, the Swiss Guard approached the road and looked both ways, wary of being observed. He didn't look out of place. To a casual observer, he was like a thousand others from the St Gallen capital: just another citizen on his way home from a bar or nightclub in early morning Switzerland at the end of a long week. Nothing about him was conspicuous.

Nothing revealed his purpose.

He checked once more for signs of life before crossing the street undetected. He moved quickly, stopping before reaching the entrance.

Shaded behind the wall, he gazed carefully at the banker walking up the ramp with his back to the entrance.

Slowly he removed the weapon from his jacket.

Al Leoni continued through the car park, gripping his briefcase tightly. The air felt warmer now that he was sheltered from the wind, accompanied by the heat of his lighted cigar burning gently against his face. On reaching the top of the ramp he veered to his left. Up ahead, the orange glow of the nearest wall light revealed a new Jaguar occupying the only in use parking bay. He was the last to leave but that was not unusual. It was a routine that had shaped his entire career. If lucky, he would get back in time to sleep for three hours.

He shuffled his trouser pocket for his car keys, still distracted by his thoughts. He pointed the remote at the car and pressed the unlock button; a quick, bright flash radiated through the darkness accompanied by the sound of his car unlocking.

A second sound followed, this time coming from behind him.

He stopped. Footsteps that were not his own were moving in close proximity. He turned around instinctively and scanned the surroundings for signs of life. As far as he could tell the car park was deserted and silent except for the echo of dripping water down a nearby gutter. The orange glow of a barely working wall light lit up the ramped entrance, creating distorted shadows against the walls. He squinted. In his confused state he thought he saw movement.

A red light flickered before him, lasting less than a second.

Washington D.C.

The Chairman of the Federal Reserve was still in his office at 8 p.m. Unsurprisingly as chairman he was the last of the seven governors to leave and usually the first to arrive, often before seven-thirty.

Jermaine Llewellyn was the most important of the seven. As a registered Democrat, he was one of four from that party currently in office, and at sixty-nine years of age he was also the oldest.

When nominated to replace the former chairman, a Republican, many slated him for his pro-Friedman views on monetary policy, the opposite of his predecessor, and being the first black chairman his appointment was something of a landmark. Despite his credible reputation as a former tenured Professor of Microeconomics at Yale and having over five years experience among the governors, his appointment was met with opposition on both sides, including the other governors, and even after three years in office he still had enemies. In the past, many had slammed his decision to cut interest rates, but thanks to the support of the President he was now looking odds-on for re-election in the autumn.

Inside his office, Llewellyn was still at work. Standing near his desk, he wiped his forehead with the sleeve of his right arm and shuffled various papers in his hands. The telephone receiver clutched precariously between his left shoulder and head slipped slightly as he juggled the papers.

Seconds later, Llewellyn hung up the phone and turned away from his desk. The light on the fax machine started to flash and the sound of printing dominated the otherwise quiet office.

Within seconds the first sheet came through.

The sound of the incoming fax could be heard outside the office, despite the door being closed, eliminating any chance that the intruder would be heard. In an otherwise deserted hallway, the intruder tiptoed silently towards the office and paused before the door.

Slowly, he opened it. Through the smallest of openings, the intruder surveyed his surroundings. The soft glow of a 40-watt light bulb created shadows throughout the office that was relatively modern and not without ornamentation. In his limited vision, he saw a flat screen computer monitor dominating a large oak desk, the main feature of the room. The blinds on the main window were down, confirming no light could get in or out – even the sparse rays of moonlight from the cloudless night didn't penetrate.

He knew he could not be seen.

In the corner of the room, the Chairman of the Fed stood with his back to the door, his concentration solely on the incoming document.

Slowly the door inched open.

With his anxiety at peak intensity, Llewellyn picked up the first sheet and scanned the information with intent. The news he had received from the banker in Switzerland only seconds earlier had not sunk in over the phone, but now it struck him clear as day. The content of the document was disturbing.

This changed everything.

The fifth sheet came, then the sixth. There would be seventy in total.

Engrossed in his awkward wait, he didn't detect the red laser pointing at the back of his head.

Blood covered the bulb.

With the intended recipient lying dead on the floor, the intruder removed his gloves and picked up the newest sheet of the incoming document. The final threat had been eliminated.

What needed to be done was done.

1

Rome, five days later

The young man paused, taking a moment to scan the ancient Ponte Sant'Angelo in front of him. The bridge, usually heaving with Romans, tourists, and lined with street vendors, was deserted, its ornate features hidden by early morning mist rising from the Tiber.

Directly in front of him, the Castel Sant'Angelo stood prevalently, its thick fortified walls looming up out of the grey air. Through the mist, he could just make out the silhouette of the famous bronze angel atop the summit, its sword held aloft and its sightless eyes fixed on the bridge.

This was hardly the ideal place to hold a meeting. It was no longer snowing, but the arctic wind that had tormented the city for the past few days showed no signs of relenting. Thick black clouds had given way to dull stratus interrupted by the vaguest hint of early morning sunshine distorted by the mist.

The young man tightened the zipper on his coat as he walked, his eyes focusing on his feet. Thin layers of snow had developed into a dangerous black slush, a combination of melting snow and the sub-zero temperature, causing a soft crunching sound as he trod over breaking ice. For now that was the only sound. Several feet beneath him the River Tiber flowed slowly, almost silently, surprisingly silently, intensifying his apprehension.

To most observers he was just like any other person in the city. He was tall, standing at just over six feet, dark brown hair, a handsome clean-shaven face and piercing blue eyes. The black shoes and dark trousers gave the impression of formality, while the black jacket and woolly hat suggested an American look. Nothing about him suggested he was a policeman. Nor did anything suggest that he was one of one hundred and thirty members of the *Corpo della Gendarmeria dello Stato della Città del Vaticano*, the police force of the Vatican City, who as of ninety-six hours ago was investigating a murder on behalf of arguably the most important organisation in Christendom.

The young man continued across the bridge, making a mental note of every angel that lined it. The statues were unnerving, their appearances almost ghostlike behind the mist. He stopped momentarily before the Angel with the Throne, and again briefly at the Angel clutching the Crown of Thorns, examining their inscriptions for confirmation of his location. He continued towards the middle of the bridge, stopping once more as he approached the Angel holding a Garment and Dice with its outstretched arms. For several seconds he waited. He could hear the sound of footsteps on slushy ice.

Seconds later a man appeared in front of him.

"Thank you for agreeing to see me, Agent Mäder," a polite well-spoken voice said. "I hope the location does not inconvenience you."

Mäder paused, taking a second to examine the noble features of the man standing before him. Despite the heavy clothing he recognised him immediately.

"That's quite all right, Monsieur Devére," he said. "Although if you prefer we can always go somewhere warmer."

Devére let out a sound, not quite a laugh but not unfriendly either. "I am sorry about the cold," he said quietly. "But I think it best we meet in a location that is unsuspecting. The city has many eyes and ears."

Devére looked over his shoulder, seemingly concentrating on the nearest angel, its lifeless head looking out towards the east. Mäder waited, seeing if the man was going to continue. This was not the first time the pair had met. Before his retirement, Mikael Devére had famously served for over twelve years as President of France, and before that six as prime minister. As a Catholic, the politician had enjoyed close friendships with the Popes.

Markus Mäder, or Mark as he was better known, had been a Vatican Policeman for almost four years. His job was Vatican security, including visits from key national figureheads. For nearly three and a half years the two men had known and respected one another, a by-product of Devére's frequent visits to the Vatican.

Nevertheless, it was with some surprise that the former President of France had called him less than eight hours earlier to request a private meeting at 6:30 a.m. on the Ponte Sant'Angelo.

"It must be a very busy time at the Vatican," Devére said; "I remember the last time the Church faced a crisis of this magnitude."

Mäder did not respond immediately. He shuffled his jacket uncomfortably, attempting to keep out the cold.

"Presumably you didn't invite me here for a history lesson?"

Devére sighed, his breath visible. "I have urgent information regarding your investigation into the death of Monsieur Leoni. It is vital it finds its way to the ears of your superior."

Mark's heart missed a beat. This was hardly what he expected.

"What kind of information?"

"The circumstances behind the killing of Monsieur Leoni might still be a mystery to you, Monsieur Mäder, but when viewed in the cold light of day it is no coincidence that Messieurs Leoni et Llewellyn were killed so quickly. Should the truth become known the effect would be devastating. The media reaction alone would cause unprecedented panic."

Mark eyed him curiously. "I'm sorry, I don't understand."

"When a policeman investigates murder there are always two sets of circumstances, monsieur: those on the surface, and those that are planted deeper. To the wider world, what happened to Messieurs Leoni et Llewellyn may seem obvious on the surface: when a man is discovered dead with a bullet in his body, it is only natural to accept that he was shot. But they are not the only men connected to the Vatican whose bodies have recently shown up in a mortuary. Only others display less visible symptoms."

Devére paused briefly.

"I understand you were personally responsible for investigating the passing of your Major von Sonnerberg."

Mark's facial features remained unflinching. "Yes that's right." Secretly he wanted to ask how he knew, but he chose against it.

"And what of Cardinal Faukes? His death was investigated thoroughly?"

Mark cleared his throat, his jaw tightening as he breathed. He glanced to both sides; the normally visible St Peter's Basilica lay veiled behind the wintry mist.

"Cardinal Faukes died in his sleep two months ago. He was seventy-eight years old, and had been in ill health."

Devére smiled humourlessly. "That may be so, Agent Mäder, after all such events are not uncommon. But I am afraid it might be more serious than you realise."

The Frenchman opened his coat and removed a large white envelope from an inside pocket. He offered the package to Mark, who collected it with an outstretched hand. With raw fingers, he opened the seal and examined the contents with alert eyes. There were seven sheets of paper enclosed: each one included minimal writing and a bizarre logo at the top right corner. Every page included one name, and seven official stampings.

Mäder looked at Devére after examining the first two. The names Cardinal Faukes and Major von Sonnerberg were the standout features.

"The Rite of Larmenius?" Mark said, recognising the society's logo in the top right corner. "Why would the Rite of Larmenius have intelligence files on a Swiss Guard and a Vatican cardinal?"

"Agent Mäder, you misunderstand. These are no ordinary intelligence files. Monsieur, these are death warrants."

Mark's eyes widened, the seriousness of the comments registering immediately. He scanned the remaining sheets. The names Al Leoni and Jermaine Llewellyn were also present, as were two others he did not know and one other he did.

"Sadly there are many influential figures who would prefer the circumstances of their deaths to remain secret."

Mark focused on the names he did not know. "Who are Martin Snow and Nathan Walls?"

"Monsieur Walls was an American accountant found shot in his office, a gun by his chair and a suicide note on the desk." The Frenchman smiled wryly. "I am sure you will find it particularly odd that the note was computer typed."

"Takes care of the problem of handwriting."

"Monsieur Snow was found dead in his compartment on a train to Chicago. He had been dead for over eight hours – a heart attack according to the official accounts. As far as I am aware no suspicious circumstances were reported. Exhumation, of course, would be out of the question."

Mark nodded, his eyes continuing to examine the sheets of paper in his hands. He focused on the logo.

"Why would the Rite of Larmenius order the deaths of these men?" the policeman asked, aware of Devére's connections with the society. "I assume you know who's responsible?"

"It would be unwise to jump to any rash conclusions, monsieur. The Rite of Larmenius is unlike any organisation in existence. No two members are alike. Most of its members probably do not even know one another, and would be appalled if they ever learned what you have learned. But sadly some of its senior masters seem to favour personal gain over honesty and integrity," he paused. "I am sure you are now aware, Agent Mäder, of my reasons for not wanting to draw attention to this meeting."

Mark nodded emotionlessly. After several seconds of silence he broke eye contact, examining both entrances to the bridge, ensuring that they were still alone.

"I assure you, Monsieur Devére, I have told no one of this meeting."

Devére offered a vague smile. "But still, it is only a matter of time before certain people become aware of what I have done. Their influence spans far and wide."

"Monsieur, even if what you fear is true, I fail to believe that they would dare hurt the former President of France. For starters they'd have to get past your bodyguards."

Devére laughed, again without humour. "Believe me, monsieur, they are capable of much and have done far worse. And as you are now aware, their methods are rarely obvious. The Rite of Larmenius has many fine qualities – and none more so than discretion. An ordinary policeman will never find individual culprits on surface evidence alone; its members are far too clever for that. Scapegoats are found, cover-ups are made, and important questions are dissuaded from being asked." Devére shook his head. "But I will not stand by while faceless men use its good name to carry out such villainy. I can help you identify the killers, but it is those who give the orders who are the real murderers. And proving their guilt, monsieur, cannot happen overnight."

"If you can help provide evidence of their guilt then the Vatican can protect you. There is no security in the world better than that which guards the Pope."

Devére smiled gratefully, shaking his head at the same time. "Maybe. But first we must be sure what we are dealing with. You must find out for sure, Agent Mäder, that Messieurs Faukes, von Sonnerberg and Snow were murdered. Only then will this be confirmed," he said, tapping the envelope in Mark's hand. "Or at least satisfy my fears that they were not."

Devére turned away, walking slowly in the direction of the castel.

"But also give thought to this, Agent Mäder," he said pausing. "What is your greater duty as a policeman? Solving crimes that have already been committed? Or preventing ones that are still to occur?"

Mark nodded, immediately aware what he meant. Of the seven death warrants present in his hand, only six he knew to be dead.

2

Vatican City

The Vatican City is a landlocked sovereign city-state located within the Italian capital of Rome and has a population of fewer than 900 citizens. Since 1377 the Vicars of Christ have resided almost continually within this walled enclave whose origins date back to the life of St Peter.

According to the Gospel of Matthew, it was Peter who was chosen as the first Vicar of Christ after being handed the keys to the Kingdom of Heaven in recognition for his faith. Catholic doctrine holds that the passing of the keys marks the first moment of Apostolic succession, which continues uninterrupted to this day and provides one of four undeniable Marks that define the Catholic Church as the one true church of the Son of God. Tradition states that the original church was built around the tomb of the first Pope that in time led to the formation of the current basilica: a physical representation of Christ's promise that "upon this rock I shall build my Church".

Of the millions of tourists who visit the Vatican every year, few are aware that the modern Vatican City is all that remains of the longstanding Papal States which once covered the Italian regions of Lazio, Umbria, Marche and parts of eastern Emilia-Romagna that lasted from the 8th century until the invasion of Napoleon I. Despite its revival in the following years, the rise of Italian nationalism and the culmination of the Franco-Prussian War saw the Papal States fall to a unified Italy, leaving the Vatican City as the only remaining territorial power of the Church, officially recorded as the world's smallest nation both in population and size.

In a bedroom inside the Vatican City, Swiss Guard Mikael Frei awoke from a dreamless sleep. From the east side of the room the morning sun caused an unpleasant burning sensation on his face as it pierced through the gap in his curtains. In a dazed state, he untangled the sweat-soaked covers from around his feet and pulled them over his unguarded face, blocking out the sunlight. With his vision once more in darkness, thoughts returned to sleep.

Yet something was still disturbing him. Somewhere in the room he could hear a strange ringing. It was a familiar sound: it was distant yet somehow quite near. Now awake, the Swiss Guard pulled away the covers and squinted at his surroundings.

The telephone on the bedside table was ringing.

Slowly, the Swiss Guard rolled over. He rubbed his eyes and blinked incessantly. The bedside clock confirmed it was after ten but to Frei the hour was still early after a night on duty. He did not expect contact today.

After the fourth ring he picked up the receiver.

"*Allo?*"

"Wachtmeister Frei," a man replied with a voice of authority.

Dazed only seconds earlier, the soldier's mindset suddenly changed to one of alertness. He recognised the voice of his commander on the other end of the line.

The Swiss Guard sat up in his bed. "Yes, sir."

"I apologise for calling you off duty. I need to speak with you most urgently."

The soldier paused. His mouth felt dry and his skin sticky from the sweaty sheets.

The voice spoke crisply. "My office. Ten minutes."

The voice gave way to the dialling tone, accompanied by vague ringing noise as his ears adjusted to the silence. Replacing the phone, he adjusted the sheets and sat up on the side of the bed.

In the last year this hadn't been a complete rarity. During his first six years in service, Mikael Frei had never been asked to open a door let alone be approached for matters of importance. General audiences and official visits had come and gone with the twenty-nine-year-old providing little more than a ceremonial role in the proceedings. But that all changed when he was promoted to wachtmeister, the Swiss equivalent of sergeant. His excellent abilities as a sharpshooter, and his dedication to the martial art of kung fu eventually led to frequent duties alongside the other sergeants guarding key officials, including the Pope.

Yawning, he looked around the room, taking in the sights. It was a familiar room, its furnishings offering a reminder of both his present vocation and his American upbringing. A large certificate was mounted on the wall, signifying his Bachelor of Science from the Annapolis Naval Academy. Several photographs from his time at Annapolis also lined the wall, mostly of his friends, graduation or dressed in full battle gear playing cornerback for the Goats.

Lining the next wall were pictures of his family, accompanied by some of him in service, alongside the other guards. He gazed with interest at the most recent, an official photograph, taken by the Pope's official photographer. Located in a large frame, he was walking across St Peter's Square with four other sergeants, talking with the President and Vice President of the USA as they arrived on their recent visit.

He yawned again, this time deeper than before. He looked once more at the clock on his bedside table and saw two minutes had already passed. His skin felt sticky, but the shower would have to wait.

He knew he could not be late.

The barracks of the Swiss Guard lie in close proximity to the Tower of Nicholas V and the Finestra del Santo Padre at the north of St Peter's Square. It was Pope Sixtus IV who approved barracks for the guards in the 15th century prior to the decision by Pope Julius II in 1506 to recruit mercenaries from Switzerland to aid the Vatican as a token of appreciation for the valour shown by Swiss mercenaries who had once saved his life in battle. The building that survives from that time offers residence for all 110 guards, the entire military force for the Vatican and celebrated as the oldest military unit in the world.

Frei left the barracks immediately. Despite the sunlight it was bitterly cold outside and the faintest falling of snow settled picturesquely on the ground and melted on impact on his uniform. It was not the traditional uniform. Instead he was dressed in the regular uniform: a blue version of the famous Medici tri-colour gala, which still provided the image of a soldier. A dark blue cape took the edge off the wind and a traditional black beret covered his short dark hair.

Even without the uniform he looked like a soldier. Standing just over five feet ten inches in height, with bright blue eyes, clean-cut dark hair and a near clean-shaven face, Mike Frei was a soldier in every sense of the word. Although not good-looking in the sense of being a pretty boy, a deep strong voice and well toned muscles from regular gym work provided the look of authority while an approachable smile made him a regular target for tourists craving a photograph of a uniformed guard. At the height of the tourist season he was used to having flocks of pilgrims gather around him and his colleagues requesting a keepsake of themselves standing next to a guard dressed in Medici uniform. On the more relaxed days it was flattering.

But today was not about ceremony. He walked rigidly, his mind focused on the imminent meeting.

He checked his watch.

*

Eight minutes after hanging up the phone, he stopped before the door leading to his commander's office. He walked the last corridor quickly before easing his pace. The various markings that surrounded the door seemed to provide a guarantee of privacy.

He sought to knock but hesitated. Even outside he could sense an atmosphere in the room. The muffled sound of a harsh, broken voice barking incessantly at a person or persons unknown was audible from outside and instantly recognisable as the voice of his commander. There was another person in the room, yet at present it was unclear who this was.

A sudden knotting sensation was forming in the pit of his stomach. He was unaware what the meeting was about, but even standing outside the door it was obvious that this was no ordinary situation. He considered knocking but decided to wait; hoping the sound of the voice would stop. He checked his watch. The time was now 10:39. Still only nine minutes had passed.

At least he wasn't late.

Taking a deep breath, he waited till exactly ten minutes had passed and knocked three times on the door. They were not loud knocks but in the deserted corridor the sound of his knuckles on the door seemed to travel, adding to the apprehension. He waited for what seemed like several seconds for a response.

The sound of heated discussion gave way to silence.

"Come."

The Swiss Guard breathed out heavily as he opened the door. He entered the room slowly, respectfully, allowing himself time to take in the new surroundings. The flag of the Swiss Guard, hanging like a glorified banner, decorated the nearest wall that was bathed in sunlight penetrating through a large window behind his commander's desk.

Thierry de Courten was standing behind his desk when Mike entered. As usual, he was dressed smartly in the uniform designated only to the commander of the Swiss Guard. Three gold stars signified the rank of colonel, or oberst, the highest rank in the Swiss Guard. He was nearing six feet two inches in height with short dark hair and green eyes. A well-trimmed beard covered a strong jaw line and continued down his neck. He was clearly a strong man with an imposing presence, something that the Swiss Guard had once found intimidating.

The other man Mike also recognised. Dressed in a smart suit, Commissario Pessotto, Inspector General of the Vatican Police, smiled grimly. His dark hair was slightly unkempt, unusually for him, and his face unshaven, indicating to Mike that he had not slept that night.

Mike closed the door to the office and exchanged salutes with both men. The oberst forced a grateful smile.

"Thank you for meeting us here, wachtmeister," the oberst said, his smile fading. "I appreciate you are on leave today."

"Yes, sir," Mike answered, feeling incapable of saying anything more. In reality he assumed he didn't have much say in the matter. Since his promotion he had become quite familiar with the oberst but it was difficult to be friends with a man in that position. For over seven and a half years he had known only this man as head of the Swiss Guard, yet today he noticed something different.

Purple bags were gathering under his eyes.

The oberst placed two paracetamol tablets to his lips and swallowed them down with mineral water. The throbbing sensation that had lasted all morning continued to burn through his head. A near empty bottle of water was present on his desk, sitting next to a large grey folder concealing what Mike assumed to be military files or something just as important.

Commissario Pessotto eyed the Swiss Guard with purpose. "Now, Frei," Pessotto said slowly, gesturing for Mike to sit down. "Does the name Al Leoni mean anything to you?"

Mike sat down opposite the oberst and removed his beret, passing it through his fingers as if it were a tea towel. In all honesty it didn't.

"Very well. How about Leoni et Cie?"

The Swiss Guard looked back blankly. "Only that it's a Swiss bank."

Thierry nodded. "Let me explain, wachtmeister . . ."

"Leoni et Cie is one of the most profitable banks in Switzerland," Pessotto said, interrupting. "Not only that but it is one of many in which the Vatican Bank owns a considerable stake. Al Leoni is . . . or was, I should say, the bank's chief executive."

Mike nodded, his eyes focused on the chief of Vatican Police. He was vaguely aware of the bank's connections with the Vatican, but he had never been privy to specific details. He waited until he was sure that Pessotto had finished before replying.

"But not anymore?" Mike asked

Pessotto eyed Mike curiously. "No. Mr Leoni was found dead in St Gallen in the early hours of Friday morning. His body was found in a car park, fifteen yards from his car and within three hundred yards of Leoni et Cie's main office. He had been shot in the forehead, estimates range from forty to forty-five yards. His car was unlocked, the key still in his hand. His briefcase was also found at the scene – empty."

Mike nodded, his expression serious. He didn't need telling that a bullet to the forehead from that distance indicated a professional job. His first instinct was to ask what this had to do with him. For now he decided against it.

"The exact circumstances behind his death are presently unknown," Pessotto continued, walking closer to him as he spoke. "The matter is already under investigation but unfortunately there are complications."

Mike raised an eyebrow. What did he mean: complications?

"I don't understand."

The oberst shook his head. On his desk a walkie-talkie buzzed into life, providing him with his usual updates. A pause followed before the oberst returned a message.

Mike eyed him curiously. It seemed strange that the Swiss Guard would be interested in this man's death. Officially the military of the Vatican only existed to guard the Pope, including security of the Apostolic Palace and the gates of the Vatican City.

Pessotto: "Leoni et Cie is particularly important to the Vatican Bank, and also to the Vatican. The Roman Curia also has funds invested in Leoni et Cie. For over two hundred years the family have donated significantly to the Church and to the Holy See. Eventually the bank will need to appoint a new chief executive but the process is not a straightforward one. In the past the role would fall to his eldest son. Until a replacement is found, the bank will legally be in the hands of Mr Leoni's next of kin who remain the largest shareholders, followed by the Vatican Bank. His wife divorced him over five years ago. His holdings in Leoni et Cie will fall to his daughter."

Pessotto paused briefly.

"As I'm sure you will appreciate, she is currently in a state of shock. After all, it is not everyday your father gets shot."

Mike nodded. In reality he knew that he could not possibly imagine. He wasn't very close to his father, particularly since his parents had divorced.

Silently he wondered how anyone could understand.

"What's more, we have another matter to consider," Pessotto said. "Al Leoni was also the nephew of Cardinal Tepilo."

The revelation surprised him. He knew the man well, everyone did. The cardinal had served for over five years as Cardinal Secretary of State, effectively Prime Minister of the Vatican. In the eyes of many, he was almost certainly the man who was to be the next Pope.

"Well, Frei, as I'm sure you are aware, this puts us in a tricky situation," Pessotto continued. "Until further arrangements are made it is vital that the safety of the rightful owner of Leoni et Cie is assured. Now, highly irregular I know . . ."

"It transcends the purpose of our entire organisation," de Courten interjected.

Pessotto looked briefly at Thierry. "The oversight commission of the Vatican Bank are most concerned," Pessotto said, resuming eye contact with Mike. "Mr Leoni's death has caused quite a stir among certain elements of the Roman Curia. The Camerlengo is understandably heartbroken. Until the identity of Leoni's killer becomes known, they have requested that a guard be assigned to ensure that nothing of this kind happens to his daughter. I'm sure you will agree: a short-term solution is necessary." Pessotto turned to the oberst as he spoke.

Mike's expression was rigid. He didn't need telling that he meant him. "Wouldn't an ordinary bodyguard be more appropriate?"

"Ordinarily, yes," Pessotto agreed. "However, this is, shall we say, complicated."

Mike remained silent, his facial features unflinching. It was clear to him that there was more to this than met the eye. Whatever it was, he assumed they were not going to tell him.

Pessotto: "The family are currently residing in their château in the Canton of St Gallen. You are from St Gallen, yes?"

"I was born there, sir."

"You know the area well?"

"I visited my gran most summers when I was a kid."

"And you also hold American citizenship, allowing you to perform duties in America if the situation requires."

Mike hid his frustration with a calm façade. "May I ask what exactly these duties would involve, sir? Are you asking me to work as an employee of the bank or are you asking me to be a babysitter?"

The comment made Thierry smile.

Pessotto allowed himself a vague grin. "What you must understand, Frei, is that Leoni's ex-wife is a fifty-four-year-old woman who knows nothing of running a bank. His brother, an academic I understand, lives primarily in America. His daughter is now the official owner of the bank. In the past, Leoni et Cie was simply family owned: it had been that way for over two centuries."

Mike nodded. He knew the way Swiss banks were modelled. "Is she experienced?"

"Unfortunately no. These days she's more of a socialite than anything else."

Mike hid his surprise. "And she's running a major Swiss bank?"

"As I say, wachtmeister, she is the majority shareholder. The activities of the bank itself are taken care of by professionals, experienced professionals. In theory, she is little more than a figurehead. Both the supervisory councils of the Vatican Bank will meet with the senior directors of Leoni et Cie and in due course permanent changes will be made. Until that time, we have a problem."

Mike nodded, his teeth pressing gently against his lower lip. Silently he struggled to digest the information. He looked at the oberst, watching his expression. The commander stood quietly, a rare sight, clearly nursing a throbbing headache. He paid particular attention to the dark patches under his eyes, also a rarity. The situation had clearly made him lose sleep.

"Sir, if this is what the Swiss Guard asks of me . . ."

"Yes we do," Pessotto replied, beating Thierry to a response.

Thierry's expression was philosophical. "You will be given a short period of leave from your regular duties. During that time you will no longer be officially a Swiss Guard, although you will still be paid on the same terms, of course. Plus expenses," Thierry said dryly. "The funeral is scheduled for Friday. You will meet her on Thursday evening at her château. I shall be going, along with members of the Vatican Police. At least half a dozen cardinals will be present, including the Camerlengo. From then on you shall take over responsibility of guarding her."

Mike nodded. For the briefest of moments he looked through the window at the pale sky. Despite the sunlight, the snow was falling more heavily than before. It was hardly the best news he could have hoped for. If he wanted to babysit an only rich child he could have made far more money as a bodyguard.

He looked at his commander. Under the circumstances he felt strangely sorry for him.

"I'll guard her as if she was the Pope."

3

St Peter's Basilica was closed by 6 p.m. The site that had earlier welcomed countless pilgrims and sightseers captivated by its famous artefacts and architecture was practically deserted. A small gathering of nuns walked slowly in the direction of the stairwell near the centre of the church that led down to the grotto, their footfalls and quiet chatter echoing softly throughout the immense surroundings. Outside the main doors, two security guards stood rigidly at attention, watching as the last flurry of visitors ambled leisurely across the square, discussing their surroundings and taking photographs of the illuminated basilica against the darkening sky.

Five pews from the main altar an ageing cardinal knelt quietly at prayer, the only occupant. Purple bags were present under his eyes and a worried expression crossed his face. He looked at the watch on his left wrist and then once quickly over his shoulder. Light footsteps belonging to the nuns descending the stairs gave way to quietness disturbed only by the vague echo of singing from one of the distant chapels. There was a beautiful sense of harmony about the building that despite the troubling recent events that dominated his mind he found of great comfort.

Of all the Vatican buildings it was the one place where he could find tranquillity, if only momentarily.

Cardinal George Utaka of Niger was one of the most important cardinals at the Vatican. Formerly Bishop of Toulouse in France, the man currently held the title of President of the Administration of the Patrimony of the Apostolic See: an organisation located within the Roman Curia, formed in 1967, responsible for dealing with properties of the Holy See and providing funds for the Curia to operate. Officially, the office was made up of two sections, one formed to manage the properties of the Holy See following the loss of the Papal States, the other for the funds awarded by the Italian government under the terms of the Lateran Treaty of 1929. Although separate from the Vatican Bank, Utaka was one of five cardinals currently sitting on the oversight commission of the Vatican Bank.

Prior to a week ago he had never seen such chaos. Over seven years on the oversight commission had taught him the extremes of being involved with the Vatican's most controversial asset, but until now the role had been plain sailing. The bank had changed since the P2 scandal, and thanks to the commitment of his predecessors, so had its image. Two decades of worldwide stability had provided the springboard for controlled long-term growth and the capabilities of those on the board had ensured control remained firmly in the hands of insiders. The clean up operation was in many ways still a work in progress, but at least being part of the current administration he was never likely to face the same difficulties.

Or at least he would have thought so two days ago.

His thoughts were disturbed by the sound of footsteps. Dressed in a black suit, rather than the uniform of the Vatican police, Markus Mäder walked confidently. He continued along the centre aisle and stopped on reaching the cardinal's pew. He genuflected before the main altar and took a seat next to the cardinal.

At first the cardinal didn't acknowledge his presence. Instead, he maintained the illusion of being at prayer. Several seconds of awkward silence passed. In the immense surroundings, the silence seemed strangely loud in nature to the American-raised policeman as he waited for any sign of acknowledgement. He could feel his pulse beating quickly, a rare sign of nerves, and his throat dry from a combination of fatigue and several hours without refreshment.

The day had been anything but straightforward.

The cardinal made the sign of the cross and ascended slowly to the seat. He moved closer to Mark but remained silent. For several seconds the Vatican policeman watched.

After what seemed like an eternity, Mark broke the silence.

"Eminence, I have received word from my contacts in Prague and New York," he paused before completing the sentence, "I'm afraid it is as we feared."

For several seconds he remained still.

"Ah," the cardinal said softly. He bowed his head into his hands and closed his eyes.

Mark had seen the noble face of Cardinal Utaka many times before, but never had he seen him look so stressed. The grey streaks in his beard seemed almost to have whitened in recent days.

The cardinal removed his gold-framed lenses and rubbed his tired eyes with his right hand. His hand trembled slightly.

"We must assume the worst case scenario."

"Eminence, Mr Devére was clearly not of sound mind. There may be other possibilities."

The cardinal shook his head despondently, replacing his glasses. "No. It is certain. This is serious: a warning to the Vatican."

Mark's expression was equally serious. "Eminence, I have spoken with my colleagues in the Vatican Police, the St Gallen Feds and even the FBI in America and as yet none have been unable to find any leads or connection to the other three. The deaths of Walls and Snow have both been written off as suicide and heart attack. An autopsy for Martin Snow at this stage is out of the question."

Cardinal Utaka nodded philosophically.

Mark watched the cardinal closely. Eight years of experience told him no man gave more to the Christian cause than the cardinal. He remembered hearing a rumour that a beggar once asked him for alms in Southern India. The cardinal, remembering the story of Francis of Assisi, emptied his pockets and gave the beggar everything, including his handkerchief. It was no surprise this was the man silently dubbed second favourite to succeed the pontiff, whenever that should be.

Behind them, the sound of footsteps echoed once more. Cardinal Utaka looked over his shoulder.

Oberst de Courten was walking towards them.

Thierry continued to within five paces of the pew and waited for both men to stand. Mark stood to attention and saluted, his gesture returned by the oberst. Slowly the cardinal ascended to his feet.

"I hope you have a plan, oberst," the cardinal said. "It is your job."

Thierry lowered his salute. "My job is to protect the Apostolic Palace, eminence."

"Do not be naïve, de Courten; you did not get those three gold stars by being naïve. When you protect the Pope you protect the entire Vatican. Do I really need to remind you?"

The cardinal eyed both men closely.

"We must fear the worst and hope for better."

"We still do not know all of the circumstances," Mark said. "Walls, I understand, was in a lot of debt. Leoni might have been mugged."

"A couple of days ago I would have probably agreed with you," the oberst said grimly. "But now things have changed. Commissario Pessotto gave me this. Received from Washington D.C. not one hour ago."

Thierry passed a faxed document to Mark and then to Cardinal Utaka. The cardinal's facial expression became one of confusion.

"It appears that Jermaine Llewellyn received a fax of some

description around the time he was killed. The source of the document was the Leoni et Cie headquarters in St Gallen."

"Of what nature?" Utaka asked quickly.

Thierry's expression remained neutral. "I'm afraid its contents are still to be found."

Mark looked seriously at Thierry. "Leoni's briefcase was empty when his body was found."

An awkward silence lasted several seconds.

Utaka shook his head. "Why would Leoni and Llewellyn be killed at the same time?" he asked rhetorically.

Thierry shook his head.

"We cannot ignore this any longer," the cardinal said. "The evidence is indisputable."

"But this makes no sense," Mark said. "The Rite of Larmenius have not carried out anything of this kind for three decades. Why would they start now? As far as we know none of the victims have links with them? Nor do any of the society's present members survive from the last time."

Utaka looked seriously at Thierry. "What do we know? What have you been told?"

"We have been told only what we have been shown," Thierry said. "Six dead – no connection."

Utaka shook his head. "If we are not careful this could destroy everything we have worked so hard to create." He pointed his finger at Thierry. "That girl's a sitting duck."

"I have already taken precautions there," the oberst replied. "Come Friday, daughter, mother so long as she is there, and uncle, should he return, will be put under the care of Wachtmeister Frei."

"Oh Mike," Mark said without excitement.

"Is he able?" the cardinal asked.

"Mike is an excellent soldier, eminence," Mark said. "We've been friends since we were four; I used to share a room in barracks with him when I was a halberdier. He's loyal, strong, a great marksman . . ."

"And most importantly he will be stationed in St Gallen. It's his home canton," Thierry said, echoing Commissario Pessotto's earlier words. "The man has been trusted to guard His Holiness himself. He shall accompany us to St Gallen. I have instructed him to watch over Ms Leoni until we know the facts behind the killings. Who knows, perhaps when he returns he might be able to shed some light on things."

"On your head be it," the cardinal said, pointing his trembling finger.

The three men separated, making their way along the main aisle heading towards the stairs that lead down to the grotto. Kneeling near the high altar under Bernini's Baldacchino, nobody paid any attention to the hooded man, who was listening to their every word.

It was no longer snowing in Rome but the temperature was still bitter. The evening air appeared motionless; the blanket of steady cloud that had engulfed the sky above the city for the past three days was at last beginning to disperse. A stunning full moon shone brightly against oceans of black sky, its glow hindered intermittently by occasional passing cloud.

On the streets below, hordes of people walked quickly, wrapped up in thick clothes, heading towards the metro or one of the city's many bars or restaurants. In the heart of the city, the Trevi Fountain, the site that would be swarming with tourists in summertime, soaking up the atmosphere drinking glasses of red wine or sitting relaxing on its famous steps, whiling away the time watching water trickle among its famous statues, was practically deserted, its elegant façade coated in a thin layer of ice.

At just after eight-fifteen, Mikael Frei walked past the Trevi Fountain and entered a restaurant, located just off the square. The warmth of the central heating hit him instantly as he entered from the cold. The interior was finely furnished, comprising several two-, four- and six-seater tables lined with white tablecloths, most of which were in use. A long bar was located immediately to the right offering lagers on tap while various bottles of wine, spirits and other drinks occupied the fridges or hung from the wall behind the counter.

The Swiss Guard stopped before continuing towards a four-seater table some twenty feet from the entrance. Two seats were already taken. Both occupants were men, both he recognised. The more relaxed of the two smiled at him.

"Hey, Mikey, what's happening, baby?" He removed his left foot from the nearest seat.

"Sandro," Mike said shaking hands with his friend.

Alessandro Vogel was one of the youngest members of the Vatican Police. Aged twenty-seven, he had joined the corps two years earlier after serving in the Italian Police and before that the NYPD. As an American born of an Italian father and an American-Swiss mother, he was technically acceptable for membership in the Swiss Guard or the Vatican Police and he had the looks, the wit and the accent to prove it. To an outsider, he was a typical native of Manhattan.

Everyone loved him from the start.

The second man sat opposite Alessandro. He had a shaven head, unlike his face that showed stubble, and large biceps reminiscent of an Olympic discus thrower. Stan, or Johann Studer, as he was christened, was over nine years older than Mike and had served both the Swiss Army and the Swiss Guard off and on for over twenty years. The man held the rank of hauptmann, the equivalent of a captain, making him the fifth most senior member of the Swiss Guard. Following the sudden death of Major Pius von Sonnerberg in Prague, he was looking likely to be promoted.

"How's it going, buddy?" Alessandro asked.

"I'm okay," Mike said taking a seat next to him and removing his black woolly hat. A waiter passed almost immediately, offering the Swiss Guard a menu. A large bottle of Chianti was already present in the middle of the table, surrounded by four glasses, two of which were half full.

Stan picked up the bottle. "What's this I hear about you meeting with the oberst?" He poured wine into an empty glass and pushed it across the table to Mike.

"I thought that guy only went on dates with cardinals."

Mike grinned at Alessandro. "He wants me to go on vacation."

"Vacation? I'm going on one myself next Wednesday," Stan said.

"It's not one of them," Mike said, putting his hands through his short hair. He looked briefly over his shoulder. The sound of IL DIVO was playing through the speakers, loud enough to drown out the general level of conversation from the various tables and eliminating their chances of being overheard. "They want me to protect a banker's daughter in St Gallen."

"Oh," Stan said, looking slightly surprised. "It's one of them."

"Stan's going on one of them this Thursday."

Mike looked at Stan. "You're going too?"

"The Leoni funeral? Yes. Several foreign diplomats will be present, paying their respects. Cardinal Tepilo will be there, of course. Half the Vatican seem to be going."

Mike nodded, digesting the information seriously. "Who are these guys?"

"Leoni et Cie?"

"Yeah."

Stan shrugged. "Guys in suits, guys with money."

"Guys married to red hot mamas who spend all their hard earned cash while dreaming of running off with a gorgeous Swiss Guard," Alessandro said.

Mike smiled.

Stan laughed. "I never had you down as a babysitter, Frei."

"It didn't feel as though I had a choice in the matter."

Stan sought to reply but stopped. The waiter returned, placing a selection of breadsticks, bruschetta and cold meats on the table.

"*Grazie.*"

The waiter smiled and turned immediately. Stan picked up a breadstick and started eating. "You'll like his daughter," he said, checking that the waiter had definitely left. "I hear it on good authority she's a right little party animal."

Mike looked up, his mouth displaying a vague hint of a grin.

"Oh yeah," Stan continued. The breadstick crunched loudly as he chewed. "Spoilt little bitch I heard. Her daddy was worth zillions. And it's all hers."

"God bless Switzerland," Sandro said.

"So who is she?" Mike asked, picking up some bruschetta. "Commissario Pessotto said she's more a socialite than a banker."

Stan nodded. "Like I said she's a party animal. She thinks she knows it all. She's very posh. Loves her art . . ."

"Oh nice."

"Very, very posh," Stan said putting on a humorous accent that made Mike and Sandro laugh. "Apartments in Manhattan, Paris, Madrid, London, a mansion in Boston, and a château in St Gallen; dinners with the English Queen, that kinda thing."

"Ask her if I can use the one in Manhattan," Sandro said, moving his hand through his blond hair.

Mike grinned, taking the first taste of his food. He loved the way the tomatoes blended with the crunchy bread. He could just picture her now: dressed in designer clothing that would cost him a decade to put down even a deposit, a study full of credentials that weren't even hers, a house big enough for a five-star hotel and enough cars to fill a showroom. He knew the sort. St Gallen had a few of them when he was young.

"Who told you this?" Mike asked Stan.

"Markus Mäder told me."

"Does he know her?"

"He's been there already," Stan said, finishing the breadstick and reaching for his wine glass. "He met Al Leoni a couple of months back."

"Pity he wasn't there the other night," Mike said pausing. "Hey, where is Mark anyway? I haven't seen him for weeks."

"Word on the street says he's been meeting Cardinal Utaka in secret."

Mike smiled at Alessandro.

"I think he was in Turin or Venice or something," Stan said. "He was in Prague after the major was killed. I just texted him; he'll be here soon."

Mike looked across the table, wondering exactly what he meant. He studied Stan's reaction. His hard face gave little away. As far as he was aware the major had died of natural causes.

The door to the restaurant opened and Mark entered. He removed a woolly hat from his head and tidied his hair with his hand. He paused momentarily, searching the restaurant with quick eyes.

Mike raised his hand and Mark noticed. He walked quickly in their direction, shaking hands with Mike and Alessandro as he passed.

Of everyone at the Vatican, Mark was his favourite. Both had been sworn into the Swiss Guard on the same day but their friendship had begun over twenty years before that. Their mothers had been bridesmaids at each other's weddings in St Gallen and both had moved to the States before either boy was old enough to remember.

Mike monitored Mark as he circled the table, moving in the direction of the one vacant chair. Three weeks had passed since he had seen him last, but in a way it felt more like hours. Even though he was dressed casually, a black fleece covering what now appeared to be dark jeans and a jumper, somehow Mark always presented the appearance of someone of military pedigree.

At least in the eyes of those also of military pedigree.

Both men were descended of Swiss Army and Swiss Guards going back four generations and both experienced their first aircraft carrier before leaving the womb. Nineteen years later both enrolled at the Annapolis Naval Academy, sharing dorms throughout. While Mike continued in the Swiss Guard, Mark had left after his service as a halberdier was up. Less than two years after leaving for Florence, fate led him back to the eternal city.

The Vatican policeman took a seat by Stan and pulled it up to the table, the wood scraping against the floor.

"Frei was asking about Leoni's daughter," Stan said, shaking Mark's hand.

"Yeah, oberst told me you're gonna be her babysitter for a while."

Mike forced a smile. "Gee, good news sure travels fast, doesn't it? I hear she's just my type."

"Sure. Brunette, blue eyes, nice selection of cars, debatable sense of humour. Height: approximately one hundred and sixty-five centimetres. Weight: one hundred and fifteen pounds give or take . . ."

"And value: one and a half billion euro," Alessandro interrupted.

All present smiled.

"She'll be okay," Mark replied, smiling. "Just don't argue with her; or question her; or disobey her; or look at her . . ."

"I'll bear it in mind," Mike said. He shook his head, but failed to hide a smile. He looked at Mark. "But seriously, what's it like holding the baby?"

Mark hesitated deliberately. "Well, it pretty much sucks yeah."

"At least you won't starve," Sandro said.

"Sure," Mark replied, covering his mouth. "Well, probably not to death."

4

Washington D.C.

The rain was falling relentlessly in the American capital. Pedestrians walked with uncomfortable determination through Union Station, jackets buttoned or zipped up, scarves wrapped tightly around their necks, and briefcases and bags hanging like dead-weights from their arms as they waited impatiently for their trains. Although the station was crowded the peak of passengers was over and the carriages were sparsely populated in comparison to a couple of hours earlier.

A loud bell-like jingle from the PA system preceded the announcement of the 20:45 service departing to New York. Among the gathering passengers waiting to board the train was Ludovic Gullet. He was dressed in black jeans, matching his jacket, and he carried a small suitcase in the manner of a tourist. His lengthy dark brown hair was done up in the usual ponytail and a serious expression crossed his face. He had been waiting for over an hour and boredom had set in. Given the choice of sitting at one of the bars or on a bench, the competition was non-existent, but on this occasion he chose the takeaway cappuccino.

He knew the seriousness of his forthcoming meeting couldn't be underestimated.

The doors to the train opened automatically and several people alighted onto the platform. After waiting for the outgoing crowd to depart, he entered the train in the company of several and took an aisle seat in an unoccupied area. He placed his suitcase beneath the seat and waited patiently for the train to start moving.

Five seats down on the opposite side of the aisle, the bearded man sat quietly. A copy of the *Washington Post* was spread out across the table and an empty takeaway coffee cup was present on the side. He had read the paper umpteen times already and pretended to read it once more. Not for the first time in recent days, the topic of Jermaine

Llewellyn's possible replacement was dominating the early pages. He glanced at the newcomer as he boarded the train but continued to focus on the paper. He was quite specific about not drawing attention to their appointment: to the outside world they were just two nobodies heading to New York. But in reality the instruction was an unnecessary precaution. The concept of anonymity was not lost on either.

And that, itself, was good.

At 20:46 the train began to move. As the train gathered pace, the bearded man left his seat. He deposited the coffee cup in the rubbish bin and walked slowly towards the newcomer. Neither made eye contact. Gullet gazed momentarily at the man as he took a seat opposite him but displayed little interest, giving the impression they were strangers: just another commuter working 25 hours a day, time was money et cetera et cetera. He certainly looked like a workaholic.

But looks could be deceiving!

The bearded man dropped his copy of the *Post* on the table and sat down with a rigid awkwardness. To Gullet, the man's facial expression was one of perpetual seriousness. It was the beard that did it: that enigmatic symmetry of black hairs that seemed to shrivel uncontrollably, as though always giving the impression he was annoyed, even when he was content.

Several moments passed in silence. About ten seats down, a ticket inspector was doing the rounds, walking slowly in their direction. He glanced briefly at their tickets lying neatly on the table as he passed before moving on. Although efficient in nature, the inspector clearly lacked interest, particularly at this time of night. Even if he recognised the bearded man from his publicity photos or occasional interviews on Fox or CNN he didn't show it. He was hardly a celeb! Even if he was the President he was unlikely to attract much attention.

He was a master of discretion.

Gullet looked up but remained silent. The bearded man didn't make eye contact straightaway. He removed his scarf and folded it four equal times before placing it on the table in front of him, a trademark of the man's reputation for efficiency. Gullet knew his real name but he never called him by it. He was aware that he had other names in certain quarters.

The most notable being the 'Grand Master'.

The bearded man surveyed the carriage, examining the features of every passenger in turn. Eight seats down, a black man in his early twenties was listening to an iPod, his earphones partially hidden by a woolly hat with a Redskins' logo. Next seat on, a black woman was sitting opposite two balding white men who were dressed badly, although they didn't know it. Two seats down from them, a white woman in her early forties was reading an Agatha Christie novel, sitting opposite a suited man in his fifties who was texting on his mobile. None of them looked to have a dynamic interest in politics. It was essential their conversation not be heard by interested ears.

"The council are pleased with your work," the Grand Master said quietly.

Gullet remained silent, his eyes alert. A white man dressed in heavy clothing was walking towards them, heading in the direction of the toilet at the end of the next carriage. He was not going to draw attention to the subject matter in these circumstances. The bearded man watched him intently, waiting until he was out of sight. He didn't have a reputation for being an anxious man. No, it was not that. He was tired. He didn't show it but he sure felt it. Recent events were taking their toll.

The Grand Master waited until the man was inside the next carriage before continuing. He removed an envelope from his inside pocket and slid it across the table.

"I have another assignment for you."

Gullet picked up the envelope and checked the contents without removing them. A surprised expression crossed his face.

"You're quite sure?"

"Quite sure," the bearded man replied. As usual he spoke slowly. His voice seemed calm and calculated, almost hypnotic in tone that Gullet always found disturbing and somehow unnatural.

"The terms of your contract will be in keeping with the last. Once the council is satisfied that your duties have been fulfilled you will find your payment in the usual place at the usual time."

Without further examination Gullet placed the envelope inside his jacket pocket. He would study the content in further detail later but he had seen all he needed to see. In many ways it was just another job in a different location at a different time for the same reason. In his profession, he had learned to cope with shock but nothing could have prepared him for this. In his mind he considered the public reaction should he succeed. Wars had been fought over less. He remembered the reaction after he'd carried out his last high-profile assignment.

"People will ask questions."

The bearded man folded his arms. "People always ask questions – it's in their nature. Fortunately for you the press will blame the incident on a one-off disgruntled patriot or a protest to the economic downturn, as they are now," he said, pointing at the front page.

"Why would they?" Gullet asked, lowering his voice. "Why would they take him out? He always acted against that stuff."

The bearded man shrugged. "People are stupid. They believe what they are told to believe."

"I thought Llewellyn had a lot of enemies. Strange the press are suddenly backing him."

"You know what people are like. Anyone who gets an obituary is suddenly a hero in the eyes of the media."

Gullet smiled. "I remember when that guy first made office. I thought the Klan may've made a comeback."

"Well in your case, I suggest you do nothing to convince people otherwise."

Baltimore/Washington International was announced and the train began to slow down.

"I suggest you make your way from here."

Gullet nodded. He waited for five passengers to disembark before ascending to his feet. He would not go on to New York. As he sought to leave, the bearded man grabbed his arm.

"And tell him that Mr Broadie wants his manuscript back."

Gullet made lengthy eye contact. He released his arm and continued towards the door. He exited the train as the doors began to bleep before walking along the platform in the direction of the exit.

Several minutes later he entered the airport.

5

Canton of St Gallen, Switzerland

Not for the first time, an expensive Jaguar made its way past the luxury château located in the heart of the St Gallen countryside. Stopping briefly for its immensely wealthy passengers to disembark outside the stone steps leading up to a pillared entrance, the driver continued along the seemingly endless driveway, lined with woodland on either side, towards the garage area, allowing the next wealthy guests to arrive. The timing of the arrivals was done with military precision: in keeping with the host's own insistence for punctuality.

And it was not just Jaguars they arrived in. The garage area was cluttered with luxury motors of all kinds. Most of the guests arrived in pairs. The men dressed in dark suits and the women in designer dresses, their fingers and wrists lined with various items of jewellery often found in the windows and catalogues of upscale retailers in Paris and New York. The occasion matched the location. On first inspection it was just another social gathering of the rich and well connected in a close-knit society of businessmen, bankers and hereditary fortune earners.

The château was impressive. Viewed from the outside, an imposing façade of stone in the medieval gothic style rose to a great height, its features including ornate carvings and high windows. Inside, eighty-three rooms spanned five floors, less than fifteen of which were in use, and decorated to maintain a historical feel. Technically the building belonged to Al Leoni's brother, as Mike understood from Mark, and dated from the 13th or 14th century, with extensions added in the 16th, 17th, 18th, and after the Second World War. From what Thierry had told him it had been in their family for over two centuries after being bought by his great, great, great, great, great, grandfather, the original founder of Leoni et Cie, from an exiled French duke back in 1793.

Most of the guests frequented what was once the great hall, the main attraction. A large tapestry depicting an epic battle scene covered much of the main wall that was predominantly brown in colour, matching the stone and oak combination. A large fireplace was set into the lower wall, and spanning the room were various pieces of art, mainly Renaissance, and artefacts dating from twenty years ago back to the Middle Ages. A loud humming sound engulfed the room, the accumulated noise of countless individuals chatting in small groups.

Among those present, Mike and Mark chatted quietly, standing in close proximity to one of three buffet tables that offered sandwiches and snacks of various descriptions. A glass of mineral water was present in Mike's hand that was feeling vaguely restricted by the arm of his brand new suit that had been bought for him especially for the occasion. Although he had been complimented on his appearance he never enjoyed wearing suits: he was used to the suited look from his role guarding the Pope on official visits, but at the Vatican he rarely needed to. He'd never understood the fascination with the lavish lifestyle. His father had been a sheriff in the Deep South while his mother was a nurse. Neither was blessed with much money, but growing up doing without had never really bothered him. His goal in life had been to become a soldier.

And he'd succeeded.

He had never felt so out of place. The room was larger in height and width than some three-bed apartments. Large paintings of people and places of significance decorated the room that was illuminated by a pair of spectacular twelve light crystal chandeliers that dominated the ceiling. Standing next to a piano, not to Mike's knowledge the piano was a Steinway, a large man in an expensive dark suit was engaged in conversation with a blonde-haired lady who was about half his age and weight and a thousand times more attractive. They discussed the fine array of art and tapestries hanging from the walls in the manner of a collector and every so often she laughed quietly, and probably falsely, at his anecdotes. Small groups of women, aged thirty to fifty, chatted near the door to the corridor, their conversation clearly one of catching up, while near the double doors leading to the courtyard a man with dark greasy hair and a malevolent looking face was standing facing a man with white hair and an equally malevolent face. Not to Mike's knowledge they were both British Members of Parliament.

Although the occasion smacked of opulence, there was also an overwhelming sense of sombreness about it. Every guest was dressed appropriately for an occasion of mourning, and had arrived in preparation for the funeral of Al Leoni, due to take place in St Gallen the following morning. Most would be staying at the château for at least one night. Many of the guests had attended Mass earlier that evening: marking the occasion where the body of Al Leoni was brought into the main church of the Abbey of St Gall.

Several key Vatican officials had attended, all of whom were also standing in the great hall. On the other side of the room from Mike and Mark, the Cardinal Secretary of State and Camerlengo, Cardinal Tepilo, an elderly white-haired and bearded Italian with a kind heart, stood near Stan and talking to a smartly dressed gentleman facing in the direction of an impressive collection of medieval armour. Cardinals Utaka and del Rosi were also present, standing in close proximity to the fireplace and chatting freely with a crowd of four. The glorious red of their zuchettos and fascias against their black cassocks shone like a supernova in the oily sea of black and white that filled the room.

From a distance it looked like a house of penguins.

"Imagine living in a place like this," Mike said, looking up at the chandeliers.

"I know," Mark said stuffing a sandwich into his mouth and spilling crumbs onto his suit jacket. It was a different make to Mike's but it was very smart all the same. "Just wait until you see her place in Boston."

Mike laughed quietly, probably in amazement. Although he was aware that the château technically belonged to her uncle, it certainly coloured his preconception of the woman he had been assigned to protect. He had seen the château once or twice from a distance in his youth but he never imagined he would visit it. It was large enough to house an army. In fact, according to Thierry, it once housed a band of mercenaries led by a famous Italian condottiere.

He looked around for Thierry but couldn't see him. The oberst's absence was frustrating but he assumed there was a reason. Quietly he was nervous: not of fear but the situation. The main point of Mike's presence was to become acquainted with Ms Gabrielle Leoni, or whatever her name was, and the sooner he met her the happier he would be. He guessed from the general atmosphere of the gathering that she would have enough on her plate without being guarded by a stranger. The thought silently concerned him. Knowing his luck she was probably just some spoiled brat intent on making his life a misery.

His eyes wandered the great hall with interest, attempting to take in everything as it happened. As he examined every face of the ever increasing attendance he couldn't help wonder if she was one of them. When he asked Mark about her he said he hadn't seen her, and that figured. Mark told him there were two types of women present: the real ones and the wannabes. And there would only be one real one.

And he would have the pleasure of guarding her.

"So why are you here tonight?" he asked Mark, sipping slowly from his mineral water. He decided to keep off the wine, at least until after the introductions were over. "Don't tell me she invited you."

Mark laughed, also sipping mineral water. "Are you kidding? She wouldn't spit on me if I was on fire."

Mike laughed quietly, shaking his head. He continued to sweep his eyes across the great hall. He eyed each woman with interest. Soon he would meet her.

But which one was Gabrielle Leoni?

"I'm gonna keep my ear to the ground," he said, surveying the guests with circumspect eyes. He paid most of his attention to the male guests, some of whom he hoped to question off the record. Most were aged forty-five to eighty, and armed with glasses of expensive drink and trophy wives or girlfriends, or in some cases both. Their attire suggested wealth and power, yet none of the faces were obviously famous or recognisable.

"So who are these people?" Mike asked. "Don't tell me they were all his buddies."

Mark placed three pieces of shrimp into his mouth and answered as he chewed. "Not exactly," he said, swallowing. "But most of them knew him."

"Paying their respects, huh?"

"Exactly," Mark said, wiping his mouth. "Interesting gathering though. Some of the men are members of a society called the Rite of Larmenius."

"Rite of what?"

"Rite of Larmenius. It's an appendant body of the Masons, but only for the really high-up guys. Its members include some of the most influential men on the planet. Practically every major President of the USA or president or prime minister from Europe is a member, at least honorary. Basically it's a society that can only be joined when you reach a certain level of influence. They meet in lodges every month and have a three-week bender in the Alps at the end of January. No one really knows what goes on. Most did a lot of business with her father."

Mike nodded. "Oh good, I love skiing."

Mark smiled, continuing to scan the room. Mike did the same: half in habit and half through boredom. In his profession he was used to keeping an eye out for anything suspicious. Although he considered it unlikely that he would be called into action tonight, he knew the possibility was not out of the question. In many ways the large number of people would make it easier for any potential assassin to wander in undetected.

He watched the crowd, particularly the men. He paid special attention to their body language, attempting to judge their personalities. To Mike the night had a unique atmosphere: it was merrier than a wake, yet far drearier than a wedding. Without question, this was the atmosphere of a gathering of people uncertain how to react to the death of the château's owner.

In close proximity to the piano, cardinals del Rosi, Utaka and Tepilo were now all standing together. Thierry, who had appeared from nowhere, was with them and talking to a very beautiful brunette.

Mike raised an eyebrow at the sight of the elegant lady. Like many ladies present she wore an expensive dark dress and exuded an air of confidence. She had the persona of a princess and, by the looks of her, also the wealth.

But what struck him was her face, particularly her eyes. The subtle shade of her dress seemed to bring out the brightness of her stunning blue eyes that looked capable of lighting up a room of their own accord.

Like most ladies present she was about five feet six inches in height, a slender figure of maybe eight and a half stone at the most, a perfectly rounded chest and to top it all off a naturally beautiful face. She wore two rings on her left hand and one on the other, none of which lined the marriage finger. Expensive earrings hung from both ears, shining like pearls behind jet-black hair, bearing an uncanny resemblance to the Belgian chandeliers, and lining her neck was a heavy necklace that reminded Mike of the one from the Titanic movie. On face value, she must have been wearing more in monetary terms than the average person earned in a lifetime: if not ten lifetimes.

"Here we go!" Mark said.

Mike continued to watch the mystery woman. Although he heard Mark speaking, for now he failed to respond. For the first time in what felt like a long time he was captivated. His last girlfriend was Tracey, an all-American girl of great taste but varying intellect. Had Mike have stayed in Annapolis maybe things would have turned out different, but the calling of the Vatican was never going to be defeated. As a Swiss Guard he was used to being married to the job. In recent years romance was a side of his life that had practically shut down.

"You what?" Mike said, returning to reality. He spilled some water down his suit. He cursed under his breath and turned to find a serviette. He picked up two together and brushed vigorously against the spill.

"I said the oberst is calling you."

Mike looked across the room, his focus on the colonel. Indeed Thierry was waving him over. The beautiful woman standing close by was looking aimlessly in his direction.

Suddenly Mike felt warmer than before, his tight shirt stifling beneath his jacket. He felt his breathing heighten slightly, his heart rate increasing with each breath. He threw the serviettes onto the nearby table and adjusted his cufflinks as he walked. His legs were moving but without conscious thought.

Finally he began to concentrate. He gently brushed his right eyebrow with his index finger and cleared his throat quietly, placing particular effort on his breathing. He walked slowly through the crowd, taking care to avoid contact with any of the guests. The air was warmer when the crowds were together.

He came to a halt before Thierry. Three of the cardinals were also present. To Thierry's right, Cardinal Utaka stood elegantly with his hands together, whereas on his left, Cardinal del Rosi stood silently. His facial expression was imposing, his arms folded across his black and red garments. As much as Mike liked the cardinal, he was the one man he feared more than any other. His neatly trimmed moustache and goatee beard below a full head of curly greying hair, partially hidden by his zucchetto, always made him look angry. Cardinal Tepilo was also present, standing next to the mystery woman, a kind smile crossing his wintry beard.

Mike greeted the cardinals individually, paying particular attention to Cardinal Tepilo, before greeting the oberst. For the first time the mystery lady was staring directly at him. Her face seemed preoccupied but she also displayed an empty expression that was vaguely provocative. For now the Swiss Guard could not tell whether it was friendly or unfriendly.

"Gabrielle," Thierry said, turning to her, "I would like to introduce Wachtmeister Frei. He will be acting as your guard for the next . . . well . . ."

Mike's heart missed a beat. Surely he wasn't serious.

"I've told you before, oberst," the lady replied, now facing Thierry, "I do not need a babysitter. I am quite capable of taking care of myself."

Cardinal Tepilo smiled kindly. "Gabrielle, my darling, recent events have been tragic to us all. I do not wish to risk the safety of my remaining family . . ."

"I am well aware what happened, Uncle Roberto," she replied, turning to face him. "Besides, he was your nephew too."

The Camerlengo's smile faded and his eyes seemed to water.

"Even the Pope has guards, my dear," Utaka said, making brief eye contact with Mike. "Think of him as extra security. Whatever you need he's there."

"Wherever you go, he will follow," del Rosi added.

She looked at Cardinal del Rosi and then at Mike. "Wherever I go," she said with a unique expression, vaguely playful but also serious. Thierry smiled at that comment, whereas Cardinal Utaka shook his head. She looked directly into Mike's eyes and then surveyed him from head to toe as if he were a work of art, or worse. He felt as if her eyes were looking right through him, almost as though she could read his thoughts or emotions. For the rarest of moments the bizarre thought unnerved him and time seemed to take an eternity.

Finally she held out her hand without further comment.

Mike hesitated before slowly accepting it. When he did, he held it softly. Unsurprisingly it was cold and slender, as if she were a delicate flower petal that should not survive any great force. With her right hand still holding his she approached him. She brushed her left hand down his suit and squeezed gently against his chest. Slowly she smiled.

"That's a nice suit," she said at last, stroking him in the area where he had earlier spilled water. "Did you go swimming in it?"

Cardinal del Rosi laughed, whereas the other three looked on uncomfortably. The Swiss Guard broke eye contact momentarily, drawn to Cardinal Utaka shaking his head. As quickly as his eyes left her, he resumed eye contact with his new host.

For now he remained focused, attempting to control his breathing. Nobody was speaking but the sound of chatter throughout did little to alleviate the tension. As he looked into her eyes he saw something had changed. That gaze that only a moment ago appeared warm and bright now displayed only the cold arrogance of a spoiled child. If there was any hint of a warm, loving smile it had now withered into a snobbish frown. The aristocracy may have long since died out in these parts but the transition had clearly bypassed her. Had the situation been normal, he would probably have given a retort, but on this occasion discipline took over. Finally, he forced a smile and turned to the oberst.

"Wachtmeister Frei is one of my most loyal soldiers. I would trust him with my life," Thierry said. "Only last year he provided a guard for the President of the USA. He regularly serves as guard for His Holiness."

"Really," Gabrielle said. She looked at Thierry, then once more at Mike. She looked him up and down and finally in the eye. "Well the Pope may need you, but I don't. Farewell, Mr Frei."

Gabrielle Leoni moved quickly to one side and walked in the direction of a man of ancient features accompanied by a lady young enough to be his granddaughter. Utaka and del Rosi also separated, moving in opposite directions. Thierry smiled at Mike and patted him on the shoulder before following Cardinal Utaka. Cardinal Tepilo also patted him on the shoulder caringly and smiled warmly before walking away in the other direction.

Mike bit his lip, concealing his frustration well. He walked slowly in the opposite direction, heading back to where Mark was still standing. He failed to notice a man walking past. Red wine spilled over the stranger's white shirt.

"Oh man, I am so sorry," Mike said hesitantly, surveying the gentleman. The man was elegantly dressed – more so than most, and that was saying something. He was fairly tall with medium length hair and a neatly trimmed beard. He monitored Mike for what seemed like an eternity, his face a dull expression, a clear sign of disapproval. His dark eyes felt threatening to him.

For several seconds they watched each other silently. Then, surprisingly, the man's facial exterior softened.

"Not to worry, fella," he said, his face breaking into a smile. "I have a spare shirt in my room. I'll change into it; it's no bother."

"You need to get that out soon," Mike said, wiping his shirt with his hand. "That'll leave a stain."

"Right, thanks. I'll bear that in mind. Thanks again."

The man departed in the direction of the corridor, heading towards the main stairwell. Mike's eyes followed him until he left the room. Now alone, he paid attention to his surroundings before walking carefully through the crowd, returning to the buffet table. Stan was standing by Mark, piling up a plate of snacks.

Both tried to conceal their laughter.

"Do you like her?" Stan asked.

Mike looked at Stan, a look of irritation crossing his face.

"Oh, sure," Mike said, wiping his hand vigorously with a serviette. "I like her more than food poisoning."

"I told you she's a treat," Mark said.

"Oh she's special," Mike said, throwing away the serviette and picking up a piece of shrimp from a nearby plate. "I tell ya . . . if someone were to attack her with one of these right now I'd jump right in front of it."

Stan laughed and turned away.

Just as he made the comment, Mike heard his name being called, the voice unmistakably Thierry's. He chewed the shrimp quickly and about-turned. He walked briskly, passing a crowd of eight or nine, carefully navigating the ocean of black suits.

He followed Thierry through an open doorway and along a winding corridor.

6

It was clear to Mike that the great hall was not the only impressive feature of the château. Countless valuable artefacts and works of art, mostly dating back to the 17th century, lined the left wall of the long corridor, spaced evenly and coordinated by size and colour.

The right side was no less of interest. Priceless works of art hung from the walls, accompanied by gothic carvings, etched into the stonework, many of which had faded over the years. A random carving of cupid, bow at the ready, stood out from a cluster of other carvings that lined the next section of corridor, mostly depicting scenes from the classical era. Continuing around the next corner, several large portraits lined the walls, unbeknown to Mike, all depicting male members of the Leoni family dating back to the first owner.

Mike ducked his head as he passed under an open archway and stopped next to Thierry in front of a heavy door. Like most he had seen so far, it was made of oak and was one of many lining the main corridor. Thierry opened it with a struggle and held it open politely for Mike. The door creaked loudly as it moved on un-oiled hinges.

He entered slowly and closed it as quietly as possible, failing to prevent further prolonged creaking.

Once inside, he surveyed the room. The main light was already switched on, the only light entering the room. In comparison to the other rooms he had seen, this one was by far the barest. An antique desk was placed near the windows, overlapping the closed curtains, and surrounded by four wooden chairs and an empty bookcase, the only furniture in the room. A peculiar smell permeated throughout, suggesting to Mike the room had not been used recently. He assumed it was not the only room in the château to appear this way.

The oberst sat down in close proximity to the desk and offered Mike one of three vacant seats opposite. He breathed out heavily and slowly rubbed his eyes. Mike watched him. It was clear the oberst was not enjoying himself.

He wasn't the grandest of men. As leader of the Swiss Guard some might have forgiven him for flaunting his rank, but in Mike's experience that never happened. In the past it had been customary for the oberst of the Swiss Guard to be of Swiss nobility, and while that may have been true of Thierry's lineage once removed on his father's side, he never displayed such links.

He wasn't a privileged man, as Mike understood, although in comparison to many his progress through the ranks had been an easy ride. As a law graduate from Oxford, he was all set to follow in his father's footsteps, a Swiss banker. It was surprising in many ways that he didn't. He certainly had the capability, and guys with his background were hard to come by.

But he hated banks and, furthermore, he hated bankers. Perhaps it was because his father spent more time reading contracts than reading him bedtime stories when he was younger. Like Mike, he wasn't particularly close to his father.

No, it was his uncle to whom the oberst was closest. He, too, had been a soldier: in fact, he, too, had been a Swiss Guard. After making the rank of major it was most unfortunate that he was killed in a car crash in the early 1990s. Rumour had it the event changed the oberst. For as long as Mike had served, he had never seen him show much emotion.

Tonight was no exception.

Mike's eyes began to wander, examining the room through boredom. For the first time he noticed a man of hard features captured in a portrait behind Thierry. The portrait was the only artwork in the room. This man was far less elegant than those he had seen in other paintings that night. He was dressed in the attire of the 19th century, and was portrayed as having a crooked nose. Nevertheless, the man's facial appearance was vaguely in keeping with some of the others that lined the walls. Yet, this one was less dazzling. In Mike's opinion, his face was repulsive.

"Is that one of her relatives?"

Thierry turned around, examining the painting without interest.

"Who cares," he said.

Mike smiled briefly.

Thierry shook his head and brushed his finger and thumb over his tired eyes. The purple bags were less evident on this occasion, possibly hidden beneath thin layers of makeup.

"You know, Frei, everybody here is an expert," he said, making eye contact with Mike. "But there are two types of expert here: those who have studied art their whole lives, and those who once visited a museum."

Mike smiled, his eyes once more on the painting. He had seen the oberst talking to several mourners that night, putting up with their stories. He was doing a very good job fitting in.

"And neither are really experts. Just have varying degrees of ignorance."

A quiet knock on the heavy door stole their attention. Thierry answered come in and the door opened slowly, creaking on its hinges.

The newcomer was Mark. He nodded at Mike as he entered, heading in the direction of the desk. He removed a set of photographic prints from his inside pocket as he walked.

Thierry ascended to his feet and helped him organise the contents across the unused desk. Meanwhile, Mike waited patiently. Less than a minute later Thierry signalled for him to join them.

Initially what he saw made no sense. There were six photographs laid out evenly, each one printed in black and white. Every photograph was of a different man, their ages, physiques and ethnicities varied. On face value they were all seemingly without connection.

Mike recognised the first man immediately. The man was white, mid to late seventies in age, and slightly overweight. His facial expression suggested he was a kindly individual.

"I'm sure you will recognise our lately departed Cardinal Patricio Faukes," Thierry said.

Mike nodded, his attention on the photograph. As far as he was aware, the Spaniard had died in the Apostolic Palace some two months earlier: a combination of poor health and old age.

"This man also," Thierry said, pointing to the next photograph.

Mike nodded, his eyes now focused on the handsome face of Major Pius von Sonnerberg. For as long as Mike had been a Swiss Guard, the man had been his superior.

"These men, I'm sure, will be less familiar."

Mike made brief eye contact with Thierry before looking with interest at the next man. He was also white, perhaps late fifties and clearly overweight. As far as Mike could tell he had never met the man.

He scanned the others. "Who are they?"

"That man was Martin Snow," Mark said of the third individual. "A former employee at Starvel AG, and a respected business analyst – found dead on a train nearly five weeks ago."

Mike nodded. He immediately made the connection that these men were all deceased. Silently the thought unnerved him. As the seconds passed, the atmosphere within the cramped room, devoid of fresh air and light, seemed to grow heavier. It was clear to Mike why Thierry had chosen this room. It was a room where they were guaranteed not to be disturbed.

"Next to him is Nathan Walls, an accountant for GPLA, based in North Carolina," Mark said.

"Their names are not important," Thierry interrupted, "what matters is that each man was found dead between November and six days ago. Indications suggest that each man was murdered yet none of their deaths were witnessed. As far as we know, none of these men knew one another."

He exhaled deeply.

"What's more, until recently there was no reason to suggest that three of them had even been murdered."

Mike rubbed his clean-shaven face and looked inquisitively at his commander. Although it was obvious certain circumstances were still to be revealed to him it was evident from their tone that the matter was of profound importance. He looked at Mark, for now remaining silent. Until that point Mike had assumed Major von Sonnerberg and Cardinal Faukes had died of natural causes.

Mark bit his lip. He could tell from Mike's expression that he was confused.

"Take a look at the guy on the far right, Mike."

Mike looked at the print closely. Until now he had paid it little attention. The image was similar to the others: a white male aged somewhere in his sixties. Although he had never met the man he recognised him immediately.

"That's her dad."

Thierry nodded. "Yes, Frei: that is Al Leoni."

Mike nodded, continuing to examine the photograph. A smart grey beard lined his face, common for a man of that age. His eyebrows were bushy, at least compared to the men in the other photos, and the jaw line was strong, his features unmistakably Swiss. Yet his expression was strange: it seemed blank, unnaturally blank, as if it was the expression of a dead man, despite the photo being taken several years earlier. It was strange the way the black and white played havoc with his thoughts.

He paid particular attention to the man's eyes. He felt drawn to him. He had seen those eyes before, recently.

His daughter also had his eyes.

He examined his other features. On face value he saw less evidence of a family resemblance. His nose was stronger than hers and his lips thin and thoughtful. In a way it reminded him of Cardinal Tepilo but the resemblance was by no means clear-cut. The photograph made him feel uncomfortable. All of a sudden he felt particularly aware that he was a guest in the man's lifelong home.

The door to the room opened with a familiar creaking sound. Mike turned instinctively and relaxed immediately. Cardinals Utaka and Tepilo entered together, followed by Cardinal del Rosi. Once inside, the last cardinal closed the door behind him with excessive force, causing the sound to ricochet around the room. The ground shook for a couple of seconds, though having no effect on the long unused desk.

Cardinal del Rosi looked inquisitively at Thierry. "You have informed our man of the task at hand, oberst?"

"I was explaining to Frei that these men had been murdered . . ."

"It is not clear, wachtmeister, why these men were murdered," Cardinal del Rosi interjected, facing Mike for the first time; "unfortunately it is equally unclear who murdered them."

"We have some idea, eminence," Mark interrupted.

Cardinal Utaka looked at Mark, then del Rosi. "Even if we knew who was responsible it would not make the situation any less important."

Cardinal del Rosi gazed at his colleague. He folded his arms slowly, exploring the room with his eyes. A look of frustration dominated his face.

"Both Guiliano and George are quite correct, wachtmeister," Cardinal Tepilo said of del Rosi and Utaka, now facing Mike. "It is not known why they were murdered, nor is it clear who was responsible. This leaves us with a great, great problem."

Mike watched the cardinal closely, his attention on the man's beard. He wore a thoughtful expression, as he always did. It suited the man's reputation as a great thinker and theologian.

Cardinal del Rosi's expression changed. "You are aware of what happened to Jermaine Llewellyn?"

"Not really," Mike answered. "Only what I read in the papers."

"Llewellyn . . ."

"Jermaine Llewellyn," Cardinal del Rosi said interrupting Cardinal Utaka, "was the Chairman of the Federal Reserve. Being raised in America you are no doubt aware he was chiefly responsible for supervising banking policy in America . . ."

"Frei doesn't need an economics lesson, eminence," Thierry said, raising his voice for the first time. "Frei is already well aware that Leoni et Cie is of vital importance to the Vatican Bank, holding more than a 20% stake. He is willing to ensure that the bank's most important shareholder – that Cardinal Tepilo's niece . . ."

"Thank you, Thierry," Tepilo said.

Mike nodded, returning his attention to the desk. What did the other three have to do with it?

"Do all of these murders concern the Vatican?"

No one answered straightaway. Cardinal del Rosi looked curiously at Mike. "That remains unclear."

Mark walked slowly across the room, stopping a few metres from Mike. He removed a selection of papers from his inside pocket.

"So far we have only one lead," Mark said. "Three days ago I was asked by Mikael Devére to meet him privately in Rome."

Mike's eyes displayed nothing but surprise. "The former President of France?"

Mark nodded. "It was Devére who told me of his suspicions that Cardinal Faukes and Major von Sonnerberg had been murdered. He also suggested that their killer or killers were under orders from someone, or some people, involved with the Rite of Larmenius."

Mike looked at him, all the while remaining silent. The cardinals all looked on with neutral expressions.

Mark unfolded the documents and passed them to Mike. "Take a look at this."

Mike accepted the documents from Mark and slowly began to search them. Unbeknown to Mike they were photocopies of the documents that Mark had received from the Frenchman on the bridge. Mike scanned the content quickly, his eyes alert as he examined the top corner of each page. There was a logo present. The logo was unique: consisting of a red cross, almost identical to the cross of St George, intercepted by a bizarre skull and crossbones at its centre.

"Based on the evidence we have, each of these murders were decreed by this society," Mark said quietly. He paused, making sure that nobody was going to walk in. "Take a look at this."

Mark directed Mike to the last page of seven. Each page was identical in style and similar in content. Yet the final sheet disturbed him. The name Gabrielle Leoni appeared in the centre.

"Oh my!"

Thierry edged closer to the desk and picked up two of the original prints. "Major von Sonnerberg was found dead in his hotel room in Prague on Christmas Eve," he said seriously. "Until now we have kept details of his death under wraps. In fact, we only knew for sure ourselves a few days ago."

Mike nodded despondently, his eyes focused on the death warrants. "What happened?"

Thierry sought to answer but Mark got there first. "The Vatican Police have been investigating but at present no definitive leads have been uncovered as to why he was killed. Cardinal Faukes is even more unclear. An autopsy was never carried out. It was simply assumed that he had died of natural causes."

Cardinal Tepilo nodded. "His Holiness himself performed the funeral Mass."

"Three days ago the Vatican Police received a tip-off that not only were the deaths of these men connected, but also that they had in fact been murdered," Thierry said. "As I'm sure you will agree, judging by what's in front of us, it seems probable that they were all murdered by the same people."

Mike nodded at his superior. If nothing else, at least it made sense of Mark's recent absence. As he considered the web of intrigue that was unfolding before him it was clear that he was part of something big. This was never a babysitting job for a heartbroken daughter, not that she showed it.

He was acting as bait.

He looked at Mark. His manner was serious, more so than at any time Mike had known him.

"The Rite of Larmenius is one of the most secretive societies on earth," Mark said. "They are the most exclusive appendant body of the Freemasons: the highest form of Freemasonry there is. No one knows exactly what they do, or officially who their members are. For all we know the men responsible for all these killings could even be in this château right now."

Cardinal Tepilo looked seriously at Mike. "Wachtmeister, please do not mention any of this to my niece. She is suffering so much."

Mike nodded slowly, his expression one of sympathy. Turning, he studied every face one by one. The worried expressions were unlike any he had ever witnessed.

But at least now he knew what he was in for.

Even if he didn't know why.

7

Washington D.C.

Senator Daniel D'Amato was not a regular attendee of social gatherings of the upper crust; in Montana he hardly had the opportunity. Rubbing shoulders with the social elite: lazy bastards who never did a day's work in their life. No, what appealed to him was money – and power.

With his background, growing up with money should have been a given. As the eldest child of seven to a Spanish immigrant and a Texan son of an oil baron, the last thing he lacked was stability – and money. Yet that all changed following the early death of his mother, and escalated thanks to the business incompetence of his father. While an inheritance of millions would have awaited him should his father have inherited the genius of his grandfather, chronic gambling, alcoholism, and a bitch of a stepmother left the future senator fighting his own battles.

In the early days he lost, often badly. While such setbacks might have finished a lesser man, in many ways it shaped his character. What he lacked in stability he gained in determination and as his personality developed so did his initiative. At twenty-three he graduated from Duke and by twenty-seven he had set up his own construction company. By thirty-five he sold it for millions and in time moved into banking and eventually oil and mining. As a result of his commitment came the money – and power.

When elected to the Senate seven years ago at the age of fifty-eight, he was thought to be a strict Republican with strong Keynesian beliefs and a preference for Christian families working in primary and secondary sectors. With his background it would have figured. His election had been a landslide despite rumours of dodgy dealings in his days as a banker, but as far as the voting population knew such rumours were without foundation. Even if there had been an element of truth to the stories, his reputation since being elected had been beyond credible. On the east coast he wouldn't have had a leg to stand on, but Montana was a different story. On political issues he always appeared strong and whether right or wrong he always stuck to his guns.

His re-election had been an even greater triumph and in both terms pre-election promises had largely been kept. What he gave the people was stability. And what they gave him was power – and money.

He claimed to represent the people, and he did. His credibility had been proven and in certain circles whispers of approval were turning into loud voices of hope.

Yes, this was the man who would lead the Republican Party at the next Presidential election.

D'Amato arrived back in D.C. three days earlier and had spent most of his time since on Capitol Hill. At seven that evening he arrived at a prominent restaurant, in close proximity to the National Mall, accompanied by two other senators with connections to the Rite of Larmenius where they racked up a bill of over $500. At half past eleven he took a taxi to the Reflection Pool and continued on foot past the memorials for Roosevelt and Mason to the Thomas Jefferson Memorial. Although it was raining he decided against taking the taxi to his precise location. It was vital his meeting remained secret.

He was a master of discretion.

The monument was the perfect place to meet. Being so far removed from the mall and the metro, lying on the Tidal Basin of the Potomac, it was far quieter than the other monuments and despite the floodlights it was unlikely to attract attention at this hour. The rangers had gone home at least half an hour ago and the vague hum of cars in the distance and boats crossing the water were rare disturbances to the silence.

Silence was golden.

The rain had eased but it was still to stop altogether. The steps leading to the monument were soaked from the earlier downpour but the floor remained fairly dry under the shelter of the roof. The outline of wet footprints from earlier in the day had dried under the floodlights, leaving little more than vague messy imprints on the floor.

It was the first rain for three days in the city. The fresh aroma of water on nearby greenery felt pleasant on his nostrils but there was a chill in the air, causing his breath to appear visible when he exhaled. He hated the cold, but given the choice it was always solitude before comfort. As usual, he dressed in a heavy overcoat, protecting his suit from the rain. A black umbrella was resting against the base alongside an empty brown briefcase.

It was now just before midnight and he was alone, his presence hidden by the frame of the former president. The eyes of the former president, looming above him, were the only threat to his privacy. The expression on his face somehow suggested concentration.

He turned away from the statue, concentrating on the various inscriptions on the walls. He had read them many times before but they never failed to captivate him.

He focused on one section in particular:

No man shall be compelled to frequent or support any religious worship or ministry or shall otherwise suffer on account of his religious opinions or belief, but all men shall be free to profess and by argument to maintain, their opinions in matters of religion.

He smiled to himself as he continued to panel three.

God who gave us life gave us liberty. Can the liberties of a nation be thought secure when we have removed a conviction that these liberties are the gift of God? Indeed I tremble for my country when I reflect that God is just: that his justice cannot sleep for ever.

The senator nodded, his attention on the final line.

This it is the business of the state to effect and on a general plan.

He liked this one. Mr Jefferson was reading his mind.

The sound of coughing from nearby stole his attention. The senator turned away from the wall, his attention now on the steps at the entrance. A man had emerged from nearby. He carried a black briefcase and an open umbrella in one hand and a lighted cigarette in the other. He came to a standstill at the bottom of the steps and carefully examined his surroundings. After several seconds he noticed the senator standing behind the statue.

The newcomer approached him slowly.

Smiling, the senator held out his hand. "Howdy, partner, put it there."

The newcomer exhaled smoke from his mouth and nose and hesitantly shook D'Amato's hand. He was dressed in a grey jacket, accompanied by black trousers and matching shoes. A bushy moustache, predominantly black with vague strands of grey, matched the colour of his hair that was sprawled untidily as a result of walking in the rain. Without further eye contact he walked across to the other side of the statue and placed his briefcase by D'Amato's.

This was the most concealed part of the monument.

"Nice of you to show up, Ged," the senator said.

The man named Ged Fairbanks threw his cigarette to the ground and stamped on it. "GPLA is inundated with work, Danny. Do I really need to remind you?"

The politician from Montana smiled at him, an arrogant and smug smile. It was almost as if to say I'm in control and there's nothing you can do about it.

Fairbanks shook his umbrella violently, causing drops of water to fall to the floor, accompanied by a sharp rattling sound as the frame vibrated against the fabric. He placed it down against the statue and looked around at the memorial. He had seen it many times before without paying particular attention to its features.

"There's a rumour going around Charlotte that Nathan Walls was killed by the same guys who killed Leoni and Llewellyn," the accountant said seriously. "But you wouldn't know anything about that, would you?"

"Where do they come up with these wild accusations?"

"The media has papers to sell, Danny."

The senator removed a cigar from his jacket pocket and put a light to it. He smiled as he smoked, blowing the smoke in the direction of the accountant. He paused momentarily. Across the Tidal Basin, the sound of sirens roared loudly before fading to a distant hum. The sound unnerved Fairbanks. In a worried state, his eyes darted across the nearby surroundings, concentrating on the Japanese cherry trees that moved frantically as the wind picked up. The image was like something out of a horror film.

"Let's get this over with."

D'Amato nodded, his eyes focused on the accountant. Fairbanks picked up his briefcase and placed it against Thomas Jefferson's foot. A grim expression dominated his features. He entered the combination from memory and opened it.

He passed D'Amato a large document.

D'Amato searched the document with quick fingers, satisfied by what he saw. To Fairbanks it was clear that D'Amato was enjoying himself. The senator took a seat on the base of the statue and inserted the document into his own briefcase.

"I thought you'd be on vacation in Switzerland with your pals."

"I can vacation when this shit is over," the senator replied. "It's cold in the winter."

The accountant remained silent, forcing an awkward smile. He focused his gaze on the nearby pathway as an act of caution. Despite the poor weather, he knew it was possible that a passer-by could stumble on their meeting. The rain was starting to ease and moonlight penetrated through the dense nimbostratus clouds above, casting ethereal shadows among the cherry trees. Although the location was

54

deserted, the foliage offered no shortage of hiding places. He failed to shake the feeling they were being watched.

D'Amato removed a sealed envelope from his jacket pocket and passed it to Fairbanks. "Everything you need is there."

Without looking at the content, Fairbanks placed the envelope in an inside pocket, never breaking eye contact with D'Amato.

"Don't spend it all in one go."

A sharp sound from the nearest road caught him unaware. It was the sound of tyres cutting through puddles accompanied by a gear change from an unseen motor. Fairbanks looked in all directions nervously. D'Amato smiled, continuing to smoke. He used the pause to flick ash to the floor near the accountant's feet.

"And that concludes our business, Ged . . ."

Another car passed unseen. Without waiting for further invitation, Fairbanks descended the steps and accelerated into a jog. He headed in the direction of the George Mason Memorial, neglecting to put up his umbrella. Water splashed off the pavement as his shoes landed on the hard ground.

The senator laughed to himself. He threw his cigar to the floor and extinguished it with his size nines.

Justice cannot sleep for ever.

"Sir, I shall bid you adieu."

8

They left the room shortly after midnight. Not for the first time that evening Mike passed a man slightly worse for wear leaning the majority of his weight on the fed-up woman on his arm who acted as the only barrier between him and the floor. Along the corridor, a group of the women were talking quietly, while some of the men discussed business as they sipped brandy or port, some smoking cigarettes or cigars. A peculiar stench of smoke and perfume had combined to create an unappealing odour, overwhelming the pleasant lavender fragrance that had scented the building only a few hours earlier.

In his mind Mike continued to replay the recent episode in the small room. The sight of the men in the photographs still flashed vividly, accompanied by the various Masonic-approved death warrants. Silently that had shocked him, even more than he'd expected. Although he was experienced as a Papal Guard this was the first time he had ever been included from the start on any potential terrorist attack or conspiracy against the Vatican or its affiliates. Secretly the idea that the people behind the recent killings might be present in the same building unnerved him.

But in other ways it made him more vigilant.

Mike followed Mark along the corridor, walking in the direction of the great hall. Mike nodded briefly at one of the Vatican bankers before entering the great hall. Mark, meanwhile, continued along the corridor to another part of the building.

Despite the revelations, Mike's appetite had returned. He navigated his way past a small group of well dressed women and continued in the direction of the buffet table. Without intention, he made contact with the arm of a stranger going for the same plate.

"Excuse me," Mike said, addressing the person who he now noticed to be a woman. Like most women present she was blonde, perhaps five feet seven inches in height, and wearing a stunning black dress. The woman smiled politely as she took a small bite of her sandwich. It was a tiny bite, in keeping with her miniscule figure: she was no more than an eight USA size: not that Mike knew what an eight was.

"I'm so sorry," Mike said, forgetting about food. "I didn't see you there."

The woman remained silent, her eyes focused on Mike. She held her smile. Although she was not the only woman who he would describe as beautiful, she was one of the few who appealed to him. She struck of elegance, but not opulence; confidence, but seemingly without the surface arrogance that many of the attendees seemed to possess. She was not without mystery and her eyes were simply dazzling. In a weird way it reminded him of the first time he saw Gabrielle Leoni – that stuck up bitch – but they were somehow more playful: more friendly. To Mike, they depicted a somewhat wilder side, also illustrated by the curls in her hair that partially covered her pretty face. Her face was whiter than most and seemed to be freckled on both cheeks, concealed by makeup.

The stranger slowly held out her hand, her smile widening. "I'm Rachel," she said, her voice quiet, her tone friendly. She was clearly American, possibly from Connecticut, Mike guessed from living in Georgia and Maryland.

"Mike," the Swiss Guard replied shaking her hand gently. She had a ring on the middle finger of her left hand but her marriage finger was naked.

"So," she said, flicking her hair away from her face, "are you a friend of Gabrielle's?"

"As a matter of fact I only met her tonight."

The woman's eyes lit up. "Oh, my God, are you her Swiss Guard?"

The accuracy of her assumption was surprising. Less than two hours had passed since meeting his hostess for the first time. He knew he had made a bad impression: perhaps an awful one.

"Gabrielle told me all about you."

Mike looked at her awkwardly, for now remaining silent. Her smile widened, slowly turning into a laugh. It was a playful laugh, almost as if she knew a secret that she was unable to tell him.

"So what's it like being a Swiss Guard?"

"It's . . . it's . . . pretty hard to describe," Mike stuttered. "I mean it's mostly for show."

That was a lie but it made him feel good.

"So if someone was to aim a gun at the Pope would you have to, like, throw yourself in front of him?" she gestured with her hands as she spoke.

Mike smiled. "Yeah, maybe; I never thought of it like that."

"Wow. That would be so brave."

Mike held his smile, failing to disguise his reaction. Although she was slightly older than him, maybe early thirties he assumed, she could have passed for late twenties. More importantly she was unlike the others, the ones Mark called the wannabes. Without question, this one was different.

"So I take it you know Ms Leoni?"

"Sure. We went to Dartmouth together. Her uncle was a professor there. He's at Harvard now. He's here somewhere," she said, looking briefly around the room. "I expect you'll see him sometime soon."

"You must be pretty smart to go to Dartmouth."

"Well, I don't know about that," she said.

He looked either side, scanning the room out of habit. Stan had returned, standing close to Cardinal Tepilo. The man who Mike had earlier spilled wine over was walking by, stopping as he approached the cardinal. He listened to Rachel ask about his past and smiled in response, disguising his embarrassment.

"So what are you like a model or something?"

She laughed. "Yeah, something like that. I used to work in banking, but I gave that up once I got married. I'm divorced now."

He wanted to know more about her former husband but decided the question was off limits.

"I still live in America but I come out here a lot. Gabrielle's my best friend. We spent lots of time together. I'm gonna be staying here for a while after the funeral."

Mike nodded, his eyes focused on hers. He was unaware he was staring. At least he wouldn't just be guarding Gabrielle Leoni.

"Sounds great."

"Well not as great as guarding the Pope. Who knows, maybe you could guard me when I'm around."

She walked nearer, touching him cutely on his left arm. He watched her as she approached, all the while remaining still. In a way he felt guilty bearing in mind the reason for his presence. He broke eye contact again, taking the opportunity to examine the guests. On the other side of the room Thierry and Cardinal Utaka were standing next to a man with grey hair while Stan was in close proximity to the other cardinals. Mark was in conversation with two known Rite of Larmenius members, including a lawyer from Germany, and was surrounded by three smartly dressed socialites. He smiled to himself. He had never met a lady who didn't like Mark.

He turned once more towards Rachel and saw that she was distracted. Gabrielle Leoni was walking towards them.

"Hey, how are you holding up?" Rachel asked nervously, hugging her and kissing her cheek.

"Good," she replied, turning her face to Rachel's lips. "Pedro just invited me to visit his new yacht in the Galápagos."

Mike turned around, looking to where she had gestured. He assumed she was referring to the ageing Spaniard standing by the fireplace. Despite the grey streaks in his flamboyant hair and the smart suit, he had all the sexual innuendo of a porn star and was surrounded by a horde of wannabes aged anything from nineteen to sixty. It wouldn't have surprised him to learn the man owned a selection of gentlemen's clubs.

"So," Gabrielle said, "I see you've met Wachtmeister Fritz."

"Frei," Mike interjected. He wasn't used to being insubordinate, but she was hardly the Pope. She stared at him piercingly for a few seconds, each one seeming an eternity.

"You're so lucky having your own Swiss Guard," Rachel said. "I wish I had one! He was just telling me how he'd dive in front of the Pope and take a bullet for him."

Gabrielle turned to face Mike. Not for the first time she looked at him as though he was a dog that had pooed on the lawn.

"I'm sure his absence will be a major loss to His Holiness."

Rachel giggled playfully. Meanwhile, Mike looked at her seriously. In a strange way he felt guilty, knowing the true severity of the situation while she was in the dark. He thought back to earlier that night, the first time he saw her, unaware of the death warrant that existed. It was strange to think that very document was currently located in the inside pocket of a suit currently being worn by his best friend, standing in that very room. For the briefest of moments he considered telling her.

Immediately, he dismissed the idea.

"By the way," Gabrielle said to Rachel, "Alexei was asking after you."

"Oh, okay, well, I'll no doubt see you around, wachtmeister," Rachel said, failing to pronounce wachtmeister correctly. She winked at Mike and shook his hand before heading off in the direction of the main doors. Just as she did, a man dressed as a waiter passed by carrying glasses of champagne: a toast to Al Leoni's life and greatness! Mike took one, his first of the evening.

"I see you've met Rachel."

"I like your friends," Mike invented. He was secretly pleased with that comment. Not for the first time his eyes circled the room, taking in the flurry of activity. Strangely, the evening had no flow to it, no obvious occasion. Slowly, the size of the gathering was beginning to dwindle.

"Don't get your hopes up. She's like that with all the guys."

Mike sipped his champagne, his eyes momentarily on Gabrielle. The bubbles felt pleasant on his dry mouth. He swallowed half the glass before returning his attention to his host. Her piercing stare continued to focus on him.

"Well I'm sure you'll get to see a fair bit more of her. She's my best friend. She'll be staying here for a while."

Mike nodded. Although he showed no emotion, spending time getting to know Rachel would certainly not be a bad thing. Anything was better than just guarding her. She was certainly beautiful; no one could deny that. In fact, she was magnificent, even compared to Rachel, but she knew it. The more he focused on it the more it bothered him. Why did she have to be so uptight? Was it her father? Possibly. But something didn't ring true. She was an actress, no doubts there. But what role was she playing?

"So, Frei: is that short for something?"

Mike loosened his tie. "Frei is my second name."

"So what's your Christian name?"

Mike hesitated. Only his closest friends called him by his first name.

"Come on. If you're going to be my guard I need to know your name."

"Mikael," he replied. "My friends call me Mike."

"Am I your friend, Mikael?"

Mike laughed but not on purpose, fearing that he might have given away his dislike of her. Maybe it was a test, although somehow he doubted it. He smiled philosophically.

"By all means please call me by whatever name is best for you, Ms Leoni."

"Very well, Mikael," she replied, placing extra emphasis on Mikael. "We'll be staying here for several weeks. My mom is flying in right now for the funeral, but will be leaving soon after. I, on the other hand, will be staying to see to Leoni et Cie. After that we may return to Boston, however by then your time here will probably be at an end."

"Fine."

"There are fifty-three bedrooms in the château, so take your pick, as long as it's not on the fourth floor: they're strictly for guests and family."

"Thank you, Ms Leoni."

"In a week or so I'll need you to take me to St Gallen?"

"What for?"

He grimaced, instantly regretting his comment. Her answer was surprisingly generous.

"I need to make some arrangements at Leoni et Cie. Besides, my father left some stuff there. And I want it. Understand?"

Mike nodded, his expression slightly awkward. "Sorry."

The briefest of nods was followed by the quietest muttering of good. She didn't respond after that: instead she headed off in the direction of the Spaniard and his wannabes. He watched her for several seconds, examining her every characteristic. She walked slowly, but confidently. As she walked through the crowd he couldn't help notice she dazzled all present. She had an aura about her that he found strangely transfixing.

Yet he couldn't help feel that Mark was right. She walked with a sense of arrogance, almost as though she was walking through a park on a warm summer's day, totally oblivious to everything and everyone, without a care in the world. It was as if she was unaware that her father had just been murdered.

But there was something about her. She was snobby, yes, but no worse than any of the other women present, including the wannabes – especially the wannabes – but who could expect any different bearing in mind her background? There was not another like her in the room. Sure, they all dressed the part and pretended to know the lifestyle, but she made it all seem so natural. Without question the rest all loved her, and admired her and wanted to be just like her.

But none of them could. She was different. She was unique.

She was . . .

"She's just as I imagined," Mike said to Stan as he devoured a sandwich. Two men were standing next to Mike.

"Mike, have you met Mr Velis?"

Mike looked at the man, allowing himself a moment to examine his features. It was the same person he had spilled wine over earlier that night. He was clearly wearing a different shirt.

"Yeah. Hey, I'm sorry again about your shirt."

"Not to worry," the man said smiling. "I did what you said. The other shirt is being washed as we speak."

Mike grimaced, remembering the uncomfortable coming together less than three hours earlier. It seemed like a long time ago.

"Mike, this is Mr Louis Velis, chief executive of the Starvel Group. And this," Stan pointed to the other man, equally well dressed with flat dark hair, "is Mr Gilbert de Bois, a media baron from Canada. Mr de Bois is also the chairman of Leoni et Cie."

Mike: "Oh right. Well it's a pleasure, Mr Velis, Mr de Bois."

"Please, please, call me Louis," Velis said shaking hands with Mike and patting him on the shoulder. The man held a cigar in his other hand and was smoking intermittently. "Mr Velis is so formal."

Mike forced a smile, continuing to take in their features. Although he had never heard of either man the name Starvel struck a chord. He found himself thinking back to earlier that night: the cramped room, the ugly man in the portrait, the six photographs. He remembered Mark mention that one of the six had been a Starvel AG employee: Martin Snow, white, mid-fifties, overweight. Silently the thought intrigued him. He was familiar with the Starvel Group as a brand: they were famed as the world's oldest and largest Swiss bank. He assumed the man was in someway responsible for their incredible success. In the last ten years they had become one of the largest multinational conglomerates in existence. It seemed no matter where he went in the world Starvel had a branch, or office, or even a hotel.

"Mike is one of the best guards we have," Stan said. "He's going to be providing a guard for Ms Leoni . . . you know what with everything that's happened."

"Oh I quite agree," Velis said nodding. "I'd expect nothing less of the Gardes Suisses. Terrible business," he said, tutting and shaking his head. "It's very reassuring, Wachtmeister Mike. You must protect her with your life."

"I will, sir. Thank you."

"I'm sure we can," de Bois said, putting his hand on Mike's shoulder. A glistening white smile shone across his teeth, appearing all the brighter against the backdrop of his dark goatee. "An unnecessary precaution though I'm sure. As soon as the situation with Leoni et Cie is done and dusted she'll have nothing to worry about. She'll be free to live the life of luxury."

"Yes, she'll be able to have a party every day," Velis said laughing.

Mike smiled.

Stan punched him softly in the arm. "Won't that be great, Mike. Whilst we'll be off guarding His Holiness, you'll be getting down with socialites."

Mike forced a laugh.

"I suppose this is a bit like work for a professional socialite," Velis said, puffing on his cigar. He smoked slowly, the red glow lighting up his face momentarily.

De Bois looked at Mike then Velis. "Now be fair, Louis. You know that girl. She loves her board meetings."

Velis laughed softly. "Yes, but still, nasty business. Let us hope your presence is indeed an unnecessary precaution, wachtmeister. And let us hope that nothing happens to His Holiness while you are away."

Stan laughed, while an awkward grin crossed Mike's face. Inside he felt distracted. Without conscious thought his eyes wandered across the room. Not for the first time his gaze settled on Gabrielle. A rigid expression crossed her face as she spoke with a white-haired banker. A glass of champagne was present in her right hand and she was surrounded by four wannabes. For the merest of seconds she looked at Mike, emotion once more absent from her eyes.

Then she looked away.

"Tell me, old boy," de Bois said, his hand on Mike's shoulder, "am I correct in my understanding that Ms Leoni is looking to offload her shares in Leoni et Cie?"

The question caught him off guard.

"Gee, you'd have to ask Ms Leoni. That has nothing to do with me really, sir."

"Of course, of course," he said, patting Mike on the shoulder. "Just what with everything that has happened . . ."

"Mike hasn't really spoken to her yet," Stan said to de Bois.

An awkward silence fell. He looked at Velis and the man smiled.

"No, of course, well, jolly good," Velis said, placing his cigar between his lips and pulling at his expensive cufflinks. "Now if you'll excuse me, gentlemen, the hour is late. A pleasure, Wachtmeister Mike."

"A pleasure meeting you too, sir," Mike said, shaking hands with Velis then with de Bois. Velis turned away and walked with de Bois through the crowd in the direction of the corridor. It was the same corridor that Mike had earlier walked with Thierry. It was approaching 12:30 a.m. and people were starting to head off to bed in preparation for the funeral in the morning.

"Nice guys."

"Yeah they're all right," Stan said, taking a large gulp of champagne. "Unlike the others here."

"Yeah?"

"Look around. The joint's full of wannabes."

Mike nodded, turning around to see a young woman practically asleep on Mark's shoulder. Rachel was near him, no surprises there. Gabrielle he noticed was not: instead, she was now talking with Cardinal Utaka.

"Wannabes and piss heads."

"And cardinals."

"And bankers."

"And Swiss Guards."

"Vive la Gardes Suisses."

"Vive les wannabes."

9

Mauritius

The hired Jeep thundered along the deserted road at speed. Thick tyres kicked up dust as they bounced over the rocky tarmac like a jet ski against the waves. The road had become increasingly uncomfortable over the last few miles and bruises were beginning to materialise beneath the driver's dusty combats.

He had been driving along the isolated stretch for almost six hours and boredom had set in. The dull landscape, merely a passing blur on the horizon lit only by sparse rays of moonlight passing through moderate cumulus cloud partially covering the black sky, was becoming more and more open as he approached the coast. Up ahead he could just make out the glorious sandy beach.

It was nearing midnight and time was precious.

Mikael Devére yawned vigorously. With the final paragraph of his memoir completed he selected the spellchecker and saved the document without a filename. He yawned for a second time in quick succession. Several hours of staring at the computer screen had left him fatigued.

He clicked the print command and the laser printer sitting dormant on the far side of the room sprung into life.

Devére breathed out deeply before downing the remainder of his coffee. The coffee, now stagnant and cold after standing for well over an hour, tasted bitter and sickly on his dry throat made all the worse by the mugginess that enveloped the room. Ever since the air conditioner had broken three days earlier the heat had become almost unbearable. And living in seclusion on the far side of the island, away from the large towns, he was in no position to fix it.

He peered at the clock on the wall. In his dreary state he had been unaware how late it was.

Yet despite the late hour sleep was the last thing on his mind. The last few days had been the most turbulent of his life.

And he knew that things were possibly about to get worse.

He was one of the most influential men in the world yet he was in hiding. During his days as President of France he had become used to security threats, but not like this. Five days earlier he had nearly been killed and he knew that they could try again at anytime. He wondered how long it might be until they found him.

An hour? A week? A year?

In some ways he wanted to be found. It is better to die than live in hiding.

Yet part of him wanted to hide forever – tucked away on one of the most secluded beaches in the world. The views of infinite sand and blue sea under crystal clear skies were inspiring. It was truly paradise.

But now was not the time to appreciate it.

He ascended to his feet and looked around the room. It was a basic room compared to most in the house. Three large filing cabinets dominated the far wall that was painted white, matching the carpet. A large walk-in wardrobe was located in one corner, used primarily as an overspill for the master bedroom down the hall, next to a glass door leading to a small balcony that offered breathtaking views of the coastline.

As he looked at the far wall he caught a glimpse of himself in the mirror. The vision looked strange to him: it was as if he was seeing a total stranger. The normally handsome and noble face of the seventy-two-year-old from Bordeaux looked more like a phantom than a politician. Beads of sweat covered his forehead while his hair, bald in the centre and framed by messy unkempt strands of grey, seemed to be turning white before his eyes. His eyes, surrounded by shades of purple, seemed less vibrant than usual. A thin beard covered his face, the result of a week without shaving. The rough hair went some way towards covering the cut on his right cheek, a tangible reminder of the surprise encounter that forced him to flee.

As he looked away from the mirror he noticed a framed photograph on top of a nearby cabinet. It was a family photograph. He was standing against the wall alongside his wife, and surrounded by his four children and three grandkids. He walked towards it and picked it up longingly. He paid close attention to his youngest granddaughter. She would be three next week.

His sigh was interrupted by the sound of the printer informing him the job was done. After replacing the frame on the wall-side cabinet he walked towards the printer and picked up the newly printed sheets. He scanned the contents quickly for clarity.

This was his last gamble. Perhaps the young policeman was right. If the world knew, then maybe he would survive.

Time was precious.

The battered Jeep continued through a clearing and descended at a sharp angle over the brow of a hill. The road was now bumpier than before yet conveniently flanked by trees on either side. Dust covered the tyres and much of the bodywork, ruining the overall appearance of the vehicle that had been painted a smart green colour when he hired it seven hours earlier. Stones flew up from the tyres as they made contact with the hard ground, made crumbly from several weeks without rain, causing further wear and tear to the tyres now lacking in grip and making it difficult to keep to the road.

Up ahead a solitary villa stood overlooking the coast. A light from an upstairs window shone like a beacon through the darkness, illuminating large stretches of the beach. Another two kilometres and he would be there.

He had found him.

With his task completed, Devére slid open the patio door and eased outside. He walked a yard or so across the balcony and leaned despondently against the metal railing.

From there he looked aimlessly across the darkness. The moon, now brighter than before as the cloud dispersed, illuminated the horizon in a ghostly haze that reflected its light magnificently across the calm waters of the Indian Ocean. To his left, the gentle tide swayed pleasantly against the shore in the still air.

Devére lowered his head into his folded arms. He felt his eyes filling up with sorrow. In his mind's eye he imagined the faces of his family as they celebrated his granddaughter's birthday, still without knowing where he had gone. The thought of them sitting at home waiting for that phone call letting them know he was okay had played on his mind ever since his sudden departure. The situation tortured him, the grim realisation that he knew he couldn't contact them or risk putting them at risk.

How had it come to this?

He looked out across the countryside, his attention on the horizon. Out of the corner of his eye he noticed something strange. Something was moving across the horizon. Suddenly he felt a choking sensation in his throat. It was not the dense air that caused sudden panic. Lights, headlamps, cut the darkness focusing in the direction of his house.

As his eyes focused on the road, his mouth opened and vague elements of drool fell to the ground below. The lights were unmistakable.

They had found him.

The Jeep came to a halt outside the house. After switching off the engine, the driver killed the lights. He closed the door without consideration for any need of silence and surveyed the house. The upstairs light that had illuminated the coastline like a lighthouse only moments earlier had been extinguished in a poor attempt to outfox him. It really was a poor attempt. There was nowhere to hide.

After concealing his face with a balaclava he walked towards the door. Unsurprisingly it was locked.

He took a step back and surveyed the building. He paid particular attention to the glass door of the once lighted room. The sliding door that led to the balcony was closed and devoid of any sign of disturbance.

Slowly he exhaled. The prickly heat, burning like hot coal against his hands as he rubbed them together, felt somehow satisfying. His ears strained for any sound of life but he heard nothing. The soft swaying of the tide was the only disturbance to the silence.

He approached the entrance and removed a crowbar from his jacket.

Not wasting a second, Devére unlocked the door to his safe using combination. It didn't look like a regular safe. The true nature of the device was concealed by its casual appearance as a cabinet. Gathering together the printed sheets of the document, the ink barely dry from printing minutes earlier, he placed the document on the top shelf. In his hurried state, his skin prickly from panic and heat, he placed the laptop and a memory stick atop the pile of printed sheets and closed the door. He locked it hastily and closed the second door, hiding the safe from view.

Suddenly he heard a bang coming from downstairs. Then silence.

Devére stood motionless. Straining for any sound of life he heard footsteps, male footsteps, unmistakable, sand boots, possibly of a soldier, walking confidently across the tiled kitchen floor. Then they were muffled.

He had reached the lounge.

*

The intruder continued through the darkened room. He walked cautiously, careful not to alert the owner by knocking over any items of furniture. The room was well furnished, its many items lit only by the sparse rays of moonlight penetrating the open curtains to the large windows overlooking the sea.

The intruder moved towards the stairs and slowly began to ascend them.

He removed his SIG P75 from his pocket.

As the footsteps became louder, Devére realised he had to act fast. He looked at the balcony. No chance. There was no other way down. He gazed at the safe and considered the files he had just hidden.

At least he would never find them.

Faced with no other option, he eyed the walk-in wardrobe at the far corner of the room. On the stairs, the footsteps were getting louder. He gently opened the door and closed it noiselessly.

Holding his breath . . .

Suddenly the door to the room opened widely and the Jeep driver entered. At first he was surprised to see that the room was deserted. Switching on the wall light, he scanned the room for signs of life and saw there were none. The door to the balcony was closed. Looking through the glass, he could see that there was nowhere there to hide.

Pondering his options, the intruder stood in silence.

Inside the wardrobe Devére's view was good. Through narrow slit holes he could see the intruder standing motionlessly, surveying the room.

Hidden only by the door and some of his wife's coats, he stood as quietly as possible.

The intruder paused. He thought he sensed something. It was a peculiar feeling, but one he often felt on a mission. Had his senses deceived him? Something was drawing him towards the wardrobe.

Inside, Devére's breathing quickened, the sound almost audible. The intruder moved forward, pausing in front of the door. The door opened in a flash and Devére felt a kick to the stomach. The Frenchman fell from the wardrobe and hit the floor, a metre or so from the intruder. Pain shuddered through his kidneys.

The intruder eyed Devére curiously. This was not the man he knew. The first thing he noticed was his hair, usually so smartly combed, now appearing frizzy and sweaty in the unpleasant air.

Next, the intruder examined his face, that famous face. His appearance was now more reminiscent of a drunken tramp than a former president.

Then he looked at his clothes. Gone were the expensive suits. Instead the tatty polo shirt looked like he had been wearing it constantly for days on end.

Devére looked at the intruder. The first thing he noticed was his face, covered with that stupid balaclava.

The intruder spoke first. "So this is where you've been hiding."

Devére felt vomit slowly float up to the top of his throat. In the heat it hurt to swallow. "Take the mask off, Ludo. You embarrass us both."

The man smirked. He was right, of course. He placed his right hand to his head and removed the balaclava. A grim smile crossed Ludovic Gullet's face as he walked in a circular motion, resembling a shark monitoring its prey.

"Remain on your knees, Mikael. I am not going to tell you again. There is no point in trying to escape. We are quite alone here. Any silly games and I shall have to hurt you very badly."

Inhaling at irregular intervals, Devére remained silent. He adjusted his sweat-soaked shirt, sticking uncomfortably to his body. Silently he considered his options, all the while gazing with malice at his unwelcome guest. The intruder did the same. Both said nothing for a time and this seemed to suit Gullet. He was right and Devére knew it.

They were quite alone.

"Well, Ludo? What do you want? I have no money."

The intruder spat on the floor, phlegm sticking to the lush carpet. "Do not be absurd, Mikael. I have not come halfway around the world to pinch your wallet."

Devére shrugged. "Then why are you here?"

Gullet removed a pack of cigarettes from his dark combat trousers and opened it. He placed the first available cigarette to his lips and lit it. The foul smell filled the stuffy room. The still night air remained unpleasant, reflected by the noiseless sea, the tide now almost motionless.

"We don't have much time, Mikael," Gullet said, removing the cigarette from his mouth and blowing smoke in his face. "I have some questions to ask. I think you know what they are."

Devére looked at him blankly. Then he gazed at the clock on the wall. It was now 12:12 a.m. It seemed an age ago that he last looked. Time was no longer on his side.

"I have not the faintest idea."

The intruder smirked. He knew Devére was lying.

"This is a nice place," he said, exhaling smoke once again in Devére's direction. "The only question on my mind is, why come here now?"

Devére looked back sternly. "What do you want?"

There was a thoughtful yet arrogant smugness about him. "I have been sent here by a man with no name who is very upset. He says that you are out to destroy his business."

Devére remained unflinching.

"He seems to think that it was you who leaked the findings of Nathan Walls to Al Leoni and Jermaine Llewellyn."

Devére shook his head. As a politician he was used to defending his cause but this was hopeless. Agonising.

"I have never spoken to Jermaine Llewellyn in my life."

That was true. The intruder probably knew it. Still no answer.

"Ludo, believe me."

For several seconds he remained silent. For Devére this was worse than any possible torture Gullet could have offered.

"The man also instructs me to tell you that Mr Broadie wants his manuscript back."

A jolt of understanding informed Gullet that what was said was understood. The intruder smoked with a sick pleasure as he saw the man's shoulders slump, sound in the knowledge that he was not in a position to put up a fight.

Devére shrugged at Gullet. He considered stalling for time, but what good would it do? He wondered how he would die. It could be any number of ways. There was no chance of the intruder being witnessed. Suddenly courage came to him.

"Well you can tell Mr Broadie he can kiss my mutha-fucking ass. I do not have it."

Gullet stepped forward and pistol-whipped the politician across the cheek – the scar that was beginning to heal suddenly slit open. Blood seeped down his face, sticking to his skin.

"Why?" Gullet barked. "After all we've been through together, why does it have to end this way?"

The intruder wiped his mouth and took another drag on his cigarette. Smoke escaped from his mouth and nose. He blew with fury and kicked Devére with his right foot.

"Now listen carefully, you filthy piece of shit. I want to know: where is it?"

Devére rolled over, coughing in the dryness. The feeling of being winded felt excruciating on his dry throat and stomach. He looked up at Gullet and felt a strange satisfaction knowing that he would never find what he sought. He started laughing and the intruder punched him once again. He began to lose feeling as the cheek began to numb.

"Where is it?"

Devére gazed once more at the photo of his family and nodded philosophically. Finally he smiled.

"You know, Ludo, I always thought that you were an ass. You can tell Monsieur Broadie, you're also a failure."

The intruder looked at Devére, his expression resembling thunder. Finally he forced a laugh. He threw his cigarette to the ground, scarring the carpet. He extinguished it with his boots and raised his gun.

10

St Gallen

Mike had visited the City of St Gallen on many occasions during his youth. Although it had been over ten years since his previous visit, he remembered it as though he had never left.

During his school years he often spent the months of summer with his Swiss mother and grandmother in the small town of Altstätten near the foot of the Alpstein Mountains close to the Austrian border and would visit the city quite frequently. He never disliked Altstätten, a fairly unspoilt and charming town in the Rhine Valley unchanged despite the passing of time, but the lack of entertainment often left him bored.

Even when he was a kid he dreamed of seeing the world. He remembered vividly being required to speak about his ambitions during his interview to join the Swiss Guard. He recalled one Sunday when he was nine: he was leaving church with his grandmother and the locals were saying goodbye to a young soldier who had completed his army training and was set to become a Swiss Guard. Even now he had not forgotten the looks on the people's faces as they said farewell to the brave young man. Although Mike never found out what happened to the young man, perhaps he served with him now, something happened to him that day that would go on to shape his life. For what seemed like hours the wannabe Swiss Guard spoke of his lifelong desire to serve, only to learn that of the required two-hour interview, only seven minutes had passed.

It was ironic that fate had led him back to the city as a Swiss Guard so many years after he had dreamed of being one. It was also rather bizarre that Gabrielle Leoni's château was in such close proximity to his grandmother's old home.

But that, according to Commissario Pessotto, was precisely why he was chosen.

Today he didn't look like a Swiss Guard. Replacing the historic attire, his Reebok trainers, dark tracksuit bottoms and black fleece hardly stood out from the crowd. He was armed but no one could tell. A SIG P75 was hidden by zip-up leggings and another was concealed in the glove compartment. He had never fired either, except in training, and doubted they would be needed today. St Gallen was hardly a violent area during the day.

Gabrielle didn't approve of his dress sense. It was bad enough that she had to be babysat, let alone by someone who dressed like he did. She promised to take him shopping in the coming days, and she had already made a long list of things for him to buy: or to put it a better way – for her to buy for him. Her attitude since his arrival had been consistent. She was the princess, he was an intruder. But he wasn't only a guard: he was also her driver.

Of course, he assumed that her lavishing attention on his appearance might not have been so straightforward.

The funeral was an occasion unlike any he had ever witnessed. He had attended the funeral of the late Pope John Paul II, but the funeral of Al Leoni was, in many ways, even more elaborate. Over twelve hundred people attended the service in the Abbey of St Gall. His uncle, Cardinal Tepilo, led a moving ceremony, joined in various parts by Cardinal Utaka, del Rosi and four others of prominent status. A famous folk singer that Mike had never heard of performed a moving rendition of Ave Maria, followed later in the proceedings by an overweight tenor in his fifties singing Amazing Grace in Italian.

Other people of interest appeared. Louis Velis was present with Gilbert de Bois, along with their partners, accompanied closely by others who Mike didn't know.

All the key officials of the Vatican Bank were present, as was Thierry and several other key personnel from both the Swiss Guard and the Vatican Police. He didn't have much chance to speak to Thierry, but the oberst nodded at him from time to time to acknowledge his presence.

Many other wealthy figures that had not appeared at the château also attended the Mass. Throughout the ceremony the Swiss Guard couldn't help wonder who they were, how they came to be there. Not for the first time the expressions on the faces of some of the mourners looked doleful – yet another smartly dressed individual offering condolences to a departed brother whose only mutual characteristic was their bank balance.

Rachel was there, in the company of no one in particular. She sat in the pew behind Gabrielle, looking very beautiful in an elegant black dress. Gabrielle's mother was there, sitting alongside her daughter, but for the most part remained anonymous, tears flowing from time to time.

And, of course, there was Gabrielle. She certainly looked like a weeping daughter. A black veil covered her attractive face, and she made a continued attempt to conceal the tears. She walked slowly that day, although he couldn't tell how much of it was real. Not for the first time there was a distance to her, but, despite this, there was something about her that made him feel a strange genuine ache for her loss. She may have been from the upper crust, yet there are some things even the wealthiest can't buy and in no way was that more perfectly portrayed than in the moment when she read her specially written tribute to her father. Diamonds hung around her neck, three fingers were ringed and pearls dangled from her ears – even the veil was worth more than his monthly pay packet. But as he stood at the back watching her every move a void that wasn't visible before now existed: it was a strange void, a hollow emptiness that could only be explained by losing something or someone irreplaceable. Behind the façade of a lady in her early thirties, entrepreneur and socialite swimming in elegance unrivalled even by some Hollywood actresses, stood a frightened child, all alone in the big wide world. For the only time since his arrival he felt closer to her, despite the gap of over a hundred yards, than he had done to anyone for a long time.

But that was then. Al Leoni was buried in the family mausoleum, located in the grounds of the château. Everyone stayed for the lavish banquet, somewhat more sombre than the night before. Then everyone left and they were alone.

All that needed to be done was done.

Mike turned right on reaching the city centre, heading in the direction of the Abbey of St Gall. Sleet was falling against the tinted windows of the silver Lexus, dripping down the glass and melting on the pavement. He remembered times when he had walked the pavement before – a very long time ago. The thought made him smile.

After turning another corner he drove past the Abbey of St Gall. The location was deserted and lying silent, a far cry from the last time he was there. He looked briefly into the rear-view mirror: partly to make the turn and partly to see if the site of her father's recent funeral had left a mark on her.

It hadn't. She seemed oblivious to its appearance, and to his. As usual since his arrival, he drove and she rode in the back. It was as if he was an actual chauffeur and she his employer.

For Mikael Frei, becoming a wachtmeister was suddenly the worst thing that had ever happened to him.

It was approaching noon when he parked the Lexus in central St Gallen. By the time he had switched off the engine and exited the car she was already descending the ramp of the Leoni et Cie employee car park that led to the street. To her credit she didn't need to be waited on hand and foot but that was hardly what he was there for.

If the role of doorman were added to his list of duties then he'd most probably have pointed the SIG P75 at himself.

Gabrielle walked so quickly that he needed to burst into a jog to catch up with her. Her high heels were hardly the most convenient footwear for the slushy underfoot, but it was otherwise in keeping with her appearance. It amazed him how she could walk so fast in such footwear. She was not the only person walking the street dressed as she was, but that was hardly shocking: it was a street of wealth and status. From her facial expression alone Mike couldn't tell whether she loved it or hated it. She pulled off the businesswoman look but it didn't quite suit her. She wasn't into the whole Carrie Bradshaw thing either. She was used to cocktails and designer clothing but boardrooms and business meetings weren't really her.

Not for the first time she made a good actress.

They walked the street carefully, heading in the direction of the bank. The four-storey building dated back to the early 1790s, and had been built specifically for the new private bank. It didn't look like a typical commercial bank. The grey stone looked dirty in the gloom, and what the tinted windows gained in privacy they lost in appearance. Overlooking the door was the bank's eminent logo, a gothic castle, identical to the one she lived in.

Leoni et Cie was one of the oldest banks in Switzerland. Like many private banks in St Gallen it was founded as a partnership in the late 18th century and for over two hundred years had remained under the control of the same family.

As Mike understood of the family history, Banque Leoni was founded in 1783 by Jean-Antonin Leoni, a thirty-three-year-old native of Zürich who had moved to Paris fourteen years earlier to pursue a career in banking having earlier studied in Geneva. Following the outbreak of the French Revolution, Leoni returned to Switzerland with an impressive fortune already amassed from his new bank and moved operations to St Gallen while the French banking sector shut down.

According to family tradition Leoni, a devout Catholic, used the bank as a mechanism to help fleeing aristocrats escape from France during the Reign of Terror and even funded some military operations for the Papal States against Napoleon I following his triumph in France.

Even before the formation of Banque Leoni the Leoni name had been intricately linked to the political, economic, cultural and religious life of Europe. According to accounts from the 15th century, a Sébastian Leoni had been a Burgher of Zürich in the 1450s while in the two centuries that followed the family distinguished themselves as bishops, priests, surgeons, theologians, members of the Zürich Grand Council, one composer, and from 1710 onwards concentrated their efforts on trade and commerce.

Although Jean-Antonin Leoni returned to France in 1796, once banking had resumed in Paris, his stay lasted only until 1804 when he became a target of Napoleon I for his role assisting aristocrats fleeing the revolution. Despite managing to flee to Palermo, Leoni was eventually captured by an Italian mercenary on Napoleon's behalf and guillotined in France less than two months later. With Banque Leoni now in the hands of his son, Jean-Sébastian, operations resumed in France during the reign of Louis XVIII before the bank was later outlawed on the orders of Napoleon III, leading to Banque Leoni concentrating on establishing trade links with much of central Europe and the new United States of America from its base in St Gallen.

For his gallantry in assisting the Papal States in their war against Napoleon I, and his later death, Jean-Antonin Leoni was made a venerable by the Church in 1886 and in 1921 was beatified.

Gabrielle entered the bank through the four-pronged revolving glass door and walked confidently across the spacious atrium, followed immediately by Mike. It was his first visit to a Leoni et Cie bank and he didn't really know what to expect. Behind the reception desk a woman of plain features sat with her eyes fixed on her work, her demeanour resembling the efficient manner of a 19th century Victorian headmistress. Gabrielle stopped at the desk and stood quietly in front of her. The woman looked up inquisitively but at first remained silent. She glared at Gabrielle, although still giving the impression of looking down her nose.

"*Oui?*" she said. "*Comment ça va?*"

"I'm here about a deposit box," Gabrielle replied, choosing English rather than French or German.

"Do you have an account?"

"Of course."

"And your name?"

"It's a numbered account," Gabrielle replied, almost as if to say mind your own business. "I phoned an hour ago."

She pointed to an electronic keypad. "Enter your account number here."

Gabrielle placed her empty briefcase against the desk and entered the digits from memory. The receptionist softened her stance.

"Of course," she said, pointing to the lift. "Third floor."

The smartly dressed concierge standing by the lift acknowledged her presence and ushered Gabrielle and Mike inside. He pressed the button on their behalf and exited before the doors closed. The journey continued uninterrupted until the third floor at which point the branch manager, dressed in a smart suit and well polished shoes, was there to greet them.

"Ms Leoni, how nice to see you."

She forced a smile. "Philippe."

He smiled politely and pointed to a palm screen. He informed Gabrielle of the usual procedure, which was nothing new to her, and demonstrated the use of the fingerprint scanner, an alternative to needing a key. She pressed her right hand on the screen, which scanned her fingertips biometrically. The word *Beglaubigt* flashed, informing her that she had been authenticated.

"Follow me please."

The dark-haired manager retrieved the safe deposit box before leading her to a private cubicle, cloaked by a red curtain. Mike walked slowly after her, stroking his SIG P75 through his fleece and examining the location with interest. On either side of the room countless deposit boxes lined the walls like a gigantic filing cabinet. He had seen many similar ones in the American banks but somehow these seemed more secretive. He had seen countless movies where deposit boxes like these concealed unimaginable secrets, hidden away like pirate treasure. He had been in the Vatican Secret Archives and this was in some ways quite similar.

The safe deposit box was of metal construction, approximately twelve inches in width and breadth and twenty-four inches in height. Inside the cubicle, a desk was fixed in the corner and a chair was tucked neatly underneath.

Gabrielle pulled the curtain closed and slowly opened the box. It was not particularly different to the contents of years before. Inside, she found several documents, birth certificates et cetera, ad hoc selections of various currencies but nothing out of the usual. A few contracts of significance, including various property rights and ownership documents were recognisable by the logos, perhaps twenty in all, some of which dated back two centuries. Finally she located a large envelope, brown in colour, sealed with the official stamp of her lawyers. This was what she had wanted:

It was her father's will.

She knew what was inside. A few scraps would go to distant cousins, nephews and nieces, et cetera; a certain amount would go to her aunt in Frankfurt. Some would go to her mother, and the majority to her uncle and her.

Unsurprisingly that would include a forty-three per cent controlling stake in Leoni et Cie PLC.

She opened her briefcase with two distinct clicks and slipped the envelope inside. Once finished, she returned her attention to the box and scanned the remaining documents.

One in particular caught her eye. Unlike the others, it was a small white envelope that had been officially sealed with a Leoni et Cie logo. She moved her painted finger and thumb gently across the envelope, unveiling a single sheet of white paper. It was clearly the information for another bank account. The Leoni et Cie logo was also present at the top right corner and the account number began with three zeros. Unsurprisingly, no name or any other details were present. More surprisingly, a key was also present in the envelope, indicating another deposit account, but of the older pedigree.

Her heart rate increased as the sound of footsteps outside the curtain suddenly became more vociferous. Unbeknown to her a white Frenchman in his forties was being escorted by an employee to a faraway cubicle. Returning her attention to the other account, she closed the deposit box slowly and placed it on the desk.

The key was still present in her hand.

Mike had become quite used to waiting outside a cubicle over the last two weeks. She was always running errands. She shopped, she visited other banks, she visited other institutions of which she was patron, all of which helped endorse the feeling that he was an outsider. It was clear she loved her privacy, but not just against him. Everything was an intrusion.

He looked for several seconds at the red curtain, doing his best to concentrate on the task at hand. It was funny that the curtain, such an inanimate object not unlike those used in changing rooms at clothes shops, somehow seemed to separate him from her like some great impenetrable force field. He had seen it happen in several films: someone was abducted from a changing room or toilet or similar and the thought silently amused him yet at the same time also unnerved him. He glanced quickly at the clock above the reception desk.

The sooner she was out, the happier he'd be.

He looked around the bank out of ritual and saw that it was practically deserted. Behind the desk, about ten feet away, the man named Philippe continued to stare, but until now he was still to speak to him. He was only doing his job, Mike mused, but maybe he could sense the firearm. The man didn't know he was a Swiss Guard, but something told him he knew he was a soldier. Maybe it was the way he stood, or the way he carried himself. Who knows? It takes one to know one and this guy possibly used to be one.

More than five minutes passed before the curtain opened and Gabrielle walked out. The black briefcase under her arm, empty on arrival, now carried the weight of one small document.

"I'd also like to see this," Gabrielle said, waving the other key at the manager.

The man named Philippe nodded. "Of course, Ms Leoni."

He asked for the key and she passed it to him. He had never worked with her personally but he was well aware who she was, and what she was known for.

Gabrielle stood silently, giving the impression of calm and patience.

"If you would put in the numbers, please."

She inserted the numbers from memory and calmly held her breath. Her relaxed persona was in keeping with her usual demeanour, but inside her head was filled with curiosity.

Her father had never mentioned this account.

"Would you like to use the same cubicle?"

"That would be fine."

Without looking at Mike she followed the employee to retrieve the box and re-entered the cubicle. He placed it on the same desk as before and closed the curtain on leaving, returning the original box to its rightful location. The second box was identical to the last one, which was no surprise. The weight was also the same; that was no surprise either. The content's weight was insignificant to the build of the box.

The box was definitely the same, same height, metal clasps and a handle. Yet somehow this one was different. It was somehow more mysterious. It reminded her of a time ten years earlier when she was in Peru with her uncle, working with him on an excavation in the City of

Ica, around the area where a series of bizarre stones had once been found suggesting man once lived alongside the dinosaur. She hesitated but decided to continue.

She checked the curtain before slowly opening the box.

It was the last thing she expected. Located at the bottom of the box, paper casing, brown in colour, surrounded what felt like a box or a heavy manuscript, possibly several hundred pages thick.

A look of confusion crossed her face.

She picked it up slowly, attempting to ascertain its significance by feeling the cover. The strong casing gave nothing away. She placed the peculiar item into her briefcase before double-checking the box. It was the only item.

Moments later she left the cubicle breezily and smiled at the manager. After handing over the now empty deposit box she walked behind the desk and stopped before a computer monitor.

"May I check something?" she asked looking at the screen.

Considering himself in no position to argue, he moved out of her way, allowing Gabrielle access to the desktop. She clicked several times in succession on the mouse and typed numbers on the keyboard. She waited several seconds. Finally a bemused expression crossed her face.

"When was this last used?" she asked, referring to the second deposit box.

The man thought for a moment. "It must have been four weeks ago."

Gabrielle nodded.

Shortly before her father's death.

11

St Peter's Basilica had been closed for over an hour. Not for the first time in recent weeks, Cardinal Utaka had entered the church at its quietest and was kneeling silently at prayer. For the cardinal it was a time for quiet reflection at the end of another day of chaos. The purple shades under his eyes were seemingly larger than they had been the previous day, and his mind continued to be plagued by dark thoughts.

Life may have been a struggle at present, but he had known worse. There had been times when his whole life had been burdened by constant pressure. Ever since his birth in a now destroyed shantytown in Niger, the only boy of five, all products of the same father, a teacher, and mother, a cleaner, his life had been plagued by poverty.

Then at the age of nine his life became even worse.

Following the destruction of his home, he was exposed to the realities of the nation's capital of Niamey. Living in a one-bedroom house during the peak of the Diori Regime, following the country's independence from France in 1960, Utaka learned the harsh circumstances of a nation suffering severe drought and famine at a time of rampant corruption. During his teens his aim had been to become a physician, but his parents couldn't afford the cost of education. After working for a time as a teacher, the young man moved to France in 1965, just as the nation's hold on its former colony began to diminish.

Until his arrival in France religion had never been a big part of his life. Officially he was recorded as a pagan, a survivor from Niger's pre-Muslim past that was barely relevant to the harsh realities of the new regime. But he never considered himself spiritual. Death, corruption, famine and drought left little time for the traditions of the desert and what little faith Utaka had was dampened by the circumstances of the time.

But in France that changed after meeting a local priest, Father Abidal, the only white man who treated Utaka like a white man. Niger still reeked of its colonial past, yet Abidal illustrated to him the true meaning of Jesus Christ. Love thy neighbour seemed lost on Utaka after witnessing so many years of tyranny, but soon he became enthralled by the ways of his new friend. Within a year he chose to be baptised and within four years he was ordained a Catholic priest. He began as a missionary in the shantytowns of Peru and Bolivia, but fate took him back to Niamey. His parents passed away, but his mother lived to see him become a bishop. It was one of his lasting regrets that when she died he was away in the Philippines. Yet it warmed him to learn that in her last days she entrusted to his eldest sister that knowing his success had made the last years of her life the ones she regarded as her proudest.

For ten years now the man who came from absolute poverty had defied the circumstances of his early years and found a home in the house of St Peter. Despite a life sapping in energy and hardships his motivation for his vocation remained undiminished. He had beaten cancer once and struggled with pain to the joints, but still found the energy to undertake all the roles placed on him by the Church. Some he cherished; some were great hardships.

At present, it was the latter.

The echo of heavy feet disrupted his thoughts. The cardinal opened his eyes slowly and turned in the direction of the noise. After seeing Thierry approach from the back of the church, he struggled to his feet and genuflected towards the main altar. He placed the pressure of his frame onto the nearest pew and came face to face with the oberst.

Neither spoke to begin with. The Swiss Guard knelt reverently before the cardinal who placed a hand on his shoulder. The cardinal uttered a blessing in Latin and removed his hand, placing it on the pew for support.

Thierry kissed the cardinal's ring and rose to his feet. The tiredness in his eyes remained – something also present in the cardinal. Both had needed time to reflect on what was now an escalating problem. In many ways their lives would have been so much easier if they could have struck back with violence. But even if they were so inclined, they were still not sure exactly what they were dealing with.

"Tell me, de Courten," the cardinal said slowly, "is what I hear true?"

Thierry didn't respond immediately. Yet an answer was clear from the seriousness in his eyes.

"I'm afraid it is, eminence."

The cardinal seemed to shake slightly on hearing the news. He closed his eyes.

"I spoke to Commissario Pessotto not one hour ago. Mikael Devére was found in his home in Mauritius. He had recently been holidaying there."

Utaka mumbled something, possibly the man's name, something that to Thierry seemed an act of compassion: that by acknowledging the deceased man's existence the cardinal felt sympathy for his passing.

"What happened?"

Thierry chose his words carefully. He spoke of Devére being found shot in Mauritius where he owned a holiday villa on the eastern shore. He spoke of him being found in his study: the condition of the house, and the room, largely unaltered. Nothing seemed to be missing; no obvious signs of struggle except for forced entry via the back door. The blood found on the floor was confirmed as Devére's, not that there was any other likely possibility.

Only one strange feature was present. Graffiti marked the wall, the logo of the party in opposition.

The cardinal nodded despondently, confirming that he had understood.

"You really think they were responsible?"

Thierry paused. It was obvious to the oberst the graffiti was a smokescreen.

"We cannot ignore this any further, de Courten. It is indisputable."

Thierry nodded. A grim realisation began to sink in. All of the deaths so far had had a disturbing pattern, yet this one had one obvious motive. In order to clarify its significance it would be necessary to uncover who was behind it. The new circumstances complicated things. The press reaction in France was already referring to Devére's assassination as the end of the world.

Ironically, in time, it might save it.

12

The drive back to the château occurred mostly in silence. She didn't value his company – that much was clear from her decision, once again, to ride in the back rather than up front with Mike. He had already become used to her ignoring him. But he was used to working in silence. As a Swiss Guard he was forbidden from talking in the ranks and, despite not being on parade, the atmosphere felt quite similar.

He was able to choose his own bedroom and that was an advantage. The sixteen on the fourth floor were off limits but the remaining thirty-seven were not. The bedroom he chose was on the third floor at the rear of the building and talk about spacious: the room was larger than some one-bed apartments. A relatively modern queen-sized bed dominated the centre of the room, casting an eerie shadow across the floor and pale walls as the afternoon sun seeped in through large gothic windows.

A fine array of furniture, much of which dated back to the 18th century, lined the room, including a sturdy oak desk tucked up in the corner. A large antique mirror overlooked an out of date fireplace that was now just for show, ornately decorated with etchings of characters from Greek mythology onto a wooden panel that had been painted white in the 1990s. The room had no bathroom, but that was no bother. A fine bathroom had recently been fitted a few metres down the corridor.

The room was lavish but that was not the reason he chose it. He was there to provide protection and the room was ideal for that reason.

Rule number one: always cover the rear.

As a large gate and an effective CCTV system monitored every corner of the building, Mike decided to concentrate on the gardens. The room's large windows, including double doors leading to a balcony, provided a perfect view of the well-maintained gardens: without question the most beautiful he had ever seen.

A large fountain was situated in the centre of a hedged courtyard, distributing its water along four separate channels flowing to the north, east, south and west, and lined with small statues and topiary of characters from the classical period. The garden extended over ten acres in total and was walled from every corner of the first two thousand square metres, helping to protect the plants from the wind. Various plants and trees, bare due to the time of year, surrounded countless other minor water features which were placed seemingly at random. In the summer, the garden would host a wide variety of plants not usually found in St Gallen, but able to grow due to the garden's microclimate made possible by the thick wall.

The design was unlike any he had seen before, although as he understood from Gabrielle's gardener, much of it was typical of a walled garden dating back to the gardens of ancient Persia: the four channels that distributed the water from the fountain separated the area into four quarters, supposedly representing the four rivers of Eden.

Beyond the far wall, nine acres of greenery created an attractive setting, interrupted by three streams that flowed throughout. Towards the north-west a small sun house was located on the shore of a lake, roughly half a mile from the château. Dogs and birds roamed the garden at leisure and at the western end of the garden stood a grim looking early 18th century mausoleum, now containing the remains of Gabrielle's late father. Supposedly seven generations of the family were now entombed there. Eventually Gabrielle would join him there – whenever that might be.

Despite the pleasant surroundings, the garden disturbed him. Abundant vegetation and water features may have been a photographer's dream, but it also provided plenty of places to hide. Although there had been no sign so far of infiltration, a lingering feeling of doubt continuously scratched away at him as it had done every day since his arrival. Soldiers called it intuition. In many ways it was the reason he chose to serve in the army of Jesus, but it was also the reason why for the first time in his career even the flutter of birds flying among the ancient trees caused a genuine sense of alertness. The vision of her father and the other deceased men still haunted him, but what troubled him most was that he knew an attack on her was coming. The seven death warrants were an arrogant admission of responsibility for a string of murders, yet the identities of the individuals responsible remained concealed behind a faceless organisation. Thierry spoke of the importance of Leoni et Cie yet to Mike the story was incomplete.

Researching the matter, he'd learned that the Rite of Larmenius dated back to around 1717, if not earlier, and had a reputed 400 members worldwide, all of whom were Master Masons. Although many of their members may have been Catholic, under Vatican law Catholic Freemasons were forbidden from taking communion at Mass. Their statutes stood for good, notably pursuit of knowledge, yet their logo unsettled him. The inclusion of a skull and crossbones, in keeping with that of the Jolly Roger, supposedly represented man's mortality. The cross suggested a religious pedigree but Mike presumed the financiers in America would not have been murdered for such a reason. It was not a cross in the conventional sense. He assumed Pessotto and Thierry knew, they must have known what Mark knew, but they weren't going to tell him. He hated being in the dark and now, for all intents and purposes, the lights were out.

He looked suddenly to his left in a reflex action. The bedroom door was opening, making a quiet creaking sound. Gabrielle had entered the room. Unlike earlier, she was dressed casually in a blue top and her hair was scattered untidily. She walked across the room slowly and stopped on reaching the bed.

"My mom thought you might be hungry."

Now on his feet, he eyed her closely. The mascara under her eyes was smudged slightly. It was clear that she had been crying.

"Thank you, I am."

"Dinner will be ready in an hour."

Mike nodded, forcing a smile. He watched her, expecting her to leave, but for now she remained still. She stood silently, her eyes focused on a selection of photographs covering the eastern wall. He looked at them briefly, his attention on a man in Swiss Army uniform, aged somewhere between 25 and 30.

He looked again at her and she looked at him, her thoughts once more returned to reality. She offered the briefest of smiles before leaving the room. It wasn't a warm smile but strangely affectionate nonetheless: as though she was satisfied with his performance.

"I nearly forgot," she said, stopping in the doorway. "Thierry called when we were out."

"Thanks, I'll call him."

She didn't say anything else. It was clear to Mike that her eyes were filling up once more, and she didn't want to cry in front of him. He reasoned it was probably at least partly for that reason she had pretty much avoided him since his arrival. After closing the door he heard the vague sounds of sighing as she made her way down the corridor. For the briefest of moments he almost wanted to comfort her, not that she would allow it.

Thoughts turned to Thierry. He hadn't spoken to him since his arrival and that had been irritating. He reached for his mobile phone and dialled Thierry's office number. It was probably a routine enquiry, he guessed, but he wanted to speak to him, if only for reassurance.

He dialled the phone, his attention once more on the wall. He looked closely at the photo again: the man in question was probably about six foot, handsome and, based on the clothing, of NCO rank. The man looked vaguely familiar to him, but not in an obvious way. He wondered briefly whether he was a relation, or else a former lover. As far as he knew she had never married. Everything else was a mystery.

He waited for the ringing to go to voicemail and decided to hang up. After getting no reply the first time, he tried again ten minutes later. On this occasion the oberst answered and was clearly pleased to hear from him.

"Ah, Frei, how are things?"

It was clearly a question of courtesy. He was not interested in Stephanie Leoni's ceaseless mourning, or her daughter's autocratic treating of Mike. No, his only concern was Leoni et Cie.

"All quiet, sir."

"Any problems?"

Any problems? What he really meant was has anyone tried to murder the owner of Leoni et Cie?

"No problems, sir."

The conversation changed. Thierry spoke about Mikael Devére.

He spoke for over thirty minutes.

Gabrielle walked slowly down the long corridor of the fourth floor and stopped in front of her father's study. A sense of anticipation overcame her on entering the room, causing her to stop. It was a strange feeling, not common but also not unfamiliar: it was almost reminiscent of checking a supposedly deserted room after hearing the sound of footsteps from within.

Inside, the room was largely unchanged since her father's death and many of his possessions still occupied the desk. Although momentarily distressed by the many reminders, it was not that what troubled her.

The object wrapped in paper was lying in a cleared space in the centre of the desk.

Still to be opened.

Using a penknife, recently retrieved from downstairs, she fought determinedly against the surprisingly tough outer shell. There were at least three layers of packaging in total, each an efficient barrier, protecting the item from the outside world.

Finally it opened.

She removed the casing carefully, scattering it across the desk. The package itself, excellently preserved from perhaps several decades without use, would have been an enigma in itself had it not been for what was inside. The item in question was indeed a manuscript, possibly a chronicle, beautifully preserved and on initial inspection appeared to date back to the Middle Ages. The protective casing had clearly done its job, perhaps not only protecting a heavy item from wear and tear but also concealing one of the strangest things she had ever seen.

When it came to history, she considered herself an expert. In addition to her history degree from Dartmouth, the many years she had spent investigating various items and areas of historical and archaeological interest in the company of her uncle had taught her the basics of understanding items of historical pedigree. But her uncle was the real expert.

Her immediate thought was that it was genuine. All the key signs were there. The manuscript was handwritten in Italian on vellum parchment, once smooth and untainted, dented in several areas, possibly in part by use of a knife. The manuscript was limp vellum bound, the front cover formerly illustrated, though the title had faded over the years. The cover was an extensive piece of vellum, wrapping over twelve hundred pages in length, sewn together with a single stitch at the spine. The binding was damaged in part but still attached the content together effectively. Water stains were present and some of the edges were shrivelled due to evidence of fire sometime in the past.

The manuscript was heavy, weighing perhaps 16 kilograms, and contained a barely legible title or author details on the cover. Marks on the cover suggested the past inclusion of gold-plated letters, but what little remained offered limited indication of its meaning.

But this meant something.

She opened the tome slowly, examining the early pages with naked fingers. The corners of most of the pages were shrivelled from centuries of use and damage; she instantly regretted not using protective gloves. Nevertheless she continued, taking care to touch only the very corners of the pages.

She turned them slowly. Although she was fluent in Italian she was unable to understand the words in the current light. The early pages contained what seemed like large essay type entries in keeping with a chronicle, yet many were broken up by dating, suggesting perhaps it was a diary.

She closed the manuscript and looked once more at the cover page. Taking a clean tissue from an open box, she attempted to clean the cover, successfully removing elements of debris and unveiling letters slightly more visible than before. Squinting, she moved the tome towards a desk lamp and plugged it in at the socket. She turned on the lamp, her pupils contracting as they adjusted to the light of the 40-watt bulb.

The letters: Vat. Ross. 342 were stamped across the lower section of the cover.

But even that was not the biggest surprise. Written across the cover, formerly covered with gold lettering, was a cross, opening widely in the style of a pattée, yet not joined in the centre. The void accommodated a symbol that was hard to distinguish due to its age.

Yet surprisingly it was recognisable.

She had seen it many times before.

13

Vatican City

Cardinal Utaka was a regular attendee of meetings of the Vatican Bank. Although officially the assets of the bank were not considered property of the Holy See, he was one of five cardinals on the Vatican oversight commission responsible for running the bank, alongside a supervisory committee of five professional bankers.

He walked with Cardinal del Rosi along a wide corridor and stopped momentarily before closed double doors. Two Swiss Guards were standing to attention, specially posted for the meeting on the orders of the oberst. The guards opened the doors and saluted, unveiling a well lit room, instantly recognisable as the usual meeting room of the Vatican Bank, located in a tower near the Porta Sant'Anna. Inside, five people were seated unequally around a long table. There was an atmosphere in the room: not oppressive or even unpleasant, but one befitting a meeting of importance.

Cardinal Tepilo was sitting at the nearest end, dressed in his usual black cassock and red zucchetto.

Next to him was Randy Lewis, the most recent addition to the supervisory committee and at the age of fifty-four also the youngest. Prior to his appointment over two years earlier, Lewis had served two four-year terms as Chairman of the Federal Reserve in the United States and before that six as a governor. Born in Massachusetts to Italian immigrants, he had the facial appearance of an Italian-American with bright blue eyes and an elegant head of silver grey hair. He merely nodded at the cardinals as they passed but otherwise remained quiet.

Two empty seats on from Lewis, the American from Louisiana, Irving Swanson, smiled and held up a welcoming hand. His chubby face and belly, the result of sixty-nine years of fast food, sugary desserts and lie-ins drew comparisons with Fred Flintstone, with glasses, except for a smart suit replacing the orange vest and turquoise tie from the prehistoric era.

In many ways Irving Henry Swanson was the most experienced figure in the room, including the president. An economics degree from Yale followed by a masters in law from Keble, Oxford had proven the springboard to a distinguished career in the banking sector which included over ten years working as a manager for investment bank Starvel until the Wall Street crash in 1987. He left on redundancy with money to spare and used most of it to form his own hedge fund company. Nine years later a company of rising profits and infinite potential sold for £30 million on the UK AIM, an act that caught the eye of incoming Starvel CEO, Louis Velis. In 1997 he returned to Starvel, now as a director, and was praised four years later for helping steer the company through its troubled period in the late 1990s.

Opposite Swanson, Giancarlo Riva was the only non-cardinal Italian and was facially a man of sharp features who could pass for ten years younger than his age. Like most present, Riva had a proven track record in banking, including twenty-five years working in management roles for some of the biggest banks in Europe, including Banco Ambrosiano in the late 1970s. Over the next decade his experience had caught the eye of seemingly every major bank in Europe, including Leoni et Cie and Starvel. Despite some accusations from various journalists of insider dealing, his close friendship with Cardinal Tepilo led to his surprise appointment as a Gentiluomo di Sua Santità, a Gentleman of His Holiness, effectively an attendant to the Pope, and also as a councillor on the state council of the Vatican City in 2008. He smiled politely at the cardinals as they sat down next to him.

Seated at the head of the table, the President of the Vatican Bank, Angelo Rogero, leaned forward on his elbows and nodded without emotion. Prior to his involvement with the Church, the Colombian banker had served for over twenty years as CEO of the highly successful LABCC, the Latin American Bank of Credit and Commerce, through to his early retirement in 2005. Under his direction, LABCC not only survived the Latin American currency crises but also capitalised on the financial uncertainty. TIME Magazine dubbed him man of the year in the early 1980s: a financial genius, particularly for someone in his early thirties. He was deep voiced, ambitious and pragmatic and had a reputation for efficiency, even by Thierry's standards. A full head of wet gelled black hair sat atop his clean-shaven Latino head, perfectly complemented by his white suit and yellow tie. A large golden ring encircled his marriage finger and two identical rings covered both middle fingers.

Two seats on, the President of the Pontifical Council for Interreligious Dialogue, Cardinal del Rosi took his seat. Cardinal Utaka sat down next to him.

Moments later Cardinal Tepilo ascended to his feet, followed by all present. He led them in the sign of the cross before returning to their seats. There were no handshakes or pleasantries. The first topic on the agenda would be obvious: the Vatican Bank was in crisis. A cardinal had been found dead within the last two months and a key banker had been killed within the last three weeks, leaving a key Vatican asset without a chief executive.

Cardinal Tepilo spoke for the first time. "The Archbishop of Santiago de Compostela, Cardinal Torres, is presently in Madrid and sends his apologies for not being present this evening."

Rogero nodded. Three of them were missing in total. Rogero's close friend, Juan Pablo Dominguez, the Vice President of the supervisory committee was absent, while the Archbishop of São Paulo, Alberto Atri, due to replace the recently deceased Cardinal Patricio Faukes, had failed to return in time from Brazil.

Utaka spoke quietly. "As you are all undoubtedly aware, a series of murders have taken place in recent weeks and this has led to a series of speculation. I feel it only right to inform you what is known. The Vatican Police have recently uncovered evidence that the people who killed Mr Leoni are also responsible for the death of Cardinal Faukes, and perhaps many others. As yet they have no evidence regarding the actual killers."

A bitter silence descended on the room. No one looked particularly surprised.

"The Vatican Police have a talent for telling us what we already know, eminence," Lewis said.

Cardinal Utaka didn't respond straightaway. He looked briefly at Lewis before eyeing the other members of the council.

"The Vatican Police and the American FBI believe that the attacks on Mr Leoni and Mr Llewellyn were carefully coordinated," the cardinal resumed. "They both occurred when they were about to leave their offices and both are thought to have been alone. The American FBI and the police force of St Gallen have identified that both men were shot by similar weapons although we are unsure as yet who is responsible. In the meantime, let us move on to banking issues."

Irving Swanson spoke for the first time.

"Now, eminence, president," Swanson said in his typically spirited tone of voice, "in the light of recent events, might I suggest we begin by clarifying the position of chief executive at Leoni et Cie?"

Rogero nodded. "Such matters are indeed most important, Mr Swanson. But let us not forget, no decision can be made without the agreement of the majority shareholder."

Cardinal Tepilo sat up rigidly. "Angelo, I have spoken with my niece. She has agreed with a sad, sad heart that the appointment of her father's replacement should be made by the Vatican Bank."

A strange silence engulfed the room.

"This is good news, eminence," Rogero said, cupping his hands together. "Very well, let us then proceed to the matter at hand. Suggestion for candidates to become the new chief executive of Leoni et Cie can now commence."

"Now, president, eminences, looking at the present structure in place at Leoni et Cie worldwide, personally I have my doubts as to whether any members of the current staff are up to taking on the mantle. If the council is looking for a temporary replacement I would be more than willing to take on the responsibility, at least until such a time that a more permanent appointment can be made," Irving Swanson said.

Cardinal Utaka nodded but Tepilo shook his head. "Thank you, Mr Swanson, your offer is most welcome. However, having spoken with my niece, she is most happy for Mr Riva to work alongside Mr de Bois with the running of Leoni et Cie."

Lewis looked at the Camerlengo, surprised. "I was unaware such an appointment had been verified."

Silence filled the room.

"I trust that is no bother, Randy?" Cardinal del Rosi asked.

"No bother, eminence, just a bit . . . unusual . . . wouldn't you agree?"

"This situation is unusual."

Lewis eyed the cardinal closely. "Speaking for myself, I'd have thought Irve was the obvious choice."

"With all respect, certain members of the management team were unsure Mr Swanson had the experience necessary," Cardinal Tepilo said. "Without question, Mr Swanson's past record is truly inspiring, but Leoni et Cie are traditionally private deposit bankers, not investment."

Lewis shook his head. "These days there's very little difference."

Swanson eyed the Camerlengo with an irritated expression. He loosened his collar with his right hand.

Cardinal Tepilo turned to Rogero. "If it is experience you are looking for, my personal belief is that Giancarlo is most well qualified. He has many years experience managing banks of this nature and has acted as adviser to the bank for over ten years. As a director of Leoni et Cie I have worked alongside him first hand and will continue to do so."

Riva smiled gratefully. "Thank you, eminence. If the council is in agreement I should be most happy to take up the role until a more permanent solution is found."

Rogero sucked on a biro as if it were a cigarette. "All in favour of Mr Riva's appointment as temporary chief executive of Leoni et Cie?"

The hands of Cardinal del Rosi and Cardinal Tepilo rose. Riva nodded, his expression remaining unaltered.

Rogero: "Not quite a majority."

"Cardinals Atri and Torres both offered their support for Giancarlo," Cardinal Tepilo said. "My niece, Gabrielle, also."

Rogero looked inquisitively at the Camerlengo. "It is a shame that none of them are present to pass on their support in person."

Lewis smiled, shaking his head simultaneously.

"If you would like to contact the Camerlengo's niece, Angelo, I am sure she would be very happy to speak with you," del Rosi said.

Rogero leaned back in his seat, eyeing each member of the council in turn. "Very well. Mr Riva shall take up his duties as the new chief executive of Leoni et Cie until such a time that a more permanent appointment can be made."

Riva nodded. "Thank you, eminence. Now, Mr President, members of the council, may I also take this opportunity to suggest that the Vatican Bank considers increasing its shareholdings in Leoni et Cie."

A strange silence engulfed the room, broken by Randy Lewis. "You want to increase our stake?"

Riva: "I realise such action may seem unwise at such unsteady times, but I feel the thought is worthy of adequate consideration. After all, it seems likely that Ms Leoni has little intention of continuing the work of her father."

"Angelo, I do not feel comfortable discussing action that abuses the trust of the majority shareholder after it was her own good grace that allowed us to have this meeting. The recent fluctuation in share price has only occurred as a result of present turmoil. Let us not forget her father was a loyal ally of the Vatican, and Gabrielle Leoni is in no fit state to negotiate," Utaka said.

Rogero nodded. "I agree."

Riva shook his head. "I apologise, eminence, if my comments appear insensitive, but we must consider the reality of our situation. It seems to me significantly unlikely that Ms Leoni will want to maintain such a high stake. Without question, Leoni et Cie has been a good investment for the Vatican Bank. A strong move at such an uncertain time could help capitalise on the temporary turbulence and lead to significant long-term growth."

Rogero: "I sometimes wonder, Mr Riva, if your reputation was built on careful decisions or flippant fortune. To me, you are the foolish man who built your house upon the sand."

Randy Lewis looked up in amusement. Rarely did a meeting end without a run-in between these two: although it usually happened far later in the proceedings.

Tepilo: "Giancarlo, I am sure, has no intention of taking advantage of a grieving daughter at a time of mourning, Angelo, but let us consider the situation from a different point of view. Should my niece decide to sell, perhaps it is in the interests of the Vatican Bank to increase its stake, rather than allow it to be bought by a third party. It seems likely, after all, that Mr Gilbert de Bois will be thinking the same thing."

Rogero sucked his pen.

"President, if it's all the same to you, frankly I would be somewhat reluctant to recommend the Vatican Bank continue to hold stake in Leoni et Cie if Mr de Bois were to increase his present shareholdings, or for that matter in any other company that he should hold a majority presence," Swanson said.

"A strange thing to say of a former colleague," del Rosi said.

"Not really, eminence," Swanson said, "after all, was it not former Chairman of the Federal Reserve, Mr Lewis, who once ordered an investigation into Mr de Bois's dealings at Starvel due to concerns of his."

Cardinal Utaka's ears pricked. He remembered vividly how accusations of mismanagement at Starvel throughout the 1990s had created such a scandal. What's more, he remembered the Banco Ambrosiano fiasco.

Cardinal Utaka sought to speak but Lewis beat him to it. "President, it is true that back in '99 I was somewhat dubious of a bank in which both Mr Swanson and Mr de Bois were directors and their activities abroad . . ."

"Starvel and Leoni et Cie are not the same bank, Angelo. If there had been any truth in these allegations Mr Swanson himself would not have been here for the past six years," Cardinal Tepilo said. "Nor, I am sure, Mr de Bois as chairman of Leoni et Cie."

Rogero nodded.

"I'd certainly agree with that," Lewis said.

"Frankly I am also somewhat concerned of your disaffection for Mr de Bois," Cardinal del Rosi said. "It may, how you say, cloud your very sound judgment."

Soft laughter filled the room.

"The reason for the investigation, president, was down to the activities of the bank, not specific individuals," Lewis said with his arms folded.

"That may indeed be so. However, I am also dubious that a man who was once accused of such fraud may be in control of significant Vatican funds," Cardinal del Rosi said. "I would also sooner see increased Vatican control in what is otherwise a most sound investment."

Rogero cracked his knuckles, his eyes focused on Riva. "Mr Riva, your suggestion that the majority shareholder is looking to offload her shares seems to me to be invalid speculation. Do you have any foundation for your speculations?"

Cardinal Tepilo beat Riva to a response. "Angelo, at such times my niece has much to consider. But my own feelings tell me that Leoni et Cie is a part of her life that sadly died with her father. Let us be clear, gentlemen, these are tough, uncertain times. But let us also not forget, my own family history aside, Leoni et Cie has been a valuable asset for the Vatican and can continue to be so, both now and in the future. Until we know of my niece's intentions perhaps it would be unwise to linger on the subject."

"It would be equally foolish to let such a rare opportunity pass," del Rosi said.

Lewis: "In the situation at present, such activities cannot arise until they are approved by various committees."

All present nodded.

"Very well," President Rogero agreed. "Let us now concentrate for a time on the here and now. If Ms Leoni does decide to sell her shares then we shall meet with her and discuss whether the Vatican Bank will increase its interest up to a point of an overall majority. The Vatican has never banked publicly before, but until 1999 few had. The wind is changing, and the Vatican may need to blow too."

"Just so long as it is made clear, president," Lewis said, "regardless of Leoni et Cie's past performance, any future success would require a new chief executive being of the calibre of Al Leoni. We, the Vatican bankers, have never acted as more than advisers."

"And that, Mr Lewis, can still happen," Riva said.

"Perhaps you would like the job?" Swanson said, leaning over to Lewis.

Lewis folded his arms and smiled with sarcasm. "Irve, you know what your problem is? You're a saint."

In a quiet area near the Porta Angelica, the head of the Vatican Police spoke quietly with the driver of a black Mercedes. Within seconds the car was gone, heading north.

It was approaching midnight when the blue hatchback driven by Mark made the turn off heading towards Zürich. He was tired but the hot coffee contained within the polythene cup placed in the cup holder was beginning to kick in. He still had a long drive ahead of him.

Ever since he'd joined the Vatican Police his duties had been befitting someone in the secret service or even someone working for Britain's MI6. He was used to following orders when he was a soldier, but his current role was more what he had signed up for. He despised the long journeys behind the wheel on the lifeless roads, but he always wanted to work in intelligence. Stan often joked he had none to work with. If only he could see him now.

He had been driving for over five hours. The City of Milan was glowing brightly in his rear-view mirror, the lighted windows of its famous buildings distorted by moderate rain. Up ahead was almost total darkness, the blackness of the unlit road disturbed only by occasional traffic heading in the opposite direction. He would soon be passing into Switzerland. It had been his intention to finish the journey that night but fatigue was setting in. He would stop somewhere *en route* and finish the journey to Zürich tomorrow. At least that would give him ample opportunity to consider his new leads.

These leads were in the form of several documents contained in two large boxes that currently resided on the passenger seat. Both Commissario Pessotto and Thierry de Courten knew what was in them but Mark was still to examine them himself. There were nearly fifty files in each box, all of which were potentially of relevance to the murders, or at least the best information available, according to Thierry.

Truth be told, Mark didn't know much about the Rite of Larmenius. He had heard whispers, but nothing concrete. Stan had told him that they were the most powerful secret society in Europe and America and in the past they had had possible links with the KGB. Their members were supposedly primarily wealthy businessmen who may or may not have used the society as a medium to accomplish political or personal aspirations, but either way this was still to be confirmed. The Rite of Larmenius, he thought to himself.

Where do they come up with these names?

First of all he needed to confirm that Al Leoni was dead, despite the fact that he had attended the funeral. No, he had to trace the bullet and, if possible, the possessions he had carried the night he died: at least the few that remained. He had to talk to strangers, check that he left alone, all the duties of a good cop.

There had been many dead ends over the past two months.

He had a feeling this would not be the last.

14

The door of the 18th century library had not been opened for a long time. Gabrielle herself had been the last to use it nearly two years earlier. The slow disturbing creak of the opening door, lasting several seconds before coming to an abrupt silence, unnerved her slightly as it turned on its hinges, presenting a depressing room lacking fresh air and light. From the doorway the inside looked abandoned: cobwebs covered the ceiling and twelve rows of old texts lined the bookcases, many of which were coated in dust.

It was the ideal location for a horror film.

She entered the room slowly, leaving the door open to allow light to enter from the corridor as she searched for the nearest light switch. The light failed to respond when she pressed it, unclear whether a bulb was absent from the dated lampshade in the middle of the ceiling or whether it had simply failed through lack of use.

She inhaled deeply. The oppressive air felt unpleasant on her lungs and an overwhelming stench of dust dominated her nostrils. In the poor light, she attempted to focus on her surroundings. She removed a torch from her pocket and shone it directly in front of her. Across the room, heavy velvet curtains were closed, unsurprising given the lack of use. Even when they were open she recalled this was always the darkest room in the mansion, and for that reason she'd always disliked it.

Guided by the light of the torch, she walked slowly towards the nearest window. She stopped as she neared it and pulled on a large rope. Sunlight pierced through the gaps, shining on long unused bookcases and creating distorted shadows that further unsettled her already troubled frame of mind. Inhaling, she shone the torch in the vicinity of an antique desk and walked towards it, turning on the desk lamp. The low 40-watt bulb lit up the vicinity, identifying another long rope attached to the nearest curtain. She walked towards it slowly and pulled it. The curtains squeaked as it parted and light shone through, identifying a large gathering of dust motes floating in the sunlight.

She turned her attention to the shelves of books, now visible. Most of what was there was left to her. This was no major shock. Her mother had no use for them. Her uncle made use of most when he was there, but for now he was still abroad.

There was a certain text she wanted: one that she believed might offer some insight into her new discovery. She walked along the various shelves, pointing her torch at the books as she passed, attempting to ignore the incessant creaking of the wooden floorboards. Most of the books were library bound, identical in size and colour and smelled typically 19th century. After passing the fourth row of books, she stopped. She pointed the torch at one row in particular and studied the titles one at a time. The books were stacked by subject, and alphabetically by author.

She was in the history section.

She knelt down on one knee and began to examine the books on the bottom shelf, failing to avoid dirtying her blue jeans. All of the names were European, and most of them were unrecognisable to her. Most of the books were originals and some of them exceedingly valuable. Her uncle often boasted that they had the greatest collection of rare books and manuscripts in Europe.

She identified a heavy text and looked carefully at the title. After realising it was not the one she wanted, she moved onto the next row: the first of five rows of a medieval European History sub-section. On first inspection this section was dustier and dirtier than the previous batch. It looked as if it had not been used in two centuries, let alone two years.

She shone the light at the various texts, attempting to read the words along the seam. Suddenly she shuddered. In a reflex action she pointed the torch to her left. The antique clock standing against the wall next to an elegant portrait chimed softly as it confirmed the time of 10:00 a.m. Seconds later the door closed with a loud echoing bang, its vibrations fading slowly.

For several seconds she remained motionless. As best she could tell no one had entered the room. She inhaled deeply, convincing herself it was merely the wind. She had always hated that door.

Regaining her composure, she knelt down by the far wall and cast her eyes on the various texts that lined the bottom shelf. After examining several, she removed a heavy tome. It was more delicate than the last one but heavier in weight. She pulled it out carefully and shone the light on the cover. Unsurprisingly the text was printed, dating from the late 18th century. It was written in English by a man named Drummond, a Scottish writer, and entitled: European History 1300-1650. She returned the book to the shelf and slowly pulled out the one to its left. Neither were the one she wanted.

Replacing the manuscript, she froze. A series of creaking footsteps occurred suddenly to her left. She flashed the torch.

Through the poor light she could vaguely make out the silhouette of a human.

The figure retreated, dazzled by the torchlight. The figure raised an arm and squinted through the light, incredibly managing to avoid spilling the warm liquid from either mug of coffee in her hands.

"Rachel," Gabrielle said, getting to her feet and lowering the torch.

"Hi," she replied.

As Gabrielle emerged into the light Rachel looked her up and down. Gabrielle's blue Levis were now almost brown in colour, covered in dirt and dust.

Rachel controlled her astonishment well. "Your mom asked me to give you this," she said, offering Gabrielle a cup of coffee. "We thought you might be thirsty."

"Thank you," she replied, stepping away from the bookcase, without taking the mug. Although the door was wide open and the curtains no longer closed the room was still dark. At least being nearer the window she could make out the face of her friend. She was dressed in a grey Dartmouth hoody, blue jeans and flip-flops.

"I thought you'd gone," Gabrielle said, giving Rachel a hug and partially covering her in dust.

"I got back thirty minutes ago. You said we'd go shopping, remember . . . last week . . ."

Gabrielle's hands covered her mouth.

"Oh, wow, honey, I'm sorry, I . . ."

Rachel smiled warmly. "That's okay. I know you've got a lot going on right now, and . . . you know . . . if you want we can just stay here."

Gabrielle looked at Rachel. For so many years they had been best friends.

"Oh, no, don't worry: it's nothing to do with that."

Rachel looked at her sympathetically. She didn't want to push the subject of her father.

"You know, I'm glad you're here," Gabrielle said changing her tone. "I've got something to show you."

Without waiting for a response, Gabrielle accelerated through the open door. Rachel hesitated before following. Walking on uneven carpet and balancing coffee mugs was difficult. The carpet was Persian, dating back to the 16th century. The last thing she wanted was to leave a stain.

The door to the study was open when she arrived. In the corner of the room, the desk area was surprisingly empty aside from a large manuscript. Unbeknown to Rachel, the ancient tome discovered not twenty-four hours earlier was still sitting on the desk. The gold-plated lettering on the cover was slightly more visible than before, but any meaning was still unclear.

Rachel entered tentatively, passing the coffee mugs to Gabrielle. She placed them down on coasters several feet away from the manuscript and wiped her wet hands on her dirty jeans. Her eyes focused on the tome, standing alone like a lost treasure in the centre of the desk.

Rachel looked blankly at the mysterious book. She waited for an invitation before turning several pages – even in the improved light failing to understand the handwritten Italian text. She turned her head and made eye contact with Gabrielle.

"Where did you get it?"

"My dad had it in a safe deposit box."

"Wow," Rachel said, returning her focus to the text. She had seen the style before. The writing was in keeping with that of many chronicles from the 14th and 15th centuries. She closed the book and looked at the title. An expression of confusion dominated her face.

"What does that mean?"

"I don't know," Gabrielle replied. "But have a look at this."

Gabrielle pointed at the front cover. Rachel looked closely at the symbol.

"Oh, my God."

Mike yawned vigorously, his vision slowly coming into focus as he rubbed sleep from his eyes. It was approaching 10:30 a.m. He wasn't used to getting up as late as this, but since his arrival his routine had been anything but straightforward. After two weeks he was beginning to identify the usual patterns of the family and their neighbours, making it easier to notice anything out of the ordinary.

He went to bed later than normal. Something was bothering him. He was aware that a black Mercedes-Benz had pulled up twenty metres from the electronic gate and stayed there all night but it had left by the time he awoke. He decided he would keep an eye on it but he wasn't convinced it was a problem – probably just another visitor to one of the family's flamboyant neighbours, he guessed. No, the disturbance he felt was different. It was almost as though he was being watched, but he couldn't work out why, or from where or who.

It was nearly 2:40 a.m. when he finally fell asleep and his body felt all the worse because of it. He was still to shower, but that could wait. The first agenda was coffee.

Without thought to his appearance he exited his room dressed in tracksuit bottoms and a basketball vest revealing nicely toned muscles. He walked in the direction of the stairs, paying passing attention to every room. At the bottom of the spiral staircase he changed direction, heading along the corridor he first walked with Thierry the night he met Gabrielle.

It already seemed like a long time ago.

As he passed the sitting room something caught his eye. The room was different, noticeably different. A large collection of books were scattered across the cream carpet.

He entered the room cautiously and walked slowly around a pile of handwritten manuscripts. Some were written in Latin, others in Middle English, some written on parchment, some printed on paper, others on goodness knows what. Scattered across a large coffee table was a more modern collection. As best he could tell all of the books and manuscripts were history related, but seemingly connected to nothing in particular. Two empty coffee mugs were placed on coasters on the edge of the table and a cigarette lay perched over an ashtray. His first impression was that she had emptied her entire library down onto the floor.

Knowing her that was probably it.

Shaking his head, he left the room, thoughts returning to coffee. Without paying particular attention to his surroundings, he entered the kitchen, failing to see Rachel sitting at the table.

"Good morning, sunshine."

The voice startled him, but he didn't jump. He was rarely shocked. Seven years in service had taught him to expect the unexpected.

He turned around, looking at the kitchen table. In keeping with the sitting room, the table was covered by at least ten history books, one of which she was reading.

"Hey," Mike said, his tone of voice slightly whiny, humorously whiny. He was suddenly aware of his appearance. Rachel smiled as she studied him, almost admiringly, her face partially hidden behind the large manuscript.

"I thought you'd left."

"Obviously," she responded, closing her book. "I've been in Zürich for the last few days."

Mike nodded. An awkward silence overcame them.

"If you're looking for Gabrielle she's in the lounge."

Gabrielle – or Ms Leoni as she liked him to call her. She was the last person he was looking for. At least this was a welcome change. Every now and then he caught her looking at him. He was glad to see her, not because he thought it would come to anything. Any company was better than just guarding her.

The atmosphere in the room changed as Gabrielle entered, armed with another large book. She was hardly her usual self: her Levis were still partially coated in dust and she was not wearing any makeup. She was still beautiful, he had to admit that, but she was different. She was almost normal.

"Aren't we a little overdressed," Gabrielle said, clearing some space at the table for the newest book.

He considered saying the same about her but thought better of it. He had to admit she wasn't wrong.

"I'll go take a shower."

"You do that."

He sought to leave, but something made him stop. In the periphery of his vision he caught sight of something strange. The ancient manuscript Rachel had been reading was now set down on the table, the front cover showing. He didn't recognise it: as far as he could tell, he had never seen it before. Yet he couldn't help feel as though he had.

Despite the relative warmth of the mid-morning sun radiating through the château, the hairs on the back of his neck were standing on end. Gabrielle was still to tell him about what she had found in the safe deposit box only a day earlier, but in his mind a connection was already made. It was indisputable. The mysterious logo on the cover was identical to the one Mark had shown him only a couple of weeks earlier.

He walked towards the table and picked up the manuscript, his attention focused on the cover. Although the markings were faint, there was no doubt it was the same. He studied it for several seconds before opening the manuscript to a random page. He squinted, a vague attempt at understanding the Italian text. After living in Italy for so long, he had learned to speak and read Italian fluently but he found the penmanship painful on the eye. The 14th century text was harsh, probably a thesis of the time, written by what Mike assumed to have been one of the great chroniclers. The lettering was elegant but tough to comprehend.

Ideally, this needed a translator.

Gabrielle had been staring at him for almost a minute. He turned to face her, placing the tome carefully down on the table. He put his hand to his chin – a hint of a beard had grown from five days without a shave, the short hairs burning slightly against his hand. He wondered how much she knew; he also wondered what to say, what to tell her: he wasn't going to tell her more than she needed to know.

The time for playing games was over. Maybe it was a good thing. Maybe she knew something, some snippet of information that could prove helpful. If luck was to hold, the identity of the murderers may be obvious. Maybe that was why he was posted there.

It was a clue, perhaps even a definitive lead to the identity of those responsible for a heinous series of crimes. There was a connection between the murders, there had to be. Somewhere, anywhere in the world, they lay silent, plotting, contemplating, considering their next move.

But who were they and what did they want?

Mike looked at Gabrielle and addressed her with authority.

"Where did you get this?"

The black Mercedes hardly looked out of place. To the untrained eye the luxury motor was yet another flash car that lined the leafy street in one of the richest areas of St Gallen.

The man with blond locks sat in the front seat as he had done for over three hours. He certainly felt like a rich man. He may not have been the owner of the car, the suit or even the designer sunglasses, but he certainly looked the part. Not that fashion was an issue: fitting in was an issue, and he was doing a very good job fitting in. The sunglasses not only went with the suit but they also hid a large part of his handsome face. But that wasn't the most important thing: anyone can forget a face when it's not looking suspicious. That was the real purpose: they also concealed where he was looking.

He couldn't see into the château. Three car spaces from the electronic gate was far enough to avoid suspicion and, more importantly, allowing reasonable observation of the entrance. Not that he had a perfect view: he was still over quarter of a mile from the nearest wall and he certainly couldn't see through stone.

Boredom was already setting in. He would have a long, long wait.

In a quiet room located somewhere in the Vatican City, the Italian cardinal typed quickly into the keyboard of a desktop PC. The instruction was in German, as usual, the numbers slightly larger than what he was used to.

The confirmation from the bank in Zürich would come at 10:00 a.m. the next morning. It was always the same time, always the same date. Then he would receive the second confirmation, this time from the man in America.

This was the way it had been for over eight years.

15

Mike sat quietly, his vision fixed on the bizarre manuscript. Despite the relatively good light from the nearby window his eyes were hurting. The elongated writing of the Italian manuscript was difficult to read, practically illegible in parts. Located next to the tome was an accompanying notebook, now over one hundred pages long and written in bullet points.

Five days had passed since Mike had learned of the discovery of the peculiar tome. The initial surprise he had felt on seeing the manuscript for the first time had now subsided, replaced instead by a unique blend of curiosity and anxiety as he considered its significance: in particular what appeared to be the symbol of the Rite of Larmenius marking the cover.

For the first day he questioned Gabrielle continuously, his focus on the exact circumstances behind its history and ownership. He was now aware that the manuscript had been found in a safe deposit box at Leoni et Cie and that Gabrielle had been unaware that the account even existed. He wondered silently whether the identity of the book's original owner might also be of significance, but that in turn had created a new problem. As Gabrielle's suspicion of the Swiss Guard for the reasons behind his newly found interest heightened, surprising interest for a Swiss Guard, he found himself susceptible to an inquest of his own, notably his own knowledge of the Rite of Larmenius. Though he was reluctant to go into too much detail, he finally relented in telling her of the Vatican's suspicion regarding the order, in particular the death warrants for six individuals including her father.

The explanation made no sense: Al Leoni had never been a member of the Rite of Larmenius: at least as far as Gabrielle let on. Although she clearly knew more about the society than Mike did it was equally clear she didn't take them seriously. It was Mike's fear that news of the discovery might have a negative effect on her. The last thing the Vatican needed was Al Leoni's niece going off at the deep end after making a snap conclusion. It was for that reason he decided not to tell her the exact circumstances of Mark's meeting with the former President of France, or the existence of a death warrant with her own name on it.

The next day had been largely uneventful. Early that morning, Gabrielle's mother departed on a plane to Ottawa, leaving the running of Leoni et Cie in the hands of her daughter. While Mike was still to see Gabrielle display any interest in the bank he frequently found her speaking about it on the telephone. Thierry called later that day, informing him that Giancarlo Riva was to take over as interim CEO and would remain so for the foreseeable future. While the oberst was largely unspecific about what the foreseeable future meant, it was clear to Mike that he would not be leaving anytime soon.

Although Mike was anxious not to allow Gabrielle's emotions to get the better of her, the manuscript troubled him. And seeing the unexpected turn of events as a productive way to pass the time, the Swiss Guard had spent every free minute investigating the text.

As best Mike could tell from his limited grasp of 14th century Italian handwriting, the manuscript was a diary written by an Italian seafarer named Nicolò Zeno, cataloguing the events of one of his journeys. According to the diary, Zeno had been sailing in northern Europe in 1390 and became shipwrecked on an island somewhere off Scotland, although Mike was unable to translate the name. Following his arrival, the Italian was surrounded by natives of the island, and feared he would be killed. Luckily his life was spared on the orders of a prince named Zichmni. From then on, Nicolò Zeno remained in Zichmni's company, and was later joined by his brother Antonio who took up a position of command in Zichmni's navy in his ongoing war with Norway and his explorations of the North Atlantic.

For Gabrielle, the diary was a tease: an irrelevant fairy tale, probably not even factual, that had nothing to do with anything. For Mike, the content was equally confusing. From what he had read so far, the explorer's entries mentioned nothing of the Rite of Larmenius, leading him to wonder whether the symbol on the cover was different to what he had earlier assumed. Nevertheless, he was convinced enough to continue reading, leaving less than eight hundred pages to finish it completely.

He looked across the room, his attention on Gabrielle. Her attitude towards him had softened in recent days, but moments in her presence were still uncomfortable. Rachel returned to Boston two days after her mother left, leaving Mike and Gabrielle the only people living in the château, the first time that had happened. She spoke to him more frequently but conversation generally centred on the same subject. She largely avoided his bedroom, but on the rare occasions when she did enter it she always appeared distracted. She seemed to stare: not at him but at one particular photograph on the wall, the same photograph. There were several photographs in the house, but only one of that man. He recognised no one, except for the odd one of her, her mother and her father while they were still married and he assumed the rest were of relatives or friends. The more Mike focused on the man's appearance the more he noticed the little things. The setting was familiar: Mike had one of himself and Mark that was quite similar, taken after they had completed their initial six months training in the Swiss Army. Evidently this man had gone through the same process. The face meant nothing to him, but the more he looked at it the more it seemed somehow familiar. A blurry blot in his memory from the distant past that he couldn't seem to recall.

She entered his bedroom again that morning but on this occasion her mood was different. She carried a large cup of coffee and for the first time since his arrival she seemed pleased to see him. She told him that her uncle, one Henri, or Henry, Leoni would be returning to the château later that day after a two-year absence and would need to be collected from Zürich. On this occasion Mike agreed without argument. In principle it was a good thing.

At least she would have someone else to keep an eye on her.

Henry Leoni arrived at Zürich Airport around midday. Mike had seen him once before, but it wasn't until Gabrielle introduced him that he realised. The man had appeared at the funeral, delivering a moving tribute to his brother. As best Mike could recall, Henry Leoni had spent much of the occasion in the company of others, but he did spend one night at the château, one of forty or so guests who did so, before departing briefly back to his job at the University of Harvard.

Since their return they had spent most of the time in a large ornate room on the fourth floor overlooking the garden that Gabrielle's uncle used as a study. Of the few rooms that the Swiss Guard had seen so far in the 83-room château, the study was one of the most spacious and definitely one of the most finely decorated. A varied portfolio of artwork hung from the walls where space allowed, although most of the room was occupied by large bookcases holding hundreds, if not thousands, of curious books: most of which were to do with history. Original pieces of medieval armour and broken tapestries hung from the walls throughout, creating the bizarre impression that he was in a library or even a monastery. A large globe dominated an antique desk that was placed near the room's large windows that offered appealing views of the garden and the surrounding countryside.

Gabrielle sat quietly, slumped into an elegant easy chair situated about five feet from the desk. She sat facing her uncle, at times making eye contact while at other times drifting as she listened to him.

Conversation centred on the Zeno manuscript. When the topic arose she spoke of her discovery with the authority of a scholar and that was amusing to Mike. Only days earlier, her knowledge of the book, her knowledge of anything, seemed limited yet on this occasion Mike was impressed as evidence of her Ivy League education became apparent for the first time.

Gabrielle's uncle on the other hand was a scholar, and he, too, was an expert. As a Professor of History at Harvard, he was generally thought of throughout the academic world as a fine mind but also something of a loose cannon. His theories, particularly with regard to archaeology, were often met with opposition from other historians, especially as he seemed to centre his research on the mysterious, unlikely and implausible. In his youth he was fascinated by the stories of Robin Hood, King Arthur, and the Pied Piper of Hamelin and concentrated much of his early career on the Greek legends, Aesop's fables, and claims of Viking crossings to America. Myths and legends had a romantic portrayal, not like the well documented later years. As a religious scholar, Christianity was central to his life, and many of the unique items lining the walls were religious in nature.

At sixty-three years of age, he was now semi-retired but continued to lecture at Harvard. He was fluent in eight languages and spoke perfect English with a hint of a Massachusetts accent rather than the expected German-Swiss. He was now on sabbatical from Harvard. He reassured Gabrielle the break was overdue, but it was obvious to Mike that his return had a more serious purpose. Every Leoni was included in the sphere of their ancestral bank: it was a custom that had originated over two hundred years earlier. Since the death of his brother, he had decided to return to St Gallen where he would spend some time organising family affairs, including his largely ceremonial role as a Leoni et Cie director.

Without question there was something about Henry Leoni that Mike liked and it was immediately clear what that was. Whereas his niece was uptight and demanding, he was like a young boy in a toyshop. Since his return the atmosphere in the château had been calm and relaxed.

Equally, there was something disturbing about him. He looked exactly like his brother. Physically he was a man of fine features, a thick beard, grey to white in complexion, striking green eyes below a full head of predominantly grey hair. Unlike Al, Henry possessed something of a potbelly, but many of their features were shared. To Mike, Henry Leoni seemed somehow warmer than his brother. Not that he knew, but perhaps because the first picture he had seen of Gabrielle's dad was the one he saw that first night at the château. Without question Henry Leoni was very much alive. As far as he knew the death warrant was for Gabrielle and her alone.

Still elusive was the motive.

Five feet from the desk, Mike sat in comfort, his attention still focused on the manuscript that lay open on the desk. He sipped fine port in the manner of a connoisseur and spoke openly with his new host. He listened to his opinions with interest, not because he had any fascination with the subject, but any opinion Henry Leoni had about the symbol would certainly be worthwhile. Gabrielle thought he was intruding, but on this occasion Mike won. He had already informed Henry Leoni of his suspicions regarding the Rite of Larmenius but refrained from going into specific detail about the Vatican Police. On face value the Harvard academic seemed more interested in the historical impact.

The academic spent over ten minutes looking through Mike's notes and translations of the diary, scanning the original intermittently. He made notes of his own from time to time, but was impressed by Mike's work so far. His excitement had built steadily throughout the last hour as both Mike and Gabrielle talked him through what they knew. The academic was hanging on every word.

Mike had never seen anyone so excited by a book before.

"Fascinating, Gabrielle, fascinating," Henry said, removing his glasses and rubbing his beard. "You say this was found in St Gallen?"

"Yes," she said, offering a vague hint of a smile. She fiddled with her hair as she spoke. She had been doing so regularly, practically every time she answered a question, and Mike had noticed. "It was in a safe deposit box."

"Fascinating," he said again, replacing his glasses and looking with interest at the tome. "And to think. Lost for all these years . . . incredible."

For several seconds Gabrielle looked at her uncle, then aimlessly across the garden. Her curvy posture was slumped comfortably and a strange smile crossed her face. It was Mike's opinion that this was the first time she had relaxed in a while.

"So what is it?" Gabrielle asked.

"It will take time to uncover all of the secrets," Henry said, "but, God willing, it may offer genuine historical support regarding one of the greatest enigmas in history. Take a look at this."

Gabrielle leaned across her seat and looked down at the open page.

"Now unless I am very much mistaken, the manuscript appears to be some kind of diary which provides a most unique insight into the life of the legendary Prince Zichmni," Henry said, validating much of what Mike already knew. "And judging by these markings on the front," he referred to the stamped reference Vat. Ross. 342, "it was once part of a significant collection, perhaps a library of some form."

He turned several pages with gloved fingers.

"Now Mr Frei appears to have uncovered the gist of the story," he said smiling, turning to both Gabrielle and Mike. "You are both familiar, of course, with the story of the Zeno brothers?"

Mike couldn't help notice a twinkle in his eye as he said that. It was almost as if he was Father Christmas and he was about to give a good little girl the doll she had wanted all year. He finished every sentence with a laugh, not in the comedy sense but almost a chuckle, or even, a ho-ho-ho.

Gabrielle shook her head, obviously confused.

Henry smiled and looked at Mike. "And our friend here surely?"

Mike paused as he raised the glass of port to his lips. "Only what you see in my notes."

Henry looked at him, almost in disbelief. "You mean you had never even heard of them?"

"Sorry," Mike said. He sipped the port slowly. The taste felt brilliant on his tongue.

"Astounding. Quite astounding," Henry said, adjusting his glasses. He returned his attention to the diary, turning to the first page. "Well, we will not know for sure what secrets the manuscript contains until we have translated the text in its entirety, but we can go over the basics."

He placed the book on the desk and continued. "Now, historically, Nicolò and Antonio Zeno were brothers of the great Carlo Zeno, the famous Venetian captain general in the war against the Genoese. During the Middle Ages, the Zenos were among the most distinguished families in Venice. At the height of the Crusades the family are recorded as being the chief franchise holders for transportation between Venice and the Holy Land. However, the brothers themselves had another claim to fame."

Mike placed the glass of port down on a coaster, waiting in anticipation for the academic to begin.

Henry began his story. "Now, according to a book published in 1558, written by one of their descendants, the author stumbled across a series of letters in the family home in Venice written by the brothers in life. Now, we understand that there were at least two sets in total, the first of which were addressed from Nicolò to his brother Antonio, while the second was from Antonio to their other brother Carlo."

Leoni paused to check his notes.

"In the first set of these letters we learn that Nicolò set off in 1390 on a voyage to England and Flanders but somewhere on the way becomes stranded on an island somewhere between Britain and Iceland known as Frislanda. A superb place, even larger than Ireland."

Mike looked up. He had seen the word Frislanda written in the diary, but despite his best efforts he had been unable to translate it.

Gabrielle was confused. "Frislanda? I've never heard of it."

"Precisely," the scholar replied. "It is a complete mystery. It has baffled historians for centuries. It is of course important to remember that they lived at a time when mapmaking was still in its infancy; much of the world was still uncharted. But according to the letters, Zeno was stranded on Frislanda after being lost in a storm. The natives there were about to kill him and take his goods, but as luck would have it a man named Zichmni, a prince of some kind, found Nicolò and rescued him and his men. Now, the letters refer to this prince as having a significant presence in the Orkneys and was the owner of some islands known as Portlanda."

Gabrielle's eyebrows lowered. "Where?"

"Near Frislanda, perhaps Pentland in Scotland – I'm afraid no one knows exactly," he said, sipping his port. "Now, the letters go on to confirm that Nicolò invites Antonio to join him there. Antonio raises a crew to make the voyage and stays for fourteen years. Under the command of this Zichmni fellow, Antonio is treated well and pledges allegiance to the prince. Antonio later uses his own fleet to attack an island called Estlanda on Zichmni's behalf. Now, some historians believe this may have been the Shetland Islands."

"The Shetlands?" Gabrielle asked. "What in Scotland?"

"Precisely. Now, Zichmni then attempts to attack Iceland but fails. After this he attacks seven other islands in close proximity, named in the letters as Bres, Talas, Broas, Iscant, Trans, Mimant and Dambere," he counted each one off with his fingers, "none of which can be definitively placed. Now, after building a fort in Bres, the prince puts Nicolò in charge of his fleet and he later makes a voyage to Greenland and founds a monastery."

Henry paused momentarily.

"Now, Nicolò then returns to Frislanda where he dies in around 1402 AD; a claim disputed by historians, I might add. But soon after his death, Zichmni receives word that a fisherman, one of a lost group from Frislanda, has returned after an absence of twenty-six years. The fisherman tells the prince that they made landfall in a faraway country known as Estotilanda. Estotilanda we understand as being the areas of Labrador, Newfoundland and Nova Scotia."

"You mean Canada?" Gabrielle asked.

Henry nodded. "Well now, Zichmni then decides to explore for himself, and, taking Antonio with him, travels west. But instead of reaching Estotilanda he reaches an island called Icaria?"

"Where?" Gabrielle asked.

"We are unsure exactly where. As I say, this has perplexed historians for centuries. But the letters suggest that the inhabitants make them unwelcome. After making their escape, they sail to the west and eventually encounter an island called Trin situated south of a place named Engroneland. Engroneland we assume also to be Greenland."

Gabrielle shook her head vigorously and exhaled with impatience. "You've lost me!"

Henry laughed. "There, Antonio takes the crew home leaving the prince to explore."

"Let me guess, he was never seen again?" Mike said.

Henry laughed, this time louder than before. "You're forgetting, my friend, he was never seen in the first place."

Gabrielle huffed, rising to her feet. "Great. So a guy no one has heard of went somewhere but no one knows where. So what? What does this have to do with anything? What the hell was this doing in a safe deposit box and why was it left to me?"

"Well," Henry said, leaning back leisurely in his chair, a smug but at the same time light-hearted grin crossing his features, "I cannot answer the question of why it was left. But these letters are the only proof of the matter that is otherwise regarded by many modern day historians as a hoax perpetuated by the fellow's descendant."

Gabrielle looked through the window, her attention scattered. A ghost of a smile crossed Mike's lips, as though enjoying her confusion.

"My dear, do you not understand what this means?"

Gabrielle shrugged.

"If this diary is indeed what I think it is, it may offer genuine historical proof that these gentlemen made a trip to North America in the late 1300s."

Mike looked at the academic with renewed interest. "But America wasn't discovered until . . ."

Mike broke off mid-sentence, immediately understanding his point.

Henry nodded. "Most historians now accept that the Columbus voyage was in fact one of many later voyages to the continent previously reached by sailors from China, Scandinavia, and perhaps even the Middle East: the first rediscovery of America, if you like. But question marks still remain over the authenticity of many that came before."

He smiled at the manuscript.

"Hidden for all these years in a bank."

Mike forced a brief smile. "I feel you have no real interest in banking."

Henry reached for the bottle of port, already nearly a third empty. He leaned towards Mike and refilled his glass. "No," he said pouring. "My passion is history."

"I'm beginning to understand why," Mike said. "Cheers."

"Cheers."

Mike sat up as he sipped his port. His facial expression hardened. "Sir, with all due respect though I feel you're missing the big picture."

Henry looked at Mike with interest. "A diary that may provide genuine evidence of the greatest historical find of the century, sir – now that is one big picture."

Mike nodded. He had to admit it was amazing.

However.

"Personally, I am more interested, and more concerned, by this symbol on the cover. A symbol, I hate to remind you, that just so happens to belong to a secret society presently viewed by the Vatican Police as prime suspects for the murders of seven good men, including your brother."

Henry Leoni looked philosophically at Mike through his glasses and then at his niece. He moved a little uneasily. He collected some ice from a container on his desk and dropped it into his glass. He mixed it with his finger and reached for the bottle of lemonade.

"The circumstances remain largely unknown to me."

"I'm afraid that's one thing we have in common."

Mike hesitated.

"Sir, what do you know about the Rite of Larmenius? I mean as a scholar."

Leoni shrugged, ascending to his feet. "Freemasons: elderly gentlemen acting out meaningless rituals about long dead stonemasons, if they even existed at all." He smiled, shaking his head. "Am I wrong?"

"Right or wrong, this symbol is an exact match for the logo used by that order. And from what I've heard they might be responsible for several hundred murders of this kind."

"You never mentioned this," Gabrielle said, looking at Mike. Her expression was one of frustration.

Henry laughed ironically. "You really think the Freemasons killed my brother?"

Mike looked at the academic with serious eyes. "I'm pretty sure someone did. And whoever it was has killed at least six others in recent months. Three of which were poisoned – cleverly poisoned."

Henry shook his head. "Walking in the footsteps."

"Excuse me."

Henry looked thoughtfully at Mike, returning to his seat. "The Rite of Larmenius are not evil, Mr Frei; that much I am sure of. I know some of its members myself. Perhaps a few individuals have killed over the years; such a possibility is plausible for an organisation of such a size. But as for this," he said, referring to the manuscript. "This has nothing to do with Freemasonry."

The comment was intriguing. "You sound pretty sure."

"Over the years this symbol has been used by several organisations," he said, offering a vague smile. "It has been adopted by armies; banks; even ships. It is not as uncommon as you believe."

Mike nodded.

"Historically, these were logos used by the Knights Templar."

A confused expression crossed Gabrielle's face. Mike, meanwhile, looked at Henry Leoni with an intense expression.

"The Knights Templar?"

"You've heard of them?"

Mike nodded. The Swiss Guard placed his hands to his mouth and rubbed his unshaven face.

"Who were they exactly?" Gabrielle asked.

Henry laughed. "Now that is a good question," he said; "and I am afraid even after thirty years of research not an easy one to answer. In the beginning they were a group of nine French knights, all related by blood and all committed Christians. Following the recapture of

Jerusalem in the early years of the Crusades, the nine knights set out to the Holy City in about 1118 on a mission to protect pilgrims *en route* to the Holy Land, or so the historian tends to claim. For over two hundred years they fought valiantly in the Crusades and also became bankers, exceptional bankers, leading to their becoming highly wealthy. Upon their arrival they were accepted by the King of Jerusalem and set up their headquarters in the stables of the former Temple of Solomon, leading to their famous name: The Poor Fellow Soldiers of Christ and of the Temple of Solomon, the Knights Templar for short."

He paused, considering his words.

"However, that is only one aspect. The real question is what happened next," he said, raising an eyebrow.

Mike sipped his port. He wasn't particularly knowledgeable about the Templars, but he was well aware of their reputation in both history and conspiracy theory. He had read *The Hiram Key* in college and remembered thinking at the time how such ideas could send shockwaves through the Vatican. He knew from his time at the Vatican the subject was a sensitive one. He remembered seeing the Chinon Parchment with his own eyes after it was discovered in 2001.

"Now history indeed tells us that the Templars fought actively in the Crusades from 1129 right up until the fall of the port of Acre in 1291. But then in the early 1300s, after two centuries of loyal service to Christianity, they found themselves excommunicated by Pope Clement V. The King of France had turned against them and many of the order were executed."

Mike laughed. "I've heard this one. Their final leader, Jacques de Molay, cursed the King of France and the Pope to join him in the afterlife within one year. Then, by two separate acts of God, both die."

Henry also laughed. "Indeed."

The academic sipped his port and placed it down on a coaster. The circular mat was cleverly decorated with an illustration of a Cavalier soldier from the English Civil War. Mike had seen many similar coasters, all history related, scattered around the study.

"The dissolution of the Poor Knights of Solomon remains one of history's greyer areas," the academic said. "While it is clear discrepancies in their practises did exist, what is also clear is that the King of France had an agenda."

"What kind of agenda?" Gabrielle asked. Mike watched her from across the room. Not for the first time she seemed preoccupied.

"He was severely indebted to them. The treasury was dry and the Templars' wealth would have been most appealing."

Mike nodded whereas Gabrielle was far more subdued. Her earlier confident state had been replaced by an overwhelming sense of unease.

"So what have the Knights Templar got to do with this?" Mike asked.

"Well, officially, the Templars were disbanded, their members excommunicated by the Church. Many of the order in France were executed. No one really knows what happened to the other individuals themselves."

The Swiss Guard eyed the academic curiously. "You think some of them survived?"

A wry grin crossed the academic's features. "History recalls that the order ended in 1312 after a Papal Bull, the *Ad Providam*, was sent out by Clement V," he said, his focus on Mike. "However, after the Templars were dissolved and the final Grand Master executed in 1314, there is unsubstantiated evidence that what remained of the order survived. According to a certain charter, the Larmenius Charter as it has been dubbed, de Molay, knowing he was going to die, passed on the reigns to another. A man named Jean-Marc Larmenius."

"Larmenius?" Mike asked. "As in Rite of Larmenius?"

Henry's facial expression changed. "Funnily enough that is one thought that hadn't occurred to me," he said, laughing softly. "Freemasonry itself dates its formation to around 1717, but there is plenty of other worthwhile evidence in France, Scotland, Switzerland, and across the sea in America that suggest they might have survived. The charter itself is less enlightening. It is merely a manuscript, discovered in France in the 19th century. Most historians doubt its validity."

"Just like the letters?"

Henry chuckled. "But legend has continued to persist that the order may have continued. It seems unlikely they should disappear completely. There were as many as 20,000 members at the time of its demise. Less than a thousand faced trial. But as far as history is concerned."

"If they can't see it then it doesn't exist?" Mike said.

"A little extreme, but I suppose."

Gabrielle looked at her uncle with interest, only now more agitated than before. It was clear to Mike that the subject was upsetting her.

"What was the Templar logo? I thought it was two men to a horse," Mike said.

Henry left his seat and removed a book from the nearby bookcase. "Yes that's right, but they also had a unique cross. A cross that is also present here," he said, pointing at an example of the symbol. "What's more, it was they who first used the Jolly Roger on their ships. A reminder of man's mortality, apparently."

Mike nodded, immediately seeing the resemblance. Henry replaced the book on the shelf and walked slowly towards the corner of the room. A black shoulder bag was lying on the floor with its flap closed. Mike had noticed him carrying it at the airport.

Henry opened the bag. In between the wealth of booklets and random books was a particularly large and heavy textbook.

"My father had a copy of that. I was looking for it in the library," Gabrielle said. It was clearly worse for wear. The author was a man named Florent Domme and entitled: *Volume III: The First Great History of Europe*. The text was almost two centuries old and printed in French.

"A most interesting text; and you are a very perceptive young lady," he said, forcing a smile from his niece. He turned the pages. "Your father lent it to me to loan to a friend of mine at Harvard. Here we are."

For the first time in what seemed like hours Mike left his seat. The printed text was murky and difficult to understand despite a sound knowledge of French.

"What does it say?" Gabrielle asked.

"It refers to the French Revolution," Henry said, "nothing new as such. Yet strangely it includes the briefest mention of this Larmenius Charter – particularly remarkable because the charter was not officially discovered for another ten years or more. The text here speaks of an unnamed band of conspirators existing among the revolutionaries, possible connections to the Freemasons. According to Monsieur Domme, many of its members were descendants of the enemies of Philip le Bel who had just completed a long overdue revenge. It talks little about their role in the proceedings, mainly financial. But here is the symbol."

The symbol was exactly the same: not in golden lettering, but a printed illustration by the man who had written the original book. Mike eyed it for several seconds, his focus hardening. The more he focused the more he found his sight became blurred, as though he was attempting the art of scrying.

"The symbol itself was found on a chain hanging around the neck of an unnamed revolutionary, apparently," Henry said, closing the book. He placed it down firmly on the desk, the sound reverberating momentarily.

"Strangely there is another legend that supports this claim. After the execution of King Louis XVI, a man supposedly jumped up onto the scaffold, put his hand into the royal head, flicked the blood and shouted at the top of his voice 'Jacques de Molay thou art avenged'."

Mike looked at the academic. "Meaning what?"

"Well, the Templars were dissolved by the King of France and the Pope," Henry said, adjusting his glasses. "With the present King of France dead, a Capetian no less, the revolutionaries had murdered Philip IV's last living descendant."

Mike watched the historian. He kept a straight face, yet inside he felt troubled. It was as if he had just heard a ghost story.

"So you think these Templars survived and brought about the French Revolution?"

Henry laughed. "Many historians have sought evidence of a genuine Templar survival. But the trouble is that no one has ever found any definitive evidence. The signs are potentially there but always lacking that final link. However, the legend of the Zeno brothers always suggested that Zichmni was none other than the historical Prince Henry Sinclair, Earl of Orkney. Supposedly this man's ancestors were in league with and even assisted a number of Templars who had fled to Scotland to escape the Inquisition and eventually made their way to America."

Henry looked at Gabrielle then at Mike.

"How my brother came to find this I cannot imagine. Very interesting."

Gabrielle bit her lip. "The safe deposit box belonged to Mikael Devére. I checked. I found the key and the details in one of dad's safe deposit boxes."

The eyes of both men landed on her. Mike's facial expression changed.

"What?" Mike exclaimed.

Gabrielle looked at Henry, remaining quiet.

"You never told me that!" The Swiss Guard's voice was quite loud, his tone serious.

"It's private: it's against the law to divulge a client's secrets."

"Then what are you doing right now?"

Gabrielle looked at him, anger crossing her features.

Mike's expression hardened. "You have no right to withhold this kinda stuff. Every clue is important."

"Don't tell me what to do."

"The Vatican think it's important for me to be here, the least you can do is tell them anything you know. The smallest of clues might be significant. Someone leaves this in a Swiss bank account at Leoni et Cie. Your father is found dead. Then Mikael Devére confesses a link to the Vatican Police. Next thing Devére flees and is also found dead."

Gabrielle's eyes opened widely. "Mikael Devére gave the Vatican a tip-off? You said it was anonymous."

Mike inhaled deeply. Gabrielle meanwhile remained silent. Both retained eye contact for several seconds.

Henry spoke to break the tension.

"I'll be able to translate the text, of course," Henry said, an expression of calm crossing his bearded face. "However, it may take some weeks to uncover all of its secrets."

Gabrielle nodded, forcing a smile. "That's okay. I mean it's not like we're going anywhere," she said calmly. She turned her attention to Mike, her expression like thunder. "You don't mind if he stays, right?"

Mike grimaced, the sarcasm not lost. Potentially his knowledge was invaluable.

"As long as Henry doesn't mind me drinking all his port."

Henry laughed. "Come. I'll get us some food."

16

The evening passed uneventfully. Talk of the mysterious book faded as Henry Leoni recounted the last two years of his life and activities in the space of two hours to which Gabrielle listened sparingly. As the hours passed she spoke less and less and as the sun began to set, she departed for the garden where she had remained for almost an hour.

She sat alone on a wooden bench located in a beautiful setting amongst the greenery on the eastern shore of the lake, approximately half a mile from the château. The bench was protected by an elegant 19th century sun house that revolved on a wooden stage, allowing the occupant the opportunity to catch the rays of both the morning and evening sun. In the comfort of her secluded location she sat quietly, squinting across the utopian setting. In the brightness view was difficult, despite sporting an expensive pair of Chanel sunglasses. To her left, twenty metres of greenery led to a small stone bridge that crossed the stream flowing away towards the south. Statues of the archangels lined the bridge, inspired in part by the Ponte Sant'Angelo, standing like lookout guards, their stone faces concentrating on separate areas of the garden.

By her feet a Great Dane was sniffing playfully. She stroked the adoring animal. For her eighth birthday, her father had bought her a bizarre collection of animals – the culmination of several months of constant nagging. She smiled as she reminisced. There had been five dogs in total, a pony and many other animals including a cobra that gave her nightmares after it escaped. Even sitting alone in the tranquillity of the early springtime evening, her naked heels felt insecure.

She had always loved the sun house. Coffee in the morning in the gardens with a selection of newspapers was the way her father used to start his day and he would always finish with a brandy in the study while planning the activities of the next day. Gabrielle was the opposite. A swim in the morning and relaxing in the garden with a magazine in the company of her faithful companions was a necessity to help unwind. In past years her mother would join her and they would talk about clothes, shoes, and celebrities as they planned their next social engagement.

Suddenly the dog began to bark. Less than fifty yards away, a figure was breezing along the winding path that circled the shore of the lake, his features concealed by the sunlight. She pulled on the dog's collar, struggling to keep it still. The force of the tame animal became too strong, allowing the dog to escape her grip. Seconds later she heard a voice speaking playfully at the dog. She smiled as the features of her uncle came slowly into focus.

"Hey," Henry said, approaching with a warm smile.

She didn't respond with words. She merely smiled and lowered her head, her sunglasses veiling the emotion in her eyes.

"You okay?"

"Uh huh," she said, nodding.

Henry took a seat beside her and adjusted himself for comfort. Almost immediately the dog started jumping playfully around him. A mixture of white and black hairs affixed themselves to his smart trousers. He stroked the dog as it sniffed around the bench, howling softly before curling up around Gabrielle's feet.

"I always liked this place," he said, relaxing and admiring the view. Ripples on the lake reflected the setting sun, appearing orange and red as it danced on the water. Close by, a large oak tree cast a long shadow across a winding gravel path that Gabrielle used as a riding trail in her youth when her father kept horses in the stables at the most eastern point of the garden, overlooking mile after mile of pastoral beauty.

"It reminds me of our youth," he continued. "In our early days your father and I often played hide and seek amongst the shrubbery. I always won," he smiled as he reminisced. A warm expression of tranquillity overcame the man when he smiled. His beard seemed to give his face an extra calm and thoughtfulness, almost constituting the appearance of being wise. His eyes seemed to twinkle as his thoughts wandered back to a distant and faraway time when he and his brother had passed the time carelessly amongst the greenery as if it were Robin Hood and his Merry Men.

Gabrielle remained quiet. Stray tears gathered in her eyes, which were still shaded by her Chanels. The shades provided the appearance of calm and confidence, yet silently angry thoughts dominated her head. Until now she had thought little of her father's murder, but now she considered the plausibility that her father had been lost as a result of a planned assassination. The thought was eating away at her, tormenting her. Feelings of anger mixed with those of dread had resulted in a dry bitterness as she realised for the first time that the grief was still too much to bear.

It was a strange feeling, one she had never experienced. The presence of the Swiss Guard may have offered security but it was not in the non-uniformed guard and his SIG P75 where she found peace of mind, but the presence of the man who had cared for her like a second father since her youth.

They had always been close. Her mother always said that Gabrielle took after him. She was never like her father. While Al swapped his free time for the boardrooms, a strenuous and unending mission at adding to the foundations of his ancestors, Gabrielle was content. While Al wanted status, Henry drifted. Even when Henry was at college their parents had accused him of slacking off.

But it was not until his early twenties that life started to make sense. Heading off on various expeditions to South America, Africa, Asia, Europe, wherever, made life seem so real. Even when he was a child he loved adventure. For Henry, growing up in a house of formality had increased his desire to escape. And having a paradise of Edenic proportions in the garden only whetted his desire further. His life only had meaning when he was exploring. The thrill was in the expedition, not the reading and the libraries that the other historians seemed to flock to. The past was to be lived.

Life was not always perfect. He had lost his wife to cancer after thirty-three years. She was also a teacher of history and often worked alongside him.

But he rarely worked alone, and many of his later trips included Gabrielle. She was not a banker and she knew it. He knew it and what's more her father knew it. Money was one thing but the search for buried treasure was not the search for accumulation of capital.

It made her feel alive.

She turned to face her uncle and smiled. Henry returned her smile and placed his arm around her. His face illustrated complete harmony.

In the background he recognised the sound of a male Little Bustard making its calling sound, almost as if his childhood self was blowing a raspberry at his brother. He opened his eyes and smiled with delight as it made its way along the path.

A rustling in the trees caused the creature to hesitate.

He laughed softly. "Incredible thing nature: whenever it's disturbed it runs."

Gabrielle didn't respond immediately. Instead she gazed at the bird.

It was brown and white with a white streak for a collar, below a black neck and a grey head. Suddenly it began to run, unnerved by the possibility of a nearby predator.

"If you ask me it's stupid. It's got wings but it still chooses to run."

Henry laughed, his eyes still focused on the pathway. A group of five other identical creatures appeared at the end of the path near where the first Little Bustard was running.

"Your father always said you had a fine mind."

"No. That was you."

Another rattling in the greenery, somewhat louder than before. Something had spooked the pheasant-sized birds.

"Well I was right."

A pause followed as the birds regrouped on the ground in close proximity to the stream.

"Little Bustards are gregarious. They choose to stay in packs. Out in the open rather than flying alone."

"Safety in numbers you mean?"

"Not just that."

"What then?" she asked, more interested than before.

"Some enjoy the company. For others the best way to hide is in a crowd."

"Sounds like the Knights Templar," Gabrielle said.

He looked at her, confused.

"You said yourself they were among the rebels of the French Revolution."

Another of Gabrielle's dogs, this time a Finnish Lapphund, almost wolf-like in appearance, coloured predominantly black and white with orange and yellow colourings around its head, made its way to the bench. Gabrielle stroked the dog, her facial expression lifeless.

Henry smiled philosophically. "You mustn't upset yourself."

"The Vatican Police think the murders were connected. That the cardinal, the Swiss Guard, the Chairman of the Fed, Mikael Devére and the others were all carried out by the same people."

"I'm afraid I don't know anything about them. The killing of Mikael Devére I must say was particularly shocking. I knew him well. He was a good man."

"Even more so than dad?"

"No," he responded with sorrow. "He was a good brother and a good friend. I miss him dearly."

"Me too," she said, leaning her head on his shoulder. As the sun set behind the château, a glint of moonlight gleamed down peacefully on the lake. The dogs barked at the moon as they played together along the path before running out of sight.

"I'm thinking of selling our stake in Leoni et Cie."

A thoughtful expression crossed his face. "It's been in the family many years."

Gabrielle's lips formed a thoughtful smile. "You think I should keep them?"

Henry looked philosophically at his niece. "I think you should do what feels right."

Gabrielle nodded. "I'm going to see Uncle Roberto next week. I'll discuss it with him then."

Henry hugged her closely and Gabrielle smiled.

"I'm really glad you're here."

Over two hundred yards away, Mike watched them, vigilantly anticipating any sign of disturbance.

He walked slowly, keeping to the path that circled the lake. He licked his lips as he walked. The delicious taste of Henry Leoni's unique Fondue, succeeded by a rich tasting Carac, still dominated his tongue. It was clear to the Swiss Guard from growing up in America that the Harvard academic had given the traditional Swiss dishes something of an American twist.

His intention since his arrival had been to remain as distant as possible. If nothing else it was a token gesture at attempting to respect her privacy. It was his job to monitor her closely, but he could never shake the feeling he was intruding, even stalking her.

The garden was particularly difficult. He had become used to her taking long walks in the garden over the past few weeks. Occasionally they walked together, but most of the time he kept his distance, though keeping her in his line of sight. She was always aware that he was there, even though she never showed it.

At night the setting became distracting. Strong rays of moonlight created shadows across the greenery, causing images to appear distorted. There was no wind but greenery was never completely motionless. Leaves on trees fluttered, rattling sounds occurred among the vegetation as the animals moved, practically invisible. Up above, the darkening sky was bathed in starlight, partially polluted by lights from the château. If his job had been different perhaps he would have enjoyed the setting.

Instead everything was a threat.

As he came to within 150 yards of the sun house, he turned and slowly walked in the other direction, his focus still on the sun house. Gabrielle remained unmoved. Even in the moonlight he couldn't help feel that she was watching him, her stare penetrating gaps in the greenery. Her eyes had that effect on him, an effect like no other.

He focused his attention briefly on the lake, walking away from the sun house. He would continue back to where he started and then when he finished start over again.

He would remain invisible.

That was the way he was trained.

Less than quarter of a mile from the château, the driver of the Mercedes typed quickly into his BlackBerry, his view intermittently focused on the rear-view mirror. Within seconds the message was sent. Moments later he drove away. Nobody saw him leave.

17

The New Temple of Solomon: Headquarters of the Knights Templar

Seven times in the space of two hours the large metal gateway opened, allowing another smartly dressed individual driving a luxury car to make his way up the driveway towards the grandiose colonial summer mansion. Their arrivals did not arouse curiosity. With the thunderstorm that had lasted all day pelting down all the heavier on the prestigious street located close to the New England coast, they were unlikely to be seen. Even if they were, the area was famed for its privacy.

Most of the property owners on the street ruled their own empires. The residents included media and oil barons, investment bankers, venture capitalists, and CEOs of various multinational corporations, and those who weren't were lawyers, esteemed professionals, minor royalty, former politicians or members of some other highly paid profession.

All of the locals were multimillionaires. The house prices were a barrier to entry, the smallest starting at a couple of million, and this kept out outsiders.

Despite the wealth they lived without arrogance and that was good: they didn't attract attention – and the last thing they wanted was to draw attention to themselves.

Being so far from the major cities provided anonymity, and anonymity was good – the activities of those present might have attracted suspicion if there was any suggestion of their true purpose.

The high gates, walls and trees, despite lacking greenery at this time of the year provided seclusion, and seclusion was good – a meeting could continue for hours away from watchful eyes and this enabled progress.

On the whole, the neighbours took little interest in each other's affairs. They respected their neighbour's privacy, and privacy was good. A person could go missing for weeks and no one would care, or perhaps even notice. This would be handy, and, at times, necessary.

The location was ideal for its privacy, but there was one even more appealing feature. The address did not show up on any database. Nor were there any glorified keep out signs or guards walking the perimeters. This was the most important guarantee of secrecy. High security apparatus might serve its purpose of keeping out outsiders, but such things could themselves be a magnet for suspicion. Sometimes, effective privacy required presenting one face to the world to hide one within or the concealment of a secret truth with a public lie. Supposedly all things are built on lies and all lies are based on truth. Therefore are all things built on truth? As these men certainly knew: the answer was no.

In the eyes of history, the achievements of men whose legacy had helped shape a nation or industry were frequently susceptible to exaggeration or false prestige. Should one be the subject of enquiry by a curious writer, the truth should it be revealed was more than likely to be out of line with the way their image had hitherto been portrayed. Though such revelations were usually not disastrous, on the rare occasions when the effects of enquiry were more than they bargained for, particularly when the person under investigation was still living, the attention of the press could be explosive, at least until the next sensation. Such media focus seldom resulted in world changing events, but their world was not all encompassing. In the case of these individuals, members of a society whose very survival throughout history had depended on discretion, they had no such luxury. Should the truth of their endeavours be uncovered the repercussions of disclosure were limitless. The possibility was unimaginable. Should it be necessary for the truth to be concealed from the public with a lie then so be it.

The real truth must remain private.

As the seventh car disappeared behind the north-west wall of the summer mansion, the driver changed direction. Instead of joining the three fine cars, all belonging to the owner, neatly parked outside the garage area, he descended at an angle over a wooden bridge, stopping on the other side of a brook. Once parked, the driver exited and walked calmly towards one of four doorways, leading into the rear of the property. The route had been pre-designated, not just through careful planning, but regular routine. Even before the invention of the motorcar the principle was the same.

It had been this way at the property for over three hundred years.

The house didn't look like the headquarters of such an organisation. The mansion was surrounded by trees and contained a beautifully kept garden that boasted several water features set amongst the trees and elaborate statues of the ancient muses. Inside, the rooms on the ground floor were impeccably decorated, the ceilings high and the furniture opulent. Much was in the colonial style, in keeping with the character and age of the house. Priceless art and antiques from the time of the British occupancy up until the civil war lined the living room that was located next to the dining room, which was in keeping with the character of European royalty. The kitchen was practically a dining room, consisting of a high modern breakfast bar and large glass doors that offered access to the forested garden.

The upstairs was in keeping with the downstairs. Thirty large lavishly furnished bedrooms spanned three floors, offering scenic views along the coast and the four acres of garden through high windows. The master bedroom was the most extravagant. A king-sized bed dominated the wooden floor that was flanked with antique furniture and walk-in wardrobes in close proximity to an ensuite bathroom that resembled a small spa.

But hidden within this lavish façade was something somewhat bizarre. An inconspicuous doorway that led from the sitting room down carpeted stairs to the basement that one would immediately assume to be a wine cellar or a basement cluttered with unused suitcases, washing machines and toys once belonging to the grown up children of the occupant in fact led to something different.

No, this was no ordinary basement. Heading down the carpeted stairs the witness would suddenly be greeted by the inexplicable illusion of stone cloisters from the medieval era in Europe. Black and white tiling covered the floor like a giant chessboard stretching across a large room that was mostly unfurnished except for a large circular wooden table surrounded by six leather armchairs, one large wooden chair and another even larger, appearing like a throne at the head of the table. An ancient stone altar lay at the opposite end of the room situated between two stone pillars and covered by a large white linen sheet, different from any other due to a large red cross that originated from its centre.

Three unusual relics stood atop the altar, flanked by two lighted candles.

The first relic was a long wooden staff, protected by a glass container.

The second was a mummified human skull, sitting atop two thighbones in the manner of a Jolly Roger.

The final relic was an idol, ungodly in appearance, its face in keeping with that of a goat with arms crafted from alchemist's gold from the 7th century Before Christ. One hand held a sword, while its clawed feet were fixed on top of a round ball, depicting the world, concealed by a serpent – half snake, half skeleton – coiled up around the base. A vulgar pair of angel's wings supported the idol that stood naked except for a gold medallion covering the gap between its breasts. A hideous expression dominated its face illuminated by the sparse flickering of the candles, the only light entering the room, thus hiding the identity of the eight silhouettes in the shadows near the altar.

The facial features of seven of the eight present lay concealed not just from the lack of light but also the iron helmets that shielded their faces with the exception of their eyes, partially visible through eye slits. All seven were dressed in identical attire: chainmail vests, white surcoats, and tunics, identical to that worn during the Middle Ages, and white mantles with red crosses, similar in manner to the linen sheet covering the altar. To an outsider the bizarre gathering was out of time and geographically out of place: instead in keeping with a time when the Holy Land was plagued by hostilities over seven hundred years in the past.

The eighth individual stood isolated in the middle of a circle formed by the positions of the other seven. Unlike the others he was not dressed in the attire of old but rather stark naked bar his underpants. His sight was restricted by a blindfold, wrapped tightly around his eyes and shaven head, and a noose around his neck. A crucifix, nearing eight feet in length and two in width, had been placed on the floor in front of the man who was reciting a long-winded speech from ritual while being continuously whipped by five of the seven.

". . . So help me God and keep me unswerving in this my grand and solemn obligation of an entered Preceptor of the Temple."

With the vow complete the brutal behaviour stopped. The nearest man removed the blindfold and the garrotte, allowing him to tend to his wounds. Blood seeped continuously from his back, causing an unpleasant warm sensation and incessant itching. For the first time in over five minutes he breathed in deeply, his passages no longer restricted by the noose. At last came the final part of the ceremony. The most senior present returned before him carrying the head and thighbones from the altar on top of a glass container. The eighth individual kneeled before the final man. He kissed the relics and muttered words in French.

The remaining present removed their outer clothing and took their seats around the large table. In the centre of the table was a manuscript, though its appearance was unlike any other that existed in the known world. It was a strange assortment of papyrus and various types of ancient parchment bound together more recently, consisting of thousands of entries, some dating back to the 10th century Before Christ. Most of the early pieces were written in Hebrew or Egyptian, whereas other more modern pieces were written in Latin, French, and a mixture of middle and modern English. The content was incomprehensible to an outsider, and even to some present, but its relevance was central both to their organisation and its very formation. Everything that was to be discussed was to be written in keeping with the earlier records in the manuscript. And should such records fall into the wrong hands, their relevance in the eyes of an observer would be meaningless. This was a custom that dated back to the Crusades. If the game of life were a game of chess then these men were the chief players of the most important yet ominous game of all involving an organisation whose existence in the eyes of the common folk was assumed to have ceased over seven hundred years ago.

"And so let it be noted for the record," the bearded man said, removing his helmet, armour and outer garments, revealing an elegant suit, "that on this night the 214th Preceptor of Switzerland was witnessed within these cloisters to take up the 'grand and solemn obligation' of a Preceptor of the Temple."

The bearded man spoke slowly and clearly as he always did. He was the most important, working under the title of Grand Master. He took his seat at the head of the table, opposite the Sénéchal, the second-in-command. He said all this as he wrote on paper with a gold fountain pen. The other men watched, allowing the dim light of the candles to illuminate their faces, making them recognisable to one another. The new Swiss Preceptor was the last to take his seat, his back still bleeding.

"Following the unfortunate death of the Chairman of the Federal Reserve, it is vital a replacement be quickly appointed," the bearded man said, firing up a cigar and exhaling immediately. "All this could hardly have come at a worse time for the President. The economy has enough problems without this. This is the ideal time to answer his prayers."

"It's just a shame that he's praying to the wrong god," the American Preceptor said with a smirk.

Brief laughter filled the room.

The bearded man spoke. "As we have previously agreed, Rudolph Kodovski of Seattle will be appointed to replace the previous governor. Nominations to take over the role of chairman include established governors Ian Harte and Hans Schumer."

The American Senator looked carefully at the documents on the table, scanning the content in the dull light. He would study them in more detail later, but he had seen all that he needed to see. Both of them were male, early fifties, happily married with children, white and had solid backgrounds in finance. Both were Christian: one a Republican, the other a fairly right of centre Democrat.

"I have a meeting with the President tomorrow," the American Preceptor, Danny D'Amato, said quietly. "His personal preference seems to be for Schumer over Harte and he is hopeful he can persuade others that his choice is the right one."

The French Preceptor nodded. "Personally I thought he might have preferred Harte to Schumer."

"Ah," the Scottish Preceptor said, also smoking a cigar, "you're forgetting the President is also a Republican."

"Yeah. But how many other Democrats can the guy meet who loves Nascar as much as he does?" D'Amato said.

"Enough," the Sénéchal interjected, his eyes appearing red as the light of the candles reflected off the red glass placed in front of him. "You talk of hicks and cowboys. This is important. There is much to discuss."

The American smiled. "Now, eminence, you need to learn to relax."

The cardinal eyed him scornfully. "I will relax, senator, only when our task is completed."

D'Amato shrugged. "Both are good men. I have no preference either way. Both men support our cause and both are aware of our needs. They both appear to be family men and both are. The people will approve."

"People approved of Mr Llewellyn," the Englishman said, sitting alongside D'Amato. A thick head of hair, grey to white, covered a large head, making him appear distinguished. The man spoke with a pronounced accent, the product of four decades living in Westminster.

"And now they can approve of Schumer," D'Amato said.

The bearded man nodded in agreement. "Excellent. Hans Schumer shall be appointed to the position of Chairman of the Federal Reserve, recently vacated by one Jermaine Llewellyn, where he shall chiefly oversee banking policy for the United States of America which shall include satisfactory supervision of its institutions."

His pronunciation of institutions was slow and with emphasis, and brought with it intentional and ironic laughter. He wrote neatly on the paper as he spoke and continued to smoke freely.

"In addition to Mr Schumer's forthcoming appointment, our new Sénéchal informs me that Mr Giancarlo Riva has been appointed as interim chief executive of Leoni et Cie International Bank, replacing the long serving Mr Al Leoni who recently suffered an equally unfortunate death," the bearded man continued. "Gentlemen, I am sure you will join me in wishing Mr Riva the best of luck in his new job and live in the hope that he will avoid a similar fate to that of his predecessor."

All present nodded.

"But now, gentlemen, to more pressing matters. As we are all aware, it has recently come to light, although still hidden from the outside world, that the health of His Holiness is deteriorating. The best medical projections indicate that he will not last beyond the next year. It is now time to prepare for the reality."

"Such news will be distressing to many, even of other religions, I should imagine," the Scot said. "He is seen as such a warm and loving man. It is perhaps not unjust to say he will be tough to replace."

The English Preceptor, Lord Parker smiled. "I never knew you were capable of compassion, old man."

The Sénéchal nodded. "I, too, bear no ill feeling towards him. Dare I say: he is my very good friend."

"It is the irreconcilable differences that have caused the problem," the German said.

"I blame his predecessors more than I would blame him," the Scot said.

The bearded man nodded.

"Such is the will of God in this modern Godless world," the Italian Sénéchal said. "Alas, it is time to take matters into our own hands. We live in desperate times, and such times call for likewise measures."

"These are not as yet desperate times," the bearded man said with an air of authority unrivalled by any of the others present. "Any course of action must be in keeping with the normal set of circumstances. As a man of God you know better than any that the Devil's greatest trick was to teach the world he doesn't exist."

The new Swiss Preceptor nodded in agreement. "The Vatican Police and the Swiss Guard are being unusually vigilant. The deaths of Faukes and von Sonnerberg particularly shocked them."

The Sénéchal looked at the new preceptor with piercing eyes. "Do you forget why you are here?"

"No he doesn't," the bearded man said. "And don't you forget why he's here either."

The bearded man leaned forward across the table, glaring at the Italian. It was clear by his reaction that the Italian was not used to being disagreed with.

The Frenchman nodded. "If history has taught us one thing it is that everything must be fitting of the normal series of events. Kings reign, empires crumble but the consequences of their actions dictate the world for decades, if not centuries. People live and people die but wars don't start by accident."

The bearded man nodded.

The new Swiss Preceptor spoke. "These guys aren't fools, eminence. Ever since the Vatican has learned that Major von Sonnerberg and Cardinal Faukes were murdered they've been smelling rats everywhere. And now that De . . ."

"Do not mention his name!"

The American looked up with renewed energy. Blasphemy. If there was one thing this man could not stand it was blasphemy.

"You take me for a fool?" the Sénéchal asked with venom. "I speak not of murder. Attempts to infiltrate the Papacy have been occurring for over two hundred years; the concept is as old as the order itself. Our predecessors saw it fit to march on the Papal States. They thought they had won, but they were foiled by their own misplaced arrogance. Any mistakes could result in unthinkable problems."

"The natural series of events will eventually bring with it the inevitable," the bearded man said. "The only aspect of importance is the timing, and that we can only predict within reason. We have already lined up his replacement," he said pointing to the Italian.

"There is more to consider than merely the man," the Frenchman said. "The most important consideration is the bank."

"That and Gabrielle Leoni," the German said.

"What? That silly girl?" Danny D'Amato said.

"The owner of Leoni et Cie, yes," the Preceptor of Germany said.

The bearded man nodded in agreement. "Gentlemen, as you are now undoubtedly aware our associate in Washington D.C. completed his business with the former Chairman of the Federal Reserve while our new preceptor was in St Gallen. He completed his search and he took care of the outcome. I hope there is no need to talk about how he did it."

The remaining seven shook their heads. No stupid questions. Careless talk must be eliminated.

The Grand Master cleared his throat. "The former owner of Leoni et Cie became aware of a leak from a source that we now understand to be our former Sénéchal. A problem, I think it is fair to say, surprised him."

The Italian stiffened his neck, his gaze concentrating on all present.

"Where did the leak come from?" the Scot asked.

"Nathan Walls," the German Preceptor, Jurgen Klose said.

"Walls has been dead for weeks."

"Yes. But the former Sénéchal was aware of his findings," the Frenchman said. He placed a black briefcase on the table and opened it, its locks clicking together with precision. "The former owner of Leoni et Cie carried this in his briefcase the night he died."

He distributed the content to the Italian.

"Turn on the lights."

The American left his seat and strolled across the room towards the light switch. His gait was almost leisurely – as though he hadn't a care in the world. The American had a habit of irritating the Italian. *Bloody Americans*, he always said. *Nothing but arrogant sons of bitches*! D'Amato knew the Italian disliked him, but this was business. D'Amato hated half the people he did business with.

He was a master of discretion.

Several minutes passed in silence as the Italian read the document.

"Is this the only copy?" the Italian asked.

"Of course not," the bearded man said. "He faxed one to Llewellyn."

"And where is that?"

"Right here," the French Preceptor tapped on his briefcase. "Courtesy of our friend Ludovic Gullet."

Smiles crossed the faces of most present.

The French Preceptor resumed. "Nathan Walls was in the process of recommending certain irregularities to the Federal Reserve before he was cut off. Llewellyn was informed of the same findings by Al Leoni."

"And you are sure no one else knows?" the Italian asked.

"Well Martin Snow did . . ." the German said.

"Gee, that was unfortunate," D'Amato said sarcastically.

"That has been taken care of," the bearded man said. "Once Mr Schumer is sworn in the findings of Mr Walls will no longer be of concern. In time, Leoni et Cie will come to be controlled by the Vatican Bank and the process of evolution will continue. What's more, this will all take place under the watchful eye of our own Vicar of Christ."

"May I also take this opportunity to remind the council that we will soon be approaching the seven hundredth anniversary of the formation of our order in its purest form and yet due to such incompetence it was very nearly our last," the Sénéchal said, his voice rising, his eyes taking in the facial expressions of all present. He centred his attention on the Preceptor of Scotland. "This is not acceptable. It seems your expertise is misplaced."

Eyes focused on the Scottish Preceptor sitting opposite D'Amato. The man had a fine head of once brown but now whitening hair that was combed neatly. He looked strongly at the Italian through rimless glasses.

"Your explanation?" the bearded man asked coldly.

"I have no explanation," he replied with confidence.

The Scot straightened his posture. He was an academic, and of high regard. Many of his close acquaintances would have been shocked to learn how he was spending his sabbatical.

"The portents of our former Sénéchal will never come to light. While I am aware that mistakes have been made in the past, both by myself and those who came before us, I am supremely confident that we shall have what is required in our possession very soon."

The former Foreign Secretary, Defence Secretary and Chancellor of the Exchequer, Melvin Parker, looked at the Scot closely. "This is good news."

"Indeed," the bearded man agreed, nodding at the Sénéchal. "Very well, the second attempt at gaining control of Leoni et Cie, including $3.7 billion of investment from the Vatican Bank and a further $245 million belonging to the Roman Curia, is soon to be accomplished. This will be further confirmed with the appointment of our own Vicar of Christ and the natural process of evolution can continue."

"This sounds rather familiar," D'Amato said with a smile, feeling more excited than before. Now was a chance for some real power – and money.

The Italian folded his arms, staring at D'Amato. "Being an American brought up away from the turbulence of European history it is difficult to understand the true suffering of our ancestors. We are merely the descendants of the original Knights Templar, a phoenix risen from ancient flames by those fortunate enough to escape with their lives after being so wrongfully condemned in 1307 AD. We ourselves exist to carry on the purpose, the meaning and the agenda of those who came before us."

"And what exactly is that agenda, eminence?" D'Amato asked. "To guard pilgrims in the Holy Land?"

All present laughed. The Italian may not have liked it but the American was right. His background wasn't privileged like the Italian's.

Being underprivileged was not a bad thing. In the past its members were always underprivileged. It was an organisation of charity: poor in money terms but certainly not lacking wealth of spirit. Once what they had went to the order. That was the way it was then, but it was not the way it was now. The organisation was built on the donations of their predecessors. Following in such footsteps was a privilege. But with privilege comes great responsibility.

"Our agenda, Danny, it seems you already know," the Englishman said. "It is our new preceptor who does not."

He referred to the new Swiss Preceptor in the manner of a disposable item. He was new, as opposed to them being old. They were the masters and he was the apprentice. It was their way; it had always been their way. Eventually he would be the master and those whose time had not yet come would be the apprentices. Heck, they would not even know the organisation existed: or to be more precise, continued to evade the glances of the wider world looking down upon them. Hidden in a forest, hidden in time, yet out in the open for all to see.

The Italian spoke for nearly forty-five minutes, his concentration firmly fixed on the Swiss. The other six did not speak during that time. As the speech continued the Scot and the Frenchman nodded from time to time.

The words that left his mouth were staggering. Had he been responsible for all this? Maybe it was all of them. D'Amato's role was obvious, the rest, less so, at least for now.

"Do you understand?" the Italian asked.

All present gazed at him. Their gazes were strong: it was as if they were piercing right through him. He knew why they needed him but nothing could have prepared him. How? Why? So many questions he wanted to ask, too many questions, questions that must remain unanswered, at least for now. All matters were private, some private even between the individuals. There would be some secrets between them, but most of the secrets were shared. And all the secrets that were shared must remain completely private.

"It is agreed then," the Grand Master said, "Mr Kodovski shall take over the duties of former Chairman of the Federal Reserve, Llewellyn, as the seventh governor, and with it Mr Schumer will take over as chairman. Giancarlo Riva will become permanent CEO of Leoni et Cie which shall in time become fully incorporated into the Vatican Bank, including all funds connected with the Roman Curia. In time, the Knights Templar shall oversee the election of our own Sénéchal who shall replace the present occupant on the throne of St Peter. This will bring the start of a new era, a chance to right the wrongs of his predecessors brought up not privy to the sacred mysteries entrusted to our predecessors long ago . . ."

"And if we should fail?" the German asked.

"We shall not fail!" the Scot interrupted.

The Sénéchal shot the Scottish Preceptor a piercing stare before finishing his master's speech.

"And if we should fail our lives shall become forfeit and the Temple of Solomon shall burn to the ground like our predecessors before us until such a time when a new phoenix is born arising from the flames. And may the Lord have mercy."

"Jacques de Molay, thou will be avenged."

18

For the second time in three weeks, Mike parked Gabrielle's silver Lexus in the multi-storey car park in close proximity to the Leoni et Cie headquarters in St Gallen. After locking the car behind him, Mike escorted Gabrielle through the car park and across the city towards the Abbey of St Gall. Outside, the weather of three weeks ago had been replaced by moderate rain that had fallen all day, washing any lingering remnants of recent snow down the roadside drains and forming puddles on the pavement. Water sprayed from the road as cars passed by at low speed in both directions while individuals in suits walked with open umbrellas along the soaked concrete heading to various finance institutions that lined the street.

Cardinal Tepilo was standing alone at the front of the abbey when Mike and Gabrielle entered. Stirred by the sound of the opening door, the elderly Italian walked with enthusiasm towards his great-niece, embracing her some eight pews from the altar.

"Gabrielle, my darling," he said with a beaming smile. "How are you?"

"Good," Gabrielle said kissing him on both cheeks. She stood silently while Cardinal Tepilo placed his hand over her head and muttered a blessing in Latin. She remained motionless throughout. Once it was over she looked over her shoulder at Mike who was standing with folded arms by the large doors.

"You can wait for me outside."

Mike nodded before turning away, closing the door behind him.

Gabrielle turned to face her great-uncle. "You remember Wachtmeister Frei?"

Tepilo nodded. "Of course, how is everything?"

"Totally unnecessary."

"I am very pleased to hear it. Please sit."

Gabrielle returned his smile as she took a seat in the nearest pew. "I understand Mr Riva is the new chief executive," Gabrielle said, a statement not a question.

"Both the supervisory and oversight committees of the Vatican Bank have asked him to take over purely on an interim basis. I hope this pleases you."

Gabrielle forced another smile. Honestly, she was quite surprised by Riva's appointment. While most at the Vatican, her father included, viewed him as a hardworking and talented banker with a reputation for pragmatism, in her opinion his record was less distinguished than the other four. His reputation for devotion and charity had earned him few enemies, yet to Gabrielle this seemed somewhat at odds with his appearance that was seemingly always abundant in jewellery and accompanied by luxury suits – a strange feature for someone so close to the pontiff. Rogero or Dominguez were never likely candidates, but it disappointed her Swanson or Lewis had not put themselves forward.

"Sure."

Tepilo smiled warmly, his hands cupped together thoughtfully around his chin.

"So how are things? You would like to check the books?"

"No," Gabrielle shook her head, reaffirming eye contact. She adjusted herself in her seat.

"My father's strength was efficient forward planning and an ability to minimise risk. Now he is dead. And I am the owner of a bank."

A look of pity crossed the Camerlengo's face. "My darling, your father's death has come as a shock to many. It would warm your heart to know of the many tributes I have received of him. It seems from every corner of the world he has touched hearts."

Gabrielle smiled warmly. "I'm sure it would," she said, attempting to maintain composure. "But that doesn't really take care of the problem."

Tepilo nodded, forcing a brief smile.

"Uncle Roberto, I am not a banker. Neither is Uncle Henry. So I have decided to sell our family's holdings in Leoni et Cie."

Tepilo's facial expression didn't alter. He shuffled in his seat, his eyes fixed on the floor.

"I see."

Gabrielle studied her great-uncle. She arched her neck, allowing her eyes to take in the abbey's exquisite frescos. The ceiling was painted in a consistent style and colour and supported equally throughout by strong white pillars, some decorated. The interior was different from the last time she had seen it. In the position where five weeks earlier her father's coffin briefly lay there was only empty space providing a clear view of a painting of Christ's crucifixion, one of three paintings located at the front of the church, one of which was covered by a thick curtain behind the main altar.

"I informed my lawyers this morning that I wish to sell my 43% in Leoni et Cie."

Tepilo nodded, his facial expression thoughtful. "My darling, this is a difficult time – for us all. You must reflect before you make decisions of hurt."

"Being majority shareholder of a bank like Leoni et Cie is a heavy commitment. Sadly, that is something that neither myself nor anyone else in our family feel we can do."

The cardinal ascended to his feet and walked slowly in the direction of the altar. After ten metres he changed direction and walked towards a nearby statue of a saint. He paused momentarily before lighting a candle.

"It may be difficult for you to find a buyer in the present climate," Tepilo said, peering towards the nearest stained glass window. Through the coloured glass he could see the sun was beginning to shine sparsely through the dense cloud that dominated the sky. "The world economy still suffers its terrible hardships."

"So I've noticed," Gabrielle said coldly. "However, if I am to sell, I would want it to be to the Vatican. I'm sure my father would agree."

Tepilo didn't respond straightaway. Instead he maintained his attention on the flickering candles.

Gabrielle rose to her feet, walking towards him. "Gilbert de Bois has already called me to enquire of my future intentions. If he gets his way he will acquire a majority stake. I would fear for the Vatican if Leoni et Cie were left in the control of a mercenary like him. Not to mention our family heritage."

Tepilo smiled at his niece. "I am pleased to see you value your Church and family heritage over profit."

Gabrielle's expression was harder. "For whatever reasons, both my father and the Vatican Bank have allowed Mr de Bois a fair amount of influence in recent years. If it were not for his desire for increased lending and high-risk investments Leoni et Cie, and perhaps many other banks, would have performed much better throughout the recent turmoil. The last thing you want is to give him any encouragement. Without the influence of the cardinals and the supervisory committee he could ruin that bank."

Tepilo turned, slightly animated. "The trouble is that the entire banking sector is affected and this is proving problematic all around the globe. Such a decline is the fault of no one man. Leoni et Cie has been a useful asset for the Church, and both your father and Mr de Bois useful allies. But these are uncertain times. The Vatican Bank is overstretched and our resources thin. It would be unwise to put so many eggs into this one basket."

"If Mr de Bois gets his way then you may find he is not so much an ally but a competitor."

"You talk of him as an enemy."

"Just because someone is on the same team as you does not mean his best interests are the same as yours."

Tepilo nodded. "That is true," he said, walking slowly in front of the altar.

Gabrielle watched him as he moved. "I thought as a member of the oversight commission you could use your influence to convince the Vatican Bank to make a bid for our family's stake in Leoni et Cie. My accountants recommend a value of $3.73 billion. However, I am prepared to let it go for less than that, but only to the Vatican."

Tepilo paused before answering.

"Such a decision cannot be made by one man. The Vatican Bank is not only made up of ten members on the Vatican Council, we have officers, a directorate, statutes, regulations. Remember, my darling, the Pope himself would have to approve such an offer. No matter how good an opportunity for the Vatican."

"If Leoni et Cie is bought by an outsider then the bank will become just like any other." Gabrielle walked towards her uncle, gently taking hold of his cassock. "Leoni et Cie could become something new. The first Vatican owned multinational corporation. No religious institution has control of such a company. Think of all the good it could do."

Cardinal Tepilo paused, taking his time to digest the information. He nodded timidly. "Such potential is otherwise unheard of," the Camerlengo agreed. He moved closer to her, taking her hand. "My darling, please, no decision need be made in the blink of an eye. Rarely is the sale of assets made solely out of concern of family heritage."

"My father fought to preserve the bank to honour the work of his father. I would never undervalue the importance of family heritage."

For several seconds the Camerlengo failed to respond. Then he nodded slowly, his expression one of joy and at the same time pride.

"Very well," he said, again nodding. "I shall speak with my colleagues at the Vatican Bank over the coming days. I shall inform them of your decision and attempt to find the best way forward."

Gabrielle smiled briefly. She hugged him and smiled as he blessed her reverently once more, before leaving the abbey. Outside, Mike was standing in the company of Giancarlo Riva, chatting freely. The conversation centred on recent activities.

Riva smiled as she approached. "Gabrielle, how are you?" he asked, standing with his arms open.

"Good," Gabrielle replied, air kissing the banker, and shaking hands briefly.

"I am honoured to see you again."

Mike laughed as he monitored her expression, but Gabrielle largely ignored it. She knew that Mike would have had a comment, but she never gave him the opportunity.

They chatted briefly before she called for Mike to follow her. She walked at a quick pace, heading back in the direction of the car park.

"You okay?" Mike asked, zipping up his jacket to protect himself from the rain.

"Sure."

Mike looked briefly over his shoulder, his attention on the doors. Riva had disappeared, now inside the abbey. He turned and looked at Gabrielle for a second time. It was clear to him that she was distracted.

"Did your meeting not go well?"

"No, the meeting was fine. I just can't believe that they made him chief executive of Leoni et Cie."

Mike eyed her curiously. "You don't like him?"

She shrugged. "It's not that. I just don't trust him."

The Italian waited until he was alone before picking up the telephone. He dialled quickly, balancing the receiver between his head and shoulder as he punched in the numbers. Through the slightest of gaps in the blinds he monitored Gabrielle and Mike as they walked swiftly through the rain in the direction of the car park, disappearing from sight as they crossed the street.

The ringing tone continued with regularity: eight times, nine times, ten . . . eleven . . . twelve and still no reply. It was most unlike him not to reply.

Finally it connected.

At just after 1:10 a.m. a relatively modern Toyota Corolla parked in a motel car park located less than twenty miles from Zürich. He had been driving for nearly three hours and fatigue was setting in. The road leading to Zürich was quiet at that time of night and that suited him just fine.

It did not bode well to be conspicuous.

The motel was quiet for a weekday. Outside, four hookers in their late thirties smoked fags, drank gin and smelt of both, mixed with a cheap perfume in a poor attempt to overwhelm what they consumed. Such behaviour hardly enhanced the reputation of the establishment but it was in keeping with the general setting. It was hardly the Ritz: just a convenient journey breaker for businessmen stopping off on their way to Zürich, hoping to avoid the rough and tumble of the city and perhaps indulge in a cheap thrill without judgment or a heavy hit to the finances.

The driver exited the car and surveyed the location. In front of him, two storeys of red brick motel housed forty-six double bedrooms, most of which were vacant. On the opposite side of the street, a KFC was still open approximately fifty metres from a petrol station. He needed petrol but that would wait. He was there for a reason.

He locked the car electronically and made his way past the whores up metal stairs to the second floor. The prettiest of the whores gave him a come-on as he approached, but he walked on without reply, shielding his face with his baseball cap.

He stopped at the top of the stairs. Directly in front of him an unlit sign informed him rooms 201-211 were to the left and 212-223 to the right.

At this time of night the rooms were quiet. The darkness escaping through windows on his right informed him that most were either not in use or the occupant was asleep. Only two rooms had lights on. The faint sounds of a television escaping through the open window of 218 in addition to the light shining through a small gap in the curtains informed him he was in.

He walked towards the door and knocked quietly.

Mark was fully clothed, lying on top of the covers of his double bed. An empty pizza box was leaning against the bin and a half full bottle of local lager was still in his hands. The television was on but his eyes were closed. The pay-per-view movie was entertaining and just his type. He had always loved the Die Hard movies and Die Hard 4.0 was no exception. Mike once joked that all he was good for was mindless mayhem.

Awakening to the sound of gentle tapping at the door, he opened his eyes and gazed across the room. Bruce Willis's daughter was trapped in an elevator and his beer was still in his hands. The clock on the TV informed him that it was after one in the morning.

A further sound of knocking followed. He yawned vigorously as he rolled off the bed, placing the beer on the bedside table. He walked towards the door and opened it as far as the chain would allow. He viewed a familiar face.

The visitor unzipped his leather jacket and removed a package. Neither said a word, but Mark knew what it was. The visitor handed it over, tipping his baseball cap in acknowledgement before departing in the direction of the stairs.

Mark closed the door and dropped the package on the desk.

At last he had a lead.

19

"So why don't you trust him?" Mike asked Gabrielle as he adjusted his position in his chair. Both sat facing the open window of Henry's study, watching wildlife as it scampered across the large garden. It was a pleasant morning in St Gallen, the best since his arrival. It was almost 11:30 a.m. on the ninth of March and the sun was approaching its highest point, beating down on the nearby countryside.

"Because he's a banker," Gabrielle said, swivelling on her chair.

Mike laughed. "Are all bankers untrustworthy?"

"Yes," she said, continuing to swivel. "Except for my dad, of course. And our ancestors."

"You don't trust anyone do you?"

Gabrielle placed her feet down against the floor, slowing the chair to a standstill. "I don't trust him."

"What makes you think that a Vatican banker is untrustworthy? Particularly one who has the approval of the cardinals? A Gentiluomo di Sua Santità, no less."

Gabrielle shook her head. "That means nothing." As usual there was authority in her answer. "And it was very foolish of you."

"How do you mean?"

"Outside the abbey: you were talking to him about . . . things."

His eyebrows lowered. "Oh yeah, what kinda things?"

Gabrielle stuttered. "You know what things . . . things that have been happening . . ."

"Oh yeah. When?"

"Just when I was leaving. Right after you shook hands with him."

A broad grin crossed Mike's unshaven face. "You mean right after he said he was honoured to see you again? After you air-kissed his cheek?"

Gabrielle tried not to smile but to no avail.

"Don't be cheeky."

"You ladies, suckers for an Italian."

"Yuck. Riva is no charmer. He's slimy." She shuddered slightly.

Mike shook his head, continuing to smile. A strange feeling overcame him as he looked at her. Her attitude had certainly changed since the return of her Uncle Henry. Whereas the Gabrielle he had began to know was bossy, obsessive and up herself, as Mike had recently said on the phone to Stan, the new Gabrielle was different. Not all that different he had to say, but for the first time since meeting her he was no longer in awe. The pain of losing her father was still great but at least she was no longer trying to fool anyone. In many ways she was what he expected of a grieving daughter. At least there was one person she could trust.

Even if it wasn't him.

He continued to watch her, her attention also focused on him. They had only known each other for six weeks but in many ways it was starting to feel like a lot more.

"But seriously, you have to be careful. Just because the Vatican Police decide to tell you something it doesn't mean they tell everyone."

Mike watched her, his eyes giving nothing away. Finally he shrugged. "I told him nothing."

Gabrielle fidgeted, lost for words. "Well that's okay then."

The door to the study opened and Henry Leoni entered. He carried a cup of coffee in his left hand and a selection of papers under his right arm. As usual he had a beaming smile on his face.

For the last few days Mike and Gabrielle had not seen much of him; in fact Henry had not seen much of anything. Day and night had passed him by as he continued with his attempts to understand the curious manuscript.

Henry took a seat at his desk and began to organise his notes. To an outsider they were incomprehensible.

"After several days, countless hours, minutes and seconds of constant research," he began, "I have made a brief translation of the manuscript."

Gabrielle smiled. She knew her uncle had the excitement and giddiness of a schoolboy on Christmas morning when he had something important to discuss. His enthusiasm excited her.

"Now, as yet we do not know all of the secrets that the text contains – to do so shall require further research in detail. But from early translations it appears that the manuscript is indeed a diary written by Nicolò Zeno concerning the activities of both he and his brother from 1390 right up until around 1398.

"Now, as I mentioned several days ago, historians have long been aware that Antonio and Nicolò Zeno reputedly wrote of an incredible voyage in a series of letters, which were later found by one of their descendants. However, until now there has been no way to validate their authenticity."

"Is this about the letters?" Mike asked.

"Shhh!" Gabrielle said. She placed her finger to her lips, her expression stern.

Henry nodded and smiled. "After going into limited detail of his initial voyage, leading to his being stranded on Frislanda, Nicolò points out numerous observations, some of which were also included in his letters to Antonio. He goes into specific detail about his first meeting with Zichmni following his arrival in Frislanda. Roughly translating, it says:

"And when he learned that we came from Italy and that we were men of the same country, he was overjoyed. Promising us all that we would receive no discourtesy, and assuring us that we had come into a place where we would be well treated and very welcome, he took us under his protection and pledged his word of honour for our safety. He was a great lord and possessed certain islands called Portlanda, lying not far from Frislanda to the south; these were the most richest and populous of all these parts. His name was Zichmni."

The historian paused before continuing.

"Interestingly, the diary also confirms that Nicolò had written to Antonio, potentially confirming the authenticity of the first set of letters while also adding support to the claim by their descendant that many papers regarding the trip were accidentally destroyed in his youth. Moving on, Nicolò says of Zichmni:

"I have heard that he is a great lord from a great and ancient family of Sorano, lying over against Scotland: Sorano, of course, being Caithness.

"Now, according to the letters, Zichmni had recently taken the island from the King of Norway. Interestingly, the historical Henry Sinclair had not beaten the King of Norway in a fight, but he did inherit the earldom of the Orkneys in 1379 beating off competition in the same year mentioned in the diary. What's more, Sinclair's seal on a document now located in Copenhagen spells his name Zinkler, noticeably similar to both the Venetian spelling of Zichmni and Sinclair."

Henry adjusted his glasses.

"Now, some seven years after Antonio's arrival the brothers make a very interesting observation:

"Following my return from Engroneland, we were treated most

warmly, and after many months in his company we were included in Zichmni's full confidence. Over a period of several months we were made welcome among his followers, some of who were outlawed soldiers also under excommunication from Rome. I have heard that their ancestors had fought alongside the King of Scotland against the English at Bannockburn earlier that century. The identities of these men, I was never then nor in the years that followed made fully aware, yet I have heard people say that they include survivors of that great chivalrous order excommunicated by Rome."

Henry turned, facing Gabrielle and Mike. "Now, the Battle of Bannockburn was in 1314. Officially the Templars were excommunicated in 1312 but the arrests began in 1307. Now, the brothers then go on to tell of a fascinating account that occurred later in 1397:

"I accompanied Zichmni and his followers to his castle south of Sorano, known locally as Roslin. At this time I thought it good to make diagrams of the surroundings and I was later granted a full tour of the castle including a grand chamber away from prying eyes. In this dark chamber, as I do recall, located far below the outer wall and entered from somewhere in the cliff side, I witnessed Zichmni and his followers participate in rituals and traditions unlike any other I have seen in Christendom. Dressed in the armour of a century earlier, torsos marked with a red cross in keeping with that adorning the uniforms of the famous Crusaders in their heyday, the prince and his followers I now understood were indeed the inheritors of that great order that continues to this day as it has done since the Year of Our Lord eleven eighteen. These men whose predecessors were accused of worshipping the Devil and other frightful crimes against God and man by His Holiness and the King of France continue to undertake these ancient rites that are mysterious in form and unholy in appearance. I have heard it said that these men are gifted with wisdom of the ancient time and with it possess hidden knowledge of the dark arts, science, alchemy and even the power to speak to the departed. Central to their ritual, the armoured men gather in the celebration of a curious object contained within a tomb more splendid than any other throughout Christendom. Located before a raised altar, decorated with angels and etchings of a bygone time that glow reverently in gold, lining the tomb below a strange winged statuette of an unknown demon standing atop the tomb, vulgar in appearance, great dark eyes appearing like coals in a sea of blood, this strange object I have seen to glow mystically in the torchlight. Of its significance, I do not know though I have heard the knights say that it is capable of granting almighty power to those who possess it. Of its true origin I cannot possibly comprehend, though I do believe it to be the very source of their great torture and heresy. In my time there I was never again invited to bear witness to this ungodly event, yet in my curiosity I returned to the chamber where this item once came. While the location remains to the wider world untold, I do believe that to this day it remains, under the perpetual watch of eight knights, who stand around this splendid tomb."

The historian replaced his notes on the desk.

"Now this is fascinating," Henry said, turning in his seat. Gabrielle's hands covered her face that now harboured an expression that displayed both fear and amazement.

"If this is true," Henry continued, "not only did the order continue, but they did indeed participate in strange rituals, probably those accused by the Pope and the King of France, leading to their excommunication."

"Oh, my God," Gabrielle said, removing her hands from her mouth.

"Furthermore, this account matches those that cropped up in the trials, stories of worshipping heads and idols."

Mike exhaled loudly, rubbing his hair with his hand. He sought to speak but Gabrielle beat him.

"Roslin? Where is that?"

"Scotland," Henry replied. "Just south of Edinburgh."

Gabrielle nodded.

"The diary also provides a further invaluable insight. Now, according to the Larmenius Charter, the Templar Grand Master between 1381 and 1392 was a chap named Bernard Arminiacus, however there is a gap between 1392 and 1419 until Jean Arminiacus takes on the mantle. The Grand Master at this stage is not named. Now, according to Mr Zeno in 1397," he said, turning through his notes, "Bernard Arminiacus is noted as having died five years previously, in keeping with the dates in the charter. Zichmni was sworn in as his replacement."

Mike raised his eyebrows, his attention on Henry.

Henry: "Now, according to the diary, shortly before this time, with Antonio in Frislanda, Zichmni attacks Estlanda, which we can assume is the Shetland Isles. However, Zichmni gives up on this because it is too well defended. The story ends soon after with their return to Frislanda, around the same time that Nicolò returns from Greenland. The diary goes on to tell of the return of the fisherman from his voyage across what the author calls the 'Green Sea of Darkness', as mentioned in the letters, although this I'm afraid seems to be where the diary ends."

Mike looked on, concerned. There was something about Henry Leoni's enthusiasm that disturbed him.

"Why was this diary left by the former President of France to your brother?"

Henry looked at Mike, the question catching him unprepared. "I'm afraid I cannot possibly begin to guess."

Mike monitored the academic curiously.

"So you think these Knights Templar still exist?" Gabrielle asked.

"I'm afraid such a question seems difficult, if not impossible, to answer," he said, turning to his niece. "But this Zichmni is described in no uncertain terms as being a Templar Grand Master. And such a fact fits in perfectly with the omission of this period in the Larmenius Charter. And what's more there is a legend, which originated in France so I understand, that fleeing French Templars found refuge at the Isle of Mey in Scotland, in close proximity to what is now called Rosslyn. Now if we can find proof that the events described in the diary are true, then it seems almost certain that this legend has a basis in history after all."

Not for the first time, Henry scanned his notes with interest.

"Not only does this seem to confirm that the famous Zeno letters were genuine but it builds on them. And Rosslyn Castle in Scotland is mentioned as Zichmni's base, almost certainly confirming that Sinclair was the man in question. There is even a diagram outlining the exact layout of the vaults and how to enter them."

Gabrielle's eyes lit up. "You think they may still be there?"

"It seems doubtful. The castle is little more than a ruin these days."

Gabrielle nodded. "Well maybe the vaults are still there," she said, rising to her feet. "If there is anything still there at least it might provide an insight into what the diary means."

"Gabrielle, don't be absurd," Mike said.

Gabrielle turned to face Mike. "Excuse me."

The Swiss Guard hesitated. "I'm sorry, Ms Leoni, but with all due respect . . ."

Gabrielle turned to her uncle. "How can we get to Roslin?"

"Getting to the village is straightforward enough. As I say, it's near Edinburgh. In fact, the curator is an old friend."

"Awesome. You'll come, right?"

"My dear, this is incredible."

Gabrielle smiled before exiting the room. She walked quickly along the corridor, heading in the direction of her room.

Mike exhaled forcefully. After six weeks in her company nothing surprised him anymore. It didn't seem to occur to her that she might be in danger.

The question was how to stop her.

Rising to his feet, he sprinted through the open door and chased her along the corridor. He turned on reaching her bedroom and entered unannounced.

"Look, with all due respect, I can't let you do this."

A piercing stare, somehow made all the more painful by an aching silence, made him feel very cold and insignificant. Only now was he aware that this was the first time he had visited her bedroom. It looked fit for a princess.

She slammed the door to her wardrobe. "I beg your pardon."

For what felt like several seconds he stood in silence, his eyes taking in the extravagant and lavish furniture that lined her room. A king-sized bed dominated the centre of the room, lined with purple sheets and elegant cushions, surrounded by modern wooden furniture and walk-in wardrobes. A widescreen TV was mounted on the wall over several cabinets filled mainly with clothes. An open door, leading to an ensuite, presented a luxurious setting, mostly silver and white, in keeping with those found in health spas.

He turned to face her, still captivated by the room. For the first time he realised that she had taken off her Dartmouth College jersey, leaving only a t-shirt. He looked at her revealing figure and turned away awkwardly.

"With all due respect, I think you should stay here until this has blown over. It's not safe."

"Think. You're not here to think. You're here to guard."

Silently, Mike considered his actions. He hardly felt the need to remind her that her father had just been killed, perhaps even in connection to this diary. He was aware that a threat existed, although he was still to tell her of the death warrant that existed on her. The last thing he wanted to do was to tell her.

"I don't think Cardinal Tepilo would approve of you going too far from home."

"Well too bad, I'm going and you can't stop me," she said turning her back on him. She opened her wardrobe for the second time and began searching her clothes. The sound of coat hangers banged with fury.

He placed his hand against the wood, hitting the door closed. "In case you've forgotten seven people have been murdered in the last three months. We don't have a clue what we're dealing with here, and until we do we're doing this my way. I'm here to protect you, at least this way you'll be safe. We're staying."

Her mouth opened widely. For the briefest of moments it was unclear who was the more surprised.

Mike, meanwhile, stood in silence. He watched her face, reality sinking in. He expected a stern response, heck he expected an all out battering, but he was glad he had said it. Leaving the château was bad enough, but attempting to locate lost vaults that were possibly affiliated with the people who murdered her father was madness. Deep down she probably knew he was right although she would never admit to that.

She approached him slowly. Her expression suggested dented pride and her eyes seemed angry yet at the same time uncertain. He knew she was uncertain; in fairness it was why she wanted to go in the first place.

He held his breath. He felt the warmth of her breathing on his neck as she exhaled. Every second seemed like an eternity to the waiting soldier. He had never faced physical danger and he knew he would never truly understand how it would feel until he did. This seemed like danger. Men had died, he knew that, but for the first time he imagined a different danger, a very real danger that he could not escape.

A tear trickled down her face and he suddenly regretted shouting at her. She swept her hair away from her face, trying to compose herself.

"I'm not used to being spoken to like that," she said calmly. "I didn't ask for any of this."

Mike sighed deeply, his facial expression softening.

"I know. But the Vatican seem to think my presence is necessary. The Vatican Police have been investigating this for over a month but still they have no leads. People have been killed: they think it's to do with Leoni et Cie. Now, I'm starting to wonder. But going to this place – it's like running from a lion and hiding in a cage of tigers."

"Uh huh: and what about you? Do you think your presence is necessary?"

Mike shrugged, the question catching him off guard. What about him? He didn't have a say in the matter. Even if he thought his presence was pointless he had orders to follow.

"I've been assigned here to protect you and that's exactly what I intend to do."

She curled her hair with her finger and forced the briefest of smiles. Somehow the tension in the room alleviated.

"Right. And wherever I go, you go."

"I never said that."

"No," she replied sweetly, "Cardinal del Rosi did. Wherever I go, you must go, he said. Think of him as extra security. Whatever you need he's there, Cardinal Utaka said. Remember?"

Suddenly he did. She had only just met him but she remembered. His mind wandered back to that night. Then he remembered the suit comment.

"I don't think he meant for me to take you to Scotland."

"Well that's too bad," she said walking him towards the door. "Now pack your bags. We'll be leaving in two days."

"What about Leoni et Cie?"

"Mr Riva can look after Leoni et Cie. Now come on."

The driver of the Mercedes had not slept much the night before. Boredom had struck days ago, and it was starting to affect his concentration. He looked at his reflection in the rear-view mirror. He looked tired. His face displayed the suggestion of a beard due to several days without shaving.

He blinked rapidly. Was he seeing things? In the corner of the mirror a car was reversing out of the driveway of the château. Finally there was action. He switched on the ignition and slowly followed in pursuit.

20

Vatican banker Juan Pablo Dominguez had returned to the Vatican City earlier that day after a two-month absence in Venezuela. Feeling no ill effects from his flight from Caracas to Rome via a brief layover in New York, he walked the grounds of the Apostolic Palace in the company of Cardinals Utaka, del Rosi and Tepilo.

The banker walked slowly alongside the cardinals chatting briefly, a recent catch-up between good friends after a lengthy period without contact. On reaching a low wall they stopped momentarily, taking in pleasant views of the evening sun glistening down on the greenery.

Despite the pleasant surroundings it was clear that the cardinals were troubled. Not for the first time, purple bags shadowed Cardinal Utaka's eyes. He faced the garden with an empty expression, using the wall to support his frame.

"The Vatican Bank will need to make a decision soon," the Colombian said. "Even in the present climate it will not take long for a rival bidder to be found."

Cardinal Utaka shook his head, his expression despondent. "This could not have come at a worse time. It is bad enough the market suffering as it is without everything that has happened."

He turned and looked at Dominguez and Tepilo.

Cardinal del Rosi also nodded. "Our resources are stretched enough already."

Dominguez grimaced philosophically. Cardinal Utaka arched his back, walking slowly away from the wall. He looked briefly behind him. In the near distance Stan walked slowly, his eyes on the cardinal. This evening it was his task to escort the cardinals. From time to time he spoke on a walkie-talkie.

"For many years your family have been a key ally for us," del Rosi said to Tepilo. "They have often acted as the peacekeepers between Mr de Bois and ourselves. I hate to think what would happen if she should go."

Tepilo nodded. "Alas, recent weeks have caused her great sadness."

Dominguez listened with interest. "The markets will pick up in time. These things always work in cycles."

Utaka shook his head. "It is not that what worries me."

They passed two on-duty Swiss Guards who saluted efficiently as they turned towards the basilica. The dome glowed brightly as the setting sun shone down on the orange stone. Stan saluted as he approached, continuing thirty feet behind.

"I feel Gabrielle Leoni can still be a useful ally for us," Cardinal Utaka said. "She may not have the capabilities her father had but she has always had our best interests at heart."

"A new CEO will need appointing anyway," Dominguez said, the slightest hint of a Latino accent on his pronunciation of CEO. "I would personally recommend Mr Lewis or Mr Swanson. Honestly, I am a little surprised that neither was appointed in the first place."

Cardinal del Rosi nodded. "Giancarlo is well qualified. Leoni et Cie is in good hands, for now."

"Of all the Vatican bankers it is he who Mr de Bois and the other directors fear the least," the Colombian said. "If you ask me, his long-term appointment would be of great benefit to Mr de Bois."

"He has been my close adviser these many years," Tepilo said. "I trust his counsel."

Utaka nodded. "And what of you, Juan?" he said. "What would you do?"

Coming to a standstill, Dominguez replied immediately. "Personally, I would attempt to persuade Ms Leoni to keep her stock. After all, many a rash decision can be made without careful consideration: particularly financial. However, if she could not be persuaded, I would recommend that the Vatican Bank make her an offer for some of her shares: giving us enough for control of the bank but no more. Perhaps she will agree to keep a stake, perhaps between six and fourteen per cent, which will ensure that she is still the third highest shareholder in the business."

Both Cardinal del Rosi and Cardinal Utaka smiled. It was as though they had received their first bit of good news in a long time.

Del Rosi turned to face the Camerlengo. "I see no reason why your niece cannot keep matters in her own hands."

"I shall discuss the matter with her soon," Tepilo said.

"Any takeover would still require high leverage," Dominguez said. "It is pivotal the bank not overstretch."

Utaka nodded. "We will discuss the possibility in detail at the next meeting. In the meantime, let us pray these things do not become any worse."

21

Roslin, Midlothian, two days later

The sound of ringing bells from a nearby church echoed in the wind as the morning light broke over the small village of Roslin. The early March weather was predictably damp and the underfoot slippery. A white mist originating from the river had replaced the overnight downpour that finally ceased around sunrise. Groups of elderly women, accompanied by equally aged men, walked along the drenched pavement towards the church, overcoats zipped up, umbrellas at the ready, walking sticks at their side as they battled against the dreary Scottish weather.

The village was sleepy: a quaint Scottish community in the Edinburgh commuter belt largely unspoilt by the passing of time. There were very few cars on the road and the area surrounding the castle was almost completely devoid of life, unsurprising for a Tuesday.

The castle was located on a quiet road, adjoining the chapel, and the car park was equally deserted. A black Renault had come and gone from outside the gate of the chapel, its place taken by a Jaguar driven by a white-haired man in his late eighties whiling the time away waiting for his wife. At 11:00 a.m. the driver of the Jaguar looked across the concrete without interest as a relatively modern minibus pulled up in an empty bay. Its passengers, a party of tourists from the USA paying homage to the Magdalene myth, entered the chapel slowly, many stopping on the way to take photographs as they prepared to rack their brains attempting to solve the chapel's ancient enigmas. Three cars lined the car park, each one locked and uninhabited.

Ten minutes later the driver of the Jaguar paid equally little attention as another car pulled up in an empty space. Its arrival did not arouse suspicion. Seconds later a bearded man opened the driver's side door and exited the car, walking in the direction of the chapel. He was dressed sensibly for the weather: a heavy blue raincoat protected him from the cold and rain, while dark waterproof leggings ended with heavy hiking boots.

The driver was Henry Leoni. Meanwhile, Gabrielle and Mike stayed in the car.

From his position sitting in the front passenger seat, Mike surveyed the location. The area was depressing: the grey stone, a prominent feature of the area, looked desolate in the poor light, brought about by a combination of weather and time of year. The misty air was a distraction, making it difficult to focus. He was pleased so few people were present.

He hardly approved of the setting, but at least he was prepared. He dressed in dark combats, heavy boots, anticipating the muddy environment, and a grey rain jacket decorated with the Navy Goats logo that he used for American football training, effectively concealing his firearm. His face, clean-shaven after orders from Gabrielle not to look scruffy, was partially hidden by a black woolly hat, acting as an efficient barrier against the cold. Despite the heating in the car still being on, he was cold. This was his first visit to Scotland.

They had flown out from Zürich early that morning and the journey was over in two and a half hours. The flight had been easy enough, but he never enjoyed flying. At Edinburgh Airport, Henry Leoni collected a hire car from a local dealer and took the wheel on the thirteen-mile journey to Roslin. The car was the dealer's standard model, a blue Ford with quarter of a tank of unleaded petrol and two thousand miles on the clock. A small scratch, un-noted by the staff, lined the passenger side door that was otherwise clean. Not that its appearance was a worry. Not being bulletproof was more of a worry. The hire car was hardly what Mike had become used to in recent weeks but luxury was never the priority today. Today was about answers: answers to private questions: questions that had long remained secret.

Gabrielle had been quiet and Mike had noticed. As usual, she sat in the back and spent her time scanning through her uncle's notes and photocopies of various extracts from the Zeno diary. They had not brought the original diary with them.

A blue and white Yamaha motorbike entered the car park and pulled up in an empty bay on the opposite side of the minibus. Mike looked at the helmeted driver with interest although failing to identify any facial features due to the presence of a black visor. He assumed the driver was probably just another tourist or a visitor from the nearby village seeking solitude in the medieval holy site. Mike watched him for several seconds before diverting his attention elsewhere, continuing to explore the near vicinity through the rain covered windscreen.

He rubbed his neck and this bothered Gabrielle.

"What's the matter?" she asked.

"My neck's sore; it always gets sore on flights."

Despite showing no obvious sympathy, at least on this occasion she believed him. She could tell on the plane that he was uncomfortable. She sensed his discomfort was more psychological than physical.

"I take it you don't like flying," she said. "What are you, claustrophobic or something?"

Mike grimaced as he massaged his neck. "Not exactly."

"What then?"

Mike looked through the window, concentrating his attention on the entrance to the chapel. Henry was walking across the wet concrete with enthusiasm and purpose. Mike switched off the ignition.

"Your uncle's coming."

Mike opened the passenger side door and pushed the seat forward for Gabrielle. She ducked her head on leaving the car and walked towards her uncle. Despite enduring another sleepless night, she showed no obvious signs of fatigue.

Mike breathed in the dense air and immediately felt the cold. Although the rain had largely stopped, drizzle continued to fall intermittently from the overcast sky. There was a distinct chill in the air as the wind blew in from the east. The Swiss Guard removed his gloves from his pocket and pulled them onto his hands.

Attempting in vain not to shiver, Mike adjusted his woolly hat and zipped up his jacket to his chin. "You wanna see the chapel?" he asked as Henry locked the door.

"No," Gabrielle replied. "We're here on business; not vacation."

Mike shivered, his eyes continuing to explore the surroundings. He sought to reply but Gabrielle had already stormed on ahead. She walked determinedly along the path that led to the castle, slippery from the earlier downpour. She followed the path to the left, disappearing momentarily from sight, hidden by the dense foliage. Mike started to jog in a bid to catch her up, careful to avoid losing his footing.

Several metres behind them, the man on the motorbike removed his helmet and watched with interest as they walked towards the castle. Drizzle fell on his long blond locks that had remained dry under the helmet.

*

"Where are we heading?" Mike asked, now walking alongside Henry.

"The bridge to the castle entrance is straight ahead," Henry said, struggling to keep up with his niece. "The curator offered us the traditional route into the known vaults, but we'll follow the instructions of Mr Zeno. The diagram is excellent and offers magnificent plans of the castle and its vaults. Personally I think this may be the only diagram of its type still in existence."

Mike nodded, his breath visible in the cold. They quickened their pace as they followed Gabrielle along the pathway before stopping in front of the approach bridge. The view was inspiring. Dense forestry sloped down into the glen, surrounding the River Esk to the castle's side, its water flowing away to the west. Puddles of dirty water had formed on the muddy paths below the approach bridge that they would later need to walk through. The possibility was unappealing.

Gabrielle crossed the approach bridge slowly, careful to avoid losing her footing as she neared the wet grass of the ancient courtyard. The smell of water on greenery filled her nostrils.

Mike and Henry followed. While Mike continued to focus on Gabrielle, Henry studied his photocopies as he walked, using the map to navigate. To his left, a relatively modern house had been built from the ruins, whereas directly in front of them the remains of the keep were located beyond the west curtain wall. Although the jagged ruins looked grim and sombre below the dreary sky, the red brick structure that remained was not without its charm. To Mike the design was like something out of a fairy tale.

"You're sure this is the place?" Mike asked.

"Yes," Henry confirmed, looking at a photocopy of the diagram. A plastic folder protected it from the rain. "There is very little left now. The castle was gutted on at least three occasions up until 1688."

"Any idea . . ."

Mike stopped as a middle-aged couple crossed the bridge behind them. He smiled and said "good morning" as he waited for them to pass. Once they were out of earshot he whispered to Henry.

"Any idea where we are?"

"I believe the vaults may have been over there," he said, pointing vaguely in the direction of an area of ruins several metres below the keep. He removed another photocopy from his jacket pocket and scanned it with interest. Mike looked at the printed text over his shoulder. The diagram was effectively an architect's blueprint of the site comprising both the castle and parts of the surrounding glen.

"You see there," Henry pointed to an area to the right of the keep: "that was once the postern."

"What's that mean?"

Gabrielle returned from the other side of the courtyard. "It means the way to the vaults must be down below. Come on."

The man with blond locks walked on undetected past the entrance of the chapel. Through the gap in the trees, he scanned the surrounding area for signs of life. Over two hundred yards to the south the castle was largely deserted, the silence disturbed only by the muffled sound of the rain falling on the soggy ground. He placed a woolly hat over his head and covered his locks.

Mike and Henry followed Gabrielle back down the steps that led to the approach bridge and continued along the path to the west side of the castle, several metres below the keep. The forestry was dense and the presence of caves in the near distance unveiled an unappealing desolate void multiplied many times by the dull light. The muddy pathways were deeper and wetter than those above as the ground continued to soak up the rain. Shrubbery and vegetation was growing out of control at the foot of the former wall, dangerous from years of dilapidation.

Mike walked slowly, a growing sense of apprehension causing his breathing to heighten. Up ahead the various caves and gaps in the greenery that cut into the glen gave him the genuine feeling of being lost, not just geographically, but also in time. The castle's craggy remains were unsurprisingly devoid of any modern amenities.

"The caves were used by soldiers at the Battle of Roslin," Henry said, his eyes fleeting between the location and the photocopy in his hand. "My word, I believe one of these caves could be the entrance to the vaults."

Gabrielle sprinted ahead, nearly stumbling. "I wonder if this is safe?"

"Probably not," Mike replied. "Nor legal."

"It's legal. Come on."

They continued walking for over five minutes. The academic led the way, walking alongside the river and then through greenery towards the entrance of an ancient cave cutting into the landscape. The cave was approximately a quarter of a mile from the castle and on face value looked too remote to be connected to the building itself.

But the photocopy in his hand suggested otherwise.

Gabrielle paused, examining the rock. Without waiting for further direction she removed a torch from her pocket and entered without hesitation.

The Swiss Guard exhaled heavily, peering into the gloom. In the poor light he could make out greenery seeping through cracks in the rocks. Water dripped like clockwork from the stone above his head, forming puddles on the ground below. He walked forward several steps and stopped to look down at his combats. They were already marked by dirt.

Gabrielle walked on carefully, using her hand to guide her along the left wall. Henry followed slowly. They continued for over thirty metres. Suddenly Gabrielle came to a halt. There was a gap in the wall, unveiling a fork where the cave offered two separate routes.

Henry considered the way. "I think left."

Gabrielle smiled. She turned her head back towards the entrance. Mike was still standing in the daylight.

"Are you coming?"

Mike inhaled deeply. The coldness felt bitter as it seeped down the back of his neck and along his spine.

"Mikael."

"Everything okay, sir?" Henry asked.

Mike entered slowly. "Sorry," he said shaking his head. He zipped up his jacket to the top and covered his mouth. The light material did little to combat the thinness of the air. It was tough to think that an army once sheltered there.

Gabrielle pointed the torch at the wall, slowly edging closer to the left tunnel. Concentrating on the nearest wall, she noticed the presence of several symbols, unrecognisable in form, continuing for several metres before ending with a second fork in the wall of the cave, offering a second tunnel up ahead. To Gabrielle the markings were incomprehensible: a forgotten memory of a history long lost in keeping with those often found in an Egyptian pyramid. She focused on the mysterious symbols for several seconds before heading further inside.

Henry followed, continuing through what appeared to be a narrow clearing, now over two hundred metres from the entrance to the cave. He led the way, now heading further to the left, potentially back towards the castle. The ground sloped downwards from there on and the light faded.

Gabrielle and Mike paused before entering. The area ahead smelled of damp and decay.

"Ladies first," Mike offered.

"Age before beauty."

"You're older than me."

"What's the matter?" Gabrielle asked. "Scared?"

He was but he couldn't admit it. He looked at her. A smile crossed her face, vaguely visible in the poor light. Using his torch, he examined the floor of the next tunnel. A large skull, possibly that of an animal was present at the start of a new passageway.

"Oh this is nice," Mike said.

"No guts, no glory."

High up above, the biker's view was perfect. Through a telescopic lens he looked down at a middle-aged couple crossing the approach bridge below.

For now his targets had disappeared from sight.

He adjusted his dark woolly hat and moved closer to the nearest tree. His outfit blended in well with the vegetation. He knew he wouldn't be seen.

22

Deep within the catacombs they walked on. Water continuously dripped from above, landing in unseen puddles close by. The sound caused echoes, each one reverberating in time with the beating of Gabrielle's heart, enthralling her, yet terrifying her of what unknown terrors lurked ahead. In the poor light she found her sense of hearing heightened, making sounds seem louder than normal. It wasn't only her sense of hearing that had increased. A dank smell, overwhelming in nature, was consuming her nostrils and affecting her breathing. As best she could tell the cave was a product of natural formation, its age probably going back to the last ice age.

Still the ground sloped downwards, continuing in a relatively straight line. Fragments of debris caused distorted shadows in the torchlight, making them appear obscure and possibly threatening. She shone the torch at her feet, using the light to carefully navigate the unstable ground. She knew any mistakes could have dire consequences.

Eventually they walked through a clearing. For the first time the area seemed more open than before, though still slightly confined. The feeling of dampness escalated. Several metres on they came across a ruined tomb, surrounded by floodwater.

Gabrielle shone the torch, concentrating her attention on identifying the name and date of the tomb or sepulchre in front of her. Several carvings were barely visible on the verge of its stone lid, the name illegible. One thing at least was certain. They had reached the castle vaults.

"Of course we're not totally sure what we're looking for, are we?" Henry said, practically whispering. He shone the torch in front of him, lighting up Gabrielle's face.

"Presumably you have some idea?" Mike said to Henry.

"The diary talks of a tomb."

"What kind?"

"The kind that people are buried in," Gabrielle said.

A rebuke would have been too obvious. "I meant what kind of

tomb?" Mike said. "Is it underground, above ground? Is someone of significance supposed to be buried there?"

"Oh," Gabrielle said sarcastically. "It's above ground and we don't know."

Mike shook his head, momentarily distracted. He looked at Henry. "What's so special?"

"The diary says that an object of some significance was used in a room in the vault and was contained in a tomb more splendid than any other."

Henry laughed to himself.

"Funnily enough the castle is famous for another tomb. An old superstition, the tomb of the sleeping lady."

Mike walked on slowly. An overwhelming stench of decay, probably the product of the nearby graves, was becoming heavier on his lungs.

"Superstition? What kind of superstition?"

"Well, according to a very old legend, a treasure worth several million pounds is buried beneath the castle vaults, guarded by one of the St Clair ladies, who, like sleeping beauty, sleeps through the centuries. If she can somehow be awakened she points to the place the treasure is buried and Rosslyn Castle shall rise again."

Mike paused before answering. "You're searching for treasure now?" he asked dryly. "Does it say that in the diary?"

"Not exactly, but this tomb is probably the same one mentioned in the diary."

Mike nodded, moving forward cautiously behind the academic. Unbeknown to the Swiss Guard they were now almost exactly below the keep. Aside from the torches, the light was almost completely gone.

"We could be going anywhere," Mike said, the pace of his words affected by his breathing.

"We entered from the south-west, and we've been going north-east the whole time," Gabrielle said. "We're heading in the right direction."

"Are you sure?"

"Uh huh. Just keep going."

Biting his lip he followed, tiptoeing through the wet catacombs, trying to avoid stepping on the fragments of debris that covered most of the ground. There were puddles beneath their feet, accompanied by the vague sound of dripping water landing in a puddle or puddles from some unknown area.

"I wonder where the water is coming from?" Gabrielle said.

"We're near the river," Henry replied. "There must be some seeping in from somewhere." He turned and looked at Mike. "Also, it is raining."

Mike forced a smile, minor relief in the dilapidated underground devoid of air and light. Led by the glow of Gabrielle and Henry's torches they continued past another tomb, this one greatly damaged by floodwater. It was not of a lady.

Henry pointed the light along the corridor, now slightly less cramped than before. Shadows moved up ahead. In the torchlight they made out an archway, cut into the rock and largely covered by cobwebs.

Approaching the archway Mike stopped suddenly. The area was ruined, dilapidated stone and brick strewn on the ground some ten metres from the next wall. He walked slowly, careful to avoid losing his footing. The debris was obviously flooded and potentially susceptible to further damage from above.

Gabrielle eyed him closely. "What is it?"

Mike didn't respond straightaway. Now kneeling, he moved closer to the rubble, his attention on what was beneath. A bizarre pattern was visible, its outline unlike anything else he had seen so far, though in the darkness he assumed more was still hidden.

Mike looked over his shoulder. Henry moved closer.

"Pass me your torch."

Mike collected the torch and moved closer to the rubble. Beneath it was a grave, unmistakably damaged. There were markings on the grave, difficult to determine after centuries of ruin.

Some things were evident. A skull and crossbones was present, in keeping with other Templar graves in northern Scotland.

"Can you see a name?" the academic asked.

Mike remained silent. Under the light of the torch he could see the markings.

"Zen."

Henry smiled.

"Zeno."

For now Mike's attention remained focused on the grave. He waited for Henry to examine it himself, his eyes lighting up at the sight of the markings.

For over a minute the academic studied it. His bearded face broke into a strong smile. "I think we've come to the right place."

Mike retreated away from the grave, standing beside Gabrielle, less than ten metres from the cobweb-covered archway. He eyed it closely, aware that the opening was deliberate and obviously made by man.

Mike entered first, careful to avoid losing his footing. Through the archway was a large chamber, its interior brighter than the corridor, its walls illuminated by sparse rays of light entering through cracks in the ceiling. It was obvious from the layout that the chamber had once been used frequently although not in recent years. It was more finely decorated than the other crypts, and was vaguely reminiscent of the inside of the nearby chapel, though not as complex. The torchlight uncovered various symbols decorating the walls ranging from that of pagan origin, such as the Green Man, to depictions from the Crusades and those seemingly belonging to the time of ancient Egypt. Whatever they were they seemed to have been made by the same people responsible for the markings on the wall of the cave.

In the centre of the room was an altar raised onto a stone platform. A chequered floor, almost resembling a gigantic chessboard, covered the ground whereas several stone pillars were assembled in equal measure. In the centre of the chamber, below the altar, was a tomb. High up on the wall behind it was a symbol etched into the stone, significantly faded, and yet instantly distinguishable as a skull and crossbones with a Templar cross flanking it. Other illustrations accompanied it, though their appearance was practically unrecognisable due to centuries of decay.

Gabrielle came to an abrupt standstill, her senses heightened by a sudden sense of panic.

"Oh, my God," she said loudly.

Mike walked closer, his eyes lighting up at the sight of the symbol. Was this why they were here? Was this why seven men had been murdered? Somehow the thought didn't ring true. Several metres before the altar, a bizarre statue stood atop the tomb. It looked like a goat, but also an angel or a demon carrying a sword. A grim expression lined its face, both morbid and evil. Underneath it was an inscription. A strange etching of what seemed to be the Rite of Larmenius symbol was also present in the ancient stone.

"What does it say?" Mike asked.

Henry approached the stone, peering in for a closer look. The smell of the stone felt dank on his nostrils. He smiled as he read.

"She sleeps through the centuries."

"Some woman," Mike said, his eyes transfixed on the strange object.

"This is Asmodeus," Henry said smiling. He eyed the object curiously before examining the remainder of the room. The chequered floor, the pillars, the carvings on the wall: it all pointed to one thing.

"This was a Masonic lodge."

Mike retreated a few steps and examined the room in further detail.

A former stairwell, leading to where the house was now located, was present in the east side of the chamber, covered in part by an identical logo. By now the feeling of coldness was starting to turn to numbness, heightened in no small part by the significant revelations that lay before them. For several seconds Mike stood still, awestruck, gazing intently at the strange logo that now seemed to hold the key to so much.

"This is it," Gabrielle said, her body shaking with excitement. She shone her torch on the inscription of the tomb, carefully examining what remained. A smile crossed her lips. "Wow. I wonder what it means."

"It's a riddle," Henry said. "The sleeping lady sleeps through the centuries. Something of importance must be buried inside."

"Open it."

"We can't," Mike said.

"Come on," Gabrielle said trying in vain to open it alone. "Help me lift it."

Mike walked slowly around the tomb and examined it under the torchlight. Patterns of angels were carved into the lid, flanking the original Templar symbol of two knights to a horse. He placed his hands on both corners of the lid. Finding a grip was difficult. With gloved fingers he gripped it tightly. It was heavy but not screwed down. Gabrielle tried to lift it but failed. Henry smiled at her. He moved in alongside her, taking a position opposite Mike.

"On three," Henry said. "One, two . . ."

After a few seconds of struggling it came free. Wasting no time, Gabrielle shone the torch inside.

Henry gazed inside. His smile withered at the sight of an empty tomb.

In truth Mike was partially relieved. Using his torch he peered inside, examining the 14th century grave from top to bottom. It looked like a tomb but where decaying remains should have lain in rest, there was nothing: a dark void cut only by the shining of the torch. He checked everything thoroughly, satisfying himself that it was empty.

Gabrielle looked blankly at her uncle for inspiration.

"The sleeping lady," he said. "If she can somehow be awakened Rosslyn Castle shall rise again."

Gabrielle shrugged.

"Medieval tradition says a great treasure worth millions is buried beneath the castle vaults. It never says what this treasure is. Clearly, once upon a time something was buried in this very tomb; something of intrinsic meaning to the castle's purpose," Henry smiled philosophically, his eyes continuing to survey the chamber. "Very interesting."

Gabrielle looked around, a lost expression dominating her face. "How do we get out?"

"How about the way we came in . . ." Mike said.

"You want a piece of me . . ."

"Shhh!" Henry put his hand to his lips.

A strange silence followed. Close by, water fell from the dizzy heights, echoing briefly then leaving nothing but the vague sound of rain falling against sodden ground several metres above. Henry walked slowly around the chamber, paying particular attention to the walls. He walked towards the archway, his eyes focused on the area directly above it. He shone the torch. For the first time he noticed another painting on the stonework. It was vaguely familiar. It was of a knight, possibly lying down. A strange emblem marked his shield. It appeared to be a ship sailing on a starry moonlit night.

Gabrielle was also looking at the image. "Take a photo."

Henry searched his pocket and removed a small digital camera. A quick sound followed as the built-in lens escaped from inside the camera. For several minutes he photographed the area in detail. The initial sense of excitement returned as he captured various images on the portable memory card.

"Right," he said. "Let's go."

Over twenty minutes later they exited through the same cave, walking slowly in the direction of the approach bridge. The ground was muddier than before as it continued to absorb the rain.

Mike breathed deeply. The first thing he noticed was that the heavy atmosphere inside the tunnel had lifted only to be replaced by a different type of oppressiveness. The chilly rain was falling heavily, only now the cold delivery felt somehow refreshing on his dusty face.

Gabrielle walked quickly, heading back towards higher ground. Following the path, she led the way tirelessly up the slope and within a few minutes reached the car park.

Several bays along from the hire car, the man with blond locks had returned to his bike. He saw that the Swiss Guard had noticed him but not for the first time his face was covered by his helmet.

Moments later, he watched as the academic reversed slowly and turned right on leaving the car park. Within seconds the biker followed.

They were the only two vehicles on the road.

23

The GPLA headquarters in Charlotte, North Carolina, was deserted by 8 p.m. For the last two hours Ged Fairbanks had been the only person in the office. He rarely stayed beyond six but tonight he was in no rush to leave. Neither was he in the mood to work.

With his back to his desk, Fairbanks swivelled on his chair and gazed through the window down at the road. Several feet below on the opposite side of the street, a man with a shaven head and dressed in a designer suit stopped to check his watch before continuing with clockwork efficiency from one end to the other. Several metres later he stopped again, looked up at the window of the accountant's office, and made a casual about-turn at the corner before repeating the sequence for the umpteenth time. An outsider may have assumed he was waiting for someone.

The accountant, however, knew better.

Fairbanks turned away from the street and returned his attention to his desk. An empty glass was present in front of him, accompanied by a bottle of single malt whiskey. The bottle, full at the start of the evening, was at least ten per cent down. The accountant refilled his glass and downed it in one. The fine liquid burned on the back of his throat, yet in his dazed state he struggled to notice. His mind was troubled by the activities that would come to pass. Sometimes he wondered if he were a stronger man whether he would have resisted them.

Yet he was not a strong man.

At least now he could move on and life could return to normal. For far too long this agenda had dominated his life. Men he had never met phoned him at all hours, demanding everything and anything in exchange for everything from one hundred-dollar bills to villas in the South Pacific: most of which he accepted. Thoughts turned to Fiji: sand, sea . . . women in bikinis.

Perhaps he had made the right decision.

He looked at the document for the final time before replacing it in the bottom drawer of a nearby file cabinet. He locked the drawer, breathing a sigh of relief as he did so. No more people in suits would be monitoring his every move.

What needed to be done was done.

The Scottish Preceptor was snoring loudly when the phone rang. He always was a deep sleeper and it was not until the fourth ring that he finally awoke. His wife poked him a couple of times and swore at him but by that stage he was already awake. In a dazed state, he rolled over towards his bedside table, his blurry vision fixed on the clock. The red LED from his alarm clock suggested it was 2:13 a.m.

Who the hell would possibly call at this hour?

"Yes . . ."

"Hello, Alex!"

The voice was cold and precise. There was no need to ask who it was.

"Now where the Devil have you been?" the Scot asked, rubbing sleep from his eyes. "I've been trying to call you all day. And with all due respect I'm due in Baltimore in seven hours."

"I'm not interested in your social events, Alex," he said clearly. "This is important."

The Scot sat upright in bed, and switched on the table lamp. The man always sounded angry on the phone. This sounded like bad news.

It was bound to be bad news.

"Listen, I've been trying to call you," the Scot said.

"That can wait."

It was no use arguing; it was never worth arguing with him. The sooner he listened the sooner he would be asleep again.

He adjusted the phone to his ear. "Very well, so what can I do for you?"

"Our Sénéchal informed me earlier today of the Vatican Bank's intention to up their holdings in Leoni et Cie to just over 50%."

The Scot paused. "Fine. I'll read all about it in *The Times* on the way to Baltimore. You should be thrilled."

"But we have another problem."

The Scot yawned vigorously, reaching for a bottle of mineral water on his bedside table. He filled an empty glass and downed half of it in one. The cool liquid felt pleasant on his throat.

"And what about it?"

"Certain members of the Vatican supervisory council have decided that Randy Lewis should take over as chief executive."

"What about him? He's just an ignorant SOB."

"He may be an ignorant SOB, as you say, Alex, but to me he's a bloody ulcer."

The Scot shook his head, looking once more at the clock. The Scot's wife kicked him in the back.

"I'm not quite sure I understand."

"Well understand this!" the bearded man said coldly. "Former Chairman of the Federal Reserve, Lewis, has been advising the council, including our very own Sénéchal, to let him and Swanson run the board. He's made numerous attempts at reminding them that a former Banco Ambrosiano and Starvel manager is largely unopposed to make decisions and Lewis thinks the idea is a bad one."

The Scot blinked several times in succession. He rubbed his eyes but it made no difference. The situation was still there. Time was ticking. Six hours, fifty-eight minutes until Baltimore.

"Sir, that was always on the cards . . . besides, what do you want me to do at 2 a.m.? And we have a presence on the oversight commission. Shouldn't you be discussing this with him?"

There was silence at the other end. The preceptor breathed deeply.

"Besides, perhaps Lewis won't even notice."

"No, professor: Randy Lewis may be a lot of things, but he's no greenhorn. He isn't one to let things slip. He's a workaholic. People are already suspicious. It is vital there is no trail."

A brief pause followed.

"I will be meeting with our Sénéchal in Rome on Friday to discuss the matter further. I suggest you accompany me before returning home from Baltimore."

The Scot gazed once more at the clock. "Fine. Now, about the other matter?"

Silence dominated the line.

"I had an interesting phone call today from a second cousin of mine."

"Do you really think I'm interested in your family reunions, Alex?"

"Well you might be once you hear what he had to say. He informed me that he received a surprise visit today from none other than Professor Leoni, his wee niece and her wee puppy."

The Scot spoke for several minutes.

"Most interesting," the Scot continued. "It seems that Monsieur Devére had left them a wee present: something that once belonged to me, you might recall. Now, as I've told you before, we are still unaware exactly what became of some of our ancient texts. We know that Monsieur Michalak left some of them to Monsieur Devére, but what we don't know is what became of them. Remember, he was quite evasive on the subject. But it seems that one of the most important has returned to the surface."

"Superstitions, Alex, I care not for them."

"But do you not see what this means? Let's say Monsieur Devére decided to inform some of his, shall we say, close friends about a few select things. Many historians have sought for years to find evidence of a genuine Templar survival."

"And . . ."

"Well let's just say he perhaps gave someone a certain history lesson."

"Such as?"

"Well. Al Leoni."

The line was quiet for several seconds. "And?"

"Well, we now know that it was Devére who passed on the findings of Nathan Walls and Martin Snow to Leoni. It seems fairly likely that if he was going to talk he would talk about everything."

A further pause followed.

"This is good news," the bearded man said.

At the other end of the line, the Scot's expression was one of confusion. "This is not good news if these things find their way into the wrong hands."

"Such matters do not remain in the wrong hands for long," the bearded man said. "I will be speaking to our Swiss Preceptor myself in due course. Perhaps he may have a plan."

"I'll look forward to giving him my regards as well."

The bearded man laughed slowly. "Now get some sleep. You're in Baltimore in a few hours."

The line went dead and the Scot hung up the phone. He was gone before his head hit the pillow.

24

They returned to St Gallen late the next evening after spending one night in Edinburgh. The hotel was grand in nature, regarded by many as one of the most prestigious to line Edinburgh's Royal Mile, and one night's stay cost the equivalent of a week of Mike's salary.

Although it was Mike's first experience staying at this type of hotel, he didn't have the opportunity to enjoy it. The majority of people present may have accepted hordes of smartly dressed guests whiling the time away in extravagant surroundings as part of the furniture yet for the Swiss Guard each was a possible suspect. A bald-headed bearded man in his late sixties chatted for over an hour with Henry Leoni in the bar, yet another old friend, acquaintance and well-wisher of the distinguished academic, while a handsome man in his early thirties stared incessantly at Gabrielle's legs, and she had noticed, but he later vanished, not to be seen again.

In many ways the relaxing environment was the perfect backdrop: a chance for his host to escape the events of recent weeks, but for Mike the evening dragged. Sometime after nine, in the corner of the bar he saw what on first impression was a man dressed in biking gear, perhaps the man from Rosslyn, but he disappeared almost as soon as he appeared. In his dazed state of mind the Swiss Guard thought he recognised the man, but he dismissed it as implausible.

Even so, the thought lingered.

He awoke that morning slightly later than usual. Despite the relatively short flight across one time zone being insignificant in terms of jet lag, the lateness of their return had left him feeling dazed. At just after 10 a.m. he left his room and entered the kitchen, his mind on autopilot as he searched for coffee. Kopi Luwak, St Helena, Hacienda la Esmeralda Geisha and El Injerto were just some of the crazy names that lined the cupboards of the oversized kitchen, recognised worldwide as some of the best coffee brands available, most of which he had never previously heard of. Before his arrival he had never questioned the pedigree of coffee. He poured himself whatever was in the percolator and savoured the flavour: another prestige brand that would be absent from the shopping list of the Polish sisters.

The one thing he would miss was the coffee.

He paused momentarily, sipping from his coffee while looking through the windows across the landscape. The torrential downpour that had lasted all morning was showing no signs of abating. It had been raining constantly for three days in Switzerland and, not for the first time, the day's weather would see him confined to the indoors. And that was fine, if it hadn't been for Gabrielle's ceaseless thirst for hidden knowledge. What did it mean? He still had no idea.

Soon enough, it would all be beyond him.

He exited the kitchen and walked slowly along the corridor. On first inspection, the château seemed deserted, the silence disturbed only by the sound of raindrops falling against the windows and the intermittent sound of thunder from somewhere towards the north. The doors to most of the rooms were closed, as usual, though the door to the dining room was open, presenting an elegant façade typically reminiscent of that found in a European stately home. On entering the room he found it unaltered from its usual appearance and devoid of any other presence. Although there was no evidence that anything was amiss the fact that there was no sign of life disturbed him slightly. At least when he knew where Gabrielle was, he knew that nothing bad would happen to her.

On leaving the room he walked along the corridor in the direction of the stairs, checking every room as he passed. In the distance he thought he could make out the sound of somebody talking, possibly on the phone. As best he could tell it was a woman's voice, probably Gabrielle's, but at present he couldn't be sure who it was or from where the sound was coming. The lack of human presence disturbed him, his senses heightened by the sound of the appalling weather outside. Ever since the day of the discovery of the manuscript the thought lingered that someone was watching them, something that the presence of the biker at Rosslyn and the night at the hotel had intensified. While in reality he considered it far less likely that anything out of the ordinary would happen on a day like today the feeling still unsettled him. As he continued along the corridor he knocked on doors before venturing inside, intent on satisfying that uneasy feeling that lingered at the back of his mind that refused to go away.

After finding no signs of life on the ground floor he headed up the stairs. On reaching the fourth, he stopped. At the end of the corridor, the door to Henry Leoni's study was ajar. Through the briefest of gaps

Mike could hear the sound of papers being shuffled and books being stacked, indicating that the Harvard academic was at work within. Turning away from the stairs, Mike walked towards the study and entered, knocking quietly against the door as he did so.

Henry was sitting alone at his desk. A cup of coffee was placed to his lips and a half-eaten piece of toast was on a plate close to the computer screen. A large library bound book was laid out neatly in front of him.

"Morning," he said peering up.

"Morning," Mike returned, walking towards the desk. Two other books were closed, symbols and titles of various meanings and origins decorating their ageing covers, concealing ancient wisdom of various importance: each one seemingly identical in appearance, their calligraphy recognisable only to the trained expert.

"Where's your niece?"

"She's on the telephone. I think the Vatican have made an offer for some of our shares in Leoni et Cie."

"Oh really," Mike said, grimacing a smile, unwilling to intrude but keen to clarify his own position. "I thought what with everything that's gone on she might have waited a while."

"Neither myself nor Gabrielle are bankers, Mr Frei," he said thoughtfully. "The time is right. Although, I must admit, it does seem strange. After all, over two hundred years of family heritage survive in that bank." He smiled at Mike philosophically. "But I don't think we'll sell our entire stake. And at least it'll be taken over by the Church, not just some corporate vehicle."

Mike nodded, making eye contact with Henry. It was strange. He had only known the man four weeks but something had left a mark.

"Well, the sooner your business is done, the sooner I'll be leaving, I guess."

Henry looked at Mike with interest. "Well it's been very reassuring having you here. The old place won't be the same without you."

Mike forced an awkward smile. "I'm not sure your niece would see it that way."

"You can't take Gabrielle at face value."

"No?"

"No. That's just her way."

Mike sipped his coffee slowly. The taste danced beautifully on his dry tongue. He looked at Henry who continued to smile thoughtfully at him. Maybe he was right. Maybe she wasn't one to show her emotions. She certainly shouted; that was emotion. She had cried, although not in front of him. Sometimes she seemed so cold and distant, but other times he almost felt she could be kind and caring.

"Don't say anything to her yet," Henry said. "It may upset her more than you think."

Mike smiled as though he had heard a joke. Suddenly his ears pricked. Soft footsteps were ascending the stairs, becoming ever louder before stopping at the summit. The sound continued, this time along the corridor, seemingly approaching the study. Seconds later the door opened and Gabrielle entered. She was dressed in blue jeans and a black top and carried a relatively modern paperback book in her right hand. Not for the first time she looked fantastic.

"Who was that?" Henry asked.

"Renouf, Anderson and Klose."

"What did they want?" Mike asked.

Gabrielle looked at Mike sternly. "Do you always ask what's not your business?"

"Sorry."

Gabrielle turned away, placing her book down on the desk. "Since you ask, they are doing the legal work for Leoni et Cie. I'm selling 30% to the Vatican Bank."

Mike nodded, digesting the information. A peculiar silence engulfed the large ornate study, strangely loud in nature, resembling the moment following a glass or plate dropping to the floor before smashing into a thousand pieces, leaving a fading echo as the pieces come to a standstill. Several thoughts were running through his head.

"Not that this concerns you," she said, turning towards him. "Now that my interest in Leoni et Cie is subsiding, that will be the end of you."

Mike made eye contact briefly, his coffee mug partially shielding his face. "I'll stay until I'm told otherwise."

"Right. But the Vatican will no longer need to protect us. When the contract is signed, they can appoint their own permanent chief exec. I'm going to Rome a week Friday as it happens for a meeting of the new bank with the Vatican bankers. We can drop you home."

Mike nodded, his thoughts focused on the Vatican. At least he would be back with his friends, Mark, Stan, Alessandro.

At the same time he felt strangely sad. He looked at Gabrielle as she walked towards her uncle. There was a sense of despondency about her. Maybe it was about Rosslyn; maybe it was her father; perhaps the decision to sell her shares in her family bank. The thought was credible enough. Out of the corner of her eye she looked at him and instantly looked away.

"As it happens, this has come at a good time," she said, mainly to her uncle. "I need to go to the Vatican anyway."

Henry looked up. "Oh?"

"Does the name Count Poli mean anything to you?"

"Poli?"

"Yes. I found this."

She opened the book to a specific page and passed it to her uncle. He chuckled immediately.

"Ah yes. The James Jackson account."

"What's that?" Mike asked.

Henry smiled kindly. "Nothing really: just an old wives' tale. An account from 1836 in this village in Scotland."

"It's no tale," Gabrielle said adamantly.

"You don't know that."

"You don't know that it's not."

Henry relented, smiling in mild amusement. "Okay, so suppose it's true?"

"What is it?" Mike asked, walking closer and peering over Gabrielle's shoulder.

Henry: "According to a book, written in 1836, a man named Poli, a descendant of the last Provost of Rosslyn Chapel before the Reformation . . ."

"Reformation?" Mike asked.

"Yes. Of the Church."

"You mean like John Knox and Henry VIII?"

"That was they," Henry said, making Gabrielle smile. "Now a man named James Jackson from the village of Penicuik near Roslin writes in 1836 how a man named Poli came to the area two years earlier, and had in his possession a strange book that described the chapel and castle as they were at the time they were deserted."

"And what was this strange book?" Mike asked. "Kinda like your one?"

"Precisely," Gabrielle replied.

Henry shook his head, still smiling. "Now, Poli was joined by Jackson, supposedly."

"Not supposedly."

Henry shook his head once more. Resistance was useless.

"Well, Poli showed him and the rest of the party around the buildings. While visiting the chapel he bemoaned the absence of the 'Splendid Tomb' of the early St Clairs not being present in the vaults."

Mike edged closer to the desk, reading the book over Henry's shoulder. Suddenly he was starting to become interested, almost as if everything that had happened so far could be validated. Were they too late? Had they gone to the right place, only after it had been taken? Whatever it was.

What had this to do with Al Leoni and the Rite of Larmenius?

"So . . . supposedly . . ."

"Will you stop saying that!" Gabrielle snapped.

Mike looked at Henry and laughed. It was as if the professor was in school, a student not a teacher, whereas his niece was the headmistress.

Henry: "So, Poli leads these men into the vaults of the castle where the splendid tomb was housed and this legendary treasure was buried. However, it was not gold, nor silver, but books."

"Books?" Mike said.

"The castle was once used as a scriptorium," Gabrielle said.

"You mean like the Vatican?"

"Funny you should mention that," Gabrielle replied, showing him the page in question. "Because the manuscripts were taken to the Vatican and are now in the library."

"Now that is a supposedly," Henry said.

Gabrielle looked at Henry and then at Mike. "And, I looked up that symbol we saw in the vault at Rosslyn – you know the one of the figure with the shield that had an image of a ship on a starry moonlit night. Well, a near exact symbol is found in Westford, Massachusetts which is thought by some to mark the grave of one of Zichmni's men after they reached America."

Mike raised his eyebrows, convinced she was clutching at straws. "So what do you think is there? What kind of manuscripts?"

"No one knows for sure. The only one named was a copy of Rota Temporum by Adam Abel."

"And you think that book is of relevance?"

"Probably not. But if we can locate that one then maybe we can locate the others."

Mike wiped his mouth with the back of his hand and looked inquisitively at Gabrielle. A smile touched his lips.

"You think the Vatican is harbouring proof of a Templar survival?"

"Stranger things have happened."

"Name one."

She stuttered. "I don't have to. And besides, you're going home."

Mike laughed ironically, then for a moment he met her gaze. For what seemed like several seconds, Gabrielle looked at him with a despondent look before turning away and leaving the room. She headed along the corridor, continuing until reaching her bedroom. The sound of her footfalls was in keeping with the thundering wind that accompanied the rain. He heard a door slam, echoing momentarily before fading to silence.

In a large office, located on the 15th floor of a Boston skyscraper, the chief executive of the Starvel Group, Louis Velis, pondered the document in front of him. Although he was used to approving corporate loans for major businesses, this one was slightly different to what he expected. $347 million was more than the average loan, but it was not that what struck him most. More surprising was the source of the request.

He looked at the terms for the final time and signed the contract. He would ring the cardinals immediately to tell them the good news.

In a poorly lit chamber somewhere in the Vatican, the senior cardinal and the Scottish Preceptor sat quietly, their eyes focused on the rough Latin text of the ancient chronicle in front of them. Turning yet another irrelevant page, the preceptor scanned it for any sign, any possible clue hidden in the ancient Latin.

Closing the cover, he moved onto the next manuscript, still looking for the missing manuscript. As a professor of history he knew that urban legends were subject to inaccuracy, but also that ancient pages can harbour many secrets.

New truths were being uncovered. These truths must remain secret.

25

Zürich, three days later

The main office of the European law firm, Renouf, Anderson and Klose was situated in the heart of Zürich's central business district. The building had an attractive glass exterior and was entered via one of two identical automatic doors.

Mike and Gabrielle entered the building at midday. Inside, the tower seemed somehow smaller than it appeared from outside – an illusion of light on glass. A smartly dressed man on reception informed them that eight firms shared the twelve-floor building and that Renouf, Anderson and Klose were on the eighth, ninth and tenth floors, with the office they needed on the ninth. The building took all sorts, and Gabrielle could tell from the notice board on the reception of the ninth floor that this firm would be the same. Renouf, Anderson and Klose employed one hundred and fifty-four lawyers in the city according to their website, twenty-four of which were partners, all concentrating in different areas. One was oil; another was insurance; then there was also property, foreign affairs, litigation and, of course, banking. She caught sight of the name Jurgen Klose as the partner for banking.

Mike had become used to the sight of men in suits recently. The waiting area consisted of white walls, countless artificial pot plants giving the false impression of natural environment, and was frequented by men wearing black suits and worried faces with arms attached to perpetually unopened briefcases. There were twelve available chairs, separated into groups of four by two small glass coffee tables offering newspapers and magazines from the *New York Times* to *Heat Magazine*. Of the twelve seats, three others were in use. A bald-headed bespectacled man in his fifties seemed oblivious to everyone's existence with his eyes staring with constant attention at the newspaper on his lap, interrupted by the regular glances at the clock. Two seats along a bearded man seemed more interested in Gabrielle's legs, whereas on the other side of Mike sat a vastly overweight Swiss lady in her forties clearly suffering from stress.

Mike sat down, preparing himself for a lengthy wait. He picked up a motor magazine and began flicking through pages of sports cars. Less than two minutes after their arrival a young associate dressed in a smart suit appeared from a nearby corridor. He smiled at Gabrielle.

"Ms Leoni, they are ready for you."

Jurgen Klose studied the document for the final time and once more found nothing obvious he disliked, at least according to this paper.

The accounts were impressive: a customer base of over half a million people worldwide, mostly in Switzerland, central Europe and the US, including a steady clientele of millionaires from St Gallen. Worldwide assets of over $75 billion, mostly made up of small loans; market capital in excess of $6.5 billion or approximately 6.4 billion Swiss Francs, at current share price, not bad for a bank of that size in the current climate; profit after tax for the last fiscal year just under $334 million; amount owed on financial derivatives contracts just under $1.1 billion was quite acceptable and the 200,000 contracts on put and call options in Japan and Asia were proving quite profitable. Yes, on face value, this was fine.

No one could fail to be impressed by the performance of Leoni et Cie, the former Banque Leoni. What fifteen years earlier had been predominantly a privately owned retail bank, before its floatation and merger with US investment bank, Rosco, with a capital base of $1.5 billion, had now flourished into a real contender. The Glass-Steagall Act had been lifted in the United States in 1999 – the act which prohibited bank holding companies from owning other financial companies – and had that not occurred their recent success would not have been possible. Derivatives, insurance, mergers and acquisitions and even the emerging markets all became obvious targets and success in one seemed to lead to success in another. In two hundred years the fourth oldest private bank in St Gallen had become one of the top fifty most successful banks in the world, the fourth largest in Switzerland.

By the 1980s the firm's image was starting to develop. As the decade progressed over one thousand branches had become assembled for their purpose, branches shot up throughout France for the first time in two centuries and even the Canadians had climbed aboard the Leoni et Cie bandwagon. Secrecy was still a passion, as was customary of the Swiss nation, and as growth continued, so did the lending. Every new branch saw the privilege extended to a new generation of happy customers.

It was a combination of Leoni et Cie's fine financial footing and the religious pedigree of the Leonis that convinced the Vatican Bank to invest in the bank in the early 1990s. The Banco Ambrosiano scandal had rocked the organisation and most in the business had long memories. But Al Leoni was a colossus. Leoni et Cie was alive with activity but without arrogance. It thrived on confidentiality and did not advertise strenuously. This suited the Vatican just fine. Marcinkus had left a void that was still growing and the last thing his replacements wanted was to follow the same path. A reputed $1.7 billion had been invested by 1994 and that had more than doubled by 1999. Even the Roman Curia had funds invested there.

What had begun in the 1780s as a private deposit bank had turned into a multinational conglomerate, yet still maintaining the family feel and remaining in private ownership. In 1996 they floated on the SMI, the Swiss Market Index, and the acquisition a year later of another private Swiss bank resulted in even more success. Leoni et Cie was going places.

The merger with Rosco in 2002 was a surprise and one of the first since new American legislation had been passed. Throughout the nineties Starvel and three other banks had failed to acquire them but that had not dissuaded former Starvel director, Gilbert de Bois, from attempting to do the same with his new bank. Leoni et Cie, now the fourth largest bank in Switzerland, was already a success, whereas Rosco was still growing. Since its formation in 1989 under the direction of oil tycoon, Mark Antonio Careca, the bank had grown quickly. Extended lending had led to rapid growth and this concerned the then Chairman of the Fed, Randy Lewis, prior to the merger but such issues were no longer a problem. Leoni et Cie was the bigger bank, but only just. Rosco was still extending its wings. Had the merger not gone through perhaps in four years Rosco may have overtaken Leoni et Cie as the bigger bank.

By the time the merger had been agreed, Al Leoni was considering retirement and the bank needed a new agenda. At the beginning of his life he was a multimillionaire; at the end he was multiple in dollar billions. And Rosco would ensure continued success for his legacy. They were young but ready to flourish. And they had what Leoni et Cie didn't have: an established corporate presence in America. Equally, Leoni had what Rosco did not: a firm retail client base in Europe.

The Feds initially took their time but this was largely due to complications over the new legislation. The Swiss FINMA took less time to decide. They were still only the fourth largest bank in

Switzerland. Increased supervision would come as a result of its increased size but that was to be expected. They were still a fraction of the size of the heavyweights.

Although a merger, Klose noted that it was officially billed as a stock swap. Leoni et Cie purchased every share of Rosco for around $1.9 billion of its own stock and issued approximately 1.9 new Leoni et Cie shares for every old one. Before 2007 the bank had become a $32 billion revenue firm with assets nearing $115 billion, although both numbers had since fallen. The chairmen of both companies, de Bois of Rosco and the late Al Leoni, both became board members with Leoni appointed as chief executive, de Bois as chairman, with the Vatican Bank owning the second highest stake behind Leoni. It remained to be seen how the management styles of de Bois and Leoni would coexist, but they had done so peacefully.

Even the tree huggers approved. For every customer who converted to online banking, forsaking the paper statements, the cost of the paper was given to the GREEN Foundation, set up by Gilbert de Bois in Boston, aimed at preserving the rain forests.

And that wasn't the only good cause. De Bois had set up charities in Africa, Asia and Latin America. It did not bode well to take sides in matters of religion but Leoni et Cie seemed to take Christianity by example. And America and Europe's Christians responded.

Yes, this was Al Leoni's legacy.

This really was God's bank.

Next to Jurgen Klose, the chairman of Leoni et Cie, Gilbert de Bois, sat patiently. His dark hair was combed back smartly, yet not disguising some vague streaks of grey. His green eyes seemed all the more powerful against the backdrop of his rugged face. Supposedly in the media industry image was everything but his seemed less extravagant than many. What he lacked in extravagance he made up for in success.

Irving Swanson was present on behalf of the Vatican Bank, as was Cardinal Tepilo on his left. Swanson yawned vigorously. He checked his watch for the umpteenth time in quick succession before strolling across the lavish office towards the coffee dispenser. He removed a cardboard cup from the pile and poured himself a straight black cup of coffee with two sugars, an act of boredom as much as thirst. He blew on it and swallowed.

"Can I get one of them?" de Bois asked.

Swanson turned and looked at him. "Go fuck yourself, Gile."

"Will you two please show some decorum," Tepilo said, getting to his feet. His ageing frame hunched slightly as he addressed the bankers as if he were a headmaster telling off two of his pupils. Swanson looked with malice for several seconds before pouring a warm coffee for de Bois.

Jurgen Klose adjusted his glasses, his dynamic eyes on de Bois. Over the years he had seen it all before. A mutual dislike was fairly common in banking but he knew their feud had different issues. Childhood rivalries between friends seeing who had the best bike, the best toys, whose father drove the best car was fairly typical. It was not as if de Bois had shagged Swanson's daughter, and bragged about it all over the Internet. Rather, de Bois's Ferrari could go faster than Swanson's Jaguar, de Bois's château in the Loire Valley had a swimming pool large enough for a football pitch, and Swanson's toilet smelt of poo.

Empires crumbled on feuds. Couples bickered, marriages ended, men got shot and dollars lost and the finger was always pointed at the one who was not man enough to handle the pressure. Their rivalry was beneficial in the old days. As directors at Starvel both men oversaw leftfield returns and the shareholders basked in the success. It had been over six years since Swanson had worked for Starvel, ten since de Bois sold his stake to Louis Velis. De Bois was never a banker. But he was a businessman through and through and had his fingers in many pies, mainly media. He sold his stake in Starvel to concentrate on new ventures but Swanson was tired. His wife died from cancer and that hit him hard. His daughter was his rock and his pleasure in life came from babysitting his seven-year-old granddaughter. De Bois remained happily married but he never really spoke of such matters. Only the Vatican could have tempted Swanson back. And five years ago that happened. Past income fed the wallet. But this fed the soul.

At precisely noon there came a gentle knock at the door. Swanson swallowed his coffee. A lasting burning sensation resonated down his neck, partially concealed by layers of flab that almost resembled a double chin.

Tepilo answered come in and Gabrielle Leoni entered the room.

The dynamic of the room changed immediately, all eyes watching her every move. As she entered she saw a large airy room, abundant in wooden furniture mostly containing shelving and books. She smiled as the gracious figure of Cardinal Tepilo stood slowly to greet her. Swanson remained seated, sitting alongside Klose. De Bois stood by a large coffee table and offered his hand.

"Gabrielle, my dear, how are you?"

185

"Good," Gabrielle replied, kissing de Bois on each cheek. She turned to face her great-uncle.

"Gabrielle, my darling," Tepilo said, "you are quite sure about this? The future of Leoni et Cie does not need to rest on decisions made of hurt."

"No," she replied with a smile. "I'm ready. And please don't get up on my account."

Her great-uncle smiled thoughtfully, remaining standing. She smiled at Tepilo before turning to all present in turn. Secretly she was quite disappointed that Cardinal Utaka was not present. Swanson forced a smile from his position on the couch and Gabrielle shone one back. Klose watched with interest. It wasn't every day he was treated to such a sight.

"Have a seat, my dear," the lawyer said to Gabrielle, motioning towards a leather sofa around the large wooden table. Despite the German his English was crisp and without accent. They offered her coffee, she declined; they exchanged pleasantries, and she laughed and smiled; Klose was staring and that pissed her off, but she was used to that. She faked a smile and waited for him to act.

"Now," the German said, walking towards the table, clicking the pen in his hand. "You've seen the contract? You are happy with the terms?"

"Yes," she said, referring to the estimated $2.39 billion she would receive over the next five years for her share. "Yes I am."

Klose smiled briefly. "Whenever you're ready."

The lawyer laid out the contract before her on the table and offered her the pen. She glanced at it quickly but she had already seen all she needed to see. She would personally see a $33 million golden handshake if profits went as planned over the next year. 31% of her 43% stake would go to the Vatican Bank, leaving her with 12% that she was in no hurry to lose. All profits and liabilities would remain with Leoni et Cie PLC, all future profits and liabilities would remain the responsibility of Leoni et Cie PLC, et cetera et cetera.

Inhaling deeply, Gabrielle signed the contract. Images of her father flashed before her and were gone in an instant. She looked at Cardinal Tepilo and smiled.

Tepilo took her hand. "May the peace of Christ be with you always."

Gabrielle smiled briefly at all present before leaving the room. Jurgen Klose signed the document on behalf of Renouf, Anderson and Klose and the cardinal signed it for the Vatican Bank. De Bois signed it as chairman; he'd have signed it a hundred times if he could. Swanson was left till last. De Bois picked up a fountain pen and handed it to his former co-director.

Swanson looked at Tepilo. "You're making a big mistake, eminence."

"Irve, come on," De Bois said.

Tepilo looked menacingly at Swanson. "Enough of this childish nonsense."

De Bois removed a cigar from the inside pocket of his suit and lit it immediately. He looked at Swanson, his expression one of clear hostility.

"Just sign it, jackass."

"Now we've been over this before," the cardinal said. "This does nothing positive."

"Fine, don't sign it. Like it matters."

With a resigned grunt Swanson swept the fine nib across the paper, almost ripping it. He threw the pen on the contract and looked at his former colleague. De Bois broke into a smile. He offered his hand.

"No hard feelings."

Swanson declined. "Asshole."

De Bois exhaled on his cigar, directing smoke roughly in the direction of the cardinal.

"Arrogant, arse," the cardinal said, turning to leave.

De Bois laughed as he turned towards Jurgen Klose. He removed his cigar with his right hand and patted the lawyer's shoulder.

"Thank you. We are all very grateful."

The German raised his eyebrows and left the room, leaving Gilbert de Bois alone. He removed his mobile phone from his trouser pocket and dialled.

26

Vatican City

Gabrielle had visited the Vatican on many occasions throughout her life. Although she was no stranger to the famous buildings, the sheer scale of St Peter's Basilica never failed to captivate her. Even though she was not as religious as some of her ancestors, she loved the architecture of the Vatican City and regarded the location as one of her favourites.

She walked alongside Mike across St Peter's Square, approaching the basilica. Its giant dome dominated the clear blue sky. It was 8 a.m. and the site that would be populated by thousands of pilgrims the next day – as it was every Wednesday when the Pope gives his famous general audience – was empty, delivering a quiet eeriness that made her feel nervous despite the presence of the Swiss Guard walking alongside her.

They were completely alone, yet she didn't feel it. The famous fountains trickled gently, echoing as water hit water. Across the skyline she noticed the presence of several pairs of eyes looking down, each belonging to the stone faces of the great saints of old, lined up one by one, seemingly watching their every move.

Twelve days had passed since signing the contract in Zürich. Gilbert de Bois's unavoidable return to Canada meant the first meeting of the new bank since the takeover would be delayed, forcing them to return briefly to St Gallen before making the journey to Rome.

They had departed the previous morning. Mike's intention had been to complete the journey in one day, but that was foiled by the weather, forcing them to find a hotel some thirty kilometres north of the Italian capital. The site he chose was circumspect, a small bed and breakfast in an unspoilt town less than five minutes from the main road. Despite the objections he booked one room with two beds, determined not to allow for the possibility of a surprise attack. There was tension as usual, but different to what Mike was used to. She was despondent, more so. In the circumstances he almost wondered whether she might miss him, whether perhaps Henry Leoni was right.

Then he dismissed the idea.

The weather had improved by daybreak, allowing them to return to the Vatican in time for her meeting. Then she would leave and he would stay.

And what needed to be done would be done.

They crossed the square, approaching the steps leading to the Maderno façade, passing the famous statues, instantly recognisable as St Peter and St Paul. They walked on unimpeded until they reached the security guards. Mike saluted as he approached and explained that he was a Swiss Guard, not that they would have guessed from his blue jeans and black t-shirt. They walked through the metal detector unhindered, catching a piercing stare from a very masculine looking female security guard as they entered the basilica.

Mike led the way through the open doors, heading through the church in the direction of the main altar. The site was practically deserted, unsurprising given the early hour. A small group of Spanish tourists were heading in the opposite direction, probably towards the square, and a group of early risers on a pilgrimage from San Antonio were standing with stiff necks, gaping in awe at the inside of the dome. Within an hour the site would be heaving with tourists.

Side by side they walked in silence: strange and awkward in nature. For Gabrielle it was a proud attempt at strength at the end of an association that was, at least in her opinion, ultimately unnecessary.

For Mike it was bittersweet. Throughout his eight weeks at St Gallen he couldn't help replay that first night over and over in his mind. It was impossible not to dislike her after the way she was to him, but the situation was hardly straightforward. He remembered the way she looked, even the way she had looked at him, at least before the suit comment. It was strange. It seemed man was never destined to have it easy with women of unattainable beauty. Never in a million years would he have predicted the weeks that followed. In many ways the strange series of events had brought them close together, possibly in pity or circumstance. He doubted she viewed his being there as obvious friendship.

For her it was the same. She never admitted it but it was there. A strange connection established not by friendship but purpose: purpose and fear. But that had led to affection and respect. As they made their way past Bernini's Baldacchino she smiled briefly at Mike.

They walked slowly, heading in the direction of the main altar. Several lesser altars lined the interior, decorated by sculptures of Popes and other religious figures, portraits of the Apostles and random depictions from the Bible. The altars were largely deserted, whereas those in use were occupied by various priests, mostly alone, carrying out early morning Mass, some assisted by altar boys.

Several metres above them the early sun radiated brightly through that window of yellow alabaster, illuminating the dove of the Holy Spirit in its centre, penetrating through Bernini's Gloria and shining on the Cathedra Petri, the Throne of Peter, the chair that was said to have once been used by the first Pope and Apostle of Christ. In the light, the throne, enclosed in bronze casing, emitted a bright angelic image as it stood supported effortlessly by the hands of four doctors of the church, standing proudly on equal sides, illustrating expressions of adoration and joy from their sculpted faces. Gabrielle couldn't help look up in admiration and awe, not just from religion, but the exquisite calibre of the man who created them.

On reaching the front of the church Mike stopped to examine his surroundings. There was no sign of Thierry.

"He's probably in the Chapel of St Columban. He goes there sometimes to pray."

Gabrielle nodded, pausing before following him back in the direction from which they had come from. He dragged his suitcase along the floor behind him, causing a loud echoing sound to resonate throughout the church. He turned on reaching the stairs in the middle of the basilica, leading down to the grotto.

The grotto of the great basilica was located between the former floor levels of the old Constantinian Basilica and the nave of the modern church. The present grotto comprised a labyrinth of chapels and snaking corridors lined by the sarcophagi of various Popes and ancient doctors of the church, the only physical remains of the ancient basilica that existed between the 4th and 15th centuries.

Mike led the way down the stairs to the grotto and stopped before the original tomb of Pope John Paul II. A solitary candle burned by the side of the grave, illuminating the white stone slab in a heavy tint of purple through the coloured glass that surrounded the flame. To his left he saw the chapel of St Peter and directly behind it the tomb of the famous Apostle enclosed by a grated window, solid walls and decorated by ornate paintings. He genuflected reverently before the tombs and

Gabrielle did the same. He forced a smile and she flashed one back. A group of nuns, five in total, walked past them, heading away from St Peter in the direction of St Longinus. The side chapels were mainly empty and quiet bar a ghostly enunciation of Gregorian chants from one of the distant chapels.

Mike led the way to the left of the former tomb of John Paul II, passing the Polish Chapel and entered the chapel of St Columban next on the right. The chapel was pleasant in atmosphere and largely undecorated. Four pews dominated its centre, situated before a stone altar. A green mosaic of Saint Columban and five others decorated the wall behind the altar, reflecting the light brightly as it bounced off the cold stone. In the second pew Thierry sat alone.

The oberst made the sign of the cross before turning to face Gabrielle and Mike. Mike jumped to salute with military precision and Gabrielle laughed loudly. Thierry smiled at her and raised his hand slowly to salute Mike. To Mike it was obvious he had not come to pray as such. It was probably the only chance he would get that day to have some peace and quiet.

"Wachtmeister."

"Sir."

Thierry turned towards Gabrielle who smiled warmly. "Gabrielle," he said taking her hand in his. His broad hands felt warm and prickly. "How are you?"

"I'm good," she replied, quietly appreciating the moment when her hand became free again.

"I hope Wachtmeister Frei has been of comfort to you."

Now on the spot, Mike brushed his eyebrow with his left hand. The last thing he wanted was an assessment, but already this felt more like an autopsy: slow, painful, and on the whole unenlightening.

But in many ways the last eight weeks had been useful. Later that day he would report his findings to Thierry and the Vatican Police.

"Mike was a true gentleman and an excellent soldier," Gabrielle said without making eye contact with Mike. "My mother, uncle and myself felt vastly more secure in his presence."

Vastly more secure. *Jeez, she was worse than Riva.* As he looked at her he noticed the hint of a grin had graced her lips. For a moment he thought she was going to look at him, but instead she maintained eye contact with the oberst. The perfect actress!

"I'm very pleased to hear this," the oberst said. "How is your mother?"

"She's okay. She's with my aunt in Ottawa now."

"And yourself?"

"I'm okay. My uncle is back home in St Gallen. He's gonna stay for a while."

"I'm very pleased to know your safety will be assured."

Gabrielle smiled. "Thank you, Thierry."

Not for the first time no eye contact was made yet to Mike what sounded like one thing insinuated another. Standing in silence, he couldn't help but think back to what Henry said. What began as a front ended as a front only somehow less convincing than before. Eight weeks had come and gone but it seemed like a lot longer. And as Mike flipped his suitcase onto one side, it was as though he had just finished a lengthy holiday.

"Wachtmeister, why don't you escort Ms Leoni to the Sistine Chapel; the council of the Vatican Bank are meeting there."

"Wow, I love that place," Gabrielle said.

"Wachtmeister. I'll be in my office."

Together, they walked side by side through the long and deserted passageways that made up the Vatican Museums. The wheels of Mike's suitcase echoed loudly in all directions as they rolled across the floor, making Gabrielle smile. Although she had walked this floor before she found herself in awe of the incredible array of art that covered the ceilings and walls.

They continued through several large arch-shaped doorways and entered the Gallery of Maps. She arched her neck as they walked, her mind failing in every way to take in the inspiring scenes covering the curved ceiling above her. On the walls, the atlas paintings seemed almost three-dimensional: an artistic illusion that made the islands seem to protrude from their position surrounded by glorious blue seas harbouring navies of painted ships while ancient muses, floating above the water, decorated golden plates on which the name of the country was written.

While Gabrielle was totally captivated, Mike had seen it many times before. On some days he would walk the corridors several times. Strangely he had never really appreciated them. Tourists came from all over the world to see the famous art, yet to him they were just a passing wall mark: almost like a cheap print in a 5 x 7 inch frame hanging on a bedroom wall. He smiled to himself as he watched Gabrielle study the room in detail. She really was an expert in everything she did.

"So what happens to you now?"

She delayed, continuing to focus on the walls. "You mean now that the Vatican have bought Leoni et Cie or now that you've left?" she asked with a smile.

"Both, I guess."

"Well, my family still owns shares in the bank but I won't be involved in running it."

Mike nodded. "Right."

"Yeah."

They entered another corridor lined with art from the Middle Ages. One particular picture caught Gabrielle's eye. Many of the characters were on horses ascending a mountain, evoking scenes from Exodus. Moving on, she looked at another, this one a scene of war: men, some on horseback, fighting on a green field before a castle on the coast. The Latin title meant nothing to her.

"And how about today?"

"Well seeing as I'm here I might as well check out the library."

Mike looked at her. "You know there are like a million books in there. And besides, you need special permission from the librarian. Only scholars are allowed in there. And that's just the non-secret one."

"I know," Gabrielle replied. "But I'm sure the cardinals won't mind. I mean I'm about to have a meeting with the Vatican bankers. And my great-uncle is the Cardinal Secretary of State. The Camerlengo, after all."

Mike had to admit she had a point. It was one thing some atheist scholar from Massachusetts trying to obtain a copy of some manuscript while researching a class on the Second World War. Gabrielle Leoni was no ordinary person. Billions of dollars of the Vatican's money was tied up in her bank, her family's bank.

Gabrielle Leoni: socialite, banker, and scholar.

"And then what?"

Gabrielle shrugged. "Who knows? You won't be around to find out."

They came to a standstill outside the Sistine Chapel and looked one another in the eye. Behind exquisite doors people were talking loudly, confirming that the meeting was still to start.

"Well," Mike said.

"Yeah," she replied, breaking eye contact and fiddling with her hair. She cleared her throat and looked away.

Mike sighed and an awkward smile reached his lips. Secretly he almost felt choked up but retained the soldier's calm.

"It was a pleasure."

Gabrielle laughed. "Shut up, you hated it."

For once Mike's façade let him down and Gabrielle smiled widely.

He searched for words that never came. Finally she broke the silence.

"Thank you."

"What for?"

"You know. Rosslyn. Driving me to St Gallen and places. Taking care of my mom. Trying to protect me even though I was always yelling at you, arguing with you, telling you what to do . . ."

"Telling me what not to do."

Gabrielle smiled. "Precisely."

Mike laughed. "Yeah . . . well . . . that was nothing."

"Yeah."

Further seconds of silence passed awkwardly. The sound of Gilbert de Bois laughing was audible from the chapel. It sounded like he was speaking to Cardinal del Rosi.

Mike laughed and so did Gabrielle.

"Sounds like quite a party in there."

"Who knew cardinals and bankers had a sense of humour."

Mike let out another brief laugh, leading to further silence. Then inexplicably a sense of decorum took over.

He looked her in the eye.

"You take care."

"Yeah. You too."

Mike reached out his hand, not knowing what else to do. She smiled as she reached for it and leaned forward to kiss him. He leaned in himself. Both sets of lips felt contact with one another's cheeks and without intention their lips partially met. For what was only the briefest of seconds if not less the soft touch of Gabrielle's hand behind his head accompanied by the faintest brush of her beautiful lips on the side of his felt like a moment of perfect bliss. As she released her hand, her eyes opened and they looked at one another, all this time without speaking a word.

She forced a smile and raised her right hand before turning away. She entered the chapel and like a true actress did not look back. As the door closed behind her Mike stood alone. He placed his hand to his clean-shaven face, and for several seconds continued to watch the door.

Finally, he picked up the handle to his suitcase and walked back the way he came, accompanied only by the echoing of the wheels as he dragged the case behind him.

27

Oberst de Courten had been sitting in his office for over ten minutes. What began as a brief escape from the hustle and bustle of being commander of the Swiss Guard had become a rare period of quiet reflection. The Vatican was never quiet but today had been a chore. Under normal circumstances the Vatican Bank was relatively unimportant, yet recently, other than the Pope himself, it had become his key responsibility.

Nine Vatican bankers, usually ten, in the Sistine Chapel, two outsiders, was rare but not altogether out of the ordinary. To him it was just another get-together of the people in suits congregating in God's holiest of chapels to participate in the worshipping of a different god: this one with an earthly presence consisting of millions of churches throughout the world whose logos differed from £ to $ to other stupid signs that looked more in place at the bottom of an ancient Egyptian sarcophagus. Everyone seemed to worship this god and even the Vatican was acting as an altar to him.

To Thierry, the room was his sanctuary. Like many of the rooms in this part of the Vatican City, it was elegantly decorated with Renaissance art, artefacts, and a flag of the Swiss Guard, incorporating the crest of his tenure. His walkie-talkie sat on his desk next to the phone that echoed from time to time with yet another message.

By the desk lamp was a three by seven inch frame enclosing a beautiful photograph. He was in it, standing, not formally, but casual. It seemed strange, distant and vague, despite being taken less than two years ago. He seemed much younger then. In his arms was a five-year-old girl: medium length locks of golden blonde hair and smiling blue eyes, a characteristic shared by the other three in the photograph. Next to her was a slightly older version of the child, perhaps three years her senior, with an equally cheeky smile befitting an eight-year-old. Next on was a ten-year-old, also a girl, also a blonde, also smiling. Their cuteness displayed trickery of youth while their clothing, despite lacking in prestige, suited their appearances. To an outsider the photograph was a vision of warmth: a happy family kept together by the final member of the family, Eliza de Courten: forty-two years of age, mother of three, devoted child of God, wife of the oberst and image of perfect loveliness. Her prettiness, clearly sharing the family attributes inherited by her children, was still visible despite signs of forehead wrinkles and isolated streaks of grey in her otherwise natural blonde hair, partially covering her ears, lined with department store earrings, potential cost £80 the pair. Her bright blue eyes demonstrated a wild side illustrating reminders of lost youth and adventure never to be tamed despite twelve years by the side of a soldier.

He smiled to himself. Seconds later he heard a knock at the door.

"Come."

The door opened and Mike entered, now dressed in the traditional blue uniform of the Swiss Guard and minus his suitcase.

"Wachtmeister," he said, rising to his feet. He saluted Mike and offered him a chair.

Mike sat down, taking a second to examine the room. As usual it was a tidy office, an important office in keeping with the character of the Swiss Guard: eternally lacking in wealth but abundant in humility and natural prestige. Bankers in suits may earn all the dough but, as Alessandro once said, all women dream of a Swiss Guard.

Seconds later there came a second knock at the door. Commissario Pessotto entered quickly, dressed sharply. He smiled briefly at Mike before taking a seat next to Thierry.

"Now, Frei," Pessotto said, his hands clasped together and his expression thoughtful. "How did it go?"

For over quarter of an hour Mike recalled the activities of the past two months. He referred to the funeral, which was nothing new. He referred to the bank and the circumstances surrounding it, then the return of Henry Leoni and his observations regarding the recently discovered manuscript. Rosslyn came last.

Thierry's reaction was difficult to determine. As the commander of the Swiss Guard nothing shocked him. Mike emphasised the importance of the manuscript being found in a safe deposit account at Leoni et Cie which may, or may not, have belonged to Mikael Devére and the alleged content of the diary. In general he centred the topic on the logo and its inclusion in the vaults at Rosslyn, including the grave of one of the Zenos.

Commissario Pessotto sat quietly. His dynamic blue eyes moved quickly as he digested the information. Although he didn't show it he was a man with the weight of the world on his shoulders. Every few minutes Mike's telling of the story was interrupted by the sound of Thierry on his walkie-talkie, dialogue both brief and intense.

As usual, he received a string of constant updates.

"I made no secret of the fact that I was unhappy about going to Rosslyn," Mike said. "But as Ms Leoni never ceased to point out, I was to guard her, not imprison her."

Thierry forced a considerate smile. "She is party to a difficult situation. Sometimes people do not know what's best for them."

"Without divulging information about the exact threat on her it was difficult to persuade her," Mike said. "She made it quite clear that she did not want me there. After all, she is a grown woman."

"Sadly even grown-ups don't always know what's best for them," Commissario Pessotto replied. He looked thoughtfully at Mike.

Mike nodded and grimaced simultaneously. He expected to be reprimanded. He referred briefly to the Mercedes that continuously reappeared outside the château and the biker at Rosslyn but the conversation didn't last. Pessotto concluded that it was probably a coincidence.

Their conversation was interrupted by a knock at the door. It was Stan.

"Oberst. Cardinal Pedrosa seeks a moment of your time."

Thierry nodded without interest. "Very well," he said. He rose to his feet slowly. Every second it seemed someone, usually a cardinal, wanted a moment of his time. He informed Mike that he would return shortly before exiting through the open door. His footsteps echoed loudly as he departed with purpose and impatience.

Pessotto looked at Mike and smiled. "Excuse me, wachtmeister."

Mike nodded as the head of the Vatican Police also left the room, leaving Mike and Stan alone. For the first time Mike noticed one gold star on each of Stan's shoulders.

"So they made you a major, huh," Mike said, sounding impressed.

"Yeah," Stan said modestly, leaning against the door. "So, how's it feel to be back?"

Mike stuttered a laugh. How did it feel? He could hardly describe it. Familiar surroundings helped create the illusion that he had never even left: as if the last eight weeks, the château, St Gallen, Zürich, Scotland was all a dream.

But the walls seemed somehow strange to him. He had always felt quite at home at the Vatican. He never imagined himself being at home in a grand house.

"Weird."

"I can imagine."

Mike raised his eyebrows. *Imagine what?* Mike thought to himself. They say as soldiers you should never get attached but for him it was unavoidable. Not just to her, but the situation. The symbol, the diary, it was still there in his mind, as it was on the walls of the crypts of Rosslyn.

He was missing something.

"So how's it all been going?"

Mike laughed and shook his head simultaneously. As a major in the Swiss Guard he knew that Stan's clearance was far above the norm.

"You wouldn't believe me if I told you."

Mike sat back in the chair, clasping his hands together thoughtfully. To an outsider the conversation was out of character with usual Swiss Guard procedure: instead it was more in keeping with casual tongue wagging between friends idling away time over a cappuccino. Mike always knew Stan was one of the least formal officers in the army. It was partly for that reason he liked him so much.

Stan scratched his head, struggling to respond to what he had heard. His response was not immediate. When it came Mike expected it to be calculated, the way in which someone of greater intellect digested the information before composing an elegant solution. In this case it was not.

"That's some shit," Stan said.

"Tell me about it."

Stan spoke to Mike in fluent German, the official language of the Papal Guard. His harsh voice was reminiscent of a Luftwaffe officer barking out instructions to his fighter pilot before launching another lightning strike over war-torn Europe. His Swiss descent was complete on both French and German sides and he was fluent in every language of the confederation.

"So what happens now?"

"About what?" Mike asked.

"About the rich bitch."

Mike looked up, almost in disgust. He was quite surprised at his own reaction. For the briefest of moments his mind wandered back to his conversation with Stan that night in the restaurant near the Trevi Fountain, before he met Gabrielle. He suddenly felt strangely defensive.

Mike shook his head. "It's no longer my concern."

Heavy footsteps echoed loudly along the corridor.

"I best be heading off," Stan said, preparing to leave. "Oh, Mike, got an extra ticket to Lazio-Roma tomorrow night. Wanna come?"

Mike smiled and nodded. Thierry re-entered the room and walked slowly around his desk. He exhaled with frustration before taking a seat.

Stan saluted Thierry as he approached, leaving the office through the open door.

Thoughts returned to the matter at hand. He wondered whether the meeting in the Sistine Chapel was over and whether Gabrielle was in the library.

Was it really possible she could be onto something?

Thierry turned to face Mike. A stranger facing the oberst for the first time may have confused his state with stress. To Mike his demeanour was like that of a prison warden who had just inspected a consignment of new scumbags sent down after being convicted of knife attacks on women or pensioners. His concentration was waning, unusually for him. In a strange way Mike respected him more because of it. Mike knew that both Thierry and Commissario Pessotto valued their jobs above their lives. To him, there were no men alive better qualified for the responsibility of guarding Christ's representative on this earth.

"I find your story a little hard to believe, wachtmeister."

Mike looked seriously at his commander. "Sir, I swear . . ."

"I'm not referring to your integrity, Frei," the oberst said, rubbing his face. "What you are suggesting goes against all rational thought."

Mike nodded, remaining silent. Eight weeks earlier he would have said exactly the same thing.

There was a question he wanted to ask. For the past few weeks he'd continuously had the feeling that he was missing something, something other people probably knew:

The cardinals? probably.

The oberst? surely.

Mark? definitely.

Even the Pope?

"Sir, to tell you the truth this whole experience has been a little hard to believe. What with the symbols at Rosslyn matching those in the death warrants, the diary, what Henry Leoni said . . . sir, is there any chance that the Knights Templar still exist?"

The commander didn't respond immediately. He downed a glass of mineral water with a paracetamol and savoured the flavour of the water, using the opportunity to consider his response while alleviating the dryness on his tongue. The humidity in the city was often unbearable in the summer, but summer seemed to have arrived early that day. Outside, thick cloud dominated the sky, its water falling at irregular intervals. Three days of consistent rain and thunder had done little to help the comfort levels and more thunder was forecast for the next day. At least the meeting was today.

"Throughout history there have been countless organisations claiming to be descendants of the Knights Templar," the oberst said, pausing. "You know even the Swiss Guard units are said to have been formed by Swiss mercenaries taught by fleeing Templars."

Mike shook his head. "No, I didn't."

The oberst smiled, probably the first for a while. "I have never heard of this."

He paused momentarily to refill his glass.

"The Vatican Police have been investigating the murders for two months now and still have no leads. The murdered men have no obvious connection to one another. Four have some connection to the Vatican, but no obvious motive for their deaths. Martin Snow was found dead on a train. No CCTV. Von Sonnerberg was in his hotel, seemingly having died of natural causes, surprising for a man of thirty-six. However, the presence of barbiturate, paralytic and potassium solution from the autopsy suggest otherwise. Nathan Walls was also in his office; again, there was no CCTV. Commissario Pessotto is convinced that the suicide note found beside the smoking gun was a decoy. Devére was found in his holiday villa in Mauritius. You know about Llewellyn and Leoni."

Mike nodded.

Thierry shook his head, exhaling deeply. "Why anyone would want to murder poor old Cardinal Faukes is beyond me."

He paused briefly for water.

"All were alone. There were no witnesses. No description of the killer. And that's what makes this confusing. Remember, Frei, Devére's comments alone are not proof."

"Presumably Devére must have had some idea. His own death seems evidence of that. Mark mentioned he had his own connections with the Rite of Larmenius."

"The Rite of Larmenius are a strange organisation, Frei. They are not accessible to the average man and they do not give out lists of members. No outsider even knows for sure who its members are. They do not advertise, yet allegedly they can be found when you know where to look. By being a member of the Rite of Larmenius you are merely rubbing shoulders with the well connected. They have no obvious cause as a whole, nor do the Freemasons. Individuals, perhaps groups, may provide for financial gain, but that's a drop in the ocean compared to the size of the organisation worldwide."

The walkie-talkie on his desk buzzed.

"All the Vatican Police have is rumours," Thierry resumed. "Such rumours can often disguise the true event. Supposedly thousands of murders have been attributed to the Rite of Larmenius, the Freemasons or other secret societies, at least in the eyes of the media or conspiracy theorists. Never has a murder been officially credited to an individual who is a confirmed member: and none on behalf of the organisation. Only a few have been tried in a court of law: and even if one was found guilty of a crime it would be as an individual. The group has never formally been tried. How can it be?"

Mike nodded. That made sense.

"We do not even know for sure that these murders were done by the same person or even for the same reasons. And that makes Mr Devére's comments rather inconclusive, don't you think?"

Mike nodded. "Who do you think is behind this, sir?"

Thierry shrugged. "Our job is the security of His Holiness and the Apostolic Palace," he said. "Commissario Pessotto thinks we could be dealing with hired killers. In the past various members of the Rite of Larmenius have not been overly friendly towards the Vatican. They were particularly vocal at the height of the Lateran Treaty and their members are known to have had some involvement with the P2. They haven't denied involvement in this, but very little comes from them these days. It's like they've vanished off the face of the earth."

The oberst rose to his feet. He walked across the room and inserted a key into the lock of a drawer. The key turned slowly, making a loud clicking sound. He retrieved a collection of photographs and returned to his seat. He passed Mike a photograph of three men eating at an outside table.

"Who's this?"

Thierry smiled. "Daniel D'Amato, Senator for Montana: in certain circles he's being touted as the next President of the USA, God help them. I've heard some interesting reports but nothing concrete."

"Is he a member?"

"Yes. One of the few we know for sure and just their type. The man alongside him also: Lord Parker, former UK Chancellor of the Exchequer. As I say, they're mainly just a rich boys' club for the extremely wealthy. Not only bankers: academics, politicians, that kind.

Former presidents, prime ministers, even monarchs have become members. Supposedly they are ritualistic in nature, a bit like the regular Masons. Some accuse them of Devil worship. Bollocks if you ask me."

Mike studied the photograph. "Who's the other man?"

"Ludovic Vladimir Gullet," Thierry said raising his eyebrows, "former KGB, communist sympathiser and lone wolf terrorist. He is one of the world's most famous assassins. That man, Frei, was involved in the assassination attempt on His Holiness John Paul II."

A look of horror crossed Mike's face. For several seconds he fought to control his hatred.

"You think that he's responsible for the murders?"

"Not much is heard of him these days. He is exceedingly wealthy. He owns a chain of casinos and lives as a tax exile in Campione d'Italia. Commissario Pessotto's intelligence informs us that he was present in the correct locations the nights of the murders of von Sonnerberg, Walls and Snow. There is some suggestion he was also in Washington the night that Llewellyn was murdered."

Thierry looked seriously at Mike.

"If he was involved, he could not have been in St Gallen to kill Al Leoni as well could he?"

"How about Cardinal Faukes?"

"At present we have been unable to confirm that one either way."

Mike nodded, allowing himself to take it all in. "Could he and possibly others be acting on behalf of the Rite of Larmenius?"

Thierry paused. "Gullet seems to have left the business, but that cannot be ruled out. And I'm glad to see recent weeks have taught you lateral thinking, wachtmeister. The Vatican Police have a man working at Gullet's casino in Campione. Off the record, of course."

Mike looked up, a hint of a smile on his face.

Thierry passed Mike two other photographs. "Murder by Gullet in connection to the Vatican is not altogether unique, wachtmeister. It is almost certain that he was involved in the killings of these unfortunate souls."

Mike looked at the photos. Both were men: mid-forties, Italian, dark hair. One had a moustache and flat hair; the other, clean-shaven, round glasses, hair combed neatly to a side parting. Mike recognised neither. An answer came before he asked.

"Alexei Nesta and Gianluigi Calveccio."

"Who were they?"

"Bankers; very good bankers," the oberst replied. "They were both connected to Banco Ambrosiano prior to 1981 and both had regular dialogue with the Vatican Bank. They were killed shortly before the deaths of Calvi and Soisson, although what with the later furore they received very little press coverage."

Mike nodded. He was vaguely aware of the happenings of Banco Ambrosiano and Clearstream at the height of the P2 scandal.

"What do you think are their motives?"

"Who knows? I'm sure the victims' deaths are of benefit to someone. We must assume that the murders are connected and we also cannot rule out the possibility that a powerful body has decreed them. The Rite of Larmenius are seemingly the most likely. Yet there are too many members to make the organisation itself worthy of suspicion."

He swallowed more water.

"Officially the fraternity is merely an appendant body of the Masons that spans every continent. Most of its members have probably never met one another. Yet within the organisation there is secrecy. Meetings take place between people who most of the six billion people on this planet have no idea even exist. What goes on in them?" Thierry shrugged. "For several years rumours have circulated that someone may rule them from down below. It is unlikely that Gullet or any other could carry this out alone. Why the Rite of Larmenius should do this remains unknown."

He paused for breath.

"Secret fraternities and religion often have a strange relationship. Many of their members could even be Roman Catholic. But their views on religion are certainly not consistent with yours or mine. No two individuals are alike. Their mercenaries themselves probably do not know. But whoever is behind them . . ."

"Sir, I know this may sound strange, but Henry Leoni spoke of a strange legend. Apparently before the last Templar Grand Master was executed he passed over the reigns to a man named Jean-Marc Larmenius. If there is any substance to this continued Knights Templar, could they be connected to the Rite of Larmenius? It seems too big a coincidence."

Thierry didn't reply straightaway. The sound of footsteps, soft footsteps, was coming from the corridor. Then there was a gentle tapping at the door.

28

Gilbert de Bois had been talking for nearly an hour and forty-five minutes by the time his presentation came to an end. What had started off as a general meeting on logistics, investment portfolio and the usual quarterly performance update, had developed into a full-scale exhibition and corporate biography highlighting the phenomenon that was Leoni et Cie. Thighs were being slapped, backs were being patted, asses were being kissed, and compliments and pleasantries were being passed around the table like a plate of biscuits as all present were in turn praised by the Chairman of Leoni et Cie for the indispensable role each had played in the proceedings.

De Bois owned the floor. He walked with a vague swagger and dressed in a brand new bespoke suit. To Gabrielle his façade presented the profile of an astute, hard-nosed businessman yet on this day strangely mixed with the baby kissing, tree hugging, shaking-the-hands-of-the-dying-to-cure-them-with-his-royal-touch bravado of a dodgy politician.

The presentation ended and the interior of the chapel came into view. Gabrielle yawned vigorously. She never enjoyed these occasions and this was one of the worst. Man, de Bois could talk. It made no sense her being there from a business point of view, but it was her whose behind de Bois was kissing the most: or Al Leoni's as the case might be. Most of his presentation was used as an opportunity to praise the deceased magnate for his service to the bank and the Church.

Throughout the presentation her mind continued to wander. Mentally she rehearsed her request for permission to enter the Vatican Library, her thoughts continuing to linger on the possibility that something of interest might be hidden within its ancient rooms.

Yet that was not the only thing on her mind. Thoughts of Mike kept entering her head, strange considering the importance of what might await. Her eyes had remained wide open throughout but her attention was divided. She couldn't stop thinking about him, particularly that moment in the corridor. Did they kiss? Did he mean it? Did she mean it? Did she like it? Surely not: he was her guard, he was a jerk and why did he never wear those clothes she bought him? He looked like a bum. Yet there was something suddenly appealing about him.

A hint of a smile crossed her face.

With the lights on, her thoughts returned to reality. The memory of the slide show that had illustrated cash flow forecasts, expected turnover, expected outgoings, long-term debt financing and all that other stuff that had sounded like it was being spoken in a different language, gave way to awareness of the chapel's exquisite interior.

Lining the lower tier: painted drapery, coloured silver and gold, hung above the walls marked with papal crests at their centres.

On the central tier: masterpieces by Ghirlandaio, Signorelli, Botticelli, d'Antonio, Perugino, and Rosselli displayed a visual history of the life of Moses opposite scenes from the life of Christ: depicting the joining of the old covenant and the new, as illustrated by Moses receiving the Ten Commandments proceeded by the coming of Christ, leading to the formation of the new Church.

Gabrielle felt her neck stiffen as she looked up at the Popes of old, lining the upper tier, positioned above the images of biblical times. A certain irony spun through her mind as she saw the Popes appear above Christ and Moses: a positioning used to demonstrate the new political role of the Church, as emphasised by Peter receiving the Keys to Heaven from Christ, as depicted by Perugino. What was initially painted to represent Saint Matthew's vision of the keys illustrating Christ's power to forgive his friend who betrayed him also constituted Christ's passing on his power to the new Pope who would later pass it on to each successor since.

Above the Popes, images of the ancestors of Christ then slowly merged with the ceiling. Leaning back on her chair, her neck almost horizontally back, she gaped in awe at God's perfect creation as portrayed by Michelangelo. Scattered across the ceiling like stars across the sky, the scenes of Genesis were mapped out, almost like an epic cartoon strip, revealing God's creation of the perfect world tainted by humanity as illustrated by Adam, whose separation from God led humanity into disgrace. The ambiguity of the image was clear as Christ appeared in the same cycle: representing the lineage of Adam as an ancestor of Christ, also painted by Michelangelo, but also identifying humanity's need for salvation and leading to the coming of Jesus born to redeem the world.

She rubbed her neck as she adjusted herself in her seat. Looking beyond two of Gilbert de Bois's flowcharts and behind the stand on which the projector was aimed, her attention now moved on to the final miracle of Michelangelo, perhaps the most intense imagery contained within the chapel.

Dominating the entire wall at the altar's end were a collection of muscled figures, some originally painted naked, instantly recognisable as the key characters of the bible returning at the coming of the Last Judgment. High above six candles and a crucifix at the altar's centre, a sea of blue interrupted by visions of men and women on land and cloud illustrated an intimidating view of Michelangelo's Apocalypse where earth waited in fear for the Second Coming of Christ as depicted in Revelation. The humans on clouds, Gabrielle could see, were ascending to heaven whereas others fell in the opposite direction. Interestingly, the wall somehow became more threatening as it increased in height in what was a stark contrast to other frescos lining the walls and ceiling that despite being elegant and awe-inspiring in appearance failed in every way to rival the natural power given out by the figures who are humble before God.

Gilbert de Bois thanked all present for their attention and applause filled the room. For the first time in almost two hours de Bois stood in silence, his demeanour somehow fitting beneath Christ's stance in the Last Judgment having dominated the proceedings since the beginning. He folded the pages of the flowcharts and took a seat at the end of the table.

Every member of the council was present today, the exception being Cardinal Tepilo who had travelled from Zürich to join up with the Pope on his tour of Scandinavia. At the head, de Bois lowered himself into his seat, a seat he was not used to occupying. To his left was an empty chair, usually taken by Cardinal Tepilo.

Next on, Giancarlo Riva applauded quite loudly.

To the Italian's left, Cardinal Torres applauded more gently and nodded his head politely in acknowledgement of what he had just seen and heard. His appearance was youthful, despite approaching his fifty-sixth year. Below his zucchetto, long locks of curly blond hair, lined with sparse streaks of grey above a partially wrinkled forehead and freckled face, successfully brought out the warmth in his deep blue eyes.

Next on from Torres was Swanson. Like de Bois, his suit was purchased only a few weeks earlier and he wore a bright red tie against the backdrop of a white shirt.

Next was Cardinal Utaka, sitting opposite Gabrielle. Ceasing his applause, he removed his glasses and rubbed his eyes gently. Shades of purple were still present under his brown eyes that always seemed to radiate warmth.

Opposite de Bois, also next to Gabrielle, was Rogero, sitting with his fingers grasped loosely together. As usual, he dressed in an elaborate white suit more like that of a Colombian drug baron than a banker. His calm façade illustrated composure and tact, displaying a foolproof poker face. He nodded philosophically as his dynamic mind digested the activities of the past two hours. De Bois had focused most of his attention on the president, at times giving the impression that he was talking directly to him.

Next to Gabrielle was Cardinal del Rosi. His goatee beard was neatly in trim and his hair smartly combed. In Gabrielle's opinion he always seemed angry, despite being one of the most pious men at the Vatican.

Sitting alongside del Rosi was Juan Pablo Dominguez.

Also Colombian, Dominguez had an impressive résumé. His role at the Vatican Bank had begun in earnest five years ago after taking early retirement. Like Rogero, he had thrived in the Latin American turbulence of the 1980s. Following on from his training as an accountant in the United States, he acted as a financial adviser for many of the big banks and businessmen, including Rogero, and many regarded him as 'Rogero's lieutenant', whereas Rogero usually said it was the opposite.

Like Rogero, he wore jewellery and had a fine collection of suits including his present choice, a black label by Marc Wallace, complemented by a cream shirt and matching tie. A gold watch adorned his left wrist and a single earring on his left ear, partially hidden by his long dark hair, kept in place by a hair band that kept the greasy fringe away from his handsome Latino face. A wedding ring lined his fourth finger representing a thirty-four year marriage to his childhood sweetheart.

Next was the balding, bespectacled Archbishop of São Paulo, Cardinal Atri, the newest member of the oversight commission having been appointed to replace Cardinal Faukes. Atri had come to prominence slowly following two decades of work in the shantytowns of Brazil, a man who commanded affection for his love and generous nature, strangely not affecting an ability to budget.

Last of those present, Randy Lewis grinned with amusement as he ceased his applause and loosened his collar. He had met de Bois before, many years ago when he was still working for the Feds and de Bois was a director at Starvel, although their paths had not crossed since. Lewis never envisioned he would like de Bois. On paper he possessed the attributes of a modern day saint. In all his years in the industry Lewis knew finding a businessman with a conscience was one thing, but a Mother Teresa was something else. De Bois clearly wanted the world to know of the causes he supported: everyone knew of the causes he supported.

And de Bois never let five minutes go by without another reminder.

Over the years Lewis had seen it all. When he was Chairman of the Fed it was his job to make sure policy was implemented and while a job was a job he was sure as hell going to enjoy it. During his tenure anti-trust and monopoly procedures were tightened. The excessively rich were foiled in their attempts to get significantly more powerful and kudos came from every corner. Competition was steadily increasing throughout the 1990s and following the amendment of Glass-Steagall, which he had been strongly against, a new stage had been created. No longer was the industry the playing field of retail banks or investment banks, but companies whose services crossed the entire spectrum: in his words, 'Monsters'.

Gabrielle yawned vigorously, her eyes continuing to pursue the visual narrations of Genesis high above her as a welcome distraction from what was going on below. For the others it was a chance to reflect. Numbers had been plucked from the air as though it was an epic game of bingo. De Bois spoke of forecasts in the manner of a weatherman and Lewis acknowledged many with isolated bouts of laughter accompanied by countless shakings of the head. Rogero and Dominguez made notes from time to time, usually at the same time. Every so often they would look at one another and make facial gestures, a practice devised from two decades of friendship that allowed instant communication without giving anything away to the rest.

De Bois had covered every aspect with an in-depth identification of how every penny had and would be invested, how every procedure would be undertaken, what this meant in terms of profit for the bank, what it meant for the Vatican and how Leoni et Cie would fair in terms of its industry.

At face value it seemed pretty good. Leoni et Cie was extremely resourceful, with market capital soon expected to pass the $7 billion mark again, catering for a global client base.

Profits were rising and predictions were good.

Rogero leaned back in his chair. "We are all grateful to Mr de Bois for taking the time to prepare a most enlightening presentation," Rogero said. "You like to talk about numbers, chairman. But I fear your figures for future growth do not add up."

Silence descended as all eyes focused on de Bois.

Juan Pablo Dominguez nodded. "Your calculations for extended investment portfolio seem to be very heavily based on accelerated growth, chairman," he said with accented English. "Such feats can only be achieved with heavily speculated investments and high levels of lending. Investments of this type have no guarantees. It would be unwise to overstretch our resources at a time of global uncertainty."

Del Rosi: "Over the years the Vatican has tended to concentrate on less risky strategies aimed at steady growth strictly within countries with established economies. The purpose of the Vatican Bank is supplementing our extra costs at minimal risk for the purpose of helping the poor. Not to buy an NFL franchise."

A brief outburst of laughter followed, including Gabrielle and Utaka, his first smile in a while. As the laughter faded, silence descended. Gabrielle watched Rogero. Already things were turning into a major tussle between the heavyweights.

"Eminences, president, vice president, I cannot deny that there are aspects of the strategy devised both by myself and our late chief executive that include sailing our ship into uncharted waters, but the suggestions you have heard today are little different from what I oversaw at Rosco," the French-descended-Canadian said. "As you are all aware, gentlemen, the performance of Leoni et Cie since 2002 has been outstanding. The last few years aside, we have achieved leftfield returns in excess of anything else the bank has ever recorded. Both Al Leoni and myself were at the forefront of this. But if we are to continue to build, it is essential that we explore new avenues. The economic turmoil makes it even more essential that we look for new opportunities."

"Mr de Bois, forgive me," Cardinal Atri spoke up, "but your proposals leave me confused. It seems that many of your recommended investments are to occur in companies who operate primarily in many of the world's poorest countries: Peru, Bolivia and El Salvador to name but a few. Such locations seem not only risky from an economic point of view, but you also seem to be concentrating in nations where regulation and supervision by the authorities is generally lower than the wider world."

Cardinal Torres nodded. "Sadly, many of the companies on your list have a reputation for somewhat questionable business practices: particularly regarding environmental issues and conditions for their employees."

Cardinal Utaka also nodded. "The Vatican has never endorsed companies who employ child labour."

De Bois chewed on his pen before using it to gesture.

"Eminences, please do not misunderstand my proposals. Cardinal Atri, as a newcomer to the oversight commission, perhaps it is fair to say you know less about me than some of your colleagues. I assure you, I too am a man of ethical consideration. The investments I have put forward are merely some of many, giving an all-round portfolio, thus protecting the bank from risk. Over the last twenty years I have seen with my own eyes the negative consequences of reckless investment. For that very reason I have never chosen to invest in companies of questionable pedigree, nor would I advocate providing loans to new businesses that fail to meet the necessary criteria. The recommendations I have given specifically avoid investing in companies whose primary gain is from deadly sin such as gambling and gun production. I have even agreed to give up smoking."

Vague laughter followed.

Torres shook his head. "Chairman, it is not only a questionable approach to business morality that I find concerning. By investing in companies who also have links to governments of questionable actions, particularly in South America where drug cartels are so prevalent, it seems difficult to tell with certainty that our paths and those of spurious pedigree cannot cross."

Del Rosi nodded. "The Vatican Bank cannot afford to risk backing individuals of dubious nature."

A brief silence followed as all eyes focused on de Bois.

"Mr de Bois, I'm afraid certain members of the council do not share your confidence for future growth," Lewis said. "Either that or they do not trust you."

Rogero laughed. It was obvious that Lewis was being a deliberate ass.

"Mr de Bois, isn't it true that while a director at Starvel you were once accused of fraud?" Cardinal Atri asked.

Hush descended. De Bois paused before answering.

"Yes, eminence, that is true, but the allegations you refer to were confirmed to be false. As a matter of fact Mr Lewis was Chairman of the Fed at the time of the allegation. If anything you probably know more than me."

A brief outburst of laughter swept around the table, briefly taking the emphasis off de Bois. He looked briefly at Swanson, who sat with an expression of boredom.

Cardinal Torres looked with interest at Lewis. "Well, Randy?"

Lewis stuttered, unusually for him. "Mr de Bois's performance with both Starvel and Rosco was certainly remarkable, gentlemen. His fine business record crosses many industries," he said, shuffling papers in his hands. "But I was certainly somewhat sceptical of certain elements of Starvel's business model. Looking at your proposals here, I cannot help but notice similarities, particularly regarding potential privileges to attract wealthier clients from Europe and America."

Lewis pointed at the paper in front of him.

"One of the biggest problems with Starvel was a tendency to assist the richest clients moving funds across borders undetected. In the past, Leoni et Cie have made a good effort to avoid this kind of practice. The days when Switzerland hid the resources of the rich from the authorities of a host nation are over."

De Bois removed his pen from his mouth. "I understand your concerns, former Chairman, but as I am sure you remember, Starvel, even the parts where I was not involved, was never found guilty of breaking any laws." He paused momentarily. "Assisting our own clients in establishing tax effective investments is not, nor has it ever been, in any way illegal."

It was intriguing to Gabrielle how de Bois referred to Lewis in the context of his former role. She was vaguely aware how Lewis had investigated Starvel back in 1999 when de Bois was a director. She remembered her father and Louis Velis had even discussed the possibility of a takeover of Leoni et Cie, not that it went ahead. De Bois clearly disliked Lewis and this did not faze Lewis.

Lewis nodded. "Be that as it may, as President Rogero and Vice President Dominguez have quite rightly pointed out, many of your projections here are all very well when the market is going well."

Rogero nodded. "Frankly, our former chief executive was rather more particular in his financial strategy."

Former chief executive? These guys seemed to think Al Leoni did all the work. Tact and diplomacy were both gifts he had been blessed with and he knew when to use them.

He smiled warmly. "President, eminences, on the contrary. These forecasts you have seen today were also the belief of our former chief executive. He shared the vision of Leoni et Cie. He believed, as I do today, that if Switzerland and the US can cooperate and coordinate our strategies, share our strengths and amalgamate our resources, then we can consolidate our position as a front-runner in our industry. He, too, shared my vision for a better world, and also agreed that the future of

Leoni et Cie lay not only in walking the well trodden paths, but in forming new ones, including those of the inaccurately dubbed Third World."

Dominguez hid a smile.

"While I have no doubt that your desire to end world poverty is noble, Mr de Bois, I do have my doubts as to whether Mr Leoni acted without contingency," Rogero said. "And I am also quite concerned that much of your investment portfolio includes such heavy speculating on oil, gold and currency futures."

Rogero turned to face Gabrielle.

"Ms Leoni, your family have been involved with Leoni et Cie since its beginning. Do you believe that your father would have acted so much on speculation?"

All eyes turned to Gabrielle.

"Well, my father personally believed that speculating was a lot like gambling. He made it a rule not to speculate or lend more than a certain percentage of revenue."

A series of nods and agreements followed. De Bois replaced the pen in his mouth and removed it once more.

"Ms Leoni, with all due . . ."

"Shhh!" Utaka said. "Go on, my dear."

She hesitated. "My father favoured less risky strategies such as gold deposits, arbitrage and hedging. While he did not neglect futures completely, he was more concerned with long-term stability than accelerated growth. Also I was largely under the impression that both investing in companies in LEDCs and the opening of new branches in South America would only occur in moderation."

Rogero nodded and Gabrielle felt silently pleased. She had justified her appearance.

"Speculating is a grey area, Gile," Swanson said. "We all know that. When it comes off it's fantastic. But the Vatican Bank is not a typical investment bank. Nor do our directors have the morals to act like one."

"I thought as an investment banker you would favour speculating," Riva said. "Every investment banker I've ever spoken to believes it combats market inefficiency."

Lewis laughed, De Bois exhaled on his pen.

Dominguez: "Mr de Bois, I am also somewhat intrigued by your proposals regarding the establishment of new branches, particularly, again, in countries whose economic measures, particularly its attitude towards supervisory policy and regulation are, how should I put this: underdeveloped."

De Bois smiled. "Vice president, I do not deny that I have always advocated more relaxed measures with regard to regulation and favoured a strategy that accommodated such action during the infant years of Rosco. The companies of the British AIM have thrived for this reason. Please be under no illusions, banking has changed since the 1980s when banking secrecy and dangerously low levels of supervisions resulted in criminal misuse. Speaking purely from my own experience, I favour them only because, historically speaking, companies who have adopted similar strategies have gone on to make better returns. LABCC I seem to recall enjoyed great success in such ways."

Rogero shook his head. "LABCC was operating at a time when Latin America was constantly under speculative attack from the nations of the West. We never operated in nations outside our own continent and even those outside Colombia were under extreme supervision."

Swanson nodded. "Even Starvel's greatest weakness was susceptibility to bad loans given to poorly run companies."

Dominguez: "Leoni et Cie is no ordinary bank, chairman: particularly now that Ms Leoni has decreased her stake. This bank now belongs primarily to the Vatican Bank. The Pope himself would have to agree to any changes in strategy."

"What do you suggest?" Giancarlo Riva asked, arms folded. "That we fail to capitalise on reasonable investment opportunities simply because it's against your conscience? The Church has learned to adapt in all elements of banking. In the past the Vatican forbid usury, but that, too, has adapted with time."

Lewis laughed to himself, his attention on Riva.

"The emerging markets have always been a popular target amongst the successful banks. With successful planning, the strategy of Misters Leoni and de Bois could be correct," the Italian continued.

"As you're undoubtedly aware, vice president," de Bois said, his eyes on Dominguez, "times have changed. It is not like the old days when a bank was simply a bank. Mr Lewis, you know that better than most, it was you who oversaw the change in American legislation. If Leoni et Cie is to continue to be profitable then it must continue to adapt. The primary agenda of the Vatican Bank has always been first and foremost to make a profit. The mission of the Catholic Church has always been to promote a message of peace and charity. The Bible says love thy neighbour: not to become a Communist."

Widespread laughter filled the room.

"Nevertheless, I do not believe in speculating," Rogero said strongly, his smile fading. "For many years LABCC followed the ideals of the traditional great banks of Switzerland. I even paid our employees a little more when they avoided such tomfoolery. Futures contracts are never easy money – Barings has taught us that much."

Lewis: "Overstretching in a bull market might have worked before the crunch, but it was also over reliance on that what caused it. I am also concerned that investing heavily in companies operating in nations of questionable government, and in particular opening multiple branches in these countries increases the risks of effective supervision on our part. Particularly as such branches would be under the management of local individuals with questionable backgrounds, and forced to rely on a loan portfolio of companies and individuals susceptible to default. If Mr de Bois wishes to run the bank in accordance with his vision, I suggest he forms his own bank. Either that or he make us an offer for our shares."

The room fell silent. De Bois again removed his pen from his mouth as though it were a cigar.

Dominguez raised his hand. "Mr de Bois, I understand the board at Leoni et Cie recently granted you corporate loans of up to $40 million to cover your margin calls."

"Yes, vice president that's correct, what's wrong with that?"

Dominguez: "Nothing, Mr de Bois, do not misunderstand me. But such an occurrence might seem strange at this time."

Torres: "In the eyes of the council, it seems such an occurrence is somewhat at odds with your confidence for future growth."

De Bois prepared to answer but Cardinal del Rosi beat him to it.

"I can assure my fellow cardinals and members of the supervisory council that the Vatican Bank is under great assurances that these loans are temporary necessities to help ensure that Mr de Bois can cover his costs on other businesses and will be repaid at the agreed time. It would undermine confidence further should our chairman be required to sell large amounts of stock."

Another brief silence followed. Gabrielle studied each face in turn. It was tough to predict what they were thinking. Dominguez wrote something down, Lewis folded his arms. Del Rosi stared at de Bois.

Torres: "Such assurances aside, the future of the bank is something that cannot be left to chance. Since the 1980s the strategies of the Vatican Bank have succeeded on careful investment and in this way our past and that of the original Banque Leoni have much in common. Investments in retail have brought assets of significant worth over several decades of steady worldwide growth; investments in currency have been hit and miss with an overall emphasis on the hit; decision to invest in foreign companies have often been rewarded, but even then we have determined to invest in companies of reputation. But nothing has been so effective as the client-friendly, hedging and arbitrage strategy of Leoni et Cie. The banks of St Gallen have long succeeded on catering for low numbers of clients with deposits of over a million Swiss Francs. In your time alone this has already fallen. Why should we change a winning formula?"

De Bois forced a smile. "Gentlemen, you are smart people. And being smart people you don't need me to tell you that there is no such thing as risk. Every business faces risk. The profitable banks, they face risk," he said with his hands out wide. "But risk is not a barrier – it is an obstacle to be overcome. The past success of Rosco and Leoni et Cie came from not just a strong client base, but identifying opportunities and profiting from them, and avoiding those that are not. If the proposals I have put before you are implemented effectively then not only can we achieve increased profits for the bank, but also provide a much needed boost to areas where average incomes are low and mortality rates are high. And that, gentlemen, after all, is the purpose of the Vatican Bank, is it not?"

De Bois looked around the table. The poker faces were keeping their cards close to the table.

Utaka: "Bearing in mind that the Vatican Bank has recently acquired an additional 31% ownership in Leoni et Cie, and also bearing in mind that Ms Leoni and her family have been the majority shareholder for so long, it is at our discretion to identify the best way forward."

Rogero shook his head. "You claim to be a man of morals, Mr de Bois, but you are far too reckless in your assumptions. Speculating on futures must be closely monitored and be balanced by less risky investments. And while it is true that the Vatican, and Leoni et Cie, has at times benefited from investing in traditionally poorer regions, such matters cannot be taken lightly. The Vatican Bank exists on low risk ventures that satisfy our needs over time and that I am not prepared to gamble."

"I would also wish for strict guarantees from Mr de Bois," Torres said, "that should his proposals be implemented that he would not as time goes by allow any desire for personal gain to affect his judgment."

Riva: "Eminence, we are all professionals. We do not need every activity to be placed under some kind of surveillance."

Rogero: "You speak of trust, Mr Riva, but we cannot stray from who we are. We are all religious men, not immune to threats coming from a higher power. If some unlucky circumstance should cause Leoni et Cie to lose its hard earned gains, or profit from the hardship of others by investing in companies whose desire for greed is greater than their respect for human rights, then I would see it as a clear sign that God is personally laying the blame at the people in this room. I know from the Vatican's good relations with the old regime at Leoni et Cie that Mr Leoni and Ms Leoni only ever had our best interests at heart, whereas you, Mr de Bois, are still to earn this trust. Your background is very impressive and your desire for charity is warming, but your strategy is not without flaws. Therefore I feel that while speculations in oil and currency can occur up to a point, and increased investing and the establishment of new branches is essential for future growth, we must keep them under strict observation. And for that reason, I feel that we are unable to support your proposals in full. And taking into account that a change in ownership has now been established, I must move for you to be removed from your position as Chairman of Leoni et Cie and from now be assigned the role of deputy chairman, as appropriate for your level of investment in the bank."

Silence filled the room. No one seemed to object.

De Bois maintained eye contact with Rogero for several seconds. He eyed the faces of everyone present slowly, before looking up at the visions of God's earthly paradise above him.

"If that is the will of the council, then so be it."

All present nodded. A smile crossed Swanson's face.

Rogero cleared his throat loudly. "Perhaps now we can move on and open the floor for suggestions for a permanent chief executive of Leoni et Cie."

Riva: "Mr President, if it pleases the council, I would be most pleased to continue with the role I have recently been undertaking."

Rogero bit his lip, a rare sign of irritation. "Any objections?"

There were no objections, but a few unsatisfied expressions.

"Any other nominations?"

Swanson: "President, I would be more than happy to participate in some capacity in the running of Leoni et Cie. However, if you want my personal opinion, then the best candidate and the most qualified would be Mr Lewis."

Lewis forced a brief smile.

Rogero put a pen to his lips. "All in favour of Mr Riva continuing with his duties as chief executive of Leoni et Cie?"

Cardinals Torres, del Rosi and Gilbert de Bois all raised their hands. Riva nodded.

Rogero: "All in favour of Mr Lewis?"

Rogero, Dominguez, Swanson, Utaka, Atri, and Gabrielle all placed their hands up. Rogero removed the pen from his mouth.

"In that case, I propose that Mr Lewis takes up the position on behalf of the Vatican Bank." He looked at Lewis. "Mr Lewis, do you accept?"

Lewis looked at Rogero, giving little or nothing away. Finally he nodded.

Del Rosi: "Angelo, personally I feel that it would be wise to have at least one cardinal on the board."

"Cardinal Tepilo is still a director for Leoni et Cie," Gabrielle suggested.

Rogero nodded. "Very well, his experience of your bank as a member of your family would undoubtedly be a valuable asset. Perhaps he would agree to take up the position of chairman."

Gabrielle nodded, clearly approving.

"Very well," Rogero said, "Cardinal Tepilo shall remain as a director for Leoni et Cie and, should he agree with the outcome of today's meeting, take up the role of chairman. That concludes our business for today. May the peace of the Lord be with you all."

29

Every member stood in unison and the pleasantries resumed: hands were shaken, the rings of the cardinals were kissed, and both of Gabrielle's cheeks were kissed by de Bois, a little awkwardly for her liking. She shook hands gently with Cardinal Torres, and kissed Rogero and Dominguez, far more bearable. She shook hands briefly with Atri and Swanson as she passed and walked towards Cardinal Utaka.

"May I have a moment?"

The cardinal ascended to his feet and looked at Gabrielle with interest. Judging by her facial expression and the tone of her voice he decided it was of importance. He tucked his chair under the table and guided her to a seat at the side of the chapel.

Around the table, the bankers assembled their belongings quickly and exited in small gatherings. The Swiss Guards on temporary duty for the meeting, taking the place of the usual museum guards, saluted as they opened the doors and allowed them access to the corridors. Gabrielle smiled at the departing council, and said goodbyes to no one in particular. De Bois passed them as he exited. He kissed Gabrielle once more and kissed the cardinal as well.

Utaka shook his head.

The final members departed and the doors were closed behind them. A pleasant hush descended on the chapel, out of keeping with the atmosphere of recent hours. This was how she remembered the chapel. It had a pleasant ambience, one in keeping with a location of holy importance.

Now alone, she started to relax. She inhaled a few times deeply and raised her eyes to make eye contact with the cardinal. He smiled warmly at her.

Besides her great-uncle, Cardinal Utaka was her favourite cardinal. Leoni et Cie's financial affinity with the Church dated back to the early 1990s and the friendship between them had lasted most of her life. A strange sense of mischievous happiness overcame them, followed by a fit of giggling that lasted several seconds. Utaka laughed aloud, perhaps for the first time in weeks.

"Well. A day well spent," he said.

"I'm sure the appointment of Mr Lewis is good for the Vatican."

He nodded. "Both he and your great-uncle have our interest at heart. I personally find Randy to be most agreeable."

Gabrielle forced a smile. "My dad always spoke highly of Mr Lewis."

The cardinal nodded. He paused momentarily, not an awkward pause but an act of calm concentration: a chance to digest the activities of recent times. A look of serenity overcame him when he smiled.

"Thank you," he said. "Without your support it would have been difficult. Now is the opportunity for sound financial planning. While I don't agree with Mr de Bois's methods, I do agree with his sentiments for the poor. Think of all the good the bank can do."

Gabrielle smiled. Perhaps it was the cardinal's non-religious upbringing that made him somehow more human than the others. He had witnessed hardship, that was obvious, and he had conquered. Yet there was no anger, nor animosity towards the past. Instead he radiated warmth: perhaps even more so than the pontiff.

"And how are you?" he asked softly. There was a genuine interest in the question that Gabrielle found reassuring. Since the day of her father's death she had faced countless general courtesies and made up pleasantries such as "so how are you holding up?" or "I'm sorry for your loss".

But his manner was different. He spoke to her in the manner one would use to address a relative, taking the time to digest the response before sharing in the activities of their life.

"I'm okay," she replied. "Sergeant Frei has been amazing."

Not for the first time a strange feeling overcame her as she thought of him. For a second she wondered where he was. Whether he was thinking about her.

"Good," he said. "I'll speak to him myself afterwards."

Gabrielle nodded and forced a smile. Despite the smile, the cardinal detected all was not well.

"I feel something is troubling you."

She considered her reply carefully. "Cardinal, I know this is not usual but there is something in the Vatican Library I need to see."

Utaka's response was one of calm. She remembered back to the meeting where his poker face had kept de Bois guessing. She expected a no, followed by an explanation, followed by a justification. His answer was pleasantly surprising.

"Only scholars are allowed to enter the library and archives," Utaka said with his hands together. "However, I'm sure that in the light of your devotion to the Vatican over the years we can allow that. Your great-uncle, I'm sure, would have no objection. We can rely on your discretion, of course."

"Of course, thank you, eminence."

Once again silence followed, this time more awkward.

"I sense something else is troubling you."

Gabrielle fiddled with her hair, considering her response. This was potentially dangerous territory. She still didn't know how to explain the Templar story, if there was such a thing. Yet something else worried her, something even more terrifying. Perhaps people died for knowing too much. How much could she safely tell?

She grimaced intently and eventually decided to tell him. She began tentatively, focusing largely on the discovery of the diary. The cardinal remained silent for over ten minutes, allowing Gabrielle to complete the story without interruption. She told the same story that Mike had told Thierry. She finished by telling him of the possible significance of the Vatican Library.

The cardinal remained silent for several seconds. He rubbed his eyes, possibly in shock as much as anything else.

"I am surprised at you, Gabrielle," he said, rising to his feet. "The Vatican did not post a Swiss Guard so you could jeopardise your own life," he pointed his finger at Gabrielle. "I'll see Frei myself."

"No, no, don't blame Mike."

"He disobeyed a strict order."

"No. He obeyed your every word," Gabrielle said, rising to her feet. She spoke slightly louder than she'd intended. "Wherever I go, he must go. That was what you told him."

The cardinal put his hands to his face. Remembering words was difficult. Perhaps that was the instruction. The world seemed to thrive on technicalities these days but that was no excuse for flippancy.

"He should have known better," Utaka said. "Someone may have . . . you could've been killed. We have no idea who is behind these murders. Whatever possessed you?"

"Mikael Devére told the Vatican Police that the Rite of Larmenius killed my father. I want to know who it was and why. I have a right . . ."

"They, they . . . even the Vatican isn't sure who's responsible."

"That's a lie and you know it."

Gabrielle hesitated, ridden with guilt for her outburst. She could tell by the cardinal's expression that he harboured feelings of deep uncertainty and worry.

"I think there's more to this than the Vatican realises. I think the Templars may be real."

Utaka forced a laugh, not of humour but frustration and perhaps denial. He returned to his seat, his eyes staring at Gabrielle. In Gabrielle's opinion he knew more than he let on.

"I take it you have heard of them?"

Utaka shook his head but on this occasion made no eye contact. "There are millions of organisations that claim to be the Knights Templar," Utaka said. "Impossible. It's been seven hundred years."

"Eminence, it's indisputable. I've seen the proof. They're out there, they have to be." A couple of stray tears fell from her eyes. "They killed my dad."

The cardinal looked upon her with sympathy. "Nothing is known," he said seriously, "not for sure. And endangering your own life will not bring him back. This is not the time for recklessness. This is the time for compassion, and mourning."

"If my father's death and the others are connected then this could be vital – for the Vatican too. It's here! I know it is. We have to find it."

There was no denying the strength of that statement. Too much had happened to dismiss the whole thing out of hand. This was perhaps a vital lead.

"Why don't I take you to Cardinal Marcelos."

30

The Archivist and Librarian of the Holy Roman Church, Cardinal Rafael Marcelos, had spent most of the day working quietly in his office. With his tasks for the day nearing an end, he relaxed momentarily.

After taking a few seconds to gather his thoughts, he picked up a freshly printed letter and inserted it into an envelope that had already been named and addressed. Although the library was officially closed for refurbishment, that had not stopped the requests. A history professor from Wales had written asking to see a manuscript located in the secret archive concerning the Vatican at the time of the Second World War: his request was denied.

Another, this one a theology academic from a university in Oregon, applied for permission to see a copy of something regarding Theology and Philosophy in the 12th century: his request was accepted.

And now he was writing to someone named Jones from Sunderland in England who had written to him looking for something that he had never even heard of that was hidden in the secret archive. How did he even know of this? It takes all kinds.

He was unlike any librarian in the world. Over 75,000 manuscripts lay hidden within the incredible architectural labyrinth in the company of over 1.1 million printed books, more than any other library in existence in the West. Every day, scholars throughout the world would write to the library, requesting a brief glimpse into the fountain of knowledge and in theory every request had to be approved by him.

It had been that way for over eighteen months. He had previously spent over eight years as Prefect of the Secret Archives: that curious location adjacent the library on the via Di Porta Angelica, which existed as the central repository for all acts passed by the Holy See. He had heard rumours regarding some of the manuscripts that allegedly lay hidden there but even he did not know for sure. Although open to the public, very few people were allowed to view its content. An estimated 4,000 scholars every year were granted access to both and then only for a specific book at a specific time for a specific reason justified by occupation and reasonable intent. A researcher with relevant qualifications and reason for their research could request permission in writing or in person and acceptance was still only a matter of chance. To get into the secret archive without reason was like breaking into the Pope's bedroom, only the Pope was likely to be more welcoming.

Marcelos sealed the envelope, yet another rejection to a nobody who should mind his own business instead of digging up stuff that didn't concern him, and threw it down into his out tray. He shuffled some papers in his hands and looked with interest at his computer screen, anticipating his next task.

Suddenly there came a knock at the door, a gentle respectful tap, perhaps one of the two surviving Archivist Emeriti rather than the abrupt manner he associated with the non-clergy. He paused before answering.

Cardinal Utaka was the first to enter. The librarian monitored him momentarily before rising awkwardly to his feet.

"George, I assume the meeting is over."

"It is, Rafa," Utaka returned. Gabrielle entered beside him and smiled awkwardly at Marcelos.

Marcelos looked at her judgingly, secretly not knowing what to make of her. On first impression he assumed she was a businesswoman of some kind, probably a female lawyer, or something less impressive.

Likewise, Gabrielle did not know what to make of him. He was unlike the cardinals on the oversight committee. He was smaller than most, perhaps five feet two inches in height, with round glasses surrounding large green eyes that seemed almost owl-like below a semi baldhead. His crooked nose reminded her of the goblins from the first Harry Potter.

"Rafa, this is Ms Leoni," he gestured to Gabrielle. "Ms Leoni would like to examine a manuscript from the library."

Marcelos looked at Gabrielle as if surveying an object. "I see," he said slowly, walking around the desk towards them. "And does Ms Leoni have a reasonable purpose?"

Gabrielle sought to respond but Utaka beat her to it.

"The document is of relevance to my own position as well, Rafa."

The librarian remained silent. His pretence of all subjects was imposing, but Utaka clearly knew how to match the man. Marcelos walked a couple of paces forward, his eyes still focused on Gabrielle.

He nodded slowly. "And tell me, what qualifications does Ms Leoni have for viewing this manuscript?"

Neither responded.

"Because every scholar must present evidence of need and purpose. Otherwise everyone under the sun would want to search our possessions."

"I'm aware of our laws, Rafa."

The librarian ignored him. "We can't have one rule for some and one for others."

"Nevertheless, the oversight commission of the Vatican Bank have agreed that she be allowed access. Ms Leoni is a significant shareholder in Leoni et Cie. She is also Cardinal Tepilo's great-niece. The Camerlengo himself was most adamant."

That was a lie but it stomped him. Rules or no rules, the 'next Pope' was hardly likely to be argued with.

The Brazilian motioned towards his desk. "This contains a catalogue of every manuscript or book currently located in the Vatican Library," he said pointing at the screen. He gazed at Gabrielle as if he had asked a question. A vague silence, a peculiar silence, engulfed the room, strangely appropriate for a library.

"Does Ms Leoni know the name of the manuscript?"

The atmosphere made Gabrielle feel uneasy. She realised this was a test of her credibility.

She smiled. "Yes."

The librarian's expression remained neutral. In Gabrielle's mind it hid disappointment. His fortress had been breached. Without further word he gestured with his left hand, offering her the chair behind the desk.

Gabrielle sat down slowly, edging closer to the desk. The chair was heavy; it amazed her how the librarian managed to concentrate in such discomfort. She looked at the cardinal who stood silently, gazing intently over her shoulder. She looked at Utaka and forced a smile. He placed his right hand to his bearded chin and waited in anticipation.

Gabrielle examined the instructions on the screen.

Vatican Library.

Language: Italiano.

"Printed books or manuscripts," the cardinal said.

Manuscripts surely. Go to catalogue.

A series of instructions appeared before her, written in Italian.

Catalogo Manoscritti della Biblioteca Apostolica Vaticana. Catalogo Manoscritti or Accedi.

Ricerca per indice: autore, titolo, soggetto, segnatura, incipit, explicit.

Surely she wanted subject, or title.

Titolo.

She inserted the name: Rota Temporum.

The cardinal gazed over her shoulder.

Cerca.

The search displayed countless results, none of which were obviously relevant. Quickly, she considered her actions.

She removed the word Rota; this was no better. She tried several alternatives; again, similar results. She looked blankly at the names and their references, checking some in more detail.

She tried a different search, this time the name of the author.

Again nothing.

A sudden feeling of apprehension overcame her. Sitting silently, she could feel the librarian's eyes fixed on her from behind, monitoring her every move. She made eye contact with Cardinal Utaka, looking for inspiration. This was going nowhere.

"In order to accomplish a successful search we must be sure we possess all the correct details," the Brazilian librarian said. "It would be most unfortunate should someone be searching our catalogue and finding something they shouldn't."

On first reflection this sounded incriminating. What did he mean, find something they shouldn't? Finances, perhaps? Records of Nazi gold lying hidden and gathering dust? Or maybe that legend about the pornography collection was true! Surely the other stuff would be in the secret archive.

The secret archive?

"What about the secret archive?"

"Impossible."

"You have access to the catalogue on your desktop," Utaka said.

"That is irrelevant. The secret archives are restricted access."

"Cardinal Tepilo . . ."

"Cardinal Tepilo did not agree to that, I'm sorry . . ."

"If the manuscript is there then I'm sure he'd be most displeased that Ms Leoni was not granted access."

The Brazilian exhaled loudly. He leaned over Gabrielle and clicked a couple of times on the mouse. A new catalogue emerged.

"Type in the name of your manuscript please."

Gabrielle looked at the screen, her concentration intent. Her heart began to thunder, her optimism heightening with each passing second. She looked at the flashing cursor and typed in the relevant letters. The Brazilian looked over her shoulder.

The result was the same.

"I'm sorry."

"But it's there. I know it is."

"Now if you'll both excuse me, I must continue . . ."

"Is this catalogue complete?"

She looked longingly at Cardinal Utaka for guidance. He paused, nodding at the archivist.

"Thank you for your time, Rafa."

Cardinal Utaka escorted Gabrielle outside and closed the door behind them, the sound echoing momentarily.

Gabrielle struggled to control her breathing. For several seconds she stared at the closed door. It was there, it had to be, somewhere, hidden away, long since forgotten. She looked at the African cardinal and shook her head. Almost apologetically, he forced a smile.

"Come," he said. "I have to see Thierry."

31

Mike watched with interest as Cardinal Utaka and Commissario Pessotto entered the office, followed a few minutes later by Cardinal del Rosi. Mike could tell from the cardinals' manner that the meeting in the Sistine Chapel had been stressful. He sprung to his feet and saluted each man on entering, his facial expression hardening in their presence. He assumed that Gabrielle had already told them at least of some of their exploits, and silently that worried him.

He expected to be grilled.

The office felt stuffy, and Cardinal del Rosi's face reflected the temperature. He paced the room like a general, eyeing all present curiously for several seconds before focusing his attention on Mike. His expression hardened.

"Enough of this hand waving."

Mike's eyes remained focused on the cardinal. He stood silently, waiting for a question that was still to come, slowly lowering his hand.

"I hope you have some good news, gentlemen," del Rosi said. He eyed each man in turn, finishing with Mike. Mike remained silent. His throat felt dry, forcing him to swallow. He cleared his throat quietly, careful not to make a vomiting sound as catarrh formed in his gullet.

"You can dispense with the formalities, Frei," Utaka said. "Tell us everything."

Once again Mike reverted to the role of storyteller. Utaka had heard the story once from Gabrielle in the tone of a uni student intent on revealing political corruption, whereas del Rosi remained in the dark. His facial expression remained unflinching throughout.

Mike spoke for nearly ten minutes. He spoke faster than normal, struggling at times to disguise his nerves. Inside he felt flustered, a feeling that intensified every time he saw Cardinal del Rosi shake his head. Unlike Gabrielle, Mike said nothing of the Poli account and ended with Rosslyn.

Cardinal del Rosi slammed hard on his knees. "Did you really think we would approve?"

"Come now," Utaka said.

Cardinal del Rosi pointed his finger at Mike, his face reddening. "You were assigned to guard her, wachtmeister, you disobeyed a strict order."

Mike's resolve strengthened. "Eminence, with all due respect, I obeyed it precisely. I was told to go where she goes and that was exactly what I did."

"Don't you use that tone. Remember to whom you speak."

Thierry: "Eminence, Frei informed Ms Leoni of his views on countless occasions that she should keep a low profile. None of these murders have been related by geography. The risk was the same no matter where she went. At least she was in the care of her family."

Del Rosi turned to face Thierry, his expression unaltered.

Thierry looked seriously at Cardinal Utaka. "Ms Leoni was very adamant that Frei should not keep her against her will. Frankly, I believe her uncle should have been more persuasive. Frei was in no position to stop her. Unless he was to have pointed a gun at her head . . ."

"And let's thank God no one else did," del Rosi shouted.

Silence descended: a hush so firm that all present could hear the passing of the air.

Commissario Pessotto looked thoughtfully at Mike. "George tells me that Ms Leoni was most adamant that the library held something of importance, wachtmeister. What was this?"

"The library?" Thierry asked, surprised.

Cardinal Utaka raised his hand and the room fell silent. To Mike, Cardinal Utaka commanded respect that was otherwise unrivalled in the room, even by Thierry.

"Frei?"

Mike took a deep breath, attempting to gather his thoughts.

"Well, the vaults at Rosslyn had clearly not been used in centuries but the remnants of painted markings on the walls included the same symbol found on the diary. I also saw evidence that at least one of the Italian seafarers was buried there. Several days later, Ms Leoni spoke of a story dating back to 1834 regarding a man from Italy who returned to Rosslyn to remove a chronicle from the castle vaults and deposited it somewhere in the Vatican. Apparently in the past, the vaults at Rosslyn were used as a scriptorium. Ms Leoni believed the story to be true and that a manuscript of importance had been deposited somewhere among the Vatican collections. Her uncle also validated the story."

Further silence fell, less awkward but still unsettling. Cardinal Utaka looked thoughtfully at the Swiss Guard, seemingly more interested in the account than Cardinal del Rosi. Thierry's walkie-talkie crackled in the humid air. He answered and del Rosi spoke.

"The Knights Templar, I've never heard such rubbish."

"Ms Leoni seemed fairly convinced," Utaka replied.

"And that proves it, does it? You said yourself, there was nothing in the archives."

"They are not all catalogued, the ancient manuscripts."

Pessotto: "Professor Leoni sounds quite convinced also, and he's more advanced in his field."

"Hearsay, Gianluca," del Rosi said. "If all of the world's scholars were to be lined up from east to west they still would not find the south."

Mike bit his lip, his gaze centring on Pessotto. "Professor Leoni did show me proof of his claim. He had in his possession an old manuscript, similar to the Zeno diary. He showed me a reference to an organisation that was allegedly active behind the scenes in the French Revolution. The writer referred to the descendants of the Templars and they also had the same logo as the Rite of Larmenius."

"I have never heard of this," del Rosi said.

"Jacques de Molay thou art avenged," Pessotto said.

Curious stares followed.

"What did it say, wachtmeister?"

Commissario Pessotto's comments were surprising to Mike. His mind wandered back to the day they showed Henry Leoni the diary.

"Very little, sir," Mike said. "Only something to do with the French Revolution and the role of a so-called band of conspirators."

Pessotto nodded. "Did Henry Leoni give any indication of how the initial manuscript was given to his brother by Mikael Devére?"

Mike shook his head. "No. He seemed completely clueless."

Cardinal Utaka looked thoughtfully at Pessotto. "Did Leoni know Devére?"

"Devére banked with Leoni et Cie," Pessotto said.

"Devére was certainly friends with Henry Leoni," Mike said.

Cardinal Utaka nodded.

"This interests me," Pessotto said. "Wachtmeister, tell us everything that Henry Leoni said."

A Swiss Guard in Medici uniform stopped Gabrielle as she approached the Sistine Chapel. Like most Swiss Guards he was well-presented, some five-eleven in height and of Swiss complexion. He eyed her curiously as she attempted to enter the chapel and after recognising her from the meeting, allowed her access.

Within twenty minutes the chapel had changed dramatically. Its interior, earlier more reminiscent of a New York boardroom than a church, once again resembled the sacred site of religion. The long table in the middle of the floor was still present but most of the chairs had been cleared away. Three whiteboards lay folded up by the far doors awaiting collection but the majority of the apparatus had disappeared. It was strange to think that less than an hour ago this very room had been a site of constant deliberation between the banking heavyweights of the suit and the cloth.

Gabrielle took a seat by one of the walls, within a few metres of where she had spoken to Cardinal Utaka. Not for the first time, she focused on the images of biblical times lining the walls and ceiling above her, only now desperation and frustration had replaced her earlier feelings of boredom.

She felt like kicking out or screaming in anger. Biting her lip, she inhaled deeply, allowing the air to frequent her lungs. The air was cooler with the far doors open. The location that had earlier constituted privacy and secrecy would be opened to the public later that afternoon and life would move on. Soon she would return to her car, then the long drive home.

Alone.

She thought of Mike, then the manuscript that didn't exist. Then that made her think about Marcelos: that asshole who made her feel like a criminal, or worse. It was like being back at school, accused of cheating by a teacher. It was there, dammit. It had to be.

She thought about Rosslyn. Then she thought about Poli. Perhaps it was all just a legend. Perhaps there was no Poli. Perhaps the book never existed.

No, dammit. It was there. It had to be. It fitted.

If the Templars continued they went to Rosslyn. Sinclair had connections with Rosslyn. Zichmni was Sinclair, Zichmni was a Templar, she knew that much.

She kept thinking about Rosslyn. The splendid tomb, if it was a tomb, whatever it was. The markings on the wall, the Templars: something existed, or still did: once hidden in an empty tomb, as suggested by the diary.

Maybe there was more to the diary. It had the cross and it provided an in-depth guide to the vaults of Rosslyn. She had seen them; she knew they were accurate.

And there were those markings. Vat. Ross. 342. Whatever it meant. It was meaningless. Dammit.

She looked up once more at the far wall of the chapel, her eyes concentrating on Michelangelo's Last Judgment. The illusion stimulated fear. It was incredible the way the wall seemed to become more intimidating the higher up she looked. It reminded her of Rosslyn . . .

Then it hit her.

Jumping to her feet, she sprinted instantaneously towards the door.

Outside the doors of the Sistine Chapel, the Swiss Guard appeared an image of goodness. Four hours carrying out duties to ensure the safety of people he despised did wonders for his patience.

The beautiful melody from Beethoven's Ninth Symphony was playing loudly through his head as if on a continuous loop. He loved the way the brass and strings seemed to rise to an unattainable height at its peak. Even in his mind they reached epic proportions, giving himself a much-needed lift. It took a strange kind of patience to idle away the time dressed in the circus costumes that he loathed.

He had always despised the bankers but he despised the cardinals even more. And now he had found someone he hated even more than them, if that were possible.

Being born into a poor family perhaps gave him a reason to hate her. They say poverty is unavoidable: no one can alter the hand they are dealt. But the so-called elegance of the wealthy was avoidable. It didn't exist: it was nothing but a superstition: a selfish insult to those who had nothing. He had learned to hate them.

He would enjoy breaking her.

In his mind the sound of Beethoven became louder. That was when he saw her, running past him in the direction of one of the corridors. She did not see him. She never saw him.

He was just a guard.

But he was not her guard. It was a skill to kill. It was a skill to investigate. But it was a master class to investigate and possibly kill at a moment's notice without being seen.

He was a master of discretion.

32

Gabrielle sprinted, her footfalls echoing along the ancient corridor. Despite wearing high heels she somehow managed to retain her balance.

At last she was concentrating. It was there. It was there all along, right before her eyes. Was she blind? Was she stupid?

How could she have been so stupid?

She stopped before the door of the librarian's office and took a few seconds to gather her thoughts. She inhaled a couple of times, taking the opportunity to smarten her appearance and catch her breath. She adjusted her shoes, which had nearly slipped off as she ran and quietly cleared her throat. Finally, she tapped gently on the door.

"Come."

Cardinal Marcelos monitored the door expectantly. An enquiring stare changed to one of disappointment. Now what did she want?

"Ms Leoni . . ."

"These books, they have references," she interrupted.

The cardinal looked back blankly. "Forgive me."

"The books, the manuscripts," she went on, "you can look them up by their specific reference."

He looked at her with a lost expression. He was used to being bombarded with requests from various scholars but this was stupidity. Was she an idiot? probably. What did Cardinal Utaka, or the Camerlengo for that matter, see in such lunacy?

"This is a library, Ms Leoni; of course the books have references. That is how we know where they are."

"No. They have references like Vat. 14570."

Still meaningless.

"The manuscripts are catalogued according to subject, title, author and that is how we identify them. It is common practice in any library to catalogue their stock. Now if you please . . ."

On any normal day his patronising tone may have led to a rebuke, if not worse. It didn't make sense, not even to her, but she was too excited to care.

Far too excited.

"So if I knew the reference for the manuscript I wanted then you could find it?"

The cardinal huffed. "Ms Leoni, I am very sorry that your manuscript does not exist. If it did it would have been on the catalogue."

"Can you try anyway, please?"

"Sorry, I do not have time."

"Please, eminence, this is really important."

The Archivist and Librarian of the Holy Roman Church huffed. Perhaps if he could prove to her that it did not exist she might leave him alone.

"What is it?"

Gabrielle recited the reference. Vat. Ross. 342.

The cardinal typed the reference into the catalogue without interest and waited several seconds for the search to complete. He shook his head.

"Sorry. No such reference exists."

A cold icy feeling overcame her. It was as if she was consumed by an indescribable sense of despair.

Suddenly the cardinal's tone changed.

"Interesting."

Gabrielle looked up instinctively. "What's interesting?"

He looked at her curiously, as if taking notice for the first time. The way he looked at her unnerved her: it was almost as though she was sitting in an interrogation room waiting to be questioned by the FBI for possible murder. Only he was not asking any questions, not yet anyway. He just looked, looking as if he was listening, but listening to silence.

"How did you come across this?"

"I . . ."

"Wait here, please."

The cardinal ascended to his feet and exited the office.

Twenty minutes later, Cardinal Marcelos returned through the open door and stopped a few feet in front of Gabrielle. At first he remained silent. He gazed at her with interest, seemingly friendlier than before.

Then she noticed it.

The cardinal was holding a box containing several manuscripts, perhaps seven or eight in total. The front cover of the top one was partially torn but the title was still legible. Decorated in gold writing, the title Rota Temporum was present above the author's name of Abel.

The cardinal looked at her inquisitively but remained silent. His expression suggesting interest rather than judgment.

Gabrielle herself was gobsmacked. She opened her mouth, desperately wanting to break the silence, but failed to find any words.

"This is what you need?"

Gabrielle grimaced. "Would it be okay if I looked at all of them?"

The cardinal eyed her closely. His judging eyes returned.

"I shall take you to the manuscript room. No. I shall take you to the study room. You may study what you need there."

33

Mike looked on despondently as the row between Cardinal del Rosi, Commissario Pessotto and Thierry continued to escalate. What began as a frank exchange of views offering three complete differences of opinion had now developed into a verbal assault on the oberst for his handling of the situation.

This was aimed at Mike: that was obvious but Thierry defended him. This in turn led to criticism of Thierry and Mike had become practically a spectator.

It started innocently. Mike recited the story of Rosslyn for the second time. He included the legend from 1834 in detail, and Gabrielle's vain obsession in validating its existence through the discovery of a further manuscript. Thierry blamed Henry Leoni for the recent activities and so did del Rosi but del Rosi also blamed Mike. And that in turn led to criticism of Thierry. Although the oberst continued to hear what the cardinal was saying, he listened sparingly. Both Commissario Pessotto and Cardinal Utaka had stopped talking. In the corner of the room, Cardinal Utaka sat quietly, his glasses off, his right hand rubbing his tired eyes.

Meanwhile, Mike's attention wandered, thoughts of Gabrielle dominating his mind. He imagined the archivist denying her permission. He imagined her fuming. Perhaps she would resort to force. He could just imagine the ageing librarian struggling, well and truly beaten by his fiery glamorous opponent. He thought of her refusing to accept that it wasn't there, then having to be carried away kicking and screaming by the guards.

Then he thought of her outside. Returning to St Gallen.

Alone.

He may never see her again.

The more he thought about the situation the more he blamed Henry Leoni. Perhaps if he had shown more sense none of this would have happened. In some ways he wished he had concentrated more on convincing him to stay. But that was never likely: the man had based an entire career, an entire life, on discovery, excavation and adventure.

Perhaps, after all, it was his fault: he should have kept Gabrielle quiet. He shouldn't have let the excitable Henry Leoni run amok. It was foolish, reckless.

They could have been killed.

He inhaled deeply, looking to his left. Cardinal del Rosi had finished his attack on Thierry and was now slating Commissario Pessotto for his lack of leads.

Silently, he considered the possibilities. Although technically the role of the Swiss Guard was security of the Apostolic Palace and the Vatican City while matters of criminal investigation were left to the Vatican Police, the possibility enthralled him. Devére. The diary. Devére must have known, perhaps Al Leoni knew, but how did he have the original in the first place?

He knew Leoni was friends with Devére, he knew Devére banked with Leoni et Cie. Perhaps Devére had connections to the Templars. Then in that case why was he killed?

Political? Made sense, but in that case what about the others? How would a cardinal, a Swiss Guard and several bankers know of the Zeno diary? They couldn't. Dammit. Why?

The ringing of the telephone broke his concentration. Thierry raised his hand to Cardinal del Rosi and the astounded cardinal fell silent. The oberst answered the phone.

"Yes, cardinal." He looked at Cardinal Utaka. "Cardinal Marcelos for you."

Cardinal Utaka rose timidly to his feet and collected the receiver from Thierry. He spoke quietly, leaning his weight against the desk. The conversation between del Rosi and de Courten continued at whisper level.

"Our precise orders were for her to be guarded in St Gallen," the cardinal said to both Thierry and Mike. "Not to gallivant across medieval Europe."

Thierry sought to respond but was interrupted by the change in tone of Cardinal Utaka.

"That was Cardinal Marcelos," he said, replacing the phone. "It seems Gabrielle Leoni is cleverer than you think."

The cardinal looked at Thierry then at Mike.

"Frei, walk with me."

The deserted corridors of the Sistine Hall were the perfect decoy. With nowhere else to run she would be completely at his mercy. He was still a Swiss Guard but she would never know which one. Besides, by the time he had finished she would be in no position to tell anybody.

He removed his beret and replaced it with a balaclava.

In his mind, the track changed to Handel's Freedom to Move.

The Old Study Room of the Vatican Library was empty apart from her. Its appearance was reminiscent of a classroom from the last century, basic and enclosed, and was set aside as a study area for scholars wishing to view documents and manuscripts.

In Gabrielle's opinion the room lived up to its name. Ten rows of desks and chairs lined up in columns of five across the wooden floor: three-person desks on the left separated by a small aisle from smaller two-person desks on the right. Every desk was equipped with a lamp and a wooden stand for the manuscript or book to rest on.

The room was less appealing than most in this part of the Vatican but it was still impressive.

On the right side of the room, a statue and two paintings she didn't recognise covered the walls that had been painted white.

On the left, elegant arches separated five large windows, veiled by translucent drapes at regular intervals, one of which was decorated with a charming photograph of the current pontiff.

At the front of the room, another statue stood dominantly, located in an alcove over the door in the middle of the wall, while at the back of the room three silver filing cabinets flanked another door connecting the room to the library.

Above the doorway, an extravagant crucifix was nailed to the wall, marked by a plaque reading PIVS XI PONT MAX. The upper part of the room was painted in glorious white, whereas the lower part was a duller more skin-coloured shade. The arches, which separated the windows, continued upward all the way to the summit before spiralling inwards towards the centre which was decorated by an emblem she didn't recognise.

Gabrielle entered the room respectfully and sat down three desks from the back on the right hand side of the room. The smell of the wood accompanied by the typical smell of the ancient tomes dominated her nostrils, reminding her of days gone by. It even smelt like a classroom.

She placed the box down on the desk next to her and removed the first manuscript.

She began with Rota Temporum. Equipped with plastic gloves, she placed the tome delicately on the wooden book-holder and opened it slowly. Turning the pages was difficult. The manuscript felt rigid after over a century without use. She felt squeamish holding the text, not out of fear of the book, but the wrath of the archivist should she damage it. Marcelos had provided her with a pair of tweezers and gave her strict instructions on how to handle each manuscript. She picked them up with confusion and suddenly felt as though she was at a Chinese restaurant.

This was going to be a hassle.

She inhaled deeply, using each breath to compose herself. Inside, she felt the excitement begin to buzz. She turned the heavy cover and looked with interest at the early pages. On early inspection there were several hundred in total.

As predicted, it was written in 16th century Latin and was difficult to read under the naked eye. The writing style of Adam Abel was in the form of an ancient thesis rather than the smoother modern Latin of later scholars. Her uncle had already given her a vague idea of what to expect. She was aware that the book was a history of Scotland from the beginning of the world to 1535 AD. She scanned the early pages and on first impression considered them irrelevant: stories of a Scottish version of Gathelus of Greece as the early constructor of Scotland dominated the early pages, a common myth at the time. Unconcerned, she turned several hundred pages in one go. The language, seemingly the same as the early pages to the untrained eye, was slightly less easy to read than before, the pages evidently damaged by fire and water. She turned several more pages, still wearing the gloves but neglecting to use the tweezers. She had reached the reign of James II of Scotland, now in the 1440s.

She had gone too far.

All five left the office, walking with intent in the direction of the Old Study Room.

The walk was no better tempered. The booming voice of Cardinal del Rosi sounded like a judgment from biblical times as it echoed endlessly through the corridors. To a passer-by, the sound of raised voices may have aroused interest, but today that was less of a problem. The hallways were still deserted and would remain so for over an hour.

Thierry considered a response but decided against it. His lack of fight might have provided a perfect example of turning the other cheek, potentially proving a sensible ploy at dampening the situation, but in the circumstances it gave del Rosi more leeway. With every passing second the cardinal's voice became louder, his words largely a repetition of his earlier points.

"Will you shut up," Cardinal Utaka said, finally showing some emotion. He looked at his fellow cardinal with blood red eyes and then at the oberst with a somehow more forgiving stare. Cardinal del Rosi glared at his fellow cardinal but remained silent. He huffed as he walked, slowly calming himself.

Mike's face was rigid, thoughts concentrating on Gabrielle. He felt his pace quickening, far too quick for Cardinal Utaka. He forced himself to slow down. The last thing he needed was a further backlash.

It was strange to think that he had walked the same corridors not four hours earlier with Gabrielle. The awkward parting now seemed like a distant memory, faded following the passing of time. When he thought about it he thought about their embrace. It didn't seem real.

As they entered the Gallery of Maps, they saw Cardinal Marcelos walking towards them.

"Your eminence," he said mainly to Cardinal Utaka, ignoring Pessotto and the Swiss Guards. "This is, how you say, a most strange matter."

"What is it?" Utaka asked.

Mike held his breath.

"It seems your banker knows much of the content of our archives."

"Go on," Utaka nodded.

"She returned not long after you left, only now with a precise location for a non-catalogued manuscript."

How the hell did she know that? Mike thought. *Gabrielle, dammit. What have you done?*

"She knew the reference? How?"

"She did not say. I think it particularly strange. You see, most references are ordered categorically, yet this was out of sequence."

"How? How was it out of sequence?"

"It was not catalogued at all."

"An error, surely," Utaka said.

"I think not," the archivist replied, shaking his head timidly. "It was . . . disguised."

Mike's attention intensified. *What the hell did he mean – disguised?*

"The reference suggested that the manuscript had not been archived properly."

"It was in the secret archive?" del Rosi asked.

"Not only that, but its reference is seemingly linked with the location from where these books once came. The entry was old and contained only one keyword. Roslin."

Suddenly it hit him. Vat. Ross. 342. Devére's diary was previously kept in the Vatican Secret Archives.

Utaka's stance hardened. "Take me to Ms Leoni."

Failing to master the tweezers, Gabrielle delicately turned the pages with gloved fingers and scanned the text for any kind of meaning. The era was now at the beginning of the House of Bruce, the early years of the 14th century. Zichmni would still be nearly one hundred years away, if it was even included. Realistically if she was to uncover all of the secrets of the tome, it would be necessary for her uncle to study it in detail.

Something, she figured, Cardinal Marcelos would undoubtedly be against.

Although she wasn't reading the content with an air of authority, it was obvious that she was going nowhere. She closed the manuscript and placed it on the desk beside her, turning her attention to the next one.

This was untitled.

She turned several pages in one go and the book ripped slightly at the seam. She grimaced, studying the rip in detail. Slowly she opened the manuscript. This, too, was history related. She scanned the pages with interest and made out the period to be at the beginning of the House of Balliol in Scotland. She skimmed the pages quickly and decided it was irrelevant.

She opened the third book.

Awarding himself a moment of silent reflection, the Swiss Preceptor walked slowly along the corridor. In his mind, he watched with satisfaction as his victim dangled before him: her face turning from scarlet to purple as he smothered her with his hands; her feet kicking above the ground; saliva covering the palm of his busy hand, and his knuckles warm from the sickly discharge of blocked nasal capillaries. He looked down with morbid pleasure as the victim soiled herself. With her life at an end, he lowered the lifeless body to the floor. It would be hours before she was seen.

The truth would remain private.

Cardinal Marcelos led the way through the deserted corridors, heading in the direction of the study room. They walked in silence. Not for the first time, a look of frustration dominated the face of Cardinal del Rosi.

Mike hid his anxiety with a firm expression. In his mind he

continued to consider the recent events that were continuing to unfold. For the first time he considered the possibility that Gabrielle was right. Something of significance was there, deposited by the Italian over a century earlier. He was desperate to know what it was.

He was desperate to make sure that she was okay.

At the end of the passageway two guards stood at attention, unflinching as they waited for the cardinals to arrive. They opened the doors and saluted as one. Ignored by the cardinals.

The third manuscript was a 15th century chronicle entitled the Orygynale Cronykil of Scotland, written by a canon from Loch Leven named Andrew of Wyntoun. She recognised the title immediately as one of seven or eight copies from the time and decided it was of no relevance to the Zeno diary. The same was true of the next two. Both were well-known chronicles of the 15th and 16th centuries written by respected chroniclers, John Fordun and John Mair, and both were concerned with the history of Scotland. She paid brief attention to the following book: a thin manuscript regarding Gothic architecture. After skimming the first few pages she moved onto the next.

This left two manuscripts to consider. One was another chronicle by Fordun, whereas the other manuscript was untitled. In keeping with the Zeno diary, it was approximately six hundred years old and damaged by fire. It comprised over seven hundred pages and was also written in Italian on vellum parchment.

For the next three minutes she concentrated incessantly, turning pages at infrequent intervals. The text, although easier to read than the previous manuscripts, hurt her eyes, causing her to lose focus. She squinted at the text.

Realistically she needed a translator.

Yet what she saw was reassuring. Its layout suggested it was a diary, its content separated into various segments by dated entries. As best she could tell the content concentrated on the same time period as the Zeno diary, although she was unable to clarify who wrote it.

She skipped up to one hundred pages without consideration and squinted vigorously at the text. After scanning the next eight pages at rapid speed she realised the time period was around the late 1390s, documenting events that took place in the months of August and September. For the first time she began to read with interest, taking in every line as best her eyes would allow. The more she concentrated the more she recognised certain names and places. She read words slowly and turned the next page more carefully.

She continued for a further three pages. Then, inexplicably, she smiled.

A large map crossed two pages – strange considering it was drawn on vellum. The map was equally strange. It was definitely a world map but different from any modern map: any other she had ever seen. The map concentrated on Europe and Asia with some reference to America, surprising given the date of composition. The layout differed from modern maps, east placed as north, yet to her this was reassuring. Common practice at the time placed east at the top.

She focused on the map for more than a minute, taking in the names as best her eyes would allow. On closer inspection the names of certain locations were in keeping with those of the first diary.

Exhaling, she turned back towards the start. She began again at the first page and scanned the early content slowly, turning pages with regularity. The early pages were tough to turn, some stuck together.

She turned the next one carefully, making sure the pages didn't rip when they separated. Only fifteen pages in she saw the symbol.

The Swiss Preceptor slowed, practically coming to a standstill. In his mind he moved to the soundtrack of the Jaws movie, the sound becoming louder as the shark prepared to annihilate its prey.

He approached the study room.

At first she struggled to believe her eyes. These pages told a history, a different history, a history that until now was confined to hearsay and legend, hidden for over six centuries, and lost in the archives for over a century without being catalogued. The hairs on the back of her neck stood on end and her eyes began to water. This was what she had been looking for.

She needed to find her uncle.

Suddenly she stopped. Something had unsettled her. She could hear a sound, soft and vague. It was coming from the nearby corridor.

She seemed incapable of moving. She felt cold, its impact strongest at the base of her upper ribs.

For several seconds she remained silent. She looked down at the book and then over her shoulder. Concentrating on her hearing, she identified what sounded like light footfalls echoing softly outside the room. Although they say that all footsteps are unrecognisable, she was aware the sounds belonged to a man. With imperfect knowledge they sounded like the footsteps of a soldier, probably a guard. They were heavy, yet disguised by a strange almost inaudible softness that filled her with dread as the realisation hit her that she was no longer alone.

Straining her concentration for the faintest of sounds, her heart began to thunder as she realised the sound had stopped just outside the doorway. Visions entered her mind of a lingering presence, perhaps the very person who murdered her father, stalking her every move.

Inside she felt panicked, glued to the spot in anticipation. With hurried breathing, she turned away from the chronicle, and ascended to her feet. The chair made a slight scraping sound against the floor as she reversed, further unsettling her already unsettled frame of mind. She tiptoed lightly in the direction of the doorway, all the while struggling to control her breathing. Her heart palpitated with increasing velocity and beads of sweat began to form at the top of her forehead. She blinked, her eyes remaining closed for over a second. Nearing the corridor, she took a deep breath and gazed bravely into the passageway.

Nothing.

The corridor was deserted, presenting only a long narrow void. She checked to her right, and then her left, and then once more to her right, her eyes focusing on the empty passageway.

Still nothing: only silence.

The silence seemed loud, almost as though she could hear the sound of the air moving in front of her. She was aware of her breathing. She noticed the beating of her heart. She noticed noticing these things.

Looking both ways, she inhaled deeply.

Finally she exhaled in relief.

She didn't sense the presence behind her.

34

Her first reaction was to scream but the sound was inaudible. Hairy masculine fingers covered her mouth, restricting her passages. A horrible burning sensation dominated her lungs, forcing her to gasp for air. Her legs dangled above the floor, kicking frantically in every direction, knocking over desks as they made contact with her feet.

She lost all sense of balance. She blinked, almost in desperation, her vision centring on the ornate crucifix above the door that seemed to sway from side to side. The image of Christ, though pinned to the wall, seemed to float in front of her.

Other objects flashed by. She could see colours, almost as though she was seeing a rainbow. Unmistakably it was the uniform of a Swiss Guard, yet she couldn't see his face. As the assailant tightened his grip her vision began to blur.

For him it was beautiful, just like he had planned. The face that he had come to despise now resembled a gigantic beetroot, comically drowning in its own juice. His hands felt warm and moist: drool perhaps vomit as well oozed onto his hairy palms.

Just a few more seconds . . .

The strength of the man was overwhelming, depleting her energy. She fought, guided by panic. In desperation, she reached for a bookstand from the nearest desk and picked it up with difficulty.

Gripping it tightly, she smashed it against his head.

The walk to the Vatican Library continued. Their speed had picked up, their minds filled with purpose.

Without breaking step Mike's attention picked up. In the distance he thought he heard the sound of a heavy object fall to the floor.

The impact was little more than a nuisance. The assault had taken him off balance, but that was not enough to defeat him. The wooden material bounced off his head and shattered on hitting the floor. He reaffirmed his grip tightly, obstructing her every nasal passage with sweaty palms. Below him, her breathing began to relent. Her eyes closed for what seemed like an eternity, but in reality it was less than a second.

A burning sensation dominated her chest. A shooting pain, perhaps similar to what her father felt when he was murdered: probably by the same man. It shot through her arms and legs, and even her head. With seemingly her last vision, she saw the ancient manuscript in front of her. Not that it mattered now.

It was nearly over.

Swaying vigorously, her eyes saw what was directly in front of her. Those tweezers were on the table: that complicated tool that she had earlier failed to master. With one desperate reach she stretched for them. Her index finger barely reached, but she felt the slightest touch of metal. Next she was falling backwards. The Swiss Guard had stumbled, but remained on his feet.

Momentum brought her forward, his movement dictated by the fall. Inch by inch she was getting nearer. Her lungs burned with fire and her vision began to fail. With her other senses also failing, she felt contact with the tweezers with her index and middle finger. As she fell backwards once more she felt the cold feeling of metal between them.

She adjusted her grip. With little to aim at, she used them where it would hurt the most.

She opened her legs and squeezed.

Mike stopped in his tracks. An echo reverberating with urgency and despair dominated the lengthy corridor.

His eyes widened as he realised that it was coming from the direction they were walking.

Then it hit him clear as a bell.

Without conscious thought he was running.

A gasp of anguish dominated her ears as excruciating pain dominated his scrotum. Although still in his grasp, she was looser than before. She felt air enter her lungs.

Gabrielle screamed incessantly but failed to escape the attacker's grasp. Her direct hit had allowed her the chance to breathe but the setback was only momentary. Seconds later the Swiss Preceptor reaffirmed his grip. He shouted obscenities at her in German and punched her twice on the right cheek, making an instant impact on her already reddened face.

She gasped for air but felt choked. As his strength took over, the smothering sensation returned. Now she could see his face. A Swiss Guard, disguised in a balaclava, was looking down on her. His face may have been hidden but she could see from his eyes that there was hatred. Ice cold, silent, he reached for her throat.

In the background she thought she heard the sound of a door opening.

He was sure from the scream that it was Gabrielle's voice and it was clear from her tone that she was in trouble. Cardinal del Rosi shouted at Mike as he began to sprint, but the Swiss Guard didn't reply. The oberst had responded to his change of pace immediately and was less than ten metres behind him, followed by Pessotto.

Mike thundered through the corridor, his heart racing, images flashing through his head. He heard another scream, this time unmistakable. It was Gabrielle but her voice was softer than before. Something was restricting her. Experience told him she was being gagged, but instinct told him it was a hand. A morbid groan, definitely male, was also audible, coming from beyond the doors in front of him. His pace increased, the doors appearing nearer and nearer. Conscious thought left his mind and instinct took over.

He sprinted at the doors and forced them open.

The doors opened violently. Filing cabinets wobbled and a picture came off the wall. The first thing he saw was a man in Medici uniform standing in the centre of the aisle, surrounded by desks. He saw that his face was covered with a balaclava, and his hands strangling Gabrielle over a desk.

Their eyes met and without breaking step Mike sprinted towards him. The traitor dropped Gabrielle and hurried towards the front of the room. Mike pursued him. His feet lost momentum on the slippery floor but he managed to keep his balance.

As he closed on the attacker, he dived at his feet.

Mike brought the traitor to the ground and, with a powerful right arm, punched his side. The man groaned on feeling the impact, but kicked back immediately.

He struggled to his feet and scurried towards the door.

Mike wasted no time. Back on his feet, he made his way through the small gap between the desks, struggling to avoid hitting them. The Swiss Preceptor passed the final desk and picked it up with ease. Turning quickly, he threw it at Mike and exited through the open doorway.

The first thing Thierry saw was a room in shambles. The picture above the doorway to his right had smashed to the floor and the filing cabinet to his left was leaning on the next. Tables and chairs were scattered across the room as though a category five hurricane had descended. Several bookstands and lamps were lying broken on the floor.

Three desks on, he saw Gabrielle gasping for breath and holding her throat. Her face was bright red, mascara dripping from her eyes. Less than five desks away, Mike was lying flat out with a desk on his torso.

A slight stinging sensation dominated Mike's chest: a mixture of a hard right-hander from the man in the balaclava and the weight of the table. He felt his muscles twinge as he moved.

He threw the table off his chest and struggled to his feet.

He studied the room in detail, looking at Gabrielle for the first time. The sight made his heart ache. He had once seen a prostitute being questioned by police in Atlanta after a sexual assault and this was much the same. Her designer suit was torn and her face was still heavily red. Colour was slowly returning as she breathed without restriction but she did so with difficulty. Tears fell down her eyes, forming a sticky substance as they mixed with her makeup and elements of blood on her right cheek. Her appearance was unrecognisable, her body shaking. He walked slowly towards her. The tears fell faster from her eyes the closer he came and as he neared she lunged into his arms.

He looked down at the back of her head. From this alone all was normal. He felt her breath frequent his chest through his uniform and her tears on his neck. She trembled, whereas he was solid. He held her tightly, gently stroking the back of her head.

The first thing Cardinal del Rosi saw when he entered was enough to make his face red, but for a completely different reason. A picture was lying broken on the floor by the doorway; a file cabinet was turned onto its side; tables and chairs were tossed randomly across the room and directly in front of him one of his Swiss Guards was cuddling a woman while the oberst was leaning against one of the desks watching.

"What in heaven's name happened here?" del Rosi fumed, looking at Thierry and then at Mike. Mike made eye contact with the cardinal but didn't answer. He spoke softly to Gabrielle and gently laid his head on top of hers.

Del Rosi walked closer, still looking at Mike. Gabrielle released herself from his grip and turned to face the cardinal.

The remaining two cardinals entered soon after, surveying the room for the first time.

Both looked in disbelief at Gabrielle.

Cardinal del Rosi's expression changed to one of kindness. "What happened?" he asked. "Who did this?"

Cardinal Utaka looked at Gabrielle with warmth in his eyes. He approached her quickly, placing his hand to her cheek.

"Who did this to you?"

Commissario Pessotto exited the room via the rear right doorway, carefully avoiding the broken picture frame and peered with interest along the empty corridor.

Whoever was there was now gone.

He entered the study room again and walked towards Gabrielle. Cardinal Utaka was comforting her and Thierry was asking Mike about what he saw. Commissario Pessotto walked towards Cardinal del Rosi. Both he and Marcelos stared at the desk where Gabrielle had once sat.

It was not the desk as such. It was what was on the desk. He had noticed that half a dozen or more of the manuscript holders were scattered across the floor but the one on Gabrielle's desk had not moved. An ancient manuscript lay before them, still open to the page she was reading.

Commissario Pessotto's eyes lit up, his gaze focused on the vellum. The first thing he noticed was the symbol. Suddenly his blood ran cold.

Cardinal del Rosi hesitated, clearly taken aback. He looked at Gabrielle. "Who did this to you?"

Gabrielle shook her head quickly, visibly shaking. Mike continued to hold her but more softly than before. She turned her face and wiped her eyes. "I didn't see his face."

"It was one of us," Mike said sternly. "It was a guard. His face was veiled."

Cardinal Utaka's facial expression hardened. He looked at Thierry. "Search your men, oberst. We must ensure that this monster does not leave the vicinity."

"It's too late," Pessotto replied. "He's gone."

Utaka eyed the Vatican policeman curiously.

"The Swiss Guard are here to protect!" Cardinal del Rosi shouted menacingly, his voice echoing. He looked at Thierry then at Mike. Gabrielle was still shaking, clinging to Mike.

Utaka: "I think under the circumstances, oberst, perhaps you might spare Frei a little longer."

Thierry nodded, as did Commissario Pessotto, their eyes serious. Utaka nodded at Mike and then smiled at Gabrielle.

Gabrielle turned and looked timidly at Mike. He smiled at her. Beyond the fear he saw gratitude, even though she never said a word.

The Swiss Preceptor closed the door to his apartment quickly, his limp worsening with every step. Once he was sure that the door was closed, he squealed in agony.

At least he had not been seen.

The throbbing in his genitals was horrendous. The pain dominated every feeling in his lower body, restricting his movement.

Now inside, he removed his balaclava and slowly took off his garments. He was no longer bleeding, but his underwear was stained all around his scrotum. He needed to remove the stain.

Otherwise all would be revealed.

35

The intruder closed the door of the unlit room as silently as possible. With gloved hands he locked the door from the inside, making sure the key didn't rattle in the lock, and placed it carefully into his trouser pocket. These were not his usual trousers. The camouflage combats that he usually wore on operations were hardly necessary on this occasion. This was a different kind of procedure.

Tonight was about blending in.

He tiptoed carefully across the darkened room, slowly approaching the desk. Despite the darkness, he did not care for risking torchlight. Sparse rays of moonlight shone through partially open blinds, identifying outlines of furniture, allowing reasonable observation of the room.

Markus Mäder scanned the room, reacquainting himself with the surroundings. Orientation came naturally to him, but this place sure looked different at night. The water dispenser by the door gurgled quietly and a red light flickered from the fax machine, perhaps the only items in the room operating. He contemplated helping himself to a cold glass of mineral water to rid the dryness in his throat, but dismissed the idea immediately.

Even with the gloves it did not do to leave a trace.

In his early days he always did things like this. Working in intelligence sometimes meant operating as a detective or a spy, but in this case what he did bordered on burglary. Officially he was not there, and officially they could know nothing about it. In and out unseen.

No one would know he was there.

The situation could not have been more different to the last time he was there. Three days earlier it had been a quiet and more formal affair. His appearance, dressed in a smart suit and dark tie, identical to what he was wearing now, did nothing to suggest his true profession: to the unsuspecting Ludovic Gullet, he was Garfield Van der Haatz, a potential descendant of an illegitimate branch of a famous family of Austrian nobility whose loyalty had always been to the Reichs, who came with the intention of opening a large and high-profile account at the casino. He approached Gullet with noble arrogance and spoke abruptly in fluent German. His needs were Gullet's needs, business was business, and all else must be put off. What he wanted, he wanted yesterday and what he wanted next week he wanted now. He spoke with interest about spread bets, poker and other bullshit: it was vital to make the meeting relevant. After all, Gullet owned the casino.

He afforded himself a brief smile in recollection of the gullibility of the man, but discipline soon took over. From the nearby corridor he heard the sound of a light switch followed by the shining of a hall light outside the office. The door, glassed in the centre, was covered by a metallic blind, prohibiting light from entering or escaping the office. There was no chance of him being seen from the corridor.

If luck held out, the office would not be used tonight.

The meeting itself had been useful. While Gullet completely reassured him of the account, he had also achieved a good look at the office. He learned that Gullet would be away for the next few days and he had also learned a valuable piece of information about the safe. The safe was a combination lock, preceded by a lock that could only be opened with a key, which conveniently Gullet always kept by his side. Not convenient to the intruder, but even on the back of his chair it was susceptible to light fingers. He was already aware of the combination.

God bless Vatican policeman Agent Gregore.

There was no CCTV. He knew this after trying to obtain footage of Gullet's activities. He knew all of the activities that took place within the room would be private and that included his visit.

To the casual observer it didn't look like a safe. Tucked away below a series of folders in the far right corner of the room, it appeared more like a regular filing cabinet. The cabinet consisted of one neatly varnished wooden panel and had a small keyhole on the left hand side.

He removed the key from his pocket and knelt down gently in front of the first door. Exhaling deeply, he inserted the key into the lock. It turned with a clanging sound. Thankfully there was no alarm.

With the first phase over, he inserted the combination under torchlight and it opened with the first attempt. Again there was no alarm.

Inside, the contents were scattered. A series of papers were located in one plastic folder on the lower shelf while a large ring binder occupied the top. He assumed that most of the files for the company would be found in the metal filing cabinets on the other side of the room. Surely Gullet would not risk putting anything incriminating where the staff could find it. Nor would he risk hiding them in his home. If they existed they would be here – along with the other incriminating stuff.

The intruder inhaled deeply. The eighth commandment states thou shalt not steal, but stealing was not an option. Gullet would notice and that would be dangerous. He just needed to know what was included. He removed the files from the safe and shuffled them in his hands. Reading was difficult, but under the light of the small torch he could tell that the content was relevant. He fumbled his inside pocket and removed a small digital camera. He paused, taking a second to adjust himself. Then he pressed the on-off switch gently. The small lens inside the camera sprang into life, accompanied by a quiet mechanical noise that lasted less than two seconds.

He inhaled deeply. Aiming the camera at the first sheet he adjusted the focus and clicked to take the photo. For less than a second the flash of the camera illuminated that corner of the room, its light protected by both the blinds and the safe door. He checked the quality. Despite the small size of the screen he was satisfied the key information was readable.

He exhaled in relief. The heat felt prickly on his skin and a hideous itchy feeling made him uncomfortable.

The sooner this was over with the better.

He leaned closer to the documents and surveyed them one at a time under the light of the torch. He photographed the first sheet three times and then proceeded to do the same for the rest. It took eleven minutes in total. Once over, he replaced the files in the safe exactly as he had found them.

Finally, he switched off the camera and placed it safely inside his jacket pocket.

The intruder surveyed the room in detail, making sure everything was as it had been when he'd entered. After locking both doors to the safe, he eased slowly towards the door, straining for any sound of life.

Silence.

He inserted the office key into the lock as quietly as possible and opened it a few inches. As best he could tell the corridor was still deserted, the darkness interrupted only by the briefest hint of light from a faraway corridor, probably coming from a small desk lamp or a reflection from the main casino through a glassed door. Holding his breath, he opened the door fully and sought to exit the room.

Suddenly he froze. Something other than himself was moving. In the distance to his right he made out the faintest sound of footsteps echoing against the hard carpeted floor.

He inhaled deeply. He had time, but he had to be quick. Acting on instinct, he returned to the office, closing the door but without locking it, not daring to chance the sound of rattling the key in the lock. He crouched down low, his back to the door. From inside the office he was completely unsighted and the sound of footsteps had faded, its sound blocked by the door. He knew that any sound of movement would rouse the attention of the approaching person. His heart rate increased slightly.

Outside, the footsteps had become audible. From his position crouching behind the door, he looked as best possible through the metal blinds that crossed the door. Using caution he eased them open, taking care to avoid making any noise. Through the small gap he could see a smartly dressed male walking in the direction of the office, a white coffee mug swaying backwards and forwards from his right hand. Unsurprisingly it was a casino employee.

On the opposite side of the corridor a coffee dispenser was resting on a table, a red light emitting from the standby button. The employee stopped a few metres away from the door, looking first in the direction of the office, then the coffee dispenser.

Mark moved his eyes away from the blinds, nervous that the employee would check the door. He crouched down as low as physically possible, his eyes focused on the metallic blinds covering the main window of the office directly in front of him. He held his breath.

Silence.

Seconds dragged. Pain tore down his back. His instincts instructed him to shuffle for comfort but discipline took over. He knew he could not be seen or heard. Behind the door all was silent. Instead his attention focused momentarily on the main window. The lights of what he assumed to be a truck reflected against the metallic blinds followed by the sound of heavy revving.

Outside the room he heard a shuffling sound, perhaps less than five feet away. The employee was standing motionless in front of the coffee dispenser. He looked casually in the direction of the blinded office doors but unknown to Mark he moved on without taking interest. The employee eyed the coffee dispenser and stopped to place his cup under the tap. Espresso, latte, cappuccino, macchiato, hot water, and hot chocolate were just some of the choices written in Italian and German. He pondered the choices for several seconds and decided on the espresso. With the faint promise of dawn still distant over the horizon he needed the caffeine.

Outside the building, the sound of voices became louder, stealing the intruder's attention and causing him to consider his exit. As the seconds passed, the sound of conversation became louder before fading, the direction of their voices indicating that they were moving, probably walking along the side of the casino. As best the intruder could tell the voices belonged to customers searching for the entrance to the casino, disappearing as they continued to walk away from the window.

Suddenly he heard a sound coming from the corridor. An object of some description had fallen to the floor and rolled towards the office door, hitting it and rebounding in some unknown direction. Unbeknown to Mark it was a coin. The employee cursed in German and bent over to search for it, his search guided by the vague light coming from the next corridor. The anxious wait was now unbearable for Mark as it came in such close contact. He flinched involuntarily.

The employee froze.

For several seconds neither moved. On the other side of the door Mark waited silently. Unseen to him, the employee located his coin. He dusted it down with his jacket and returned to the machine.

Patiently the intruder waited, a merciless wait, the thundering of his heart making it difficult to control his breathing. Suddenly he heard a different sound. On the other side of the door the machine buzzed into life, the night-time silence broken by the sound of filtered coffee being dispensed into the mug perched on the metal grating. The employee waited. Seconds later a single bleep informed him it was finished. He gripped the cup with his stubby fingers and sipped the liquid slowly.

No sugar.

He looked down at the nearby tray and ripped open a packet of sugar, pouring it without care into the cup.

No stirrers.

Feeling frustration, he searched for several more seconds and decided to make do with a plastic knife. He stirred the coffee gently and threw the packet of sugar and the knife into the rubbish bin. He sipped the liquid as he walked, slowly returning to the main casino.

Mark inhaled deeply. His heart was pounding and his breath short, but he knew it was over. He would wait for another three minutes then follow the employee the way he came.

If his luck held out he would not be seen.

In a deserted part of the Vatican City, the man with blond locks and the head of the Vatican Police spoke urgently.

Targets would be back on the road tomorrow.

He exited, this time behind the wheel of a BMW.

*

Vatican banker Randy Lewis was still at his desk at 1 a.m. In his tidy office, lit only by the dim glow of the 40-watt desk lamp, he pondered the document before him.

He was largely familiar with the financial performance of Leoni et Cie. Millions of minor shareholders, a few more significant shareholders and one main one, the Vatican, due to receive leftfield returns on their original investments. It was a good investment for the Vatican. The share price of the bank had hardly fluctuated at all: impressive in times of economic uncertainty.

Yet something worried him. Removing the lid from his Caran d'Ache fountain pen, he circled the one major irregularity. He had missed it the first time but the second time it failed to compute. He wrote a note in the margin.

What the hell was going on?

36

Mike and Gabrielle left Rome late the next morning. Following the activity of the previous day, Thierry and the cardinals agreed that Gabrielle was still in significant danger, despite her no longer being the majority shareholder of Leoni et Cie, and that Mike would remain as her bodyguard for the foreseeable future.

This was welcomed all round. Unsurprisingly, Vatican security had been heightened since the attack and a full inquiry was to be launched into the Swiss Guard. Thierry was charged with the responsibility but this did nothing to appease Cardinal del Rosi. After hours of persuasion, he and the returning Camerlengo, furious at the attack on his great-niece, declared their intent to conduct their own inquiry, external of the Swiss Guard but also subject to the laws of the Holy See and the Vatican City.

The other major topic of interest was the second diary. After initial attempts by the cardinals to understand its significance failed, Cardinal Marcelos reluctantly agreed that Mike would also become the guardian of the recently discovered manuscript after suggestion from Cardinal Utaka and Commissario Pessotto that Henry Leoni's knowledge might be of value. Nevertheless, they also firmly ordered that Mike was under no circumstances to pursue any leads it might give without further instruction. The cardinal's assumption was that the recent ordeal would dampen Gabrielle's interest, yet Mike quietly wondered whether it would whet her desire further.

The journey north took place in little traffic and passed mostly in silence. For the first time since they had known each other Gabrielle travelled in the front. At just after one-fifteen they stopped at a small café, located discretely off the main road, somewhere between Florence and Bologna. Mike entered first, quietly surveying the location as he walked towards the counter. Gabrielle, meanwhile, took a seat at a booth-enclosed table and looked despondently through the window at the deserted road. The gravel car park outside the café's entrance was practically empty apart from three relatively modern hatchbacks with Swiss licence plates and a gathering of motorbikes that lined the wall near the outside toilets, two of which belonged to the long-haired, bearded Americans dressed in blue Levis with holes around the knees and tight leather jackets. She hardly approved of the setting but Mike had his own views on seclusion. On this occasion she was in no mood to argue.

Mike returned with two cups of coffee and placed one in front of her. She raised the cup to her lips and sipped it slowly, the flavourless liquid barely registering on her taste buds. It was hardly the stuff she was used to. Her hands shook slightly as the heat resonated uncomfortably from the substandard china, leaving a red imprint on her palms.

But it was not just the heat that affected her. She was shaken, evidently so. Her fingers trembled significantly less than the previous day but it had not stopped altogether. The night that followed was difficult. After a thorough examination by the Vatican's medical staff she kept to herself, refusing to eat or drink anything but the odd sip of water.

Sleep was also out of the question. Every time she closed her eyes evil visions entered her head, some real some not, almost like a vivid recurring nightmare where the masked Swiss Guard continued to attack her: his masculine fingers still clenched firmly around her neck that was still hurting from the attack. For the first time in years she feared the dark: every time the light faded, she saw him: those eyes of pure malice staring down at her. Could she ever trust a Swiss Guard?

Could she afford not to trust one?

Mike returned from the counter for a second time and took a seat opposite her. He removed his sports jacket and placed it down on the red cushioned bench, part of which was punctured and oozing yellow foam rubber.

He slid along the seat and forced a smile. Like Gabrielle he drank coffee, equally weak, and placed a white plate with a ham baguette on the table before her.

"In case you get hungry," he said.

She didn't reply; her gaze remained fixed on the barren stretch of road. To Mike it was unclear whether this was an act of vigilance or whether she was simply in a daze. With shaking hands she sipped slowly from her drink, some splashing onto her fingers.

"You okay?"

She placed the cup on the table and rubbed her hand.

"Sure," she said, without making eye contact. Instead her eyes returned to the road.

Mike nodded. She clearly wasn't but he let it pass. He took a bite of his own baguette and rubbed his hands together to remove the crumbs. Noticing tears in her eyes, he removed a serviette from the dispenser on the window ledge and passed one to her. She accepted it without eye contact, her gaze remaining on the road.

Mike's attention, meanwhile, remained focused on her. She was not the woman he had met several weeks earlier. The bruising on her cheek was starting to swell, poorly disguised despite several layers of makeup. For the first time since they met she wore a baseball cap and her hair was done up in a ponytail. Today her head seemed lower than usual.

She clearly didn't want to be seen.

"That guy was not one of us. He was an impostor."

Gabrielle's attention remained elsewhere. Outside, the roaring of two motorbikes dominated the otherwise quiet location. The bikers parked next to the others and entered through the glass door. They walked towards the counter and ordered coffee.

Mike looked at Gabrielle.

"It's okay," he said, his focus intense. "I'm here."

She blew on the weak coffee and sipped it slowly. The sickly liquid felt unpleasant on her stomach. The doctor had explained that she was in shock and it could remain for days if not weeks. He told her seriously that shock could affect sleep patterns, appetite and taste buds among other things, but she was aware that it was not shock that was responsible for the appalling flavour that afflicted her tongue.

She replaced the cup on the table and stuck out her tongue in distaste. Mike smiled.

"What?"

He shook his head, still smiling. "Nothing."

She continued to gaze at him. For several seconds her eyes remained unmoving. Finally, a smile reached her lips and she forced herself to laugh. She knew it was the first genuine laugh she'd had that day.

"That is one shit cup of coffee."

Mike smiled at her. "Yeah, well, at least we can get some proper coffee when we get back to St Gallen."

"Yeah. With real beans."

"And sugar."

"And food," she said, looking with disgust at the baguette. She held a smile for several seconds before it faded into a serious frown. She turned around nervously as the newest bikers took a seat at the booth directly behind her and slurped loudly on watery coffee, their senses suggesting indifference to the lack of taste. She glanced over her shoulder at the rugged back of the nearest biker. Little things scared her. The flaming skeleton tattooed into one of the biker's necks; the half dozen piercings in the larger man's ears; the ruggedness of their beards, and even the way the larger of the two put down the cup and burped.

"I've made reservations at a hotel about one hundred and seventy miles north," Mike informed her. "It's hardly the Hilton but it's still pretty okay."

She turned around to face him and muttered the word "fine" without argument. The idea of the great Ms Leoni, billionaire, philanthropist et cetera, et cetera, staying in a three-star hotel quietly made him laugh but the gravity of the situation called for seclusion. Taking every precaution he booked the room, one room, two beds, under the name Scarlet, his American grandmother's maiden name and decided he would pay with cash. He never liked to take chances but nerves still got the better of him: whatever it was. With a hawk-like intensity, not obvious to anyone else, he scanned the road for signs of action. Nothing. Just another biker: this place seemed to collect them. Moments later a blue BMW pulled up outside.

He looked at her once more. She looked lost, not physically but inside. Her eyes, normally shining with enthusiasm, were now empty and dim, colour somehow faded from each iris. It reminded him of the day of her father's funeral.

"It's okay," Mike said.

"The Swiss Guard were here to protect from outsiders," she said, her attention still on the car park. "Nothing was said about protecting from inside."

Another sip of the flavourless coffee.

"I thought I was going to die."

"They don't let anyone join the Swiss Guard. I know all of them. Believe me, none of them are capable of . . . that."

"And how would you know?" she replied emphatically, colour returning to her eyes but without warmth or optimism. When he looked into her eyes he could see something had changed inside her. He knew the day he met her that she was still living a childhood: an extended lease of innocence and pampering that could only happen to a spoiled daughter of a rich man, or a member of the nobility. Yet that had been lost in the blink of an eye at the hands of an impostor dressed as a Swiss Guard.

"I'm sorry. It's not your fault."

Mike grimaced. "That's okay. You're right, I don't know, not for sure. All I saw was the back of him. Just call it a hunch."

Silence followed. He glanced out of the window. The BMW was still outside.

"Did you see his face?"

She shook her head. "No. He wore a balaclava the whole time."

Mike nodded. A cold, sober thought emerged in his mind. What if he was wrong? He doubted himself, his friends. Surely none of them would be capable of such monstrosity.

"Someone wanted your father dead," Mike said. "Someone clearly wants you dead as well. Now perhaps we're looking at this the wrong way. Now maybe this has nothing to do with banking."

Gabrielle looked at him, surprised. "What do you mean?"

"The oberst showed me something. He said the Rite of Larmenius had killed before, most recently two people connected to Banco Ambrosiano in the 1980s: two bankers to be precise. Both were Italian; both killed without explanation and the killer never brought to justice."

Mike looked out of the window. Suddenly it dawned on him. The driver of the BMW hadn't moved.

His attitude changed instantly. "We should leave."

"I haven't finished my shit cuppa . . ."

Suddenly a chilling sensation overcame her. She looked at the car park, then at Mike.

"Maybe he's just checking the map or making a call."

"That's what worries me," he said. "Come on."

Mike stood nonchalantly and headed towards the counter, putting on his jacket as he walked. He passed some euros to the bald-headed Italian behind the counter and whispered something in his ear. Gabrielle saw him heading towards the outside toilets at the end of the corridor. He looked back at her and she in turn looked at the BMW through the window. Tinted glass gave nothing away.

Gabrielle rose from her seat and moved slowly away from the booth. She looked at Mike, not for reassurance but to know where to follow. She followed him down the corridor towards the fire escape. He pushed firmly on the metal bar in the middle of the door and opened it loudly. Now outside, Gabrielle's Lotus was directly in front of him, parked three empty bays from a diesel Volkswagen. Mike had deliberately parked it out of sight from the main road.

Once inside he switched on the ignition and the engine sprang into life. He pressed down gently on the accelerator and edged towards the road, waiting for the traffic to clear. Within seconds the café was out of sight.

He breathed out loudly, hoping his precaution was simply an overreaction. Checking his mirrors, he accelerated to forty-five miles per hour before taking his foot off the pedal.

As far as he could tell no one was following them.

For several minutes neither of them spoke. Although it was unclear whether there was even a threat, Gabrielle chose to assume the worst. The possibility overwhelmed her, causing a tight claustrophobic sensation to engulf her chest. For several seconds, perhaps ten and each one an eternity, she felt as though she was going to pass out. She searched for the button that opened the electric window.

The revving of the Lotus was overwhelmed by the sound of blustery air. Gabrielle leaned her head over the door and inhaled gratefully, closing her eyes as a reflex against the gale. The unpleasant sensation, a mixture of the sickly coffee and nervousness slowly left her and was instead replaced by the harsh sensation of fresh air blowing in her eyes and filling her lungs. After several seconds she closed the window.

"How did you know?" she asked.

Mike glanced in the rear-view mirror. Nothing.

"I didn't," he said. "I just don't like taking chances."

"You don't say."

"I live longer that way."

"Well lucky you."

An awkward pause followed. Mike maintained his concentration, eyes on the road, then the rear-view mirror. Still no one was following.

Nothing. Relief.

Gabrielle bent down and reached for a bottle of mineral water that was rattling beneath the seat. The un-chilled flavour was unpleasant, but she drank for several seconds, intent on ridding her mouth of the taste of her recent coffee.

Mike looked over. "It's gonna be all right."

Gabrielle swallowed and replaced the cap on the water bottle. "What do you know? You know nothing about me."

Mike straightened up as he decelerated into the bend. "Fair enough," he replied. "But you're not the first person to have to deal with this . . ."

"There you go again . . ."

"I'm just saying . . ."

"Well don't!"

He checked the rear-view mirror once more and was satisfied there was no immediate danger.

Several hundred metres behind, the BMW followed. A single bleep made its sound intermittently, marking their position on the tracker. As far as he could tell they were unaware of his presence.

37

For over twenty minutes the ride continued in silence. The Swiss Guard drove quickly. The light touch of the accelerator felt like the weight of a feather against his foot, making it difficult to avoid breaking the speed limit on the deserted road. Although he loved driving sports cars, for Mike the tense atmosphere coupled with the long drive was becoming a chore. His eyelids felt heavy after a night of little sleep guarding Gabrielle.

If luck were to hold they would arrive before nightfall.

For Gabrielle the journey dragged by even more infuriatingly. She sat with her eyes closed, her rigid body leaning back against the headrest. In her dazed state her nostrils gave little sense to the pleasant smell of the new leather seats.

Despite her eyes being closed she was in no mood to relax. Every time she tried, her mind continued to linger on her ordeal the previous day. The last thing she wanted was another night away from the château: particularly having to share a room. She was aware that he had stayed with her that night at the Vatican but she barely paid his presence attention. She wasn't in the mood for company.

From time to time a refreshing breeze blew across her face from the air conditioner. The moderate temperature felt perfect on her face. The electronic display suggested it was 17° Celsius, at least eight degrees warmer than the temperature outside the car. She opened her eyes fully and looked at Mike, his hands adjusting the fan level. He asked her if it was okay for her and she replied that it was.

She looked at him and offered a smile.

At that moment her mind began to wander. For the first time since the attack she remembered the way she felt before entering the Sistine Chapel. After everything that had happened it seemed like a long time ago. She thought about yesterday, before the attack. Then she thought about the way he charged through the doors. She smiled inside but her face remained neutral.

"You saved my life."

Mike looked at her, his expression suggesting surprise. "Excuse me?"

"If it hadn't been for you . . ."

Mike laughed, slightly hesitantly. "Look, Ms Leoni, with all due respect . . ."

For several seconds he remained lost for words. She looked directly at him, her expression warmer than before. He wanted to know what she was thinking, but her expression gave nothing away. He looked at the road and then at her. He forced a smile.

"It's what I'm here for."

She smiled to herself, allowing her mind to wander once again. Maybe if things had been different. She wondered how things would be if they were meeting for the first time, under normal circumstances.

He looked American, yet definitely Swiss complexion. Short dark hair, rough rugged stubble, about one day without a shave that seemed strangely more appealing than usual. His skin was rough but not in a bad way. His rippling muscles were not the biggest but nicely toned, perhaps capable of benching his bodyweight. If he were a wrestler he'd be a middleweight. He looked like a football player, perhaps one who played for Roma or Lazio.

He was handsome but that alone was never enough. It was the way he came for her. Perhaps it was the look of determination in his eyes. Or maybe it was the way he threw the tables aside to get to her assailant. Or the way he held her after scaring off the attacker.

Despite the wealth she had always been starved of love. In the eyes of most she was like a Hollywood actress: completely unattainable. She was beautiful, and she knew it. She knew men were afraid of her, perhaps too afraid. In many ways that was a problem. She knew he was afraid of her, but she liked that. Men always loved her.

Did he love her? Maybe, she thought. She liked the way she could use her sexuality as a tool. It had always worked for her. She had her heart broken once, by a banker, and vowed that she would never do so again. She hated bankers. She hated cocky men.

Coming from a family of ancient lineage, her one regret was that she hadn't been alive in the distant past. Then maybe she could have married a real knight in shining armour. He was like a knight. Better yet, a stable boy who had risen to a knight. He would have made a good stable boy. She tilted her hair to the left and smiled

"Didn't you say your dad worked on a farm?"

Mike looked at her, perplexed. "Nope. He was a sheriff just outside of Macon."

"Were you close to your father?"

Mike shook his head. "Not really," he said without interest. "Why?"

"No reason. I've never asked about your family."

"Why?"

"I'm interested."

"Really? Why?"

"Just am is all," she said coyly. She smiled at him as she shuffled in her seat for comfort. "What made you become a Swiss Guard?"

He shrugged. "I dunno. I guess it was always my dream."

"Uh huh. And you weren't close to your dad?"

"Not really."

"He was never there to protect you?"

He looked back confused.

"Or maybe it was not you who needed protecting."

He took his eyes away from the road, his concentration momentarily lost.

"What?"

She shook her head. "Nothing. You were saying about the Rite of Larmenius?"

Mike looked at her blankly.

"Before we left. You were saying something."

Mike shook his head, thoughts returning to the road. He considered the question.

"Right. Yeah. Oberst told me that the Rite of Larmenius could be responsible for over two thousand deaths since the Second World War. Most recently they are alleged to have been involved in the killings of two bankers connected to Banco Ambrosiano."

"Was this before or after Calvi and Soisson were murdered?" Gabrielle asked.

"Before, I think, but only just. I think what with all the attention that happened after with P2 most people forgot all about them."

Gabrielle nodded. "Right. And you were going to tell me that you don't think they wanted me or my dad dead because of anything to do with banking."

He felt stupid but still managed to force a laugh. "I didn't mean it like that," he said, shaking his head. "The first diary was found in a Leoni et Cie safe deposit box registered to Mikael Devére, right?"

"Right."

"Right. We also know that it was Mikael Devére who provided Mark with the tip-off regarding the murders."

"Right."

"So presumably not only did Devére know about the Rite of Larmenius being involved in the deaths of your father and the other five, but he also knew something about Zichmni and the continuation of the Templars."

"Assuming he could read the text."

"Right. And you were attacked when reading a manuscript that just so happens to have been lost for God knows how long. And, better still, judging from the fact that the first diary was also once located in the Vatican someone must have retrieved it."

"So you think they wanted the manuscript and nothing else?"

Mike paused in contemplation. "I think it's possible. Surely if this was banking related they'd have attacked you before you sold your shares."

"So what about Jermaine Llewellyn? Cardinal Faukes? Your major in the Swiss Guard, the other ones?"

Mike bit his lip. The more he thought about it the less convinced he felt.

"I don't know. But what I do think is that someone wants proof of a Templar survival to remain secret. Let's face it, the Vatican Secret Archives are as difficult to break into as a Leoni et Cie vault. Yet you find this book that even the Fila hadn't earmarked."

Gabrielle was confused. "The what?"

Mike looked at Gabrielle, briefly taking his eyes from the road. "The *Fila*."

"What's that?"

"That's what they call Marcelos. The Fila. As in the Fila Brasileiro."

Gabrielle's face broadened into a smile. "You mean the guard dog?"

"Yeah. He's Brazilian."

Gabrielle laughed hysterically. Her facial expression changed: everything about her changed. She laughed for several seconds.

"Oh, my God. That's so funny."

Mike looked at her and laughed, not at the joke but at her. Tears streamed down her cheeks but they were happy.

She laughed for several seconds.

"Oh, my God," she said again, wiping her eyes. "I can just imagine him digging a hole for his bone and guarding it." She laughed again. "That's funny."

Mike remained quiet as she regained her composure. He shook his head, failing to hide his smile.

She poked him in the arm. "Oh, man. You're funny."

A brief pause followed, a pleasant one. She looked at him, her face returning to normal.

"You were saying?"

Mike braked around a corner. As the road straightened out of the bend he began to accelerate. He looked at her again, confused.

"You were saying, before?"

"Right, so you find this manuscript that must have been in the archives for over one hundred and fifty years yet it had never been catalogued. You find it after receiving a clue from the first Zeno diary that we now know had also been in the Vatican collection. Then after finding this second diary, you were nearly killed. Devére must have been aware of the first one and it stands to reason your father also knew. How else would the key and the account details have found their way into your own safe deposit box?"

"So you think this has nothing to do with banking?"

"I'm not saying that, I'm just saying perhaps this stems deeper. No one really knows what's in the Vatican, and, let's face it, no one really knows what's hidden in the vaults of any of the major Swiss banks."

"I'm a little old for believing in monsters in the closet, Mikael."

"I didn't mean that. I meant, like . . ." he shook his head, leaving his sentence incomplete. "I don't know."

"Secrets?"

"Well, maybe."

Gabrielle shuffled in her seat as she considered a response. "And you think the Rite of Larmenius or whoever they are want it to be kept hidden?"

"I don't know. I don't even know what you were looking for. But even Commissario Pessotto was impressed by the symbol in the manuscript."

Gabrielle nodded, silently considering the possibilities. Somehow talking about it made her feel better. The spine tingling sensation of adrenaline mixed with anticipation enthralled her and more importantly distracted her from the troubling events of the day before. She tilted her head away from Mike and slowly closed her eyes.

The hotel was located in the Canton of Ticino and less than ten miles north of the City of Bellinzona. The building was secluded, situated just off E35 and commanded outstanding views of the mountains and the famous Castelgrande, the largest of the city's three famous castles.

Gabrielle had been asleep for over two hours by the time they arrived. Mike woke her after parking the car before opening the passenger side door to help her to her feet. She yawned heavily, her body disorientated by the drive.

Time and location were strange to her.

She looked with interest at the surrounding area. The City of Bellinzona glowed in the near distance against the darkening sky. She recognised the city immediately: its famous walls instantly familiar from their position on top of a hill. Finally she turned to survey the hotel. The building was painted white and was relatively modern in appearance, perhaps no more than twenty years old. The logo was displayed above electronic doors, leading to a carpeted atrium.

Hands on hips she looked at him. It was not the most luxurious she had ever seen but it was not without its charm. More importantly it was quiet. Therefore it was secluded.

Their room was on the first floor, which in this case was the top floor. Two basic double beds dominated the room, separated in the middle by one large bedside table. Switches at the headboard activated both the main wall lights and two lamps situated above each bed. An ironing board was leaning against the main wardrobe, next to a long fixed table that included a kettle and a TV. A small ensuite bathroom was accessible just inside the door and contained a sink, a toilet and a bath with an electric shower. At first sight the room was pleasantly comfortable but stains and cigarette burns on the cream carpet quickly limited its appeal.

She surveyed the room and looked at him. "If I get nits it's your fault."

He smiled. "Nits can be washed away."

"So can blood."

He smiled awkwardly. Gabrielle, meanwhile, turned away and walked towards the window. Outside, stunning Alpine views took the breath away. A glowing crescent moon rose above the mountains to the east. She looked for a few seconds at the view across the landscape before sitting down on the bed, as if testing it.

Mike looked at her nervously. "Okay?" he asked, almost as if seeking approval.

"Uh huh."

He looked at her for several seconds. "Well, I'll take a shower. You gonna be okay?"

She looked up and forced a smile. "Sure."

With a sense of unease he retrieved his suitcase and entered the bathroom, closing the door behind him.

Although Mike was only in the next room she felt alone. She inhaled deeply and felt her eyes water. The lingering smell of cigarette smoke teased her nostrils, somehow made worse by the curious smell of WD-

40 or something similar coming from the direction of the ensuite, feebly undermined by the lemon air freshener.

She looked around the room. It was basic but okay. It was the type of place adequate for a couple in town to see the castles or enjoy the scenery. A print of a painting, medieval in setting, modern in date, overhung the bed. The painting illustrated a battle in the St Gotthard Pass centuries earlier. The sight of soldiers carrying halberds unnerved her but also reassured her as her mind wandered again to the man in the next room.

She walked once more towards the window. The pleasant moonlight cast a warm glow over the peaceful landscape, disturbed only by the faintest sound of traffic heading towards Zürich, Vaduz or Milan. In the distance, she thought of St Gallen and the château. As she daydreamed, she thought of her father, standing in the garden, then standing before her and smiling. For a moment the thought reassured her.

Even though it was nothing more than a memory.

The Swiss Guard limped across the floor of the deserted church. Walking in his condition was difficult, and he struggled to make out objects in the poor light. The hour was late and the church was consumed in darkness, illuminated only by the faint glow of moonlight that filtered eerily through the window above the Throne of Peter.

He approached the confessional and pulled the curtain to one side. He knelt down on the cushion, partly in comfort but also in reverence to the man behind the lattice.

He couldn't touch him, but he knew he was there, merely centimetres away. His presence shook him. He could hear the audible sound of his impatience illustrated by his short breathing.

The Swiss Preceptor waited. He wanted to speak, but more importantly he wanted it over with. After several seconds the silence was broken.

"There is a rumour going around the Vatican that we have a snake in the grass," the Sénéchal said calmly, his voice penetrating. "Do you know what this means?"

The preceptor hesitated. His words were meaningless, pathetic gossip, as if a glossy magazine or a tabloid was dishing the dirt on some lowlife politician's affair with a skank. Yet his tone was serious. The Swiss could not see the other man's eyes but he felt them staring at him through the panel.

"It means nothing."

"It means you failed."

The Sénéchal's voice was startling. The notion itself was ridiculous. The Swiss Guard were the epitome of integrity, loyalty, bravery, esteem, and much more. No one would believe this could be true.

"You were under no orders to carry out such an attack."

"I had to do something. Our entire existence was at stake. Your compassion clouds your judgment, eminence."

The cardinal bit his lip. "Your rashness clouds yours."

Silence followed, lasting several seconds.

"Thankfully for you the committee are unsuspecting. It seems the Lord favours you. I have been asked to carry out the investigation myself."

The preceptor smiled.

The cardinal shuffled in his seat. Vulgar. Indignant. He felt such contempt – not only for the man's incompetence, but his very being. The smell from his neck, some kind of cologne, made his skin crawl. It somehow smelled of treachery. It also smelt of ineptitude.

The Swiss Preceptor inhaled deeply. It was a mistake; he knew that. It takes a certain type of man to become preceptor. He was stepping into big shoes, old shoes, shoes that perhaps predated where he now knelt.

Plan A was over. Next comes B.

The courtyard was well lit, not unlike the hotel. It was clean, surprisingly clean: no graffiti, no litter. The same was to be said of the car park. The good lighting may have served to put off vandals and thieves but the cars were hardly worth stealing.

Except for one.

Parked in a secluded corner in between a ten-year-old sedan and an SUV was the woman's Lotus. Parked to avoid attention.

No one saw the BMW emerge. No one saw the driver exit the car, survey the vicinity or enter the hotel. No one saw him leave.

38

St Gallen

Henry Leoni polished the magnifying lens using the lens cleaner and breathed gently on the glass. After removing countless fragments of dust and smudge marks that had earlier distorted his view, he replaced the 8x zoom lens and peered with one eye through the microscope. Adjusting the zoom, he focused on a certain line of the second diary. The content was mind-blowing. The more he read the more convinced he became that he was dealing with something of intrinsic importance.

Centuries of use had left countless marks on the page but it was generally in good condition for its age. Around the edges colours ran thanks largely to contamination of the fingers. Minor burn marks and evidence of shrivelled corners backed up his belief that the manuscript had once been moved from Rosslyn on the outbreak of a fire. The Italian handwriting was fairly easy on the eye, particularly one as trained as his, but reading it was one thing, comprehending it another. Never in all his years had he been treated to such a find. He concentrated on the section where Gabrielle had discovered the symbol and was amazed at what he found. He praised her profusely. He worried about her but the magnitude of the find dominated his thoughts. It was incredible. Lost for all those years.

The thought made him shake.

Behind him, the door to the study creaked open and Gabrielle entered slowly. Her jet-black hair was parted at the middle, partially covering her carefully made up face. Bruising around her cheek, purple in colour less than two days earlier, had now faded to a dull yellow colour concealed by three layers of makeup. She carried three full coffee mugs in her hands: one for Mike, who had disappeared, one for her, and one for her uncle. She placed two cups down on the desk and the final one on a coaster near the computer monitor. With her hands now free, she slipped coasters under the other two and moved them away from the manuscript.

"Thank you," Henry replied, looking up briefly. He adjusted the lens before continuing to focus on the manuscript.

Gabrielle leaned over his shoulder, looking with interest at the diary. She had read parts of it already although she failed to understand it. The night at the hotel had been plagued by fear, and reading the text had passed the time productively. Sleep was hardly likely: every little noise had spooked her, every light frightened her and every passing car unnerved her.

Four days had passed since their return. Mike took up occupation in his old room, his mind concentrating on security, while Gabrielle brought her uncle up to speed with the second diary. Her hands still trembled slightly but far less than they had in previous days. A façade of confidence had returned.

Everything about her suggested focus. Instinct told her to move forward and she was determined not to let the memory of the attack trouble her. Her father had always told her that the past never mattered: everything was experience; if it's bad, learn from it. The only past that mattered was that which was recorded in the second diary. Although she still had no idea what it meant, it continued to dominate her thoughts. Mike wasn't fooled. She told him not to worry; he didn't buy it. She told him she had moved on; he didn't buy it.

Maybe he wasn't as useless as she'd thought.

She looked with interest over her uncle's shoulder at the top right hand corner of the page, approximately fifteen pages in. On closer inspection it was the same page that had the symbol on it.

"The inclusion of the symbol is intriguing."

"Yes," he said, still looking down. "Fascinating. Most unique."

Henry looked away from his work and made eye contact with Gabrielle. She smiled at him. Despite her calm façade it was obvious to him that she was putting on a show.

"You need to take it easy."

She looked away briefly, taking a sip from her coffee.

"I'd rather concentrate on this," she said, replacing the cup. "I'd rather keep busy. You know."

He smiled. "Just like your father."

Despite offering a wide smile, secretly her thoughts continued to wander. She couldn't help but feel that the man who attacked her was the same man who had killed her father, perhaps others as well. She hated him more for her father's death than the attack on her. The thought angered her.

"Gabrielle."

She shook her head, returning to reality. "Sorry."

Henry looked at her with concern.

"I'm fine." She flashed a smile. "Seriously. I'm fine."

Henry sipped his coffee, gazing thoughtfully.

She changed the subject. "So what do you think?"

Henry replaced his coffee mug on the coaster. "The story of Zichmni picks up again around late 1398," he said, loosening the manuscript from the microscope and turning back to the beginning of the text. "The manuscript seems to be the second instalment of diary entries, this time written by Antonio Zeno. Early indications suggest that they cover both the end of the first set of letters, all of the second, many of which were written by Antonio to their other brother Carlo, and other elements otherwise unheard of."

Gabrielle looked on with interest. A smile broader than the occasion merited spread across her face. The magnitude of the statement, something the Harvard professor was still unable to clarify, met her with a sudden sense of purpose and excitement. To her it was progress: clear evidence that the pieces of the puzzle were fitting together.

History was being revealed before her eyes.

Henry: "The surviving letters are known to tell the story of four fishing boats from Frislanda whose men accidentally landed in a country named Estotilanda, somewhere to the west, after becoming lost in a storm. According to the letters, one of them managed to return twenty-six years later in the company of natives from the island. After learning that it was a rich country, Zichmni declared his desire to travel there himself. Unfortunately, three days before they left, the fisherman died, leaving them without a guide. However, Zichmni decided to proceed anyway in the company of men who returned with the fisherman. Interestingly, this diary suggests that a historical voyage took place, plotted out by Zichmni in around 1398, therefore supporting the content of the letters. It doesn't say who Zichmni was I'm afraid, but according to the diary members of the same order joined him."

Gabrielle nodded. "What else does it say?"

Henry sipped his coffee. The way he did so was almost ritualistic, as if it offered some sort of intellectual benefit.

"The diary confirms that Zichmni and his men set off to find Estotilanda, somewhere beyond what the writer refers to as the Green Sea of Darkness, meaning the Atlantic and Arctic Oceans. However, instead they reached an island called Icaria, somewhere west of Frislanda. This was also mentioned in the letters."

Henry replaced his mug on the coaster. "Interestingly, the diary continues in the same way as the letters. It explains how they were forced from Icaria and continued across the ocean and in time made landfall, and named the area Trin. But then things become less easy to follow."

"How do you mean?"

Henry retrieved a 19th century hardback book from his desk and opened it on the penultimate page. The book was a historical investigation into the original sets of letters on which the diary seemed to be based.

"What you must remember is that many of the letters discovered by the fellow's descendant are alleged to have been destroyed," Henry said, showing Gabrielle the book. "But, interestingly, in the last letter to Sir Carlo, Antonio confirms that he was keeping records. He writes:

"Concerning those things that you desire to know of me, of the men and of their manners and customs, of the animals and neighbouring communities, I have documented in a separate book, which, please God, I shall bring with me."

"You think this diary is the book he spoke of?"

"I would be astounded if there was more than one – particularly bearing in mind many of the events included here do not appear in any of the letters."

He paused momentarily.

"Look at this for example," he said, turning several pages of the diary. "According to the diary, after arriving at Trin, Zichmni and Antonio formed a colony there but they continued further south after the men failed to warm to the conditions. However, rather than finding Estotilanda, they landed at a country named Drogeo where they became shipwrecked – something not mentioned in the letters. Unable to replace one of the ships, Zichmni headed off to explore. Meanwhile, the remaining sailors formed another, this time more permanent, colony in the location where they became shipwrecked, somewhere on the coast. Eventually Zichmni returned having spent time exploring during which time his men had constructed a circular church on the coastline and a small settlement of basic huts. The diary confirms they were assisted by many of the natives."

Gabrielle looked over his shoulder. A diagram depicted the structure, drawn by Antonio Zeno. The church was portrayed in detail. It composed of a round stone tower, incorporating eight legs, with a wooden dome at the top and surrounded by a vaulted ambulatory. The entrance was located on the west side through an arched doorway.

"It looks like the Church of the Holy Sepulchre," Gabrielle said.

"Yes, and probably no coincidence: the Templars themselves are alleged to have built an identical one in Cambridge, England."

Gabrielle nodded, her eyes still focused on the diagram. On closer inspection she realised that this church also included an underground vault, curiously reminiscent of Rosslyn.

"Where is it?"

Henry shook his head. "I'm afraid it doesn't say. Somewhere in Drogeo, wherever that is."

"Do you think it still exists?"

Henry shrugged. "If it ever existed at all," he said sombrely. "The diary still refers to make-believe places. Frislanda, Estotilanda, Drogeo . . . not much help if you don't know where you are going."

Suddenly she remembered reading the manuscript at the Vatican.

"Maybe it says in the map."

Henry looked up, confused. "Map?"

"Sure, it was about halfway in. Like the famous Zeno map of 1558 but bigger."

The academic looked at her, noticeably intrigued. Readjusting his glasses, he carefully placed the text in the nearby manuscript holder and started to go through it page by page. He turned the pages slowly, his hands covered in protective gloves in order to spare the vellum from further harm. He continued until they were approximately halfway in.

"There!" she said.

The academic raised his eyebrows, his focus on the map. He studied it for over a minute.

"This is remarkable," he said, smiling. "This predates the Zeno map in Venice by over one hundred years."

Gabrielle looked at the map. "Look here," she said, pointing at the location just above Scotland. "Have a look at the place names."

Henry looked down at the map. He viewed it on its side, allowing north to face upwards. The drawings were crude in comparison to those of modern day maps. The location of the islands had been determined without reliable equipment, but latitudes and longitudes alone seemed reasonably plausible when compared to present day knowledge. The map was more in keeping with a modern one than the other famous Zeno map of 1558 and covered a wider area. France, England, Spain and the majority of Europe fitted perfectly. America was present but not the way he had expected: it was divided into several parts. Scotland was there as predicted, though the areas to the north were more scattered than he'd expected.

"Have a look at this," Gabrielle said. "Frislanda comes below the Faroe Islands. They are where Fair Isle should be."

Henry smiled widely. "I don't believe it."

Gabrielle smiled. She looked further afield. As she looked across what was confirmed as the Atlantic Ocean she saw things that she hadn't noticed before. Or at least not remembered noticing.

"Icaria is very nearby. Very small."

"St Kilda," Henry said, nodding. "Well bless."

Gabrielle continued to scan the map. Towards the west she recognised various place names. Iceland and Greenland were where they should be under the names Islanda and Engroneland.

"Estotilanda," Gabrielle said. She examined the area around Greenland and Canada where the name was located. "What's that? Labrador?"

Henry nodded. "Labrador, Newfoundland, Nova Scotia . . ." He smiled to himself.

"And Drogeo?"

Henry double-checked the content. Finally he nodded.

"North and Central America."

Gabrielle looked carefully at the map, seeking to determine Zichmni's exact route in her mind. "If Zichmni and Antonio were searching for Estotilanda but only found Icaria, later to travel south-west, then surely they found the Caribbean."

"Perhaps. But south-west of St Kilda is still a long way north. South-west of St Kilda may lead to Nova Scotia or even North Carolina. It really depends on their exact course."

"It sounds as if they hadn't a clue."

"Navigating by the stars is not an exact science," Henry said. "Just one degree out could misdirect by some 600 leagues."

Henry concentrated on the area that comprised modern day North America. Gabrielle did the same, paying particular attention to a strange feature. She had noticed it a few days earlier but been unable to study it in detail. A figure, appearing to be a knight in armour, was standing just off the coast of Nova Scotia, his sword pointing at an area of coast. A second, larger, knight was also present some seven or eight hundred miles to the south, standing over what the map referred to as Drogeo.

"What does this mean?"

Henry concentrated on the first knight. "The knight is standing over what the map refers to as Trin. This would be close to modern day Nova Scotia."

Henry's smile widened. He paid closer attention to the second knight.

Gabrielle also looked at the second knight. An outline of what seemed to be a castle was also present.

"It seems to be somewhere in New England," she said. "Nantucket?"

Henry left his seat and walked across the room. He examined the antique globe on his desk before moving over to a large world map crossing the far wall of the study. He examined it in detail before double-checking it against the map in the diary.

"It appears to be Rhode Island."

Gabrielle looked once more at the map. "Newport?"

The academic removed his glasses and smiled, practically laughing.

"Newport, Rhode Island, of course." His mind wandered back to the drawing of the stone church. "The church must be the Newport Tower. The Newport Tower is a circular structure with eight legs."

The professor smiled peacefully. Few historians believed in the authenticity of the famous Zeno map. He had always doubted its validity. To him it was a 16th century hoax: a clever attempt at convincing the believing of a possible pre-Columbus crossing of the Atlantic in an age typified by fraudsters attempting to pass off the improbable as genuine. But now its relevance was clear. The place names were not make-believe. Only the worthy would be capable of seeing them.

Suddenly a thought came to him. "As luck would have it I think I know someone who may be able to help us. A colleague from Harvard."

"Really?"

"Yes. A fellow history professor, he's been investigating it for years. He's fascinated by it."

"Can you trust him?"

"Certainly. His cousin is the curator of Rosslyn."

Gabrielle smiled, her eyes again wandering across the map. As she looked once more over Drogeo she noticed something else, something she had also noticed back in the Vatican. A star marked the north.

"What does this mean?"

Henry looked. "What's what?"

She pointed at the text. There was a name included.

"La Merika?"

"Hmmm. Yes, I noticed. Very curious."

A brief silence followed. To a rookie it was innocuous: a bizarre yet inconsequential collection of words.

"What's curious?"

Henry shook his head, still smiling. "Nothing," he said. "Just an old myth."

Gabrielle looked at him, her eyebrows narrowing. "What kind of myth?"

"Well, a Templar one, actually."

"What was it?"

"Well, there is an old story, completely unsubstantiated, from the early days rather than the latter. But the story goes that deep within the Temple of Solomon the original Templars made a startling discovery."

Gabrielle waited impatiently as he paused once more for coffee. "And?"

"Well, according to the story, the original Templars found an ancient document hidden beneath the Temple Mount. Supposedly it described stories of ancient Phoenician knowledge, including the location of a continent called La Merika. The new world as it were. It was a land that could only be approached from the east when following the western star. Curious."

Gabrielle nodded, not really knowing what to make of it. She monitored her uncle. It was as though a strange calm had overcome him.

"Well I best take Mike his coffee."

The professor nodded and smiled. He stretched, almost comically. His attention returned to the map. Double-checking it, triple-checking it, quadruple-checking it. Each time he looked it seemed more conclusive. Who would have thought it? Proof of perhaps the greatest historical enigma had resurfaced. Hidden for years beneath a rock in the earth. And no one knew.

No one remembered.

39

Mike adjusted his position in front of the desktop PC and double-clicked on the mouse. The waiting time, usually merely milliseconds with the rapid broadband connection, was taking longer than usual.

He had made several searches already that day, but he was still to find anything of interest. In reality, he was not entirely sure what he was looking for. Ever since his conversation with Thierry regarding the murdered bankers in the 1980s his mind had continued to wander. Two murdered bankers: both alleged victims of the Rite of Larmenius but without a known motive. Bearing in mind what was known of the Banco Ambrosiano scandal he assumed they were in some way involved, but the lack of leads bothered him. Surely if the Rite of Larmenius had been involved in similar activities their actions would have left a record: even if only a vague one.

Finally the page came up. The search engine provided 34,084 results, none of which were relevant. He tried a different search, this time 54,867 results, none of them relevant.

In reality he could have deemed the society's past unnecessary. Criminal investigation was not his responsibility. Yet by now he was hooked. He was in too deep not to be affected. For the first time he considered the possibility that the events of the past were connected to those of the present, even though the people involved might be different.

As best he could tell from the Internet, the Rite of Larmenius was just one of a number of secret societies whose reality was officially vastly different from its alleged activities. He found some of the legends, notably the possibility that they had once been in league with the Communist Bloc, but there was little evidence to prove it. He found little evidence to validate any of the murder stories, although references to the Banco Ambrosiano scandal were numerous. The more he seemed to discover about the murdered bankers the more similarities he saw to the current situation.

Could history be repeating itself?

Devére was no banker, but the Rite of Larmenius, possibly Ludovic

Gullet, may have killed him. Based on Devére's revelations to Mark, the Rite of Larmenius must have been directing whoever was responsible. Was there a connection between them and the Templars? Do these Templars even exist? If so, what was the significance? Was there a connection with what Gabrielle had found? There were so many questions he wanted answering.

He entered a new query into the search engine and clicked twice on the mouse. The search was useful. The first result was an old newspaper article dated 17th May 1982. Then there was another: this time 21st May. Another click of the mouse followed. On the second page there was another, dated the following day. At the bottom of the page he found a fourth article. 23rd September 1989.

Seven years and four months after the event, the trial for the double murders of Italian bankers Alexei Nesta and Gianluigi Calveccio has ended with the defendant being found not guilty.

Despite ongoing criticism of the snail-like progress that the case has seen since the discovery of the bodies in Rome within a week of one another in May 1982, the jury yesterday unanimously agreed not to convict the 35-year-old Ludovic Gullet for the double murder of both bankers due to insufficient evidence.

Regarded in the city as two of the most talented bankers in Italy, it was an Italian newspaper reporter on his way to work who spotted the deceased body of Nesta in close proximity to the Castel Sant'Angelo, merely one hundred yards from where Calveccio was later found in similar circumstances. Calveccio himself had been wearing an expensive suit and was carrying over nine hundred pounds, dollars and lira that had been untouched by his murderer.

While it is still unclear as to why they were murdered, strong suspicions connecting the manner of the killings with similar terrorism acts attributed to the controversial Masonic fraternity, the Rite of Larmenius with whom Gullet himself is known to have had involvement in the past, refuse to go away. While no spokesman for the Rite of Larmenius has commented since the murders, heightening rumours that the group has ceased to exist, both the Grand Lodges of Freemasonry and the Grand Orient have spoken out strongly against the group with both claiming that the Rite of Larmenius is in no way affiliated with either branch, and does not represent the order. According to some commentators the Rite of Larmenius may be responsible for over two thousand deaths worldwide since 1945 and were rumoured to have been involved in the possible murder of Pope John Paul I and the assassination attempt on Pope John Paul II.

An honoured soldier and former captain in the Swiss Army, Gullet's fall from grace is still viewed with sadness in his home country. Famed for his patriotism and loyalty, Gullet became a Swiss Guard in 1973 and remained so until 1981. After rapidly rising through the ranks since beginning his career as a private, a staunch Catholic throughout his life, Gullet had enjoyed a colourful career with the Swiss Guard before being expelled by the order for an alleged breach of discipline.

Despite the trial finishing yesterday, the exact reason for the murders and the extent of any connections Gullet may have had with the Italian bankers remains uncertain. Throughout the trial Gullet repeatedly denied any responsibility for the murders or that his actions were taken under orders, but continued rumours of connections with the Rite of Larmenius has convinced many that the murders were part of a wider conspiracy involving the failings of Banco Ambrosiano.

Aged 42 and 44, respectively, no evidence has yet come to light regarding the activities of Nesta and Calveccio and what they were doing in Rome at the time. Both individuals worked as analysts for several banks throughout Europe, including Banco Ambrosiano. In 1973 Calveccio was accused of currency law violation, which, if found guilty, would have resulted in a suspended four-year prison sentence, but of this he was acquitted. Nesta achieved fame in 1977 in his role as a columnist for the Italian Newspaper, Verità, and frequently appeared on television as a financial commentator.

"What are you doing?" Gabrielle asked, leaning over Mike.

Mike turned instinctively, unaware that Gabrielle had entered the room. Coffee dripped down the mug onto the carpet.

He looked at her, exhaling. "Sorry. I didn't hear you come in."

"Obviously," she returned, putting down the mug before wiping her hands on her jeans. "I've been looking for you everywhere. I made you a coffee."

Feeling like a fool, he smiled and thanked her. He took the moderately warm cup of coffee and sipped it gratefully. The temperature felt ideal on his dry mouth.

Gabrielle gazed with interest at the monitor. "What are you doing in here anyway?"

"Sorry," Mike said, placing his coffee on a coaster. "I should've asked."

"Don't apologise. What are you looking up?"

"Nothing really: just something oberst said to me."

"Oh yeah. What was that?" she asked. She sat down gently on the armrest and placed her right arm just behind his neck on the comfy chair.

As usual, he considered his actions. It was potentially classified information. Then he remembered the article was public knowledge anyway.

"There's an article here. It's on the Rite of Larmenius."

"Let me see."

She sat down on Mike's knee and leaned in to read the article. Mike inhaled slowly, attempting not to be affected by the gentle presence on his leg. It was a nice presence, accompanied by a swift and soothing fragrance of lavender. As she leaned back he felt her naked shoulder against his arm.

"Ludovic Gullet," she said, turning to face him.

For the briefest of moments their faces came into close contact. Gabrielle broke eye contact immediately, making the excuse to clear her throat. She rose to her feet.

"You think Ludovic Gullet is involved?"

Mike eyed her with interest. "You've heard of him?"

Gabrielle looked back awkwardly. "As a matter of fact I have. We've met once or twice."

Mike looked at Gabrielle curiously.

"Don't look at me like that; I never said I liked him," she said, putting her hands through her hair. "He knew some of my dad's friends."

Mike nodded slowly, his mind examining the possibilities. Gullet may have known the victims.

"He owns a chain of casinos. My dad used to go on the odd occasion."

Mike nodded, grimacing. "Sorry."

"What's it say?"

"Not much, just that he was a Swiss Guard turned bad."

A Swiss Guard turned bad, Mike thought to himself.

Thierry never mentioned he was a Swiss Guard.

"Sounds like the guy who tried to kill me."

"I doubt that," he said, shaking his head. "Like you said, he owns a series of casinos now. However, it looks as if you were right. This has happened before."

"How do you mean?"

"Perhaps I was wrong. If Gullet went bad, then . . ."

"You think it was a Swiss Guard, not an impostor?"

Mike shrugged. "I guess I don't know."

Gabrielle nodded, turning back towards the monitor. She spent several seconds reading the remainder of the article.

"You think Ludovic Gullet murdered these bankers on behalf of the Rite of Larmenius?"

"Well, it looks like one of their guys did. And apparently Gullet was in the correct location for the murders of Snow, Walls, Llewellyn and von Sonnerberg."

"You never mentioned this before."

"I didn't know. Oberst only told me the other day. He also showed me photographs of Gullet speaking with a US Senator named Danny D'Amato and a former British politician named Lord Parker."

"Never heard of them."

"Oberst thought it was potentially of connection. He also said the Vatican Police have someone working undercover at Gullet's casino trying to sniff out any evidence. Oberst wouldn't have told me this if he wasn't worried. Commissario Pessotto, Mark and the Vatican Police are working flat out."

"Of course he's worried, Mike. Everyone is."

Mike nodded. "He was prepared to admit that he thought that the murders might have a genuine connection to the Rite of Larmenius. But he feels that the Rite of Larmenius are different from other organisations or terrorist groups."

"In what way?"

"Apparently they have no definitive cause, nor is it obvious even who their members are. They don't use violence as a tool to get any political objective achieved, or at least not as far as we know. As far as the world knows they're just an appendant body of the Masons who are very select when it comes to taking on new members. According to this article they don't even have any direct connection with the Masons themselves."

"So he thinks that this organisation which consists of some of the wealthiest and most influential men on the planet are just a rabble."

"He didn't say that, he just said the organisation is too diverse to have one specific aim."

Gabrielle nodded. That made sense.

Mike frowned. "However, if the Rite of Larmenius are responsible for recent events then there must be some purpose. If Gullet is killing on behalf of the Rite of Larmenius then these murders must be connected. As, most probably, were any others that occurred in the past, including those two bankers in the 1980s. Why would he kill two bankers for no reason?"

"So you think the murders of these bankers are connected to my father? And Llewellyn . . ."

"Probably not, at least not directly, but if Gullet was responsible then their deaths must have benefited someone. And this article confirms public suspicion that they killed in connection with the Vatican in the past. And possibly at least one former Pope."

Gabrielle was confused. "You maybe wanna explain?"

"If Gullet is responsible for the recent murders then why is he doing it? As far as we know, Ludovic Gullet is only an assassin, therefore someone or some people with a substantial amount of money must be calling the shots. The Rite of Larmenius have the money and the influence, as do their individual members."

"So you think this has nothing to do with the Templars?"

"I don't know. Maybe they're connected."

"You think the Templars formed the Rite of Larmenius?"

Mike shrugged. "They have the same logo . . . and your uncle said the first leader was a man named Jean-Marc Larmenius. Kinda coincidental."

"Hardly conclusive proof. Maybe the Rite of Larmenius is just inspired by the legends."

Mike shrugged again. "Well, if the Templars have survived for whatever reason, perhaps they evolved into something bigger than we know. If they do exist, they are undoubtedly capable of pulling off several murders. Who they are exactly, well that's another matter."

A brief silence fell.

"Anyway, you'll be pleased to know we won't be staying here much longer. Next week we'll be returning to my place in Boston."

Mike nodded, a smile crossing his lips. "I think it's a good idea. The further away you are from this the better."

"Exactly," she agreed. "Also, we need to visit Newport, Rhode Island."

Mike's eyebrows narrowed. "Why?"

"Uncle Henry has been working on the diary. He thinks further proof of a Templar survival exists there."

"Gabrielle . . ."

"No, it's okay. He knows people high up in the city."

Mike breathed in and out loudly. "I don't like this."

"We're going to Harvard to see his friend. We can stay at our home in Boston. We're leaving in three days."

The driver of the BMW typed quickly into his BlackBerry.

Subjects are on their way to America: Request permission to follow.

Seconds later he received an answer.

Permission granted.

40

Vatican City

The silence that had lasted less than twenty seconds felt more like the same in minutes to Markus Mäder as he watched Cardinal Utaka scan the photographs that he had just placed before him. Small in size and comprising seventy-three in total, the images were of several documents, not original but just as important. It was clear from their content that the information was private: not meant for outside eyes to read: particularly when the outsider reading it was in some ways a victim of the events described.

Mark leaned forward in his chair, his vision focused on the cardinal. Less than three feet away to his right, Commissario Pessotto did likewise, attempting to read the cardinal's facial expression. To his right was Thierry, not behind his desk but sitting in a chair in front of it. The chairs of the four were located at 90-degree angles. All present were in a position to view one another's facial expressions and everyone could be addressed with eye contact. No one was in the dark. At least no more than the other in a meeting concerned with matters of privacy.

The cardinal's concentration was strained. His hand shook, partly due to the aching arthritis from which he had suffered for over a decade, but more due to shock at what he was seeing. After examining the final print, he removed his glasses and gently rubbed his eyes, placing the photographic prints down on his lap. The purple bags around his eyes had subsided slightly in recent weeks but the stress was starting to rebuild. A serious expression crossed his face, yet to an outsider it was still relatively neutral. There was no anger or even resentment in his expression – only concern.

"What does this mean exactly?" he asked, replacing his glasses.

Commissario Pessotto grimaced, taking the pause to make eye contact with Mark. Mark breathed deeply; an expression of hesitancy and uncertainty crossed his features. What he had captured in the photographs taken eight days ago had not produced a clear result until earlier that day. This was no hoax.

New truths were being uncovered.

"What this means, eminence," Commissario Pessotto said calmly, "or what it confirms rather, is that Ludovic Gullet was present in Mauritius the night of Mikael Devére's death and that Gullet now has a possible connection with five of the seven murdered men. Also, it confirms that the same people responsible for the deaths of the first six also issued a warrant to Gullet for the murder of Mr Devére."

Cardinal Utaka nodded, aware that most of the prints were of documents: either the same or similar to those given to Mark by Mikael Devére two months earlier.

"We now have confirmation as expected that Gullet was in Washington D.C. the night of the murder of Jermaine Llewellyn," Thierry added. "Only Cardinal Faukes and Al Leoni are the odd ones out."

Commissario Pessotto nodded. "Leoni is hardly surprising considering the small time lag between his own death and that of Chairman Llewellyn."

Mark: "We now believe that Ludovic Gullet was responsible for at least five of the seven murders and that he is working under orders from members of the Rite of Larmenius."

Utaka looked at all present with widening eyes. "That is quite a statement."

Mark nodded. "This is quite a find, eminence."

Utaka looked once more at the first three prints, all of which concerned the same document. The document was not large but extremely complicated. Strangely there was very little text: most of the information came in numbers.

"I want this plain and simple," the cardinal said, his facial expression unflinching. "What are we dealing with here?"

Pessotto and Mark exchanged glances. Thierry retreated a few inches, placing his pen between his lips. He had not smoked for fifteen years but he felt the need right now.

Pessotto: "Both the Vatican Police and the Swiss Guard have long been suspicious of Ludovic Gullet's past involvement with the so-called Rite of Larmenius."

"He was a soldier once," Thierry said without emotion.

"A guard?" Utaka asked.

"Yes," Thierry replied. "He was born in Zürich. Served in the Swiss

Army before leaving to pursue a career in the Swiss Guard in the early 1970s."

Utaka looked seriously across the room. The aroma of falling rain seeping through the open window felt vaguely refreshing as it served to combat the overall mugginess of the room. He looked again at the prints and huffed loudly.

"I am not interested in history lessons, gentlemen. What has this to do with anything?"

"Although Gullet was once a member of the Swiss Guard, his involvement ended in 1981 when he was expelled," Thierry said.

"Why?" Utaka asked.

"Breach of discipline," Thierry replied.

Utaka nodded. "I see."

Another pause followed. Thierry threw his pen down on the desk and turned to the cardinal. "We understand countless ex-Swiss Army and ex-KGB found employment with the Rite of Larmenius."

"Not just KGB," Mark said. "Rogue militants from all across Europe."

"For what cause?" the cardinal asked.

Pessotto shook his head. "If the objective of the organisation was obvious then perhaps we would be closer to finding answers."

The cardinal nodded.

"Unfortunately," Pessotto began, "we still have no idea who their members are."

"Randy Lewis has been most cooperative there," Mark said. "His role as former Chairman of the Federal Reserve has provided him with a unique position of insight. He has given us positive IDs on several of their known members, both past and present. I've managed to question a few off the record, but as yet uncovered no leads."

Utaka said something under his breath, possibly a religious mumble that was inaudible to all present.

He sat up as straight as his posture allowed. "What do we know about Gullet now?"

"A fair bit," Mark said. "He lives as a tax exile in Campione d'Italia where he owns a casino – one of many. He owns several businesses worldwide."

"Mainly casinos," Thierry said, "casinos and hotels. He inherited some from his father."

"Makes sense," the cardinal said. "It takes several million just to start one."

Pessotto nodded. "It is also a good way to cover your tracks."

"Precisely," Thierry said.

Utaka nodded. "But what of him now?"

Mark: "Only rumours really. According to some sources he is still a member of the Rite of Larmenius, yet they have never broadcast their activities: they have been largely quiet since 1982 following the murders of two bankers."

Thierry: "Officially that was never proven as them. Nor was it proven as him."

Mark nodded. "No, it was not. Yet, surely we can agree that the probability is strong. Judging from our knowledge of the man."

Pessotto nodded.

Mark: "Before that the last Rite of Larmenius murder came in the late 1970s."

"You mean the last alleged Rite of Larmenius murder?" Utaka said.

Pessotto nodded. "Very well. There is little or no chance that the murders of the past have any connection to the present. But the evidence suggests the same culprits."

"There is one connection," Mark said. "The Starvel Group."

Thierry forced a smile. "Their activities have never been straightforward."

"If you remember from earlier," Mark said, leaning over to identify five specific prints, presently sitting on Cardinal Utaka's lap, "these were also found in Gullet's safe."

The cardinal adjusted his glasses. The photos were of five single sheets of paper, mainly blank with the exception of writing on two lines in the centre of the document. On face value they concerned ordinary banking transactions: recording $4 million being transferred into one account and subsequently out into another one. Each receiving account was slightly different.

"What is this?" Utaka asked.

Mark: "This confirms that Gullet . . ."

"We do not know for sure that it is Gullet," Pessotto said. "The accounts are numbered."

"I checked, sir. I have a buddy at Starvel," Mark said. "Each one of them opened and closed by Ludovic Gullet. From what I can gather each payment was immediately sent on to another account and then immediately closed straight after."

Thierry and Pessotto both smiled.

Utaka looked anxiously at Mark. "So what does this mean?"

Mark: "It means that Ludovic Gullet has recently received five payments of $4 million for unknown reasons at infrequent intervals."

Cardinal Utaka was unconvinced. "What makes you sure this is not business related?"

"If it were then why does he not use his regular accounts?" Mark said, looking at Utaka, then Pessotto and Thierry. "We know from receipts that he hired a Jeep in Mauritius not six hours before the murder of Devére."

Utaka didn't respond. Pessotto nodded.

"A large sum of money entering a Starvel bank account and leaving it instantly clearly suggests that this was not meant to be seen," Pessotto said. "Particularly as the amount seems to occur on such a regular basis."

"Particularly as it's an unpublished account," Mark added.

"Where did the money come from?" Utaka asked.

"A numbered account that we have been unable to identify," Mark responded. "Never the same one. No clue of ownership other than the account is always with Starvel."

Utaka looked at Mark, a serious expression crossing his features. He paused to examine each of the prints, some more than once, as though trying to work out an algebraic equation. The pattern was recurring.

"What does this mean?" the cardinal asked.

"This is self-explanatory," Mark said.

"You really think he murdered them?"

"He may not have killed Leoni or Cardinal Faukes but it suggests he was involved."

Thierry nodded. "It seems Mr Gullet is at least partially responsible for all of them. Regardless of the reason."

Pessotto: "The possibility cannot be ruled out that Mr Martin Snow was murdered for connection in this."

Utaka cleared his throat. "May I offer another suggestion?"

Thierry nodded.

Utaka: "Based on the events of the past few days. The Knights Templar."

Pessotto breathed deeply.

Thierry shook his head. "The Knights Templar have been extinct for centuries."

Pessotto nodded. "I suggest we concentrate on the here and now."

Utaka looked at all present with a nervous expression. "The Vatican has a long history with the Rite of Larmenius. It has an even longer one with the Templars." He breathed in deeply. "Perhaps those rumours are true after all."

Mark shook his head. "Whoever they are, they must be willing to pay millions of dollars to eliminate the murdered men."

"It is not that what worries me," Utaka said. "There are people on this list who are still alive. This threat cannot be ignored."

Pessotto nodded. "I agree."

Utaka: "I want every person presently sitting on either committee of the Vatican Bank to be assigned security. And from now on, all business related to the bank takes place within the confines of the Apostolic Palace."

Pessotto and Thierry nodded.

"Good," the cardinal said.

"I spoke to Mike the other day. Henry Leoni helped me locate Mikael Devére's widow. We've finally made contact," Mark said. "She disappeared following her husband's murder. Scared stiff."

"Good. At least that way we might uncover what in God's name he had got himself into," Pessotto said.

"Gianluca," Cardinal Utaka said to Commissario Pessotto.

"Yes, eminence," he replied.

"Make sure you and Thierry do as I say. I want each member of the council under around-the-clock supervision."

"Yes, eminence."

41

Cambridge, Massachusetts

The Honourable Alexander Broadie was one of Harvard's most distinguished academics. Such a term was not to be banded around lightly, but even in this day and age his reputation spoke for itself. If reputations were to be formed on achievements rather than words then his may have been rather modest, but when coming from such famous lineage, other stuff could do the talking. Rumour had it he was a descendant of one of the great Scottish families, the St Clairs, whereas others claimed his ancestry also went back to Robert the Bruce. He had never been sure exactly where he came from but he never worried about correcting people who took the assumptions as accurate. It never did any good to downplay one's esteem; particularly when it was not easy to prove otherwise.

At least he looked like a distinguished academic. Not that a distinguished academic had a precise description but whatever it was, he was it. He wore an elegant brown tweed jacket with the stereotype elbow patches on either sleeve. He wore a tie despite the informality of the day – most of the students had already gone home for spring recess – smart black trousers and an expensive watch on his left wrist.

Perhaps he was once good-looking but that was now gone. His balding head, flanked by brown hair that was slowly beginning to turn white looked like a poorly attempted comb-over as it crossed in the middle. A pair of rimless bifocals sat perched upon his nose, suiting his face.

He may not have been good-looking in the classical sense but women still liked him. Perhaps it was an attraction to status that had earned him the approval of his wife, but equally the same approval of others that had twice nearly led to divorce. He had a history of preference for his female students, which was frowned on by those who knew, but discretion was a useful tool, particularly in such a prestigious location. Having a family pedigree brought approval, certainly in the eyes of those who mattered, but others clung to what he represented. He was an Ivy Leaguer, but one of a dying breed. His dress, his manner and even his general appearance was thirty years out of date. His reputation was one of an old campaigner. And old habits died hard.

His office was in keeping with his character. An antique globe sat atop a large ornate desk, in the manner of a Victorian study. Historical prints, charts and maps lined the walls of the office, located in the elegant Robinson Hall, the history faculty of Harvard. The fax machine and inkjet printer were neatly tucked away in the corner of the room while a modern sink was fitted neatly between two filing cabinets to the side of the door.

Broadie sat quietly at his desk, his eyes concentrating in the direction of the window. As he stared out across the Broadway stretch that was usually heaving with students making their way towards Harvard Yard, he smiled. It was sure peaceful with the students gone. Another seemingly endless term was at an end and there would be no more knocks on the door from disappointed students whinging about his overly harsh marking. This was the way he liked it. No marking, no students, and no distractions: no one to watch what he was doing.

The gentle chime of the elegant antique clock informed him it was two o'clock. He stretched in relaxed mood. With it came a gentle knock at the door.

Broadie turned around and looked up at the door.

"Come in."

The door opened and Henry Leoni entered breezily. A tweed jacket covered his torso and a brown briefcase hung from his right hand. There were no handshakes when they entered but not out of ill humour. Remaining seated, Broadie raised a glass of port to him.

"Straight out of Douro Valley, Henry. Ice and lemon?"

Henry laughed loudly. "Sir, I thank you."

Broadie placed ice into two glasses and raised his left hand to Henry with a showman pose. "Vintage stuff."

"I'd expect nothing less."

"Cigar?"

"Thank you."

Broadie removed two cigars from a brown container and leaned across the desk to light Henry's before doing the same to his own. Smoke swirled upward towards the ceiling and out through the open window.

"Have a seat, Henry."

If only their students could see them now. Like Broadie, Henry looked like an Ivy League professor, but Henry had always been more popular with his students. He enjoyed a drink; so did the students. He loved to joke; so did the students. All in all there was a likeable informality about Henry that won him affection. His beard and potbelly gave female students a certain teddy bear innocence feeling around him whereas Broadie was the opposite. Whereas Henry encouraged students to live life to the utmost what Broadie preached and what he did were often at loggerheads. A student entering one of his lectures hung over or skunked from the night before could be met with severe disapproval or even a firm dressing down whereas the opposite was true if he did it.

He returned to his seat.

"So, Henry," Broadie said, exhaling on his cigar, "how's life been treating you?"

"All things considered, Alex, I can't complain."

"I'm pleased to hear it," he said, continuing to smoke. "I've been meaning to have a wee chat. May I say how most sorry I was to hear about your brother."

Henry offered a sombre smile. "Thank you, Alex, I'm most grateful."

Broadie nodded. He decided to sidestep drawing further attention to Al Leoni's death.

"So, what's so big it couldn't wait?"

Suddenly the mood changed, almost as if a switch had been flicked. Henry's bearded face turned to a childlike smile. He leaned over the right hand armrest of the leather armchair and opened his briefcase. He removed a set of photocopies and handed them over the desk.

"I'm sure this is right up your street."

Broadie removed the cigar from his mouth and set it down on an ashtray in the centre of the desk, allowing ash to fall as it burned away from the tip. There was a photograph of his eldest daughter near the phone, dressed in graduation attire, standing alongside both him and his son.

Broadie accepted the photocopies from Henry and immediately began to scan them with interest. The images were largely of text, Italian handwriting, and as best he could tell written on some form of parchment. Making a note of the detail with his near photographic memory, he grabbed his glass of port with his right hand and touched it to his lips. The vintage taste was fine on his tongue. He swallowed it slowly, savouring the flavour.

"It's a shame you only brought copies, Henry," Broadie said, replacing his drink on the coaster.

"I thought it best to conserve the find itself. After all, we don't want these things to get damaged do we?"

Broadie looked up at Henry, reaching once more for his cigar. He looked at his old acquaintance through his glasses before returning his attention to the papers in front of him.

"No we do not," he agreed, placing the cigar to his lips. "Incredible, nevertheless! You say you discovered it recently?"

"Yes."

"I see. And the map?"

"In the diary."

"I see," Broadie said again, his focus on the photocopies. There was a casual manner about him, far more so than Henry remembered of him. The way he smoked and drank. It was almost as if he was high.

"So, may I ask how you came across all this?"

"No one place, Alex. Scattered fragments here and there."

Broadie smiled casually, realising it was unwise to pursue the matter. His gaze returned to the prints. "The Zichmni voyage is one of history's true grey areas. The Zeno letters are regarded by many as a hoax."

"And what do you believe, Alex?"

The Scot laughed loudly. "As you know I once wrote a book on it. My only bestseller."

"I remember."

Broadie held his smile, replacing his cigar with his port. "So you feel the location of the mysterious Frislanda has been revealed? And this diary achieves this?"

"This is, Alex, without question, exactly what many historians have long been looking for."

Broadie raised his eyebrows. The strength of the statement was profound. "Well, well, my friend. It sounds like you've done some good work."

"You'll notice the significance of the map, Alex. Just as the Drogeo legend goes."

Broadie looked down. A feeling of apprehension gripped him as he focused on the photocopy of the map with maximum interest. The text itself was not legible from the photocopy but this did nothing to detract from the scope of the find.

"Pay particular attention to the position of the knight," Henry said.

Broadie looked as closely as possible. In reality he would need the image to be blown up several times to know the location for sure.

"Looks like New England," he guessed. "Cape Cod?"

"Close. Newport, Rhode Island."

Broadie's eyes demonstrated complete interest. The potential effects of the find were magnificent. To think, after all these years concrete proof supporting the Zichmni legend was emerging. Perhaps even with connection to his kin. Whoever Zichmni was had passed that way.

"So what exactly are you looking for, Henry?"

Leoni paused. "Well, according to the diary, the surviving Templars built a round church there: a new Church of the Holy Sepulchre, so to speak. Of course, we don't really know much about this Zichmni or what happened to the outlawed Templars, do we?"

Broadie smoked, his expression pensive. "No. Okay, I see. Well I don't see what you're going to find in Rhode Island that you don't already know. Over the years hundreds of excavations have already taken place."

"Ah," Henry said. "But none of them had this."

Leoni leaned over the desk and handed Broadie another photocopy, this one of the diagram of the church. Henry drew attention to the presence of an underground vault beneath the tower.

Broadie examined the photocopy with intent. His heart missed a beat. A purple mist, accredited no doubt to the way it was captured by the Xerox, swarmed around the diagram almost like a halo.

"The Newport Tower?"

"That was my first inclination," Henry said, nodding.

Broadie paused, his focus intense. For several seconds he studied the diagram, paying close attention to the layout. Finally he nodded, practically smiling.

"This is incredible. If it's genuine."

Henry nodded, his eyes on his colleague. Silence followed, not awkward but still intense as Broadie allowed his mind time to digest the immensity of the find. This was why historians became historians. This was not necessarily the search for treasure but the search for truths long undiscovered, or, as the case may be, forgotten.

"I must admit when I came into possession of the first diary I never realised its true significance. But since the discovery of the rest . . ."

"So what do you ask of me, Henry?"

Henry shuffled in his seat, removing his cigar from his mouth. "From you, Alex? Nothing. Only a kind courtesy to use your influence with the good City of Newport to allow me permission to work on the city's estate."

Broadie exhaled with the cigar still fixed between his lips. An expression of hope and triumph disguised his true feelings.

"Henry, if you think you can pull this off . . ."

"I assure you I shall do my very best."

"I'll make a couple of calls."

"You can reach me in Boston."

Broadie ascended to his feet and shook hands with Henry, broad smiles crossing their features.

"Keep the copies," Henry said, walking towards the door. "Once we're through you might have another bestseller on the cards."

For over thirty minutes Gabrielle had sat quietly in the rear passenger seat of her uncle's 4x4, gazing aimlessly at the surroundings. The windows on either side of the car offered sparse relief from the cramped conditions. It was exceptionally muggy for the time of day, and the time of year. The interior of the SUV was luxurious, but it was hardly what she was used to. Several weeks of being chauffeured around by her guard, who was currently dozing in the front passenger seat, had left her complacent. Yet she loved driving: particularly 4x4s across dirty terrain. Her last boyfriend had been a touring car driver and that was the appeal, not that it lasted.

Sitting quietly in the parked car currently located on Broadway outside Robinson Hall, she watched the campus for activity, or, as the case was here, the lack of it. She remembered from life at Dartmouth the hustle and bustle of life at Ivy League.

But today was different. The campus, normally heaving with brainiacs and 'gifted' students strutting or ambling across campus to the buildings of various faculties, now delivered an eerie silence almost reminiscent of a small city following a nuclear holocaust. As she gazed across the deserted streets she couldn't help feel she was being watched, although that was nothing new of late. The faint wind rustling through the green leaves of the trees, the echo of an empty coke can trickling along the concrete street, even the squawking of birds overhead left her nervous.

She looked in front of her and saw Mike was looking through the passenger side window, ever vigilant despite the lack of threat. He had been on the computer until 3 a.m. She had heard him: not because he was loud, but sleeping had become difficult since the day of the attack. He suggested she take tablets, she refused. Her uncle suggested seeing the doctor, she refused. Rachel suggested they go away together.

Maybe next year.

She yawned but still felt awake, her anxiety at fever pitch as she awaited the return of her uncle. She looked at Mike, yawning loudly. She giggled as he inhaled.

"What?"

She shook her head. "Nothing."

Mike watched her, following her eyes before looking away. He had seen her smile more since their return. Something had definitely changed. To him it was an honest smile: one that after his first night at the château he thought he would never see.

Yet somehow it was one he had seen before, many times, if only subconsciously.

The front door to Robinson opened. The heavy frame swung backwards and forwards in the breeze before coming to a stop against the weight of the other door, closed on its hinges. Henry walked briskly towards the car.

The Harvard professor took a seat on the driver's side and smiled at Gabrielle as he entered. She looked at him apprehensively, as if waiting for an exam result or worse. The feeling of the campus brought back memories of a history exam in her sophomore year. She was certain she had failed it. Sure enough she had passed easily. Yet the not knowing was vastly worse than the result.

"Well?"

"Well what?" Henry said with a smile.

"Uncle Henry, come on."

Henry shook his head, an act of pretence. For several seconds the look in his eyes was one of uncertainty and disappointment. Then the academic began to beam.

"He said he'd have to make a couple of calls but he didn't see a problem."

"Oh, Uncle Henry that's awesome." Gabrielle hugged him. A warm sense of gratitude overcame her, aimed at the man who her uncle had just visited.

Mike, meanwhile, leaned back against the headrest, forcing a smile. Inside he felt nervous. It didn't do well to tempt fate.

As he looked up through the tinted sunroof of the car, the sun seemed to dance on the glass as if it were light hitting the ocean. He thought of what the Templar church might look like, if it even existed. He thought of the darkness of Rosslyn, surely an omen or portent of what might exist in another vault.

Slowly he closed his eyes.

42

Washington, D.C.

At forty-six years of age, Tamie Louise Jacobs was the youngest of the seven governors currently serving on the board of the Federal Reserve. The only independent in office, she was one of only two women, and following the death of Jermaine Llewellyn, she was the only black.

Despite her relative youth, Jacobs was now the second longest serving governor of the Federal Reserve. When nominated to become a governor five years earlier, no one really knew what to make of her. The first black woman on the board was itself a talking point in what was traditionally a white man's domain, and while her predecessor was just that, the initial assumption in some quarters that she was a staunch feminist had yet to find solid ground. Before coming to office her skills were company law, first as a lawyer, rising to partner, at three firms in New York, and later six years in the Attorney General of New York's office, rising to Deputy General where she acted on numerous occasions before the Supreme Court. Her speciality was anti-competition and that eventually caught favour with both former Chairman Randy Lewis and the President of the United States when choosing to replace Eddie McGoldrick of Boston as a governor of the Federal Reserve.

Jacobs was still in her office at seven that evening, her head firmly planted over a large document, as it had been almost continuously for the last four hours. At just after seven-fifteen a gentle knock at the door stole her attention. She looked up from her work and invited the visitor to come in. Her facial expression turned to one of surprise as she looked upon the face of her former colleague. Dressed in a silver suit, perfectly matching his hair, Randy Lewis smiled from the doorway.

She removed her gold-framed reading glasses, putting the tip to her lips and looked at him with fake malice.

"Why of all the nerve . . ."

Lewis laughed as he walked towards her. "Tamie, you look wonderful."

Jacobs placed her glasses on the desk and rose to her feet. Her rigid expression turned to a smile as she walked towards Lewis with open arms. Formality consisted of a kiss on both cheeks, but they kissed once and hugged. For several seconds they both smiled widely. She offered Lewis a seat and asked about his family. Lewis followed, asking meaningless questions about husband, wife, kids and banter.

Of all of his former colleagues, Tamie Jacobs was his favourite. Unlike the other governors, her independent status left her free of the Republican and Democrat ideals and that in turn allowed her to act without discrimination. Although in the early days she was kicked from both sides, he knew she was never one to allow herself to be beaten. The first eighteen months were the most difficult, and after two years in office she was accepted as part of the furniture. It was no surprise when he turned on the news one morning to learn that she would be serving as Llewellyn's Vice Chair.

For over five minutes they reacquainted, talk centring mostly on family, before their conversation faded to awkward silence. A strange feeling overcame her as she looked Lewis in the eye. She remembered him as a workaholic but there was an obvious tiredness in his eyes, yet strangely different from what she remembered. Despite being her former boss their relationship had always been one of friendship rather than professional courtesy.

"So what brings you back home?" Jacobs asked. "You know Hans just loves it when you drop by."

Lewis laughed. "So what else is new?"

"You back on vacation?"

"I'm never on vacation, Tamie – you know that."

"Ain't that the truth? So it's business then?"

"Kinda."

"You're not pissing in someone's pool are you?"

"Actually, Tamie, I'm taking one in my own."

"I don't think Cardinal Tepilo will like that," she said, accompanied by the briefest of cheeky smiles.

Lewis folded his arms and scanned the walls of her office. Whereas other governors made their walls a mark of honour to their degrees and qualifications, Tamie Jacobs was a refreshing change. Instead of degrees, awards and diplomas, she covered hers with photographs of her children when they were children, and her eldest daughter graduating high school. Standing either side of her daughter were the beaming parents. Randy had never met her husband but he could tell from the photo he would like him. He faced the camera with a beaming smile and thumbs up. Facially he looked like one of the singers from Boyz II Men.

"So what can I do for you?"

Lewis breathed in deeply as he pondered his options. He chose his words carefully.

"What do you know about Leoni et Cie?"

Jacobs sat back in her chair. A confused expression crossed her face.

"Well, they're a bank from Switzerland: one of the rising hot shots on the global scene; market capital well in excess of $6 billion; worldwide assets of over $70 billion; listed on the SMI in the mid-90s, formerly controlled by the Leoni family until their recent sale to the Vatican Bank who are now the majority shareholder and, last I heard, had made you their new chief executive."

Lewis nodded.

"Why are you asking me?" Jacobs asked.

Lewis grimaced. Distinguished wrinkled lines on his forehead seemed deep and thoughtful. The lines seemed a permanent feature, equally on par with a thick side parting which had not receded a centimetre.

"I was looking through Leoni's accounts recently and found this," he said, removing a small folded document from the inside of his jacket pocket and passing it to Jacobs. "And that's just one of them."

"What is it?" she asked, replacing her glasses.

Lewis grimaced again, unsure where to start. "Leoni et Cie has many irregularities."

Jacobs looked back with interest.

"How have you found them? How did they come up in recent audits?"

Jacobs shrugged. "Fine, as far as I'm aware; at least as far as America is concerned. It's not within our jurisdiction to see for other countries."

"I'm well aware of that, Tamie. I was only in office for fourteen years."

With that she smiled. For a second she forgot whom she was dealing with. She missed the days when he had acted as chairman before being replaced by Jermaine Llewellyn. Both men were of the same mould. Both taught many of the other governors much of what they knew and they in turn passed it on.

"Who audited the firm itself?" Lewis asked.

"As far as I'm aware it was delivered by GPLA from the Charlotte office and all was normal. In comparison to the size of other banks it was hardly important. Leoni is only about the fortieth largest in the States all considered."

She eyed him closely.

"Do you mind telling me what this is all about?"

Lewis hesitated. Looking into her brown eyes he could tell that he could trust her.

"Leoni et Cie has a large number of unpublished accounts, even for a Swiss Bank. In fact, they have far more than I've ever seen for a firm that size. What's more, they have far too many unpublished accounts with Starvel AG."

Jacobs removed her glasses and put the tip to her lips. Her golden earrings, hanging like lampshades from her ears, swayed slightly below her neatly combed ponytail. "Most banks have unpublished accounts with Starvel AG, Randy. You know that. That's what Starvel AG is for. It's a clearing bank."

"Not like this."

"I thought you knew Leoni et Cie inside out."

Lewis shook his head. "Not really, only what I did with the Vatican Bank. I was good buddies with Al Leoni, but in recent years Leoni did very little. It was mainly de Bois and his managers who ran the show."

Jacobs rested her chin on her hands. "You don't trust him?"

Another shake of the head. "What do you know about de Bois?"

Jacobs turned her hands over. The rings on her fingers dazzled as sunlight shone through the gaps in the drapes. "I've only met de Bois once. All I know is that he's one shit-hot businessman. Attracts money better than Midas. But you know him better than me. What was he like at Starvel and Rosco?"

"Never really did much at Starvel. He was involved more in the PR side than the AG area. He left, then it was mainly Velis."

"You ordered an investigation into their dealings once."

"That was different."

"In what way?"

Lewis pondered a response. "Starvel as a complete organisation are a monster. If they were left to their own devises they would have been a . . ."

"Big monster."

Lewis laughed. "Yeah. The kind that cooks you up real nice and eats you with pasta."

Jacobs smiled inquisitively. "So there was nothing in those rumours back in '99 then?"

"That alone was never an issue of the present ownership, although the old Starvel has been in the Velis family a long time. And bearing in mind Starvel AG is a part of the Starvel Group I'm not prepared to gamble. I'm sure you've heard about the trouble we've been having."

Jacobs nodded sombrely. "Good news travels fast, Randy."

Lewis grimaced. He still didn't know exactly what was troubling him, but it was there, eating away at him. Something he had stumbled over sometime during the distant past: during his tenure, perhaps even before.

"So what's the real problem, Randy?"

"Call it a hunch."

"Uh oh!" she replied. "When you get hunches stockbrokers start jumping from windows."

"Tell me about it."

Jacobs looked directly at Lewis, considering her response. There was a certain distance to him, not unfamiliar but not in keeping with his usual self either. When Chairman of the Fed he rarely looked like a man who carried the weight of the world on his shoulders but this was a different sort of pressure. It seemed almost personal.

"Personally, I feel that Leoni's performance may not be as strong as it appears. I've been over the accounts time and again and there are holes that can't be accounted for," Lewis said. "As I say, there are far too many unpublished, and even unallocated, accounts, some of which go back to the original Rosco."

He hesitated before continuing.

"What do you know about the GREEN Foundation?"

Jacobs laughed. "Now there's a humdinger." She left her seat and walked across the room towards a large file cabinet. She removed a file labelled classified from a middle drawer and passed it to Lewis. "Only because it's you."

Lewis looked with interest at the file.

"Apparently he put the foundation together with help from retired venture capitalists. A great capital base to begin with."

Lewis nodded. "I've seen some of the accounts myself. De Bois is very active there. Al Leoni and the board at Leoni recently granted de Bois over $40 million of corporate loans, yet his other businesses have paid over $70 million to GREEN in the past two years. What's even stranger is that GREEN is unlike any foundation I've ever come across: it has links with countless other companies, particularly banks. Now call me crazy, but I think it's nothing more than a special purpose entity deliberately put forward by de Bois to act as a subsidiary for Leoni et Cie, and perhaps others, for accounting purposes. What's more, many of the people connected with GREEN have strong links with the Rite of Larmenius."

The Vice Chair of the Federal Reserve eyed him closely. "I thought you said the rumours weren't valid."

"They aren't, but they're hardly the kind of people I'd trust with a company affiliated with the Catholic Church."

Jacobs raised her eyebrows. At that moment Rudolph Kodovski walked past the door with Schumer, a file in one hand and a cup of coffee in the other.

"Well, I'll be. Now he's making his coffee."

Lewis turned back to face Jacobs whose expression had become more serious.

"There are other things as well," Lewis continued. "Last time I saw de Bois he was talking about Leoni et Cie spreading its wings, opening branches in South America, Asia, et cetera – hell there were places he mentioned I'd never even heard of . . ." Lewis paused momentarily. "But going through the accounts Leoni et Cie has over sixty branches more than I realised: most of them are in the last places anyone would even think of opening a bank."

He paused again.

"Tamie, this may sound way outta leftfield . . ."

Jacobs raised her eyebrows.

"Tams, I have a real nasty feeling that de Bois has been using Rosco and since the merger Leoni et Cie to launder for the Rite of Larmenius."

Jacobs was concerned. "I don't like the sound of that," she said. "But from what I've seen from GPLA, the bank is fine."

Lewis nodded.

"And remember who you're dealing with, mister. If something was going on, I'd know."

An awkward smile reached his lips. "Well thank you, Tams, I won't bother you with this any longer."

Both rose to their feet. He hugged her goodbye and sought to leave. Preparing to exit, she called for him.

"Yo, Randy."

"Yeah."

"When have you ever been wrong about a hunch?"

Lewis shrugged. "I'd say never."

Sitting alone in his prestigious office, the new Chairman of the Federal Reserve, Hans Schumer, picked up the phone and dialled. He waited several seconds for it to connect. Finally a man answered.

"It's Schumer here. Something big's come up."

43

The New Temple of Solomon

No ceremony took place on this occasion: the high intensity of the last gathering was replaced by a more urgent and volatile atmosphere, out of keeping with the religious surroundings. The hidden location consisting of mock medieval cloisters in the basement of the bearded man's lavish colonial summer mansion, out of reach of the average man, serious and foreboding in appearance, was curiously offset by the breezy fragrance of lemon accompanied by the melodious sound of Beethoven's symphony #5 in C minor, op 67 – 3 allegro that drifted through the seemingly endless passage. Once again the curious idols stood forlorn on the altar, reflecting the light of two ornamental candles.

For now, only six were present. D'Amato sat quietly, looking out of boredom at a copy of the *Washington Post* on the table in front of him.

Two seats along, the French Preceptor, Gilbert de Bois, sat dressed in a silver suit, his face partially concealed by the shadows. The seat opposite him, where the Swiss Preceptor normally sat, was empty and would remain so. The seat belonging to the Scot was also empty.

Parker and Klose were present, as was the Sénéchal, sitting in his usual seat at the far end of the table. The features of the ageing Italian second-in-command were still and stubborn. Not for the first time at one of these meetings he seethed with contempt, something that he was unable, if not unwilling, to hide.

Directly opposite the Italian, the bearded man sat patiently. They had been sitting in silence for nearly twenty minutes but his posture suggested he was relaxed. A bright orange glow briefly lighted up the room as he smoked his cigar and exhaled slowly, creating rings of smoke that rose towards the ceiling before vanishing into the darkness where an unlit light bulb hung.

Six hours ago they had all received word that an emergency meeting was to be called. In this world an emergency was just that and all emergencies needed dealing with immediately and efficiently.

And all emergencies must remain private.

Sounds from the floor above ended the silence. Reverberations, sounding like footfalls, resonated loudly, identifying direction and pace. The heaviness suggested running and running suggested urgency.

The door leading to the stairs opened. A brief shuffling followed by the sound of echoing on the stairs confirmed the latecomer was approaching. At the bottom of the stairs the sound of footsteps stopped. Out of the darkness a figure appeared, his features partially concealed in the poor light. He walked slowly towards the table, crossing the black and white floor as he had done at least a hundred times before.

All eyes were on the Scottish Preceptor as he took his seat without nerves or guilt. No words were said but eyes and facial expressions did the talking. The Italian's face seemed somehow more red than usual as the light of the candles reflected off the various glasses lining the table, illuminating the lines on his forehead that seemed indescribably vicious in the poor light.

As yet no one spoke. The beautiful sound of Beethoven remained the only sound, its soothing melody filling the seemingly endless room. It was not physically endless, but endless in terms of possibility. Soon another key moment in the history of the New World would be decided by these men.

The bearded man left his seat and walked across the tiled floor towards a small stereo, hidden from sight on a small table. He removed the cigar from his mouth, smoke rising in all directions. With one press of the middle finger of his left hand the room fell silent.

In that split second time seemed to linger, almost as though they were disconnected from the wider reality. The airiness of the room somehow seemed to have vanished and the darkness seemed almost tangible. The cloisters, almost in keeping with that of a monastery in setting, now seemed more like a desolate and foreboding dungeon from which there was no escape.

The bearded Grand Master returned to his seat, the echo of his footsteps giving way to the sound of wood scraping against the hard floor as he inched closer to the table. He exhaled once again on his cigar. For the briefest of moments the end lit up his face as if he were Belial emerging from the depths of hell before vanishing inexplicably back into the void from where he had come. He eyed every member in turn but as yet no one spoke. Alert eyes focused on the head of the table.

"Well," the bearded man said to the Scot, his concentration total. "It seems that you were correct after all."

The Italian studied his superior. This was not the usual passage of play. Mind games had become customary for these critical games of chess but the mutual courtesies were rare. When one bombarded the other the other retorted. Words would fly from either side and both would always get burned with the Sénéchal forever infuriated at another's shortcoming. For him it was maddening: but this was the price for his involvement with the Church. He was a pilgrim in an unholy land. And for a place of pilgrimage, the setting had all the key ingredients of a passage from Dante.

"You seem to be forgetting that the key points of history are still to be resolved," the Italian said. "Even for us."

"Yes," the bearded man said, rising to his feet. He walked slowly around the table as if he were a shark encircling his prey. "Thank you."

The bearded man moved closer to the Scot. "Alex, please describe to the council, in your own words, what these photocopies looked like."

Alexander Broadie cleared his throat quietly, causing him to hesitate slightly. "There was no mistake. They were clearly of pages included in a diary once written by Antonio Zeno."

The bearded man nodded. "Excellent," he said calmly. He flicked ash from his cigar into the ashtray before Parker and walked slowly in the same direction.

D'Amato shuffled in his chair, his eyes on the Grand Master. Of all present his historical knowledge was the most limited.

"So what's all this have to do with anything?" the American asked. "I thought all the Templar loot had been found."

"Loot, ay. We're not speaking of pirate treasure, old boy," the Englishman said.

The bearded man looked at both men in turn.

"That may be true of the cargo that went to Switzerland," the bearded man said, still smoking, "salvaged by men thanks to whom our organisation survived. It was from that the great banking network was born."

The Italian watched the Grand Master closely, turning his attention towards D'Amato. "Perhaps it is difficult for someone such as yourself to appreciate the problems of our ancestors."

D'Amato smiled. Not this horseshit again. He always spoke like that: ancestors and stuff. The Scot was just as bad. He spoke as if he knew them. Or he was descended from them: a prince or lord or something.

"Well why don't you explain?" he asked.

The bearded man made eye contact with the American. He inhaled on his cigar, the end lighting up the room like a flame from a fire, before blowing out smoke in all directions. "The plight of our ancestors is not recorded in any history book . . ."

"Except this one," Broadie interrupted.

The bearded man eyed him curiously, walking slowly. He walked with arrogance, each stride an act of purpose that carried an air of dominance unrivalled by any other man in the wider world.

"Yes," he said, smiling briefly. A pensive expression dominated his face. "Following the dissolution of the first Temple that left many thousands of our brethren homeless, wanted men, some fled to the mountains to lay the foundation of the Swiss banking system."

"Like yours?" D'Amato asked.

The bearded man exhaled. "Precisely."

D'Amato smiled as the Grand Master continued to walk and smoke: he smoked elegantly, making him appear noble. He stopped momentarily between Gilbert de Bois and the Sénéchal to tip ash into the ashtray before returning the cigar to his mouth.

"While some indeed made their home among the mountains of Switzerland, many other members, rich in spirit but poor in wealth, went to Scotland where they defeated the English at Bannockburn. The new order in its purest form."

He looked at Broadie when he said those words. Purest form: it had a nice ring to it. What did it mean to be pure? Perhaps being a direct descendant; he was that. Perhaps being chosen represented it; he was also that. With both he could appreciate it. And that made him appear distinguished.

"Following this, some went to the New World. Lead by your ancestor no less," the bearded man continued.

"Prince Henry Sinclair," the Scot said.

"Zichmni," the Englishman said.

The bearded man continued to walk and smoke. "And that, of course, is why we are here."

He said the last bit slower than before as if he were calculating a possibility in his mind: as if plotting the latest move of his opponent before making his own. He walked over to the altar and placed his hand on a large chronicle.

"The foundation of our very being."

A brief pause followed, one the Italian found unsettling.

"Where was the diary found?" the Italian asked.

"He did not say," Broadie said. "But based on recent events I would think it fair to presume that it is the same book found by his niece in the secret archive of the Vatican. And it would appear that there are two books. One of which I believe to have once been in the possession of our former Sénéchal."

D'Amato looked at the Scot with dismay, his arms folded. "I always said I never trusted him."

The bearded man nodded. "It appears you were correct."

De Bois shook his head. "Our order has continued to survive for over seven hundred years in secret. If we are to survive it will be necessary to conceal fragments of clues."

The Scot shook his head. "That name tells them nothing."

"Baphomet," the Italian said.

Broadie did not answer.

Klose also smoked, his facial expression suggesting no interest. "What good is the diary? Even if proof is found of the Zichmni voyage it still doesn't prove anything. What good is a key if people don't know what door it opens?"

"Who said anything about doors?" the Scot said. "The map of the Zenos is well known to us. I have spent the last twenty years researching it myself."

"But what good are Frislanda and Drogeo to the outside world? As far as the people know the world is made up only of what exists on an atlas!" Klose said.

"Ah, but they do," Broadie said. "Deutschland, Germany, Allemagne: the same country by three names."

"And what say you of these fantasies?" the Italian asked, his expression stern. "What say you?"

Broadie shook his head. "I say nothing. The location of Newport has always been important to this order. We know that ourselves. We, too, have seen that with our own eyes."

The Englishman watched with uncertainty, the subject of the conversation transcending his expertise. The bearded man nodded, otherwise neglecting to reply. Taking a couple of steps towards the light he put the cigar to his mouth, perching it between his lips. Removing a lighter from his trouser pocket he flicked the wheel with his right thumb and put the flame to the cigar, reigniting the dying fire. He allowed himself a smile.

Private matters do not remain secret in the wrong hands.

Broadie sat silently as if he were under a jinx. Eyes were fixed on him, gazes of judgment, ill deserved and firmly directed. Their expressions suggested it was his fault. An answer was staring him dead in the face, shining like a beacon, almost blinding to look upon.

"Our former Sénéchal once owned the diary," the Grand Master said finally. "Now the diary has found its way back."

Silence filled the room. The bearded man eyed all present.

"The survivors of the original Knights Templar founded a colony at what is now Newport, Rhode Island, as they sought to escape the brutality of their persecutors. For six centuries we have known this. What knowledge our ancestors inherited was passed on to us. But the legacy of our predecessors did not exist in gold and silver. And heaven knows we have enough of that."

Laughter echoed around the room.

"Our legacy is more than money," the bearded man said.

"In the wrong hands this diary could ruin everything," de Bois said.

"For over five centuries our legacy has remained secret from the wider world; we know of its value, yet even we, the present Knights Templar, do not know all of the secrets of the past," the bearded man said, continuing to smoke. "If the manuscript is really that once owned by Antonio Zeno then the location of Rosslyn was obvious."

"Which we have already seen," Broadie added.

The bearded man nodded. "The voyage of Zichmni is legendary. If they indeed discovered the vaults of Rosslyn, then there is reason to believe that they successfully found the next piece of the puzzle. If the map is correct then Professor Leoni's reason for suspecting Newport is obvious. This is indeed a dangerous trail."

The Sénéchal shook his head. "I tell you, you are wasting your time. The Vatican have already heightened security following the mistakes of your Swiss Preceptor. We must proceed with more important matters."

The American's expression was rigid. "It seems your compassion on the matter clouds your judgment, eminence."

The cardinal eyed the American with malice. "To uncover the secrets of Zichmni uncovers history; none of this concerns the present. To succeed, they would still need to discover a way into the vault. It would take a miracle. I tell you the Leonis know nothing."

The bearded man walked. Smoke escaped from his mouth, rising towards the ceiling. "For over six hundred years our order has continued the traditions of long ago: we all know it, and we accept it. It was thanks to the bravery of our predecessors that led to our continuation. Such a miracle took time. The secrets of banking have been passed on – as have many other things. The knowledge that made the original Temple so great: true wisdom long since forgotten. But the vault at Newport is a dangerous place – particularly for those who know nothing of how to get in or out. Gentlemen, you ask me for miracles: I give you Professor Henry Leoni."

Broadie nodded, a worried expression crossing his face. The Sénéchal joined his hands together and shook his head.

The bearded man returned to his seat, his eyes fixed on Broadie. "Do what you need to do. Tell the good professor he can investigate, and that he has our very best of wishes."

Broadie nodded, his facial expression awkward.

"But enough of ancient legends," the Grand Master said, "our concern is not with the past. For over six hundred years the Poor Knights of Solomon have sought to right the wrongs of history. The empires that opposed us have crumbled and now only one remains. This, gentlemen, is where our concerns must lie. Less than four hours ago I received a phone call from Mr Schumer telling me that one of his fellow governors happened to receive a recent visit from former Chairman Lewis. Apparently the new chief executive of Leoni et Cie seemed quite interested in some unpublished accounts."

De Bois's fist hit the table. "Fool. Why didn't you say?"

"Such a discovery could be devastating in the wrong hands," the German said.

The Grand Master smoked. "You are quite right to react this way. I will contact Monsieur Gullet this evening. Our concentration lies with other matters."

44

Mauritius

Mark rang the doorbell of the luxury villa that overlooked the perfect blue sea and waited patiently for a response. The six-hour journey along the bumpy road had left him tired, but at least he had avoided getting dust on his clothes. The meeting he had come for was potentially invaluable and the last thing he wanted was to devalue it.

An elegant red-haired woman answered the door. She seemed different to what he expected, but she was definitely the woman he wanted to see. He recognised her from her years in the public eye but he was surprised just how small she was in real life: he estimated less than five feet two inches. The woman was dressed mainly in black, accompanied by a heavy pearl necklace that hung around her neck and silver earrings from her ears. She was not unattractive, particularly for a woman of sixty-nine. Countless facelifts had left her able to pass for fifteen years younger. She was thin but fine boned and graceful in manner and appearance. Her hair, possibly a wig or otherwise dyed and styled, was red and curly and in keeping with her brown eyes partially hidden behind tinted glasses. She was revered in her profession as something of a goddess and silently he was quite daunted by her.

"Mrs Devére," he said to the former actress.

"Yes."

"My name is Markus Mäder. We spoke on the telephone."

She looked at him, judging him. Mark, meanwhile, focused on her. At first glance her persona was that of a glamour icon but the façade was blown on closer inspection, particularly around the arms and neck. There was a visible sadness about her, as one might expect of the recently widowed. She offered her hand, which Mark gently shook: cracks in her skin became more obvious.

"Well, come in."

Mark followed her into the hallway, wiping his feet on the welcome mat. He surveyed the interior as he walked and made a mental note of the surroundings. He was aware that this was the building where Devére had been murdered and any possible clue could be vital, even though the crime scene had long since been cleared.

Awkwardly, he followed. The actress continued into a spacious living room with white walls and furniture that reflected the light. She pointed at a two-person couch.

"Sit won't you."

Mark forced a smile. For the first time he noticed her voice was huskier than it had been in her heyday: brought on no doubt from age and her habit of thirty cigarettes a day. He thanked her and took a seat opposite a second couch, gripping his hands together thoughtfully.

Despite the luxury surroundings, he felt uncomfortable. Although he was used to interviewing relatives of victims or even victims of crimes themselves, it was the part of the job he hated the most. Since he had joined the Vatican Police it had become a rarity, and this was the first time he had ever had to interview someone famous. In many ways it was easier to interview the scumbags. In his experience interviewing relatives was never easy. He was surprised that she was so welcoming, but experience taught him that the polite ones were usually the most vulnerable.

Mrs Devére walked into the adjoining kitchen and returned with a collection of biscuits, tea and coffee and a large box of Belgian chocolates. Although he was not in need of refreshment, he accepted a coffee out of courtesy and took it without milk or sugar. When offered a smoke he declined. Offered something to eat he declined. When asked if he required anything else he declined.

Mikael Devére's widow took a seat opposite Mark on a three-person couch and instantly lit a cigarette. She looked at him briefly, her gaze vaguely provocative. Mark watched her for several seconds, all the while remaining silent. In his mind he rehearsed his first question.

"Thank you so much for agreeing to see me."

Although seemingly oblivious to the comment she nodded. Smoke left her mouth like a chimney, partially through her nose.

"So, you say you're a Swiss Guard," she said, adjusting her position in her seat and crossing her legs. The angle of her skirt revealed several inches of stocking.

"I'm an investigator for the Vatican Police."

"I never knew Mikael knew any Swiss Guards."

Mark grimaced a smile, not knowing what else to do. As he looked across the room he noticed that much of the furniture was dated, though it suited the woman's character. It was like he had stepped into one of her movies from the '60s.

"So," she said, exhaling smoke. "What can I do for you?"

Mark contemplated his first move. He considered his words extra carefully. This was no ordinary investigation. This was the widow of the former President of France.

"Mrs Devére, if you don't mind I'd like to ask you a few questions about your husband?"

"I've already told the police everything I know. I really don't know what further help I can be."

Mark nodded, forcing a smile. This was clearly an honest answer.

"Well, I was hoping we could focus on your husband's activities in the days before he died."

She shrugged. "They were nothing unusual. Mikael lived a busy life. As I told you, I don't see what I can tell you that I haven't told the police already."

Mark nodded. She seemed determined to underline the point. Was she being evasive or genuinely unsure?

He paused briefly. "I understand he had been travelling recently?"

He was pleased with his wording.

"Mikael was a busy man. He was always up to something. You know what you men are like. Business, business, business."

"Did your husband have many business interests?"

Diana Devére shook her head. "Not really – although he was never short of offers. He knew lots of people; everyone wanted to know him. That's what happens when you're President of France."

She paused briefly.

"Most of his activities were charity related."

Mark nodded, no surprises, not yet. "Is there anything in particular he had been involved in recently? Anything new perhaps?"

"Not really." She moved forward, her attention on the Belgian chocolates. "Do help yourself."

He forced a smile. "How would you describe your husband's relationship with other people? Did he have any close friends? Away from politics?"

"Mikael was a likeable man. Most of his social engagements were with similar people."

Mark nodded. Hopefully he might find an opportunity.

"Do you know these people? Did he ever mention any names? Any companies?"

"Maybe. But I never took an interest in that, boys and their toys."

"Was your husband a member of any fraternities or societies? Attend dinners et cetera?"

"A couple."

"What can you tell me about his relationship with the Rite of Larmenius?"

She shrugged. "Nothing really. He was always receiving invites, but mostly he declined. He used to be a Mason but that was a long time ago. Once a year he would meet with that silly ski club."

He eyed her closely, his neutral expression hiding his true feelings. "Do you personally know any of their members?"

She laughed loudly. "They say anyone who's anyone is a member . . ." she exhaled extravagantly and looked him up and down. "So you say you're a Swiss Guard?"

Mark considered her first statement. Perhaps all of them were members?

"Did your husband spend much time in their company? Did he attend lodges? Did he spend time with any of their members outside of the society?"

She shook her head again. "I don't go in for all that rubbish."

The ageing actress and supermodel shot another glance at Mark, this time more seductive than before. She blew smoke towards the ceiling.

"Are you sure you won't have a smoke?"

Mark shook his head, his eyes focused on the floor. Her movies and photo shoots confirmed she had been a stunner in her day. He felt sudden pity for the widow.

"I feel it's important to identify your husband's exact activities before he died. Perhaps that way we might be able to identify who could have known where he was." He paused again. "Is this location known to any of his acquaintances?"

She left her seat and poured a clear alcoholic liquid into a glass. "Enough of the past," she waved a drink at him. "Are you sure you won't join me?"

"No. Thank you."

She looked back disappointed.

Mark hesitated briefly, contemplating his next move. "Mrs Devére."

"Diana."

Mark forced a smile. "Your husband made contact with me four days after Al Leoni and Jermaine Llewellyn were murdered. He was most insistent that their deaths had been decreed by members of the

Rite of Larmenius; furthermore, he suggested that the same people had murdered many other men, including, I must add, two key Vatican officials," he said, taking a breather to allow her to digest the information. "How could he have known this?"

"I assure you I don't know."

Mark bit his lip. "How would you describe his behaviour in the week before he died? Anything unusual? Was he excessively worried?"

"Not that I noticed."

"Is there anything else you can think of that may be able to assist us. Any reason you can think of as to why someone may have wanted to kill your husband?"

Devére blew smoke violently. "I think the markings on the wall of his study confirm the culprits, Mr Mäder. He was the President of France, deary. Or perhaps you had forgotten?"

He looked her in the eye and relented. He was getting nowhere: he was getting nowhere fast.

Mark nodded, forcing an acknowledging smile. "Well thank you for your time."

He rose to his feet and sought to leave.

"He was writing his autobiography," she said quickly. "Before he died. It was due for publication next spring. I can show you if you like."

His eyes focused on the Frenchman's widow. She was holding the box of Belgian chocolates in her hands.

"Chocolate?"

He took one and nodded.

"I found a printed version in his safe. Lord knows how it got there. Come. I'll show you to his study."

45

Newport, Rhode Island

The silver hatchback pulled up in an empty parking bay in a car park just off Pelham Street in the City of Newport, Rhode Island. Henry Leoni was the first to exit, leaving through the driver's side door, closing it behind him. Mike was the second to depart followed, finally, by Gabrielle. Mike eyed Gabrielle as he opened the rear right door for her, before diverting his attention to the surrounding area.

The car, a silver E-Class Mercedes-Benz, was one of only five cars parked in the car park, situated across the road from the tree-lined Touro Park to the north. The area to the west and south comprised largely of housing, relatively modern in nature, while an ageing building, now belonging to a private club, was located several yards to the east, apparently closed and devoid of any signs of life.

Henry led the way, heading north towards Pelham Street. He looked both ways before crossing it, followed closely by Mike and Gabrielle, heading in the direction of Touro Park. There was a slight chill in the air, not unpleasant but enough to warrant a jacket. It was not yet raining but the sky above was overcast, threatening anything from steady drizzle to a heavy shower.

Despite the weather it was quiet, surprisingly quiet, even for a Wednesday morning. High above them several seagulls flew in circular motions over the nearby harbour, their cries echoing almost endlessly as they reflected down over the walls of historic buildings below. To their right, at the corner of Pelham, Bellevue Avenue was largely deserted bar the occasional passing car heading south towards the shopping centre or north to where Bellevue Avenue merged with Kay Street, continuing in the direction of Green End Pond.

Although it was early April and the tourist season was still to hit its height, the city's numerous historical inns and guest houses were open for trade, their car parks lined with motors of all sorts, usually belonging to single businessmen in town for meetings, or retired married couples soaking up the sites of Newport's colonial past in peaceful solitude before being run out of town by the mass onslaught of holidaymakers throughout the months of summer and the fall.

Across Bellevue, the Redwood Library and Athenaeum appeared gloomy in the dull light, its four pillars presenting an elegant façade in the style of an ancient Greek temple, while the nearby Newport Art Museum was frequented with locals and tourists alike walking its corridors respectfully, examining the impressive legacy of some of New England's finest artists. Despite the cloud, the city's picturesque harbour was decorated with elegant white sails as boat owners enjoyed a peaceful morning on the calm waters preparing their boats for the sailing season ahead.

Henry led the way east along Pelham Street before turning left and entering Touro Park. A long pathway headed north-west from the south-east entrance, passing a statue of Newport hero Matthew C. Perry, and continued to the park's centre.

Henry walked slowly, carefully examining the grassy area. It was lonely in nature but not unpleasantly so. An abundance of trees lined the park from every corner, providing seclusion from the surrounding roads, and delivering a fresh aroma, intensified by recent rain. He paused momentarily on reaching the middle of the park, at which point six separate pathways joined together to circle the centre point. A large sign had been placed there, highlighting the park's formation in 1865.

Mike glanced briefly at the sign, reading it quickly. He gazed intently at the gaps between the trees, keeping a sharp eye out for any signs of life from any passer-by or passing car.

After several seconds of careful surveillance he turned his attention to the far end of the park where the path spread out in two directions: one to the south-west, passing a statue of the Unitarian pioneer William Ellery Channing, while the other continued north-west towards a partially ruined stone tower.

Mike looked at Henry, the academic's focus on the tower. It was evident from his expression that he had found what they were there for.

A black Toyota pulled up in another car park, some two hundred yards north of Touro Park. The driver exited the car quickly and jogged with intent across Bellevue, heading south towards the park. Unlike the Swiss historian walking through the park less than two hundred yards in front of him, he had been told the exact location of the vault and the way to get in. Secretly he doubted whether such a place even existed, but he knew his knowledge came from a special source.

Equally important, he knew that the only way to get in was also the only way to get out.

The man with blond locks watched as the driver of the Toyota crossed the car park. Although he had never met the man personally, he recognised him instantly from his long ponytail.

He waited until the driver of the Toyota had crossed the road before removing his helmet, placing it safely under the seat of his motorbike.

Keeping his distance, he followed him.

The Newport Tower was one of the oldest structures in America. Situated near the north-west corner of Touro Park, close to Mill Street, and surrounded by metal railings, it stood approximately 28 feet in height and 24 feet in exterior width.

Despite its circular appearance, the tower was one foot and one inch longer when measured from east to west compared to the same from north to south. Its eight strong columns formed round archways in keeping with that of a medieval cloister, measuring 37 inches in thickness, equivalent to one Scottish ell, while the inner chamber reached a diameter of six Scottish ells. Four windows, located at equal points some 16 feet up, also provided evidence that the tower once incorporated at least one upper chamber that had long ceased to exist.

The first thing Mike noticed on encircling the tower was that there was no plaque or guide providing information on the structure. Based on first impressions alone, he couldn't guess what possible purpose it ever had. According to its official history, the tower was used as a windmill by former governor Benedict Arnold, ancestor of the famous American general who defected to the British in the American War of Independence, sometime between 1661 and 1677 and located on land once belonging to the former governor.

Yet from what Mike had gathered from Henry Leoni, the tower had already been marked as a 'Norman Villa' on a map composed by the Italian navigator Giovanni da Verrazano in 1524 and, according to excavations made in the past decade by, among others, Alexander Broadie, potentially dated back to the late 1300s.

The site met the necessary criterion. The round structure supported by eight legs was in keeping with countless former Templar churches in England, Scotland and Scandinavia dating back to the 12th century while the pathway area surrounding the tower offered good evidence that an ambulatory had once encircled what was formerly the rotunda of a church. Any possible views the tower had overlooking the nearby sea were blocked on each side by the abundant trees, yet according to Henry, a clear view would have existed back in the 15th century.

It was Henry's view that the tower was probably built by followers of Zichmni at the time stated in the diary, not only as a church, but also an observatory, calendar system, and lighthouse marking the first Templar colony in the land described as Drogeo, and, of more significance, cementing their status as the first non-indigenous discoverers and settlers of what is now the United States of America.

Henry Leoni looked in awe at the mysterious tower. Although the structure was well preserved, he guessed from its condition that the outer shell had once been coated in white plaster that had peeled away over time. After pausing for several seconds to review the tower's exterior he walked enthusiastically towards the metal railings and entered the interior, a special privilege following his meeting with Alexander Broadie. He walked slowly across the grass beneath the tower, paying close attention to its eight legs and inner wall.

Gabrielle followed, diverting her attention up towards the cloudy sky through the empty void where a roof once existed. She was dressed in dark combat bottoms, a yellow Newport sailing jacket which she had purchased earlier that day and wore a rucksack over her back.

Gabrielle paid attention to the structure. Two of the legs were stronger than the other six, possibly indicating that they had previously served as the entrance to what was once the rotunda. Towards the summit there were a further three small windows, probably put in as lookout posts, potentially further validating the hypothesis that the tower had once served as an observatory. Opposite the western window of what was formerly the first floor were the remains of what appeared to have been a fireplace.

Gabrielle looked at her uncle with disappointment. Based on the evidence in view, the tower offered no obvious significance.

Henry surveyed the interior for several seconds. At the west end he observed a strange egg-shaped stone, which he assumed was once used as part of an ingenious ancient calendar prior to the invention of printing. For over a minute he stared intently at the void once used as a fireplace, his eyes narrowing the harder he concentrated. He unzipped his jacket and removed a series of photocopies from an inside pocket.

Mike shook his head. After walking around the tower for the second time he diverted his attention towards other areas of the park.

It was an attractive setting. The surrounding area was an historical residential area whose buildings included an inn, a Unitarian Church and a 17th century synagogue. Although the park was heavily secluded by trees the buildings of the nearby streets were visible, their empty windows providing an unnerving reality check that their presence could be under observation.

Still he saw no one, just Gabrielle and Henry standing close together by the ruins of the tower. He watched silently as Henry walked slowly towards a nearby tree before returning with a thick leafless branch, measuring over sixteen feet in length. Gabrielle, meanwhile, walked back in the direction of her uncle. Seconds later she disappeared from sight.

Ludovic Gullet entered the park undetected. After making his way along the same path that Mike had earlier walked with Gabrielle and Henry, he changed direction, heading past the statue of Matthew C. Perry and the nearby Japanese fountain. He waited there for over a minute, examining the area surrounding the statue.

He looked up suddenly. Someone was moving towards him.

Gabrielle passed the statue of Matthew C. Perry and froze. Instinctively, she looked over her left shoulder, paying close attention to the strange fountain next to the statue.

It looked out of place to her – almost as though it had been placed there by accident. She examined it closely, paying careful attention to the body.

Then she moved onto the statue of Perry. On closer inspection she noted the presence of several figures from Japanese history and folklore carved into the body of the statue's tall base, a tribute to Perry's naval record in that part of the world.

She gazed at the images, attempting to identify their significance but without success. Intrigued, nevertheless, she encircled the statue slowly, taking the time to read every English word on the inscription. Once she had finished, she peered in momentarily, looking at a four-pronged symbol, one of four similar symbols of what she assumed was a poppy or similar, located at the head of the base where the exterior curved outwards at its widest point.

Henry Leoni paced up and down the interior of the tower, mumbling to himself intently. With the large branch in his hand he gazed up once more at the disused fireplace. His focus narrowed.

Suddenly a strange feeling overcame him, both familiar and at the same time terrifying.

He could tell instinctively that something wasn't right.

Gabrielle froze. Footsteps were moving behind her.

"Oh, thank God," she said, turning breathlessly and coming face to face with Mike.

"Don't wander off like that," he said softly. "Stay where I can see you."

She exhaled loudly, looking at him apologetically. Without realising it she was resting her hands on his shoulders.

They stood before one another awkwardly. Mike was the first to break eye contact, taking a moment to examine the surrounding area. The location was quiet. Still he failed to shake the idea that their being there was under observation.

"Come on. There's nothing here."

Gabrielle nodded, returning her attention to the statue. She retreated a couple of steps, allowing a better view. Several feet above her Matthew C. Perry stood elegantly, leaning against his sword.

She eyed it closely – overwhelmed by the feeling that she was missing something. Something was not right about the four-pronged poppy symbol.

Finally she noticed.

"Mike."

Mike returned to Gabrielle. She was pointing at the four-pointed symbol etched into the statue on the base under Matthew C. Perry's feet.

"What?"

"Look."

Mike eyed the symbol curiously. "It's just a poppy."

Gabrielle shook her head. "No," she said. "It's a Templar cross."

46

Mike gazed intently at the symbol. There were four of them, all located at equal points: north, south, east and west. All were cross pattée, composed in the manner of a flower. It was the perfect disguise. Had she not have mentioned it, he would never have noticed.

"Come on, let's get your uncle."

Seemingly oblivious to his comment, Gabrielle stepped over the spiked railings, approaching the statue. She placed her hands against the cold figures before descending to her knees to investigate the lower area. Although it was now raining, the sky overhead leaden with expectancy, she concentrated intently on the statue, ignoring the light shower that was descending. Squatting on all fours, she shuffled in a circular movement around the base, maintaining her grip for any hint, any clue, any possibility.

When she reached the east side of the statue she stopped. Directly below her was an opening in the ground. She pushed aside the covering, attempting to find what was underneath. Then she saw it. A missing panel revealed a spiral staircase.

Gabrielle looked at Mike, her smile widening.

Mike put his hand to his chin, an action of disbelief. There was no logical reason for it being there.

"Let's get your uncle."

Before he had the chance to move, Gabrielle was already descending the stairwell.

Over thirty yards away, Ludovic Gullet looked on as the Swiss Guard disappeared from sight. He paused, making sure they did not return to the surface.

He edged closer to the statue, staying close to the trees at all times. Convinced he had not been seen, Gullet waited in the covering before moving on towards the fountain.

One thing he was sure of, if they attempted to return, he would get them.

*

The blond-haired American smiled to himself as he watched Gullet hiding amongst the foliage before sneaking towards the statue of Perry. He liked the way the former Swiss Guard looked over his shoulder with clockwork consistency, yet he was still to detect his presence.

From his position among the trees he waited patiently for Gullet to make his move.

Then, to the American's surprise, as he approached the statue he disappeared.

Less than one hour after his arrival, Mark left the house quickly and sprinted towards his rented 4x4. In his hand he carried several pages of printed document, the same document that Mikael Devére had hidden. It was a document that his widow had no interest in keeping. Take what you need, she had said.

Lady you have no idea!

He was in a daze. Was this why Devére had been murdered? Was this why the others had been murdered? He felt sickened by the thought. Still he had no idea why, but finally he was getting warm: a single ray of light in a frosty wintry garden devoid of sunshine.

Yet part of him did not want to believe it. The document, now on the passenger seat as he drove furiously along the dusty road, could potentially implicate a lot of people, people whose reputations were without blemish.

And that, itself, was disturbing.

47

The stairwell was winding, revolving around what appeared to be a circular stone column. It descended in an anti-clockwise direction, suggesting to Gabrielle that the design was probably British in origin, like those found in the towers of medieval castles. The steps were large slabs of grey stone widening the further away they got from the source.

Gabrielle led the way slowly, careful to avoid losing her footing on the treacherous stone. In the absence of natural light she waited until she knew for certain that her leading foot was safely on the next step before continuing further. Visibility was difficult. The darkness seemed almost tangible, a combination of both the blackness of the carefully constructed walls and the underground location penetrated only by the small piercing glow of their torches.

The air was damp. With each passing step it became more and more obvious that the location had been starved of fresh air for a considerable time. As she continued downwards she found her breathing quickened, a natural reaction as her body adjusted to the lack of oxygen entering her lungs. Yet to Gabrielle there was more to the air than just the damp: it was expectant, heightened by the location of the entrance.

In her mind she counted the steps. In her agitated state she feared that the stairwell would never stop – that she had become trapped forever in this secret void located somewhere between the park and the sea, somewhere between the present and the past. As she touched the wall to her right the thought occurred to her that she was touching history: history of an unknown kind. As far as she was aware, nothing like it existed anywhere else in America.

The stairwell continued for a total of thirty-three steps before coming to an end, merging with the floor. The lack of warning caught Gabrielle by surprise, causing her to stumble.

Mike followed tentatively, careful not to make contact with her feet. On reaching the bottom he shone his torch directly in front of him, revealing what appeared to be a gently winding tunnel, lined by man-made walls that supported an arched ceiling.

Gabrielle stood next to Mike, captivated by what she saw. As she shone her torch in the vicinity directly above them, she realised that the ceiling was vaulted, surprisingly reminiscent of the type found in the crypts or ceilings of medieval churches. In the deepest recesses where the walls joined, she could just make out the unappealing presence of cobwebs seemingly floating against the dark backdrop.

Despite the fear, she couldn't help but admire the genius of vault's constructors, not only operating in an area lacking air and light but also having the skill to carry out the job so far back in the distant past.

Mike eyed the tunnel apprehensively. Despite the relative seclusion of the location, and the absence of people in the park above, the lack of light made him wary. As his eyes continued to explore, aided only by the light of the torch, he realised that the stairwell was located at the far end of the vault, and that the tunnel ahead was the only way forward.

He concentrated his attention on the stone steps. In his mind he wondered whether any random passer-by could stumble across the location. He also wondered whether Henry Leoni had already uncovered it, and opened it himself. Silently the alternative worried him. Should it have been opened by any other means, the possibility hit him that they were susceptible to falling into a trap.

He blinked instinctively. Less than two feet in front of him Gabrielle was shining her torch in his face. His reflection caused a distorted shadow against the long stonewalls. Blinded by the light, he put his right arm across his face as a shield.

Gabrielle lowered her torch. "Come on."

What goes in must come out. At least that was the saying.

As Ludovic Gullet concentrated his attention on navigating the twisty stairwell, he found himself readily amused that anyone could think something so naïve.

In a way he almost felt sorry for them, both of them. Unsurprisingly she had taken the bait and now she was in place – underground in a hidden vault. It was the last place, as he believed, that anyone could come out from.

Still, the guard was a highly experienced and skilled soldier, trained for such an occasion. And such things had to be taken into account.

Mike and Gabrielle walked on slowly. The ground beneath their feet was of stone construction, surprisingly even, and extended to a width of between two and three metres, making the tunnel wide enough for them to walk side by side.

Even in the poor light, Gabrielle could see that the walls were constructed from stone. Mounted on the walls at frequent intervals were ancient unlit torches, indicating that the area might have been used frequently at sometime in the past. In her mind's eye Gabrielle imagined the enigmatic Prince Zichmni and his followers walking this same floor five hundred years earlier, their way lighted by the fiery glow on the now rotting wood. In many ways she was unsure what amazed her the most: the fact that such a place existed, or that such a place was even possible.

Yet the more she thought about its creators, the more she felt afraid. She wondered what significance it could possibly have, why this order, if that's what they were, could have carried out so much evil, even to her.

As her eyes adjusted to the poor light she thought she saw shadows lurking in front of her. The thought unnerved her, causing her breathing to tighten. She breathed deeply, realising that the shadows belonged to themselves, caused by a distortion of the torchlight against the gentle slope of the wall.

Although they could not see each other, both were aware of each other's presence. Both were struggling to control their breathing, their sounds seemingly more audible in the poor light. Gabrielle moved quickly, almost losing her footing. Without warning, she grabbed Mike's hand and held it tightly. In another time and place Mike wondered whether he might have viewed the moment in a different way, but in his overly vigilant state he concentrated on other things. He felt as though she was looking at him, but he couldn't be sure. He thought he saw her smile, a soft genuine smile, perhaps one of excitement. For the merest of seconds he thought it was the first he had seen from her, although without further attention he dismissed it.

The light must be playing tricks on him.

Mark sat uncomfortably behind the pilot, his mind focused intently on the document on his lap. Reading was difficult, not helped by the high altitude. His head hurt all the more at the thought of what had been uncovered and harder still when he considered the possibilities it might bring. They were approaching New England.

He just hoped they would not be too late.

The tunnel ended without warning. The outline of a large chamber, possibly a chapel or crypt, loomed ahead. The walls widened noticeably, revealing a more open area.

Mike breathed a sigh of relief. Although the air was dank it was more appealing than before, less enclosed. The light had also improved, but not by enough to allow complete visibility. As best Mike could gather, the area had doubled in height, and the ceiling was arched in design.

He shone the torch around the chamber. It reminded him of the one at Rosslyn: high walls and ceilings were decorated with various carvings ranging from the Green Man to others that appeared to be of Egyptian origin, or alternatively early Christian and early medieval Europe.

Gabrielle wandered away to her left, pressing the wall with her hands. The smooth stone that had lined the corridor was now rougher than before, jutting out at irregular intervals. Up above she could make out other symbols, also reminiscent of the Rosslyn vault. In the darkness it almost appeared as though they were presenting a non-Christian Stations of the Cross.

Gabrielle knelt down on the stone floor. She removed her rucksack and opened it with her left hand, holding her torch with her right to illuminate the bag. She removed two portable lamps and switched them on.

Suddenly the dynamic of the vault changed. The chamber was now revealed to be circular in shape. She considered the tunnel they had just walked and the location where they were now: she guessed that they had walked west, back in the direction of the tower, and were probably exactly beneath it. In Gabrielle's opinion the vault was almost certainly an exact match for what previously existed on the surface, a stone rotunda flanked by an ambulatory, either of stone or wooden construction.

Gabrielle's pulse raced rapidly. Aided by the improved light of the portable lamps she could make out the interior of the chamber clearly. In its centre was a circular table, wood construction, flanked by eight chairs, all of which were covered in cobwebs. The floor, initially assumed to be stone, was in fact comprised of black and white tiles in a chessboard sequence, identical to the one at Rosslyn. As her eyes continued to adjust to the light she realised that the walled perimeter was decorated by a series of carvings, many of which she recognised.

Yet at first they refused to sink in.

Following on from what appeared to be decorations from the biblical period, ranging from those described in Genesis and Exodus to the life of Christ, the scenes depicted what she instantly assumed to be the formation of the Templar order. Nine knights, each one on horseback, were riding across the wilderness, leading to their induction at the Temple of Solomon. The knights then seemed to appear together, kneeling side by side before an unidentifiable object, held aloft by the Grand Master.

That was not the only anomaly. She recognised other Templar symbols: Templar crosses, identical to the ones on Perry's statue above, four in total, each present at every point of the compass.

She blinked. Guided by the light, she recognised to her horror imagery that seemed straight out of folklore. Located prior to more modern imagery, including the logo of the Rite of Larmenius, she identified images of a Templar initiation ritual as described in the accounts of their trials. Among the symbols was an almost identical image of a man being blindfolded and whipped while another man, probably the Grand Master, was holding a skull or a head of some kind in front of the whipped man who was portrayed as being forced to kiss it.

Also on the wall were historical depictions of the Templars in their heyday, battling in the Crusades and praying in churches and cathedrals. Marking the following wall, though seemingly following on from the previous sequence, Gabrielle made out a depiction of the execution of Jacques de Molay and Geoffroi de Charny in 1314 on an island in the River Seine in Paris, followed by the curious illustration of a Jolly Roger. The words *Je me Souviens* were etched into the rock, located in close proximity to the image of de Molay's execution. Following it was a different image, this time of two historical figures who she assumed were Philip IV of France and Pope Clement V.

Following on from that particular passage things became somewhat stranger. Another symbol, reminiscent in appearance to that found at Rosslyn, depicted a ship sailing on a starry night: one that she assumed confirmed the Templar escape from arrest. Next was a knight in armour, perhaps included to portray Zichmni.

Finally she noticed the most shocking sight yet. In keeping with the legends, she saw a semi-naked man being whipped while possessing a noose around his neck and leaning over a cross.

Mike looked at Gabrielle. For the first time in his life he felt a genuine surge of panic.

Only then did he see the room's other distinguishing feature.

Flanking every wall at ground level were the effigies of deceased medieval knights, marking their graves in the ground below. Every effigy portrayed a knight in armour holding a broken sword and shield. Also present were others without effigies and displaying an engraved sword in the company of a long cross with a botonny base and a Templar cross at the top. Every effigy incorporated the words along the verge 'Knights Templar'.

He looked at Gabrielle. "Come on. We need to find your uncle."

Nodding aimlessly, Gabrielle looked at Mike then once more at the symbols, the horror of their reality still refusing to sink in. Leaving the lamps, she followed Mike in the direction of the tunnel, heading back to the stairwell.

Suddenly they stopped. Footsteps could be heard moving slowly towards the chamber.

"Uncle Henry, we're in here," Gabrielle said, shining the torch in the direction of the tunnel. Seconds later a figure appeared in the archway.

Ludovic Gullet emerged from the darkness. "I never would have guessed."

48

Mike stared at the stranger standing less than five metres in front of him. Although he had never met the man he was well aware who he was. He had seen the ponytail before, at least in photographs.

He studied Gullet intently. He carried a SIG P75, the weapon of a Swiss Guard, in Mike's opinion an ironic insult considering the people who had died, possibly from bullets fired from that very gun. Gullet stood rigidly. Unsurprisingly for a soldier he was dressed in dark colours, increasing his ability to blend in with the background. Should he have passed Mike in the street he would have been instantly forgettable. Forgettable meant anonymity. And anonymity in Gullet's business was good.

Gabrielle pointed the torch directly at Gullet's face. "Ludovic Gullet, I knew it was you, I could smell your vile stench through water."

Gullet was unimpressed. "Ms Gabrielle Leoni," he said quietly, his eyes focused, "please do not fidget. There is no one else here and I am armed."

Gullet walked slowly towards them, ensuring that the tunnel remained blocked at all times. He closed his right eye as a reaction to the torchlight.

"Lower your torch, please," he said, his weapon remaining fixed on Gabrielle. She, meanwhile, looked back, unflinching.

Finally, she lowered the light.

Mike looked vainly at the tunnel behind Gullet, praying that an opportunity to escape would arise. Through the corners of his eyes he looked without expectation for an alternative exit. It was worthless. Try reason.

"What do you want?"

Gullet removed a packet of cigarettes from his pocket and put one to his mouth. The flame from his lighter lit up his face momentarily. He exhaled immediately. Smoke blew towards Gabrielle and Mike, heavy in the damp air.

Gullet removed the cigarette from his mouth. "Stand still and follow my instructions," he said, exhaling. "No sudden movements."

Despite the hatred, Mike was somewhat in awe of what he saw. Unmistakably, the man had the efficiency of a Swiss Guard. No doubt he was impeccably trained in what he did. He spoke quietly, but with great authority.

Yet Mike detested him. Behind the militarily instilled efficiency Gullet was a traitor.

"Who are you?" Mike asked.

"Do not waste my time with pointless questions, wachtmeister. You know exactly who I am."

That was not his question. "Who are you?" was a question relevant on other grounds. "Who are you working for?" that was the real question. "What kind of person resorts to such tactics?" He had no idea who they were.

"Ms Leoni, I am so sorry, it appears the rightful owner does not want you trespassing on his property."

Gabrielle's face reddened. She exhaled deeply, her eyes focused on Gullet's.

Mike looked at Gullet with disdain. "If Mr Broadie didn't want us here then why didn't he say so?"

Gullet looked at him without emotion. "I said the owner of this, wachtmeister."

A cold realisation hit him. The man in the Merc at St Gallen, the biker at Rosslyn, the man who nearly killed Gabrielle: surely he had been watching them since the beginning.

He looked at Gullet. Was it he who attacked Gabrielle? Surely not, even with his experience it would take a miracle to infiltrate the Sistine Hall.

Had he been right all along? Had the man dressed as a Swiss Guard been trying to obtain the diary, hidden within the Vatican for over a century? Surely it clicked into place. Whatever the hidden agenda of the Rite of Larmenius and the Knights Templar, it was surely not about gold, yet it was worth its weight in it. It was the answer to many riddles: riddles that had lasted centuries: even preceded the Swiss Guard: riddles that would remain secret.

He looked at Gullet, then at Gabrielle. There was no fear: only rage.

"You killed my dad," Gabrielle said.

Gullet smoked. "He was killed, never mind how."

"You bastard."

Gabrielle charged at Gullet. The mercenary walked forward and pistol-whipped her across her face. She fell to the floor, banging her head.

"No," Mike shouted, leaning over Gabrielle. He looked up at Gullet. The Swiss's firearm was aimed at him. "Look, do what you want with me, but leave her alone, she's done nothing wrong."

"You are in a position unsuitable to give orders, wachtmeister."

Mike's concern was for Gabrielle. He cursed the situation. He cursed their being there against his better judgment. Then he blamed Henry Leoni. Was he that much of a fool or was this planned? Broadie surely knew. His thoughts turned to earlier days. Why was the diary in Al Leoni's safe deposit box? It still didn't make sense.

He considered playing for time, but what for? They were isolated. Fear and anger had subsided. He was assigned to guard her, yet he had failed. How had it come to this?

Gullet walked to within two metres of them and raised his firearm. He cocked the weapon.

Mike closed his eyes, waiting for the inevitable. Silently he prayed, his thoughts frantic. He heard a gunshot, earlier than expected. Was he still alive? Was this what death was like? He was sure it was not.

He heard a groan. Gullet lunged forward. He heard a scampering of footsteps from along the tunnel.

Mike wasted no time. Now on his feet he dived at Gullet and punched him hard in the face. Gullet groaned for a second time. Even in the poor light it was evident that Gullet had been shot in the shoulder.

Gullet wrestled Mike and kicked him hard in the upper torso, forcing him to roll several metres. Gullet rose to his feet, his firearm now on the floor beneath the table.

Gullet was gone in an instant, sprinting away from the chamber in the direction of the stairwell.

Mike looked up, shuffling quickly to his feet. He removed his firearm from his inside pocket and fired once. As best he could tell the shot missed – he saw a bright spark followed by a pinging sound as the bullet rebounded off the stone. A second gunshot followed, clearly from a different gun, then another.

Mike turned, his attention scattered. He scampered towards Gabrielle who was still lying dazed on the floor. He shone the torch in her face.

By now she was unconscious.

49

The GPLA building was identical to the other major ones in the central business district of Charlotte, North Carolina. It was impressive in both material and design, comprising over forty storeys, rising to a considerable height and forming an iconic part of the city's skyline. As with the other major buildings, it was visually a large glass tube that narrowed towards the summit and ended with a 150-feet antenna spire, pointing into the sky like a needle. In total, fifteen firms occupied the building, including GPLA, all of which were law or accountancy based, employing everybody from lawyers, accountants, bankers, and auditors who worked in seclusion behind tinted glass.

The atrium on the ground floor was both spacious and modern. The carpeted floor was luxurious in feel while high ceilings and a large selection of greenery made the room feel airy. The large tinted windows bathed the floor in a dense light, making the sun appear fainter in the sky when viewed from the lobby. At the entrance, two sets of revolving doors catered for the incessant demand of bodies coming and going from the various floors. Most of the individuals were wearing suits, strolling in various directions with briefcases hanging by their sides, while most of those entering carried takeaway coffees as they returned to the grindstone at the end of their lunch break.

At 2 p.m. Randy Lewis entered through the second revolving door and stopped on reaching the carpet. As usual, he was dressed in a trademark silver suit and a white shirt accompanied by a matching red tie although unlike most his hands were empty.

After taking a few seconds to become acquainted with the surroundings, he asked the nearest security guard for information and was directed to a desk located at the far left of the atrium where visitors were requested to sign in. He walked casually in that direction and queued for several seconds behind a man wearing a cowboy hat who was chatting to the receptionist in her mid-forties sitting behind the desk. Eventually the man left and the woman smiled at Lewis.

"May I help you?"

"Yes," Lewis replied, leaning against the desk. "I'm looking for Mr Ged Fairbanks, please. He's a director at GPLA."

The woman studied him from behind the desk. She looked away momentarily to type something on her keyboard and informed Lewis that Fairbanks was in a meeting.

"I'll wait," Lewis said, forcing a smile.

"Fourteenth floor."

She directed Lewis to one of four lifts, located twenty feet to his right at the far end of the atrium. Without further instruction, he walked across the carpeted floor to the lift and pushed the button for the fourteenth floor. The building was unsurprisingly crowded but the doors of the lift closed with no one else entering. People came and went on the fifth and ninth and Lewis exited on the fourteenth. Directly in front of him, an attractive blonde-haired woman in her late twenties was sitting at another reception desk.

The woman offered him a seat at the nearby waiting area where he sat for nearly fifteen minutes. At just after 2:15 a scrawny man with dark brown hair and a moustache emerged from a nearby corridor to greet him. It was a brilliant, warm day outside, although the man's face suggested it was raining. Lewis stood as the stranger approached and held out his hand.

"Randy Lewis," he said without enthusiasm.

"How's the wife, Ged?"

"Divorced last month."

"Gee," Lewis said, "I'm sorry."

"Don't be – I'm sorry I goddamn married her."

Fairbanks led Lewis along a deserted corridor and opened a brown door to a tidy office. It was a basic office for the standards with extensive views over downtown Charlotte through large windows. A photograph of the accountant's son and daughter was present on a busy desk that was surrounded by countless post-it notes, a telephone, a desktop PC, and a thousand-page audit of a finance company from Illinois.

Lewis looked at the photo and smiled. "How are Debbie and Cliff?"

"Debbie got married and Cliff's sophomore at NYU."

The man's negativity showed no signs of fading. For Lewis, monotonous guys in suits act as a stereotype to outsiders, often poorer in bank balance, yet richer in happiness, and Fairbanks showed it all. The expensive watch on his wrist, a birthday present from himself to himself, illustrated the brashness of an industry where nobodies became somebodies because of the clothes they wore or the cars that they drove, but to Lewis the owner's ignorance diminished all significance. A man's clothes, car, watch, house, swimming pool or wife said a lot about a man, but not as much as the man himself. Lewis had seen it all before and nothing really surprised him. He was more interested in the worried expression on his friend's face.

"Rough day?"

"Usual shit," he said. "Take a seat."

Lewis pulled up a chair and eased it towards the desk. The leather upholstery was more comfortable than it looked.

"So little Debbie got married, huh?"

"Yuh huh," he replied without a smile. "She's pregnant, too."

Lewis smiled. "Well how about that."

Fairbanks sat down and cupped his hands together thoughtfully. He twiddled his thumbs and monitored Lewis like a security guard. His moustache seemed to shuffle as he attempted a smile but Lewis could see that the smile was forced.

"But you didn't come all this way to talk about my daughter. Did you, Randy?"

Lewis forced a smirk. "You've got my number there haven't you?"

"We go back a long way."

"Yeah, we do."

"What is it you need? Money? Cigarette?" he asked removing the last of a packet and firing it up.

"Information, now you mention it."

The accountant exhaled immediately, sending smoke rising towards the open window behind him. "Yeah, well I didn't see nothing."

Lewis laughed ironically.

"What is it this time? I thought you retired from the Feds."

"My term ended, Ged."

"Same thing."

"Yeah, well, this is different."

Lewis considered his words, his attention on Fairbanks.

"I understand you guys recently carried out an audit of Leoni et Cie?"

Fairbanks shrugged. "Yeah. And?"

Lewis leaned forward, eyeing the accountant closely. "I wanna know exactly what you found?"

The accountant shuffled through his drawers, looking for nothing in particular. "Now that you mention it, I heard on real good authority that you're on the board of Leoni now."

"I am."

The accountant shrugged again. "So why are you asking me?"

Lewis eyed his friend curiously. He was clearly stressed but that was nothing new: his firm was one of the biggest auditors in the country, if not the world. Bags of purple were present under his eyes and the yellowing of his teeth revealed the negative effects of decades of smoking. His voice was raspier than usual, suggesting the presence of a cold or flu bug, also emphasised by occasional coughing. He had been a workaholic in Lewis's younger days, and this had clearly continued into the man's late fifties.

"Who audited them, Ged?"

Ged blew smoke. "No one guy, Randy. Probably the guys on the floor below."

He placed his left hand to his lips, covering his mouth as he coughed. His face reddened as he struggled to breathe.

"You oughta see a doctor with that chest."

"Thanks for the medical advice."

Lewis grimaced, contemplating his next question. Just as he did the telephone rang.

Fairbanks answered. "Hello?"

Without further words the accountant hung up. Taking a further drag on his cigarette, he turned away from Lewis and looked out through the window across the street. A man dressed in a designer suit and sunglasses stood innocuously on a street corner.

"Ged, now we've known each other a long time. Are you in any kind of trouble?"

Fairbanks turned around, his face suddenly worried, more so. His eyes were wide open but his attention was scattered. He looked vacantly at Lewis whereas Lewis sat up rigid in his chair.

"Now what in God's name is wrong?"

Fairbanks stuttered, forcing his cigarette to his mouth. He looked briefly once more out of his window and then made eye contact with Lewis.

"Listen, Randy, I've got a pretty busy schedule," he said, his face breaking into a smile. "Now, it sure was mighty sweet of you to come here and pay y'all best to lil' Debbie. I'll be sure to pass on the good wishes."

The accountant forced another smile and escorted Lewis to the door. He patted him on the shoulder and closed the door behind him.

Lewis stood outside the office. What had he just witnessed? He thought about knocking then decided against it. He considered the accountant's actions. His body language was peculiar, even for him.

He turned away from the office and headed straight for the lift.

*

At approximately 4 p.m. Eastern Time in America, a helicopter descended unobserved over the garden of the large mansion on the New England coast. One man was present to meet it and he awaited its arrival intently.

The helicopter touched down in the middle of the lawn and the doors opened. Gullet exited quickly. His left shoulder was heavily bandaged underneath his dark fleece. He walked across the garden quickly, slowing his pace as he approached the bearded man. As usual the grand master smoked a cigar and showed little emotion. He removed something from the inside of his suit as he smoked.

"I have a new assignment for you," the bearded man said calmly.

Gullet opened the package. It was a simple photograph with no other communication. He looked at it for several seconds before making eye contact with the bearded man.

"Do not fail me again."

50

The hazy shape on the horizon came slowly into focus. Shielding her eyes with her right hand, Gabrielle squinted through the blinding light that dominated her sight and concentrated intently on the image before her. There was a man standing in front of her. He was saying something to her yet she failed to recognise him or understand what he was saying.

Other colours appeared. In a dazed and lifeless state she felt a bizarre floating sensation, yet her body was otherwise earthbound. Where was she? How did she get there?

Suddenly she was aware that she was standing in a large kitchen, instantly recognisable as the one in the château in Switzerland. The kitchen looked spotless as always and in the middle of the room was her mother, looking at her and smiling.

Yet something troubled her. The vision, although real, seemed somehow dated, perhaps several years earlier, before recent events had taken their toll.

The next thing she noticed was her father. A glass of port was present in his left hand. His briefcase was laid down on the breakfast bar and a *New York Times* folded neatly on top of it. A glowing smile beamed from his bearded face.

She sighed deeply as she basked in the happiness of the situation.

Suddenly everything changed. The aura of success displayed by her father seconds earlier faded. Instead she was confronted by the dark vision of his body the way it appeared in the morgue. The Templar cross with a skull and crossbones at its centre seemed to flash in her mind as if it were a lightning storm.

Then she saw Martin Snow: his normally happy face, recognisable from countless headshots from business articles in newspapers or magazines, was now a morbid expression of chilled fear.

Next came Nathan Walls, then Jermaine Llewellyn, then Cardinal Faukes and Major von Sonnerberg. Even though she had never met any of them she felt a genuine sense of compassion for their passing as the dreamlike visions of the murdered men flashed before her. Finally came the former President of France: his charismatic figure now lying cold and pathetic on a deserted floor. A cloaked figure was looking over him. As the man turned she saw it was Gullet, instantly recognisable from the way he appeared at Newport. An expression of cold concentration crossed his face as he turned and pointed his firearm directly at her.

Next, she found herself deep within the catacombs of Newport in the company of eight Templars, dressed in the armour of old, their faces covered by helmets. Fear and trepidation consumed her as she gazed across the cold stone surroundings. Everywhere she looked she was surrounded, no exits other than the one you can't see with your eyes. In her mind, expressions of malice dominated the faces of the knights, despite their features being veiled by metal. Floating in the centre of the room she saw what she assumed was the legendary relic that the knights seemed to worship. A peculiar light shone out from its middle and all focus was lost.

Suddenly she was awake. The visions of Newport disappeared and she was aware that she was lying down. She felt a burning sensation in her eyes as sunlight attacked her retinas. Her initial reflex was to shield her eyes with her right hand. As she did, she noticed feeling in her arms. She noticed that she could notice the feeling. Then she felt the feeling in the rest of her body.

Realising she was awake, she squinted through the brightness. Every element of her nightmare faded as she saw for the first time that she was alone in a room. It was a private room, adequately furnished. From her right, sunlight penetrated through open windows that were surrounded by white walls that reflected its brightness. There were flowers in a vase on the windowsill and an unoccupied comfy chair just below it that had a clean dressing gown folded over the back. Next to the chair was a table, containing a tray with two coffee cups. For now it was unclear who had used them.

For the first time she heard sound. A vague echo in the distance from unknown sources became louder as her body regained alertness. Through an open doorway to her left she could see nurses and doctors moving energetically up and down the corridor. Further to her left she saw a panic button, placed on the bedside cabinet next to a full glass of water. Now aware that she was in a hospital bed, she realised that her combats and sailing jacket had been replaced with a white top that felt at least two sizes too big.

She heard different noises. With her focus now clear she could see two figures standing in the corner of the room, engaged in animated discussion. Their accents were American and their tone informal yet urgent. She wondered which hospital she was in. What town? How did she get there?

She recognised Mike, dressed in his usual style, blue jeans and a white jacket, the same clothes he had been wearing at Newport. Opposite him was a man she had met before. The guy she had once called stupid.

She thought his name was Mark.

She looked intently at the men who were yet to realise she was awake. Mike was the first to notice. He made eye contact unintentionally and ended his conversation with Mark mid-sentence. As their voices quietened Gabrielle was now aware that the television in the top left corner of the room was turned on, showing the Simpsons episode where Homer ran for sanitation commissioner.

Mike hurried towards Gabrielle. He smiled at her, thought about hugging her then decided against it as she deliberately looked away.

Mark walked nearer, but stopped at the end of the bed. He was more formally dressed than Mike but not in uniform. A pair of dark jeans looked like trousers from a distance and a dark jacket was somehow in keeping with his job as an investigative policeman.

Mike leaned over her with concern. "How are you feeling?"

"Just what the hell am I doing here?" she demanded, louder than she intended. "Where are we? And who the hell gave me this?" she said, pulling at her pyjama top.

Mark spoke before Mike had a chance. "Calm down, Ms Leoni, you banged your head when you fell."

Gabrielle looked at Mike with an irritated expression. "Who is this?" she asked. Secretly she knew and took no notice when Mike answered.

"Really? So you say he's not a doctor."

Mike exhaled deeply.

"Then can you please tell him to keep his diagnosis to himself. And get me out of these stupid pyjamas."

"I'll get you a drink," Mike offered.

"I don't want a coffee," she said, attempting to get out of the bed. "We're leaving, don't touch me," she shouted at Mark.

"Gabrielle, wait this is important."

"Where the hell are we? And will someone please shut that blind."

"Newport Hospital," Mike said, adjusting the blind. With the shades down the light was far more bearable.

Gabrielle looked confused. Visions of Newport were vague. Had it really happened? She remembered the underground vault. Then Gullet. Then things were a blur.

Mike told her about Mark and Agent Gregore coming over in a Vatican Police helicopter some seven hours ago. Mike's storytelling faltered from time to time as Gabrielle pressed him continuously for answers. She stared at Mike, her gaze wandering to the open door. Along the corridor various nurses and doctors continued to run every which way in a purposeful manner. Then she noticed the clock and saw the time was approaching seven in the evening. They had been there over six hours.

"What are you doing in Newport?" Gabrielle asked Mark, finally controlling her tone.

"We discovered that Gullet had a contract on you," Mark replied. "We now know that the people who attacked you at the Vatican Library were the same people responsible for your father's murder and the others. They knew you were going to Newport . . ."

"What do you mean, they knew? Who knew? Who are they? How did you know? What's he talking about, Mike?"

So many questions caught Mike flatfooted. "Mark will explain everything. Just relax."

"I am relaxed. Now will you please tell me what's going on? And get me out of these clothes."

"Mark works for the Vatican Police. He was asked by Commissario Pessotto to investigate the murders. He's been tracking the Rite of Larmenius."

Gabrielle looked up nervously. A man dressed in a dark leather jacket walked past the door.

"Relax," Mike said. "That's Gregore. He's another Vatican policeman."

Gabrielle looked at Mike. "He's what?"

Mark: "Gregore has been working at Gullet's casino for the last three months. He's been keeping an eye on his activities. Gullet has been directly or indirectly responsible for every murder."

Gabrielle looked at Mark, her expression one of annoyance. "Listen to me, you dimwit. Earlier today that man nearly killed me. He came down on me in a secret vault that was filled with dead Knights Templar. Did you really think I hadn't worked that out?"

Mark breathed out loudly. Mike put his hand on Gabrielle's right arm.

"Don't touch me."

"You have to hear this," Mike said. "Mark has been investigating every murder. Yesterday he visited Diana Devére."

She instantly recognised the name. Diana Devére, née Saylis: the beloved wife of the former President of France and a star in her own right. Gabrielle had met her on several occasions. She assumed the woman would have attended her father's funeral had her husband not gone missing.

Gabrielle looked at Mark. "You saw Diana Devére? Why would Diana Devére grant an audience to the likes of you?"

Mark scratched his head and exhaled loudly at the same time.

Mike: "Gabrielle, you have to listen to this. Mark has found out that Gullet has been carrying out these murders for the Knights Templar."

Suddenly Gabrielle felt cold. The warmth of the late spring day in Newport felt pleasant yet the sound of that name made the hairs on her arms stand like pinpricks. She wrapped herself in the soft linen covers, her vision focused on Mark.

"Tell her," Mike said.

Mark looked at Gabrielle, for the first time with sympathy. "Yesterday I visited Diana Devére in Mauritius. She has a holiday villa there and, equally important, it is where Mikael Devére was murdered. While no witnesses or even fingerprints were found at the scene, we do know that Gullet was on the island earlier that day and from the facts we have uncovered from Mikael Devére's safe, we now know why Gullet carried out the murder."

Gabrielle nodded as he finished. "That doesn't particularly surprise me."

Mark's expression hardened. "Well what I'm about to tell you certainly will. You will probably not believe me. You will be horrified, yet I assure you I am telling the truth. But hopefully, with your cooperation, we can help make sure no one else will get hurt."

He paused, his expression stern.

"For over fifty years we have believed the Rite of Larmenius to be responsible for the murders of over two thousand people since the end of the war, but until recently no one knew why. Thanks to you, however, we have finally managed to make connections. Every murder they have ever committed has been on the orders of an organisation that until recently no one knew even exists. They operate in secret, yet their members include public figures: important people, politicians, people you see on television regularly: members of the media; businessmen; even royalty. No one who has come to learn of this society has lived to tell the tale. Many may have tried but each has wound up dead. Once someone becomes a member they have no choice but to abide by the rules. They have an extensive surveillance network and have been watching you throughout. They are more than an organisation. They are the most influential figures on the planet."

Gabrielle looked at him, her focus intent.

"You see, Ms Leoni, these Knights Templar are everything you suspect. Their story begins centuries ago. It will undoubtedly continue as long as it remains secret. Its origins are said to go back to the original order and since 1307. These men have secretly been manipulating history for over seven hundred years. Even to this day. They have funded wars, assassinated monarchs: they even brought about the Declaration of Independence and the French Revolution. They have compiled extensive data on every politician, businessman, and person of influence throughout the world. They have rigged some elections, funded politicians, including many US presidents and European presidents and prime ministers. Any bribes are paid in the secrecy of Swiss bank accounts and they have ordered the assassinations of every major opponent. All for one extreme purpose."

"What do you mean elections are controlled? How can you possibly know this?"

"Mrs Devére showed me. Mikael Devére had evidence. They are a shadow government for all of the important governments of the world. Including his own tenure."

Gabrielle looked at Mark, bewildered. "You can't be serious."

Mark looked philosophically at her and nodded. "Exactly. Mikael Devére was a Templar."

Randy Lewis settled comfortably into the easy chair, located next to the bed of his hotel room in downtown Charlotte and looked with vague interest at the television. The Orioles were seven to two up against the Blue Jays at the bottom of the seventh at Camden Yards, and the MLS game between D.C. United and the New England Revolution would be on immediately afterwards. In his left hand he held a glass of whiskey, recently poured from a small bottle acquired from the mini-bar.

With his jacket folded over the chair, and his collar loose, he relaxed momentarily, sipping the whiskey slowly. Despite the fine taste the liquid offered no relief.

He picked up his mobile phone and navigated his text messages. He read the newest one for the umpteenth time. Fairbanks had something to say to him: but only in the privacy of the hotel's multi-storey car park at ten-thirty.

He had three hours to wait, but at least it was something. Maybe the day wasn't a complete waste after all.

51

Gabrielle gazed aimlessly through the small glass window of the closed door. Outside, the Vatican policeman continued to walk across her eye line. Clearly out of hearing range, the man sipped coffee from a cardboard cup at irregular intervals and ambled casually, out of sequence for a policeman, as if he was a visitor waiting for the patient's family to leave before making an entrance. His presence provided security without drawing unnecessary attention.

Gabrielle looked at Mike, as if looking for clarification. Perhaps it was all make-believe, the most horrible of dreams. Or maybe this was the best news they could have hoped for. In a strange way she was relieved, at least she had not imagined it.

"I can't believe this," she said to both Mike and Mark. "If this is true . . ."

"I can't quite believe it myself, Ms Leoni. We knew there had to be a connection between the recent murders, but nothing prepared me for this. It was only yesterday that Diana Devére allowed me to see the contents of Mikael Devére's safe. Even she doesn't know what I know. Just imagine, within this little hidden safe in Mauritius was written proof that the former President of France was merely a puppet in a scripted master plan perpetuated by financiers, businessmen, members of the common media, even academics. Imagine if people knew? Imagine if people knew that this legendary brotherhood who, according to the history books, ceased to exist in the Middle Ages was actually still carrying out the greatest conspiracy of all time."

Gabrielle adjusted herself in her bed. Without realising it she had been leaning on Mike's right arm for several minutes.

"But how?" she asked weakly. "Who on earth would join such a society? How could anyone learn about what has been done and enter willingly?"

Mark shook his head. "Firstly, I think you need to understand the immense influence of this order. The Templars were among the first people in history to voyage to the far reaches of the planet. Mike told me about this Prince Zichmni, which, if true, he was at least partly responsible for their survival. Members of their order crossed the Atlantic at a time when many people in Europe still believed the world to be flat. They have transformed the world's banking network and practically invented the idea of a multinational corporation. They have shaped man's destiny in the USA, brought down the Kings of France and even to this day they have successfully brought about many of the key outcomes of history.

"Secondly, from what we can gather from Devére, no man is introduced to this immediately. And, most importantly, they are not given a choice."

"You mean they're threatened?"

"I don't think it's quite like that. You see, you've clearly heard of the Rite of Larmenius."

Gabrielle nodded.

Mark: "The Rite of Larmenius is an appendant body of the Freemasons, an organisation apparently formed by a combination of fleeing Knights Templar and members of the ancient rite of Stonemasonry. When the Templars were outlawed they collaborated with the Stonemasons as it allowed them to travel easily across borders. The modern day Rite of Larmenius is a society for the immensely rich. Businessmen, politicians, academics, even royalty are tempted into becoming members of this very exclusive club. Yet even 99% of their members probably don't know the true nature. The Rite of Larmenius itself is for the most senior Masons and the criteria for membership incredibly strict. Its members participate in meetings that are otherwise private from the rest of the world, including an annual three-week conference in the Alps. All members are invited to be part of the wider order, but only a minority of them we understand to be Templars. The Rite of Larmenius itself has less than a few hundred. Once a member has been introduced to their ways there is no way out. Members are forbidden from discussing anything that goes on within their walls with the outside world. None who have tried have ever survived."

"So the Freemasons are the Knights Templar?" Gabrielle asked. "You have got to be kidding me!"

Mark shook his head. "The Masons are not the Templars: the Rite of Larmenius are the Templars' feeder group. Many can join the order and pay the subscription. Only a select few are invited to see the real society."

Gabrielle looked desperately at Mark. "How do you know all this?"

Mark unzipped his jacket and removed a lengthy document from his top pocket. He shuffled the papers and passed them to Gabrielle. There were twelve or thirteen pages in total.

She adjusted her position in her bed and unfolded the pages. She scanned the early content quickly, detecting several sheets of printed font.

"What is this?"

"Answers to many questions," Mark replied. "What you hold is the fourteenth and last chapter of Mikael Devére's upcoming autobiography: a personal insight into the activities of the Rite of Larmenius and the secret order of the Knights Templar through the eyes of one of its own members."

Gabrielle nodded. The look of despondency that dominated her eyes satisfied Mark that she had understood. Gabrielle looked briefly at Mike before breaking away. Her eyes concentrated on the pages before her.

Finally she started to read.

"Don't you think grand-père wears well, my love?" Yvette said to her daughter, Stephanie, as she held her in her arms. Stephanie, cuddling a small teddy won at the fair less than a week earlier, looked me in the eye and giggled. How is it, I have often wondered, that a heart so consumed in shade can be returned to the sun through the mystery of a child's laugh. How many hearts that once bore such sorrow did return through that divine friend of joy?

It was ten o'clock in the morning on the first day of November. As usual, I sat in my favourite chair, looking through the window at the fading greenery. Three days earlier my family's visit had been a quiet, more sombre affair. The chest pains that had forced me to cancel my trip to England and brought me back to hospital were fortunately benign, in truth little more than a reminder, Mother Nature is watching.

Being President of France, three days in an infirmary was never likely to go unnoticed. My setback had already caused speculation in the press. Over the coming days I read what seemed like thousands of articles. Most put the pains down to stress, the pinnacle of a series of failings that had taken its toll on my ageing body. Over forty years in the political sphere had taught me to understand the merciless tenacity of the angry press, though the months of April and May, in particular, were to me the most upsetting. A series of anonymous letters had been sent to a magistrate alleging serious misdemeanours involving four senior advisers. The press spoke of events as a second

Clearstream scandal. As a man of senior age I was old enough to remember the first one, though never could I have imagined another: and so close to people in my own administration.

In truth, I did not know whether the pains were a blessing or a hindrance. Two terms as President of France had already surpassed my ambitions, ambitions that went back to my schooling. Yvette asked me to retire. Knowing my stubborn ways she showed little surprise when I declined, but love is a powerful thing. Holding my granddaughter and looking out across the dying autumn setting I felt a sense of poetic realisation and my heart was touched by many remembrances long since forgotten. How strange it is the softest breeze, the falling of leaves, the smile of a loved one can arouse such humility; can whispers of old voices inspire the sorrowed heart.

Announcement of my intention to retire was made on Canal+ less than three days after my decision was final. Contrary to common belief, the interview was pre-recorded. The recording that went to air was not the first, nor the second, nor even the tenth. Had I gone to air without so much as a second chance I fear I would have failed to speak for sorrow.

The two days following the election was both the busiest and quietest I had experienced. It was now early April and again I sat in my favourite chair. The view this time was not of a dying autumn but a garden in young spring. As I turned away from my little paradise, I watched with both sadness and joy as the young man who was my successor entered his new realm. I knew that providence was with him. While my autumn had turned to winter, his spring was only now beginning. With my time as president now a memory, it was time to thaw out the frost. For me, a new spring was also just beginning.

Unlike six months before, the company I kept was not family. Sitting beside me in my living room were seven men whose friendship and counsel had been central both to my life and time in power. Each man was revered in his profession as something of the miraculous, and such status was not without foundation. Like me, they watched the birth of the new era with expectation. The expressions on their faces were of complete focus. Not once did the room light up with humour, nor even casual curiosity. They knew as I did that the events that were soon to take place would go on to shape a nation, and, in turn, the rest of the world. For over twelve years I had witnessed and taken on the events of my time, while others merely watched. For someone living outside the sphere of political complexity the importance of these men cannot be understood.

Nor did I understand when I was first brought into this very selective sphere.

This is the last chapter of my life.

To those who know me only as leader of Free France this is my admission.

For those who know me well this, alas, is my confession.

For those I love most, I ask not for you to understand.

Only your forgiveness.

I was twenty-five years of age when I completed my studies of the DEA's degree at the Institut d'Études Politiques de Paris and the École Nationale d'Administration. Following in the footsteps of my grandfather, and inspired by my hero Charles de Gaulle, I entered my first job, excluding six months on a coal-transporter following my baccalauréat, as a civil servant. Growing up in the inner city area of Marseille as one of five children of my father, a painter and decorator, and my mother, a nurse, I had never been blessed with much money. Higher education was far from a certainty, but after achieving the necessary grades I was accepted onto a course in Paris studying Politics and made do working in a restaurant in my leisure hours, forsaking the pleasures of university life for the employment that would keep me there. In what little spare time I had I found myself engrossed in the subject and I became actively involved in student politics. At the age of twenty-two I made my first step into the political arena when I joined the French Communist movement, participating in meetings that took place in a former prison cell.

After graduating from ENA in 1964, I initially trained in the civil service at the Court of Auditors but this held very little for me. Working in the service resembled little more than a lightless vacuum withering my youthful ambitions into a premature stagnation.

Then in the summer of 1970 fate intervened when my superior at the Court of Auditors took me along to a gathering in Rouen whose attendees included the future President, Manu Ricard. Although it was still eighteen months before his election, Ricard was already being hailed as something of a colossus among politicians, the man who could lead France to true greatness. I must admit there was a certain presence about him that was seldom seen in any other in attendance; any other I would ever meet for that matter. In many ways Ricard was revered for his ability to keep the common touch and this was evident from the very start. While few were granted the privilege that I was that night, I found my intriguing nature got the better of me and Ricard responded to me with kind humour. From *that moment my university ambitions were rekindled and after three years of determination I was appointed chief of personal staff for the Prime Minister, Jean Papin.*

A short time into my new role I began to work quite closely with the then Minister of Relations with Parliament, Alain Michalak. Nearing his seventieth year, Michalak was looking forward to the birth of his first grandchild yet still finding the energy and enthusiasm for serving his country. Despite being almost forty years my senior, our connection was instant – heightened I cannot deny by my father's past friendship with the man from their time fighting the Nazis. Over the next three years our professional relationship led to firm friendship and this I carried throughout the next decade.

I resigned the post when Papin retired and decided the time was right for a new chapter in my life. For years I had worked on the fringes of the political sphere: now I wanted to see the real thing. Following Papin's advice, I ran for election in the National Assembly and was successful. Within four years I was awarded my first high-profile role as the Minister of the Interior and my ambitions began to grow. For the first time I was empowered. My emerging friendship with the President had grown steadily over the last decade and since my election he spoke to me regularly regarding many subjects. My invitations to the gatherings he attended became rapidly more frequent and men I had never met knew my name and spoke to me as if I were an old friend. As time went by my reputation grew and, largely through Michalak and our President Ricard, so did my list of contacts.

Among my privileges, the number of these gatherings I was made welcome to increased, including a bizarre endorsement by Michalak for membership in that body, the Masons. Following his recommendation, I was inducted as an apprentice in 1983 and after only a few meetings, I had already passed to the third degree. Although I must admit with hindsight that my progression was undoubtedly planned, my fascination with the order led to increased dedication and within two years I found myself a member of five of its appendant bodies. There, my dedication to the craft intensified. In the early days perhaps as many as five evenings a week were spent attending meetings of this order. Sadly this nearly saw the failure of my marriage.

By 1988 dedication brought further reward when I was put forward once again by Michalak to a further appendant body of the organisation, the Rite of Larmenius. What I understood to be a ten-

year waiting list was achieved in what seemed to be a matter of weeks: in retrospect I realise this had been in planning years in advance. I had heard many acquaintances, some Masons some not, speak of the Rite of Larmenius but despite my experience of its sister orders I could never have understood its true nature.

In the spring of 1989 I attended my first meeting and early in 1990 I was invited to my first 'gathering' in the Swiss Alps. I had heard various reports of what goes on at a 'gathering' in my early days, but only now did I begin to understand the true nature of this peculiar event. I was initiated in the usual style before witnessing its curious opening ceremony. Soon after, I was introduced to many of the society's members.

While I understand from its history the Rite of Larmenius was created by American-Swiss Masons in the early 1700s, mainly for writers and inventors, its members now seem to be high-ranking politicians, businessmen, academics, major military personnel, bankers, CEOs of oil companies and even high ranked members of the media. Although most were Swiss or American, I was introduced to what seemed like hundreds of high-ranking officials from the world's top professions.

Yet while the members of the society conducted themselves with privacy, behind the elegant walls of its various lodges and the high security of the 3,000-acre Alpine retreat I began to see the real picture. Over the three weeks that the 'gathering' took place, meetings were frequent; the subject matter usually in keeping with that between directors of a large multinational company. Business was clearly ongoing, and continued to do so throughout my visit. In 1992, thanks to the support of many of the order's members, including Ricard, I was put forward to replace the outgoing Patrice Toulalan as Prime Minister. If only I knew then what I knew now . . .

Over the next six years I attended many of these gatherings, all of which were attended by Michalak and Ricard. During that time the faces generally remained the same and the conversations likewise. Businesses expanded and new ones were created as the logistics of many major companies, if not every major industry, was discussed within its walls. Ricard's death in 1998 had left a void and Michalak's influence extended. The faces at the meetings began to change and soon I was to learn why.

As Ricard's death was within 12 months of a general election, the proceedings were brought forward. With no obvious successor for the greatest President France had seen since the Republic, and backed by

Michalak and many other friends and acquaintances I had made within the Rite of Larmenius, I was put forward. My success was a landslide and for this now I was hailed. After more than twenty years in the shadow of Ricard, I emerged. Some even dubbed me the new Saviour. And for this now I was revered.

Following my election there was another 'gathering' in Switzerland. Only four months into my first term, the mood surrounding me was different to any I had ever witnessed. Strangers spoke to me with an air of great respect and friendship; tycoons patted my back, kissed me on both cheeks, and told me I was doing a great job. Strangers in suits at faraway tables raised their brandy glasses and cigars to me as I passed, as if I was their hero. The smiles were broader and the praise unanimous. I was now walking in the footsteps of Ricard but that itself was worthy of respect. And that now came in large quantities.

Ten days into the ceremony of 1999 I was introduced to a man of considerable esteem. I had seen his face only once before but I had met his father many times, although I was only vaguely aware of his background. To the wider world he is a smartly dressed bearded man and the successor to his father as CEO of one of the largest banks in the world. His reputation was one of the miraculous among the banking world, notably in America, and as I was later to learn such a reputation was not without foundation. He spoke with an air of integrity and, just like Ricard, possessed great inner strength. But then again very few present did not.

Over the coming days I was introduced to four others: one of whom a cabinet minister from Britain, another a businessman from Germany, the others academics from Scotland and Canada. All were included in this gentleman's sphere and I was later introduced to another of similar background: he was a retired oil magnate of legendary success. While the bearded man had very few equals, these men were among the few.

Months later, I received a surprise invitation, along with Michalak, to the man's large estate in Newport, Rhode Island. This lavish mansion, overlooking the Atlantic Ocean, was fittingly located on the same stretch as The Breakers, that esteemed bit of paradise on the long stretch of coast once owned by that famous family, the Vanderbilts.

Yet while Breakers lay dormant, this paradise, fittingly known as Redwood for the countless trees of that nature growing in the garden, was still active, yet away from prying eyes. As with the gatherings in

Switzerland, the Rite of Larmenius emblem dominated a sign outside his house and a Star-Spangled Banner waved softly in the breeze that summer's day.

Inside there were very few surprises. Priceless art hung from the walls as if one were touring the Louvre. Its furnishings of art and artefacts from all corners of the globe and history was, in every way imaginable, in keeping with his reputation as an art lover, history lover, philanthropist and idealist. If there was such a thing as idealism then Redwood was all this.

Following the tour, I was then invited to see Redwood's most unique feature. Behind a set of double doors, in keeping with the usual character of this opulent setting, the passage to what I initially assumed to be a wine cellar or basement was in truth, as it remains to this day, the most terrifying sight I have ever witnessed.

Descending the stairwell, I witnessed for the first time an area on first viewing somewhat reminiscent of a medieval dungeon. A large round table dominated the floor that seemed in keeping with a Masonic lodge. In the corner of the room a grotesque statue stood in the centre of what I am told was in fact an altar, protected by a tablecloth marked at the centre with a red cross in keeping with those used by the knights of chivalry in the days of the Crusades.

Unbeknown to me I was now introduced to the true nature of the Rite of Larmenius. Away from the flamboyant backdrop of the Alps and the swagger and the opulence of the magnates in suits, I sat around this circular table in between the oil magnate and the cabinet minister, opposite Alain Michalak. On this occasion Michalak's demeanour was more serious than at any other time in my memory – also for that matter any other time I spent with him in his remaining years. The bearded man sat at the head of the table, where he dominated the proceedings throughout. The seat, impeccable in design, I learned in later years was a throne once located in Avignon and used by many Popes and antipopes, a reality not lost in irony as I began to learn the true nature of the order. These were the true masters of the Rite of Larmenius: the most important of the important. If the game of life was a game of chess then these men are the players: everyone else the chess pieces. This was the final piece of the puzzle. Not only was I Ricard's successor as President of France, I was his successor in another way.

Of their purpose as yet I did not know, but following my forced acceptance to join this, the highest appendant body of the Masons, I was instructed to prove my worth. They removed a crucifix before me *with the challenge to avoid renouncing the crucifixion – the ultimate test for a man of the Catholic faith. They whipped me, taunted me and choked me with a rope as they told me to spit, urinate and other things to the cross, something which I avoided with iron resolve. Every man present I assumed at the time to be Christian and this was the true test of faith. For my part, I was told I had passed yet the nightmare was only just beginning.*

This peculiar ritual continued as I was introduced to the spectre of their worship. Many who attend lodges of the Rite of Larmenius and witness its statue, Asmodeus, demonic in appearance with angel's wings and serpents crawling around its feet, see little more than a lost ritual of minimal significance, supposedly in tribute to the legendary Temple of Solomon, a location that holds great mystery to all Masons. Yet only now did I learn it was so much more. They refer to it as an angel, but its inclusion is out of place with any Christian worship or any other religion known to me. Following my final challenge, reciting an oath, blindfolded, I was accepted as the new French Preceptor of this organisation known collectively as they were in their heyday: the Order of the Poor Fellow Soldiers of Christ and of the Temple of Solomon.

As time passed, my suspicions grew that these men were indeed none other than the continuation of that ancient order disbanded by His Holiness Clement V all those years ago, now returned in the curious surroundings of the mock cloisters over five thousand miles from where they once came. Its existence may remain hidden from the wider world yet now I understood that while the scattered elements of that organisation disintegrated, the survivors in turn became the founders of something bigger: a history, till now, untold.

While awaiting inevitable death in his cell, the last Grand Master of the Knights Templar, Jacques de Molay, passed over the reins to Jean-Marc Larmenius who then took control of the fleeing order. They accurately foresaw that the accusations placed upon them by the King of France and weak Pope would leave Europe in a vacuum. Following the Templar demise with so little found, the key properties were passed to the Knights Hospitallers and Philip gained little. Yet the end result was less than any expected. The gap left by the Templars caused ripples. And those who had survived could take up root throughout the world. Many of them joined with the Rite of Stonemasonry, thus disguising their true identity. They saw their mission not only as survival, but also revenge on those who had caused their downfall. Even those who had aided it were not to be spared.

The new Templars took up the portents of the last of the original masters. The king who had betrayed them was murdered: as were his remaining kin: all within fourteen years. The first act came at Bannockburn where Templars fleeing France came to Scotland, a country itself excommunicated. The King of England was punished for his cowardice and the Scottish King rewarded.

The Hundred Years' War was an inevitability following France's delicate state and lust for power. The lasting conflict developed the vacuum and the Templars flexed their muscles. The new Swiss mercenaries would prove to be an invaluable asset taking on the skills of the old order by its new members untainted by the political allegiances of the past. And once the organisation had established its political and military foundations it spread its financial ones. In the secrecy of Switzerland, the order continued to use the banking knowledge and resources of their predecessors. They were successful, but they remained anonymous. Switzerland developed as its own nation incorporating the excellence of their banking and military under the guise of the order's flag to opposite colours. It funded war, not for personal gain but to see its enemies fall.

In the coming years its wings touched all corners of the globe. They voyaged from Scotland to the New World and the new order in Portugal travelled to America and beyond using the knowledge of their predecessors. In time they put markers in place and the order slowly returned to the surface as affiliates of the Masons and its appendant bodies, notably the Rite of Larmenius.

Its corporations thrived, its founders profited. Yet was this the true nature of their being? I was assured it was not. The real motivation was unspeakable. Their demise was the ultimate betrayal.

In the 1500s their hatred of the Church they once served escalated into a bitter feud, bringing about both Reformation and the power struggle that followed. After Scotland's return to England's rule they put down the Jacobite Rebellion, cementing the establishment of a united kingdom. They had discovered America and now set about freeing it. The Founding Fathers were all inducted into the ways of the Templars and the new nation was born. Next came their oldest enemy. Secretly financing and dictating the rise of Napoleon I, the Templars eliminated every remaining descendant of Philip IV.

Their revolution brought about the true end to those who had betrayed them. France still carried the aura of its past and it was decided a new direction was needed. France had to be rid of its tainted past and the fickleness of the aristos make way for the hardened and the prudent. Under the guidance of the Templars, Napoleon was triumphant. Louis XVI was deposed, de Molay was avenged. Now the new government began with Templar control.

Yet of their other rivals only the ally of the king who caused their demise remained. Napoleon marched on the Papal States with success. Other attempts followed. The power of the Church was weakened, but Rome, for the time being, survived.

Throughout the 19th century the Templars, under the guise of others, continued. The New Order has seen to it that the world would be safe for those with the correct knowledge and this continued over the next century. But they were not without enemies. Adolf Hitler may be revered as history's greatest villain, yet for the Templars he was their biggest threat. His attempts to wipe out the order failed, and fascism, a dogma that failed to uphold their values of Liberty, Equality and Fraternity, was destroyed.

In the years that followed their attentions returned to religion. In the 1980s Banco Ambrosiano fell under Templar control and the biggest enemy of the order was wounded. The murder of John Paul I was agreed by these men long before and the attempt on the life of his successor swiftly followed.

To someone who has lived his entire political career in the shadow of the Templars, the signs of history are now obvious. And even during my short time their mission for total autonomy has moved forward. Over time the cast has changed, even in my time, and while I was once the apprentice, I am soon to be a master. Former President of the New France: first in command of the New World.

The Templars sought to remodel the world so that the errors of the past, which led to their demise, would be replaced. And they have stopped at nothing. They will stop at nothing. Their tentacles touch every great organisation and bank across the globe, and have significant influence for every major religion. For years they have attempted to infiltrate the Vatican, their methods, even to those close, not obvious.

Now, at last, it is done.

52

Nobody spoke for quite some time. The clock on the wall suggested it was approaching eight-thirty in the evening and visiting hours were nearly over. At around eight-fifteen, a pretty nurse in her early thirties came by to check Gabrielle's temperature, followed soon after by an experienced doctor for a follow-up test. He checked her eyes, nose, ears and blood pressure and confirmed she was mildly concussed. He suggested they keep her in one night for observation but all being well she could go first thing in the morning.

Despite the late hour it was still light out in Newport. The sun burned yellow and orange as it faded behind the horizon, forming shadows in the faraway distance, and reflecting its light off the calm blue ocean like a gigantic mirror.

Gabrielle's hands shook, causing some of the pages to fall across the floor. She had read it once, then again, then several more times and still it failed to sink in. She attempted to focus once more on the words she had just read, but the more she did so the more her vision became hazy: not through tiredness or as a result of any medical condition.

This simply could not be real.

She opened her mouth, struggling to speak. "What exactly does this mean?"

Mark looked at Mike but neither spoke straightaway.

"It means you were right," Mike said eventually. "These Templars are real. And they have orchestrated every one of these murders."

Gabrielle nodded. In many ways it was a relief: a strange feeling of peace of mind that the long weeks of uncertainty in blind pursuit of the murderers of her father had come to fruition. Yet in succeeding she now faced a different fear. Twice she had nearly been killed; twice the Vatican had saved her. She felt tears inside her but controlled breathing maintained outward composure.

"Why?" she asked. "Why have they done this?"

Mark looked at her. "It seems there are many powerful men who want proof of the organisation buried. Looking at Devére, the order's motives were survival and revenge, yet that has now changed. According to this they have already brought about the French Revolution. Revenge has ultimately eliminated their enemies but given them control as an outcome. Devére was, in many ways, a by-product of their success. Even from an early age he was lined up to be president."

Gabrielle: "But this was over two hundred years ago. The order ended over seven hundred years ago. How can any of this be significant? How can they still be concerned with avenging the past . . ."

"I don't know," Mark said. "Yesterday I was unaware they even existed. But let's face facts: the Vatican and the Templars have a long history. I've investigated things I never knew existed: that the world doesn't know exists. This order has been active throughout history, operating from under a cloak. Can you possibly imagine the reaction of the wider world if they knew?"

"Oh, my God, this can't be happening . . ."

"Think about it this way. If the Templars do exist, as Mikael Devére claimed, then they have so much at stake. After all, they have practically become a conglomerate claiming government of every major country in the world. Their foundations have been in place for so long, to remove it would have major knock-on effects across the entire world." Mark grimaced. "Worryingly still, it sounds as though key figures at the Vatican could be in league with this group."

Gabrielle put her hands to her mouth. She looked briefly at the clock and saw that less than three minutes had passed since the last time she had looked. The unknown Vatican policeman still guarded the door with military efficiency yet in the light of recent events she struggled to see him as ample security. Mikael Devére, the greatest President of the New France, under the thumb of these nameless men.

"I just can't believe it. It just doesn't make sense."

Mark nodded. "If it wasn't for you, we'd never have found them."

She looked at Mark, for now remaining silent. Was this a gesture of appreciation? If so, its significance was non-existent. Her mind flashed back to Rosslyn, Newport, and the Vatican. Visions turned into blurs.

Mark: "Now, Ms Leoni, we have something very important to deal with. Please answer as best you can, your answer could be vital."

Gabrielle nodded. Without realising it, she was holding Mike's arm again. She looked at him awkwardly and put her hand to her hair.

"What was your father's relationship with Mikael Devére?"

Gabrielle looked back blankly. "None. I mean they were friends but . . ."

Mark nodded, his expression neutral. "Did your father have any regular business arrangements with Devére?"

Suddenly Gabrielle's facial expression hardened. "My father was not a Templar . . . how dare you . . ."

"He never suggested he was," Mike said.

"Yeah, I bet he wasn't."

"All right, I'm not prepared to rule anything out," Mark said. He held her gaze for several seconds and inhaled with difficulty. "But Mike told me that this Zeno diary was found in a Leoni et Cie safe deposit box, registered in the name of Mikael Devére, and its details had been entrusted to your father. And, it just so happens, the diary all but clarifies the order's existence."

Gabrielle hesitated. "They were friends; that's all I know."

"Your father never spoke of them?"

"No," she held her head in her hands. "Devére came to the château a couple of times."

"Alone?"

"No. Like the night Mike came for the first time – when you were there."

Mark nodded. No surprises. "Did your father ever discuss banking with Mikael Devére?"

"How the hell should I know?"

A further pause followed, this time more awkward in nature. Gabrielle looked at both men with contempt, her frustration continuing to heighten. Somehow she managed to control her emotions. After all, she told herself, they were the ones trying to help her.

"As far as I'm aware they didn't," Gabrielle said. "I was never party to their conversations."

Mark rubbed his chin. He looked at Mike but remained silent.

Gabrielle eyed them both, now increasingly annoyed. "Do you wanna tell me what this is all about?"

Mark hesitated. "There were other things in Devére's safe. There were three letters from people who we now believe to be senior Templars. They refer to them as preceptors. What's more, at least two had a direct link to your father and Leoni et Cie."

Gabrielle's expression was one of worry. "You've known all this time? Come on, tell me."

Mike remained silent.

"Does the name Danny D'Amato ring any bells?" Mark asked.

"Vaguely."

"How about Lord Parker?"

She grimaced. "I think Mike may have mentioned him."

Mark's tone hardened. "Well I'm sure you're quite familiar with Gilbert de Bois."

A look of horror crossed her face. Mike grimaced uncomfortably.

"And perhaps another you'll also recall?" Mark said.

Gabrielle looked forward aggressively as Mark removed a further sheet from his pocket. It was simply a list of names.

"Also found within Mikael Devére's safe in Mauritius. It is a list. According to Mike, your uncle coincidentally referred to it as a Larmenius Charter: named after the man who replaced de Molay. Devére has listed every Grand Master in history."

Gabrielle scanned the list. She had seen a previous list to the early 1800s but this one went further. This included famous names right through to the present day. She recognised the famous name of Ricard, the former French President. She also noticed Prince Henry St Clair in the 1300s, presumably Zichmni. Then she looked with shock at the name of the current master.

"You recognise that name?" Mark asked.

Gabrielle nodded. She certainly knew.

"Another man associated with the legendary Starvel Group and also a known member of the Rite of Larmenius. A man Mike so happened to spill wine over the night you met."

Mike frowned uncomfortably as he reminded him.

Gabrielle nodded coldly at the list. Written in capital letters at the bottom of the sheet.

Grand Master of the Knights Templar 1996-present. The Chief Executive of Starvel.

Louis Velis.

The multi-storey car park was largely deserted by ten. Luxury motors, ranging in age from eight years to a few days, lined the parking bays of all nine levels like a trader's forecourt, providing an air of respectability in keeping with the smart hotel to which it was joined. Small groups of newly arrived guests walked with purpose in the direction of the doors that led to the hotel, heavy suitcases trailing behind them, their wheels echoing. Outside, the sky was overcast, rain falling heavily against the concrete, forming puddles on the streets below. The streets were quiet, the few people who walked its sidewalks did so with grim tenacity, wrapped up in heavy coats, hoods covering their heads, and armed with umbrellas to protect themselves from the rain. Despite the rain it was not particularly cold, yet there was wind in the air, its sudden outbursts bouncing off the concrete surroundings, causing an unappealing whistling noise to echo throughout the car park.

At just after ten-thirty, Randy Lewis advanced cautiously through the doorway of level five and headed towards the far end of the car park. He followed the markings to the end of the nearest row of parked cars and turned left at a minor crossroads, heading towards the exit ramp approximately two hundred metres away. Although the car park was clean and well lit, he was nervous, a rarity for him. The sound of silence, interrupted by the occasional gust of wind, was unsettling. Although the hour was late he was surprised how quiet it was. The five-star hotel had a reputation for its fine facilities and Charlotte was vibrant at night.

The slamming of a car door caught him slightly unaware. Pausing momentarily, he gazed across the car park but failed to find a source. For the briefest of seconds he continued to monitor the area close to the exit, for now deserted and devoid of any movement. As the seconds passed he noticed a smartly dressed married couple walking in the direction of the hotel entrance.

The situation felt threatening, strangely threatening. The adequate lighting caused shadows, providing pillars and posts with random silhouettes, shooting out in various directions. In the distance the sound of engines and brakes against tyres caused a sharp screeching sound, echoing before fading.

He tightened his jacket. The sooner this was over the better.

At the end of the stretch he reached another minor crossroad. In front of him he saw ramps leading to the floors above and below, whereas to his left and right the parking bays continued. At first he looked to his left: another endless selection of parking bays were filled with motors. To the right, the road continued to the far wall where the parking bays were largely unused.

Heading to the right, he walked across the unused bays in the direction of two pillars in close proximity to the wall. The area was darker in comparison. Fragments of glass covered parts of the floor, attributed to the broken wall light that was still to be replaced. On first inspection the area seemed deserted, yet it had one strange feature.

Puffs of smoke were spiralling upwards from behind the farthest pillar.

Clenching his briefcase tightly in his right hand, Lewis continued in the direction of the pillar. He looked over his shoulder, satisfied he was otherwise alone. The command was quite explicit that he should not encourage any extra interest. Based on the accountant's erratic behaviour earlier that day Lewis simply put it down to senseless paranoia, yet he was well aware that seven men had recently been murdered. However remote the chances: he knew anything was possible.

Behind the pillar, a figure was shuffling uncomfortably. Unsurprisingly, the figure was a man, recognisable even in the poor light as Ged Fairbanks. He was dressed in a raincoat and held a black umbrella. A black briefcase was resting at an angle against the nearest pillar and a cigarette was present in his other hand. He walked back and forth, seemingly oblivious to the wider world. Not for the first time his expression was one of concern.

"Ged," he said. "I got your text."

Fairbanks did not respond. He monitored Lewis for less than a second before peering at the floor. He inhaled on his cigarette and exhaled lengthily: smoke invaded Lewis's nostrils, a sickening reminder of the awkward visit to GPLA earlier that day.

Silence followed, broken by the sound of doors closing. Seconds later the sound was followed by the revving of an engine. Over one hundred metres away car headlamps shone brightly, briefly causing shadows across the pillar before disappearing as the car changed direction. Lewis watched the lights: they belonged to a modern sedan, heading down to the floor below.

He returned his attention to the accountant before turning away, a reflex against the smoke.

"Ged, what's this all about? Why the hell did you bring me here?"

Fairbanks exhaled vigorously and made lengthy eye contact for the first time. His green eyes seemed somehow lost in the bad light and his facial expression was in keeping. He flicked some ash away with two quick movements of the finger and cleared his throat by coughing.

"You ask a lotta questions, Randy," he said, the cigarette causing a red glow in the darkness. He breathed smoke and gazed intently at Lewis. "It don't do well to ask too many questions."

Lewis looked at his friend with a bemused expression. "What in God's name are you talking about, Ged?"

"You have to be mighty careful, Randy, asking a lotta questions and all. You never know who might be listening."

Fairbanks threw his cigarette to the floor. He stamped it out with his foot and cleared his throat without covering his mouth. For the first time Lewis noticed a stench of whiskey on his breath.

"Have you been drinking?"

The accountant breathed clean air. "Look, we haven't got much time," he said. He bent down with difficulty, almost stumbling, and picked up his briefcase. He opened both locks one after the other and removed the content. It was a large document, in keeping with an audit. He handed it to Lewis.

"Ever since GPLA started auditing Leoni et Cie people have been asking questions. Nathan Walls asked a lotta questions. Martin Snow asked a lotta questions. Jermaine Llewellyn asked a lotta questions. They didn't die from no heart attacks, Randy."

Lewis nodded, his facial expression stern. He opened his own briefcase, previously empty, and slid the document inside. When finished, Fairbanks handed him a flash drive fitting a USB connection.

"What is it?" Lewis asked.

"It's a PDF of the same document."

Lewis nodded. He placed it carefully in an inside pocket.

"Ged, come on. We've been friends a long time. What's this all about?"

Ged fired up another cigarette and exhaled immediately. "People have been following me, Randy. Ever since they got Walls they've been watching us like owls. These guys never sleep."

"Guys. Which guys?"

"You know I'm Rite of Larmenius?"

Lewis nodded.

Fairbanks smoked, this time louder than before. "Just read the goddamn document, Randy; everything you need is there."

Fairbanks looked at his watch.

"We didn't have this conversation, Randy. Now go. Leave. Don't look back."

The accountant looked nervously across the car park and satisfied himself they were still alone. Without saying another word, Lewis walked uncertainly back in the direction of the exit.

He thought about what Jacobs had said about him never being wrong about a hunch.

Only this time he hoped he was wrong.

53

Gabrielle looked blankly at the list. Had she misread it? Was this a hoax? This surely could not be true.

She felt her hands shaking. Her lips wobbled and her eyes started to water. For the first time her facial expression let her down: a façade of control and confidence that had earlier baffled Mark had now given way to one of anxiety.

Mike had seen it all before. Strangely in the circumstances he wondered what she was like when things were normal. Perhaps this was normal. What did it even mean to be normal? Could things ever be normal again after this?

Gabrielle looked up at Mark. "This doesn't make any sense."

"Well perhaps I can help you there," he said. "Over the years Starvel has grown into the largest conglomerate in the world, yet despite this it has also been at the centre of countless, shall we say, irregularities?"

"I know where you're going with this."

"I really don't think so. In 1994 a night watchman at Starvel was suspended when he blew the whistle on the bank after he stumbled on then CEO, Horatio Velis, another former Templar, and other Starvel employees burning documents, most of which supposedly dated back decades. In 1996 Horatio Velis personally failed to extend credit to the Swiss airways firm Glospar, which resulted in them having to ground their planes. Eventually they went out of business, a massive boost for one of his key buddies who is now, coincidentally, a major supporter of Danny D'Amato in his bid to become the next President of the USA. In 1997 the First Bank of America sued after three of their key employees left for Starvel, claiming Starvel attempted to steal clients and trade secrets, coincidentally an accusation that came around the time that Deputy Chairman, Richard West, also according to media speculation a member of the Rite of Larmenius, was found hanging from a bridge in Seattle. In 1998 three directors were accused of accountancy scandal after Starvel's accounts were boosted by over $25 billion. Since Louis Velis took over in 1998, they were refused the right to take over countless banks, including, you may remember, Leoni et Cie, by Randy

Lewis and the Federal Reserve due to accounting irregularities and monopoly fears. Nevertheless, that did not stop them from merging Louis Velis's own companies with that of his father's, forming the biggest conglomerate in history. In 2002 they were fined over $50 million by the Feds after it emerged they had been transferring funds illegally from a Federal Reserve account at Starvel AG to an unregulated offshore account in the Dominican Republic and there is a similar report for using IMF funds in the same way. At least five of their former employees have faced gaol time after operating without a licence, tax evasion, bank fraud and money laundering. In 2005 two of their guys were done for insider dealing. Even last year the Feds made a formal request to travel to a Starvel base in Switzerland investigating a multimillion-dollar tax evasion scheme involving several banks including Starvel. They've been accused of marketing tax evasion strategies to their richest clients: most of which are believed to be Rite of Larmenius members, and even in the last eighteen months they were fined $500 million by the Feds for conspiracy to defraud. Going back donkeys' years, Starvel has been associated with trouble and even to this day whispers still exist of their connections with the Rite of Larmenius. These men are among the wealthiest on the planet. And guess what?"

"What?"

"Hidden inside the safe in Gullet's casino were five receipts for $4 million from unpublished numbered Starvel accounts. Five days after receiving the last he hires a Jeep in Mauritius. That night Devére is murdered."

Gabrielle's head hurt – a hard throbbing sensation made a million times worse as she remembered the man's past presence in her home. Strangely it all made sense.

"Velis was one of my dad's best friends."

Mark grimaced. "I know."

"He was at the funeral. He's stayed at the château. They even talked about going into business together. Velis talked about making a takeover of Leoni et Cie. My dad said he was one of the greatest men he'd ever met."

"There's no doubting the man is gifted. But he's also a ruthless cold-blooded murderer," Mark leaned in closer. "Gabrielle, this man murdered your father."

Gabrielle's face withered. Mike put his hand around her but she shied away. She attempted to recover, but failed. Stray tears fell down her face.

"Listen to me. I know this is hard for you to understand, perhaps impossible, but you have to face facts. Your father . . ."

"No," she said firmly. "This can't be. My dad even attended his daughter's wedding. He even . . . oh, my God."

Gabrielle's facial expression changed to one of horror. Standing silently in the open doorway was Rachel.

Ludovic Gullet waited patiently behind the wheel of his dark sedan, parked to avoid attention. He waited until the newest arrival was completely out of sight before leaving the car.

Gabrielle wrapped the covers around herself tightly. The room somehow seemed colder than before and outside the clear blue sky had turned to twilight. Streetlights began to flicker in the distance like small stars lining the city and basking it in a soft halo stretching to the sky.

Gabrielle stared at the door, her heart pounding. Rachel stood quietly, her face a picture of genuine concern. Yet she was distant.

"I just heard what happened," Rachel said, walking slowly towards the bed. "I came straight from Boston as soon as I heard. How are you?"

Gabrielle unwrapped her naked legs and eased herself out of bed. Mike noticed and quickly got to his feet.

Gabrielle shook her head. "Oh, God no."

Mike grabbed Gabrielle's arm. "Gabrielle, wait, it's okay."

"Gullet was waiting for us. He knew exactly where we were," she said, her head still shaking. "They knew we were there."

Rachel put her hand to her mouth and tears began to trickle down her face.

"Gabrielle, relax. It's okay, we've been through this."

"Louis Velis a traitor. This is Louis Velis's wife."

Inside the lush hotel room a lone desk lamp offered the only light for Vatican banker Randy Lewis as he turned another page of the lengthy document. In front of him, countless sheets with various dates and titles, mostly dating back to the late 1990s, were scattered untidily. Official stamps in the top right corners, often referring to something unimportant never to be seen again after being archived in a warehouse somewhere in the middle of nowhere, gave the impression of respectability and the numbers at this point added up.

He turned the page and started to scan the text. He was not sure what he was looking for but he had a good idea. If it existed, it would be where he was looking.

After scanning the final line of the first paragraph he placed it on the side and sipped his coffee, now starting to cool after twenty minutes. Nothing had presented itself.

At least not yet.

A cold awkward hush descended on the room. Gabrielle stood rigidly, her face merely centimetres away from Rachel's. Her face was red: a combination of fatigue and anger. For the first time in hours she was standing and a sudden onset of nausea hit her. The room seemed to spin around her, making it a struggle to keep her balance.

Suddenly she was aware that she was being held back. She could hear Mike barking her name loudly in her ear. She looked at Mike then Mark. Finally she looked once more at Rachel.

"Mark has already spoken to Rachel," Mike said. "It was the first thing he did. I had no idea."

Gabrielle looked at Rachel then Mark.

Mark nodded. "As soon as I found out about Velis, I tried to locate you. Learning that Velis's former wife was your best friend, my first intention was to question her."

Mark breathed deeply.

"At first I did consider the possibility that Velis had been using his former wife to keep an eye on you, or worse . . ." he broke eye contact and smiled at Rachel. "However, after speaking with Ms Flores, I am satisfied that she is completely innocent of everything that has gone on and is in no way involved with her estranged husband."

Rachel's eyes flooded with tears, ruining her makeup and forming a messy, sticky substance that flowed down her pretty face. Almost immediately Gabrielle's mood changed. Anger finally relented and her eyes began to fill up again. Releasing herself from their grip she opened her arms and squeezed Rachel tightly.

"I'm so sorry," Rachel said. "Markus told me everything."

Mike and Mark looked at each other awkwardly as Rachel and Gabrielle mumbled words, overlain with the sound of crying yet clearly understandable to both ladies. They cried for several minutes until finally Gabrielle returned to her bed and covered herself in blanket.

Mike sat back down, his hands placed to his mouth in deep contemplation. Mark wandered towards the door and said something to Gregore. The casually dressed Vatican agent walked away and Mark closed the door behind him.

"I always knew there was something," Rachel said eventually. "The four years we were actually together were littered with irregularities.

Some nights he'd stay up all night in his study. And there were business trips he made without warning, secret bank accounts that made no sense. I assumed he was just having an affair."

Mike scratched his head, nearly laughing but controlling himself. No matter how hard he tried the reality of the situation refused to sink in.

"I understand you once worked for Starvel?" Mike asked.

Rachel nodded. "It's how we met," she said after blowing her nose. "I was twenty-two. I wanted to make it as a marine biologist but my parents kept on at me to get a real job, you know?"

Mike nodded.

"So I got in with Starvel AG, at the bottom. Then after a while I met Louis."

"And he never said anything about his activities? Nothing about the Rite of Larmenius?"

She shook her head. "No. He was very unpredictable. Loved his privacy. We had three places: one in Manhattan, one in Zürich and the summerhouse at Rhode Island. That place gave me the creeps," she said, shaking slightly. "It's one of the oldest houses in New England. There were rooms he never let me in. He was particularly possessive about the basement."

Mike nodded once more. "Why did you split up?"

She forced a laugh. "I wanted to leave him for so long but I was so afraid. Eventually he got bored of me. I got millions in the divorce."

"Less than half his stuff I bet."

Rachel nodded, forcing a smile. "I've never had to work since."

Mike smiled sympathetically and put his hand to his chin. Small amounts of stubble had returned after two days without shaving. He looked at Mark, raising his eyebrows. Then Gabrielle spoke.

"I just can't believe these guys knew we were there. How did they know?"

Suddenly the room fell silent. She looked on with annoyance as Mark and Mike exchanged further glances. Gabrielle smelt a conspiracy.

"What? You know something. What is it?"

Mike grimaced. "Look, there's no easy way to say this."

Gabrielle got to her feet and poked Mike in the arm. "What do you know? Come on. They knew we were there. Someone must have told. Come on, who was it? Tell me."

Feeling the continuous irritation of Gabrielle pushing her long fingernails into his arm he finally answered.

"It was your uncle," Mike said.

Suddenly she stopped. A cold chill breezed through her. Did she hear him correctly?

"Gabrielle, wait . . ."

"Uncle Henry? Where is he?"

"Gabrielle."

"Where is he?" she pressed, now louder than before.

Mark looked at Mike, searching for words.

"Where is he?" she demanded, punching Mike.

"Down the hall. Room 408."

Without waiting for further clarification she pushed past Mark and opened the door. The corridor, flowing with activity less than ten minutes earlier, was now practically deserted bar a small number of cleaners, busy washing the floor. The flurry of visitors had now dissipated due to the lateness of the hour.

She walked across the slippery surface, the tiled floor cold on her bare feet, causing a chilling sensation reaching all the way to her kidneys. She looked briefly at the signs, pointing in the direction of various departments such as Cardiology and Physiotherapy. The door to her room was one of many lining the corridor, all of which were numbered, each beginning with a four. She wandered the corridor with purpose, reading each number. 405. 406. 407.

Mike had caught up with her. He grabbed her arm.

"Gabrielle, wait."

"Let go of me, Mike."

"Gabrielle, please don't go in there."

Gabrielle ignored his request and pushed through the door of room 408. She entered the room quickly. Unsurprisingly it was identical in appearance to hers. A single bed dominated the room and lying on the bed was her uncle.

Suddenly her blood ran cold. Bruises marked his face and arms: all that was visible above the thin white sheets. The presence of his heartbeat was evident from the heart rate sensor on the opposite side of his bed, bleeping at regular intervals, attached to his chest by a series of leads. On the monitor she could see jumbled lines and random numbers that offered her no significance other than that her uncle was breathing.

Gabrielle's eyes filled with tears. She felt her chest tightening, her lungs refusing to take in air. Almost trancelike, she walked closer to his bedside and rubbed his hand with hers. She tightened her grip on his hand: no longer large and warm like she had remembered, but cold and lifeless. Somehow he looked older than he had the last time she saw him.

Yet there was a genuine sense of tranquillity on his face that she found strangely reassuring, as if he was oblivious to the injuries he had sustained: instead almost resembling a picture of a child lying calm and undisturbed dreaming in peaceful slumber.

Randy Lewis's eyes lit up as he examined the document before him. After scanning the final paragraph for the umpteenth time, he exhaled energetically.

His suspicions were confirmed.

Lewis removed the memory stick from his jacket pocket and inserted it into the USB port of his laptop. The file took only seconds to load.

Lightly clicking on the mouse pad, he scanned the PDF for consistency and found it was exactly the same as the paper document.

Fairbanks had done him proud on this one.

Rolling over his wrist, he looked at the time on his watch. It was approaching 2:34 a.m. The clock on the bottom right corner of the screen said 8:24 a.m. The Vatican bankers would be up, Central European Time.

Lewis opened his email account and attached the file to an email, sending it to four contacts. The first was for Rogero, the next Dominguez, and then Swanson. Contemplating his next move he added Cardinal Utaka to the list.

Two clicks of the mouse in rapid succession and it sent successfully. Seconds later he sent a second email, this time to de Courten and Pessotto. This one contained a different attachment, one that explained so much.

Lewis exhaled loudly, tightness leaving his lungs.

There was nothing more he could do till morning.

In a dark corner of the hotel car park, away from watchful eyes, Ludovic Gullet stood over the slumped body of his latest victim. After looking with satisfaction at the look of despair still etched across the accountant's stone dead features, he walked away coldly, silently relishing the familiar rush of adrenaline he felt on every occasion.

He looked at his watch. There was still time that night for his other target.

*

Deep within the mock medieval cloisters of the luxury Newport mansion, the Senator for the State of Montana, the highly acclaimed academic, the senior director of Leoni et Cie, the superlawyer, the former Chancellor of the Exchequer and the chief executive of Starvel spoke to one another with urgency.

Matters of privacy must remain a secret, the truth to the public is a lie and the real truth must remain private.

54

Juan Pablo Dominguez had spent the last four days travelling: La Paz to San Francisco, San Francisco to New York and finally New York to Rome.

At Leonardo da Vinci-Fiumicino he collected his BMW from the long stay car park and drove through the empty streets back to his apartment in central Rome. He had barely slept for two days but that was nothing new. Throughout his career he had built a reputation on endurance and often made do sleeping in cabs and on flights forsaking rest as a poor alternative to work. Despite his semi-retirement at the relatively young age of 50, six years ago, he maintained his discipline for efficiency.

By the time he sat down at an outside table of a café in close proximity to the Trevi Fountain it was approaching 14:15. Yet time and day were misleading to him. South America to North America, west to east, and then to Europe may have left him feeling slightly disoriented, but under the circumstances he felt reassuringly fresh.

A waitress delivered freshly made coffee and placed it before him on the clean metal table that was covered in a red and white tablecloth. After adding one sugar and stirring the frothy liquid, he looked around to take in the sights. The Trevi Fountain was trickling away peacefully, tourists whiled the time away pleasantly, and up above the sky was a clear shade of blue without the presence of cloud.

After taking a second to relax, he removed his BlackBerry and checked his emails. There were three in total. The first was from a man he had met in Bolivia. He scanned it: nothing important. The next was from Delta Air Lines: he had sufficient reward points for a free flight.

The final one was from Randy Lewis. Marked urgent.

There was a document attached. He opened it and began to read.

The young Vatican policeman turned away in disgust. Never in his eight years working as a detective had he witnessed such a sight. The victim had not been dead long but the unappealing stench of a bullet wound was already beginning to manifest itself.

Judging by his expression, the victim had been caught unaware. His face suggested confusion rather than fear, and the condition of his chest, ripped apart by six bullets, suggested he was shot at close range. Blood marked his white shirt, now largely destroyed and marked by blood that had clotted around the wound.

Inside the luxury hotel room a crime scene had been set up for over an hour. Forensic experts searched the room for any clue, any hint of the killer's identity. Commissario Pessotto would have to hear about this. It was nearing 8:30 a.m. Eastern Time. The story would undoubtedly catch the headlines come late morning. This left little time to prepare.

Angelo Rogero sat back in his chair. His large hands were cupped thoughtfully around his mouth and a serious expression dominated his face.

A black laptop was open in front of him, its screen displaying the content of his latest email. The attachment was a long report sanctioned by GPLA with regard to the financial performance of Leoni et Cie, conducted over five months ago by the late Nathan Walls.

Two decades in charge of the greatest bank in South America had taught him to know the signs and how to deal with them. After looking once more at the information before him, he downed the remainder of his coffee and attempted to make a call on his mobile. He had always thrived on urgency and he had always conquered. He needed to act fast.

He needed to return to Rome.

Twenty minutes later, Dominguez was sprinting through a crowded street less than a mile away from the Vatican. He crossed the street without looking both ways, darting west towards the Castel Sant'Angelo.

As he passed an electronics shop something made him stop. His rapidly pounding heart missed a beat as he turned slowly towards the television that was playing in the showroom.

The breaking news: a man had been murdered in a hotel room in Charlotte, North Carolina. The man in his fifties had been shot six times in the chest.

Dominguez couldn't hear the sound but he instantly recognised the photograph accompanying the story. Vomit came to his throat.

It was Randy Lewis.

Gabrielle sat quietly by her uncle's bedside. Despite the heat, her hands shook: the blanket, wrapped loosely around her dressing gown, failed to make much difference.

She had not spoken much to anyone that morning. Sleep was out of the question. She had refused the night nurse's offer of sleeping medication. They offered her tablets; she refused. They offered her a session with a psychologist; she refused. They offered her food; she refused. They insisted they keep her in for observation.

Mike and Mark agreed.

A nurse was leaving the room after checking Henry Leoni's condition just as Mike entered. He held the door open for her before walking over to Gabrielle. He saw that the blanket around her shoulders was falling.

Despite noticing his hand on her shoulders she didn't respond. Instead she continued to gaze aimlessly through the window at the distant horizon. She seemed so innocent.

He considered enquiring of her health but decided the question was pointless. Instead, he watched her as she maintained a lifeless stare, looking at nothing in particular, blinking from time to time.

For several seconds Mike did the same. For the first time that day he spared a second to wonder what had happened to Gullet. Was he dead? Who shot him? Did Gullet kill the man who shot him? Mike shook his head.

A few yards away, Henry Leoni lay unconscious on the hospital bed. His eyes were closed and his face bruised. An IV drip was attached to his left arm and several cables attached to his chest. The heartbeat sensor bleeped with consistency, the monitor updating at regular intervals.

"How is he?"

Gabrielle shook her head. "They say he's stable. I've never really known what it means."

Mike nodded. He wanted to help her; reassure her; anything he could.

"It means that he's in the best place to get better and that he wouldn't want you to worry."

Gabrielle turned and forced the briefest of smiles. She put her hand to her right eye as though to remove a loose eyelash, but there were no tears. Her gaze returned to the horizon.

Mike rubbed her shoulders softly and asked if there was anything else she needed. She shook her head and Mike smiled sympathetically.

As he prepared to leave, Mark entered. A serious expression crossed his face.

"We have to return to the Vatican," he said with authority. "Cardinal Tepilo, Commissario Pessotto and the oberst have summoned an emergency meeting. Randy Lewis has been murdered."

Juan Pablo Dominguez supported Cardinal Utaka as they walked side by side along the corridor before stopping in front of a closed door. Both looked at one another briefly with resigned expressions, hesitating before proceeding. Cardinal Utaka knocked gently on the door.

Dominguez exhaled nervously. A pause that lasted almost ten seconds seemed more like a lifetime to both men. The Colombian had never been to this part of the Vatican before and he always wondered how he would feel if he did. Yet never could he have predicted the circumstances.

Slowly the door opened and Dominguez came face to face with the occupant. Dressed in glorious white, reminiscent of the story of the Transfiguration, both men bowed reverently before the man, instantly recognisable as the current pontiff.

55

Vatican City

The meeting began on time. The doors to the Sistine Chapel were closed at both exits and Swiss Guards were posted at the doors, taking the place of the usual museum guards, standing with rigid authority and no hint of communication.

By 10 a.m. every attendee was present, sitting in equal spacing around the familiar table at the centre of the chapel. There were more chairs than usual.

At the head, President Rogero, dressed all in black, sat next to Juan Pablo Dominguez on one side and Giancarlo Riva on the other. Rogero remained taciturn, concentrating on the document in front of him while Riva chatted quietly with Cardinal del Rosi.

Mike was present: a first for him, sitting one empty space on from the cardinal. To his left was Gabrielle.

Alongside Gabrielle, Cardinal Tepilo sat opposite Rogero and he in turn sat next to Cardinal Utaka. Mark was next, one back from Thierry.

Next to the oberst was Swanson, who yawned for the umpteenth time. Dominguez came last, completing the table, taking advantage of the empty seat vacated by the absent Cardinal Atri.

Rogero cleared his throat emphatically and clapped his hands together with one swift bang.

"Thank you for coming at such short notice," he said, rising to his feet. With a hawk-like expression he monitored the reactions of all present, giving the impression he was speaking to everyone. "Cardinals Atri and Torres have sent their apologies. They are presently performing duties of office and have been unable to return in time."

Rogero looked briefly at Dominguez who was also scanning a large document. His face looked pale, much more so than usual. Swanson sat with his arms folded and Thierry likewise. Cardinal Utaka nodded briefly at the president but for now remained silent. He watched as

Rogero cleared his throat for a second time. The way he did so conveyed authority, causing an echo to reverberate around the chapel.

"Nevertheless," Rogero continued, his eyes darting across the room, "there are matters of extreme importance that must be dealt with swiftly. I am sure everybody is by now aware of the tragic circumstances surrounding Mr Lewis."

Heads nodded in unison.

"And I appreciate that everyone has forsaken important business to be here. I myself was out of the country."

Cardinal del Rosi nodded. "Precisely. Yesterday I was visiting a famine-stricken village in Botswana."

Cardinal Tepilo also nodded. "I delayed my trip to America as soon as I heard the tragic news."

Swanson studied the Camerlengo, but remained silent. He decided against informing the council that by attending he was breaking a promise to his granddaughter by failing to take her to Disneyland.

Thierry looked at Rogero. "I don't think we should waste time, Angelo. Let us proceed."

Cardinal del Rosi shot a look across the table at Thierry. "All right, oberst, give the president some air."

Rogero smiled, yet not altogether convincingly. "Shortly before Mr Lewis was killed, he sent an urgent email to myself, Juan, Mr Swanson and Cardinal Utaka. It appears as though Mr Lewis had made a personal visit to a Mr Ged Fairbanks, a senior director at GPLA."

A meaningless silence filled the room.

Cardinal Tepilo's facial expression suggested confusion. "The accountants?"

"Correct."

"What was that about?" asked Irving Swanson. "I'm afraid what with everything that's happened I haven't been able to check my emails."

"Perhaps it would be wise to start from the beginning, Angelo," Cardinal Tepilo said. "I am afraid I did not receive a copy."

Rogero nodded. "Very well. GPLA were chiefly responsible for auditing Leoni et Cie, in particular its American activities. Now, with prior knowledge to myself and Juan, Mr Lewis made a visit to GPLA's headquarters in North Carolina."

He paused momentarily, watching every reaction.

"We are still unsure of Mr Lewis's previous intentions and expectations. However," he paused uncomfortably. "Forgive me if I seem apprehensive. What he found is quite shocking."

Riva looked up at Rogero. Bollocks: that guy is never shocked.

"Well, president, you have told us where he went, but you are still to tell us what exactly he found," Riva said, arms folded. "I am afraid I also did not receive this email."

Rogero looked with interest at Riva. He was aware Riva had not been included on the email.

"According to this email, read by both Juan and myself," he said, gesturing to his fellow countryman, "Mr Lewis acquired a certain document, provided by this Mr Fairbanks. The document was a recent audit of Leoni et Cie assembled by Mr Nathan Walls."

Mike's ears pricked at the sound of that name. Gabrielle's eyes lit up. She turned and looked at Mark, Thierry and Cardinal Utaka. None of them looked surprised: each clearly had already been told.

Rogero inhaled deeply. There was an edge to the Colombian's expression, which was strangely out of character for him.

"I have read the document in insufficient detail to comment further," he said. "Juan has read it in far more detail. Perhaps I should leave it to him to give you a more informed overview."

This was hardly a rarity. Over the years Rogero often presented Dominguez the floor given half a chance. Yet this was hardly an act of cowardice. It was often said of Rogero that his greatest strength was that he knew when to take the floor and when to step down.

Dominguez rose slowly to his feet and gazed awkwardly at every face in turn. Exhaling slowly, he rubbed his hands together, a rare sign of nerves. He looked briefly at Cardinal Utaka and then at the glorious ceiling above him. In the eyes of all present, he looked strangely lost.

"Juan," Cardinal Utaka said, nodding reassuringly. "It's okay."

Dominguez made eye contact with the cardinal, grimacing a smile. "Thank you, eminence," he said. "Now you'll have to excuse me, gentlemen, Ms Leoni. As Angelo has said, the news is indeed shocking. Frankly I feel slightly ill."

Tepilo and Riva looked inquisitively at Dominguez. The comment seemed an understatement.

"The document written by Nathan Walls clearly was meant for the eyes of the regulators. Unfortunately it seems that the information it included never appeared before the relevant authorities. As you are all undoubtedly aware, Nathan Walls himself was recently murdered and if this is anything to go by, the reason may well be obvious."

Dominguez paused to inhale.

"Nathan Walls had been assigned the task of providing a thorough audit of Leoni et Cie's accounts, and this, it would seem, was no easy task. Yet what he did find was hardly convincing."

Dominguez leaned over the table and opened the large document to the thirtieth page. He skimmed the content at speed, turning pages at regular intervals.

"Page 37, paragraph three: Mr Walls states his discomfort at Leoni et Cie's extensive business network and declares that it could be used to move money across borders without regulation, which could in turn be used to inflate share prices."

Dominguez turned several pages.

"Page 47, second paragraph. Leoni et Cie's levels of lending in countries whose authorities are known to provide unsatisfactory standards of regulation and supervision have contributed to large levels of growth. Such levels of lending, particularly three loans to specific individuals or companies, would be illegal in US and Swiss law for a bank of their capital base. Such issues may cause liquidity problems if not properly supervised. Here, he criticises the directors for what he calls laxity with many of its loans unsecured."

A look of confusion crossed Gabrielle's face. What the heck was he talking about?

He turned another nine pages.

"Page 56, paragraph four. Mr Walls cites an abuse of depositors' trust. The bank has over two thousand and forty unpublished accounts with Starvel AG. Such practice, although not illegal in United States or Swiss law, is dubious and may be used as a platform for moving money undetected and potentially for money laundering. He goes on to suggest that there is overwhelming evidence that this has occurred."

Nervous expressions crossed the faces of most present.

"Perhaps most importantly," Dominguez said, turning to the penultimate page, "Mr Walls draws further attention to the bank's liquidity. According to the audit, if faced with liquidation the bank's reserves and cash flow would not provide sufficient coverage to pay off creditors. Over the last year alone the bank has lost over one thousand customers of multimillionaire status, denting the bank's asset portfolio by well in excess of $3 billion."

He paused briefly.

"Worse yet, there is also evidence to believe that over one hundred private accounts that include funds belonging to the Roman Curia have been funnelled inappropriately through this network. Going back to the merger with Rosco, he fears the company's bad loans could be in excess of what we first expected. Including recent losses, loss of customers and unsecured loans, in total he suggests as much as $10 billion could be unaccounted for."

Cardinal del Rosi's jaw dropped, as did Gabrielle's. Swanson looked nervously across the room at Riva, while Cardinal Tepilo bowed his head into his hands.

A serious hush descended on the chapel. The eyes of most present remained on Dominguez or Rogero as if questioning what they had just heard or perhaps waiting for a solution that was not forthcoming.

Finally, Cardinal del Rosi broke the silence. "What does this mean exactly?"

Dominguez looked at the cardinal from across the table. "What this means, eminence, is that Leoni et Cie's financial position is not as it seems. Frankly, the bank may not have the ability to survive of its own accord if faced with liquidation. If such a situation arose, unless it is recapitalised, the Vatican Bank would be dramatically undermined. Effectively, we are bankrupt."

Rogero breathed out with force while Cardinal del Rosi slammed the table.

"You expect us to sit here and swallow this . . ." del Rosi said, breaking off mid-sentence, his focus firmly planted on Dominguez. "$10 billion does not simply disappear!"

Dominguez shook his head. "I cannot answer how it did, eminence; particularly how Roman Curia money became used in this way. Nor can I answer how Leoni et Cie came to operate in some of these locations that Nathan Walls suggests. Mr Walls suggests the bank has accounts, and even branches, in the likes of Caracas, Bogotá and even many renowned tax havens of the Caribbean and the South Pacific. He even lists the names of towns and villages I had previously never heard of. I myself did not even realise Leoni et Cie had branches in South America. This could not have been achieved without the approval of the highest authority."

Suddenly all eyes fell on Gabrielle.

Cardinal Utaka looked at her without judgment. "Ms Leoni, did you have any idea what was going on?"

A couple of stray tears fell from her eyes. "I don't even know what it means."

Mark: "The manner and timings of the deaths of Jermaine Llewellyn and Mr Leoni seem in keeping with that of Mr Walls. Bearing in mind what has happened recently to Mr Lewis and Mr Fairbanks . . ."

"Fairbanks!" Tepilo shouted. "He is not dead as well?"

Mark nodded. "Yes, eminence: the story was also included on page nine of the *New York Post* and page six of the *Charlotte Observer*. Not the most important story of the day, I'm afraid."

Utaka looked at every face with an expression of astonishment. "Surely the rest of you read the papers?"

Swanson shrugged. "I was with my granddaughter."

Riva grimaced. The last thing he wanted to admit was that he was at a Juventus match.

A strange, yet controlled, argument broke out about nothing in particular. Rogero ascended to his feet and clapped his hands together loudly, ordering calm. Hush descended on the room. He gestured for Mark to continue.

Mark cleared his throat. "I have spoken to Oberst de Courten, Commissario Pessotto, President Rogero and Vice President Dominguez. Following the recent killings of both Mr Lewis and Mr Fairbanks in similar circumstances, it seems most likely from what we know that both Mr Leoni and Ms Leoni are themselves innocent of any involvement. Someone else, however, is not."

Silence followed. The silence was uncertain, somehow accusing in nature. A series of mumblings followed.

"How did Randy get this?" Swanson asked.

Rogero shook his head. "I am unaware of the circumstances, Mr Swanson. Or why GPLA did not make this public. Mr Lewis sadly was killed before we had the chance to ask any questions."

"Nathan Walls was himself killed less than a week before the audit was due. The one presented to the authorities had clearly been tailored," Thierry said.

A quiet grim realisation overcame all present. Gabrielle looked at Mark and Thierry, quietly observing their features. It was clear that connections had already been made.

"Has His Holiness been informed?" del Rosi asked.

Utaka nodded. "Yes. He is presently at Gandolfo considering the situation. In the meantime he has asked for immediate action to ensure security of the bank."

"What kind of security?" del Rosi asked. "Financial or that no one else gets murdered?"

Cardinal Tepilo bowed his head into his hands, shaking his head. Thierry grimaced; so did Mark.

"I am in a position unsuitable to discuss such unfortunate business," Rogero declared. "However, that is why Oberst de Courten and Agent Mäder are here."

Rogero gestured for Mark to take the floor. He nodded briefly at Rogero before ascending to his feet.

"Commissario Pessotto has unfortunately been called away

following the death of Mr Lewis," Mark began. "He has asked me to attend in his place; I hope this is acceptable to everyone."

Several heads nodded in unison. He looked at Thierry and the Swiss Guard nodded.

"Following the deaths of Al Leoni and Jermaine Llewellyn and my somewhat uncomfortable audience with Mikael Devére, Commissario Pessotto sent me to Prague to follow up his claims," Mark said. "Once we knew that Major von Sonnerberg had been murdered, it was only a matter of time before potential evidence was found regarding his claim for Cardinal Faukes."

Mark inhaled deeply, his eyes watching people's reactions.

"After examining various pieces of evidence we became aware of a connection between a string of murders that had recently occurred. Thanks to Mr Devére, we learned of a connection between the deaths of Major von Sonnerberg and Cardinal Faukes and also the deaths of Nathan Walls and Martin Snow, a financial commentator and one-time employee at Starvel AG. Now this report assembled by Nathan Walls was never made public," Mark continued. "Now I can only speculate but seeing as both Mr Lewis and Mr Fairbanks were murdered following Mr Fairbanks's decision to entrust this document to Mr Lewis and seeing how Nathan Walls was murdered before its content became common knowledge, the motive seems clear. This is something that none of us predicted and goes against all of our initial beliefs."

"You talk of speculations, Mr Mäder. Perhaps it would be beneficial to offer some hard facts," Tepilo said.

Del Rosi looked strongly at the Camerlengo, then at Mark. "What about the others?"

Mark: "Martin Snow was a senior employee at Starvel AG, an organisation where, according to this report, Leoni et Cie has numerous unpublished accounts. He was also respected for his regular economics articles. He frequently wrote about takeovers, finance deals et cetera."

"Quite right," Swanson said. "It was said of Snow that if a firm's shares went down one day and he wrote about it, they'd be in administration by the end of the week."

Mark nodded. "He appeared on television as an analyst. People criticised him for his negativity. Key bankers stayed away from him. Called him a liar."

"So what do you think, Mr Mäder? You think that Mr Snow somehow became aware of this problem and was killed before he made it public?" Riva asked.

Mark looked across the room at Riva. "Yes, Mr Riva, I think that's exactly what happened."

Thierry nodded. "Ok, Mäder, I think they get the picture."

Mark nodded.

"And Major von Sonnerberg?" Riva asked openly. "I am certain that man was no Starvel AG employee."

Mark: "That one remains unclear, as does a motive for Cardinal Faukes. However, in the light of recent events the possibility cannot be ruled out that Cardinal Faukes knew something that we did not. All we do know is that they were murdered and that if it had not been for Mikael Devére we would probably never have known."

Cardinal Tepilo shook his head softly. "Surely, Mr Mäder, if these poor souls really were murdered in order to keep this little situation secret, then who initiated their deaths?"

Del Rosi nodded. "Come on, Mäder, oberst, let's hear some comments."

For several minutes Mark spoke of Ludovic Gullet and the activities in Mauritius and also the deaths of Llewellyn and Al Leoni. Once finished, he returned to his seat.

Rogero's expression hardened. "You believe Starvel or Starvel AG ordered the murders of these men in a bid to keep the plight of Leoni et Cie secret?"

Thierry exhaled deeply. "If what I understand to be correct is indeed correct then I'm afraid it extends even further than that."

Rogero folded his arms. Thierry glanced at Mark and the Vatican policeman ascended again to his feet. Mark inhaled deeply and spent the next thirty minutes talking about his findings. Mike remained quiet but nodded from time to time. Gabrielle looked up infrequently but otherwise said nothing, her expression suggesting the reality of the situation was affecting her. The facial features of each member changed at irregular periods in the speech but none gave anything away.

56

Riva looked up at Mark. "That is one almighty conclusion, Agent Mäder."

"Do you really expect us to believe that the Crusades are still ongoing?" del Rosi asked. "I thought you'd given up on such superstitions."

"I assure you, eminence, this has very little to do with the Holy Land," Mark said to the cardinal. "However, what I can now confirm is that every person involved with Gilbert de Bois's GREEN Foundation, something that Leoni et Cie is officially affiliated with, are also members of the Rite of Larmenius – as are seemingly all key personnel of Starvel AG. Based on the evidence, GREEN was created specifically as a special purpose entity of Rosco, and subsequently Leoni et Cie, and several other companies for accounting purposes and to transfer, and perhaps launder, money on behalf of the Rite of Larmenius. We are now aware that Gilbert de Bois is either involved with or, more likely, is a member of the Templars himself. It would suggest he is indeed responsible for much of this mess, particularly as I understand he recently made proposals for a significant development of Leoni et Cie's structure, including the establishment of branches in some of the areas mentioned. Based on the findings, his vision was already well underway."

"I understand Mr Lewis seemed to be of the same opinion," Rogero said, gazing briefly at the document as he spoke. "Cardinal Tepilo, you are a trustee of the GREEN Foundation, do you have any comments?"

Tepilo looked astounded. "Angelo, good heavens, I always believed that the GREEN Foundation was set up to do good. It just cannot be true."

"Moments ago you referred to the Knights Templar and the Rite of Larmenius as if they are the same," Dominguez said. "What makes you certain these men even exist? And if they do, what are their connections to Starvel and Leoni et Cie?"

Mark: "Their connection to Starvel, Mr Dominguez, is that they both own and control it. Starvel as a bank officially dates back to the 17th century but if what I understand to be true is in fact true, it actually dates back further still. It is perhaps the oldest merchant bank in existence and has been in the Velis family since the beginning. The origins of the Swiss banking system have never been determined by historians and their secrecy is beyond the comprehension of many others."

Del Rosi folded his arms impatiently.

"It was Frei who first made the connection," Thierry said.

"Actually, sir, it was Gabrielle."

All eyes turned to Gabrielle.

Del Rosi spoke first. "Do not be shy, my dear. What was this connection?"

Gabrielle searched the room nervously, slightly reassured by Cardinal Utaka's kindly stare. She referred to the diary and Rosslyn, finally Newport.

Del Rosi inhaled deeply. "We've been through this."

"And we will do it again if it is necessary," Thierry snapped. "Mikael Devére's tip-off regarding the Rite of Larmenius's role in the murders has been confirmed. They have operated in similar ways before. All that was missing was a motive. Their connection in the past to Starvel is little more than rumour, but it was quite inconsequential at the time. At least, so I thought."

"Well you were wrong, weren't you?" the cardinal retorted.

"Guiliano," Utaka said, his tone strong, his voice calm. "Please, none of us saw this coming."

"Randy Lewis clearly did," he replied.

Thierry nodded his appreciation at Cardinal Utaka and continued.

"Once we had learned that every person mentioned by Mr Devére was murdered by the same individual, or individuals, both Commissario Pessotto and I felt it necessary to act with caution. The Rite of Larmenius is unlike any other organisation in the world. The discovery of a peculiar diary by Ms Leoni, once owned by Mikael Devére, eventually shed new light on their historical origin. Yet what we discovered was something none of us could possibly have anticipated."

"Mikael Devére," Swanson said, "you keep saying Mikael Devére. You mean 'the' Mikael Devére?"

"Three times elected President of France and prior to that the prime minister," Mark answered, "yes, I do, Mr Swanson."

Cardinal Tepilo hesitated. "You believe he, too, was murdered by these men?"

Mark nodded. "Yes, eminence, we do. We have been working alongside Interpol, the French Police, the forces in Mauritius and the FBI and have reason to suspect that he too was murdered by Ludovic Gullet, a known member of the Rite of Larmenius."

Cardinal Tepilo shuffled in his seat. "You feel, perhaps, that Mr Devére was aware of Mr Walls' document?"

Mark nodded at Cardinal Tepilo. "Possibly, eminence, but that is open to question. What we do know is that Mikael Devére was not only a Rite of Larmenius master, but also a member of the Knights Templar."

Cardinal del Rosi leaned back in his chair and folded his arms. He examined the facial features of every person. Somewhere he felt something was stirring.

"Very well, Agent Mäder," Cardinal Tepilo said, slightly hesitantly, "please enlighten me: how was the former saviour of France party to this?"

Mark bent over and picked up a briefcase from underneath the table. He opened the locks simultaneously, the clicks echoing loudly, and retrieved several photocopies from within. He passed them around the table, one for every member who was still to see it.

Swanson looked at Mark. "What is this?"

"It was found within the safe belonging to Mikael Devére in Mauritius. Read it and you will see."

Darting eyes scanned the content quickly. The sound of papers being turned lasted several minutes. Questions started to fly like bullets.

"This has got to be some kind of joke!" Riva said.

"Louis Velis is head of the most powerful society on earth?" Dominguez nearly laughed as he spoke. Swanson continued to look at the text, his face drained.

Cardinal del Rosi inhaled slowly, his expression one of worry. Silently he struggled to control his rage. "Mäder, I want this plain and simple. What are we dealing with?"

Mark: "From what we have uncovered, the present order of the Knights Templar are a select council, perhaps less than ten individuals, who hold the highest degree of the Rite of Larmenius. A wealthy group of businessmen who claim, so I understand from this, to belong to an appendant body of the Freemasons founded centuries ago by the original Knights Templar while fleeing persecution from the King of France and the Papal Inquisitors. The Vatican's views about the Masons have always been clear: they are considered anti religious, perhaps even a substitute for religion. The Rite of Larmenius's political ambitions are unclear, yet they have a presence in every major industry, and, as we understand from Mikael Devére, their members include respected academics, members of the American Senate, Presidents of France, and perhaps even someone in this very room."

The most awkward of silences followed. Eyes moved in every direction. Thierry watched their eyes. Would someone give the game away? Not yet.

Mark: "If his claims are valid, these men orchestrated every murder. What's more, they have ordered every murder of this type ever committed."

"Including the bankers in the 1980s?" del Rosi asked.

"Yes. And even Calvi and Soisson."

Rogero nodded. "So these Templars were connected to P2?"

"These men are the highest Freemasons in existence."

Del Rosi shook his head. "Surely these men did not see it fit to displace His Holiness John Paul I?"

Thierry grimaced.

"And surely not our beloved late John Paul II . . ."

Thierry nodded again, his features sombre.

Cardinal del Rosi's facial expression changed from that of utter hatred to one of mourning. His eyes watered as though he was close to tears.

Dominguez looked up with interest. "If the former President of France was a member of these Rite of Larmenius then why was he murdered?"

"He was murdered, Mr Dominguez, because of this," Mark said, pointing to the document. "Based on the evidence at hand, he almost certainly was aware of Nathan Walls' findings and decided to tell Al Leoni about the hidden accounts. Not only did he admit to Leoni et Cie's false pedigree, perhaps an act of friendship, he also decided to expose the order. Before he died he intimated that he knew much. Had he not been killed I think he would have attempted to bring the whole thing crashing down."

"Surely such levels of our modern government cannot be under the thumb of such tyrants," Cardinal Tepilo said. "Such promise of democracy tainted from within."

"We have always known that significant business can be achieved within the Rite of Larmenius or other groups," Thierry said. "The findings of Devére and Walls must be made public. This information will assist the FBI and many others in their dealings."

"And the Federal Reserve and the Securities and Exchange Commission will need to know about GPLA," Rogero said.

"What use will that do?" Riva asked. "If this Frenchman is correct then the commission itself is under the thumb."

Mike looked at Riva. Was this a statement of knowledge or one of fear?

"We must take advice from the IMF and the World Bank," Rogero said.

"Knowing the Rite of Larmenius they will be working on a cover story," Mark said.

Thierry nodded. "Exactly. No connection exists. Scapegoats will be found."

"Particularly dead ones," Mark added. "If these men really do exist then they survive on secrecy – just as they did in the Middle Ages."

"But if we can bring Mr Devére's statement to light, it will ask a few probing questions," Thierry said.

Cardinal Tepilo slammed the table, anger consuming his ageing face: the lines on his forehead sank deeper into his skin.

"Are you forgetting what Mikael Devére said?" the cardinal shouted, his eyes monitoring all present. "We have a traitor among us!"

There was no denying the severity of the statement or the tone in which he said it. Worried expressions looked every which way. Random chatting about nothing in particular faded into an anxious silence. There were no accusations or purposeful approaches. It seemed every person present remained sceptical of accusing their colleagues: or afraid to incriminate themselves.

Tepilo rose slowly to his feet, using his chair to support himself. He looked intently at every face as though he was walking along an identity parade.

His features hardened. He looked at them one by one: the Swiss Guard; the Italian; the Colombians, his own niece . . . somehow, somewhere, there existed a society of men intent on controlling the Vatican Bank: perhaps intent on controlling the entire world. Someone in here was a traitor.

Finally the cardinal nodded, a strange smile crossing his bearded face. As he did, he felt the familiar feeling: that feeling he always experienced at these meetings: he was in the presence of insignificant people.

"And so it would appear," Cardinal Tepilo said, "that the only people known to operate with these Templars are those connected with Starvel. Is that not correct . . ."

He turned and faced the American banker on the other side of the table.

"Irving."

57

Every pair of eyes studied the face of Irving Swanson. A shocked silence, both penetrating and judging, pervaded the room.

The American looked randomly across the table. His expression was one of astonishment, his concentration strained, his eyes panicked. For several seconds he struggled to focus on the accusation. For over an hour his mind had attempted to digest the startling revelations.

The severity of the situation was evident: if the words of this man, the former President of France of all people, were to be believed then at least one high-ranking official at the Vatican was aware of the fraud. Further than that, they had helped orchestrate it.

Furthermore, they blamed him.

Suddenly the air seemed to have become denser and he felt somewhat warmer than before. His lips wobbled and he swallowed involuntarily. Inhaling deeply, he attempted to focus his attention on those present: looks of astonishment and confusion that also harboured judgment: the facial expression of the woman was in keeping with one who had squashed an insect; the other bankers were slow to condemn but quick to voice their displeasure. They had accepted the Camerlengo's instant connection of him to Starvel.

Yet still no one spoke. Silent looks of inquisition asked the inevitable question.

Is this man a traitor?

His eyes focused on their eyes and suddenly he felt intimidated, rarely for him, as if an imaginary force field was holding him down oppressively. The Swiss Guards in their uniforms: perhaps knives or guns hidden within easy grasp. The bankers: self-made millionaires and superpowers in their field. The cardinals: the generals of their society. Everyone was suddenly an enemy.

Another involuntary swallow. Still he examined the possibilities. Mark looked briefly at Swanson, but somehow his expression was less judgmental. All the while, he remained silent.

"Irve," Cardinal Utaka said, leaning forward on the table. "You were formerly a director at Starvel. Is that not correct?"

It was an obvious and pointless question. Everyone knew everything about everyone on this committee. Everyone knew that Irving Swanson was an employee with Starvel: first in the 1970s and '80s and then the late '90s to 2004. Everyone knew he was celebrated for his role.

Swanson stuttered noticeably. "Eminence, sure, I was an employee at Starvel, twice. I even made director. But I left years ago. Everyone here knows that."

No surprises, not yet.

"But before that time you worked for and alongside Misters Horatio and Louis Velis," Cardinal Tepilo said, returning slowly to his seat, examining the document in front of him. "The second man being the present leader of this order, at least according to what I read."

Swanson watched him, his face appearing less surprised than before. He had heard Mark talk of Velis.

"How would you describe your role?" del Rosi asked too pompously.

Another pointless question! Del Rosi was stirring but that was no surprise. In his position perhaps he would have done the same.

Swanson adjusted his glasses and shifted awkwardly in his chair. "Well, eminence, sirs, I entered Starvel back in 1974, when I was thirty-two; it was only my second job in banking. Back then Starvel was mainly an investment bank, at least the American part, and Starvel AG was a separate clearinghouse. For ten years things were outstanding, but in 1987 the company was struggling; heck, they all were after the crash and all. By then I was a senior manager. Things picked up eventually, but the bank was plagued by internal struggle. I stayed till the end of '87 and after that I moved on. By then, I'd fallen out with Velis senior. I used most of my severance pay to invest and made several million as a result. I was quite content with my lot in life. I settled down, spent time with my wife and kids. Was kinda nice being out of the rat race."

A brief silence followed, no questions, not yet.

"But you did return to Starvel?" Rogero said.

Swanson nodded, his lip continuing to wobble. "Well, sir, as a matter of fact I was asked back. By 1997 Starvel was struggling again," he said, the pace of his voice quick. "Four years of overspending and unsecured loans had left them isolated in certain quarters. Other banks refused to lend to them; other CEOs avoided talking to Horatio Velis and Richard West face to face. And following West's death some depositors began to take their money elsewhere."

Swanson paused, taking the time to inhale deeply. For now they watched him but still nobody spoke.

"But Starvel also had different problems," he continued. "They cut off credit to that airline and they were slated in the press. Heck, other banks were accusing them of stealing trade secrets. But Velis senior had started other fires. Literally. Back in '94 he was accused of burning files. By that time I had left, but I was still in contact with some of the staff."

"Perhaps in your absence things changed?" Riva said.

Swanson looked at the Italian with a stern expression. Rogero considered the comment with interest. What did Riva mean?

Swanson: "Gentlemen, while I cannot deny that there were elements of Starvel's dealings that I did not approve of, the bank itself was always legit – 99% at least. Every bank has its skeletons in the closet."

Dominguez nodded briefly in agreement. He fidgeted with his fingers, now cupped together in front of his face.

Another awkward silence descended, possibly judgmental in nature. Eyes moved with regularity, but mouths remained closed.

Utaka: "You were unaware of any dubious business practices?"

The banker hesitated. "Well, sir, Starvel is a complex unit whose tentacles span many nations and networks, even more so in the last ten years. These days it's practically eight separate entities in one. As I say, 99% at least is legit, although I must admit even during my first time I was aware that certain elements of the Rite of Larmenius had a substantial presence there. Following allegations of money laundering, the Feds asked questions but as far as I'm aware a full investigation never occurred. As I'm sure you're aware, Randy was chairman at the time."

Thierry made a note on a blank piece of paper.

Swanson returned to his glass of water and finished it. "West was dead by the end of '97 and around that time two new fellas came in: Gilbert de Bois, who lasted less than three years as deputy chairman, and Louis Velis as the new chief executive. Within two years Starvel had become the world's largest multinational conglomerate incorporating four other companies."

"What happened to their directors?" Utaka asked.

"Fired," Dominguez said.

"Early retirement," Swanson corrected; "although most were given no choice in the matter. Velis and de Bois were not the easiest of fellas to work for. Most hated them from the start."

"And what of you?" del Rosi asked.

Swanson shook his head defensively. "Personally, my own dealings with Horatio Velis were limited. In '96 he offered me the opportunity to return to the bank as a director. By late '97, with Louis now in control, I was invited again to join the board, one of twelve, and this time I agreed without much thought. Most of the directors of Starvel still there approved of me and I was friendly towards them."

"So you were friends with this Mr Velis?" Tepilo said.

Another shake of the head. "No, sir, in fact at the time Louis Velis and I had met only once before. A year later his daddy was dead. He knew of my past performance and he offered me a good salary. At the time, I'd become bored. Felt I needed the challenge."

Heads turned and expressions hardened. The American refilled his glass with water. This infuriated del Rosi.

"We have listened to Agent Mäder talk, and we have all read the document before us," del Rosi said. "Do you really expect us to believe that none of this could have gone on without the involvement of all key personnel?"

Swanson felt himself become choked up, forcing him to swallow. "Well, eminence, even during my first time at Starvel I admit I was aware that the bank had its secrets. Back in the '80s, Velis senior was known to have been funnelling funds all over the goddamn shop. But back then there was no bank that didn't. And they destroyed all the evidence. As time went by I began to understand parts of their true nature. Velis and the others were not actually playing with depositors' funds. I was aware Velis senior was conducting activities on behalf of the Rite of Larmenius, but at the time it was not obviously illegal. I heard rumours that West wanted out, but that was never confirmed officially. It wasn't until 2003 that I realised every previous CEO of Starvel had been a Velis and every Velis had been a Rite of Larmenius master. Until 1977 Starvel was a private family bank, mainly Swiss based. Three quarters of its most high-profile employees are Master Masons; you pretty much have to be to get a promotion."

Another awkward silence followed. The temperature seemed to rise with every second.

Rogero: "A moment ago you said the bank was legit."

Swanson nodded. "Yes, sir, it is. However, that's not to say one or two individuals did not use the bank for illegitimate gains."

"And Louis Velis?" Rogero asked.

Swanson stuttered. "Well, sir, it's like I say, I always knew that Velis was involved with the Rite of Larmenius, though I never heard anything especially bad. De Bois, I always had my suspicions, but at the time I didn't really know him well enough. Both Louis and his daddy, I understood, were quite high up – knew a lotta people. Yet Louis had also made millions in other industries. He'd started in hotels, working for the industrialist Anthony Castlefield."

"Sénéchal of the Templars 1978-87," Mark interrupted.

All eyes turned to Mark and then back to Swanson. The experienced banker inhaled deeply.

"Well, Velis rose quickly up the financial ladder," Swanson said. "He eventually went into business himself. Best I could gather, using some funds given to him by his daddy, he was a millionaire by the time he was twenty-seven. The family was well connected; his granddaddy was also a steel magnate; word has it he was good buddies with the Vanderbilts. By thirty-five he was worth dollar billions in his own right and was looking for further opportunities. As was my understanding, he wanted to consolidate his hotel empire into a worldwide conglomerate. He took over from his daddy just before the legislation changed and merged his own companies with that of his family. He also brought in Gile for his PR expertise and merged together a few others, including a struggling clearinghouse known now as Starvel AG. He salvaged three other near bankruptcies, turned them around and sold them on, pocketing millions every time. His actions were genius. When he came to Starvel he came with a reputation as something of a hero."

Rogero's expression was stern. First he condemned him, now he praised him.

"And de Bois?" Utaka asked.

Swanson stuttered. "Well his career is media. He started with millions after inheriting his father's fisheries company and sold it on. Using the proceeds he went into business at Rosco on the back of his friendship with the bank's founder, an oil tycoon Mark Antonio Careca. He was definitely a Rite of Larmenius."

"And a former Templar," Mark said.

Swanson hesitated and took a drink. "Well, you see, Velis and de Bois began making moves when rumour had it the legislation was about to change. Within two years that happened and I was on the board when Starvel attempted a takeover of Leoni et Cie. Everyone in the industry was delighted when that one was shelved. At the time, money was siphoned off like cigarettes and Velis seemed more interested in this than anything else. This was the real reason it was refused, ironically on the advice of Randy as Chairman of the Fed. As a matter of fact Randy actually asked my advice on the matter."

Dominguez looked on, intrigued.

Swanson exhaled deeply. "It was around this time Velis offered me a role in the Rite of Larmenius."

Looks of astonishment crossed the faces of every banker.

"So you admit it!" Tepilo said with venom.

Swanson shook his head vigorously. "Eminence, no, I told him to go to hell."

Rogero looked at Swanson, his expression stern. "You chose not to take it?"

Swanson: "Velis couldn't sack me as I was too good, and by then I knew too much. You see, in 2004 a director at Starvel AG told me that every major Rite of Larmenius master had a bank account with Starvel and their businesses all had accounts with Starvel AG. I guess in many ways dealing with Starvel AG is unavoidable. Individual deposits of billionaires gave the bank a finance sheet that looked more like Fort Knox – the bank's assets alone are greater than $3 trillion. This was legal, just coincidence that practically all of the world's most influential people had accounts with the same bank. By now Starvel was easily the most successful organisation in the world bar Microsoft. Velis, however, also used Starvel and the bank's offshore subsidiaries to launder money on their behalf or as tax havens for his rich clients: Randy once told me Starvel alone costs the US Economy over $400 billion a year in taxes."

"$400 billion!" shot out from three mouths.

"Perhaps in hindsight Starvel's involvement with the Rite of Larmenius goes further. Velis was aware of his father's misdemeanours and he did not halt this: he escalated it. Gile was undoubtedly aware, but back then I never saw enough of him to know for sure. By 2004, Starvel AG was probably 95% Starvel and 5% the Rite of Larmenius bank. Starvel was legit. Rite of Larmenius was probably 95-5."

Cardinal Utaka removed his glasses and rubbed his eyes vigorously. Rogero leaned forward with a pensive expression but remained silent.

"By 2003 at least seven other board members were involved with the Rite of Larmenius, but even they probably wouldn't know what we've just been told. By then I was outnumbered. Velis asked me if I wanted more: I refused. Velis wanted me out and accused me of something, I can't remember what, something about insider dealing. But that was just an excuse. He needed me out, I knew too much about the bank. By then I went willingly."

Rogero exhaled strongly. He watched the emotion drain from Swanson's face. "Why didn't you tell anyone?"

Piercing eyes returned Rogero's stare. "See, it's against the law to reveal dealings of your clients, president."

Rogero leaned forward, his expression remaining one of annoyance.

"Besides. Had I said anything about Velis, the same thing would have happened to me that happened to Randy and the others." He stuttered again. "And how the hell was I supposed to know about all this?" he shouted, referring to the fraud. "I was never on the board of Leoni et Cie; I'd never heard of these Templars. Officially Gile was just the chairman, and not involved in the running of the bank."

The banker inhaled, struggling to control his breathing.

"But by the time I left I had other considerations," he said, his voice weaker than before. "By then my daughter was married and had recently given birth to little Millie. Things change when you have a family, sir. Things that once mattered were now insignificant. And Velis was aware of that. See, things like that don't mean a goddamn thing to guys like him. And that's where Velis had one over on me, and that was when I was fired. I mean, men like him don't give a hoot about what matters. For him, family is something to show off, or, in the case of your enemies, something to get at. And they knew that," Swanson said, pointing his finger. "And I would never let anything like that threaten my family."

Thierry rose to his feet, shaking his head. "Personally I do not believe that Mr Swanson is in anyway involved in this unfortunate scenario."

Looks of surprise dominated the faces of most present. Mark remained neutral, though his expression suggested he agreed. Swanson looked weakly at Thierry, tears falling from his eyes.

Mark rose to his feet. "Without question Gilbert de Bois's role as chairman allowed him significant insight into Leoni et Cie's affairs. Yet, as Mr Swanson quite rightly pointed out, he could not have done this alone. Nor could he have been able to move Roman Curia funds into and from the bank. Devére, himself, mentions key figures from the Vatican being in league with this organisation, and who better than one who has acted as an independent adviser for both Starvel and Leoni et Cie over the last ten years. And, it just so happens, that Mr Lewis only became suspicious in the first place after inspecting transactions that have taken place since you were appointed chief executive."

His eyes focused on Giancarlo Riva.

Gasps of astonishment filled the room, notably from the cardinals.

Riva looked at Mark with an expression of shock.

Mark: "According to Ged Fairbanks you have been a freelance consultant to Starvel for over fifteen years. He also speculates that you have been secretly assisting de Bois in manipulating Leoni et Cie's accounts for over eight years."

Riva rose to his feet. "This is an outrage. You don't know what you are doing, none of you."

"Then perhaps you would like to explain this," Thierry said, removing a sheet of paper from his inside pocket. "It seems Mr Lewis sent more than one email."

Riva's eyes widened. He looked at Swanson then Mark. "But this is preposterous," he said nervously. "Is that why you brought the Swiss Guard? You set me up? This was a trap?"

Riva looked around with awkward eyes.

"You are all so pathetically wide of the mark: you call yourselves investigators? This is slander. You have no proof."

He faced Cardinal Tepilo.

"Eminence, please believe me, this is not true. Please you must understand."

"Understand?" Tepilo said, standing, moving towards the Italian. "Understand that you are a traitor? That you're in league with the Devil himself? That a master of the Rite of Larmenius has been acting as a Gentiluomo di Sua Santità, a councillor for the Vatican City? Giancarlo, I trusted you; everyone here trusted you."

Riva banged loudly on the table and started shaking his head vigorously. His face was consumed by panic. He shouted loudly, his eyes focused on Cardinal del Rosi in the next seat.

"Eminence, please, there has been an awful mistake."

The cardinal stood and walked away from the table. Mike backed up slightly as Cardinal del Rosi retreated towards the wall. Suddenly Riva made a break for the far door.

Mike's reactions were immediate. Had it not have been for the cardinal's decision to move, his actions might not have been possible. Without giving any thought to anything else he dived across the vacant seat to Riva and sent him crashing to the floor.

58

The meeting was adjourned for over an hour. Mark and Thierry arrested Riva on the spot before summoning four halberdiers to escort the banker to the headquarters of the Vatican Police. Mark spent the next half hour chatting to Swanson about his knowledge of recent events, whereas the other cardinals and bankers talked nervously among themselves.

Thierry re-entered the room shortly after and took his seat at the table. By now every other person had returned but the order of the meeting was lost.

Dominguez looked up. "We have spoken about Starvel, we have spoken about the Rite of Larmenius and I feel that this covers these Templar people." He paused momentarily. "Yet I feel we know little about how this affects our problem with Leoni et Cie and the finances of the Vatican Bank. That is where our attention must lie. Tell us, Mr Swanson, about your relationship with Mr de Bois."

Swanson sipped quickly from his glass, gathering his thoughts.

"Well, sir, Gile and I only met back in '97 after I returned to Starvel. We never particularly liked each other, but our paths rarely crossed. He and Velis on the other hand go back a long way. From what I've been told they met back in the late '80s at what the Rite of Larmenius call a 'gathering', a three-week jamboree of sorts located in the Swiss Alps, although I never knew for sure that Gile was a member. Velis's background was in hotels, as I say, and de Bois's in media. The idea of expanding Starvel must have been in their minds for some time. Starvel went from being the world's most impressive corporate bank to a global conglomerate: its tentacles span banking, insurance, hotels, clearing and settlement, retail – you name it. By the time they met, Velis was already revered as something of a prophet when it came to business."

Rogero nodded. "Why did de Bois leave?"

"Well, sir, the official reason was that he wanted to concentrate on other ventures. Gile always has his fingers in a number of different pies. I was there for over four years following his departure and he and Velis never spoke or did business since. At least not as far as I was aware."

"If Velis really is the Grand Master of the Templars then he is the highest Rite of Larmenius there is," Mark said. "De Bois's inclusion now seems straightforward. And all of these murders must have been carried out on their orders."

Dominguez nodded. "Every business carried out by the Rite of Larmenius . . . no wonder Starvel has become so powerful."

"What do you know about the Rite of Larmenius, Mr Swanson?" del Rosi asked, his voice noticeably calmer than before.

"Only what I've been told, eminence, I was never a member. I openly admit I was once a Mason but that was a long time ago. The Masons are fine. It was actually a current Starvel AG director who asked me to become a Mason, but I only lasted three years. That was one of the reasons I was ousted the first time. I've heard some stuff of the Rite, particularly about their rituals. Nothing concrete."

Tepilo listened with interest, his eyes without judgment.

Mark: "The FBI in America is clearly aware of a possible link between certain members of the Rite of Larmenius and the murders. They have wanted to raid the secret lodges for some time. The chief reckons they could get enough evidence to open up cases on over three thousand murders between last year and the end of the Second World War. But there could be other indictments. Tax evasion, money laundering, embezzlement, larceny . . . the potential seems endless."

"Sir, I would love to see these guys crumble," Swanson said. "I will help in any way I can."

Mark shook his head. "If Mikael Devére is correct then the Templar order has pulled off every major move on the world scene since the 14th century. Tearing down an order that has survived out of view for over six centuries is hardly gonna be a piece of cake."

Thierry nodded. "I agree. However, we need not target their institutions. Just the simplest of evidence against the individuals in question could be the most devastating blow to political corruption since the war."

"Looking at the testimony of Mr Devére, and the other contents found within his safe, there are probably only about eight men on the highest council," Mark said. "Perhaps a few hundred know of them. Most members of the Rite of Larmenius are probably just powerful businessmen looking for a little more. Nothing illegal. And Starvel is just a mechanism. We can't imagine how the Templars operate, but what we are sure of is that the Rite of Larmenius operate for the Templars and them only."

"To bring them down would require cooperation from the inside. Velis must have known about Devére and acted," Thierry shook his head, allowing a smile. "What better way to bring them down than by publishing your memoirs and announcing the identity of the secret rulers of the world."

Gabrielle lowered her head, a stray tear forming in the corner of her eye.

"Who are the other members?" Utaka asked.

"The original death warrants handed over to me by Mr Devére confirm that seven people initiated the six deaths, so presumably that makes eight including him. Devére was one; US Senator Daniel D'Amato another; de Bois seems fairly likely," Mark said.

"Lord Parker of England," Thierry said.

"Alexander Broadie," Gabrielle said. "He's my uncle's colleague at Harvard."

"Harvard professor and known Rite of Larmenius master," Mark said, nodding. "Respected. Supposedly descended of the St Clairs of Rosslyn, other known Templars. Possible distant cousin of Velis."

"Very well," Utaka said. "That leaves only two."

"Three, eminence: Devére would surely have been replaced by now," Mark said.

Cardinal del Rosi and Cardinal Tepilo looked on with interest.

"How about Gullet?" Mike suggested.

"Unlikely," Mark replied. "Gullet was probably the go-to guy. Probably had no other firm connections even if he is a Rite of Larmenius master. And there's no way he would talk."

Utaka nodded. "That leaves three mysteries."

Swanson looked up. "If these guys do exist, any proof will probably be in the vaults of Starvel's main headquarters. Ms Leoni talked of old castles and churches in Rhode Island. That stuff's medieval. Maybe these Templars claim ancestry of the Crusaders but god knows that's no concern to the current members. Heck, they probably wouldn't care anyway: they've bigger fish to fry."

"What are you getting at, Irve?" Dominguez asked.

"Agent Mäder referred to these guys being hunted by the Feds, Interpol and God knows who else. Evidence that this hitman from Campione d'Italia had files on these guys and hired a Jeep in Mauritius bears no connection to the order itself. The work of Walls itself is proof of Leoni et Cie's financial failures, but it does not prove who was responsible. That and the testimony of Devére alone aren't proof."

"Not proof," del Rosi slammed. "Nine men have been murdered."

"Mr Swanson is correct, eminence," Thierry concurred. "To indict the order itself it would be necessary to dig further."

Swanson: "Now, eminence, oberst, sirs, as y'all know, I used to work at Starvel. I know the layout; I know the vaults; hell, they even entrusted me with the restricted key codes. Now I can't promise everything will be there – heck, Velis has probably already destroyed the most important stuff. But if there is anything that proves the existence and guilt of these guys, it will be there."

"And what do you suggest?" Rogero asked. "That you simply walk in and ask Mr Velis for permission to see his files."

"No, sir, I do not suggest I ask him. But every bank has records. And Starvel as a whole probably has as much as the Vatican Library. The Starvel AG vaults are more select. Now I reckon I could get enough to indict every one of these Templars."

"Absolutely out of the question," Cardinal Utaka said. "The Vatican will not condone stealing. No matter how noble the intention."

"It wouldn't necessarily be stealing, eminence," Mark said. "The FBI will get them sooner or later."

Cardinal Tepilo's expression softened. Cardinal del Rosi looked sternly at Thierry.

"I'm afraid I must agree with Cardinal Utaka," Thierry said. "Neither the Vatican Police nor the Swiss Guard have the authority to break into the vaults of a bank in America."

"Then perhaps you would explain how Agent Markus obtained photographs of the contents of Gullet's safe?" del Rosi slammed.

Mark: "Eminence, I did indeed break into the office of Ludovic Gullet's casino and I take full responsibility. It was my own decision."

Mike smiled.

Swanson: "Eminence, I know Starvel inside out. I could get in with a little help. Officially the Vatican need know nothing about it. Although maybe if Agent Mäder could come with me."

"Absolutely not," del Rosi said.

"I'll do it," Mike said. All eyes turned to him.

"Thank you, wachtmeister," Thierry said. "But we cannot allow this."

"I'll do it," Gabrielle said.

"My dear, please," Tepilo said.

"All right," Swanson said, "I'll do it myself if I have to. Now I appreciate y'all feel I let you down. Only if it were my own risk I could be fine with that." He paused to consider his words. "Just promise me you'll protect my family if anything should go wrong."

Silence followed.

"Very well," Thierry said. "The Swiss Guard will watch over your family until this has all blown over."

Swanson nodded gratefully. He removed a handkerchief from his pocket and blew his nose forcefully.

"How the heck do you intend to pull this off, Irve?" Dominguez asked. "I've been to Starvel's base in Boston. It's worse than Fort Knox down there."

"Wait," Gabrielle said, her voice echoing off the walls.

All eyes turned to her. She cleared her throat before speaking.

"My friend Rachel used to work at Starvel. In fact, she was married to Velis. She still knows people who work there. They could provide Mr Swanson with clearance."

Mark looked at her with interest.

"Out of the question," del Rosi said.

"How would she do this?" Mark asked.

"Well, as I say, she still knows people who work there. I reckon if in doubt I could offer them a pretty good deal."

A few minor laughs drifted around the table. Cardinal Utaka looked at her thoughtfully.

"You would be taking an almighty risk," Thierry said softly, "and her also. Her friends may lose their jobs. Or worse. You yourself . . ."

Gabrielle shook her head. "No. They'll be fine. They won't know. And I don't care about me," she said, inhaling slowly.

"I just want this to all be over."

59

Boston, Massachusetts

The black hatchback pulled up outside the main headquarters of the Starvel Group at just after 10:30 a.m. After identifying a vacant parking space approximately three cars down from the entrance, far enough away to avoid suspicion, the driver parked the car and switched off the engine. Seconds later, he opened the door and ambled leisurely towards the parking meter located on the nearby sidewalk. He shuffled his pocket for change and dropped the coins one by one into the meter: the electronic display suggested he had three hours. Once finished, he re-entered the car and closed the door behind him.

The driver was Mark. Replacing his official police uniform, he wore trainers, jeans, and a leather jacket over a blue t-shirt. He wore mirrored sunglasses to shade his eyes from the bright sunlight but also to disguise his regular checks in the rear-view mirror. The occasion was one for precision.

Sitting next to him was Irving Swanson. As usual, he dressed in the attire of a banker, identical in appearance to many individuals walking in and out through the revolving doors of the nearby building. On the back seat, Gabrielle sat next to Rachel who was clearly restless. Next on from her was Mike.

It was four days since the meeting at the Vatican. Since that time two further meetings had taken place and both had ended in disagreement. Nerves were setting in, the moods of all involved fragile, and accusations following the circumstances leading to Leoni et Cie's financial fraud continued to fly. After accepting that Giancarlo Riva and the recently disappeared Gilbert de Bois were in some way responsible, and accepting that the fraud itself was coordinated by people from outside the Vatican, the cardinals eventually agreed to Swanson's request to go through with his plan with the aid of Rachel who had bribed one of her friends working in records to loan her her key card during a long lunch break. She assumed that if she was discovered she would get fired but Gabrielle promised to see her okay if that happened. The risk was worth it provided nothing further went wrong and, as far as the employee was aware, nothing would. Important bankers and lawyers lose important documents and key cards with regularity in the hustle and bustle of the rat race yet that was fine provided they did not end up in the wrong hands. Such mishaps seldom resulted in ill consequence – or at least that's what the guys at the top like you to believe! Yet things marked private have a habit of doing so when privacy conceals secrets worth millions. Rachel knew that for a fact.

Rachel exhaled nervously as she looked through the rear windscreen at the entrance of the bank. She scanned every passing face for familiarity and was relieved every time to see no one she recognised. Then she scanned the next passing crowd and relief turned to fear. Then came relief again. And the cycle continued.

"I can't believe I agreed to this," Flores said.

Mike noticed that her hands were trembling. "We appreciate what you're doing. Besides, you don't have to come in."

"No," she said, forcing a smile. "It's okay. I need to operate the cards. It's fine, really."

A ghost of a smile crossed Gabrielle's lips.

"Right," Swanson said, turning the other way to monitor the road. "It is now 10:38 a.m. Now is as good a time as any."

The American headquarters of the global conglomerate Starvel PLC looked like any ordinary bank building. It was situated in the business district of downtown Boston, roughly midway along the Freedom Trail, one of several large skyscrapers that dominated the city skyline. The building comprised twenty-five storeys minus the roof, appearing cylindrical in shape and was constructed almost entirely from reinforced concrete with several glass windows reflecting the outside world like a mirror. The company's famous logo dominated both the upper skyscraper and the gable above the entrance: an almost unique assignment of a castle with a sloping roof below a cross, curiously reminiscent of one used by the Knights Templar in England in the 13th century, and also identical to the famous Templar cross.

Rachel led the way through one of four revolving doors, and surveyed the surroundings for familiarity. A lavishly furnished foyer was decorated with flora of all descriptions and twenty or more smartly dressed cashiers smiled widely from behind their booths lining the far end. Countless retail clients queued for various machines and cashier desks, while corporate clients chatted about matters of importance in the middle of the atrium. Large groups of suited individuals entered and exited the lifts with regularity whereas others stood patiently on one of two escalators that moved upwards to the eastern side of the complex. In total, four escalators went up and down to and from the first floor from the centre of the atrium, while six lifts lined the wall opposite the entrance, providing accessibility to the first seventeen floors and parts of the vaults.

Unlike most buildings of this type the whole thing belonged to Starvel. Although the company as a whole was mainly concerned with banking, the building also provided employment for over three thousand employees working in various departments including actuary, investments, mortgages, insurance, travel and currency exchange, and over eight subsidiary companies, including Starvel AG, who occupied the twelfth to seventeenth floors. The top eight floors were part of the hotel, and accessible through the opposite side of the building.

Rachel led them across the atrium, heading in the direction of the lifts. The building was typically crowded: perhaps less so than earlier in the week, but still packed with individuals, mainly in suits, hampering their progress. In many ways the high volume of people made Rachel nervous, yet Mike, Mark, and Swanson all spoke of the benefit.

The best way to get lost was in a crowd.

"Here," Rachel said, pointing at one of the lifts. "This is an employee elevator. We can get to the vaults from here."

Mike eyed the surroundings curiously, maintaining a cool façade. Mark was not part of this – nor could he be. Gabrielle should not have been but she insisted. The cardinals were against Mike being there but he had a problem.

He had to go with Gabrielle.

The lift doors opened and everyone inside got out. Rachel entered first and the others followed. She swiped the key card and clicked on the last of four symbols below the ground floor. The floor they wanted would include the archives of Starvel AG.

Fortune favoured the brave. No one saw them descend.

The archives were hardly what Mike expected. While the atrium and upper floors of the bank were opulently decorated with modern furniture, the archives were more in keeping with a large library. Despite the initial impression of airlessness as they exited the lift, an unexpected hint of lemon air freshener made the air pleasantly bearable.

Up above, panelled lights shone down from high ceilings, reflecting off white walls and cream carpet, illuminating the long corridor brightly. Lining the corridor to their right was nothing but a wall, whereas to the left, organised shelving units housed thousands of boxes, numbered and named, lined up in sequence, containing files of all sorts dating back to the Great Depression. The racks continued for over one hundred and fifty feet along and over four hundred in depth before ending at another wall.

Ignoring the majority, the three intruders followed Rachel along the corridor until reaching a metal door. The door was wired and attached to an electronic keypad, which was consistent with a top-secret military bunker or even those used to guard the doors leading to the Vatican Archives. She stopped momentarily in front of it and swiped her key card quickly. She held her breath until a green light flashed. She pushed against the door and it opened.

The door revealed a second corridor, identical in every way to the previous one. Once inside, every member followed Rachel, keeping an eye out for any signs of life. Although the area was brightly lit and surprisingly spacious, the archives seemed deserted. With a straining ear, Mike could just make out the sound of shuffling papers from one of the far shelves but he was unable to see who was making it. He hoped the important stuff would also be this quiet.

They walked through a further set of doors and down a small staircase, leading to another floor of archives, accessible only via the way they had come. An almost identical corridor followed, also ending with a metal door. They entered the final corridor.

"Okay," Rachel said, mainly to Swanson. "This is the Starvel AG vault. Whatever you need is here."

"I fear not, my dear," the banker replied. "The important stuff will have its own vault."

Rachel looked nervously at Gabrielle.

"I take it you know where," Mike said.

Swanson pointed in the direction of the farthest metal door, located over one hundred yards away. The door was larger than the others, painted green and heavily armoured. A strange smile crossed Swanson's face, somehow peaceful in nature. To the Swiss Guard, it was the smile of long overdue revenge.

Rachel inhaled with difficulty. She remembered the archives well from her previous employment but she had never been beyond the furthest door. She was aware that there were areas beyond her pay grade but she had no idea of their contents.

The appearance of the final door suggested security clearance was beyond the norm. Without any idea of how to gain access, she allowed Swanson to take the lead and followed him towards the door, passing further shelving. To the far right, partially hidden by several rows of shelves, was the nearest of three photocopiers.

Rachel looked blankly at the door, the smell of metal dominating her nostrils. "I've never been past here before," she said to Swanson.

Swanson looked back reassuringly. To the left of the door he eyed a small keypad, illustrating that the door was code operated. He adjusted his glasses and looked closely at the numbers before punching in a seven-digit code, making sure every number registered. All present waited patiently for a response. The device bleeped three times at equal intervals before a loud echo resonated as the lock separated.

Swanson opened the door widely and entered, followed first by Mike. Directly behind the door was another staircase: seventeen steps down, then sixteen more in the opposite direction. This area was less finely decorated than the rest of the vaults.

Mike followed Swanson to the bottom of the stairs and entered a small room, reminiscent of a large storage closet. The room was approximately eighteen feet by thirty, painted white and containing nothing but three lengthy rows of shelves that housed over two hundred silver boxes, decorated with coded alphanumeric labels.

Gabrielle looked at the room with disappointment, walking slowly towards the first shelf. She opened the nearest box and began to scan the contents. She removed eight thin files. They all dated back to the 1980s.

Mike wandered towards the far end. For the first time he noticed that the air was denser down here, as though they were in a vacuum. He inhaled slowly, determined to keep his composure, and peeked inside one of the boxes.

"Some of these date back centuries."

"Thankfully, the regular employees are unaware it even exists," said Swanson. "We are quite alone."

Mike looked anxiously around the room. "This could take years."

On the top floor, the secretary for the chief of security saw a red light flashing on the wall without an accompanying sound. After removing her reading glasses and taking a second bite of her apple, she left her seat to take a closer look.

The light meant that someone had entered the limited access vault. She assumed it was probably fine, just one of the directors carrying out restricted business. Still, its occurrence unsettled her. She had never known anyone use the vault in office hours.

The secretary placed the phone to her right ear and started dialling. She tried four of the senior managers and received no response from any of them. She then tried three lesser managers: all were away or on early lunch. Finally she tried Mr Velis.

Giving up, she returned to her apple.

Another black hatchback pulled up opposite the Starvel building and a smartly dressed passenger got out through the rear right door. The passenger looked both ways before jaywalking across the street and entered the building through the revolving door.

He crossed the atrium with prior knowledge of the layout and immediately headed for the lift. He swiped a key card on entry and pressed for the fifteenth floor.

Mark blinked twice in quick succession, watching the suited man as he entered the bank. His appearance was curiously familiar, although surely a coincidence.

Directly opposite, the American with blond locks looked with interest at the same man. Behind the seclusion of tinted glass he was in no danger of being noticed.

The identity of the man surprised him but he was not altogether shocked. He smiled to himself.

Over four hours had passed. Standing next to the photocopier, Mike passed another set of files to Gabrielle to photocopy and replaced the recently copied one back in the original box and handed it to Rachel. Gabrielle removed the paper clip from the original and made one copy of each before placing them into her briefcase.

They would study them in more detail later.

Each person had brought a briefcase, but four was not enough. All present had come and gone five times back to the car and this was alarming to Mike. Surely it did not bode well to keep coming and going from the lift with briefcases.

"Okay," Mike said to Gabrielle. "Only six boxes left."

With every passing second he felt his body become more and more tense. From Swanson's observations of the files he felt they probably had enough of what they needed already, yet the scale of the findings made the potential of the threat more severe. Mike knew it could be only a matter of time before someone spotted them, and such repercussions could be extreme. On the other side of the furthest metal door he heard the sound of voices and his heart began to thunder. It was most probably just some employees checking a mortgage receipt for a client or something.

Thankfully they were not coming in their direction.

Mike waited calmly for Gabrielle to finish a final photocopy. Downstairs, Swanson was still working, examining the files before deciding whether or not it was necessary to make a copy, while Rachel walked nervously over to Mike, returning from the vault.

"Okay," Mike said to Gabrielle. "You and Rachel get the heck outta here. I'll stay here with Mr Swanson."

Gabrielle looked at Mike and then at Rachel. Her nervous state, mixed with the brightness of the light, made her pale skin look almost ghostlike. She grimaced hopelessly at Mike.

"Okay," Gabrielle said, taking Rachel by the hand. "Don't be long."

Mike escorted Rachel and Gabrielle through the first metal door and continued up the stairs and all the way to the lift. Rachel swiped the key card and quickly passed it to Mike. She would no longer need it.

Rachel smiled thankfully at Mike as the doors closed. Seconds later, the lift ascended to the ground floor and the doors opened. They exited quickly and walked with composure across the crowded atrium, heading towards the front doors. Nobody noticed them. Dressed in their smart designer suits and briefcases they looked like just two young career women easily mistaken for employees. They ignored the doormen as they exited to the street and headed swiftly towards the car.

The dark hatchback was parked in the same position. At 14:27 Mark added another hour to the meter and fifty-five minutes later he added some more. At 15:41 he was back in the front seat when the rear right door opened and Gabrielle entered, followed by Rachel. She flashed a smile and placed the briefcase to the floor.

"Everything okay?"

Gabrielle smiled. "Sweet as a nut. We've got him."

Fifteen minutes later, Swanson finished examining the final file of yet another box and breathed deeply and gratefully. He replaced the original in the box and placed the copy in his leather briefcase.

There were only two boxes left.

In an upstairs office, Velis and the visitor argued loudly. While their words remained private in the luxury of the otherwise deserted floor, their emotions were highly charged.

After fifty minutes of heated discussion the smartly dressed bearded man with thinning grey hair left the office and exited the building. Moments later the Templar Grand Master entered the elevator. His destination: the archives.

Twenty minutes later they were finished. Swanson lifted the final file from the photocopier and carefully placed it into his overly full briefcase. He replaced the final original into the silver box and passed it to Mike. The Swiss Guard entered the chamber for the final time and returned it to the correct shelf.

At last they were ready to go. Swanson ensured that the door to the restricted vault was closed before heading back towards the lift. He nodded briefly at the sharply dressed Swiss Guard: only the second time he had worn his stunning suit. Silently it was beginning to grow on Mike, but the nature of the work made it feel stifling.

Swanson walked slowly. His briefcase felt heavy in his right hand and pain shot through his calves and back: a combination of several hours of photocopying and bending over to investigate files. He grimaced slightly as he walked. The sooner they were out the better he would feel.

Mike swiped the key card to the first door and walked through it quickly. The next corridor was empty and Mike breathed a sigh of relief. They picked up speed and within two minutes they reached the lift.

Both men exhaled gratefully and made brief eye contact as Mike stepped forward to press the up button. The illuminated dials suggested the lift was on its journey downwards. Seconds later the lift chimed and the doors opened.

One man was present.

It was Louis Velis.

60

The chiming sound of opening lift doors reverberated softly through the lemon-scented air. Mike and Swanson stood rigidly, practically paralysed, before its occupant standing less than three metres away.

Inside the lift, Louis Velis was dressed in an immaculate black suit purchased from a tailor in New York two years earlier. He wore a plain white shirt and matching red tie, and had a look of curiosity on his face. He stood silently, failing to hide his surprise at the sight of the man he had met once before and his former co-director.

In the otherwise deserted archives, the two intruders remained unflinching. Mike felt a thudding sensation hammering through his chest, the thought of the inevitable repercussions dominating. No one had spoken, but in his mind he considered the banker's thoughts. He remembered the night he met the man. Then he thought of Gabrielle. Had she made it out? And Rachel? To think she had once been married to this man. Suddenly he was worried.

Velis walked a couple of paces forward. His facial expression relaxed as he neared them.

"Whenever someone opens the door to the restricted vault, it activates a small red light on the security control panel," Velis said. "I also have one fitted in my office. Personal reasons, you understand?"

The first thing Mike noticed was that Velis spoke slowly. He remembered noticing the same thing the night he met him. Something about the way he spoke irritated Mike and disturbed him at the same time. It was almost hypnotic.

"Now only twelve people have the code to this door. Five, I know to be abroad; I myself am one, and the only others I know to be deceased. Therefore, you can imagine my surprise when I saw the light flickering. At first I thought perhaps it was a mistake, a power cut, a malfunction," Velis said, gesturing with his arms. "But clearly that was not the case," he said, eyeing his former colleague. "Something you left behind, Irving?"

Wetting his lips, Swanson remained silent. There was a hint of fear yet also bravery in his eyes that Mike found out of character for the banker. There was also hatred, a strange bitterness resembling a playground rivalry between the bully and the fat kid. Swanson's face slowly reddened and his breathing was becoming louder. Still he did not answer. Velis looked down at Swanson's briefcase and unfolded his arms. He raised his eyes at Swanson and walked slowly towards him, stopping within inches of the Vatican banker and taking his briefcase.

Velis opened the briefcase slowly and removed several of the copied files. His eyes seemed to open wider as he examined the content. He looked at the Swiss Guard with slight alarm. Yet any momentary expression of panic was immediately replaced by one of calm, still conveying an air of contempt that seemed a permanent feature of his noble face. Perhaps it was the beard that did it: that dense covering that seemed to thin and thicken enigmatically whenever his facial expression changed.

He looked at Swanson, his focus centring on the banker's eyes. His expression remained neutral. "Where are the rest of these?"

Swanson looked at Velis with an equally neutral expression, seemingly oblivious to any possible threat. Mike inhaled deeply, standing silently with his hands by his side, a briefcase dangling from his right arm. His focus centred on Velis. The banker's tongue crossed his lips in a strange pensive movement. Suddenly there was movement.

Velis removed a revolver from his jacket.

Velis's eyes narrowed. He raised his firearm at the former Starvel director's chest.

"Now then, gentlemen: shall we do this the easy way or the hard way?"

On the top floor of the Starvel headquarters, the chief of security returned to his desk and looked with interest at the dashboard before him. His monitor told him that the red light had been flashing earlier and had continued for several hours.

He sipped his coffee nonchalantly and after several seconds deliberating decided it was important. He picked up the phone and rang the CEO.

No response.

Although he assumed that it was probably him, he thought it best to be sure. There was no CCTV in that part of the building: as requested by the CEO. He guessed the reasons but never fully understood why.

He picked up his walkie-talkie and spoke to one of the security guards.

*

At the other end of the line the overweight security guard understood the instruction. Replying the word "Roger", he signalled to one of the other three and headed towards the elevator. He swiped his card and then pressed for the vaults.

The ageing man in the smart suit walked across the atrium with rigid determination, brought about by his recent argument with Velis. He ignored the security guards as he motored through the revolving door and walked across the rush hour traffic, entering the same car through the rear right door.

Almost forty minutes had passed since Rachel and Gabrielle had returned. Gabrielle was nervous; Rachel was nearly in tears and Mark reassured them with confidence that all was okay.

But silently he was nervous: this was taking too long.

The Vatican policeman checked the rear-view mirror for the second time in quick succession and concentrated on the entrance to the bank. He scanned the vicinity intently for almost ten seconds before returning his attention to Gabrielle. On this occasion he did not see the smartly dressed man exit the bank, heading back across the street.

Unlike Mark, the man with blond locks watched for a second time. The identity of the man was beyond doubt.

Velis instructed them along the corridor, their way directed by the movement of the gun. The Starvel magnate swiped his key card at every door, his arm and wrist slicing downwards like a knife through butter, followed by the sound of the door opening and closing as they entered another stretch of seemingly endless corridor.

They continued all the way to the door of the restricted vault, coming to a halt within twenty feet of the photocopier. Velis briskly searched both men for firearms and confiscated a SIG P75 from Mike, hidden within his suit. He lined both men up with their backs to the wall and ordered them to place their hands over their heads. For several seconds they stood in silence. No sudden movements.

Velis lit a cigar and exhaled the smoke in the direction of Swanson. His facial expression thinned as his eyes focused. He removed a handful of photocopies from both briefcases with his free hand and waved them at Swanson.

"Where are the rest of these?" he asked slowly and quietly. Some of the photocopies fell to the floor as he waved them.

"What makes you think there's more?"

Velis tipped the ash away, using the copied files as a makeshift ashtray. A soft burning smell poisoned the lemon air, causing the paper to shrivel but without catching fire. Strangely there were no fire taps installed in the ceiling of this section of the vaults.

He walked closer to Swanson. "How did you get down here?" Velis asked slowly. "Who else was with you?"

He turned his face towards Mike. "Her?"

No response.

"Yes, I might have known. But how did she get access to the vaults?"

Velis smoked for a couple of seconds. Suddenly it dawned on him.

"My wife, of course," he said, a strange smile forming across his mouth. "Probably slipped one of her peasant friends a fifty."

Although he smoked incessantly Velis hid his nerves well. This was not a man who had something to hide.

"I am going to offer you one chance to leave these vaults alive," he said with emphasis on the final word. "Where are the rest of these?"

Swanson stiffened his posture but remained silent. He muttered the words, "I dunno what you mean," and shrugged at Velis.

"Do not take me for a fool, Irving. There are over twenty thousand documents in that vault – you know that as well as I."

Velis's eyes still focused on the intruders. Biding his time he smoked. Mike's eyes all the while remained locked on Velis.

The banker blew smoke at Swanson. "Why? Why now after all these years would you risk your life? Risk incriminating yourself." A brief pause followed. "After all we've been through together."

Swanson laughed in irony. "All we've been through. You mean that you stitched me up. That you blackmailed me; threatened to hurt my wife; my daughter, you even threatened lil' Millie if I told anyone about your goddamn lies. You made me sign my own pact with the Devil."

"So that is why you took up your new position with the Church. You were worried about your salvation?"

Swanson looked at Velis. There was a resigned hatred in his eyes. The fear Mike had witnessed only days earlier had withered and flourished into a strange peacefulness. He had never liked Swanson: he always struck him as being a snob and a soulless mercenary: more interested in cash than religion. Yet images can be deceiving. Now there was a strange sense of liberation about him.

"The world knows, Louis. We know about Mikael Devére. We know about Nathan Walls' report: that you killed him to conceal the real performance of Leoni et Cie: that you've been funnelling Vatican funds and God knows what else to fund your criminal activities. That Gile is a crook; that you're a murderer. Did you kill Randy too?"

"You are a foolish old man, Irving. Do you have any idea what you are really getting yourself into?"

"Yeah I do. And I was an even more foolish middle-aged man. Ever since I met your pops I was afraid of him; West, I was afraid of him; afraid of the Rite of Larmenius; afraid of what you people would do to me if I said anything out of line."

Velis smoked, retaining eye contact with Swanson.

"I can barely forgive myself, knowing all I did of your activities," Swanson said, slightly stronger than before: "knowing that I kept my mouth shut and failed to lift a finger despite all these people being killed before my eyes. I thought it was right: right to protect my family. But what you've done is unforgivable."

"Do not be naïve, Irving. I kept you on as a favour. I even thought that in time there might be a place for you as a master of the Rite of Larmenius."

"A favour," Swanson laughed in irony. "Am I supposed to be thankful? You talked as if you were some kind of goddamn prophet; a saviour of humanity. You are not even human, you evil son of a bitch."

Velis removed his cigar from his lips and exhaled, sending smoke spiralling towards the panelled lights, the smell overwhelming the scent of lemon.

"It's over, Louis," Swanson said. "Even if you kill me it won't make a blind bit of difference. The confessions of Mikael Devére will soon be known to the world. The Vatican can work without me. Come on. Let the guard go."

Mike looked at Swanson, in surprise if nothing else. Velis looked at Mike.

"I never did get that stain out of my shirt."

Mike felt a tightening sensation in his chest.

"This is your last chance," he said to both of them. "Where are the rest of these?"

The sound of the opening door echoed throughout the corridor, followed by the appearance of two security guards. Looks of startled fear and amazement crossed their faces as they witnessed the scene in front of them. The normally dormant archives were playing host to a bearded man in an expensive suit pointing a gun execution-style at two men standing against the wall.

Velis hesitated momentarily. The security guards lifted their guns and shouted, causing the banker to panic. Velis aimed to his left and quick as a flash shot three times. Adrenaline set in and Mike grabbed Swanson and sprinted towards the racks. Ducking his head, they dived into a row of shelves, breaking them and causing several boxes to fall to the ground around them.

61

The sound of scampering footsteps gave way to that of a metal door opening and closing. Several gunshots in quick succession ricocheted off metal, bouncing in all directions, causing deafening echoes that continued for several seconds. Behind the door, footsteps sprinted in an unknown direction, while in the main corridor furniture crashed against furniture, causing files to fall, boxes to break and paper to tear, creating an image of chaos.

Now on the floor, Mike rolled over and placed his hands over his head as a protective reflex. He waited for the sound of bullets to stop and from his cramped position surveyed the corridor, still unsure what had happened. Had he been shot? He felt numb, but felt no pain. He checked his body; he was not bleeding.

He rose cautiously to his haunches and surveyed the vicinity in better detail. The sound of recent gunshots was still ringing loudly in his ears, but the activity had now ceased. As he looked around the room, he saw one of the security guards sprinting down the corridor in the direction of the restricted vault. Velis was already on the other side of the door and, not to Mike's knowledge, climbing a concealed staircase. The second security guard was running gingerly, pressing his hand to his shoulder. A gunshot had grazed the bone and left a faint blood wound.

Mike struggled to his feet. Books and documents were scattered across the floor, appearing as though a tornado had swept the room. He looked down at Irving Swanson who was lying on the floor and grimacing in pain. His smart suit jacket was partially ripped and his glasses absent from his face.

Mike looked at the security guard then down at Swanson. Moving was difficult. He tried to sit up but failed. Only now to Mike's horror did he see the patch of red across Swanson's white shirt.

Swanson growled out in pain, his back stiffening as his body rose in keeping with the movement of a seizure. His face was frozen and his breathing audible.

The Swiss Guard knelt down by his side, and grabbed the banker's ripped shirt. He pressed it frantically against the wound, but the delicate silk had little effect. Blood gushed at an alarming rate.

Mike barked at the security guard to call an ambulance, all the while continuing to focus on Swanson. The security guard nodded and walked with difficulty, edging closer to the door. He swiped his key card and continued through the door, now sprinting towards the lift.

Mike removed his own suit jacket and pressed the quality material to the wound but realised it was useless. Blood continued to ooze down from his chest. Swanson's breathing heightened.

"Just relax, Mr Swanson," Mike said. "We're gonna get an ambulance. You're gonna be fine. Just hold on."

Swanson blinked rapidly. A look of lifeless resignation overcame him as he gazed aimlessly up at the light.

Blood spread beneath Mike's sticky fingers as he continued to put pressure on the wound. The suit was covered in blood but clearly had no positive effect.

"Hold on, Mr Swanson, the ambulance is on its way," Mike said, removing tissue paper from his pocket and pushing it to the wound. The low quality paper fell apart in his hands and formed a messy substance on impact. Left with no further option he removed his own white shirt and pressed it to the wound.

Swanson looked up at Mike.

"Frei," he said weakly.

"It's okay, Mr Swanson. Save your strength."

Mike checked Swanson's pulse and realised it had weakened considerably. Swanson's face was excessively pale.

"Frei," he said once more. "You must believe that I could never have been a part of this . . ."

Swanson coughed vigorously, leaving his sentence incomplete. Mike looked down at the banker and felt he was referring to the activities of the Rite of Larmenius and the meeting of four days ago. A grim irony consumed him as he realised Swanson still believed that he was on trial.

"Please believe me."

Mike felt a stray tear come to his eye as he looked down at the banker. He blinked a couple of times, continuing to press the blood-soaked shirt to the area of impact. Swanson coughed weakly and blood seeped from the corner of his mouth. The sound was familiar.

"I believe you, Mr Swanson. Everyone does."

"I just could never let them harm my family. I couldn't do it to lil' Millie."

Mike nodded. "I understand that, sir. I promise you nothing bad will happen to them."

Swanson seemed to grimace and smile simultaneously. For the first time he felt a sense of light-headedness as his body lost all sense of feeling. As he looked up at the light, various images entered his head. In the moment they say when your life flashes before your eyes, the vision for Irving Swanson was different. In the light he thought he could see a brilliant angelic vision: perhaps marking his journey to heaven. He saw his wife as she had appeared in her younger days. Next to her was his daughter standing by her husband, cradling a child in his arms. In the distance he thought he could hear the vague siren of an ambulance, fading slowly. Then he felt the strange sensation of being underwater.

He smiled as he surrendered to the beautiful floating sensation as he lost feeling of any pain. In his final vision he saw little Millie.

Then he saw nothing at all.

Thierry de Courten killed the phone call with his finger and dialled the next number without replacing the receiver. It was approaching 9 p.m. Rome time but the commander of the Swiss Guard was still at work and would be for some time yet.

Outside, the sky was fading to blackness with faint sparkles of starlight beginning to appear at irregular intervals across the horizon. A stunning gibbous moon was glowing like a lighthouse through sparse cumulus in the area above the Colosseum, lighting up the otherwise clear sky.

The oberst put the phone to his ear and poured mineral water into a glass. He searched his desk drawer for something for his headache and found one remaining tablet among scattered empty packaging. He placed the tablet to his mouth and swallowed it down with water. He exhaled forcefully as he waited for the phone to connect.

Finally an answer.

"Get me Cardinal Utaka, please. This is urgent."

"Yes, sir," the female voice replied.

De Courten grimaced impatiently as some forgotten band from the late 1970s filled his ear with outdated trash. He inhaled slowly and contemplated what he would say. It had been another day of surprises.

Despite the tiredness, his mind instantly forgot about sleep. All thoughts centred on the news he had just heard. A senior Vatican cardinal had been seen leaving the main Starvel building in Boston. Perfectly innocent perhaps; or at least he would have thought so a week ago. Only now no chances could be taken. Strange as it sounded it made perfect sense. There really was a traitor among the Vatican bankers. Only his name was not Giancarlo Riva.

Nor was it Irving Swanson.

The music suddenly stopped and the familiar voice of Cardinal Utaka spoke clearly down the line. The oberst's ears pricked and his concentration resumed.

"Eminence, please come to my office. There is something we need to discuss."

In a modern fifth floor apartment, the ringing of a telephone offered the only sound. Within seconds, the ringing was accompanied by the creaking of a door opening followed by heavy footsteps marching across wooden flooring towards a nearby desk.

The apartment's sole occupant answered immediately.

"*Oui?*" Gullet said.

"I have a new assignment for you."

The line went dead instantly, and Gullet hung up. Seconds later he heard the bleeping sound of an incoming fax from the accompanying machine. He waited for the printout to finish and studied it with serious eyes.

The phone went again.

"And this one I want alive."

Gullet hung up for the second time in succession and exited the room. If he was quick, he could get it done tonight.

62

Mike had become fairly well acquainted with Gabrielle's mansion in Boston in recent weeks. While it was completely different to the château in Switzerland, to Mike it offered an identical level of elegance, which he had slowly begun to enjoy over the past few months.

Unlike the immense stone and gothic masonry of the château, the house was a fifteen-bed colonial mansion dating back to the late 1690s and located on a hilltop just outside Boston on the road to Salem in the Massachusetts countryside. Like many buildings of its type, it comprised four storeys of white timber with large windows and high ceilings providing the house with a pleasant airiness, sometimes missing from the château. The house was approachable along a two hundred yard oval-shaped driveway, covered in gravel and flanked by beautifully kept lawns, abundant in maple trees, and entered through one of two identical metal gateways. One of the most distinguishing features was a wide porch, comprising four pillars, supporting a triangular-shaped gable that included the name Maplewood Manor. On the right side of the porch a Star-Spangled Banner hung softly in the daytime breeze; at night four mock Victorian lampposts illuminated the driveway.

Directly above the porch, the upper storey contained an unusual looking balcony that Gabrielle explained to Mike was a widow's walk, a common feature of past centuries that provided grieving widows brief contact with the outside world at a time when it was customary for a widow to remain confined to the indoors for the first year following the death of a husband. Also, being the only place in the house with a view of the ocean, it allowed the wife of a fisherman the opportunity to look out across the sea in anticipation of the return of her husband: many of whom never returned.

The walk provided spectacular views of the ocean and also a complete view of the garden to the west. The garden was less impressive than the one in Switzerland yet it still comprised over four acres of stunning greenery. Inside the house, countless artists' impressions of the garden hung from the walls, including impressive attempts by Gabrielle, capturing the countryside at its peak and offering a romanticised portrayal of the New England fall.

Although Mike's bedroom was vastly smaller than the one in Switzerland it was elegantly furnished with items from the colonial era and managed to house a king-sized four-poster bed in the centre. Two antique mirrors lined the walls and a Victorian wardrobe, brown in colour with one squeaky door, covered much of the far wall. The white paint appeared dull in the poor light, shrouding the room in an unappealing gloom in the early hours although it caught the sun pleasantly in the evening.

Mike had remained in his room since they returned. He sat silently on the edge of the bed looking through the large window overlooking the back garden. In his despondent state his gaze became strangely transfixed on a small copse about 600 yards from the rear of the house. As the sun continued to set, he became drawn to a series of bizarre shadows that formed as the light hit the ancient wood. Across the garden several artefacts, including ancient carriages, a well, and an Amish-style barn, gave Mike the strange sensation he had ventured back in time and was witnessing the hustle and bustle of New England in its heyday. To Mike, the setting created a curious illusion of timelessness somehow heightened by the way the branches fluttered effortlessly in the breeze.

A gentle knock at the door broke his attention. As he looked to his left, he saw Gabrielle holding a cup of tea in her hands.

"I thought you might be thirsty."

Mike looked up and nodded. "Thanks."

He received the cup and adjusted his grip. The burning sensation aroused his senses, returning his mind to reality. He was now aware that he had been lost in his thoughts and that his thoughts had been depressing. In his mind he could still see the living body of Irving Swanson in front of him, blood covering the banker's shirt and even Mike's own hands.

"How are you feeling?"

Mike didn't respond immediately. His gaze now focused on the floor.

"I can't believe Velis could kill him like that. Executed in cold blood."

Gabrielle gently removed the cup from his hands and placed it on a coaster on the antique bedside cabinet. She pulled the duvet towards her to remove a wrinkled fold and sat down beside him. She cleared her throat quietly and looked at Mike. His gaze remained fixed on the floor.

"Louis Velis is evil," she said. "It wasn't just Swanson. It was all of them. He killed my dad. He may not have pulled the trigger . . ."

She stopped mid-sentence, close to tears. She took a deep breath and composed her thoughts.

"There was nothing you could do."

"That's not true."

Gabrielle inhaled slowly; an expression of genuine concern crossed her face. "Okay," she said. Then she tried reverse psychology. "What could you have done?"

Mike shook his head, his eyes fixed on the floor.

"You did everything you could. You have nothing to be ashamed of."

Mike nodded unconvincingly. "He knew he was going to die," Mike said. "He knew that Velis would find out. He knew Velis would kill him. Even if not today, he knew it would happen. Velis was never going to let him get away with it."

Gabrielle remained silent.

"After he was shot he asked me if I believed him."

"About what?"

Mike shook his head. "He didn't say."

A strange silence filled the room. Gabrielle placed her right hand to his left shoulder and stroked it gently.

"I could tell he was talking about that day at the Vatican. He was asking if I believed he was innocent."

Gabrielle's expression changed to confusion again. "He was."

"Not to him. He really thought he was on trial. That's why he did it." Mike said, turning his head to the left, making eye contact with Gabrielle. "He died because he wanted to make amends. He really thought he was a traitor."

"But we went through this. He explained."

"He was still guilty because he could've seen it coming. He risked his life because he really convinced himself he was in the wrong. He gave his life."

Mike looked down at the floor and shook his head. He forced a laugh.

"When we were down there he really laid into Velis. And when he was finished he actually asked Velis to let me go. Can you imagine? He told Velis to let the guard go."

"He knew that you were a good guy. And that you did all you could."

Mike looked at Gabrielle briefly and forced an awkward smile but remained silent. Gabrielle scratched her head.

"You know, it's funny, the more I get to know you the more you remind me of my brother."

He looked at her with sudden interest.

"My brother, his name was Stéphane. He was five years older than me. When we were younger he'd tease me and pull my hair and even beat me up," she said, forcing a laugh, her voice breaking slightly.

Mike looked at her with concern.

"Anyway, the school I went to had a lot of snobby brats, sons of legacies et cetera," she said without making eye contact. "Sometimes at school, a few of the kids used to tease me. You know, because of my dad, some of them weren't as rich . . . it was always one big competition."

Mike looked at her as if he was seeing her for the first time. Strangely, he thought back to the day of her father's funeral.

"And Stéphane always used to look out for me, you know?"

Mike nodded, his eyes remained focused on hers.

"Anyway, he went to college in the US and when he returned he was all set to join my dad at Leoni et Cie, but he changed his mind. He joined the Swiss Army and eventually became a Swiss Guard."

Gabrielle wiped a couple of stray tears from her eyes, her gaze at times on him whereas other times it wandered.

"I guess growing up with Leoni et Cie being so normal the Vatican always there in the background made a mark."

She paused momentarily.

"My dad was disappointed but strangely proud. I was delighted. See, he'd always been there for me. He made an excellent guard."

Mike rubbed his right eyebrow, thinking back to a time a few weeks earlier. "There were photos of him in my room in Switzerland?"

She nodded, smiling weakly.

"He was killed," she said, anticipating his question. "In 2004 he was on guard outside the Porta Sant'Anna. A madman ran him over. He hit his head and . . . well."

Mike nodded silently. The story was strangely familiar to him. He had only been a halberdier for a few months, but he was sure that he had known him.

"I'm sorry."

She looked at him and forced a smile once more.

"I loved him," she said. "Even now I think about him, I think about the way he was, the way he used to stand up for me . . ."

Another brief silence descended.

"I know I gave you a hard time," she said as she wiped her eyes.

"When we were at Newport I thought I was going to die, but then I think about the way you told Gullet to let me go . . . and the way you held me."

Her voice trailed off as she failed to control the tears.

"And the way you came for me that day at the Vatican . . ." she said, her voice quivering for the second time in quick succession, tears smudging her pretty makeup. "And the way you dived for Riva . . ."

Mike looked at her seriously, his eyes focused on hers.

"Look, you have no right to feel guilty about letting Swanson down. You said it yourself: they don't let anyone join the Swiss Guard . . ."

As Mike made eye contact he could see that her eyes were filling with tears. For several seconds they looked at one another without speaking. He placed his hands delicately over hers and then to her face. He wiped away the tears softly with his thumbs, keeping his eyes focused on hers. He moved his hands gently against her face and saw her smile. Then, with a sudden lunge, he put his hands behind her head and kissed her, bringing her lips to his, bashfully, then deeply. She placed her hands behind his head and moved closer to him, all the while their tongues massaging one another's. Slowly his hands wandered up and down her sides and hers on his, her body rising as he explored her waist. The strangest thing that entered his mind was how normal it felt: as though why hadn't they been like this all along?

Her the billionaire's daughter and he the guard.

The Deputy Director of the FBI listened with interest to the voice on the other end of the phone. It was the Vatican policeman in Boston explaining exactly what had happened. He would get what he needed within the next few hours.

In a hired Jeep, paid for anonymously by cash, Ludovic Gullet and three other men travelled north at speed. The meaty engine churned loudly as the driver accelerated up the hill, causing an irritating humming noise to reverberate through the open window. The early summer air was surprisingly warm despite the late hour and the powerful headlights that had been on full beam for the last half hour cut the darkness of the deserted road devoid of passing traffic and streetlights.

Gullet checked the clock on the dashboard and saw it was nearing 2 a.m. From New York to Boston the hunt was on. He had promised to keep the Grand Master posted on any new developments.

Three hours till their destination.

*

The Mercedes followed. The driver drove with dipped headlights to avoid suspicion and kept a distance equivalent of four to five vehicle lengths. As yet they were still to discover he was tailing them.

If luck was to hold, nor would they.

63

Mike awoke slowly, his blurry gaze coming slowly into focus as he looked across the twilight sky. For the briefest of seconds he struggled to grasp whether it was the hour before night or the hour before dawn. He was completely disorientated. It was as though he had been part of the strangest yet most wonderful of dreams.

Was it a dream? he wondered. Could it have been real?

No. Impossible.

As he rolled onto his left side, his body felt warm and content. He felt strangely relaxed: particularly around his head. It almost felt as though something or someone was stroking him.

Now he realised what had awakened him. He blinked a couple of times and his vision came into focus. The woman he was supposed to be guarding was lying next to him.

Naked in his bed.

She smiled. "Sorry, I couldn't resist waking you," she said, her smile widening.

Mike forced the laziest yet most content of smiles. "That's quite okay."

She laughed. "Every time you look at me, it's like you haven't seen me in years. You're like a lovesick puppy."

Knowing it was a compliment, he smiled and asked her how she was. She did not respond with words. She leaned over and kissed him: a kiss that lasted over thirty minutes.

The Jeep was parked in a secluded area off road at the rear of the mansion. After turning off the engine and extinguishing the headlights, Gullet departed the vehicle and ordered the other three to disembark.

The mansion was only nine hundred yards away.

Gullet led the way undetected over an eight-foot brick wall and across the open ground. They moved swiftly, the mansion appearing nearer and nearer: four hundred yards, three hundred, two, one.

They continued in the direction of a small copse in close proximity to an unused barn and took shelter behind its walls, less than seventy metres from the house.

Gullet looked at his watch. 4:41 a.m. Magnificent.

They would be out before dawn.

Gabrielle smiled, almost laughing, as she walked barefoot across the tiled kitchen floor towards the refrigerator. Wearing only a dressing gown, she felt a cold chill rise up her body from her feet but in her happy state she barely noticed.

She poured orange juice into two glasses and closed the fridge.

Dressed in casual clothes with the exception of dark balaclavas to veil their faces, the four mercenaries approached the rear of the vicinity with caution. Above them, the sky was slowly becoming lighter as the first signs of dawn appeared beyond the distant sea.

The first of the men approached the conservatory door. He rattled it with his right hand; unsurprisingly it was locked. The second of the men removed a crowbar from his jacket, broke the glass and slid open the inside lock.

They were in.

Upstairs, the Swiss Guard was oblivious to the muffled sound of glass breaking below. He had already left his bed and entered the master bathroom.

Gabrielle closed the door to the fridge and placed the first glass under the ice dispenser. She pushed the button for several seconds and two large pieces of ice fell into the glass, causing liquid to splash over her white dressing gown. She placed the glasses delicately on the side and wiped it with her spare hand.

There was a shuffling of footsteps behind her.

"Aw, did you miss me?"

The intruder wasted no time. He grabbed her by the mouth, prohibiting her from screaming. Familiar feelings of dread overcame her.

Glass hit the floor.

Two of the intruders ascended the stairs with caution. They knew the guard would be upstairs and assumed he would still be sleeping.

Armed with Heckler and Koch MP5 submachine guns, in keeping with the weaponry of the Swiss Guard, they walked almost crab-like:

backs to the wall, every angle covered.

Silently they approached the first door.

Mike left the bathroom suddenly. The sound of a toilet flushing followed by the appearance of the Swiss Guard, dressed in only a t-shirt and a pair of boxer shorts, was unexpected.

The first thing the Swiss Guard saw did not register to his conscious self; instead intuition directed his actions. He moved his body as a reflex, sprinting through the door of the nearest room and closing it behind him.

Gunfire narrowly missed him.

His drowsiness was gone instantly. With his heart thumping, he stood with his back to the closed door and quickly searched his memory. There were two men: both were dressed casually and their faces hidden; both were armed, clearly professionals.

And they were clearly after him.

The Swiss Guard took a step to his right and waited for the door to open. Seconds later it did.

Gunfire.

Hidden behind the door he was completely safe from the marksman's bullets. He saw a hand appear holding a Heckler and Koch, bullets spraying aimlessly across the room. Mike fixed his grip on the door handle and pushed it with fury. The intruder was caught hard on the shoulder, forcing him against the wall. The gun fell to the floor and skidded beneath the bed.

Reacting instinctively, Mike closed the door and forced the intruder to the floor, striking him twice in the face. After knocking him unconscious, he crawled under the bed.

More gunfire.

The second intruder had opened the door and was firing blankly in the direction of the double bed. He noticed the slouched body of his partner, clearly unconscious, but saw no sign of his target. Ceasing fire, the intruder walked slowly around the bed, taking care to avoid his partner although largely unconcerned for his health.

The room was a mess, the air polluted by tattered bed linen. He considered the position of the Swiss Guard. Nowhere to hide: he must be under the bed.

Mike had crawled to within touching distance of the second man. Seeing nothing but the bottom of his legs, he grabbed both of them and pulled violently.

A thumping sound was followed by a short burst of gunfire. As the intruder hit the floor the weapon fell from his grasp and bounced away several feet. Wasting no time, Mike reappeared from beneath the bed and grabbed the man's upper body. He forced the intruder hard to the floor and punched him twice in the face.

With both of his attackers unconscious, the Swiss Guard picked up one of the guns and sprinted out of the room and down the stairs. He heard footsteps then all was quiet.

The house was otherwise deserted.

Ten minutes later the hired Jeep was travelling south through early morning Boston. On the back seat, Gabrielle struggled to relieve herself from the wrist cuffs and mouth gag. Despite the seatbelt she had no way to protect herself from the bumpy journey that threw her from side to side.

In the front were two men. She could not see the driver. She could only see the other man.

The man she had met at Newport.

The man with long blond locks followed from a distance in his E-Class Mercedes-Benz. Boredom had led to contempt. He had followed the Jeep all night and now he was about to do the same again.

64

Gabrielle awoke suddenly. A cold shivering sensation was running up the right side of her body. For the briefest of moments she felt as though she was falling through the air before coming to a standstill on the solid floor.

A sudden bout of dizziness caught her unaware. With it came an overwhelming feeling of nausea, but no pain, nor any recollection of how it came about. Had she been drugged? She assumed so, though without memory of where or when or how. In her mind she recalled two men and a large vehicle, then a large house, perhaps a mansion. Yet the vision was blurry: almost dreamlike and without clarity of whether it was real or a figment of a distorted mind.

She blinked several times and her vision slowly focused. From what she could see, she was sitting in a dimly lit room or chamber, illuminated by what seemed to be a series of flickering candles. The light caused shadows and distortions across black and white patterns. Not for the first time in recent weeks the floor seemed more in keeping with a giant chessboard.

She blinked again, this time for longer. In front of her stood what looked like a large altar, like those often found in medieval churches. Strange objects lined the altar. One was unrecognisable, black in colour, perhaps some sort of skull or mummified head, and another, perhaps a statue, reminiscent of the one that guarded the tomb at Rosslyn.

The smell of burning wax teased her nostrils yet she sensed there was a stronger presence in the air. The air was cramped, as though the room was enclosed or underground. As she moved she became aware of other senses. The small of her back came in contact with the cold floor that was either stone or marble, causing her to shiver. She also heard what sounded like dripping water coming from up above, as though it were seeping through floorboards. From somewhere a vague sound of footfalls also rang in her ears, as did other sounds. There was burning: not the candles but something else.

Although she was aware her hands were tied, she noticed the gag that had earlier blocked her mouth had been removed. Yet other parts of her body felt confined. The dressing gown that she had worn earlier that morning was gone and had been replaced by different clothes: someone else's clothes, stylish but perhaps a size smaller than hers: not readily apparent to a stranger viewing from afar but noticeable to Gabrielle as it restricted her movement uncomfortably around her arms and legs.

After wriggling herself upright, she leaned her back against something solid but cold. She looked over her shoulder and saw it was a stone pillar: a strangely comforting reason for the coldness. As her eyes continued to adjust to the poor light, she noticed many of these pillars, gothic in structure and appearance, supporting a high ceiling vaguely reminiscent of an early medieval European cathedral. Where was she? What country? Had she travelled on a plane? Surely nothing like this existed in the USA. Was she in Europe: France or England maybe? Rome perhaps? It reminded her of the crypts in Rosslyn Castle and to a lesser extent the Newport Tower.

Something else unsettled her. She was alone but she didn't feel it. Through the darkness she felt something or someone watching her; perhaps guarding her. In the poor light the voids between cloisters, leading she assumed to an underground crypt or steps up to a higher church or castle, remained sealed in blackness. The voids alone were unsettling, yet the feeling of being watched was more unsettling. She considered the possibility that unseen eyes were watching her. Her senses detected something was directly in front of her.

She squinted in that direction. Distorted by the shadows, she saw what seemed to be a circular table. Eight chairs surrounded it. The atmosphere suggested importance unlike any boardroom she had ever witnessed, emphasised above all else by the inclusion of the most impressive of the chairs located at the head of the table, seemingly identical in appearance to a throne.

That was when she realised: a lone silhouette was visible in the darkness.

The figure sat with an air of authority and patience unlike any person she had ever witnessed. Although his features were hidden, the outline of his face became vaguely visible when illuminated by the glow of his cigar lighting up the area hauntingly like a vision of hell bathed in a fiery light. She saw the man was bearded but at present she saw nothing else. He spoke with a muffled voice in the direction of one of the other seats. Another was present, sitting opposite. Though she could not see or hear him.

Although the light restricted her vision her senses suggested he was looking directly at her.

For the first time he spoke to her.

"You are currently sitting in the New Temple of Solomon," the bearded man said. His words echoed momentarily before fading to a distant murmur.

A deathly hush descended.

"You were wondering where you were?"

The man's assumption was correct yet Gabrielle remained silent. A sharp stabbing sensation entered her chest, instantly diagnosable as claustrophobia. Although she had never suffered from a fear of confined spaces before, the severity of the situation enforced it. Her back itched, partly due to the cramped conditions, and partly the tightness of her clothes. She inhaled deeply and from somewhere found the courage to speak.

"Where are we?" she asked, realising her throat was dry. "Who are you?"

The bearded man spoke clearly. "We are in America if that's any comfort?"

Comfort was the last thing she felt. Using the pillar as a backscratcher, she lifted herself up and down in quick succession, relieving some of the tension in her back and allowing herself a better view of the room. As her eyes continued to adjust she felt the room was less old than she had originally thought, yet still relatively established.

"You are currently seated in the second oldest church in the New World," the bearded man continued, flicking cigar ash into an ashtray. "I understand you've already visited the oldest. I'm sure that once you grasp the story of what is behind it you will appreciate its importance."

She looked for an exit, yet that was out of the question. Perhaps someone would find her? Perhaps Mike would find her.

Where was he? Was he still alive? She felt her eyes fill up but the tears wouldn't come. Anger turned to numbness. In spite of her fear something else troubled her. She had heard this voice before.

"Louis?" she said timidly. "Louis Velis?"

The bearded man smoked but did not answer.

"What's with the clothes?"

Velis exhaled on his cigar. "We didn't want you to catch cold. They were once the property of my estranged wife. You can keep them if you like. It seems a shame to see them go to waste."

Gabrielle looked herself over, understanding he was referring to Rachel. That explained why they were a size too small.

"I suppose this all belongs to you."

Velis put the cigar to his mouth and rose to his feet. He walked slowly around the table, his eyes remaining fixed on Gabrielle.

"It was Jacques de Molay's great ambition, once the Crusades were over to develop the order in a more humanitarian way: incorporating the charity of the Hospitallers and the military and banking expertise of the Templars while remaining wholly committed to the greater good. Free of the dogmas and interference of national politics. Independent of Rome yet still worshipping similar ideals."

"Yeah. What went wrong?"

Velis forced a laugh. "The man himself was unable. After all, how could a man, weak and ailing in his seventies, ignorant of the true promises of science, politics and theology, illiterate, provide the leadership and stability needed to act independently of the most powerful king in Europe?"

He gestured with his arms.

"But as you can see: the concept was not entirely unfounded."

Gabrielle fidgeted but failed to move. The cuffs burned against her wrists.

"The Knights Templar were not evil," he said, walking slightly closer. "Talk of Devil worship, idolatry, spitting, urinating on the cross . . . seems a little strange, don't you think? After all, no one throughout the course of history has shed more blood for Christianity than the Templars."

Velis flicked ash into an ashtray. Gabrielle remained silent.

"The Knights Templar, whatever you might think of them, were exceptional," the bearded man said, his smile widening. As Velis walked closer Gabrielle could see pride in his smile: it displayed knowledge yet it was strangely appreciative: almost as though he were an apprentice praising a master.

"How could it be that a group of nine knights, related by blood, wholly committed to the cause and ideologies of Urban II would within two centuries become the strongest army the world had ever seen? That they should become so wealthy that even the richest nations of the time were in their debt and that they should master the art of banking and yet remain wholly devoted to poverty and worship of Jesus Christ. They could have been rich beyond any man's wildest dreams. Yet the promise of eternal bliss remained their choice. Remarkable. Don't you think?"

"Let me guess, they found the Holy Grail in a cupboard?"

Velis laughed. "Such a thought is amusing. Every book I read on the subject seems to think so, or that they were blackmailers or in possession of hidden knowledge. No one seems to realise they were the cleverest businessmen on the planet."

Velis smoked as he walked. There was a certain smugness and awe about him.

"By 1307 the original Templars were caught in the middle of a feud that spanned all of Europe. The loss of the Holy Land left a gap in their purpose. After all, without the Crusades they were merely a group of mercenaries funded by the world's most powerful bank. To tyrants like Philip le Bel, they had the potential to rule all of Europe. The result: they became the focus of attention for every greedy monarch in Europe, even the Pope."

Velis continued to walk. "The bitterness of rival states was focused on them rather than each other. Yet as soon as the Templars were gone, the nations who had dissolved them went back to fighting each other."

The bearded man smiled as he smoked.

"The Templars who had survived knew this. And the new order could use this to their advantage. Eventually this ensured the pacification of Europe."

Velis paused thoughtfully, continuing to walk.

"In many ways the Inquisition was a good thing. For two hundred years the Templars had operated in the turbulence of the Crusades. They had encountered bloodshed and little reward. For those who had survived, anonymity brought its own benefits. The advances made in banking, science and politics within the last century ensured that the order could no longer play second fiddle to pointless slaughter. This was the birth of Capitalism."

Velis exhaled, smoke rising from his mouth.

"Many of humanities' key advances occurred during this time – the Renaissance perhaps the most important. Yet some things never changed. According to the Templar Rule no Christian could shed the blood of a fellow Christian. This itself promoted peace in Europe. You can understand that, can't you? But once the Crusades were over it took only the arrogance of one petty monarch to jeopardise the entire continent. The result: the Hundred Years' War."

Velis paused momentarily, taking a further puff on his cigar.

"Following the dissolution of the Templars, Europe turned into a bubbling cauldron. And why: so that the incompetent and corrupt could become secure while the virtuous fell. Throughout history the rule of nations had always remained in the hands of bloodthirsty monsters and their inbred minions. Yet the future of Europe and the wider world was far too fragile to remain in the hands of men so unworthy."

Gabrielle watched in silence.

"For two centuries the Poor Knights of Solomon had been the peacekeepers; it was they who had singlehandedly united an entire continent. With the Templars gone, the conflict that existed before reignited. So now it fell to us: a small group of virtuous men to retake order."

Gabrielle didn't respond. Her vision remained transfixed on the banker and the peculiar surroundings.

"As I am sure you are by now aware, my dear, the survivors of the order did not lie in wait in the seclusion of anti-Catholic Europe to reclaim the Holy Land or serve the Pope," the bearded man said. "But it is the early generations in particular who deserve most credit for making the Templar vision possible. Through the complex banking network, billions of pounds have gone on developing our vision and ensuring stability."

"Is that Starvel's purpose?"

"For many years the great Templar banks have provided stability for our customers and some of the proceeds even go to the less fortunate: just as we've been doing since the 12th century. What you must understand, my dear, is that the dissolution of the Templars had left a vacuum: farms, vineyards, castles, churches, not to mention millions of pounds of currency and gold deposits removed from the economy. But economics is only part of it. Every day the world is advancing: technology, science, politics: all aspects of human life. It takes a particular kind of leadership to oversee such progress. This was something Europe lacked."

"Is that why they guillotined half the population of France?"

Smoke teased Gabrielle's lungs and forced her to cough.

"Republican France has indeed brought stability," Velis said. "America was born under the Templar vision and that has evolved into the world's greatest superpower. Throughout all of Europe stability is at an all-time high."

"So why all the killings?" she asked, slightly louder than she expected. "Your order has murdered thousands of innocent people."

Velis exhaled, his expression thoughtful. He delayed responding for several seconds.

"Every cause has its costs," he said quietly. "If a man gets shot in the leg, the first step towards rehabilitation is removing the dead cells. Sometimes if you want something to grow you have to cut the decaying cells away and at first make it smaller. Even the most unpleasant of sacrifices can have positive effects in the long-term. Jesus, himself, taught us that."

A brief pause followed as Velis walked slowly in front of Gabrielle, his cigar glowing as he breathed. Gabrielle's eyes followed the banker.

"You don't really believe in God, Ms Leoni," Velis said, changing the subject, his eyes focused on Gabrielle. "It is important to believe in God. Only through devotion to the Supreme Being can man ensure integrity and commitment.

"But religion can also be damaging; the Crusades have taught us that. In the 11th century Pope Urban II called on Christians from all over Europe to journey to the Holy Land and offer their lives as part of a noble cause. What you must understand, my dear, is that they really believed they were fighting for the Son of God. That this was his will."

The banker continued to smoke.

"But they were deceived. I mean, seriously, what would he have said, do you think, if he had still been alive?"

"They had to do something. Pilgrims were being slaughtered."

Velis smiled and nodded. "And it was for the protection of these pilgrims that our order was created. And why many of those who came before us gladly gave their lives to protect them. Our goal was and always shall be to serve the greater good.

"Yet how does one really define greater good?" he asked, his arms out wide. "Our order once existed to aid Christianity yet we were betrayed by the very people who encouraged the genocide of others. For two centuries the Knights Templar spilled their blood for the cause of the unworthy. Only in our latter days did we finally realise."

He turned, facing the altar.

"Jehovah, Yahweh, Allah: the same God, different names. Each concept as stupid as the next," he said smoking. "He has gone by many names. Osiris, Ra, Apollo, Zeus, it makes no difference. The difference is in one's own interpretation. Yet more blood has been shed in his name than any other. And so it continues, even to this day.

"But fidelity to prayer is excellent. Only through devotion can a man really be accepted as trustworthy. Only through embarking on the path to God can man really become whole. For two centuries no one was more devoted to this than the Templars. But as an order we learned to become indifferent. Capitalism has taught us to do business with all walks of life. This was where our future lay. Every human being is a child of God, not just some of us. But such thinking was prohibited by the very people they had given their blood to protect."

Gabrielle's eyes remained fixed on the banker. He delivered his argument as though in possession of definitive wisdom with a voice, almost hypnotic, to match. Yet it was his eyes that struck her the most. They suggested unbreakable concentration with a gaze that offered complete confidence.

"So you weren't heretics?"

Velis removed his cigar from his mouth. "Heresy," he said. "What is heresy? In the Middle Ages it was considered heresy to refer to the world as being round or that the earth revolved around the sun. Pioneers such as Galileo and even the great Christopher Columbus were savaged because of their so-called heresy. Yet none of these men were anti-God. What was it Galileo once said: 'I do not feel obliged to believe that the same God who has endowed us with sense, reason and intellect has intended us to forgo their use.' As I'm sure we can agree, much of this was unnecessary."

"So what is this about? Revenge? Is that why you've stolen from the Roman Curia? Is that why you've bled Leoni et Cie dry? Because my ancestors opposed you; that they aided the people your order had massacred? Is that why you assassinated the Kings of France? The demise of the Papal States?"

"Achieving stability is a complex problem," the Grand Master said, his expression thoughtful. "Sometimes achieving it requires disposing of those who had earlier betrayed us. That may sound like revenge but in reality it is quite coincidental:

"Our goal is worldwide integration. You have already seen the New Republic in France free of autocrats and aristos operating free of religious interference. In the past a man was judged on his beliefs. Men have even given their lives for it. But it is by actions, not beliefs, that men must be judged."

Velis walked slowly. "Love thy neighbour," he said, almost laughing to himself. "The words of Christ himself encourage integration. But the Crusades that were once presented as justified violence were nothing more than pointless genocide inspired by the greed of the corrupt and the weak. By the end the Templars realised this and Jacques de Molay knew that the King of France would betray him. In his wisdom he knew that his men would be tortured and their resources confiscated. But he wanted to ensure his vision would continue."

Velis paused momentarily.

"The problem with religion is that its practices develop on the word of self-anointed prophets and act under the rule of puppets who incite so-called justified violence. They say it is God's will. Such stupid beliefs remain at the forefront of our society and culture," he said, walking away from Gabrielle.

"Love thy neighbour," he said again. "Religion is supposed to encourage stability, not threaten it. The ideals of Christianity are magnificent yet they are invariably overlooked. Over the centuries the Templars have remained loyal to their cause and in doing so helped to ensure that the mistakes of the past will be eliminated. Social change takes time, but eventually the world will learn to accept our point of view. That is the true mission of the order."

Velis smiled. "This is where Christianity's future must lie: where every religion's future must lie. A Church that supports the true nature of religion: a devotion that unites, that encourages understanding."

A look of disgust overcame Gabrielle. "And what about your own justified violence? You know nothing about the feelings of others. What you say is twisted."

"Twisted?" Velis said, removing his cigar from his mouth. "I'm afraid you are the one who is twisted. You yourself talk as though you mourn for those who have passed yet you are a prime example of one whose own actions are tainted. You talk to me about murdering innocents. Every day you live in your grand château or luxury mansion surrounded by luxuries that surpass the wealth of many African towns and villages not giving a thought for those living on the streets on less than a dollar a day. You say every life is sacred yet the very decisions you make confirm you value the life of an illiterate child in Africa less than a scarf; or that you would substitute the health of a large family from Bolivia in favour of a handbag. The very decisions you have once made may go so far as to confirm that you would overlook helping those who die each day in favour of a private jet."

"That's not fair!" Gabrielle shouted.

The bearded man laughed. "Corrupt politicians endorse foolish and greedy policies that cause the avoidable deaths of thousands every year yet they kiss one dying baby in a leukaemia ward in front of a camera and the ignorant vote in numbers. Governments see thousands of families made homeless every year and barely lift a finger yet twelve people are accidentally killed in a riot and a full scale investigation is launched costing the taxpayer tens of millions. One teenage slut gets raped and the liberals talk of the breakdown in moral fabric yet it was their own chequered human rights movements that now allow the abortions of thousands every year and the breakdown of the traditional values which could have given the rapist a better chance in life.

"You talk of genocide and massacring innocents but what we do is not in vain. No. I wish that such sacrifices need not be required, but we both know such action is inevitable. Our vision is not without its costs but the world needs us. If only to protect it from itself."

"Including murdering my father?" she shouted. "And how about injuring my uncle? Or Mike? Did you get him too?"

"Your father was regrettable," he said, exhaling, a rare moment of sympathy. "As for your Swiss Guard, he seems to have slipped the net."

Gabrielle smiled briefly, tears streaming down her face. Almost instantly her face returned to thunder.

"Why did you hurt my uncle? What did he ever do to you?"

Velis's expression lightened. "Perhaps I am not the person you should be talking to about such matters."

Slowly the man hidden in the shadows stood from his seated position and walked towards Gabrielle. His face now visible in the dim light, he smiled warmly.

65

Mike parked Gabrielle's Jaguar on the right side of the leafy street and switched off the engine. A loud ringing sensation dominated his ears as they adjusted to the quietness.

The street was peaceful and pleasant in appearance: countless trees lined either side, deciduous in nature, green in colour as appropriate for the time of year. On the opposite side of the road three dark sedans were parked outside a long gravelled driveway, leading to one of the street's impressive mansions, hidden some five hundred yards behind electronic gates and imposing concrete walls.

The other side of the road was equally quiet. To his right, a paved sidewalk ran parallel to the street, crossing several imposing gated entrances to the mansions, also protected by walls. Behind him, a silver Audi was parked two hundred yards away whereas a black Merc was parked sixty feet in front of him, its interior veiled by tinted glass.

Mike inhaled deeply. He examined the street with eager eyes, searching for signs of life. He had seen many like it, yet none quite so opulent. Newport was famous for its summer mansions and this street was a prime example.

Even Gabrielle was not so ostentatious.

Suddenly his mobile phone began to vibrate against the passenger seat. Without delay, he checked the message and saw that it was from Mark. There had been a text from Mark earlier.

The message was brief:

Wait for the signal.

Although there was no hint as to what the signal was, he scanned the street closely for any possible sign. For several seconds he saw nothing. Then, without warning, the lights of the Merc flashed briefly.

Understanding that was the signal, Mike exited the car and closed the door behind him. He locked the car electronically and walked casually towards the sidewalk, glancing briefly over his shoulder to check he was not being monitored. Within seconds he reached the car.

Tentatively, he opened the rear left door.

He sat down on the back seat and closed the door behind him. On the rear right he saw a man dressed in a smart suit and black tie holding a biro in his left hand that was also perched to his lips. Although Mike did not recognise him he instantly twigged he was a Fed. On the front passenger side was Mark. The man with blond locks sat behind the wheel.

"Hey, Mikey, what's happening, baby?" the man asked.

"Alessandro," Mike said, unable to hide his surprise. "What the heck . . ."

"Alessandro and Markus have been assisting us in our investigation," the suited man said. He had a shaven crew cut of dark brown hair in the style of a US Marine and a clean-shaven face. Mike guessed he was early fifties in age and was of senior grade.

"That's right," Sandro said. "I've been following you all over. Been your guardian angel. I watched you at Rosslyn. Even saved your life at Newport. Pity the dipshit got away. It was so dark I couldn't see for shit."

Mike grimaced as he looked at his friend. At least he knew who had been following him.

"Mike, this is Mr Pieterson, Deputy Director of the FBI," Mark said, turning in his seat.

Mike nodded briefly and shook the deputy director's hand out of courtesy. Pieterson clicked his biro as he removed it from his mouth and leaned across the seat.

"Sergeant Frei, I'm sure this is a bit surprising for you to see me here," he said quietly. "May I call you Mike?"

The Swiss Guard sat back slightly but retained eye contact with Pieterson. "Sure."

"I'm not going to go into detail, Mike; heck we don't have the time. What you and Mr Swanson did yesterday goes deeper than you know."

For a second Mike looked worried.

"Relax, sergeant, you've done more for us in one afternoon than we've managed since the beginning. Since the early '50s we've been trying to infiltrate the organisation known only to us as the Rite of Larmenius. No one who has become a member and told of its activities has come out alive and trust me many have tried. Most of its members are rich and successful yet they choose to keep themselves to themselves. Their surveillance of their own members and the wider world is almost unrivalled."

Mike nodded, swallowing, but remained silent.

"You see, Mike, we have known for many years of their involvement and possible funding of numerous murders and other criminal

439

activities. From what Markus has told me you have stumbled onto something more: something beyond all expectation. This society are believed to have carried out over three thousand murders since 1945 and Lord knows how many before that. Each of these murders we understand to have been politically motivated by some higher authority. They call the shots, Mike. And thanks to your work with Mr Swanson, we now have enough information to pull the plug."

Mike nodded. "How about Starvel?"

"Starvel itself we believe is legit, as, I'm sure, is Leoni et Cie. The activities of Mr Velis, Mr de Bois, Senator D'Amato and countless others, however, are not. We also have reason to convict a further eighty men in connection with Starvel and for other offences. These guys don't play games. They have murdered in cold blood. I understand you have witnessed this. I'm sorry."

Mike nodded once more. It was not unexpected, yet still tough to believe.

Pieterson smiled wryly. "You've done some fine work, Mike. I'd love to have the three of you working for me."

Alessandro shook his head.

"Mike would never leave the Swiss Guard," Mark said, "not with all the privileges that come with the job. Free trips to Scotland, rendezvous with old friends in Massachusetts . . ."

"Living in châteaux with foxy ladies," Alessandro said.

Mike forced an awkward laugh. "Where is Gabrielle?"

Alessandro: "Ludo Gullet and another SOB took the foxy chick here," he said, pointing to a large mansion on the opposite side of the street. The exterior was only just visible, hidden behind the extensive covering of the wall. "I tailed his ass from your place right through Boston."

Mike nodded.

"One more thing," Mark said. "Cardinal Tepilo is in there with her. We think he's been involved with Velis from the start."

"Impossible," Mike said, dumbstruck. "He . . ."

Mike paused mid-sentence. As much as he hated to believe it, it made complete sense.

"He murdered his own nephew?"

Mark nodded. "Among other things."

Mike looked at Pieterson. "But he's the Vatican Secretary of State . . . the Camerlengo . . . the preferiti . . ."

He looked desperately at Mark and Sandro.

"I've gotta get her out of there."

"We will do, son," Pieterson said strongly. "Thanks to you we have all we need to conduct a legal search."

He pointed to three sedans on the other side of the road.

"Each vehicle contains four armed officers," he said. "Once we have the place secure from the outside we can begin."

Mike nodded and looked at his watch. He hoped they were not too late.

66

Gabrielle gaped: her expression strangely like that of a frog. Her mouth opened and closed involuntarily several times in quick succession as she sought to speak but failed.

Standing before her in the dim light of the mock medieval cloisters, her great-uncle, Cardinal Tepilo, smiled warmly. His posture was straight and his hair nicely in trim. He looked younger than he had of late. He didn't look like a cardinal; instead he was dressed suitably for a regular priest relaxing at home, or even a regular retiree. He wore a green jacket around a plain white shirt, unbuttoned at the collar, barely matching his black trousers and shoes. He had been sitting in the second most important seat: the one designated only to a Templar Sénéchal.

He looked at his niece with a warm expression but also strangely pleased with himself. Almost as though he had fooled everyone and was now about to reveal his secret.

"I am sure this must be a little difficult for you to understand."

"No," she said firmly, her facial expression hardening. "This is quite straightforward. Uncle Roberto, how could you?"

"Gabrielle, please. Let me explain."

Gabrielle tried in vain to think of a response but just ended up shouting abuse. Tepilo leaned in closer and removed the cuffs from her hands. At first she raised her hands as if to strangle her uncle before punching him several times in the chest. The barrage of fists caused the ageing cardinal to lose his balance. Regaining composure, he grabbed her arms and tightened his grip on her. Finally through exhaustion she embraced him.

"You bastard."

Velis laughed as he returned to his seat at the far end of the table; his cigar continuing to glow in the darkness.

Gabrielle released herself from her great-uncle's grip and wiped her eyes with her free hands. Mascara trickled from around her eyes, creating black marks on her cheeks. For several seconds neither said anything, but Gabrielle's eyes said everything she wanted.

This simply could not be happening.

Gabrielle shook her head. "I can't believe it," she said, wiping new tears from her eyes. A look of hatred crossed her face.

"Gabrielle, my darling, you must understand, God loves each and every one of us. Just because there is religion, does not mean there is only God."

Tepilo looked philosophically at his niece as he returned to his feet.

"What Louis says is quite correct," he said with confidence. "What our order has achieved since its foundation has been quite extraordinary. Since our beginnings at the height of the Crusades we have brought real stability to France. Our efforts have seen two centuries of relative peace in Europe. We have established the most efficient banking system in the world and we even played a helping hand in the formation of this great nation."

"Spare me your crap. You talk about it as if you were there," she shouted, louder than she expected. "And what are you talking about relative peace in Europe?"

The cardinal stuttered. "Relatively speaking there has been less war in the last two centuries than ever before."

"But record loss of life."

Tepilo frowned. Gabrielle shook her head, a look of disappointment and hatred in her eyes.

"Why?"

Tepilo looked back thoughtfully. "Why? Gabrielle, please you must understand. This is God's will."

"God's will? You had your own nephew murdered. My father . . ."

Gabrielle's eyes flowed with tears. Tepilo leaned forward.

"Don't you dare!"

Tepilo retreated. A look of remorse filled his eyes. "Gabrielle, please, you must understand. Life is full of sacrifice. The Catholic Church itself teaches such things. Nothing is ever straightforward."

"Don't tell me. He's already tried."

The Sénéchal nodded, a thoughtful smile crossing his face. "My darling, Louis is quite right. What you must understand is that the activities of the Knights Templar are virtuous and our actions have merit. If it were not for our predecessors Europe would still be a place of turmoil. France would be cursed to remain in the Dark Ages. There would be no United Kingdom. There would be no United States of America, at least not as we know it. Gabrielle, you must understand the good we've done. The European Union, the Euro, the African Union, NATO, even the United Nations . . ."

"How long?" she interrupted. "How long have you been involved?"

Cardinal Tepilo contemplated the answer, as if calculating an exact number. "Thirty-two years next January as a Rite of Larmenius; I've only had this honour for just over fifteen."

Gabrielle shook her head, tears returning to her eyes. "You oversaw the collapse of the Vatican Bank, Leoni et Cie, our family's legacy, willingly," she said, louder than before. "You bled our family bank dry. You stole from the Roman Curia, the Holy See. You killed the former President of France, one of your own."

"Gabrielle, please understand, every project requires sacrifices, just as every leader faces some opposition: even if out of vanity. Mikael opposed the decisions that needed to be made and the sacrifices along the way. None of us like them."

Gabrielle shook her head.

"Gabrielle, all people need a shepherd, not just those of our faith. What we do will change the whole of the earth. The world needs a coordinator. Every major company has a board of directors."

"And even they are just puppets under your thumb."

Velis laughed loudly, his face partially hidden in the darkness. A strange silence descended as Tepilo began to speak.

"The Knights Templar have existed for nine hundred years, but, in many ways, nothing has really changed."

"I think the Crusades ended some time ago, eminence."

Tepilo's expression was a kind one. "Did they? Truly ask yourself: has the Kingdom of Jerusalem ever really been freed? My darling, the great Hugues de Payens formed our order for the protection of pilgrims. The task is never truly finished."

Gabrielle looked up as if to hit him.

"Over the years we have reached out far across the world. The Masons cross over eighty nations and continue the good work. The Rite of Larmenius is the same. The members of the original Knights Templar were the most gifted men of their time, and the most virtuous. Imagine if they had never survived? Imagine if the French Revolution had never happened. The Declaration of Independence."

"Two world wars?"

The Camerlengo's response was animated. "My dear, please try to understand."

"Understand? I nearly got killed. Twice."

Tepilo pointed a finger, then at Velis. "That should never have happened," he said loudly. "That was his men being incapable of following orders."

Velis remained silent. His cigar glowed in the darkness, lighting up his face briefly.

"And my father?" she asked, tears once again falling down her face. "Was that his men? How about the others?"

Tepilo placed his hand to her head. "Gabrielle, listen to me, every society needs its rule of the wise. Empires rise, empires fall. History repeats itself. How long will it be before these lessons are heeded? Even Saint Thomas More wrote of the Utopian society. The great Thomas Aquinas spoke of those who knew not of God but still had great virtue. The Crusades may be over but wars continue. But for the first time we are starting to achieve real stability."

"Six billion people live on this earth. There are only eight seats at this table."

"Gabrielle, few people are destined to lead. The advancement of civilisation depends always on the gifted minority. It took only one genius to invent a light bulb. It took only one man to have us excommunicated. It took one Pope to start the Crusades. One man to die for our sins. A cabinet of a handful leads nations of millions. That is the way. Even before democracy the rule was of the minority."

"It only took the murder of one archduke to start a world war."

"Gabrielle, please understand, the original goal was to protect pilgrims and this has never changed. In the early 1300s the Poor Knights were collectively richer than every nation in Europe, better trained and led by the morally superior. Yet despite this they still chose honour and the protection of others ahead of greed. Nothing here has changed. What began as a pointless waste of life for a corrupt and inefficient government has led to so much more. That is the real protection of pilgrims. What we are doing now can ensure stability for the entire planet."

Gabrielle exhaled deeply. "You know I heard rumours about the New World Order: the pyramid of knowledge: those who ruled at the top and everyone else at the bottom. I never realised it was true. See, I thought we lived in a democracy. You spoke of it yourself not one week ago. You are such a fucking hypocrite."

The force of her words rattled him.

"Gabrielle, we have no say over voting patterns, we merely assist the elected."

"You mean you pull the strings!"

"Gabrielle, throughout history the pattern has always been the same. Monarchs and nobility continuously leech off the poor for personal gain: the rich become richer and the poor become poorer.

Whether it is the rule of monarchy or democracy the outcome is always the same. Incompetent tyrants like Philip le Bel took authority because they really believed God willed it and even my predecessors approved: being a cardinal or Pope was not about love of others: it was about love of themselves. For hundreds of years the kings of Europe claimed they ruled by divine right, yet they were not necessarily the strongest, nor were they wise. Democracy without supervision of a senior council has the same problem."

Her head was spinning.

"My darling, please understand, this has already begun to change. The world needed them; the world needs us still. For the first time we have a system that is not only rational but also sustainable."

Gabrielle shook her head. For the first time her breathing slowed to its normal rate.

"You tried to kill me – twice."

"That was never intended."

Gabrielle wiped her eyes. As she did she made eye contact with Velis. His gaze remained unbroken, almost mesmerising.

As she looked away, her attention turned to the altar. "So what did Zichmni have to do with this?"

Tepilo smiled softly. "The manuscript you found had been lost for quite some time," the cardinal said, rising to his feet. He walked slowly towards the altar. "The Knights Templar did not carry the fabled treasures that legend suggests. Yet for our existence to continue we needed complete privacy. Had the endeavours of Prince Sinclair, our own ancestor, been known then the fate of our order would be available for all to see."

Gabrielle looked at the altar. The winged goat she had seen many times before stood directly before her. The relic seemed to glow in the darkness as it reflected the light of the candles.

She looked at it nervously. "What exactly is it?"

"According to ancient legend the Temple of wise King Solomon was created by this angel, Asmodeus. Even today it is respected in Freemasonry. This particular statue was found in 1124 AD. It is the only known evidence that the first Temple ever existed."

Gabrielle monitored the object. She was particularly drawn to its eyes. Its appearance seemed demonic.

"The origins of our order are known only to a select few," he said, a hint of pride in his voice, as though he was answering long unanswered questions with accuracy. "When Moses led the Israelites out of Egypt, God entrusted unto him the secrets of man. The truth is that there is no religion but religion of nature itself, as preserved in the initiation rites of ancient Greece and Egypt. Moses himself initiated the chiefs of Israel and the Levites into these mysteries, and they later formed the basis for the Temple of Solomon. Yet even by the birth of Christ, God's own son, the Levites had separated from this knowledge, leading to Christ's own sacrifice to return to eternal life. That, my child, is the true sacred mystery."

Gabrielle looked at her uncle with wide eyes.

"You see, what Louis says is correct. There is only one God. He has many names. Jehovah. Ra. Osiris. In the earliest days of our existence, our ancestors discovered within the ancient temple a manuscript of true ancient wisdom, wisdom once passed down by God to Moses, and taught once more by Jesus Christ," he said pointing to a large manuscript on the altar, made mainly from papyrus. "The Templars called it Baphomet, meaning baptism of knowledge. Moses knew this, Our Lord taught it and died for it, but humanity since that time has taught to forget it. When the Templars uncovered this knowledge they became merely the inheritors. That, my dear, is why we were excommunicated."

Gabrielle looked at him, her eyes ever widening.

"That doesn't make sense."

Tepilo smiled warmly. "What you must understand is that Moses himself was Egyptian, the adopted son of a Pharaoh's daughter the Book of Exodus proclaims. Years later, wise King Solomon himself learned the mysteries and made his temple a relic in homage to the one true God. And take a look at this," he said, pointing to a wooden staff standing next to it. "Once the property of Moses' brother, Aaron, so we understand."

For the first time she smiled. A strange feeling overcame her, overpowering in nature: almost as though an electric charge had passed through her body.

She looked across the altar at the mummified head, situated less than three feet from the Asmodeus statue. On closer inspection she realised there were two thighbones on the altar.

"The Jolly Roger."

"Close," he replied. "When Jacques de Molay was executed all that was found of him was his head and two thighbones. Today the Knights Templar uses it as a logo of the Rite of Larmenius. A reminder: no man is immortal."

Tepilo smiled.

"What Louis says is quite true. In the days of the Middle Ages a heretic was a concoction of man's ignorance. Philip le Bel was a Christian extremist. His goal was to be celebrated as the most pious man in Christendom, following in the footsteps of his ancestor, Louis IX. See, the Templars had moved on. Our goal was integration. We had fought with Muslims, Jews, Cathars. Why? They too wasted their lives in the name of false promises. Jacques de Molay knew this. It was our dream that the sons of Abraham would unite. Christians, Jews, Muslims, everyone living in peace in the New Jerusalem. They read books written by the ancient inheritors of this knowledge. This was not black magic. Only they claimed it was possible to control one's own destiny using one's own will. They accepted other religions as our friends. This was not Devil worship."

Gabrielle shook her head. "Times have changed. The Vatican has changed. Cardinal del Rosi serves to encourage understanding. Why do you knock your own religion?"

Tepilo shook his head. "Every major religion still acts as a barrier against integration. Every religion prohibits their members from joining us. To them we are heretics. The old religions are obsolete: the moral fabric of Christianity is at breaking point. Church attendance in Europe is at an all-time low, less and less people take up the call of the priesthood and Rome has become isolated: lost in time: a cathedral to the past. Yet despite this, there are still over one billion Catholics worldwide and over one billion other Christians who remain conscripted to their Church. They quite willingly enter the Church in youth yet forsake it every day of their lives for their destructive vices without giving it a single thought. Yet as soon as someone dies or they chose to marry they all turn into amateur monks before forgetting about their newly found faith till the next time. Then as soon as their children are born they insist on a Christian baptism to ensure their place in heaven.

"My darling, nothing opposes social change like religious fundamentalism. If it were not for the old religions the Crusades would never have happened; the twin towers in New York would still be standing; we would finally have a united Northern Ireland. We would ensure pacification between the Middle East and the West.

"Gabrielle, don't you see, without religious difference there would be no hatred. That was why the empires of ancient Greece, Rome and Egypt thrived for so long. My darling, we can reignite the flame. Just imagine a Pope taking this vision forward. This is the discovery that will unite the world."

Suddenly Gabrielle felt cold. "A Pope taking this vision forward?"

Tepilo exhaled deeply.

"That's why you killed Cardinal Faukes. Not only was he on the oversight commission but he was the only cardinal more likely to become the next Pope than you."

"Gabrielle, it is our dream that the sons of Abraham will unite. His Holiness has less than a year to live. His present state of mind is dangerous. For integration to occur each religion must pull down the walls which keep them apart. Only then can the world truly unite, can every religion be united."

"That's why you were excommunicated. You really were heretics. You can't seriously be considering this . . ."

"Gabrielle, we encourage our members to worship Christ, but for integration and stability to be achieved the religions of the world must unite. Gabrielle, throughout history religion has seen the genocide of innocents."

"Don't give me all that virtuous shit," she blasted. "Your New World Order has decreed the genocide of innocents. Is that why you killed Snow, Von Sonnerberg, Cardinal Faukes, Randy Lewis, Jermaine Llewellyn . . ." she asked, counting each off on her fingers. "You talk about religion as if it were some kind of disease. You forget to mention all the good it does: charity, morals, and faith. To you, humans are just pawns in your capitalist cesspit. Religion doesn't incite violence. People like you incite violence," she said shouting.

"You know, I finally get it now. This has nothing to do with what's best for the world. This isn't even about revenge. If you succeed, everyone will have to live under your tyrannical theocracy, and you'll be the one on the throne. You really believe that if you control religion you control the people. You're just like the pharaohs. You actually believe you're God."

"Gabrielle."

Cardinal Tepilo's voice broke off as the sound of footsteps emanated from the floor above. They were heavy footsteps: mostly male and instantly recognisable as the beginning of an armed raid.

"Quickly," Velis said, rising to his feet. "Down the passage."

"Hey," Gabrielle said as Velis grabbed her arm and pushed her.

"Louis, don't hurt her."

67

Outside the mansion, two skilled officers successfully picked the lock of the ancient front door, forcing it open. After whispering commands to his squad, Pieterson followed two armed officers into the building and quietly started searching rooms. Eight more followed, lined up in four rows of two. Each officer was masked, armed and intensively drilled and said little as they scattered throughout the mansion.

Within thirty seconds the ground floor had been searched and ninety seconds later so had the first, second and third. Every room was spotless and impeccably furnished in the character of Newport ostentation, but there were no signs of the owner or any guests. Every electrical item was unplugged or turned off at the socket and all of the important doors were locked. An empty dishwasher gave the impression that the house had been unoccupied for several days or longer whereas the fully packed refrigerator confirmed that the house had recently been in use. Water ran from both taps, which also indicated recent activity, while outside three cars were parked in close proximity to the garage to the side of the mansion.

Pieterson surveyed the hallway. He commanded two officers to remain by the front doors, two to remain upstairs and another two to check the basement, wherever that was. He ordered intense surveillance of the garage to make sure that no one escaped by car, followed by an extensive search of the gardens.

Mike, Mark and Alessandro remained seated in the car. Officially they were not involved, nor could they be. From the end of the driveway they had a brief view into the vastness of the front garden and even from there Mark decided that the house was empty. Despite the well planned operation being achieved with impeccable precision, Mark guessed Velis would not be fooled, and had already planned his hurried departure.

In the distance Mike heard what he thought was shouting, yet not in keeping with the subdued commands of Pieterson. He looked at Mark.

"You hear that?"

Mark nodded.

*

Moments later, over eight hundred yards away on the other side of the mansion, the two Vatican policemen and the Swiss Guard moved like marines behind the house towards maze-like vegetation. They sprinted along a winding stone pathway intersecting an immaculately kept lawn, patterned by flowers, some forming the shape of a medieval knight, and followed winding stone steps into a nicely presented courtyard lined by hedges. Sticking to the path, they avoided countless statues depicting figures from antiquity and various extravagant water features, and headed towards the cliffs that overlooked the choppy waters of the Atlantic Ocean.

Approximately half a mile from the house, the pathway changed to gravel and was lined by well-maintained hedging on either side, connected by carefully topiary-created archways at regular intervals, leading to a walled pond. Encircling the pond, they continued through walled sections of garden, then across the grass in the direction of the cliffs, initially heading downhill then up. The sound of waves crashing against rocks below was becoming louder as they reached the coast.

In the distance they could hear the humming of a helicopter approaching from the south-west.

Standing within ten metres of the cliff, Louis Velis aimed a revolver randomly at the sky while struggling to keep Gabrielle still with his left hand. He shouted at Cardinal Tepilo in the fashion of a tyrant and even threatened his co-Templar as he refused to take the gun. Tepilo spoke to Gabrielle who gazed back fiercely. Although she shouted at her great-uncle incessantly, the sound remained inaudible as it failed to pass Velis's smothering hand.

Things were not going well. Velis cursed Tepilo for his lenience, then his niece for her petulance. Then he cursed Gullet for the delay. With each passing second the Feds were getting nearer.

Yet the echoing in his ears was reassuring. Ludovic Gullet had received the orders and was flying in across the western sky.

In the distance, Gullet could see them on the cliff side. He was less than half a mile away.

Pieterson did not need telling twice. Seconds later he was sprinting towards the garden and shouting orders in all directions. Lined up in ranks of two, the squad followed: anonymity giving way to haste and their footfalls reverberating loudly as they sprinted in military formation along the gravelled path.

The deputy director carried an arrest warrant for Velis in an inside pocket. In other offices similar ones existed for Gullet, Parker, de Bois, Broadie, D'Amato and several other masters of the Rite of Larmenius for various offences, but they had failed to find any evidence to identify any other Templars. They were still unaware of the activities of the Rite of Larmenius as a whole and while they had nothing against the other individuals personally, every man was susceptible to questioning because of past dealings with Velis.

For now, the deputy director was unable to clarify the identity of the man with Velis. Nevertheless, he was an accessory for kidnapping and assisting Velis evade arrest.

That too meant gaol time.

Pieterson barked loudly at his officers as he set them out in an arc-shaped perimeter across Velis: each man separated by an average of ten yards. The squad encroached slowly. Every officer was armed, their firearms aimed at the Starvel CEO. The deputy director shouted at Velis but the sound was inaudible due to the deafening sound of the helicopter loitering overhead. Clearly Velis was stalling for time.

Velis looked at the uniformed men, then at Pieterson, then finally at Mike some fifteen yards behind. Mike stood with his arms folded: a look of hatred in his eyes yet at the same time deep concern for Gabrielle. Gabrielle looked at Mike with frightened eyes.

Realising his chance, Velis smiled. He fired the revolver into the air and then pointed it at Gabrielle's mouth. He whispered something in her ear and her expression suggested she was frightened.

Mike's reaction was instantaneous. He removed a SIG P75 from inside his jacket and ran in to join the perimeter. Pieterson barked at Mike but the Swiss Guard failed to respond. With his firearm aimed firmly at Velis he bit his lip and concentrated on making focus. His heart thundered like a freight train. It reminded him of that day at the Vatican.

Velis looked quickly over his shoulder, examining the position of the helicopter. He turned his glance to Pieterson and smiled like a madman, pushing the gun to Gabrielle's lips. He shouted at the Feds as they continued to encroach and then at Pieterson. The procedure was simple and most of the time he knew it would work. Let them get on the helicopter or the hostage dies.

Gullet opened the door to the helicopter and shouted at Velis. Velis shouted at Tepilo then at Pieterson. With each passing second the squad was getting nearer.

"One more move and I'll fire," Velis shouted, ramming the gun into Gabrielle's cheek.

Pieterson paused momentarily then ordered the squad to cease movement. It wouldn't happen: he knew that. He, too, was a pro. Velis had a hostage but if he killed her then he in turn would be killed. This usually worked.

Compromise.

Velis fired a wild shot into the eastern sky and aimed the gun at Gabrielle.

"Louis, please. Let her go," Tepilo said.

"Get on the fucking helicopter."

Tepilo hesitated, slowly nearing the edge of the cliff. Gullet pushed forward on the controls, lowering the helicopter to less than a foot above the ground. Velis trod with care, practically carrying Gabrielle. His eyes focused on Tepilo.

"Don't do this," Velis said.

"Louis, let her go. She has done nothing wrong."

"Get on board now."

Tepilo grimaced, heading slowly towards the open door. As he neared the door he grabbed Gullet's outstretched hand and took a seat nearest the window.

"Now hear this," Velis shouted at Pieterson, "lay down your weapons or she's dead."

With his revolver jammed into the back of her neck, Velis held Gabrielle tightly. Standing not a metre from the edge, Gabrielle felt a sharp pain as she attempted to exhale against the heavy wind. Down below, she could see the waves breaking against the cliff causing rocks to fly up to a considerable height before crashing back down again at the cliff's base. The lack of air entering her lungs mixed with trepidation of peering down from the great height gave rise to a feeling of dizziness enhanced by the humming of the chopper's blades.

Showing little emotion, Pieterson reluctantly agreed. He ordered every officer to comply and all did except for Mike. Pieterson growled at the Swiss Guard but Mike's eyes remained set on Velis. His eyes suggested focus.

He could make this shot.

Mark sprinted forward. "Mike, come on, it's not worth risking her life."

Mike looked at Gabrielle. He bit his lip. With every passing second he felt his hatred for Velis becoming greater. He remained rigid for several seconds. Inhaling deeply, he eventually placed his weapon on the floor and took a step back.

Velis smiled. With his eyes focused on the uniforms, he took a few

453

steps towards the chopper. From an inside seat, the Camerlengo was leaning forward, a worried expression dominating his face. He eased towards the doorway and offered Gabrielle his hand. Then, in the blink of an eye, Velis fired at Pieterson. Gabrielle forced herself free from his grasp.

Slowly, she fell towards the edge of the cliff.

68

As motion and gravity took her towards the edge, she lost control of her legs. A strange floating sensation overcame her as she lost all composure and understanding. She closed her eyes and held her breath.

She crashed down with a thump, surely too soon to have hit the rocks. Next she heard gunfire. Instinctively she covered her head and rolled blindly. Sounds of panic followed. She heard screaming, somehow distant, then nothing but a buzzing sound.

Next thing she knew she was on her back. She opened her eyes and blinked rapidly, her vision distorted by sunlight. Up above, the helicopter was departing, flying at speed in the direction of Maine. She ascended to her knees and turned her head, her mind racing, still unsure what had happened. In the ensuing seconds the Feds had regained control and bullets sprayed into Velis's chest. As the bullets penetrated the banker's body he looked aimlessly in all directions. He lost all feeling and balance as the force of the bullets took him backwards and his gun fell to the ground.

Up above him, the sunlight was blinding. The blades of the chopper somehow seemed to turn in slow motion then in chequered movements as it moved away from the coast. Velis saw his escape route fading away. Only now did he realise he was falling, eventually coming to an end on the rocks.

Mike sprinted to Gabrielle, his firearm now safely within his jacket. He placed his hands on Gabrielle's shoulders and looked down at the back of her neck. After standing silently for several seconds, he felt the soft touch of her delicate hands on his. Strangely they were not trembling. She no longer seemed to be afraid. Instead a rigid determination had overtaken her: it was the way he had always known her and was fast coming to love.

Gabrielle turned, still on her knees, and looked up at Mike. In the background she could see Alessandro and Mark helping Pieterson remove his armour. He had caught one in the chest but the bullet-resistant vest had taken the force. Knowing he was safe, she smiled. She looked to her left. In the distance she could see the helicopter now resembling little more than a dot on the horizon.

She rose slowly to her feet and looked Mike in the eye. For several seconds they held one another's gaze.

"We have to go," she said urgently. "The Templars are planning on making Cardinal Tepilo the Pope. I think His Holiness is in danger."

A look of surprise overcame Mike. In the heat of the moment he sought to dismiss the idea, but in the light of recent events he knew anything was possible. Many had already been killed, including a former President of France. And he knew they had tried twice before: once succeeding.

He nodded at Gabrielle and grabbed her hand. It was approaching 3 p.m.

On the 15th floor of the Starvel headquarters in Boston, Gilbert de Bois sprinted back and forth around his desk, searching in vain for an escape route. Outside the office, the banging on the door was becoming louder as the four uniformed officers attempted to force an entry. All four were armed, while the leader held an arrest warrant in his hand and read off a list of charges as if he was listing the specials at a restaurant. The media mogul was facing ten years for the fraud alone, but conspiracy to murder . . .

They'd throw away the key.

Left with little choice, de Bois opened the window as far as he could and looked down with anguish at the sight of downtown Boston fifteen storeys below. He looked back at the locked door and realised time was almost up. Slowly, he placed his right leg outside the window and inhaled deeply. He remembered the words of Cardinal Tepilo.

"And if we should fail, our lives shall become forfeit and the Temple of Solomon shall burn to the ground like our predecessors before us until such a time when a new phoenix is born arising from the flames.

"And may the Lord have mercy."

In the nearby City of Cambridge, the summer's day had been warm and pleasant. On the campus of Harvard University, students walked casually in short sleeved t-shirts and girls in their summer clothes. Groups of up to fifteen sat quietly on the grassy areas eating and drinking, reading, chatting or standing tossing American footballs, frisbees or baseballs to one another as they passed the time carelessly.

Meanwhile, in a locked office in Robinson, Professor Alexander Broadie was slouched backwards in his chair. A smoking revolver lay at a random position on the floor, previously gripped in his right hand that now hung lifelessly over the edge of his chair. A strange dripping sound was occurring at regular intervals, similar to the sound of a tap. Around the base of the chair a large pool of red liquid was beginning to appear, slowly seeping across the floor in the direction of the locked door.

The Swiss headquarters of Renouf, Anderson and Klose was largely uninhabited by 8 p.m. Every office on the ninth floor was locked and appeared deserted. No one was there to hear the sound of a lone revolver coming from the office of Jurgen Klose.

In a large estate, situated somewhere in the English countryside, the butler of the former Chancellor of the Exchequer walked powerfully down the long gallery. In his hands he carried a large plate of biscuits, milk, sugar and recently made tea. His destination: the library.

He knocked once on the large wooden door and waited for a response. Seconds later he knocked again, this time calling out his master's name. It was unlike his master to ignore him in this way.

The door to the library opened, its ancient frame creaking on its hinges. Seconds later the plate hit the floor.

In the evening light the shadow of the room cast eerily across the far wall, moving from side to side. He did not need to examine the room to see the figure hanging in the noose was his master.

In Washington D.C. Danny D'Amato checked his watch for the umpteenth time in quick succession. Yawning, he slouched back in his chair and looked without interest across the Senate Chamber located within the Capitol building. The Democrat from Illinois had been talking for well over forty-five minutes and D'Amato had lost interest. There was at least another hour to go.

He watched the presiding officer sitting, gavel in hand, and looking with interest at the senator in speech. Seconds later, his phone vibrated in his pocket, catching the attention of the ageing senator to his right.

He removed his phone and looked at the text.

Suddenly he was worried.

D'Amato cleared his throat as a reflex and looked nervously over his right shoulder. For the first time he noticed uniformed guards standing inside the closed door looking at him.

He considered his options. He remained still for several seconds before ascending casually to his feet. He pushed through the crowd to his left, nearly knocking over the antique desk occupied by the Senator for Wisconsin. He passed three others before noticing the next gathering of uniformed guards waiting less than ten metres away at the end of the row.

Suddenly the air felt stifling. Now silently panicked, D'Amato turned slowly and walked back the way he came. The nearby occupants slowed his progress, causing him to make contact with their desks. Their reactions were obvious. The presiding officer glanced away from the standing Democrat and gazed up at the Republican from Montana pushing his way through the crowd.

Three men were following D'Amato, and two more waited at the other end. The American Preceptor turned quickly and searched the floor for exits.

He was surrounded on both sides.

To his right, he saw one guard closing in. As discretion gave way to loud panic, he kicked him quickly and sprinted to his left. The Democrat on the floor had now stopped speaking and all eyes turned to D'Amato as he sought to evade the passing men.

He reached the end of the row and stopped abruptly before the next guard. Five officers on either side surrounded him. He removed a Smith and Wesson, secreted inside his suit, and cocked the trigger. In the upper tier observers moved frantically, some attempting to leave as they watched in shock.

He moved quickly away from the nearest guards, attempting to think of an escape route. He pointed it in one direction, then in the other.

Finally he pointed it at himself.

Mark closed his mobile phone, frustrated. "Still no answer," he said after failing to contact Commissario Pessotto or Thierry.

Mike looked at his watch and then out through the helicopter window across the night sky. A feeling of nervous anticipation dominated his stomach. Three hours until they would land in Rome.

But that might not be soon enough.

69

Rome

The sun glowed an ominous red when it rose that morning. Shopkeepers recited the red sky at morning prophecy to their early customers as they purchased groceries and newspapers before making their way through the deserted streets to continue with their errands. By 10 a.m. the pleasant early morning coolness had risen to scorching temperatures of over 28° Celsius, and the red sun had returned to its regular yellow-orange as it continued to rise through the cloudless sky.

It was a typical Wednesday morning in Rome. Cars made slow progress along gridlocked streets: fans were blowing on the highest setting, windows were down and horns were honking as the drivers waited impatiently for the traffic to clear. On the metro, commuters stood rigidly, packed like sardines in overcrowded carriages, their arms grabbing the metal rails while guarding their pockets from thieves. An overpowering stench of coffee filled the morning air, marked with the unpleasant odours of sweat and stickiness brought about by the stuffy conditions.

In the nearby Vatican City, pilgrims were gathering in St Peter's Square as they did every Wednesday. Thousands upon thousands of faithful Catholics, both men and women from all nations and occupations, spoke with strangers, displaying friendliness and good Christianity towards one another as they soaked up the atmosphere in anticipation of the arrival of the Pope.

Across the crowd, cameras flashed, mobile phones were held aloft, hands waved and certain groups chanted and sang; women were dressed in summer clothes, while men dressed in all sorts ranging from suits to polo necks of all colours, many wearing baseball caps or sunglasses, willingly enduring the muggy conditions for the once in a lifetime Mass with the Vicar of Christ.

On either side of the courtyard, water sparkled in the sunlight as it splashed from the famous fountains creating a pleasant trickling sound. High above the square, the dome of St Peter's stood dominantly in the clear blue sky, basking in a unique orange colour that also reflected onto the many stone pillars that lined the building as it reflected the sunlight.

All in all there was a lovely togetherness and purity about the occasion that was unique to a Papal Audience. Within thirty minutes he would arrive and the tens of thousands of pilgrims would celebrate with delight.

In a large chamber nearby, Cardinal Tepilo spoke quietly with the Preceptor of Switzerland. His hands were cupped together thoughtfully as though he was in prayer.

Listening intently, the preceptor nodded philosophically. He prepared himself for the matter at hand.

70

There was no time for the official heliport. Located among gardens to the west of the basilica, the heliport was approximately one kilometre away from the square, impossible to navigate in the Wednesday traffic. Hundreds of feet below, the crowd waved expectantly at the helicopter as it flew overhead from the south-west, changing direction over the dome. From the ground, the gathering thousands could hear but not see the helicopter descend in height behind the dome, hovering for several seconds before heading off at speed towards the west.

Agent Gregore lowered the helicopter over the dome and allowed the other four to disembark. Mark came first. He opened the door and jumped from about four feet onto the flat roof, bending his knees on impact.

Gabrielle came second, jumping almost straight into Mark who stood expectantly with his arms held out wide. He caught her on impact and released her immediately.

Alessandro followed, his long locks of blond hair blowing under the force of the chopper.

Mike disembarked last. He closed the door with his right hand on landing and waved at Gregore that he was clear to move on. Seconds later the pilot climbed in height and disappeared, leaving the four passengers standing on the roof.

Mark dialled his mobile phone once more and failed to get a reply. Throughout the flight he had attempted ceaselessly to contact Thierry or Commissario Pessotto but to no avail. He shook his head. He failed to understand where the commanders would be: particularly on a Wednesday. He looked at his watch. It was nearly time to begin.

"All right," he said as the humming of the chopper faded. "Sandro, you hit the floor. Inform whoever you see that there is a genuine threat. Mike and I will search the roof."

"What can I do?" Gabrielle said, using her right hand to shield her eyes from the sun.

"Find the oberst or Commissario Pessotto."

Wasting no time, Alessandro sprinted across the roof towards an open doorway leading into the dome and made his way in the wrong direction through the one-way system. He descended several steps in quick succession and sprinted along a winding corridor past an unsuspecting guard. He continued down more steps and into the heart of the dome. Over the rail the sun shone brightly through the window of the Holy dove, causing shadows across the Throne of Peter. He checked his watch as he ran.

Time was precious.

Gabrielle followed closely, doing brilliantly to keep up with Alessandro. Unsure of where she was heading, she passed the unsuspecting guard who shouted at her. She ignored him and continued to the base of the stairs.

Mike and Mark separated immediately and began searching the outer dome. Mike ascended stairs in the opposite direction to Alessandro while Mark searched the present floor. Both kept an eagle eye out for any possible threat.

Yet what they were looking for was still unclear.

Crouched behind the ancient statue, his view was perfect. Dressed in the uniform of the Swiss Guard no one would suspect him: he was just an extra vigilant form of security aiming to ensure every angle was covered.

The Swiss Preceptor adjusted his lens and looked with interest across the crowd. In a few minutes it would all be over. Carefully he set up his sniper rifle.

In the nearby Apostolic Palace, Thierry de Courten jogged for about one hundred yards along the deserted corridor until coming to a standstill before a closed door. He waited a couple of seconds for Commissario Pessotto and the four halberdiers to catch him before lining the guards up two by two on either side of the door. He whispered instructions in a huddle before gently knocking on the door. After pausing for less than a second, he opened it without hearing a response.

Inside, the chamber was immaculate: decorated in the character of the Renaissance. High ceilings provided a pleasant airiness and brightness reflected by the light wall colourings.

In the far corner of the room, Cardinal Tepilo was sitting quietly, dressed in the pristine attire of his rank. He had a radiant peacefulness about him in keeping with his usual façade. His head was bent forward sacredly and his eyes were closed: to an outsider he gave the impression that he was at prayer.

Although seemingly oblivious to the intrusion, the ageing cardinal detected all was not well. He remained unmoved for several seconds before turning towards Thierry. He opened his eyes slowly as though struggling to adjust to the light. He presented a cold expression distinctly offering displeasure at being disturbed. He folded his arms but remained seated.

"Oberst," he said slowly.

Thierry forced a smile. "Forgive the intrusion, eminence, but His Holiness has asked for you."

Neither Pessotto nor the halberdiers offered any hint of emotion or eye contact. The guards carried halberds in their right hands, appropriate for their rank, and dressed in the famous tri-coloured uniform. Each man was smartly presented, intensively drilled and standing to attention.

The cardinal rose cautiously, maintaining eye contact with Thierry. He turned his attention to Pessotto and then the soldiers on either side. On this occasion he felt strangely threatened by their presence. He looked again at Pessotto. There was something different in the commander's eyes.

"May I take your arm to assist your journey?" Thierry asked politely.

Tepilo retreated slightly, displaying a look of discomfort. The wrinkles on his forehead seemed to thicken mysteriously as his facial expression changed.

"No, no," he said, with good nature. "Thank you, thank you, my friend."

Thierry nodded reverently and smiled at the cardinal. He raised his left hand in the direction of the open doorway as though offering the cardinal right of way. He waited for the cardinal to pass and pointed with his right hand to the guards. Tepilo fired a piercing glare at Pessotto which was returned with a smile.

Mike sprinted up the steep steps leading to the pinnacle of the dome and exited onto the ledge at the summit. His heart thundered with exhaustion and his eyes were blurred with dizziness. Over thirty-six hours without sleep had taken its toll and the physical strain of climbing the dome was unwelcome. Pilgrims came from all over the world to scale the famous landmark for the privilege of looking across the city from the centre of Christianity only to find on arrival the arduous climb was beyond them. And those that did complete it usually took their time on the way down.

Mike inhaled deeply, attempting to catch his breath. The clean air felt pleasant on his lungs and his pulse rate began to slow. His body craved rest but adrenaline forced him to concentrate. He rubbed his eyes and his vision improved.

He considered the nearby surroundings and saw nothing obviously wrong. After satisfying himself that there was no threat he inhaled once more, continuing to gaze out across the square.

Hundreds of metres below in the distance the crowd appeared as little more than smudges, marking the square with every colour of the spectrum. In the centre of the square, groups of pilgrims were gathered around the Egyptian obelisk, once part of the Circus of Nero, and hundreds more around the two fountains on opposite sides of the square. The summits of the buildings were deserted, as always during an audience, with the exception of countless stone statues lining the brownish coloured roof at regular intervals overlooking the square.

He looked across the other side and saw that it was deserted. Seeing the area was secure, he switched his attention to the roof directly below him. That was also clear.

He diverted his attention directly below, scanning the sloping roof at the centre. Carefully, he examined the outer buildings, their chimney-shaped features offering no obvious signs of life.

Finally his eyes moved onto the front area, where a further thirteen statues overlooked the square, denoting eleven of the apostles, standing either side of Christ, accompanied by John the Baptist. The stone figures stood elegantly, their backs facing him. He scanned each one, left to right, finishing at the clock.

Something was wrong, very wrong.

Crouched down on the right side with a perfect view of the square, a Swiss Guard in Medici uniform was holding a firearm.

Instinct directed his actions. Mike about-turned and sprinted down the steps at a frantic and unsafe pace. Nearly losing his footing with every step, he jumped the final seven and felt a shooting pain rise from his right ankle, travelling all the way to his knee. His bone was rigid with pain but still he refused to stop. His heart thundered and his mind raced with anticipation.

As he approached the final door, his pace quickened. Fresh air entered his lungs as he crossed the red-brown roof at speed. In a trancelike state he failed to acknowledge the presence of the Pope's helicopter flying overhead in the direction of the official heliport. A large cheer went up across the crowd as the anticipation grew.

Mike darted in a zigzag direction between the lifts before slowing to a walking pace. For the first time he felt the heaviness in his legs brought on from a combination of pain and fatigue. He took brief cover behind the final lift and looked with interest at the Swiss Guard. His mind raced with hard questions, questions that he would love to ask, answers he wanted to know. With each passing step his breathing heightened and his heart rate started to pick up.

As he approached the man he inhaled deeply to regain composure and slowed his pace to a tiptoe. He walked alongside Bernini's bell tower and came to a metal railing.

In front of him the Swiss Guard maintained his view across the square.

Mike inhaled slowly, realising that the Swiss Guard was oblivious to his presence. He used the wall to assist him across the barrier and landed with sloping feet, his footfalls making no noise on the solid surface. The hairs on the back of his neck stood on end and in his mind the noise of his beating heart resonated loudly across the square. Carefully, he removed his SIG P75 from inside his jacket pocket and pointed it at the Swiss Guard crouching less than five feet away. He cocked the weapon with a clicking sound.

The traitor blinked. Slowly, he moved his head to the left.

"Every Swiss Guard who turns bad always ends up being caught," Mike said. "I don't think you've got very good odds."

The traitor turned slowly, revealing his face. "Personally, I kinda like betting on the outsiders."

A sudden knotting sensation hit Mike all over.

It was Stan.

Gabrielle banged loudly on the office door of Thierry de Courten, arousing the attention of a nearby halberdier. She shouted incessantly at the closed door, failing to accept that the office was empty.

The Swiss Guard approached, yet he was unprepared for what happened next. The authority of the woman was unrivalled and he felt surprisingly insignificant in her presence. More disturbing were the words that left her mouth.

"Follow me," he said. Seconds later they were sprinting along the corridor.

71

Mike stood rigidly, his eyes focused on the traitor. He raised his right arm slowly and aimed his firearm squarely at his face.

Neither said a word. As Mike inhaled deeply the traitor looked up from his seated position on the ledge and tightened his grip on the rifle with his enormous hands.

"Drop your weapon, Stan."

Studer raised his eyebrows, his expression one of uncertainty. He considered his options but, for the present, remained still.

"Don't look so worried, Mike. It's not got any bullets."

Mike watched, his eyes focused on the weapon. The design was similar to most sniper rifles but the barrel was strange, unlike any other he had seen.

Stan removed the ammunition, more a dart than a bullet. "Barbiturate, paralytic and potassium solution. The effects appear harmless. But when it penetrates the skin they are like those used to execute an American convict. Pretty amazing, huh?"

Mike's expression hardened. "Drop it."

Stan eyed him closely, pausing momentarily before throwing his rifle to the floor. The worried expression on his face turned to an icy smile. He nodded philosophically.

"Well I gotta hand it to you, Frei. You found me out. How did you know?"

Mike didn't reply straightaway. Inside he was struggling to contain the shock. Of all the possible candidates none could have surprised him more.

Yet strangely it all made sense.

"Obvious really," Mike said, kicking the sniper rifle several metres away. "It took me a while to put all the pieces together. I felt pretty stupid when I worked it out."

A ghost of a smile crossed his face.

"The night I met Gabrielle. It never really clicked that you knew Velis and de Bois."

Stan nodded.

"Until now it never really dawned on me that I often saw you walking with Cardinal Tepilo."

He lifted his beret and replaced it on his head. "I tip my hat."

Mike nodded. "Plus, I saw you limping around a little bit the day after the attack on Gabrielle. I guess that must've hurt?"

The traitor's face turned to hatred. "So where is the rich bitch?"

Mike hit Stan across the face with the outside of his right hand. The Swiss Preceptor fell to the floor, his left elbow taking the impact of the fall. He looked up at Mike and spat, his spit landing just in front of him. Slowly he rearranged himself.

"Assaulting a superior," he said, spitting. "Let me guess, you're in love with her?"

"Keep still," he said, gun at the ready.

The traitor remained on his knees. He looked at Mike without speaking for several seconds.

"Well, I have to congratulate you, Frei."

Mike looked confused.

"That's right. I congratulate you. You see, the Knights Templar have continued to exist for over seven hundred years. I know; I was as surprised as you are. And no one had ever realised. But you found out."

Mike's facial expression hardened. He looked down at his friend, yet it was different. It was almost as though he was looking at the man for the first time.

"Yeah, I did."

Stan smiled. "Always knew you had an eye for detail, Frei. And I heard about your performance at Newport. Ludo Gullet was most impressed. He said we could do with a guy like you."

Mike remained rigid, a look of hatred dominating his face. "So you're the Templars' insider. You were the guy they needed. Rippling with honours and equipped with all the necessary capabilities and security clearance." Mike shook his head. "Why?"

"Come on, Frei – is it really that difficult to understand?"

"Understand? Understand that you're a traitor?"

"Traitor?" Stan said, appearing to be hurt. "Now that's an odd word, Frei. The Vatican and the Templars aren't really enemies. I mean, think about it. The Templars fought for Christianity in the Crusades. The Rite of Larmenius acts in the best interests of Christianity now. Our mission was to bring the two together again. Lunacy and greed forced them apart. In the real world, one cannot really exist without the other. Perhaps you're still too naïve to understand."

There was a peculiar smugness in his voice. It was manipulative yet also quite secure. Strangely it was not evil. To Mike, Stan probably felt he was part of a virtuous cause.

"I'd hardly call the loss of three thousand innocent lives since the end of the war as acting in the best interests of Christianity."

Stan raised his eyebrows philosophically. "I guess you are too naïve to understand."

Mike shook his head. "Ludo Gullet," he said under his breath. "Is that why you're here: to finish the job he failed? How many others have you killed?"

"Oh, come on, Frei. You look at me as if I'm a rapist or a paedo. You don't think I enjoy this. I'm a soldier, not a murderer. You know what I'm made of. We're of the same mettle, you and me. I mean, say a terrorist was driving a car into the Pope? You'd have to try and kill the terrorist, right?"

"That's hardly the same."

"Ah, but imagine the terrorist was in fact a cardinal?"

Mike raised his eyebrows. "Funny you should mention that. Because it seems that's exactly what is happening."

Stan laughed. "Cardinal Tepilo is no terrorist. Just imagine, God himself as Pope."

Mike nodded, aware his reference to Cardinal Tepilo as God was not uncommon. His reputation among the Vatican as the most pious of characters would hardly find opposition, at least until earlier that day. In Mike's eyes, only Cardinal Utaka would be more appropriate.

"Was this his idea? Is that why Cardinal Faukes was killed?"

"No. It was really more of a group decision."

Mike bit his lip. "How about Major von Sonnerberg? Was that a group decision too? Or did you just fancy a promotion?"

A wry smile. "Sonnerberg knew too much. Besides, the Pope has less than twelve months to live anyhow. It would've happened anyway, Frei."

"Then why all this?"

"It wouldn't have been necessary if you hadn't come along and spoilt everything. Fortunately the poison works fast, when fired precisely a small sharp entry into the hair leaves little trace. As far as the world will know he's died from a simple cardiac arrest. Pretty elaborate I appreciate, but thanks to you necessary. It's a shame you had to meddle in things that don't concern you."

Suddenly Stan laughed.

"But then again you did locate a few of our old manuscripts. Now that's particularly fascinating. Even Alexander Broadie didn't know exactly what had become of the second Zeno diary."

Mike nodded. "Yeah, I hear he was a bit of a dimwit. Couldn't work it out himself. He needed a socialite and a Swiss Guard to find it."

"On the contrary, my friend."

"I'm not your friend."

Stan laughed again, this time briefer than before. He shrugged his shoulders then his expression became somewhat philosophical. Finally, he held out his hands with the palms facing upwards.

"As a matter of fact Alexander Broadie was the first to twig. Remarkable man. Shame about some of his friends."

"It will grieve you I'm sure to learn that he's dead."

Stan looked up quietly. An awkward expression spread across his face.

"Committed suicide in his office; I heard it over the radio on the way here."

"Nice try, Frei."

"No, it's true. So is Velis actually. Saw that one with my own eyes."

Stan spat on the floor.

"De Bois threw himself out of a window. D'Amato shot himself in Senate. They know about Parker. Gullet. Cardinal Tepilo. As a matter of fact he's being taken away as we speak," he said – not realising his own accuracy.

Stan failed to reply. He bit his lip, notably shaken. He looked at Mike and saw rigidity in his face: a stern expressionless stance demonstrating no information or emotion.

That's the way they train you.

Stan looked at Mike and laughed. "Pretty weak, Frei."

"Stan, as of yesterday the Knights Templar no longer exists. Every member is either arrested or dead. You are all that remains."

Still kneeling, Stan looked across the roof and spat in front of Mike. Next, his attention turned to the sky.

"There are thousands of people in this square. Do you have any idea what would have happened if you'd succeeded? There would be mass panic. Rioting in the streets. God knows what else . . ."

Without warning, a cheer went up across the crowd, catching Mike off guard. With this, the traitor leapt from the traps and the Swiss Guard came crashing down. Blood spewed from the right side of Mike's head as he came into contact with the floor while a crushing sensation inflamed his pelvis.

Momentarily dazed, Mike rolled in a reflex action and launched a powerful right arm at Stan. In the confusion, Mike's SIG P75 had rolled across the roof, sliding against the rail and out of reach. With limited options the pair tussled, arms locked together. After several seconds of deadlock, Mike released his grip and punched Studer in the nose.

Blood flew on impact across Mike's face. With swift retaliation, Studer launched a left hook at Mike and the Swiss Guard sergeant rolled several metres to the left. The blow left him disorientated. He saw little, but felt coldness on his face. Turning onto his back, he scanned his surroundings quickly and saw his firearm. Without hesitation he hurried towards it. Stan jumped over him and did the same.

Both dived simultaneously.

Down below, the crowds celebrated as the Pope made his way through St Peter's Square in the Popemobile. Pilgrims cheered, cameras flashed, hands waved and smiles covered thousands of faces as the kindly figure of the current pontiff waved to the crowd.

Up above, Mike and Stan wrestled. The gun was now in Mike's hand, but attempts to aim failed; the traitor's grip was strong. Studer elbowed Mike in the jaw and the gun flew towards the ledge, coming to a stop just before the wall. Studer launched a punch. Mike rolled. Stan hit his hand against the concrete and shouted out in pain. Mike regained his composure and caught Studer off guard. Two punches to the stomach made him lose balance. With all his strength, Mike dived at Stan and knocked him to the floor. Blows to the liver, kidneys and neck left bruises. Blood seeped from the nose.

The sound of boots running in unison echoed loudly from the left side of the roof. Mike looked quickly. Thierry was sprinting in the company of Mark, Alessandro and over twenty Swiss Guards including halberdiers, korporals and wachtmeisters, each man armed with Heckler and Kochs. Thierry's face showed surprise for less than a second before turning to firmness that presented complete authority. He looked at the Swiss Guards wrestling and raised his weapon.

Studer fixed both hands behind Mike's head and headbutted him square in the face. Mike rolled. From the corner of his eye, he caught sight of his firearm less than ten metres away. Acting on instinct, he scampered towards the gun and dived, rolled and collected it in his grasp. Studer rolled and regained his feet. He removed a SIG P75 from just above his right ankle and aimed it at Mike. Back on his feet, Mike aimed his weapon at him.

Deadlock.

Time seemed to stand still as both men breathed heavily, each maintaining eye contact. Mike's face itched from Studer's blood and Studer breathed with discomfort through his bloodied nose. He sniffed noisily and spat on the floor.

Stan looked at Thierry. Next to him were Mark and Alessandro – his former friends. Between them he saw Gabrielle was also there: the rich bitch. He glared at her with malice and spat, a gesture Gabrielle realised was meant for her. She recognised from his eyes it was he who had tried to kill her that day in the Vatican Library.

With his options limited, he cocked his weapon and aimed it at Thierry.

Thierry straightened his posture and looked fiercely at Stan: almost as though he was looking down at him.

Thierry: "You are surrounded, Studer. Don't be foolish."

Stan spat once more and raised the weapon to eye level. He moved his aim slightly left, now directly at Gabrielle. Finally he went for the trigger.

A loud reverberation filled the air for several seconds before fading to silence. A flock of birds flew in formation towards the north from their positions perched near the ledge causing an ethereal echoing sound from their flapping wings giving way to the sound of a microphone from down below.

Mike looked at Stan. A volley of bullets had entered Studer's chest: each a perfect execution from Alessandro. His weapon was still aimed at Stan's chest. A cold expression crossed his face.

With the gun still within his grasp, Studer aimed the weapon at Gabrielle, then Mark, then Thierry and finally at Mike. He sought to raise his hand but all strength left him. His arm lowered involuntarily and the SIG P75 hit the hard roof with a crash. He walked three disoriented steps forward, wheezing loudly against the air. In his dazed state he thought he heard the sound of cheering coming from down below.

He coughed weakly as he attempted to breathe and spat a mixture of saliva and blood. Blood spilled from his nose, chest, and the corner of his mouth. With his balance lost, he staggered forward. After collapsing to his knees, he looked up at Mike with a lost expression in his eyes:

A mixture of resignation and fury.

Epilogue

Westford, Massachusetts

A solitary figure stood silently beside the grave. It was not a grave in the traditional sense. Its appearance was inconspicuous. To the casual observer this large glacial boulder located just off a main road in the quiet Massachusetts town of Westford, and flanked by a small chain fence, was both uninspiring and forgettable.

According to most of his colleagues the markings on the boulder were a natural phenomenon brought on by years of weathering. He had always had his doubts. And now at last he had the evidence to prove it.

Henry Leoni took one last look at the photocopy in his hand and smiled to himself softly. For all those years it had been there, in plain view, but only now did he see it. In his mind's eye he could clearly make out the presence of the knight in armour engraved on the rock, and the marking of a ship sailing on a starry night on the shield, as the engraving once did in its heyday.

As he looked to the west he could see the sun was beginning to set over the distant horizon. He felt pleasantly humbled by the feeling. Soon the whole world would be able to see it; see it and recognise it for what it was. For now, at last, he believed that he understood the true significance of the Westford Knight, or the Westford Prince, as he would have called it.

For it was said by Antonio Zeno that Zichmni was 'a prince as worthy of immortal memory as any that ever lived, for his great valour and remarkable goodness'.

*

Vatican City

Mikael Frei sipped his coffee slowly and savoured the flavour. It was hardly the good stuff, but he had little reason to complain. He had been drinking plenty of that of late.

Almost nine weeks had passed since that famous Wednesday. The papers caught wind of a security breach but put it down to an unsubstantiated bomb scare. They had heard it all before.

The deaths of the remaining Templars received sparse media attention but without connection. The circumstances surrounding Velis remained classified. If the press were accurate nothing had happened. To the wider world he was still alive: better yet, no one even realised any of them had ever lived.

Mike adjusted his position in his seat and looked across the desk at Thierry. It was late morning and Gabrielle was in conference with the Vatican bankers. The last few weeks had been hectic. Leoni et Cie launched legal proceedings against Starvel AG for money laundering and banking fraud and the case was settled out of court within weeks. Although the new CEO of Starvel, Alfred Velis, was reluctant to pay out $10 billion, the timing was awful. The Federal Reserve, the Securities and Exchange Commission, the Federal Trade Commission, plus the IMF, the WTO, the OECD and the World Bank were all gunning for an investigation into Starvel and Starvel AG's activities and seeing as the FBI were already pushing for answers in the wake of the Rite of Larmenius interrogation, the last thing AG needed was the hassle.

The terms had been agreed and Leoni et Cie's performance had improved, thanks also to Gabrielle's decision to increase her stake in the bank following Gilbert de Bois's next of kin's wish to sell. Since that time Gabrielle had shown qualities Mike had never witnessed. In recent days she had attended executive meetings with the new trustees of the GREEN Foundation, the Vatican bankers and others from Leoni et Cie. At present, Angelo Rogero and Juan Pablo Dominguez were laying out the new structure of Leoni et Cie while discussing potential candidates to replace Lewis, Swanson and Tepilo: Jacobs had agreed to future appointment when her term with the Feds ended, while the cardinals agreed that Giancarlo Riva was innocent of all involvement and would continue on the committee. No one really knew what had become of Tepilo. Officially he had suffered a heart attack and was recovering in a Benedictine Monastery on the outskirts of Leicester. Everyone bought it. After all, it had come from the mouth of the new Camerlengo.

Mike's eyes drifted, stopping at one particular photograph on the wall. It was a group photo from about four years ago when Mike was still a korporal. Stan was on the end, standing next to Mike. His face seemed to light up when he was happy. To Mike, Stan had the face of a human snowman. He could never forgive him for what he had done; still it made his heart ache because of it. Despite what had happened, deep down, he still missed his friend.

"Well," Thierry said, placing a cup down on the desk. "I'm very sorry to be losing you, wachtmeister."

Mike nodded and forced a smile. "Somehow the old place isn't quite the same."

His eyes drifted again towards the photo and he caught a glimpse of himself. He was not the man he was back then. Heck, he wasn't the man he was nine weeks ago. The face in the photo was familiar but inside he felt tired, yet at the same time full of life. In many ways the sun had been shining brighter these last nine weeks. Coffee tasted better, dreams seemed more vivid and even the air felt softer. He smiled more, and, despite the hardship, he'd never been happier.

"I still sense something is troubling you," Thierry said, peering thoughtfully across the desk.

Mike shook his head. "It's nothing really, it's just . . ."

Thierry's features shortened.

"It's just, well, something you said."

"Oh?"

Mike grimaced and laughed simultaneously. "That day I first came back, you said that the Swiss Guards might descend from the Knights Templar."

Thierry nodded. "I'm certain of it."

Mike looked at him with a perplexed expression.

"Is that such a bad thing?"

"Isn't it?"

Thierry laughed. "The original Knights Templar gave considerable service to the Vatican and to God. They risked their lives for little reward and did poor men much good. The original order befriended the Vatican. The Swiss mercenaries since have always given great service to the Vatican and to Christianity. They were selfless and brave and fought only to protect. That's what religion is all about. That is who we are, no?"

Mike smiled and nodded simultaneously.

Fifteen minutes later Mike and Thierry were walking through the Sistine Chapel. The large table was absent, but the room was alive with activity. What seemed like hundreds of cardinals, all dressed in black and red, zucchettos partially covering their heads, bishops and priests were standing around a collection of relics and artefacts as if viewing an exhibition at a museum. There were not only Catholics but also clergy of other Christian denominations.

And there were not only Christians. Senior Jewish rabbis, figures from Islam, and many other religions looked with interest at the various relics, in particular the Rod of Aaron.

Cardinal Utaka saw Mike and Thierry enter and walked slowly towards them. He pressed his right hand to Mike's left shoulder and smiled warmly at him.

"A present from Cardinal Tepilo," the new Camerlengo said, pointing to the various relics and smiling. "Soon pilgrims will be able to see them for themselves. Just imagine what effect it may have on their faith."

Mike looked across the chapel, in particular at an elderly rabbi standing next to Cardinal del Rosi and a senior Islamic imam chatting freely while looking at a curious ancient manuscript, unbeknown to him known as the Baphomet. Wide smiles lined each of their bearded faces. Finally he answered.

"I really can't."

Cardinal Utaka smiled once more at Mike and walked away. Mike looked at Thierry and forced a laugh. Out of the corner of his eye he saw Gabrielle standing by the open door with her hands on her hips.

Thierry caught her eye. "Still, each of us has our own way of finding faith," the oberst said.

Mike looked at Gabrielle then Thierry. He nodded and laughed.

"So when is the wedding?"

Mike looked once more at the door and shook his head. "You'd have to ask Ms Leoni. I just drive the car."

Thierry laughed. For several seconds a pleasant silence passed between them.

"Still. I feel this is not goodbye."

Mike shook his head. "No. I'll be here rather regularly."

"What will you do?"

"Since Gabrielle has increased her stake in Leoni et Cie she wants me to be her representative on the board," Mike said smiling. "My mom always said my degree would come in handy one day."

"Well, I feel this is good news. Juan Pablo and Angelo will have someone they can trust."

Mike forced a smile. Secretly he felt his eyes filling up. For eight years he had been a Swiss Guard. It seemed strange to know he would never return to service, yet also reassuring to know he would not leave altogether.

"And if the Vatican should ever come under fire from Knights Templar?"

Mike laughed softly. "If you don't recognise me, I'll be wearing a suit."

Mike and Thierry looked at one another in the eye. A smile crossed the oberst's face, and there seemed to be a strange twinkle in his eye. Both saluted, pausing rigidly for several seconds. Although no words were spoken, in that brief moment Mike saw pride in his commander's eyes that he had never seen before during his entire service.

The pair shook hands and Mike left through the open door and walked towards Gabrielle. She was dressed less extravagantly than she used to. Little makeup lined her face and even her hair was styled less flamboyantly. Yet, she looked more beautiful than he had ever seen her.

"What?" she asked coyly.

Mike shook his head, still smiling. "Nothing. How was your meeting?"

She pursed her lips thoughtfully. "It was fun."

Mike's smile widened as he followed her along the corridor.

"We've decided that the Vatican Bank will be responsible for the whole of Leoni et Cie," she said as she walked. "You can attend the meetings on my behalf but you won't have to be involved in the business."

"Yes, Ms Leoni."

She hit him. "Don't be cheeky."

"Sorry," he said laughing.

She smiled at him. "I have no interest in the bank. I mean the last thing I need is more money, right?"

"I guess."

Gabrielle smiled. "Anyway, we spoke about the GREEN Foundation. It turns out that despite the money laundering they were actually quite serious about helping people."

Mike raised his eyebrows. "Well, well."

"Seems a shame to let such a good idea go to waste."

"I'm sure it will make a big difference."

"Cardinals del Rosi, Utaka, Torres and Atri said they'd help run it. And Cardinal Utaka is going to do the service. Oh, by the way, we're getting married next week."

Mike came to a sudden halt as if Thierry had commanded it.

"What?" she said, pretending to be hurt.

"Nothing. I just assumed you'd need at least three years to plan it."

Gabrielle tried to fight a smile but failed. "For your information I don't need a big wedding. I have everything I need."

Mike looked at her curiously, now walking again. "Really?"

"For all his faults, Louis Velis was right. I am privileged. I don't need fancy things. I have you."

Mike raised his eyebrows thoughtfully as he quickened his pace. Perhaps the man had left a mark.

"And besides, we have to do it soon," Gabrielle said, partially covering her face. "Otherwise he might realise I'm having your baby."

Mike halted again, even worse than before. A strange feeling overcame him, as though he had received an electric shock.

"You're what?"

Gabrielle stopped and put her finger to Mike's lips. She stepped onto her tiptoes and kissed him softly.

"Love you."

From the Author

As I walked, awestruck, across the ancient floors of St Peter's Basilica in September 2006 I was blessed with one of those light bulb moments. In what seemed like little more than a moment, visions of history and religion, some real some not so, started flashing wildly before me and I was presented with the subject of my first novel. Inside the incredible labyrinth of architecture, art and mystery that makes up the Vatican City, I became trapped, yet another victim of Christianity's incredible mystique.

When I first visited Rome I was twenty-one years old, fresh out of uni and all set to travel the world. Over five years later in many ways little has changed. The images are still flashing, only now half a decade of research has run into epic proportions and what began as an idea has developed into a full scale soap opera, its characters long since taken on a life of their own. With every new idea or morsel of information taken on the backdrop has become ever slightly more real, in some cases, perhaps even realistic. The reading list has become so long its books could fill a library on its own, and over time the storylines have become all the more ambitious. The completed tale was the culmination of fiction and history collided. In doing so, the line between history and creation has long since blurred, lost somewhere between the Vatican Archives and the Internet.

Since completing the book, fate has taken me on a new quest, one that is still just beginning. Over five years researching the mysteries of the Templars and the world at large has taught me one valuable lesson. Its study presents more questions than it does answers. Its outcome has inspired me to write an additional section: one that will hopefully help answer some of these recurring questions and rediscover at least parts of that blurred line. This section is probably for my benefit as much as yours, but for the benefit of the interested reader, I have attempted to offer a small window into the unique journey that has taken place inside my mind. It is only a small window, but, an adequate one; mine is only a small mind. The themes that I have chosen are those that I believe to be the most important. I hope you find them as fascinating as I did.

The Facts Behind my Fiction

The Swiss Guard

One of the main themes of the novel is the situation involving Mikael Frei and Gabrielle Leoni. In truth, before my visit to the Vatican I knew little about the Swiss Guard. Having had the opportunity to see so many of them in real life, usually from a distance, I cannot deny that there is something about them that separates this band of mercenaries from the world's other great military units. Like the guards of Buckingham Palace they may create the illusion of being statues, though in reality behind the calm facades are highly skilled men every bit as formidable as the most deadly terrorist or the most highly trained government official of any of the world's superpowers.

Quite simply, the Swiss Guard are brilliant! For those of you who, like me, see personality traits like bravery, loyalty, integrity and valour as being among the most important any human can possess, the aura that surrounds them needs little explaining. For over five hundred years the Swiss Guard have been a model of all these things.

Yet, while their prestige is both famous and tremendous, the stories of the individuals behind the uniforms are seldom told. Their faces offer little more than a small gap in the curtain into the window of their existence. These dedicated bodyguards are matched in their talents by their unique humility, a trait that adds to their likeability. It is a strange combination of reassurance and sadness that these men have become a source of inspiration for many yet remained in partial anonymity.

The decision to choose a Swiss Guard as my protagonist for *The Templar Agenda* was for the most part my own token of respect for these incredible soldiers whose dedication to their cause can be summed up simply as the task of protecting Christ's spokesman on this earth. Every member of the Swiss Guard must qualify for Swiss citizenship and have spent at least six months training in the Swiss Army.

In the case of Mikael Frei, I opened up something of a loophole by giving him an American education, using the naturalisation clause for Swiss Citizenship, as this allowed the character easy access into other strands of the novel, such as the bits set in Scotland and America, and in my opinion allows for greater affinity with the English speaking reader. Mike's naval background is inspired by my own connections with Annapolis, and is undoubtedly very different to any other Swiss Guard in service.

The background on the Swiss Guard presented in this novel is as accurate as I could make it, and is based on both second hand research and my own time spent at the Vatican. All of the Swiss Guards mentioned in the novel are of relevance to the Vatican Swiss Guard, a group of approximately 110 males of Catholic faith employed as the military of the Vatican City. In the past several groups of these Swiss mercenaries existed, often providing military support for the kings and courts of Europe – most famously in France. The Pontifical Swiss Guard began under Pope Julius II in 1506 and, since 1970, has provided the entire military of the Vatican.

The Vatican Police

Also included in the novel are members of the *Corpo della Gendarmeria dello Stato della Città del Vaticano*, known in English as the Vatican Police. The background on the Vatican Police is as accurate as I could make it. While the duties of the Swiss Guard are military and ceremonial, the role of the Vatican Police is wide ranging, including everything from traffic control to criminal investigation. Along with the Swiss Guard, the safety of the Pope is of prime importance. Though not included in the novel, it is worth pointing out that, unlike most chiefs of police, it is the personal responsibility of the inspector general to accompany the Pope for his personal security. In the case of this novel, it would be the role of people such as Mark to investigate criminal proceedings.

The way in which Mark, Alessandro and Gregore are used in this novel is, however, fictitious. While all members of the Vatican Police and the Swiss Guard are intensively trained in counter-terrorism, exactly how the Vatican Police investigate such levels of security threat is not widely known. All members of the Vatican Police must qualify for Italian citizenship and have at least two years experience in Italian police work.

The Vatican Bank

Another important theme of the novel is banking. When I began writing the novel I was fresh on the back of a degree in Business Economics & Finance, employment with the Ministry of Defence and the economic turmoil was starting to pick up pace. One of the best things about doing a degree in finance was studying banking systems and institutions, including its failings and frauds. Sadly, the Vatican Bank is not immune to criticism here. Though Leoni et Cie and Starvel are fictional institutions, Banco Ambrosiano and Clearstream were anything but. Throughout the 1970s the Vatican Bank invested hundreds of millions of dollars in Banco Ambrosiano, heightening their 'moral' responsibility in the bank's failings.

In reality, the Banco Ambrosiano failings were the result of the people, their incompetence and an appalling lack of morals. In the case of *The Templar Agenda*, the plot is less critical of the Vatican Bank. Historically, the bank has proved both powerful and successful but its elements have remained hidden from the public eye. Everything included in the novel is as accurate as I could make it. Its headquarters are in the Vatican City, located near the Porta Sant'Anna. They have probably never used the Sistine Chapel for business purposes, but, for me, the temptation to include it was too great. The structure I believe to be fairly accurate: the bank is effectively structured into three layers, a council of cardinals, one of bankers, and finally the day to day aspects run by other Vatican bank employees and a directorate. For the purpose of this novel I have concentrated on the oversight commission of cardinals and the supervisory committee of bankers, though all of the people are fictional, their backgrounds concoctions of my imagination. All of the titles given to the cardinals, particularly del Rosi, Utaka and Tepilo are inspired by the real titles of members of the current and previous council.

The Rite of Larmenius

The chief villains of the piece, and almost entirely made up. Over the centuries there have been literally thousands of secret societies whose influence, or alleged influence, on the wider world has led to many a controversial claim. The Rite of Larmenius is effectively an amalgamation of some of these: in particular the conspiracy theories that surround the Freemasons and their high-profile appendant bodies. In the case of this novel, I have extended the theme to hypothetical connections with the Masons. This, quite simply, was inspired by the Masons' own legends, the order's alleged connections with famous high-profile figures, particularly George Washington and Benjamin Franklin and, as some readers will undoubtedly already be aware, the probable historical Templar influence on the early Masonic societies in Scotland, such as the Scottish Rite. Everything mentioned in connection with the Masons in this novel is fictitious.

The existence of the Rite of Larmenius depends solely on the premise that a man named Jean-Marc Larmenius became the historical successor to Jacques de Molay as Grand Master of the Knights Templar. Alleged proof of this is mentioned in a document known as the *Larmenius Charter*, discovered in France in around 1806. This curious piece of writing is almost certainly a forgery, though the names mentioned are interesting. In particular, it lists alleged grand masters including historical people who had a clear link to the Revolutionaries in France. For that reason, I have used it as fodder for the storyline.

Templar Survival

Did the historical Knights Templar survive their persecution and continue to exist unnoticed?

The topic of Templar survival has been of fascination for authors for at least three centuries. In particular, the last forty years has seen something of a blitz on new research, but sadly during that time the line between history and fiction has become increasingly blurred. The trend, beginning in the Middle Ages, linking the order with the Holy Grail has proven particularly inspiring, though exactly what the Holy

Grail is is anyone's guess. It is often said that there are as many grail theories as there are grails. The idea of the Templars being the guardians of either hidden knowledge or a cup of physical importance is something I have chosen to avoid in this novel. Who knows, maybe next time! *Elixir enhances mans geometric ninth unit.*

In the eyes of many mainstream historians the possibility of a Templar continuation is seldom given much respect; even its suggestion has sadly become labelled as a form of career suicide in certain circles. In reality, the argument is a positive one, an answer to which is by no means clear-cut. From a fictional point of view the conspiracy theories are fantastic, and researching them and including them in *The Templar Agenda* has been a pleasure. But proving them historically is another matter. In the case of this novel, I have stretched history to the limit. For the interested reader, it is worth pointing out that evidence to suggest that the Knights Templar continued to exist in one form or another following their dissolution is easy enough to find, even without forged documents like the *Larmenius Charter*.

The following is purely my own view, based on my own research and opinions.

The Templars in Scotland

One of the most famous examples of Templar continuation is found in Scotland. While focus in recent times has centred on Rosslyn Chapel, there are many other places that have greater claims, particularly further north. Ironically, one of the best is the nearby castle, also owned by the St Clairs. The castle dates back to around 1330, shortly after the time of the Templar demise, and continued to be used until around 1688, as mentioned in the novel. As traditional history confirms, Scotland was itself under excommunication at this time and some Templar commentators have even suggested that the Templars assisted the Scots in the Battle of Bannockburn, a claim that cannot be proven either way.

Of more interest is the known existence of vaults beneath the castle and the chapel. Exactly where and what they contain remains a mystery, probably even to the modern day descendants. The complex system of underground tunnels and vaults that are known to exist have been said to include everything from tombs of Templars in armour to stairways that lead to nowhere, adding to the location's appeal and mystique. Of particular fascination, in close proximity to both the castle and chapel is a cave, hidden by a waterfall, that can only be entered by being lowered into a well. Its existence is incredible, and certainly adds fuel to suggestion that its existence was deliberate. Who knows, perhaps the family really did have something important to hide there.

In truth, many of the legends that have grown up around Rosslyn are a result of the lack of known facts of the location's history, ignorance of which leads to more questions than answers. The location of the vaults, and the vaults themselves, mentioned in *The Templar Agenda* are fictitious, though they are inspired by many of the tales and the area's legends, in addition to my own observations from my visits. The strange tale of Count Poli is a genuine story. It is mentioned in Jackson's *Tales of Roslin Castle* – the book has not been printed since 1837. Writing in 1891 John James Wilson wrote of Jackson in his *The Annals of Penicuik* that his work 'showed considerable historical research and a ready gift of weaving together truth and romance in a singularly attractive form'. Perhaps *Rota Temporum* is hidden somewhere in the Vatican Library – my searches on their website, unsurprisingly, came up with nothing.

Templars in the New World

Another pivotal strand of the novel is the premise that the Templars were able to launch a voyage to America prior to the voyage of Columbus. Writing in 2011, I believe the chances of validating this theory are easier than it was even ten years ago. In the past, suggestion that the Templars, or even the Vikings, had ventured across the Atlantic was also met with scorn by elements of the academic community. Sadly, some of these *experts* were oblivious to what was right in front of them!

One of the locations used in this book is the Newport Tower, a curious structure located near nothing in particular in the heart of Newport, Rhode Island. The architecture of the tower is itself open to interpretation and its original purpose cannot be pinpointed with complete certainty. One of the few documented references to its existence describe it as a stone mill, owned by one Governor Benedict

Arnold, ancestor of the famous man of the same name.

On face value, the structure is strange. Its appearance is out of keeping with a traditional windmill. Furthermore, the presence of a fireplace on what was once the second storey and the tendency for many of its features to fit with astrological alignments do little to convince that it was built for that purpose. True, the structure is documented as Arnold's 'old stone mill'. However, there is no evidence that Arnold built it.

To accept the structure as a product of colonial Newport contradicts the documented facts. Sailing the area in 1524, explorer Giovanni da Verrazano recorded the structure as a 'Norman Villa', confirming the tower's pedigree as no younger than 16th century. I congratulate authors Steven Sora, Scott Wolter and Andrew Sinclair in particular for their writings on the tower. Regards the novel, the vault located beneath the tower is fictional – at least I assume it is. The descriptions of Touro Park and the surrounding area concur with my own visit and subsequent other research. Incredibly, the symbol on Perry's statue is genuine.

In recent times other evidence has come to light supporting the Templar continuation theory, not mentioned in this novel. One impressive piece of research has been conducted and put forward by Scott Wolter regarding a strange stone found in Kensington, Minnesota. Dubbed the Kensington Runestone after its location and inspired by the inclusion of several runes of Norse origin, the find was initially claimed a forgery by the academic community (another one), claims which can now be accepted as inaccurate. For the open minded, Wolter's findings provide persuasive proof that a party of Templars and Cistercian monks were present in modern day Minnesota in 1361.

The Zenos

Both Nicolò Zeno (1326-1402?) and his brother Antonio (1330?-1403?) did exist. The Zeno family were established among the aristocracy of Venice and the family did historically control the franchise of transportation between Venice and the Holy Land during the Crusades as mentioned in the novel. Both men were esteemed navigators and their brother Carlo was regarded as something of a hero for his role in the war against Genoa.

In life the brothers were noted for their talents as seafarers but not on the same scale as Carlo. This changed in 1558 when one of Nicolò's descendants, also named Nicolò, published a strange account involving his ancestor in life. According to the published account the younger Nicolò while playing in the family home stumbled across a strange map, a book and a series of letters written between the brothers in life, including some to Carlo. Sadly, the descendant claims to have destroyed many of them, not realising the consequences of his actions.

Over the centuries, the legend of the Zeno brothers has become one of great controversy. If the letters are to be believed the tale described in the novel is historically accurate. The accompanying map, giving poorly drawn locations for the islands of Frislanda, Icaria, Estotilanda, Drogeo and many others has convinced some authors that historical voyages were made by the brothers, possibly across the Atlantic over ninety years before Columbus.

Proving the validity of the map and the letters is a historical nightmare. Most scholars condemn them as hoaxes. One of the greatest arguments against their validity are contradictory accounts that suggest both of the brothers were elsewhere at the time they were said to be in Frislanda.

Another problem is identifying the location of the various islands. Frislanda is supposedly somewhere between Scotland and the Faroe Islands, though nothing obviously exists to meet the necessary criteria. For the purpose of this novel, I have chosen Fair Isle in Scotland, also suggested by Andrew Sinclair. Icaria I chose as St Kilda, as its location is close to being where Icaria could be based on the assumption Fair Isle is Frislanda, though Icaria is described as being larger than St Kilda – Sinclair suggested St Kilda or Kerry as possible answers; Sora, interestingly, refers to a sunken island in the general area rediscovered by Arlington Mallery. Estotilanda is often identified as Labrador or Nova Scotia, which I have accepted, whereas Drogeo I chose to be New England as this fits in with the location of the Newport Tower. Suggestion for Drogeo has been anything from Nova Scotia to Mexico or the Caribbean.

Zichmni

According to the Zeno letters, on reaching Frislanda the stranded sailors were rescued by a Prince Zichmni. According to most authors, the leading candidate was the historical Henry St Clair.

Historically, Henry St Clair was Earl of Orkney and the feudal Baron of Roslin. The earl also owned Rosslyn Castle, something I have used in this story. Incidentally, he was also grandfather of the builder of Rosslyn Chapel. He was prince of the Orkneys, placed in a similar role by the King of Norway – according to the legend of Zichmni the prince defeated the King of Norway in battle, St Clair merely inherited the position.

Most of St Clair's life is well documented. None of his biographies to date refer to him as being involved in any voyage across the Atlantic. According to the *History of the Orkneys* by William Thomson, St Clair's posthumous reputation has little to do with his achievements in life. Equally curious is why the Zeno manuscript should refer to a man named St Clair as Zichmni – Sinclair discusses this in detail, particularly spelling of his name as Zinkler in a document preserved in Copenhagen.

One of the greatest mysteries surrounding St Clair is confirming his exact date of death. The usual assumption among historians is that he died around 1401 when the English invaded the Orkneys. Intriguingly, his assumed date of death is similar to that of both Zeno brothers though this cannot be verified.

Speculation that Zichmni was the enigmatic Henry St Clair was first put forward in the 18th century by the historian Johann Reinhold Forster. Since that time many writers have agreed with his assertions, notably Andrew Sinclair who identified Henry St Clair as the only possible candidate. While it is true that the Earl of Orkney fits most of the criteria, there still leaves the question regarding the authenticity of the letters. According to many Templar authors, including Sinclair, Sora and Michael Bradley, St Clair's voyage, as Zichmni, was interrelated with the Templar order that may have survived in Scotland. It has been claimed elsewhere that the St Clairs were related through marriage to the de Payens family through the founder, Hugues de Payens. That said, another biography of the first Templar Grand Master suggests he married an Elizabeth de Chapps rather than a St

Clair. According to other historians there is no connection between the St Clairs and the Templars: some have even stated that members of the St Clair family testified against the order at the trials.

In the case of this novel, the life of the Zenos, Zichmni and the map is largely based on the 1558 account, though I have made much of it up. The letters suggest the explorers did indeed keep notes of their travels but any diaries they wrote are lost if they even existed. The diaries in the novel are fictitious. Regarding the tale's historicity, I believe the evidence at hand is insufficient to prove the voyage took place. Nonetheless, the evidence does concur with legends associated with the Micmac Indians, indigenous of New England and the Atlantic Provinces. Writing in 1536, Venetian Marco Barbaro, a relative of the Zenos also included reference to the voyage in his *Discendenze Patrizie* spelling Zichmni as Zicno.

Templars in Switzerland

Another theme used in *The Templar Agenda* is the premise that outlawed Templars escaped into the Alps, eventually assisting in the foundation of Switzerland.

The Switzerland theory forms the backbone of a book by Stephen Dafoe and Alan Butler, entitled *The Warriors and the Bankers*. As part of their investigation, the authors argue that around the time of the Templar demise the peasant communities who dwelled in the mountains were assisted by riders in white. The best example occurred in 1315 when the army of Leopold V of Austria was ambushed by mountain folk on the St Gotthard Pass. Other evidence includes the similarities between the Swiss flag, a white cross on a red background, almost exactly the same as the Templar red cross on a white background.

The possibility that the Templars situated in the south of France used their geographical knowledge of the Alpine region when fleeing the inquisitors is certainly plausible. Perhaps most interesting is their shared expertise of banking. The Swiss banking system has long been famous for its complex nature, its reliability and secrecy. Curiously, many elements of the Templar banking system do overlap, including the Templar use of safe deposit boxes, a prominent feature of Swiss numbered accounts.

To my mind the greatest surprise was that the duo did not mention any connection with the Swiss Guard. In addition to the Swiss expertise at banking, in the 1400s the Swiss became increasingly famed for their valour and military prowess. Throughout Europe mercenary forces had grown in importance as the Hundred Years' War continued to escalate. Historically, Pope Julius II employed mercenaries from Switzerland in his war against Naples, marking the formation of the Swiss Guards at the Vatican. The possibility that these Catholic mercenaries owe their heritage to the outlawed Templars is a theme I have picked up on in the novel and, as far as I am aware, has not been put forward elsewhere. In my opinion it is likely that members of the order did seek refuge in Switzerland, their expertise eventually making its mark on the Swiss nation, though the foundation of the nation was already well underway by 1312.

The New World Order

Perhaps the most controversial theme used in this book is the assertion that the Templars not only survived excommunication in the 1300s but also, over the resulting centuries, have used their power and influence in ways that continue to hold sway over the masses.

This is the New World Order theory: the premise that there exists a shadowy group of individuals responsible for the occurrence of many key events in history, all for the one extreme purpose: the establishment of a one-world government.

Over the years many variations of this theory have emerged. Quite famously in the 19th century a controversial text appeared in Europe entitled *The Protocols of the Elders of Zion*. Though now proven as a hoax, the shockwaves it produced were powerful, convincing many of a true Judo-Masonic conspiracy for world domination. Other secret societies and orders have been linked with New World Orders: notably the Masons, the Illuminati, the Bohemian Grove, the Bilderberg Group, and everything else ranging from aliens to the descendants of Atlantis.

In short, most of the conspiracies that have entered the public consciousness over the last seven decades range from the plausible to the stupid, usually bordering on the excessively paranoid. In the case of this novel, the idea was simple. The influence of the Templars, powered by their military wing and banking capabilities, has allowed a continuous manipulation of world events, enhanced by their ability to cloak themselves under the guise of others, in this case the Rite of Larmenius. The concept of the New World Order is itself nothing new. Nor, necessarily, is the idea that the Templars are responsible. Over the course of my research I have found finger pointing at the Templars for their role in manipulating events of history to be not uncommon but inconsistent. The idea has no obvious foundation or creator. If there is a source, it was probably the same people responsible for the *Larmenius Charter*, if not earlier still. The legend of the man who shouted out before the people of Paris that Jacques de Molay had been avenged I have been unable to trace.

For the interested reader the conspiracy theory in this novel is completely false. Its inspiration came mainly from the various Masonic conspiracy theories, the Switzerland connection and mostly my own ability to manipulate world events for my own purpose!

All of the characters mentioned as Templars in the novel, and their institutions, are make-believe. Though I do not doubt that there are some exclusive societies in the world capable of keeping extraordinary secrets, the Bohemians and the Pacific-Union seem as capable as any, I do not believe that the Templar Order continued subsequent to 1312 to form any elitist group with an axe to grind. The agenda in this book is plausible: their demise was unfair and also one of betrayal. In practice, however, the idea that several thousand people could stay in contact in war-scattered Europe and put this agenda into place is extremely doubtful. The best arguments for a new world order exists with the concept that the events and decisions of the people who lead us, and their ideologies, cannot exist without a more complex framework, and ultimately that their effects are leading to the culmination of one major outcome. To my mind, the connection exists only in the eyes of those who see what they want to see.

. . . besides, the politicians of the West have long proven that they are more than capable of incompetence on their own without the need of a new world order looking over their shoulder. As Keynes once said

'Capitalism is the astounding belief that the most wickedest of men will do the most wickedest of things for the greatest good of everyone.'

Relics and Idols

The New Temple of Solomon is fictional. The house is inspired by similar houses in Newport, many of which once existed as summer homes of the high and mighty. The basement is equally fictitious and in truth its appearance is something of a cross between Masonic lodges, church crypts, cathedral side chapels, my vivid imagination, castle dungeons while also taking account of the accusations placed against the Templars prior to their excommunication. One of the most bizarre accusations that cropped up in the trials was that the Templars worshipped a strange head, usually a painting or an animal. In recent years evidence has come to light that the Templars owned the Turin Shroud, believed by the order to be the burial shroud of Christ.

The name associated with the object is Baphomet, a meaning for which is still to be explained. In the case of this novel, the so-called demon, sometimes known as Baphomet, is replaced with Asmodeus, the mythical builder of Solomon's Temple, a figure of biblical pedigree also deeply entrenched in Masonic folklore. Instead of the Baphomet describing a head, I have swayed towards accepting the views of Dr Hugh Schofield who suggested the word was created through use of an atbash, a device used to substitute letters for numbers, forming a translation of the word Sophia. In *The Templar Agenda* the Baphomet is an ancient collection of knowledge, granted only to full Templars, entitled to participate in a baptism of wisdom. The Templar's agenda is in part inspired by the tales in this book of wisdom. The book is fictional, though it does concur with certain suggestions that arose at the time of the trials.

The other relic of note in *The Templar Agenda* is the skull and crossbones. Two alleged sources exist here. One, an old Templar legend, describes the story of an evil Templar who desecrated the grave of his mistress, only for the corpse to give birth nine months later to this strange idol, usually called the Skull of Sidon. Another legend, used in the novel, is that loyal supporters of de Molay on collecting his remains after his execution found only the skull and thighbones. Historically, the Templars did use the skull and crossbones on their ships, and graves, as a sign of man's mortality.

Swiss Banks

All of the Swiss and American banks that appear in *The Templar Agenda* are fictitious and the real ones I mention are used fictitiously. Leoni et Cie is modelled on a typical private Swiss bank from St Gallen – many private banks in this area date back to the 1790s or earlier – but every aspect of its business is made up. Their connection with the Vatican is loosely based on Banco Ambrosiano, though Banco Ambrosiano was an Italian bank. The P2 element is also mentioned, though their connection with the Templars is also fictional.

Starvel is a complete work of fiction. The Starvel model is unlike anything else in the world right now. Its size, growth and dominance is used to illustrate the scale of the New World Order influence. Their unparalleled control was also in part inspired by the present banking crisis, brought about in part by the introduction of various legislation mentioned in the novel. In short, Starvel is a company that could exist, its existence a testament to the poor regulation and relaxed political controls that have existed in the West for the past decade. As previously mentioned the subplots involving financial mismanagement and fraud are inspired by historical events, though the way they are included in the novel is for the benefit of the reader and the story rather than to resemble accuracy. Like Leoni et Cie, Banco Ambrosiano was part owned by the Vatican Bank, like Starvel AG, Clearstream was a clearing bank.

Vatican History and Architecture

All locations, artwork and descriptions of the Vatican are as accurate as I could make them. I have visited the site and researched it thoroughly. In some cases I have invented locations: the office of Thierry de Courten, for example, I have based on a combination of photographs of similar rooms mixed with my imagination. I have not visited the inside of the barracks or headquarters of the Swiss Guard or the more interesting regions of the Vatican Library or Secret Archives. Quite simply, few have. I have, however, based the study rooms on the real locations as best possible.

Other Places

All banks, bars, houses, châteaux and their insides are works of imagination based on similar locations in England, Switzerland, Italy, Scotland and America. Again, all people are made up, as are the business activities. I have attempted to make the background of the novel as realistic as possible, from the train times, car park opening times and in some cases included elements of my own experiences at these locations. Any people mentioned in the novel that bear resemblance with any historical or living person not acknowledged is coincidence.

In conclusion: all the errors in the novel are my own. The basis of the novel is fiction. Its purpose is to entertain, not necessarily to enlighten. If it is the opinion of the reader that this book is not entertaining, then it is the opinion of the author that this book should not be read by anyone.

Acknowledgements

First of all, I'd like to take this opportunity to thank you, the reader, for purchasing my novel. I hope that you enjoyed it. If so, I'd love to hear from you. Please feel free to drop me a line at www.theunknowntemplar.com. Reviews on Amazon or Goodreads are also always greatly appreciated.

I would like to say a big thank you to several people for their input, in particular Steven Sora, Graham Phillips and Scott Wolter for their kindness in agreeing to review the book prior to its Kindle release. Over the past five years I have had the opportunity to visit practically all of the places mentioned in the book. I thank everyone I have met when visiting the key locations on my travels for helping in my research.

Finally I would like to say a big thank you to my family and friends, particularly my parents for the incredible support they have shown me throughout my life.

Without you none of this would have been possible.

If you enjoyed the novel, please look out for my other titles

Fiction

The Larmenius Inheritance, 2013
The Plantagenet Vendetta, 2014
The Cromwell Deception, 2014
The Bordeaux Connection 2015
The Cortés Trilogy 2016

Non-fiction

Robin Hood: The Unknown Templar, Peter Owen 2009
Pity for the Guy – a biography of Guy Fawkes, Peter Owen 2010
The Gothic King – a biography of Henry III, Peter Owen 2013

For more on me, please check out my websites,
www.johnpauldavisauthor.com and www.theunknowntemplar.com.
There, you can also find a link to my blog.
All my books above are available on Amazon:

If you have any questions or you would like to get in touch, you can
email me at jpd@theunknowntemplar.com. You can also follow me on
Twitter @unknown_templar

As the book is a work of fiction I have decided not to include a full biography. For the interested reader, included below are a list of recommended reading on the Templar conspiracy theories and their history.

Barber, Malcolm, *The New Knighthood: A History of the Order of the Temple*, New York: Cambridge University Press, 1994

Barber, Malcolm, *The Trial of the Templars*, (2nd Edition) Cambridge and New York: Cambridge University Press, 2006

Bradley, Michael, *Holy Grail Across the Atlantic,* Toronto: Hounslow Press, 1998

Bradley, Michael, *The Columbus Conspiracy*, Toronto: Hounslow Press, 1991

Bradley, Michael, *Grail Knights of North America: On the trail of the Grail,* Toronto: Hounslow Press, 1998

Burman, Edward, *The Templars: Knights of God*, Rochester, Vermont: Destiny Books, 1986

Burman, Edward, *Supremely Abominable Crimes: The Trial of the Knights Templar*, London: Allison and Busby, 1994

Butler, Alan, and Dafoe, Steven, *The Templar Continuum*, Belleville, Ontario: Templar Books, 2000

Butler, Alan, and Dafoe, Steven, *The Warriors and the Bankers: A History of the Knights Templar from 1307 to the present*, Belleville, Ontario: Templar Books, 1998

Davis, John Paul, *Robin Hood: The Unknown Templar*, London: Peter Owen Publishers, 2009

Frers, Ernesto, *The Templar Pirates: The Secret Alliance to Build the New Jerusalem*, Rochester, Vermont: Destiny Books, 2007

Knight, Christopher, and Lomas, Robert, *The Hiram Key: Pharaohs, Freemasons and the Discovery of the Secret Scrolls of Jesus*, London: Arrow, 1997

Madden, Thomas, *A New Concise History of the Crusades*, Lanham, Maryland: Rowman and Littlefield, 2005

Mann, William F, *The Knights Templar in the New World: How Henry Sinclair Brought the Grail to Arcadia*, Rochester, Vermont: Destiny Books, 2004 (originally The Labyrinth of the Grail, Laughing Owl, 1999)

Mann, William F, *The Templar Meridians: The Secret Mapping of the New World*, Rochester, Vermont: Destiny Books, 2006

Martin, Sean, *The Knights Templar: The History and Myths of the Legendary Military Order*, New York: Thunder's Mouth Press, 2005

Newman, Sharan, *The Real History Behind the Templars*, New York: Berkeley, 2007

Nicholson, Helen, *The Knights Templar: A New History*, Stroud: Sutton, 2001

Partner, Peter, *The Murdered Magicians: The Templars and their Myth*, New York: Oxford University Press, 1982

Phillips, Graham, *The Templars and the Ark of the Covenant*, Rochester, Vermont: Bear & Company, 2004

Ralls, Karen, *Knights Templar Encyclopaedia: The Essential Guide to the People, Places, Events, and Symbols of the Order of the Temple*, Franklin Lakes, New Jersey: New Page, 2007

Ralls, Karen, *The Templars and the Grail*, Chicago: Quest, 2003

Read, Paul Piers, *The Templars*, Cambridge, Massachusetts: Da Capo Press, 1999

Seward, Desmond, *The Monks of War: The Military Religious Orders*, Harmondsworth: Penguin, 1995

Sinclair, Andrew, *Rosslyn*, Edinburgh: Birlinn, 2005

Sinclair, Andrew, *The Sword and the Grail*, London: Arrow, 1994

Sora, Steven, *The Lost Colony of the Templars*, Rochester, Vermont: Destiny Books, 2004

Sora, Steven, *Secret Societies of America's Elite*, Rochester, Vermont: Destiny Books, 2003

Tyerman, Christopher, *England and the Crusades, 1095-1588*, Chicago: University of Chicago Press, 1996

Wallace-Murphy, Tim, and Hopkins, Marilyn, *Rosslyn: Guardians of the Secrets of the Holy Grail*, Shaftesbury, Dorset: Element, 1999

Wallace-Murphy, Tim, and Hopkins, Marilyn, *Templars in America*, York Beach, Maine: Weiser, 2004

Wolter, Scott F, *The Hooked X, Key to the Secret History of North America*, St Cloud, Minnesota: North Star Press, 2009

Printed in Great Britain
by Amazon

27632519R00284